Brian William
Jan '05
★☆★

Suspension

SUSPENSION

Richard E. Crabbe

THOMAS DUNNE BOOKS
ST. MARTIN'S PRESS ⚏ NEW YORK

THOMAS DUNNE BOOKS.
An imprint of St. Martin's Press.

www.stmartins.com

Book design by Michelle McMillian

The photograph on the title page shows the Brooklyn Bridge under construction with workers and management, October 1878. Courtesy of Culver Pictures.

Library of Congress Cataloging-in-Publication Data

Crabbe, Richard E.
    Suspension / Richard E. Crabbe.—1st ed.
        p. cm.
    "Thomas Dunne Books."
    ISBN 0-312-20371-3
    1. Police—New York (State)—New York—Fiction. 2. Bridges—Design and construction—Fiction. 3. Suspension bridges—Fiction. 4. East River (N.Y.)—Fiction 5. New York (N.Y.)—Fiction. 6. Terrorism—Fiction. I. Title.

PS3553.R18 S87 2000
813'.6—dc21   00-31729

First Edition: November 2000

10 9 8 7 6 5 4 3 2 1

Acknowledgments

I am deeply grateful to my editor, Pete Wolverton. His vision, keen eye, and endless patience have been gifts beyond words and lessons beyond value.

I can never repay my debt to Rich Barber, my magician-agent, who somehow made selling a first novel seem easy. I am both proud and honored to call him my friend.

Suspension

All wars are boyish, and are fought by boys,
The champions and enthusiasts of the state.

—HERMAN MELVILLE

It never varied. Thad's brother was calling, his voice indistinct and echoing. Franklin smiled back over his shoulder, face shining with the Texas sun. He yelled for Thad to race to the pond. Franklin might have been younger, but he was faster. His feet seemed not to touch the ground, and he opened the gap with every laughing stride. Thad's feet were lead. Heavy and slow, they moved with exasperating weight. He gave it everything but Franklin pulled away with ease. His brother made no footprints in the tall grass, no mark to tell of his passing.

The sun was high and bright, closer than he remembered. Its heat filled him with a familiar warmth. He felt just about as carefree as he ever had, running in the sweet, young grass of east Texas. It felt like home. They ran to their favorite swimming hole. Thad could feel the cooling water already. He knew in his dream that he was happy and that maybe this day was the happiest he would ever know, even though his feet were so slow. He looked ahead at Franklin. The sun colored the grass with gold, setting the tips on fire. The sweetness of it made him almost giddy. He filled his lungs, drinking it in. They were getting nearer the pond now, and Franklin called back that he could see it, and to stop being such a slowpoke. A few more strides and he thought he saw it too. Water glistened in the distance, silver, white, and blue through the tall reeds and cattails. Its cold sparkle made the summer sun seem somehow hotter, and it shimmered in the heat waves and drew him on with a cool, wet promise.

He was running faster now that he could glimpse the pond. He heard a bee buzz by him. It seemed to go right by his ear. He paid it no mind at first, then there was a second and a third. They sounded like someone had kicked their hive. They didn't buzz, fat and lazy. They just flew right by like they had someplace to go in a hurry. They were fast, so fast he couldn't see them. But that wasn't possible. Bees couldn't fly that fast, not in Texas at least. He wondered if Franklin heard them too. They ran on, but they weren't getting closer to the pond. It was receding, always out of reach. The bees were thicker too, but Franklin paid them no mind. Thad looked up ahead, just as the glowing ball of the sun cast a sudden fiery reflection off the distant rippled waters. It blinded him for an instant, and in that instant his dream-world changed and became his nightmare.

The sun exploded with a deafening clap of thunder. It struck him with a shock wave that stunned him. When he looked for his brother, he could see Franklin, still running, but he was a ways off to his left now. Dozens of men were following him, running hard and yelling like demons. Franklin waved his sword and urged them on, pointing his pistol with his other hand. But Franklin wasn't old enough for such things. There were apples in his cheeks and his legs were gangly, even if they were so fast. But as he looked over his shoulder he saw men following him too. They seemed to appear behind him, materializing before his eyes. He saw Emmons, Watkins, Weasel Jacobs, and the others. He saw his whole company, ragged and splendid, trotting behind. They bent forward, their heads down, leaning into the wind of the bees. But the bees were bullets now. Thaddeus watched in morbid fascination as they bit his men. Puffs of dust and splatters of red sprouted in slow motion. Some men kept going; others seemed to melt into the yellow grass. A few whirled away to fall like leaves in their wake.

His heart clamped down inside his chest. His lungs were stone. He knew this place, and the fear of it gripped him like a vise. He thought for a moment the fear would kill him, shrivel his heart and wring it out till he lay white as a drum head. But it didn't. He could turn to his men, call to them and urge them on. He was their captain. They followed. Left and right there were long ragged rows of men in gray and butternut, fading into a blurred distance. Battle flags, scarred and ragged, advanced through the grass. Like ghosts they rose up from the fields and trotted toward the sun on the pond. But as he looked ahead, this too had changed. The reeds and cattails had the steely gleam of bright metal now. They had hardened, into rifle barrels and bayonets.

His feet were slow, while all around him things moved fast. He couldn't think. He could only move forward and hope to catch up with Franklin and his men. Maybe together they could break through the line of steel and stinging lead. Ahead, a hill rose up where the pond had been. It was a gaunt, rocky thing. Boulders littered the slopes as if cast aside by a careless child. As he looked on it he knew that this was the prize of all their dreams: Little Round Top, Gettysburg.

He watched Franklin lead his men, his face flushed and shining. Thaddeus saw his brother as a better version of himself. He was older than Frank, but age was not a good yardstick. From early on Franklin had something special, a presence and a certainty about him that were magnetic. He didn't have to command respect; it came to him like a birthright, and he wore it like a pair of old boots. His men would do things for Frank, at a word, that other captains could not command with the sword. Thad saw Frank bound ahead, heroic, fearless. It was as if they really were playing at soldiers back home. He himself was so scared he feared he'd wet his pants. The bullets buzzed past with a fury. He found himself crouching low in a fold in the land, catching his breath for the final push. Frank did the same. The lead sang over their heads. Sun sparkling off field glasses on Little Round Top caught his attention. He lay low and raised his own glass. A Union officer was looking down on their attack in desperate concentration. He turned to wave and shout to someone in his rear.

A battery of cannon and a thick blue line of infantry came pouring over the hill, the musket barrels sparkling through the smoke. It was too late. Thad knew it. It was too late. With a heart that felt like lead in his chest, he called out "Charge." His sword swung down, pointing at the officer on Little Round Top, as if the blade could reach out and cut the man down. The long line of gray leapt up out of the long, sweet grass raising the rebel yell. It lifted him like a wave. Up out of the fold of ground they rose. The yelling, louder than the guns, propelled them across the fields. Screams, curses, moans, shouted commands, shrieking horses, whining projectiles, and deafening explosions rang in his head. The enemy broke, taking cover amid the boulders. A tide of gray came after, lapping at the base of Little Round Top. Franklin still ran ahead, his feet leaving no mark. His brother called to him again, his face bright, his cheeks red, calling him to the pond where the bees bit only flowers and the cool, deep waters washed away the Texas sun.

"Hurry up, slowpoke. You'll miss the fun." Thad's legs rustled the sheets.

He saw the gunnery sergeant . . . the lanyard in his hand . . . yanking it hard . . . the colonel pointing down. He saw the flash, felt the air compress, the shock wave pass. A rain of lead and steel pelted the line, melting it, bleeding it of life and energy. A moan went up as if from the earth itself. Franklin spun in an awkward pirouette, falling with a puff of dust, like a beaten carpet. Time slowed and stretched. The world moved to a suddenly slower sun. He was at Frank's side. His brother was crouched low on his hands and knees. A tangle of fat red and gray sausage had fallen from his brother's coat. He was looking at the mess as if wondering where they had come from.

"Thad, I'm hurt," Frank said as Thad reached him. His face was white, eyes wide with shock and fear.

"Frank!" Thad cried out to the empty walls of his bedroom. He knew in an instant what the sausage was. The horror of it ripped him from the nightmare but not from the memory.

Captain Thaddeus Erasmus Sangree woke with a start, sweating. Nearly twenty years had passed in a heartbeat. He stared up wide-eyed at the ceiling, still seeing the ghostly image of his nightmare in the darkness. The sheets were soaked. He could still hear his brother: the sound of his voice, the words. Thad thought he was prepared for what he saw when he opened Frank's coat. But he wasn't then and never would be. Frank was opened up and all spilled out.

"Leave me, Thad. Nothin' to do for me," Thad remembered Frank saying weakly. His brother had been right, of course. Even now, all these years later, he could still feel the desperation, the feeling of reality slipping from his grasp.

"Thad," Frank pleaded. "Can't put me . . . together." Thad could still see the gouts of frothy blood running down Frank's white cheek into the yellow grass.

"Thad, I want you . . . do me . . . favor. Can't ask . . . others," he'd said haltingly.

"Anything," Thaddeus remembered saying. "Anything"

Reaching out, Frank had gripped the Colt Thad kept tucked in his belt. Thad hadn't understood what Frank needed his pistol for at first. Frank didn't say anything, but when Thad had cleared it from his belt, he pulled it firmly to his temple. Belly wounds could be a slow death. It could be hours or days before the wounded got help. Usually by that time they'd get wheelbarrowed to a shallow grave. Thinking back on it later, Thad realized he'd probably have wanted the same for himself if the tables were turned. Yet that didn't make it any easier. He'd been horrified, unable to even speak or move. Frank just said, "Send me home."

Thad was never really sure how it was that the gun went off. He remembered pulling it back. He never intended doing what his brother wanted, though he knew it was right. But Franklin's grip was strong for a man with his insides turned out. His brother's hand gripped the long steel barrel, and he'd pulled hard to get Frank to turn it loose. The big Colt exploded somehow, slamming Franklin into the dust, lifeless. Thad couldn't remember anything for some time after that. In all the years of looking at the ceiling after the dream had come, he never figured out how long it was before he came out of the blackness. The next thing he remembered was that Union colonel staring down at them like bugs under a microscope. He could imagine the man gloating over the spilled life of his little brother, curious to see the results of his handiwork, examining them like insects pinned for study. The hate had boiled up in him then, bringing him off his knees by Frank's side. He'd stood straight, unflinching, heedless of the spattering lead kicking up dust spouts around him. Methodically he had emptied his pistol at the officer, aiming at the reflection of his field glasses up on Little Round Top. He had fired with a will and a concentration of energy that hardly needed a pistol to project it. But there had been no effect. No bullet touched the man, and the glint of those cold glasses seemed to mock his rage. The focus of his rage had a name. The name was Washington Roebling.

Countless times he'd sworn his vengeance in the darkness. For him the name had become a beacon. He'd learned it some time after, reading an account of the battle in a northern paper by firelight. Washington Roebling and his brother-in-law, General Gouverneur K. Warren, had figured large in the heroics. Finally his hate had a name. Since then it had become a solid thing, a permanence in his life and a focus beyond all others, giving him purpose, meaning, and a cold sort of comfort in the knowledge that soon now vengeance would be served.

He thought again of Franklin as the sweat slowly dried on his forehead. His lips moved in the darkness, mouthing the words of Henry Wadsworth Longfellow he'd come to know by heart.

> *He is dead, the beautiful youth,*
> *The heart of honor, the tongue of truth,*
> *He, the life and light of us all,*
> *Whose voice was blithe as a bugle call,*
> *Whom all eyes followed, with one consent,*
> *The cheer of whose laugh, and whose pleasant word,*
> *Hushed all murmurs of discontent.*

❈ Chapter One ❈

A silvery sliver of moon hung over the East River, its light swallowed by the choppy black waters. The tide was racing out. The river tugged at ships as they lay at anchor along the shore. The black water folded in oily eddies and swirls around the granite base of the Great East River Bridge as if grudging its intrusion. The blocks of granite were square-cut, their edges not yet worn smooth. They were black below the high-water mark.

Sitting motionless in the cold March moonlight, three gulls sat perched on a cable of the bridge. Like gargoyles they seemed, formed in stone. The moon shone ghostly pale on still, gray feathers. Lost souls of the harbor, they huddled together in the dark, wing to wing. No lamplight burned to unhood the night. The bridge was not open yet. Construction equipment, piles of wood, coils of rope, stacks of steel beams and angle irons, barrels of bolts, nails, tar, cement, and a dozen other things littered the roadways. The smell of lumber, newly galvanized steel, fresh paint, and wet cement clung to the bridge. It was a good smell.

Suddenly the sound of metal on metal clattered through the night from somewhere toward the Brooklyn side, reverberating through the steel. Like a length of pipe dropped or thrown, it had a rolling, ringing, bell-like quality. The three gargoyle gulls came to life. Three heads swung in unison toward the sound. Six eyes gleamed in the dark. Wings shifted. A moment later footsteps could be heard pounding hard down the roadway. A shout in the dark and the sound of leather on wood marked the runner as he crossed the footbridge over the unfinished roadway. A few moments later a second set of feet clattered by.

The gulls stirred nervously. One man passed below them, his labored lungs huffing. He didn't dare to look back. A moment later came a second man, cursing in gasps but running hard. The gulls took flight, their shrill screams piercing the silence above the river. The bridge was not safe tonight. The sounds of pursuit dwindled toward New York.

Two days later it was clear that Terrence Bucklin was dead; that much was certain. He lay in an alley behind Paddy's bar, number 64 Peck Slip—not a place one would want to be found dead. The body cooked in the early afternoon sun that lit the narrow space between the rough brick walls. The Fulton Fish Market was just a couple of blocks away but smelled closer. Dead man . . . dead fish. Under the circumstances, Terrence was a very unattractive corpse. His mouth, set in just the hint of a grin, lent him the look of a man who had met his end with a lingering knowledge. Whatever that knowledge was, he took it with him.

Earlier that morning, at about eleven-thirty, one of Paddy's more religious patrons had come back into the bar after a visit to the alley. Joe Hamm, the barkeep, discouraged his customers from vomiting in the jakes, so the regulars knew to go out back if the drink started coming out the wrong end. The drunk had announced to all present that there was a corpse out back.

"Jaysus fookin' Christ! There's a corpse in the alley, Joe!"

The bar emptied. Nothing could empty a bar faster than a corpse. Hamm cursed his luck. After the drunk who found the body did his best double-time shuffle out the front door, Joe had gone back to see for himself what the fuss was about. Drunks saw all sorts of things. Joe had regular reports over the years of spirits, leprechauns, animals, and insects of various descriptions, especially spiders. On one occasion, the Prince of Darkness himself. Joe went to the alley expecting nothing more dramatic than a trick of the light. What he found was a hand and a leg sticking out from under a couple of packing crates from the chandlers next door. Hamm tossed the crates aside. He could see immediately that he wouldn't be pulling any more beers for this one. Joe stood for a moment, looking down at the body in morbid fascination. Maybe next time he'd pay more attention to what a drunk claimed he saw. He turned back toward the bar, dismissing the thought almost as soon as it came.

When Joe returned The bar was empty except for one man. That man had occupied the corner table at Paddy's for the last fifteen years. He hadn't left with the others. He had work to do, trying to finish the job that the rebels had started at Cold Harbor. He had left half his right leg and a sizable chunk of his left calf on the field in Virginia when a Confederate twelve-pounder came bounding through the line. Three years in and out of hospitals and the doctors had pronounced him as whole in body as they could make him. His spirit, however, was something else. Since then he had become a fixture at Paddy's. He was the sawdust on the floor and the smoke in the air and the smell of beer. Drinking an army pension was a slow death.

"Saw a cop pass down the street toward the docks a couple of minutes ago," the veteran observed laconically.

"Thanks, Bob. You've got a cold one comin' on the house when I get back."

"Hurry back, then." So Joe Hamm had gone in search of a cop. As he was leaving he couldn't escape the thought that he had really left two dead men in the bar.

Joe was not a particularly tall man so he went down the crowded cobblestone streets craning, bobbing, and hopping in an effort to see a cop over the multitude. He looked like a damn fool, he knew, with his beer-stained bar apron flapping. The thought of that body and all the business he was likely to lose because of it kept him hopping and craning past Front, and all the way to South Street, where he turned South toward the market. Joe came upon a young patrolman who was trying to supervise the untangling of two freight wagons, their steaming draft horses wide-eyed and straining. The cop was doing his official best to keep the teamsters from coming to blows and the wagons from crushing someone in their struggle to get their wheels unlocked. He waved and shouted to be heard over the cursing teamsters and the general clamor of South Street. From the look of things, he was having little luck at this. As Joe Hamm approached, one teamster was letting loose with a creative stream of curses and oaths. The driver on the other wagon was probably just as colorful, but he was cursing in Italian. Joe could pretty much get the gist from his hand gestures, which seemed to encompass the cop as well.

Hamm took all this in as he trotted up to the cop and clapped a hand on his shoulder.

"There's been a murder," he said breathlessly.

"Listen, don't bother me now. I've got a situation here," the cop snapped back.

Joe gave it another try "I don't think you heard me." He was annoyed that the cop wasn't paying attention. "I've got a dead man, a murdered man maybe, out behind my bar. He's in the alley behind Paddy's." That got the cop's attention.

"A dead man, you say? Paddy's? Where the hell is Paddy's?" asked the patrolman, looking around.

God, this kid was fresh out of the box, Joe thought. Everyone knew where Paddy's was.

"It's over on Peck Slip," he said patiently. "Right next door to the chandlers shop."

The young cop still had a blank, distracted look. The two teamsters were gathering steam.

"Stick it up your arse, ye goddamn dago," one shot at the other.

"Uppa *you* ass," the Italian sallied back in what was probably the sum of his English.

"Let's go then," the cop said absently.

"So who are you, and what's this about a body?" the cop asked.

"Name's Joe Hamm. Tend bar at Paddy's. One o' my regulars found him behind the bar."

"What do you mean, *behind the bar*?" the cop asked.

"Out back in the alley."

"Oh." The cop took a last look over his shoulder at the receding mess on South Street.

"Watch it," Joe said as he threw out a hand to stop the patrolman. He had almost walked out in front of a wagon loaded with barrels of salt fish. "You new on the force, or just new to the precinct?"

"New to the force. How'd you know?"

That didn't really take a detective to figure, Joe thought, but trying not to offend the kid, he said, "Well, you didn't know where Paddy's was. Haven't seen you around before neither. Where're you from?"

"Staten Island."

"Took the ferry there once," Joe said. "Nice ride. Never knew anybody that lived there though. What's your name, Officer?"

"Patrolman Jaffey. Elija's my given name. This the place?"

They stood in front of Paddy's, with its dying paint and its dusty windows. Jaffey looked up at the carved and painted wooden prizefighter hanging over the door and wondered if that was Paddy himself or just an appeal to the "fightin' Irish." Taking a deep breath, he dove into the shimmering gloom of Paddy's common room. He and Joe were walking deeper into the place, swirling sawdust in their wake, when from the corner table Bob the veteran said, "That's Terrence Bucklin out back."

That brought them both up short, turning. "Took a look while you was gone, Joe. Good man, Bucklin," Bob muttered almost to himself. "Worked on the bridge—mason, I think. Shared a beer with him once or twice . . . Friendly fella. Damned shame."

Joe and Jaffey stood in the sawdust, and, for an instant, it seemed, they all bowed their heads for the good man who had been Terrence Bucklin.

A septic breath of air from the alley carried a reminder of why Joe and Jaffey were there. The patrolman didn't know quite what to expect. This was his first body, and he wanted to be professional and dispassionate about it. He could handle this, he told himself. He just had to concentrate on the job. He had an important job, and it was important that he do it right and . . .

"Oh my Lord, oh my . . ." Jaffey blurted when he got a good look at Bucklin. The patrolman's stomach twisted inside him. He took an involuntary half step back and croaked to Joe, "Go to the station house and get Sergeant Halpern. He's my watch sergeant. You know where it is, don't you?"

"Yeah, I know Sam too. I'll get him."

This was to be a day of firsts for Eli Jaffey. He had never been alone with a corpse before. He couldn't count his aunt and little sister who died of the typhoid three years ago. They weren't corpses, really, they were family. They had lain in the front parlor of their house on St. Mark's Place, with flowers in their hair and the smell of lilies floating like a fog bank. They weren't dead like this, lying twisted in an alley, filling with the gases of their own decay. This was different—no lilies, no candles, no satin pillows, just stink and flies.

Jaffey stood, staring down at the corpse, for what felt like an awfully long time. Slowly Eli began to feel that Terrence Bucklin could see with his dead, doll's eyes into his most private place, where he locked away his doubts and fears. And he seemed to say "Can you do this? Can you look me in the eye?"

Bucklin's eyes were not easy to look at. Jaffey didn't want to look at them, but felt compelled to nonetheless.

"It's the flies, isn't it?" the corpse said to him. "Come on, look me in the eye and see for yourself, if you can really wear that new uniform. May as well get it over with."

Jaffey looked long and with a will at the dead eyes of Terrence Bucklin. When Sergeant Halpern arrived a few minutes later, Jaffey was doubled over, retching up the last of his lunch. Halpern was about to say something unkind but remembered his reaction to his first bloated corpse, so held his tongue. He was annoyed but a little amused too, though he tried to keep it from the kid, hiding the ghost of a grin behind frowning eyes.

Jaffey had the shine and delicate green coloring of an underripe tomato. At least he had the good sense not to puke on the corpse, Halpern thought, although God knew he had seen that done in his time.

"Go on into Paddy's and get yourself something to wash the taste out," Sam said. "And see if you can get some statements from Joe Hamm and anybody left inside while you're at it. You're doin' nobody any good here, pukin' on your shoes."

Jaffey gave Sam Halpern a hangdog look as he wiped the remnants of lumpy lunch from his shoes with a bit of rag. A cop should never be seen with his lunch on his shoes, and young Jaffey did pride himself on his spotless uniform. Without a word, he turned toward the back of Paddy's. He was happy for something to do, and he fumbled for his notebook and pencil. He tried to think of all the questions a good cop should ask of witnesses to a crime, and it helped to take his mind off the corpse on the alley floor with that grin on his face and the flies in his eyes. Jaffey's eyes strayed back to the body, and for one awful moment he could have sworn that Terrence's glassy eyes followed him as he moved toward the door. He quickened his pace.

Jaffey turned into the back door of Paddy's that opened on a storage area and hallway. It was black as coal compared to the light in the alley. The black of the hallway congealed into something very solid and Jaffey bounced off it with a grunt, dropping his pad and pencil. In the instant it took for his eyes to adjust to the sudden lack of light, he realized that it was a man he had walked into. To his credit, he recovered his composure quickly and in his best official tone said, "You've got to keep this hallway clear, we're investigating a murder here. Now move back into the bar. I'd like to ask you a few questions."

An amused "Humph" came from the shadow that was the man's face. He made no move. Jaffey put his hand on the butt of the nightstick hanging at his waist.

"Move back, I said, and do it now! Don't be startin' any trouble," he told the big shadow, "just move back into the bar and be quick about it." Jaffey gripped his nightstick tighter with his right hand. With his left he poked two fingers hard into the man's chest in an effort to get him moving in the right direction. This seemed to have no effect. Jaffey was a little alarmed at that. Boozer or not, this fellow just didn't have any give to him. The man's features were materializing out of the gloom as Jaffey's eyes became fully accustomed to the light. The stranger started to say something and made a move to get past the patrolman.

This would never do, Jaffey thought. He couldn't let his sergeant see him get pushed around. He drew his nightstick. In his hurry he missed what the shadow-man said. Jaffey thought a crack across the knees would set his man to rights. It was the last thing he thought.

"Sorry about your boy there, Sam. Hope I didn't do any permanent damage," Tom Braddock said without appearing to mean it.

"Jesus, Tommy, did you have to do that? It's hard enough gettin' the boys broken in without you bustin' em up," Sam grumbled as he bent over the prostrate patrolman.

"He was going to crack my kneecaps," Tom said defensively. "I can't abide a pup like him goin' off half cocked, thinkin' the world has to jump 'cause he's got new brass."

"Seems to me I recall you bein' pretty green when you started too." Sam hooked a hand under Jaffey's arm. "Here, help me get him up." Sam and Tom leaned Jaffey against a barrel.

"Sam, we weren't green when we started on the force. Ignorant maybe, but not green. We were green back in '62 when we enlisted," Tom said. "But when we started here that had rubbed clean off."

There was a lot of truth in that. When the war ended and they joined the force, they were a well-seasoned pair.

"Sure, you're right, I guess, but we still didn't know a damn thing about police work, as I recall," Sam muttered.

"There's some that say you still don't, Sammy," Tom said with a grin.

"Screw you, Braddock." Sam grinned back.

Halpern and Braddock stood over Jaffey as he came around. Jaffey looked up from his seat against the pickle barrel where the two had propped him. If he thought Braddock looked big before, he looked positively immense from the floor. Two sets of hands sky-hooked him onto his feet, and he saw at once the reason why the big man had not backed down when Jaffey had run into him. Braddock wore the shield of a sergeant detective. In the dark of the hallway, Jaffey hadn't noticed it, and with Tom in plain clothes . . .

"Shit," he mumbled to himself. He had botched the job again. But that wasn't what was important to him.

"How the hell did you do that?" Jaffey asked with a mixture of surprise and respect as he rubbed the base of his neck. "Feel like I was poleaxed."

Braddock was surprised. He expected indignance, or bravado, or maybe even a bit of a fight from this kid with the fresh brass. A commendable swallowing of pride, Tom figured. The kid was doing his best to recognize his mistakes. Tom wasn't so sure that if the tables were turned, he'd have the same humility. Perhaps he'd misjudged Jaffey just as quickly as Jaffey had misjudged him.

"It's a form of Chinese self-defense," Tom said. "I picked it up when I was working patrol in Chinatown. Studied under Master Kwan on Mott Street." He said this as if it should mean something to Jaffey, but of course it didn't. "I'll tell you that story some other time, Patrolman," Tom continued. "And from now on, make sure of what you're doing and who you're doing it to before you do it. You understand me, son?"

"Yes, sir, sorry, sir."

"Right," Braddock said. "Now go on into the bar and talk to Bob. That poor bastard knows everyone who's been in this place since after the war. Might have to buy him a drink to get anything out of him, though, and get one for yourself while you're at it. You look like shit."

"Sergeant Halpern said the same thing," Jaffey said.

"You should listen to your sergeant. He knows a thing or two."

Jaffey hesitated a moment. "I'm on duty," he said lamely.

Sam and Tom rolled their eyes and Sam said as patiently as he could. "Jaffey, if Tom Braddock tells you to get a goddamned beer, then you get a goddamned beer. Now be a good lad and put your rulebook in your pocket and see what Bob has to say about our friend over there."

"Said his name was Terrence Bucklin."

"Good. Get whatever you can from Hamm too. He's a decent sort for a bartender. Find out if he's seen this fella before, who he's been seen with, that sort of thing. Can you do that?"

"Yes, sir."

"Hm . . . and Jaffey, don't call me sir. Sergeant will do just fine."

Jaffey headed down the hallway toward the bar. He stopped to pick up the pad and pencil that he'd dropped when he walked into Braddock and felt himself a fool again at the small reminder.

"Well, Sam, let's get on with it," Tom said as he walked out into the alley. Sam knew what was coming. Braddock was one of the better investigators in the department by some accounts, though he did have one unsettling habit when it came to murder investigations.

"Terrence, Terrence, Terrence, look what's become of you now." Tom stood over the corpse, his head hung low and his magnificent handlebar mustache seeming to droop in grief at the terrible end Bucklin had come to.

"Who would want to do this to you, man? Or maybe you just drank too much and knocked your head when you fell? Was that the way of it?" Tom paused as if the corpse would answer. "This is Sergeant Halpern and I'm Detective Tom Braddock, and if you don't mind I'll be askin' your help as we go through this."

Halpern caught himself nodding to the corpse at the introduction. God, he hated when Tom did this. He remembered the first murder scene he and Tom had worked together and how startled he'd been when Tom started talking to the body like the son of a bitch was going to sit up and tell them all about it. He had kept his peace at the time, feeling that Tom was just trying to keep down his nervousness with the banter. Later, when the body had been carted off in the coroner's wagon, Sam had said "The dead won't answer you, Tom."

"Oh, Sam, that's not true. The dead have a lot to say. Helps to talk to them, helps them say what they have to, I think."

Sam remembered Tom telling him how he started talking to the dead. It was during the war, at the Battle of the Wilderness.

"Don't look at me that way, Sam. I know they're not really talking to me, but they were people once, and if you talk to them maybe you'll get answers you don't expect," Tom said thoughtfully. "Does no harm. Helps me, anyway. Helps me put myself in their shoes, see things how they saw them."

Sam remembered that day with a silent grin. He and Tom had seen a lot since then, but Tom's habit of talking to the dead had never left him. And if Sam had to be honest about it, he guessed it didn't hurt any.

Tom looked up and took in the place where the body lay. He turned slowly, his eyes scanning the doorway to Paddy's, the trash in the alley, the three-story rough brick walls, the high gate where the alley opened onto the street. He seemed to be absorbing the place. Like a bird, his blue eyes were unblinking, reflecting back the scene in miniature as if it all were now inside his head, shining out, photographed there and filed away. Finally, as if coming up for air out of deep water, Tom filled his lungs and sighed. "What do you make of this, Sam?"

"Not a whole hell of a lot, Tom. No bullet holes, not much blood, no murder weapon, no witnesses we know of. He looks dead though," Sam said, nodding down toward the body. "I'm pretty certain of that."

"He's been gone about two days," Tom said. "Probably died sometime Saturday night. It's been pretty warm last couple days. Wouldn't take long for him to swell up like he has."

"With the bar closed for the Sabbath that explains why nobody found him sooner," Sam observed.

"He's a worker," Tom muttered as he stooped over the body. "A mason, unless I miss my guess. Did pretty well for a while but he's down on his luck lately."

"How d'you figure that?" Sam asked, clearly skeptical.

"Cement on his shoes and his pants are worn at the knees," Tom said, pointing. "See his hand?" Tom turned Bucklin's hand palm up. "Calluses, and cement dust in the cracks . . . see? Shoes aren't the cheap kind but he's worn them clear through. That's why I guess he's seen better times. Looks to have been pretty healthy, although I'll grant you he don't look too healthy now." Tom looked at the body closely. "I'd guess he was thirty-four, thirty-five or thereabouts. Did you look through his pockets?" Tom glanced up at Sam questioningly.

"Just his jacket. Nothing in the pockets except an orange. Didn't have time to do more. You got here only about five minutes after me. I was standing off while Jaffey puked up his lunch."

"Yeah. Thanks for sending for me." Tom put a hand over his nose. "Wish that rookie hadn't lost his stomach. Smells bad enough as it is."

Sam gave a grim little laugh—It was shallow, as if the air weren't fit for laughing. "It ain't rosewater and lilies. Jaffey's all right, though, you'll see. He just needs to get his feet under him. There's something in that boy that shines." Sam looked back at the doorway toward Paddy's. "Been keepin' an eye on him."

"We'll see," Tom muttered. He wasn't convinced by a long shot.

"So, Terrence, mind if I go through your pockets?" he asked the corpse. He searched Terrence's pockets, starting with his vest. Slowly he felt inside and out, feeling the fabric for something that might have been sewn into the lining. Sometimes a man would do that with something he didn't want a cutpurse to find. The vest turned up a few coins, a cheap pocket watch, and a tattered piece of paper. Tom examined the watch, looking for an inscription or perhaps a tintype tucked into the back. It was an ordinary watch, a Waltham with a dented brass case, and nothing in or on it of any note. Tom had hoped for more but was not surprised. A working man rarely had the money for gold watches or inscriptions, for that matter. Next, Tom turned over the yellow folded piece of paper, feeling its worn edges and dirty sheen.

"Been in his pocket awhile, I reckon. Looks like it's been wet too."

"Might just be sweat," Sam said, looking over Tom's shoulder.

Tom looked down at the body and murmured, "This meant something to you, didn't it, lad? I'll just have a look at it if you don't mind." Tom unfolded the paper with surprising delicacy. His big fingers seemed to coax the yellow sheet open, and it almost appeared to unfold itself.

"Looks like a bill," Tom murmured. "Thompson's Mortuary Service," he read, stopping to glance at the corpse. "Coffins Made to Order. Embalming. Burial Services. Death Masks and Portraits of the Dearly Departed."

"Looks as though our man had a death in the family," Sam said.

"Two. Says he's being charged for two embalmings and caskets, one hearse, flowers, a burial plot, and a priest. Strange, two caskets and one hearse," Tom mused.

"Jesus, a hundred fifty-three dollars and forty cents. At those prices I can't afford to die." Sam gave a low whistle. "What's that address there, Tommy?"

"It's kind of washed out. I'd say 242 Suffolk Street, but I wouldn't bet the farm on it, the ink's run pretty bad." Tom turned to Bucklin and murmured as he crouched near the body, "Buried someone near to you a while back?" His hands slowly emptied the two front pockets of the man's worn wool pants. Their faded dark plaid confines yielded little. A folding knife with a blade worn down from sharpening, a button, and one key was all he found. The key might be useful, but there was no way to tell what it was for. It looked much like any other, a simple iron skeleton key. "Most likely a front-door key." Tom held up the key.

"Not much help," Sam observed. Half the locks in the city had keys like that.

"Help me roll him over."

Sam stooped by the body and together he and Tom rolled the corpse on its left side.

"Well, now, I guess we know what killed you, don't we, Terrence?" Tom said, looking at the back of Bucklin's head. "That's as nasty a bash on the noggin as I've seen. Neat, though, wasn't it, Sam, just a bit of blood?" Tom ran his hand over the matted hair. "Crushed the skull like an eggshell but barely broke the skin." Tom leaned close to the body and spoke so low Sam could hardly hear him. "Didn't know what hit you, did you, partner, just an unscheduled freight train smack in the back of the head. Next thing, you're looking up from the gutter, with the world spinnin'."

Sam snuck a look at Tom out of the corner of his eye. Tom was looking closely at the back of Bucklin's head, peeling back the blood-sticky hair to get a better look at the large depression. The skull was soft there, like a melon that had been dropped days before. A chill went through Tom at the feel of it. He pulled his hand away sticky with the cool brown blood of Terrence Bucklin's broken head. Tom had plenty of experience with blood, and it rarely affected him one way or the other. He stood and pulled a handkerchief from his back pocket. Tom wiped the blood away and tried to keep from scrubbing too hard. He gazed around at the alley on either side of the body, his eyes measuring the place. He measured the distance from the body to the door to Paddy's, the width of the alley, the packing crates that had once hidden the corpse. The alley was too narrow, too small. There was no way anyone could be out there and not be aware of another presence. Tom could not believe that a man could stand there and have his head crushed by surprise. The tall brick walls echoed and amplified every sound, and a step would be clearly heard from ten feet away. Then he fixed an eye on the tall gate that opened on Peck Slip.

"Caught him comin' over the gate," Tom said with certainty, his words ringing off the brick walls.

"Wha'? How you figure that?"

"Look," Tom said as he walked to the gate. A small brown rivulet of dried blood ran down the green-painted boards. Braddock stepped on a crate to peer over the top. "Thought so. Came over the gate. Got hit as he went over. See the scrapes? Killer came over to finish the job."

Sam gave a puzzled frown, nodding as if he knew what the hell Braddock were talking about.

Tom looked back at Sam. "See the cement dust? There's scrapes from two different kinds of shoes here too. A little hard to see, but I'm pretty certain. He was running from someone. Figured to duck into the alley and throw him off, I guess. Probably slipped getting over the gate. That would account for the scrapes. Lost some time and got caught going over. At least that's how I'm seein' it."

Sam nodded sagely. Tom looked back at the body. Terrence stared back up at Tom and Sam. *He* knew.

Tom walked back to the body, bending over to feel in the back pockets. He tugged a wallet out. "A few greenbacks here. Looks to be a pay stub too, from the New York and Brooklyn Bridge company."

"So Bob was right. He did work on the bridge," Sam mused. Bob was something less than reliable.

"So it would appear. Did all right. Says here he was paid twelve dollars last week. He's got, let's see, ah, three and five is eight dollars and some change, maybe nine and a quarter all told."

"So our killer didn't care for money, or got scared off before he could take it. Plenty would kill for less than nine dollars and change," Sam said.

Tom nodded at the truth of that. "Seen men killed for less: a pair of shoes, a pint of rotgut. Strange the killer left it," Tom said after a pause. "If you kill a man for money, you don't leave before you have it. I think Terrence here is dead for some other reason."

Sam gave a huff of agreement. "So what do you think? Jealous husband, revenge, debts—could be any damn thing."

"Terrence knows, but he's not talking," Tom said, looking down at the body. "Well, Terrence, my lad, anything else you'd like to reveal to us?" Terrence was mute. The silence echoed, and Tom waited. Sam shifted his feet, feeling more and more awkward as time and silence conspired. "Damn." Tom's eyes fixed on Terrence's vest. Sam gave a little jump as if Terrence had actually said something. "Why didn't I see that before?" Bending over the body, Tom looked closely at the dark wool of Terrence's work-stained vest. "This look like a tobacco stain to you, Sam?"

Halpern joined Tom, bending low to get a closer look. "Hard to tell with that dark cloth," Sam muttered. "Might be. What of it? Most every man who ever chewed tobacco ends up wearin' some of it."

Tom looked at Sam, a question in his eyes. "You find any chaw on him? I know I didn't."

"No, but . . ." Sam trailed off while he searched for an explanation.

"You look in his mouth?" Tom asked with a little grimace. The two of them looked at each other and then down at the body. If he had been chewing tobacco, there might be some left tucked in his cheek, a particularly unappetizing thought given the body's condition.

"Shit." Tom grumbled. He could have waited for the coroner to do his autopsy, but waiting to find out something he could learn for himself was not Braddock's style. "I'll look in his mouth." "Give me your gloves, Sam." He held out a hand as if he really expected Sam to give them up.

Halpern chuckled, shaking his head. "Not mine, partner." The ones in his pocket happened to be his last good pair. Fishing around in a dead man's mouth was not his idea of a productive use for them.

"Thanks a lot!" Tom said with a sarcastic twist to his mouth. "All right, now look here, Bucklin." He wagged a finger at the body for emphasis. "I've got to play dentist for a bit, so you just relax and don't go biting one o' my fingers off." Tom half meant it. After prying Terrence's mouth open, he looked inside, pulling the cheeks away from the swollen gums as much as he dared. Tom was as gentle as he could be, for he feared that Bucklin's well-aged cheeks might tear away. The thought sent a cold trickle of sweat rolling down his back. His probing fingers turned up nothing, and he stood quickly, almost wiping his hands on his pants. "Be right back."

Tom washed his hands three times in the washroom of Paddy's without really feeling clean, but he went back out to the alley anyway. Sam was twirling the end of his mustache the way he did when something bothered him. He had a puzzled look on his face, and he said, "It's odd, you know. Back when I was still chewing tobacco, I managed to spit some down my shirt and it always made sort of a dribbly run down the front. Ruined a couple o' good shirts that way. Tobacco stains are hell to get out. Funny thing is, Mr. Bucklin here just has a big old splotch on his vest."

Tom nodded and said softly. "I was thinking the same thing while I washed up. Killer spat on him. Bashed his head in and spat on his dying body. Tobacco juice don't run when you're flat on your back."

They stood over the corpse, Sam's thumbs hooked in his pockets, Tom's arms folded across his chest.

"Bucklin was probably still alive when he did it," Tom said slowly, knowing it as if he'd seen it done. Sam just nodded.

"Says something about the kind of man we're looking for, don't it?" Tom grunted. Whoever had done it was not going to like it when he caught up with him. It was both decision and promise.

Captain Sangree lowered his field glasses and, with the corner of his shirt, rubbed the dust from the lenses. It wasn't dust that clouded his vision, though there was a bit of it, catching the light like smudgy stars. It was remembrance. Watching the sergeant and what appeared to be a detective examine the body of Terrence Bucklin put him in mind of another body nearly twenty years before. Unlike Mr. Bucklin, there was no mystery about that death.

He stood a few feet back from his office window, nestled in shadow. The body was inconveniently close, with a clear sight line from his third story window to the alley where Bucklin lay. It was nearly impossible not to watch. Considering the man had been killed on his orders, it seemed wise to observe what he could. He was going to have to have a serious talk with his man about his sense of timing and locale. The man was an expert, and as calculating and cold-blooded a hunter as he'd ever seen. He was inclined to give him the benefit of the doubt, with all due deference to his skill, but killing Bucklin almost on his doorstep was something else, and he had better have a damn good reason for it. The captain raised his glasses again. At this distance he almost didn't need them. Bucklin's sprawled body was barely a block away. There wasn't much to see, just the cops standing above the body, mouths moving occasionally in mute conversation. He made careful note of the two, their demeanor and appearance, the way they acted and related to each other. The big one was the man to watch, he could see that immediately. The breadth of shoulder and trimness of waist gave him an air of physical power. He looked like a boxer. The smaller of the two was unremarkable. They appeared to know each other and seemed on friendly terms. There was no stiffness between them like he had seen in the young cop who got there first. They had worked together before, a factor to be taken into account. It wouldn't do to underestimate them, he decided.

Bucklin had been an unexpected threat to his plans. He had, by chance, come to stand in the way of Sangree's mission. His life was forfeit—a casualty of war, one in a long line, counting no more than any other. True, it was a shame, as all casualties are, but it was necessary nonetheless. The field glasses saw the body once again. It looked no different from countless bodies that populated his dreams. The well-worn pair of brass field glasses caught a glint of the sun as they were lowered. Tom and Sam might have seen it if they had been looking that way. A scarred hand lowered the shade and snapped the binoculars closed.

❄ Chapter Two ❄

Braddock and Halpern sat at the bar in Paddy's drinking cold beer. They had sent Jaffey off to the coroner to get a wagon down there to haul the body away. It seemed like a good plan to wait just where they were till the wagon arrived. They counted on it taking some time. They were both quiet, lost in their own thoughts, while Bob the crippled veteran sang snippets of "Lorena" and some other songs that had been popular during the war. It always gave Tom strange, mixed feelings to hear those songs. They conjured memories, some warm, some cold and brittle, as if some part of him might break if he held onto them too long. That kind could leave him feeling empty for hours, his head aching where a bullet had creased his skull in '63. Tom slowly sipped his beer, remembering his years with the Twentieth New York.

He remembered the endless drill, the lonely hours standing guard, long miles of marching, his feet bleeding in his shoes. He still knew how it felt when fear nearly overcame his will, and it took everything just to stay in line with the rest of the regiment, amazed that the fools weren't running. He had been ashamed of those times, still was, and he didn't like to recall them, never spoke about them either, not even to Sam. They had been eighteen, he and Sam, full of fight and itching to whip the rebs. He chuckled silently to himself. How young and stupid they had been.

Bob was singing in his surprisingly good tenor:

The years creep slowly by, Lorena
The snow is on the grass again;

The sun's low down the sky, Lorena
The frost gleams where the flowers have been
But the heart throbs on as warmly now
As when the summer days were nigh;
Oh! The sun can never dip so low;
A-down affections cloudless sky
A-down affections cloudless sky.

Tom sipped his beer and felt tossed about by his memories. An image came into his head of himself as a poplar tree, his leaves blown by the wind of Bob's old songs. The leaves were his memories, and as the songs swept through the leaves those memories sometimes turned and showed a different side. They were part of him, those leaves, and they made him what he was. It was strange sometimes the things that stirred them, but the songs always did. Always.

It matters little now, Lorena,
The past is in the eternal past,
Our heads will soon lie low, Lorena,
Life's tide is ebbing out so fast.
There is a future! O, thank God!
Of life this is so small a part!
'Tis dust to dust beneath the sod!
But up there, up there, 'tis heart to heart.
But up there, up there, 'tis heart to heart.

Tom looked up from his beer and stared at his reflection in the dusty, cut-glass mirror behind the bar. He looked older than he remembered. He had been a young man when he had sung "Lorena" around the Company D campfire at night. His face was thinner then. So was Sam's. His mustache had been a little scraggly, not like the luxurious specimen he sported now. And there was a look in his eye then that he had not seen in the mirror for a long time. It was the look that said he saw the world in blacks and whites, a look of fire and optimism. He had been so certain then when the war was new. The world had yet to color his vision in shades of gray. Though Tom still saw where the blacks and whites were, a lot of grays had crept in over the years. In some ways he missed that naïve vision of the world. It was comforting to see things so clearly. But the real world wasn't like that. That young man was gone and those days were gone, and that was all there was to it.

With a small start, Tom noticed that Sam was staring into the same dusty beveled-glass mirror, its dark mahogany frame surrounding them both in its carved embrace. Sam looked at him in silence. Tom knew that Sam was stirred by the old song too. Their silence bound them. Shared memories blew through Paddy's bar on invisible winds. Tom realized with a sudden self-consciousness that Sam was watching a tear roll down his face as it shone dully in his silvered reflection. Too quickly, he raised his beer in its sweating glass and held it to his cheek with a small sigh. It was a warm day, after all. Sam looked away.

Joe Hamm washed glasses behind the bar and served up beer or sometimes whiskey or gin to those who had the taste and the money for it. He and Bob had given Tom everything they knew about Terrence Bucklin, which wasn't much. Bucklin came in from time to time, actually more often in the last year. He didn't drink too much or start fights like some of the other bridge workers. He had been seen mainly in the company of about six to eight other men, most of whom Hamm didn't know except by sight. There were a couple though that were known to him: Rolf Mentzer, a rough but good-natured German who was fond of his pints and had a habit of booming out German drinking songs when the pints had lubricated the vocal cords sufficiently. It was Joe's understanding that Mentzer worked on the bridge with Bucklin in one of the masonry crews. Watkins was the only other of Terrence's friends Joe knew, but he wasn't sure of the first name. Watkins was tall and kind of skinny, with a pockmarked face, probably from the smallpox. Watkins was a fairly quiet sort when he was sober but loud and boastful when he had a snootful. He worked on the same crew as the rest, Hamm figured. The rest of the crew Joe knew by description only, and being a pretty observant bartender—an asset in his profession—he had given Tom a fair picture of four or five others he recalled seeing with Bucklin. Neither Joe nor Bob could recall anything odd about Bucklin recently. There hadn't been any fights, arguments, or incidents. Joe did mention that he seemed a little quieter in the last week or so—not quite his old self—but he didn't make anything of it. Tom had hoped for more, but apparently Terrence Bucklin had pretty much blended in with the rest of the working crowd that Paddy's catered to.

There had been many, hundreds of bridge workers through Paddy's over the years since the New York Bridge was started in '69. Dock workers, carpenters, caisson workers, common laborers, stonemasons, bricklayers, cable men—"riggers," as they were called—they all found their way to the dusty old saloon on Peck Slip. Most were immigrants. Most were from Ireland, although there were some from Germany and Italy and other countries. Beer was one of the few comforts for most of the men. Life was hard and the work, harder. Most lived in tenements. Ten to a room was not all that unusual. Packed into four and five floor walk-ups, one toilet per floor in the newer tenements, outhouses in the old. Tuberculosis, smallpox, measles, diphtheria, whooping cough, typhoid, and a long list of other maladies carried off the weak and the healthy alike, the young and the old alike, the good and the bad alike. With the Lower East Side housing nearly 300,000 people to the square mile by some estimates, it sometimes seemed that the dead were carried out faster than the living moved in.

For those who needed to get across the East River, the only way had been on a Union Ferry Company line. Though the boats were large and ran every five minutes during peak hours, they were still not enough. Winter months were the worst, with ice floes sometimes blocking the river for hours. The story went that in '53, John Roebling, the great bridge-builder, and his son Washington, then about fifteen, had been stuck in the ice during a ferry ride on a brutally cold winter day. It was then, during the three-hour delay in getting the ferry free, that old man Roebling first envisioned his bridge across the river. It hadn't been till '67 that the state legislature authorized the construction of the bridge he'd proposed and '69 before work actually began. In the fourteen years since, there had been more triumph, tragedy, and scandal than old John Roebling could ever have imagined.

The bridge was almost done now. The towers had been up for six years, looming over the city in monumental anticipation. Only the top of the spire of Trinity Church was higher, and that was only a needle point on the skyline, while the towers of the bridge stood massive, cathedrallike. The bridge was a colossus yet at the same time it had an almost weightless quality to the eye. The soaring roadway, now nearly complete, seemed to literally defy gravity. The slender cables, in harp-string tension, sang in the wind high above the river. Even the massive granite and sandstone towers had an airy feel when seen from a distance. Their gothic arches flew gracefully over the twin roadways. On certain days, when the sun was just right and its rays lanced through clouds above Manhattan, the towers seemed to frame the cities beyond in an almost religious way, and it was hard not to see the hand of God in it. It was altogether appropriate that the bridge was called the Eighth Wonder of the World.

Tom could see the top third of the New York tower from where he sat. It loomed over the tops of the nearby buildings. He was no engineer, of course, but he found it hard to believe that the slender cables were strong enough to support the weight of the steel-framed roadway, let alone the trains that would be running across it. Tom wondered about all the weight it was supposed to hold, the horses and carriages and freight wagons and pedestrians. A team of draft horses and a loaded wagon could top seven tons. At any one time dozens of them could be driving across the span. How could they be so sure the bridge could stand that? Sometimes in winter the East River froze nearly solid, and the surging currents and massive chunks of ice mangled docks and even iron-hulled steamers. The press had speculated that a strong northeaster could carry the span away. It wouldn't be the first time a suspension bridge had collapsed from the weight of the elements. The river could be a vicious place to fight the winds that were funneled by Brooklyn Heights and the man-made canyons of Manhattan. Once a mass like that flying roadway began to twist in the wind, no cable would be strong enough to hold it.

"It's amazing, isn't it?" Sam said. Tom turned and saw Sam looking past him out at the bridge tower. It was as if Sam had read his mind. "You know, each of the main cables has three thousand five hundred fifteen *miles* of wire in it, and they're designed to have a strength of sixty thousand tons. I've read somewhere that old man Roebling designed them to be six times stronger than needed." Obvious wonder filled his voice. "Those four cables are each attached to twenty-three-ton anchors, and they're buried under a hundred twenty million pounds of stone at each end of the bridge."

Tom looked close at Sam. Enthusiasm lighted his face in a way Tom hadn't seen in a while. "Sam, sometimes you scare me. How the hell do you know that?"

"No great trick. Just got to read the papers. Over the years I've picked up about everything there is to know about that bridge." Sam motioned toward it with his beer.

"Yeah, well, I've read the papers too, but I don't remember that stuff." Tom frowned.

Sam took a sip of beer, then said, "Tom, it's probably the most spectacular thing I'll ever see built in my lifetime, that's for sure, and I just feel kind of lucky, I'd guess you'd say, to be here to see it. I want to be able to tell my grandkids someday all about how it got built . . . all the technical stuff that most folks won't remember. I tell you, Tom, what you're looking at is like science and art all rolled into one thing." Sam paused for another sip. "You know, the truly great thing is that it'll bring people together and help get them from place to place with—" He stopped for a moment, looking out at the tower as if seeking just the right words. "I don't know how to put it." He thought for an instant more, then shrugged. "Maybe a sense of . . . of wonder almost. In three months you'll be able to cross the river while the tallest ships pass under your feet. That's a gift, Tom." Braddock could tell that Sam meant that quite literally.

"And you know, it will outlast us all. It will still be here when our children's children's children are old and gray . . . just as beautiful as it is now."

Tom just stared out the window, trying to see what Sam saw so easily.

"I wish I could have made something like that," Sam said almost reverently, "something people would look at and use, and say, you know, Sam Halpern built that. That would be something." Sam took a bite of pickled egg, while Tom gave his old friend a closer look over the top of his mug. "That's a kind of immortality, if you get my meaning, leaving something behind that the world knows you by," Sam said wistfully. "I tell you, Tom, Washington Roebling is sort of a hero of mine and the closest thing to being immortal this world has to offer. By my reckoning, he's one of the greatest men of the century, right up there with Grant and Lincoln." It was clear Sam wasn't exaggerating. "I swear, I would trade places with him in two shakes if I could say I had built the Brooklyn Bridge. Shame about the old man dyin' of lock-jaw like he did. Would've been proud."

"Christ, Sam." Tom was amazed. "I knew you liked the bridge, but I never realized you felt that strong about the thing. It does have a grace about it," Tom admitted, "like a church . . . I suppose. So I guess I know how you see it. To tell the truth, though, I can't say I've been all that anxious to get to Brooklyn any faster anyhow."

Sam smiled doubtfully. "I'm not quite sure you get my point, Tommy-boy," he said with a shake of his head.

Joe Hamm pulled another beer for them both.

The clatter of the empty coroner's wagon as it bumped over the cobbled street interrupted their unusually philosophical conversation.

"Looks like Bucklin's ride's here," Sam said as he turned toward the street.

Jaffey walked in with the driver as Bob, from the corner, now joined by two others started in with the third verse of "Dixie."

> *His face was sharp as a butcher's cleaver*
> *But that did not seem to grieve her*
> *Look away! Look away! Look away! Dixie-land.*

Bob figured "Dixie" for a damn good song, a popular favorite with both sides, so he sang it with gusto.

Sam and Tom went out back with Jaffey and the wagon driver. Tom and the driver rolled the body onto the canvas stretcher that the driver had carried with him.

"Where's your partner?" Tom asked him.

"Sick. I'm on my own today. I'll need a hand with this." He shrugged a shoulder at the body, his hands in his pockets. Tom and Sam turned to look at Jaffey, who hadn't really been paying attention. He looked back at them like an empty windowpane.

"Well?" Sam asked, nodding toward the body.

"Oh! Oh, sure, let me get an end." Jaffey hurried to hoist the stretcher, and together he and the driver carried Bucklin out through the bar. When the little troupe marched through Paddy's common room with the body looking like some sort of grotesque, Fourth of July parade float, conversation trailed off and died. Even Bob and his drinking partners fell silent, one of whom was a German, singing "Look avay, Look avay, Look avay, Dixzee." Tom stopped for a moment to have a word with Joe Hamm, then followed the rest outside. A small crowd gathered to watch the body being loaded onto the wagon.

"Jaffey, I want you to go along to the coroner's office and make sure he has a look at a couple of things. For one, that stain on Bucklin's vest, see it? I need to be sure of what it is. Sam and I think it's tobacco. I also want his best guess on what crushed the back of the skull. I want to know if he had been drinking and what was in his stomach too." Tom turned to Sam. "You don't mind me sending your boy, do you?"

"Nah." Sam shrugged. "Go on an' have fun. Nothin like a good autopsy to brighten the day and improve the appetite. Makes me hungry just thinkin' about it." He grinned at Jaffey, who seemed to turn green at the mere mention of an autopsy.

"And when you're done there, get your ass back here and canvass the neighborhood for witnesses, or anybody seen anything odd. Got it?" Jaffey just nodded, as if he'd thought of that already. Then Eli jumped up on the tall hard seat of the wagon next to the driver, who, with a flick of the reins on his glue-factory team, started a slow bounce down the cobbled street.

The captain stood on the other side of Peck Slip. It was a wide street, with lots of freight wagons and other traffic as well as laborers and men with business among the docks and warehouses of the area. He didn't stand out. Leaning against a lamppost, he watched as the coroner's wagon rolled down the cobbles toward South Street. The cop on the seat beside the driver didn't interest him. He was obviously a new man . . . of no particular concern. Mainly he had wanted to get a better look at the detective. If there was anyone to worry him in this whole affair, it might be him.

Still, as the wagon went by, Thaddeus Sangree couldn't help but remember the wagons on the retreat from Gettysburg. All through the night of July 4 and on into July 5, the wagons had rolled south. Rain had come, rivers of it. That was the lowest march he ever knew. His mangled brother lay rotting in a muddy Pennsylvania grave. Lee's army was defeated, bedraggled, bleeding. All hope of final victory, lost. Ahead lay an endless vista of sacrifice and suffering. Wagons loaded with wounded wound down muddy roads, men groaning and crying with each bump and shock. The futility of Lee's gamble echoed in the night with the screams of the wounded. The captain recalled being almost grateful for the dark, which hid the worst of it. He thought when he buried Frank that he had about hit bottom, but the retreat was worse.

The captain put the wagon out of his mind with a little shiver, turning his attention to the detective and the sergeant standing in front of Paddy's. It was wise to know your enemies. It was a principle that had served him well over the years, and he wanted to see the men up close if he could. He had the feeling that the detective would be his adversary. There was no reason to believe these men would discover his mission, but logic had nothing to do with how he felt. What he felt was that he needed to look this detective in the eye, the sergeant too. He needed to take their measure.

He walked across the street, feeling as if he stood out like a Christmas tree in July. He knew there was no fear of suspicion. He was a stranger to these two, a legitimate businessman with offices just down the street. There was every reason for him to be there and nothing to hide. He quickened his step and hurried to cross in front of a freight wagon pulled by a team of huge horses. He didn't want to catch the men's attention, so he matched his pace to that of the others on the sidewalk. Keeping his head down, as if deep in thought, he strode past, nearly bumping into the detective as he went by. Beneath the wide brim of his hat, his eyes were busy, and they took in all they could see and a good bit that wasn't visible to the eye. The sergeant was harder than he looked from across the street. He saw it in his eye. The detective was no taller than himself, but wider by half, it seemed. He looked to be a powerful fellow, and had a piercing blue eye as light as a summer sky. They smelled of beer and smoke. He could have killed them then, he thought offhandedly. There was no need though. They were simply adversaries, and he had overcome so many over the years that he saw them as nothing more. To be respected, perhaps, but his instincts told him that these two would present little difficulty. They may well be capable, they might know the city, its streets and its ways, but they had no idea what they were dealing with in him. If it came to it, he and his band would snuff them like candles and not tarry to smell the smoke. Let them live for now, he figured. They could be dealt with at his leisure, should it prove necessary. The captain smiled thinly. He was supremely confident when it came to his mission. He and his men had planned it well, down to nearly the last detail. They were professionals, not the sort of bumbling street gangsters the cops were used to. They had all the advantages of training, skill, planning, and discipline. Thaddeus walked with a confident stride. They were and always would be one step ahead of the police, and that was all they'd need.

A block farther on he stopped for a moment and spoke in hushed tones to a tall man in suspenders. They parted quickly. Thaddeus didn't want to go back

❧ Chapter Three ❧

Singing my days
Singing the great achievements of the present
Singing the strong light work of engineers.

—WALT WHITMAN

Tom dodged the traffic and flagged down a hack at the corner of Peck Slip and Front Street. He gave the cabbie the address, getting a grunt in response. Tom bounced uptown, passing under the land span of the bridge. Workers were busy adding the overhead trusses—at least that's what the *World* was reporting. Braddock didn't know a truss from a train track. He could clearly hear the hammering as it echoed under the span and through the cables overhead. Looking out over the river, he realized that he was seeing the bridge in a different way. Sam sure had a passion for the thing. He hadn't said that much on any subject since Custer got himself wiped out in '76. The hack continued, past the endless lines of ships at wharves up and down the river. The masts, spars, booms, and rigging formed a graceful geometric forest along the river, reaching up toward the March sky. There were nearly as many smokestacks as spars and sails these days.

The hack made a left on Market Street. As they rode farther into the heart of the Lower East Side, Tom was suddenly reminded of a stop he needed to make. Part of his arrangement with Captain Coffin was that he'd do a little collecting from time to time. August Coffin had quite a network of "clients" who required protection from the scrutiny of the law. Tom, as an officer who owed a debt to the captain, was expected to make collections and enforce a certain discipline on "clients" as a "favor" to Coffin. It was the part of their arrangement that irked Tom from the very beginning. The stop he needed to make now was the most irksome of all, but it was on the way, and he figured he may as well get it over with.

"Make a right on Henry, driver." He got a nod in response. They went a little more than a block before Braddock said, "Stop here." Tom got out of the hack, looking up at the dirty red brick building in front of him. It gave no outward sign of what went on within. "Wait for me, driver. I'll be out in ten minutes."

"Gotta charge ya fer the time" were the cabbie's first words to him.

"Do what I tell you," Tom said flatly. "You'll get paid."

Tom went up a short flight of stairs to an unmarked door and pushed it open, revealing a long hallway that extended halfway to the back of the building. Near the back, a tall man of medium build lounged against the wall. His bowler was cocked at a jaunty angle and he chewed on a short cigar. He didn't look happy to see Braddock.

"The mistress in?" Tom asked.

"Guess she is, Braddock," the tall man said, spitting on the floor for punctuation.

"Yeah, I love you too, Quinn. Just stay out of my way and we'll get along fine."

Quinn grunted his derision, but he moved out of the way.

A door on the right opened into a sort of parlor, set up as a bar. There were maybe ten or twelve men in the room. Braddock paid them little mind. Through a beaded curtain, he could see into the next room, toward the back of the building. The laughter of young girls could be heard above the conversation in the bar. There was a man laughing too. Braddock turned to the bartender, laid a dollar on the damp mahogany, and asked for a beer. As the barkeep was pulling it, he said, "Do me a favor and tell the lady of the house I'm here."

The barkeep nodded, set the beer down, took his dollar, and walked into the next room without saying a word.

"Damn expensive beer," Tom said to his retreating back.

As he stood, facing the bar, one of the patrons got up and walked toward the door. A big slouch hat did a good job of covering the man's features. He seemed to be in a hurry. Tom watched in the mirror behind the bar, eyeing the man over the rim of his glass. Slouch-hat was almost by when Tom whirled around and caught him by the shoulder.

"In a hurry, Grafton?" Braddock asked as he swung the man around to face him. A hand came out of a coat pocket. Something flashed at Tom, but he grabbed the arm, twisting away as he did. Braddock wrenched it by him, slamming the hand into the bar. "Happy to see me, I take it. Drop the knife, you little bastard." Tom grunted. Grafton tried to wrench away, but Braddock held firm. A quick twist and Braddock forced the arm back at a painful angle, while bringing his knee up. The arm broke with a dull snap that sounded oddly like the breaking of rotted wood. It could be heard clearly across the room. Grafton's shout rang loud in the bar. The knife clattered to the floor, skittering and spinning like a roulette wheel.

"You're lucky I don't kill you for that, you little shit." Braddock growled, glaring at him. He pointed a big finger at Grafton. "I told you what I'd do if I caught you in here again." Grafton just groaned and held his arm as if it might fall off. Braddock had warned him no more than a couple of weeks ago. There was no getting around it. "I told you then that you've roughed up your last little girl, and I meant it."

"It ain't fair, dammit," Grafton whined. "Little bitch had it comin'."

"I'll tell you what's fair, Grafton. What's fair is I shoot your worthless dick off right here," Tom said with one hand on the butt of the pistol he kept tucked under his jacket. He brought it half out of the holster, his thumb on the hammer. "Ought to do it too. You got one hell of a nerve trying to stick me." Grafton's eyes above his clenched teeth shone with pure terror. "Ought to," Tom said, appearing to think about it, "but this is your lucky day. I've got other business to attend to and no time for the likes of you." The hand came away from under the jacket. "B'sides, looks like you'll be wiping your ass left-handed for a while." Braddock smirked. "Should serve as a reminder."

A sigh went out of Grafton, and Tom turned to the bar and picked up his beer.

"Here, have a beer on me, but make it your last, you get my drift?" Grafton took the mug, an astonished look on his face. Quinn watched from the doorway, as did everyone else in the bar. Silence ruled. Grafton took a sip with a trembling left hand, a bit of foam dripping down his chin. His face was turned from Braddock. Tom didn't see the hate in his eyes that rose to smother the little man's fear. Suddenly Grafton smashed the mug on the bar, lunging at Tom again with the jagged glass edge. Tom backed off and sidestepped.

"You truly are beginning to annoy me, Grafton," he said in an almost conversational tone. A swift kick to the belly doubled the man over, and a crack across the back of the head laid Grafton on the beer-soaked carpet, groaning weakly. Braddock looked over at Quinn. "If I see him in here again, Mike, it's you I'll be havin' a talk with."

Quinn just nodded and dragged Grafton out.

"Ah, the virtuous knight, the gallant defender of the weak and pure of heart," a husky woman's voice said from the other room. "Always a pleasure, Detective."

"Wish I could say the same, Kate," Tom said, turning toward the voice. "Can't say I care much for your clientele."

"His money's as green as yours, Braddock. Besides, we've been keeping an eye on him lately. Haven't had any trouble."

Tom walked into the next room, setting the beaded curtain swaying and clicking.

"What's he have to do to be unwelcome here? How long did you figure it would be before he carved up one of your little beauties?"

The madame didn't answer. Instead she handed Tom a thick envelope. "My regards to your master, Detective." The sarcastic emphasis on *master* left no doubt about how she saw Braddock in the scheme of things. "Please leave. You've disturbed my guests enough for one day."

Tom turned and walked out without a word. If it was up to him, he wouldn't be taking protection money from a woman like that. Most of the girls in her place were no older than fifteen, some were as young as ten. For the thousandth time he cursed his deal with Coffin. Tom had been dropping hints to the captain that he wanted out. This was something that had to be handled delicately, though, and needed a preamble before he broke it off. Coffin had to get used to the idea and, most of all, trust that his secrets would remain safe. One way or another, Tom had to end it.

Tom got back in the hack, and they headed farther uptown, past Canal, Hester, Grand, and Broome streets. Slowly the neighborhood changed from warehouses and businesses that catered to the sea, to warehouses of people. The tenements were thick with people, on sidewalks, on stoops, hanging from windows, looking for a breeze, shopping from pushcarts, arguing on street corners. The babble of foreign tongues, the smells of unfamiliar foods, and the Italian, German, and Yiddish signs in store windows gave the blocks he rode through an almost carnival atmosphere. It was disconcerting, confusing, noisy, dirty, smelly, colorful, boiling pandemonium. Like it or not, it was the future. He decided to get out and walk at the corner of Kenmare and Suffolk. In spite of the noise and the smells and the press of foreign flesh, there was something he liked about these streets. They had a vitality and a life like nowhere else in the city, and in his line of work it was best to soak up the street life on foot. That's what he told himself. In truth, he rather liked the mix here, always bubbling and simmering, like a camp stew after a hurried forage. Not everyone shared Braddock's views on the vitality of the Lower East Side.

Children played in the streets, running, stealing apples, selling newspapers, or idling on corners. Tom noticed two packs of boys lazing on stoops with a menacing ease as he passed. He was sure he'd be seeing some of them in a few years when they graduated to more ambitious crime. Their eyes gave them away. Tom recognized the look. He noticed that as he walked down the street a ripple preceded him. It would hardly have been noticeable to someone not accustomed to looking for it. Eyes averted, backs turned, doorways became suddenly popular. An almost imperceptible stillness settled like snow over the crowded streets. Tom imagined that it was much the same as when a big cat prowled through the jungle. The birds still chirped, the monkeys chattered, the warthogs grunted and wallowed, but they all knew the big cat was there. They kept a watchful eye, and they kept their distance. Tom rather liked that image of himself. In this tenement jungle, a big cat was not a bad thing to be. A glance over his shoulder told him of following eyes, quickly averted, and a gradual resumption of street life. It was as if he moved in a sort of bubble that flowed from his badge. Most people weren't touched by it. But to those who were, it was as if the bubble were electric. Sparks of recognition crackled.

Tom neared the front of 242 Suffolk, a five-story walk-up with a low stoop and an open front door, gaping black. Three dirty, barefoot children, about ten to twelve years old, played with a barrel hoop on the sidewalk. They laughed as one of them sent the hoop rolling across the street in front of a vegetable cart, piled high with cabbages, carrots, and potatoes. The horse, pulling the cart, plodded along, head held low, its blinders giving it a tunnel vision of the street just in front. The hoop, with the perfect timing of obvious practice, flashed before the horse's eyes and the startled animal pulled up suddenly. Potatoes went rolling down the cobbles. What seemed like a dozen little boys appeared from nowhere and like locusts grabbed up the potatoes that had rolled farthest from the cart. The thing was done as neat as could be, and the vegetables were gone before the driver could even get down from his seat. Seeing that he was clearly outnumbered, he contented himself with cursing them roundly. "Ye damned little vermin! Don't think I don't know where yer rat holes is. I'll settle with yer parents on this. Thievin' little bastards. I'll settle wi' ye. Count on it!" He switched the reins and set the sagging horse in motion, propelled by his grumbling. The boys were laughing fit to bust when they turned to see Tom looming. He stared down hard at them, putting on his best stern-cop face. Their laughter dried in their throats faster than spit on a hot stove. Jaws fell open together as if on cue. Tom figured that was about the funniest thing he'd seen in a week of Sundays, and couldn't hide the grin that stole across his face. He tried to hold back the laughing but the pit-of-doom looks from the three street Arabs made him bust. The boys joined in when they saw that they weren't going to be thrown in irons. The other boys looked on from a safe distance. Laughing cops were a rarity in this neighborhood.

"So, which of you bright young lads can tell me where Mr. Bucklin lives?" Tom said when he caught his breath.

"Right 'ere in this buildin' 'ere, sir," piped up the biggest of the three.

"And whereabouts in this 'ere buildin' might he be found, lad?"

" 'Tis the third floor ye'll find 'im, second door back o' the stairs."

"Thank you, lads," Tom said as he handed them each a penny. "Go easy on the potatoes, now."

They all grinned like co-conspirators and the boys chorused, "Oh, yes, sir," and "We will, sir." Tom trudged up the slippery unlit stairway. He was glad for the lack of light; he didn't really want to see what made the stairs so slimy, though his nose gave him a clue. Too many chamber pots coming down the dark stairs on the way to the outhouses. Tom could hear the boys arguing out on the stoop, their words echoing up the stairwell. He had a sudden image of his younger brother, gone now so many years ago. It was like a flash of light in the darkened stairs and was gone almost as soon as it came.

"I don' know why you two should have the pennies, I'm the one what gave 'im Mike's rooms," said one.

"You ain't gettin' my warm spit" came the quick reply. "I'm the one rolled the hoop out in front of McGee's wagon."

"Yeah" came a littler voice. "An' who came up wi' the idea? Besides, that's me family's rooms. He's here about me da, I'll bet." That last even sounded like his brother's voice. Tom hesitated, a sudden sadness taking hold in the dark stairway. He stopped for only a heartbeat, then continued up the stinking stairs, thinking of their shoeless feet.

The heat seemed to weigh on him and press him back with every step. But the heat was only part of it. The smell of such concentrated humanity hit him in the gut, taking the wind out of him. Suddenly breathing didn't seem all that important. Breathing through his mouth was a little better, except he could almost taste the place. It smelled like a five-story outhouse, or worse, because the smells of cooking were mixed in with the rest. And then there was a hard-to-define smell of sickness and disease, and more than one deep, wracking cough echoed down the dark hallways. It was altogether a hellish place. The thought of living there turned Tom's stomach. But the place was full of people, even at this time of day, when men were usually out to work. He could hear the laughter of women and children, a song of the Old Country, in a voice cracked with age, and a loud, strident argument from somewhere above. Coming to a landing between the second and third floors, he passed a pair of men smoking their pipes, lounging on the stairs. They gave way grudgingly.

Tom knocked on the second door back of the stairs. He heard the faint sound of deep, fluid hacking from somewhere inside. He knocked again and was answered with a woman's voice, calling:

"Keep yer britches on, I'll be there in two shakes."

The door opened and Tom asked, "Mrs. Bucklin?"

"Ey, and who wants to know?"

"I'm Detective Braddock, ma'am."

"Have ye found my Terry that soon then? I only put in the report this mornin' down at the station house. They said it might take days, or weeks even. Didn't seem to give a damn if he was missin' or not, ye ask me." Tom watched her as she said this. She was much too old to be Terrence's wife, he thought. She must be all of fifty-eight or so but looked ten years older. Her hair was combed but oily gray. Her face showed the wear of a hard life with deep creases carved into the soft flesh. She had probably been pretty once; she had the eyes of a doe still, if you took the time to notice. Her clothes were neat, but old and frayed at the hem. Freckles and age spots blotched her parchment-thin skin.

"You're Mrs. Bucklin then?"

"I'm his mother. Is Terry in some sort of trouble? He's never been one to get on the wrong side of the law. It's a good boy, my Terry is."

"Ma'am, could I come in for a moment? I'm afraid there's been some trouble."

"Oh, bless me, sure, come in. Here you're tryin' to help me and I'm leavin' ye out in the hall."

"Who is it, Patricia?" came a voice from the back of the room. Tom could see there was a corner that was separated from the rest by a sheet draped over a line. The voice seemed to come from there.

"It's a detective named Braddock, here about Terry, it's all right," she said with a look at Tom.

"Have they found him, then?" the voice behind the sheet asked. "It's not like Terry to be out for days like this, nor miss a meal either."

"Don't worry yer head, Pa, ye'll start a fit again, an' yer weak as a kitten as it is. So . . ." she said, turning to Tom. "What's the trouble? Did he run afoul of some of them Protestant hooligans over on Hester? I've told him to keep well clear o' there. Never had any trouble before."

"No, ma'am, I'm sorry to tell you, Terrence is dead."

A low choking moan from behind the sheet curtain broke through the mist of Tom's words. Patricia Bucklin put her hands up to the sides of her head as if to block the words from her ears. Her hands were clenched, her knuckles white. She turned and wandered back to a chair, all the while holding her head, and with a soft moan she slid into it.

"Me boy, me boy, me boy." She sobbed, rocking back and forth, the chair creaking in time. Slowly Mrs. Bucklin let her hands drop to her lap, where they worked her apron into a ball. She hardly made a sound as her shoulders shook silently.

A watery groan from behind the sheet took on a bubbling quality, and a wracking, desperate coughing started. Tom knew that cough for the consumption. He had heard it often enough. From the sound of it, Mr. Bucklin didn't have many coughs left in him. Tom heard him spit up with a final effort. Mrs. Bucklin didn't seem to notice. She wilted into the old chair as if the life was draining out of her.

Tom stood silent, and at last Mrs. Bucklin said, "So was there an accident at the bridge? Been too many men come to grief on that damned job. I've told Terry to be careful, but after Julia and the baby died I don't think he cared anymore."

"No, ma'am, it wasn't an accident. We strongly suspect foul play."

"Jesus, Mary, and Joseph!" Patricia came out of the chair like she'd been scalded. "Waddaya mean, foul play? Terry never had an enemy in the world!" Before Tom had a chance to answer, she raged on, her words rushing all in a flood. "Always seen the good in people," she said, pacing around the small room. "Folks liked Terry, an' they was sorry for his troubles, what with Julia and the baby gone to the angels. What kind of bloody monster would do such a thing?" she demanded, waving her arms at Braddock. "Do you have him, this murderin' bastard?"

Tom took a deep breath. "Ma'am, we don't know much, just that your son was found in an alley, back of Paddy's saloon, on Peck Slip. It appears he was hit from behind. The blow . . . was strong enough to be fatal. There weren't any witnesses that we know of, but we're investigating, and we hope to have a break in the case soon." Braddock felt the urge to give them some hope, however slim. "I need to know more about Terrence, and I was hoping you could help me. Did he have any enemies or owe any money, that sort of thing?"

As Tom said this, the sheet curtain was parted by a frail hand, pushing it slowly to one side. Mr. Bucklin rose from his bed. Tom could see the effort etched on his face though he tried to hide it. He looked like the life had been drained out of him. He was gray as a corpse. His clothes hung loose on his wasted frame. He shuffled slowly toward his wife, who silently moved to meet him in the middle of the room. They held on to each other in their grief, drawing what strength they could one from the other. The yellow afternoon light filtering through the dirty window framed them in a sort of halo. As Tom watched, it almost seemed as if the light was coming from them, shining out from their essential selves, the spiritual beings they really were. It seemed to Tom that he saw them in a younger time, before the age and the work, the troubles and the deaths brought them to this place. They were shining and luminous, tight-skinned . . . vibrant. The years had not touched them nor worn away their beauty. It was a vision as unexpected as it was fleeting. Tom blinked, and it was gone, leaving the old couple in its wake. But Braddock knew what he had seen. He wasn't one to doubt, or sneer, or pass it off as a trick of the light.

They clung together like that for long minutes and Tom looked away. He noticed a tintype of a soldier on the dresser; his serious face, young and earnest, looked stiffly at the camera. It was Terrence. The markings on his uniform were those of the Sixty-ninth Regiment. Tom knew the Sixty-ninth and had admired their spirit on many fields. The great green flag they carried, the symbol of the country they left behind, always flew at the front. Many were the times when he had watched the Second Corps go by, with the Irish Brigade in ranks. He realized he must have seen Terence among those ranks years ago. He had a new respect for the man. Tom looked closer at the picture, noticing the new Springfield musket, its barrel polished, bayonet fixed. Tom thought he saw the look that he had seen in his own mirror long ago. He felt a certain kinship with the man in the tintype, a bond and an obligation. Tom took his obligations seriously.

Patricia and Eamon Bucklin sat in their tiny kitchen and, over the next hour or so, told Tom Braddock the story of their lives in America. They had come to New York when the "bloody-handed British" raised the taxes on their land and the rent on their house.

"Eamon's family," Patricia had said, "worked that land for near one hundred twenty years, and they threw us off like so much boot scrapin's."

"The children screaming hungry, an' the bastards drive us out our own home. The shame of it is they had Irish constables to back 'em up," Eamon said, shaking his gray head. They had borrowed money from relatives, sold what possessions they could, and took ship for New York. Their oldest, a girl named Shannon, had taken sick on the voyage. By the time they reached New York and went through Castle Garden, she was so weak she could barely stand.

"She had the look o' sickness about her, so they quarantined her and there she died. Had to bury me darlin' in Potter's Field 'cause there wasn't a penny to be had for a proper burial," Patricia said softly, opening an old wound. "Swore some day we'd bury her proper," she whispered.

In spite of their tragic start, Eamon had managed to find work and things got better.

"Always been good wi' me hands," Eamon had wheezed from the edge of his bed. He had found work at a cooperage on Canal Street. He made foreman and earned enough for them to live on with an occasional luxury. They had found two airy rooms on Spring Street, with morning sun pouring in the high windows and a bathroom they shared with only one other family. Life was good. They put away the troubles of the past.

Patricia made tea for Tom and Eamon on a tiny cast-iron stove. She wept silently as she stood with her back to them, her shoulders shaking. Tom heard the hiss of a tear as it sizzled on the hot iron. He pretended to study Terrence's picture. Looking around the room, he noticed that what little furniture they had was of mahogany, and the fabrics were fine—not like the stuff he usually saw in the tenements. She turned with the teakettle in her left hand and dabbed at her red eyes with the corner of her apron. "Terry used to love his tea," she said.

They told him of how, just short of Terry's seventeenth birthday, the troubles started at Fort Sumter.

"Terry was always one to do his duty. Brought him up to see the right of things and do what was expected of a man. Didn't know about seceding from the Union, or the legal mumbo jumbo about the territories, or Kansas and Nebraska or any such." Eamon paused for a moment, then, drawing a long watery breath, continued, "Never knew a black man in his life, but he knew that slavin's a curse on the land. He could see what the slavery was doin' to this country."

"We were never prouder of him than when he joined the Sixty-ninth," Patricia added, her head held high.

"We went over to Broadway to watch him march off with the regiment. What a day that was: the flags, an' the crowds, an' the bands. I cried to see him go, but I could've burst with the pride I had in him for goin'."

They told him of the war years, and Terry's letters home, and the tintype he had sent them. He had been in many famous battles, they assured him, coming through it all with barely a couple of scratches. Lots of his mates in the regiment left whole parts of themselves on those battlefields or didn't come home at all. When he was released from the service in '64, he came home, grown and different, but still the son they loved. He met "his Julia" at a social at the Hibernians hall, and they married in the spring of '69.

Tom sat patiently through their ramble in the past. He sensed they needed to tell their lives and make some sense of what had happened to them. He could feel their urgency to explain how they had come to this place. It was plain from the furniture, their clothes, and the way the rooms were kept that this was not where they belonged. They were hardworking people, but work alone had not been enough. Here, near the end of their hopes, they wanted it to make sense. Tom understood that well enough. He wished that life always made sense. Most times it was hard to tell. He sipped his tea and listened.

It was just after he took Julia Tompkins as his bride that Terry got work on the bridge to Brooklyn. He labored at laying up the three-ton blocks of cut stone that were to become the Brooklyn tower. Terry worked on that tower for five years, Pat had told him proudly. The family prospered, with Eamon and Terry bringing in good wages. They bought a small row house on East Third Street together, and in '71 Julia had given birth to Mary Elizabeth.

"She was the light o' his life, that little girl. You should have seen him, Detective."

"Tom . . . call me Tom," Braddock said, Terrence's tintype cradled in his lap.

"Tom. He and Julia would take her for walks just to show her off. She was a sweet one too, with beautiful eyes and a lovin' manner. We were happy then . . ." Patricia's voice trailed off.

Mikey came in '73. "He was a fine strappin' boy with a good set o' lungs and a strong hand," as Eamon had put it. Terry finished work on the Brooklyn tower that year and then started work on the approach on the Brooklyn side. He wanted to work in the New York caisson for the extra pay that was in it, but Patricia and Eamon and especially Julia had talked him out of it. If the caisson disease got him, like it got so many, there was no amount of pay that was worth it, they told him.

"Heard o' too many men crippled or dead with that caisson disease. I told Terry he had a family to think about and that was that."

Things were good till '78, when Eamon started coughing. The consumption worked fast. In six months he was let go from his job. The coughing became so bad that he couldn't hide it anymore. The bosses were afraid he'd infect the lot of them.

"Thought it was just a cold at first, but after two whole months o' coughin' I knew it was more. Doctors, remedies, laudanum, I tried it all. Just kept coughin'. Doctors told me to go upstate to Saranac Lake, wherever the hell that is, for the cure o' the good air." Eamon coughed once and spit in his bucket. "I couldn't afford to move across the street. Here's where I'll die, I guess."

Patricia looked away out the lone window and after a while she said, "Little Mikey and Mary Elizabeth were a comfort to us then. We could see the future growin', an' we had the hope that comes with children." Things were hard, with only one salary coming in, but they made ends meet and held onto the house, till the fire. It started in a house three doors down. A chimney fire got out of control. Before that February night was over, half the block was gone, and their house with it.

"At least we managed to save most o' the furniture 'fore the fire took the house. There we were with our parlor chairs, an' beds, clothes, an' pots an' pans, sittin' in the black snow. Nothin' left but a pile o' smoke."

Tom had heard footsteps, running up the hall. Mikey came into the room, slamming back the door on its hinges. He held up two potatoes and crowed, "Look what I found!" He winked at Tom, who winked back with a grin, recognizing the youngest boy from the front stoop. "Can we mash them tonight with butter, Grandma? I love them with butter."

"We'll see, Mikey. Thank you. There's a good lad. What a fine big boy ye are. Come here for a bit an' give yer old grandma a hug. Haven't had a hug since yesterday, an' Grandmas need hugs, ye know, to keep us young." Mike walked over to her a bit slow it seemed. With too much hugging a boy could lose his dignity. Patricia held him tight for a very long time. He didn't seem to mind.

Turning to Tom, he asked, "Did you find me da? When's he coming home, sir?"

Tom had started to speak, but looking over Mike's head he saw Mrs. Bucklin shaking her head, so he said, "That's what I'm here to talk to your grandma and grandpa about, Mike." He searched for something else to say to him without telling him more. He finally said, "I'm here to help, son. My name's Tom. I'm a detective."

"Do you have a gun?" Mike asked, brightening.

"Well . . . yes, Mike, I do," Tom answered, a little surprised.

"Could I see it?" Tom looked over at Mrs. Bucklin, who nodded. He pulled back his jacket to show Mike the Colt .38 in its holster hung on his shoulder.

"Wow, I don't suppose I could hold it, could I?" Mike asked, the longing clear in his voice.

Tom let his jacket slide back. "Sorry, Mike, maybe when you get older."

"I'm big for my age, everyone says so," Mike said, clearly fighting a losing battle.

"Big isn't what's up here," Tom said, tapping his chest. "It's what's in here." A finger tapped his temple. "You get my meaning?"

"I think so, sir. It's like when Tommy Gallagher stuck some hard candies in the back o' his pants down at Lasher's store, and Danny the cop standin' right behind him. Tommy's a year older than me, ye understand." They all laughed, even Eamon, whose laugh sounded like drowning.

"That's right, Mikey. Always use your head, and you'll go far, lad."

"I will, sir," Mike said over his shoulder as he went out the door, slamming it hard behind him. From down the hall they heard him call "I'm out with Mouse and Smokes, Grandma, I won't go far."

"All right, then, Mike. Be home for supper, lad."

"Thank you for not tellin' him, Detective, I mean Tom. He's had it hard with his mom and sis gone not a year yet." Her eyes welled up and Eamon held his head like it might come off in his hands. Tom couldn't remember when he had heard of so much trouble and sorrow in one family. It was like something out of a penny awful. His mother had been addicted to those things; the house had been cluttered with them. The heroes had scores of calamities to overcome, which they always did in the next installment. But it didn't look as if there was a next installment for the Bucklins.

They had been quiet for some time, when Patricia said, "The typhoid took them, you know." They had moved to the tenement not yet two years ago, and hadn't been there for more than eight months before the sickness started galloping through the building, the neighborhood too. It carried off Julia and Mary Elizabeth within a day of each other, and they were buried together in a cemetery in Brooklyn. "A big part of my Terry was buried there in Brooklyn." Patricia took a long shivering breath, then sighed. It seemed to well up right from her feet. "There's some comfort in knowin' that they'll be together there. There's that . . . at least."

"Ma'am, I want to find the person who killed your son. There must be something you can tell me that might be of some use in finding Terry's killer: a quarrel, some debts, maybe, or trouble at work. People don't get killed for nothing. Murder's a serious business. There must have been some serious reasons to kill your son."

Patricia and Eamon gave Tom the few names they knew of the men who their son worked with as well as those of his friends from outside of work—from church mostly. The list wasn't long but included some of the same names he'd gotten from Joe Hamm.

"Tom, our Terry was a good man. He worked hard, loved his family, went to church on Sundays, and confession. We've had some hard times, but he never gave in to bitterness, never let us down. He was our rock," Patricia said, turning to Eamon for confirmation. Eamon just nodded. "He's been drinking a bit more lately, but who could blame him? Sure I wouldn't keep him from that small comfort after all his troubles."

"Told me there was somethin' not right about the bridge," Eamon said suddenly.

Tom and Patricia turned together to stare at Eamon, who took another shallow breath.

"Didn't tell me much really, not in words anyway. But I could see he was worried about somethin'. Said there was somethin' not right about the job; that maybe there was some fellas up to no good. Probably just some strike talk or some such. Didn't think much more about it, and he didn't say any more, so I let it lay."

"He didn't mention any names, did he?"

"Not a one. Lots of men on that job. Could have been anyone, or maybe a bunch o' fellas. Just don't know for sure."

A bit later, after some more fruitless probing, Tom got up to leave. "Oh, I almost forgot," he said. "This key look familiar to you?"

He held out the key he'd found in Terrence's pocket. It turned out it was their front door key, and Patricia put it in the lock and turned the bolt to be sure. With a sigh, Tom told them where they would have to go to make a formal identification and claim Terrence's effects. He thanked Patricia for the tea and their help.

She came with him to the door and stepped out into the hall. "Could I have a word with you, Tom?" She hesitated as if deciding something just then. "You see, we've got nobody now except Mike, and with Eamon so close to gone, I don't know what'll become of us. It's Mikey I'm worried about."

"What about Julia's parents?"

"Gone, and Julia was their only living child. It's just that I want to be sure that Mikey is taken care of if anything . . . happens, you know."

Tom looked down into the pretty doe eyes in Patricia's worn face. She was close to the end of her rope. The need was written large across her features. After taking his card from his vest pocket, he gave it to her, saying "You can reach me here if you need me." Tom didn't know what to promise, or if he should promise anything at all, so he said simply, "I'll do what I can. I'm sorry for all your troubles, ma'am . . . and your loss."

Tom stepped out of the front door onto Suffolk Street. The street was still crowded, but there was the smell of a thunderstorm in the air, and a glance at the sky showed him dark clouds piling up to the west, over New Jersey. He hurried down to Delancey Street, where he could catch a horsecar. He didn't want to get caught in the storm. Half a block behind, a tall man in suspenders lounged against a lamppost watching with casual interest as Tom hopped on the trolley. He made no move to follow.

Mike watched Braddock go too. He was worried but when he was with the other kids he wouldn't show it. Mike Bucklin wasn't the biggest or the oldest in his gang, but he had a knack for petty thievery that kept them all pretty well fed. With his gramps laid up with the consumption, and the family having to make do on just what his da brought home, he felt he had to bring something home too. Sometimes he felt guilty about eating an apple he had lifted, thinking that his gramps could use it more than he. But his mates in the little gang were pretty much all in the same boat, just getting by, and hungry half the time, so he shared as best he could. Smokes and Mouse were Mike's two best friends, and they, together with Louie, Vince, and Jo-Jo, were the center of society for him. Suffolk Street, between Houston and Delancey, was their world. Lots of times they would venture over to Essex, or Orchard, but they had to watch it when they were outside their own territory. Almost every block had its gangs, starting with kids of seven, or eight. Usually the older kids had their own gangs, and they didn't bother the younger ones too much, because they had bigger fish to fry. They had to watch out for rival groups of their own age, though, and getting caught thieving on the wrong block could earn a kid a beating or worse. His gang defended its territory the same as every other. There were regular battles to claim another corner or another block. Sometimes even a streetlamp or a store would be fought over. These were things Mike had been learning fast since he came to the Lower East Side. It was a confusing place to be a kid, what with all the rules. He had taken a couple of beatings before he had caught on and joined in with a bunch of other boys like him. Mainly they tried to have fun, but they spent plenty of time in petty crime too. Stealing produce was the first thing they all did as sort of an initiation, but they graduated quickly to more ambitious stuff, like lifting goods from an unattended wagon or even picking pockets. Mostly they were just boys with plenty of time on their hands. They laughed, kicked balls, and swam in the river like any kids, and they tried to survive, which was only human.

Lately Mike's da had been real worried about something. He said it was a problem on the job. His father told him so he could know to look out for bad men. His da said he couldn't be certain but that there might be some come around one day. He hadn't seen any so far. He kept looking, though, because if his da said there were some that might come around, then you could count on it being so. His da was the finest man in all the Lower East Side. Mike would wait on the corner of Suffolk and Delancey every evening for him to come home. If the other boys weren't nearby, he'd run to him when he saw his da coming, and sometimes he'd have an orange in his pocket. He waited now, on the corner, hoping to get a glimpse of his father. It was three days now since he'd been home. Grandma had said he was just away to visit a cousin in New Jersey, but Mike was starting to worry. He couldn't remember having a cousin in New Jersey.

Braddock sat slumped on the downtown horsecar. Listening to the Bucklin's string of tragedies had worn him down more than he would have imagined. After years of walking beats in neighborhoods like theirs, the people and their tragedies tended to become a faceless blur. Tom figured it was the way cops kept from feeling the pain too much. Almost every cop he knew put up the same shields to keep out the human cost of their job. For reasons he wasn't even sure of himself, he'd let those shields down with the Bucklins. Maybe it was Terrence's tintype, and his having served with the Sixty-ninth. Maybe it was Mikey, or the fact that his grandfather was so sick. It was probably all those things and maybe some he hadn't put a finger on just yet. Whatever the cause, he felt washed out, drained . . . tired. He could only imagine how the Bucklins felt.

The horsecar made a stop and he gave up his seat to a woman in a wide bonnet. She sniffed at him with a haughty upturned nose, asserting her rights to his place. Cops could ride the horsecars free, but weren't supposed to take seats from paying passengers. He got up and stood at the back, one hand gripping the pole supporting the roof. He toted up the things he knew about Terrence Bucklin as the city slowly rolled by. The only angle that seemed at all promising was his father's story about something not being right about the bridge. That was the obvious place to start. Between that bit of information and his deduction that Terrence knew his killer, it was plain he needed to make Terrence's coworkers on the bridge his primary focus. He wondered idly just how many there were. Hundreds probably. He'd have to start narrowing that list down some if he was going to get anywhere. He had a feeling that before this was over, he'd know almost as much about the bridge as Sam, if that was possible. He smiled grimly to himself at the notion.

Tom's thoughts turned to the Terrence Bucklin he'd seen in the tintype and the corpse he'd seen in the alley.

"Somebody's gonna have to *pay* for that," he said to himself none too softly. A passenger near him took a half step back. It wasn't wise to be too near a lunatic on a horsecar.

❊ Chapter Four ❊

The work which is likely to be our most durable
monument, and to convey some knowledge of us to
the remotest posterity, is a work of bare utility; not a
shrine, not a fortress, not a palace, but a bridge.

—MONTGOMERY SCHUYLER

Brooklyn Heights was quiet this afternoon. It was always quiet. Home to some of the most prominent citizens of both Brooklyn and Manhattan, the Heights represented the very best of suburban living. Solid middle- and upper-class residences marched down dappled, tree-lined streets in sober respectability. Cobbles echoed with the occasional carriage. Children played. Strollers enjoyed the pleasant breezes. Across the river all was push and shove and no apology. The financial center bustled, the docks swarmed, the hungry begged. Here on Brooklyn Heights, where the famous Henry Ward Beecher intoned from his pulpit every Sunday, all was serenity.

That was one of the things that had drawn Emily and Washington Roebling to the place, that and the view. The view was critical. Nowhere else in either city commanded such a view of the East River. From Staten Island to the south, New Jersey to the east, and Harlem to the north, the panorama of the city and its harbor was spread out before the Heights. Most important of all was the view of the Brooklyn Bridge. Emily and Washington had needed a special house, one with an unobstructed view of the bridge, where quiet was the order of the day. As chief engineer, Washington needed both. Since being disabled with caisson disease years before, he had never again visited the construction site. Instead, he watched from the window of 110 Columbia Heights. It was the last house on the street, closest to the bridge, and both peaceful and ideally situated for the Roeblings' purposes. Perhaps best was the fact that it was only a ten-minute carriage ride to the site, a ride that Emily took two or three times a day. She was her husband's eyes and ears at the bridge. She was his mouthpiece, secretary, plan reader, negotiator, mediator, assistant engineer, technical advisor, and political representative. As far as most of the engineers and assistants, foremen and workers were concerned, she *was* the chief engineer.

Emily threw on a light coat before going out this quiet afternoon. Her husband seemed vaguely put out that she was leaving.

"Do you have to go this afternoon, Em?"

"You know I do, Wash," she said, ignoring his tone. She knew as well as he that there was no good reason for her not to go. They had all the important work done for the day. "You said yourself you'd need that book in the next day or so. I may as well get it now, because I certainly won't have time tomorrow."

"I suppose you're right. It's easier to go to the Astor Library than to get it from Rensselaer Polytechnic; that's the only other place I know of that has it."

"It's just so frustrating," Emily said, clicking her tongue. "A city the size of New York needs a real public library, not just one, but dozens. I'm afraid that until the ponderous Mayor Edson gets his ponderous—"

"Be kind, dear," Wash admonished.

Emily smiled. "—personage before the city council and fights for it, we won't have it. As for Brooklyn, that could take decades."

"It's a worthy cause, Em. Knowledge is the key to a better life." Nobody knew that better than Roebling, whose father had set a rigid Germanic example of devotion to higher learning and hard work.

"Unfortunately, I don't think Tammany Hall is too interested in libraries unless there's something in it for them. Look at the Tweed courthouse; thirteen million dollars! The whole bridge won't cost that much. Plenty of scoundrels got rich off that project. Tweed was just the tip of the iceberg," Washington said bitterly.

"Dear, there's no point getting upset about it. You'll just start one of your terrible headaches."

"You're right, as usual," Wash conceded. "It's just that when I think of how Tweed almost sank the bridge too, it makes me sick to my stomach."

"Those days, nothing got done without Tweed's hand in it, at least not in New York," Emily said, remembering how hard it had been to understand at the time. "Henry brought him in only because he had to." There had been no other way.

"It's true," Wash admitted. "The bond issue would never have gotten out of committee. It still burns me that Bill had to take a ferry across the river with a bag full of money to pay off the aldermen." Wash almost spat at the recollection.

Emily, who was in some ways more practical, just smiled, saying, "Not a bad investment really. It paid big dividends for Bill Kingsley over the years. Sixty thousand dollars is a lot of money by any standard, but it's been a good deal all around." It was far more than a "good deal," as they both knew. As general contractor, Kingsley had made a fortune on the bridge.

Wash grunted. "And for Tweed too, for a while. Sitting on our executive committee like a three-hundred-pound leech, looking to suck the bridge dry." Roebling shook his head scornfully.

"Well, he's gone now, and good riddance," Emily said for both of them.

"Seconded, my dear!" he said with a small laugh. "By the way, you know, I've still got correspondence to get out to Martin and Hildenbrand about the specs for the supports on the train tracks, the placement of the light stanchions, and half a dozen other things."

Emily looked at her husband with more than a little exasperation. "Wash, the bridge is almost done. It's two-thirty in the afternoon. I think you can spare my help till later." Emily rarely denied her husband anything. After all the years of work, she had only the slightest regret at denying him now. "Surely it can wait, darling, and if I tarry another second, I'll be late for my meeting with Mr. Saunders, the librarian." She came to him, her skirts rustling like a spring breeze through the treetops. She kissed him lightly on the forehead. "I won't be late, and don't worry, we'll do our correspondence first thing in the morning." She gave her husband a disarming smile. "I'll deliver it myself."

Wash smiled up at her from his seat at his desk. "As usual, my dear, you are very persuasive. I probably won't be up when you get back. It's been a long day. I may play a bit though. Could you tell Martha on your way out to start a hot bath for me in about fifteen minutes?"

Emily stopped in the kitchen to tell Martha to start a bath. She closed the solid mahogany door behind her with a thud and click as the heavy brass latch sprang into place. Just as she stepped up into their carriage, she heard the gentle sounds of Wash's violin. He had started playing again recently. Though his playing was hesitant, it was good to hear. He had been considered a very good violinist years ago, but the violin had sat in a corner of their parlor, silent since '72. Nearly eleven years, Emily mused. She had imagined more than once that it sang to him from its resting place. She knew it had pained him not to be able to play due to his illness. Every so often, he'd oil the wood, caressing the curves with longing. He'd always lay it back in its case with a cradling hand.

It warmed her to hear the violin again. He was getting better. She knew it. As surely as the caisson disease had first crippled her husband, it was the weight of his responsibility as chief engineer that heightened his illness and prolonged his recovery. Washington still worked just as hard on almost every detail of the construction, though the bridge was almost done. The immense hurdles of engineering, politics, corruption, tragedy, fraud, and near disaster were history now. As the weight of the bridge was lifted by the cables he had designed, so was the weight of responsibility suspended. He was getting better. Emily smiled to herself as the carriage pulled away, down Columbia Heights. The sounds of her husband's violin followed her, growing fainter and softer, till she had to strain to hear it over the sound of the horse's hooves on the cobbles. Then it was gone.

The carriage stopped after a few minutes, at the new Fulton Ferry Terminal, which stood almost at the base of the Brooklyn tower of the bridge. There were five different ferry lines, with service from South Street, Fulton Street, Wall Street, Catherine Street, and Roosevelt Street, all operated by the Union Ferry Company. Fulton was the busiest. Thirteen ferries chugged back and forth across the East River night and day. They were not small boats: 150 to 170 feet long, they could accommodate hundreds of passengers at a time, along with carriages and wagons, yet they were still not enough to keep up with the traffic. Why the ferry company had invested in a new terminal right in the shadow of the bridge, Emily couldn't understand. Maybe they knew something the rest of the city didn't. Building a new terminal, with a big bronze statue of Robert Fulton over the entrance surely didn't look like a good investment. She watched as the ferryboat *Winona* pulled into the dock and offloaded the early commuters, heading home from their jobs in Manhattan. Soon they'd be able to walk across the East River. She herself had done that just over a year ago.

All the suspending cables had been strung by then and the steel beams that were to support the roadway had been attached to them so it looked like a big ladder sailing across the river. A five-foot-wide plank walkway had been laid down for the workers to use during construction. It had been arranged that she and the mayors of Brooklyn and New York as well as the trustees of the bridge and a few others would take a ceremonial walk across the river. It was a great honor, of course. Although there had been many unofficial crossings of the bridge once the footbridge had been hung, she was to be the first woman officially to cross the span.

The footbridge, by contrast, had been quite a tourist attraction. It had been suspended before there were any beams, or roadway, following the same arc as the cables it was hung from. It was designed to provide the riggers with access to the various platforms, where they did the work of attaching the suspenders and beams. She knew it well, having relayed the instructions for its construction from her husband to Martin and Hildenbrand. It had been much higher than the roadway. Charles C. Martin, the second in command to Roebling, crossed on Washington's birthday 1877 along with his daughters. It made all the papers. "Beauty and the Bridge" was the headline. Emily thought that Martin was mad for taking his daughters out on the thing. She had seen men trembling and ashen after going out on it, their hands raw from gripping the rope handrails. The public was not really restricted from crossing, though, and Emily recalled Martin saying afterward that he spent nearly all morning most days just issuing passes to those who wanted to take the death-defying walk.

It had been a beautiful early December day when she had taken her ceremonial stroll. She had met E. F. Farrington, the master mechanic for the bridge, by the Brooklyn tower. She still remembered their dizzying climb up the spiral staircase. It was attached to the tower and ran clear to the top. They ascended to the level of the roadway, exhilarated and out of breath. In a few minutes Mayor Howell of Brooklyn, the new mayor of New York, William Grace, and a delegation of the bridge trustees joined them. There was much hand-shaking and congratulating, but that wasn't what Emily remembered best.

When she looked back on it now, she thought mostly of seagulls. They wheeled, dipped, dove, and sailed over the blue-green, white-capped water, their shrill cries punctuating their conversation. They were everywhere, soaring above the towers and scudding down below her feet. Their snowy, knife-edge wings danced on the wind. They rowed the air with effortless strokes. Emily almost felt she was a bird herself. The wind hummed through the cables. She could actually see them vibrate, and the low hum they made was the music of the bridge. The cries of the seagulls were its chorus. The city stretched out before her, from the Battery to Harlem. She could see the Hudson, to the west, and Bedloe's Island, waiting for the Statue of Liberty. Ferries passed under the bridge, their tall stacks belching black. Sailing vessels of every description plied the choppy waters, their sails painfully white and close-hauled against the wind. It was magnificent. For someone who had never been higher than a five-story building, it was a revelation.

She was giddy, and not a little frightened. There seemed to be cavernous gaps between the steel beams under the walkway. Emily had felt that each crack between the boards yawned wide enough to fall through. The boards creaked, the rope handrails blew with the wind. The cables sang. The gulls called, raucous and plaintive. When they reached the center of the span, they stopped to watch a clipper ship. It passed beneath them, tall masts looking like they'd catch on the roadway. Emily looked down, bending over one of the main cables as the ship slipped silently by. Sailors waved up to her, and she waved back. She could almost reach out and touch them in the rigging. Forgetting herself for a moment, she bent farther over the big cable and let her feet leave the boardwalk. She recalled Mayor Howell and Farrington looking at her with a mixture of amusement and wonder. Emily hadn't cared. She regained her ladylike composure, but the look of rapture never left her face. She looked back toward Brooklyn Heights, seeking out the window in her brownstone. Wash had been there, watching. She knew he saw her with the telescope by the window. She turned full toward the house. Straight and tall she'd stood, her hair blowing, the wind tugging at her dress. Emily remembered standing still for a long moment, oblivious to all around her. She stared at his window and sent herself over the water to him on that blustery December day, willing her thoughts across the space between them.

"Now I see, my darling. Now I see!"

Thinking about it now, as she waited for the Fulton Ferry, she remembered it as one of the most profound experiences of her life. She recalled it with a clarity she had never known before, as if the experience were somehow etched in her brain, never to grow fuzzy with time. Emily remembered feeling as if she were alone: just her and Wash. She wanted him to know that she never really saw the bridge until that moment, never fully understood how magnificent a vision it was. From the start, before a stone was laid or a cable strung, it had lived within him, fully formed. Only then, standing on the windswept walkway in the center of the span, did she know what he had always seen. She marveled at it. Emily was experiencing what Washington had only imagined. She was in her husband's dream, living the vision. She willed herself back to him. The seagulls soared and sang.

Emily was shaken out of her reverie by the crunch and creak of the ferry grinding into the dock on the New York side. The wood squealed and groaned as the captain gunned the engines to bring the *Winona* fully into the dock. The round bow of the boat slid across the tarred oak planks. Emily settled back into the velvet of the carriage's interior and returned to that December day. They had drunk champagne. It was chilled and waiting for them on the New York side. They drank to the bridge, to Wash, and to a number of other things she couldn't recall. At the last, it was Farrington who said simply, "Gentlemen, I give you Emily Roebling."

Emily could still recall Bill Kingsley, the general contractor, raising his champagne flute and saying, "A very great lady, indeed."

It had been taken up by all of them. Some even toasted her twice. She had blushed under their compliments but in her heart she knew she deserved them.

Later Farrington told her, "Ma'am, I'm not a great speechmaker, as you well know. I could have talked a lot more and said a lot less, if you take my meaning. All of us here know what you've done and what you've meant to this project. We're in your debt, ma'am. I can't say it plainer."

She had rushed home to Wash after. He had been waiting in his study.

"I watched you, Em," he had said slowly. She remembered trying to tell him what it was like for her, how it was nothing like she had come to expect. She didn't remember how she had tried to explain her feelings, only that her words were inadequate. Emily had a dreamy recollection of the late-afternoon sun casting softly glowing strands across the room. Lazy dust motes swirled and shone like fireflies as Wash took her in his arms. The New York skyline was outlined in shimmering yellows and oranges by the setting December sun, and the gothic towers of the bridge were on fire. The cables were ropes of light, gleaming and molten, as if from the forge. They hadn't bothered to draw the drapes. It wasn't important. There had been nothing outside that room, not even the bridge. It had been a very long time for both of them. They were familiar as an old flannel shirt but new as midnight snow. The cables that bound them held new wires of understanding that day. They renewed their bonds in that little study on the second floor of 110 Columbia Heights.

Sitting back in her carriage now, Emily still felt the glow of that afternoon. She thought back to how they had lain there afterward, a mist of sweat cooling on their skins. They had watched as the spire of Trinity Church pierced the setting sun, slowly splitting it as it slipped below the city canyons.

She asked him then, "Would you do it all again, knowing what you know now? Build the bridge, I mean."

Her husband had stared long at the ceiling, as if an answer could be found there. Emily had waited, knowing.

"Yes" was all he had said. It was enough.

It was incredible really, that a man would say that he would subject himself to ten years of pain and disability to accomplish what he had. But he said it, as she knew he would. She understood now, as she never had before, how rare it was to create something as monumental as the Brooklyn Bridge. It was the work of a lifetime. It was a castle in the sky for the industrial age . . . a monument. This was an age when engineers like Wash were the men of the hour. They and their creations were lauded and honored and marveled at as never before. Things were changing fast as inventors and engineers raced to create things like electric lights and telephones and horseless carriages. But unlike these things, which would change again, almost as fast as they were invented, the bridge would last. Millions would cross it, use it, admire it, and on a Sunday, strolling on the promenade, simply enjoy it. Not one man in a million has the chance to build something like that, and Washington Roebling had done it . . . *they* had done it. Such things were worth sacrifice.

Emily's carriage pulled to a stop in front of the Astor Library, at 415 Lafayette Place. She stopped her daydreaming and looked out the carriage window as Hughes their butler and driver set the brake and stepped down from the driver's seat. This had been a fashionable part of town at one time. Walt Whitman had once lived across the street in the row of town houses called La Grange Terrace after the country seat of the Marquis de Lafayette. But that was many years ago, and the street, although still respectable, was no longer home to the wealthy and famous. They had moved farther uptown. It seemed everyone wanted to live near Central Park now.

Hughes opened Emily's door, and she stepped down to the blue slate sidewalk in front of the new north wing of the library. For a moment she stopped to look up at the elegant Italianate brownstone façade. There was still the slightest scent of cut lumber and concrete to the place. The north wing had been completed just a few months before.

Something attracted Emily's attention to the street behind her. Thinking back on it later, she could never recall exactly what made her turn and look at the long row of columned town houses across Lafayette Place. She had admired those buildings before. They were so different from most of the new buildings going up now and had a classic, Greek revival style that she thought timeless. Legend had it that inmates from Sing Sing had done the stonework, but that was fifty years ago. Most had been divided into apartments now.

A tall, broad-shouldered man with an imposing mustache caught her attention for no reason she could explain. She supposed it was the way he walked, but it was hard to put her finger on it. He moved toward the front door of the Grange with an easy stride. She watched him. There was no swagger, just an ease that spoke of a man at home with who he was. He tipped his hat to a woman leaving the building. Emily liked the way he did that, especially the brief glimpse of his smile and the way his eyes crinkled at the corners. Emily wondered idly about the man as he took a first step toward the front doors of the building. Then he hesitated and stopped, turning toward her. She had been surprised to find herself staring at the tall stranger across the street. Staring at strange men was definitely not something she did. Still, he was quite handsome, she noticed as she flicked her skirt and turned up the stairs to library. Wickedly she couldn't resist one last glance before she went in the front door. To her amazement, the man was still watching her, the ghost of a smile playing on his face. She couldn't help but smile too. Thank God Hughes hadn't noticed. It was embarrassing enough to be caught staring like some streetwalker. But in truth she rather enjoyed it. He had looked at her in a way she hadn't been looked at in some time. She had the feeling that somehow they had known each other before. Odd, how a glance from a strange man across Lafayette Place could do that.

Her step was light as she entered the big central hallway of the library. Emily took the stairs to the second floor. She had been around hundreds of men almost constantly since she had been assisting Wash. Every day she had been at the construction site, the only woman in a manly world. Emily knew just how unique that was. For Emily to be treated as an equal where men ruled was extraordinary indeed. She remembered how at first every man's eye had been on her and how nervous she had been. The workers sometimes had stopped what they were doing to stare as she got out of her carriage. On occasion she felt that those stares had been not quite appropriate. She had gotten used to it, though, and to a lot more. Stares from strange men were not all that uncommon for her. Still . . .

Tom opened the door to his apartment. It creaked on its hinges in a familiar, homey sort of way. He knew he should put some oil on the thing, but the squeaking hinge was a kind of "welcome home" to him, and he never did seem to find the time to oil it. He went on in to the kitchen and put the small bag he carried down on the counter near the sink. The squeaking hinge did serve some purpose after all. Tom's two cats, Grant and Lee, trotted into the kitchen with an urgency they usually reserved for catching mice or fighting. Lee rubbed against his leg, arching her back and straightening her tail. She purred as if he were a long-lost lover. Grant took a more direct approach, jumping up on the counter, mewing pitifully, as if he hadn't been fed in weeks. Tom stroked Grant's neck and rubbed him behind his ears. The big cat twisted his neck and closed his eyes, soaking up the attention. Tom's thoughts started to drift to the woman he had seen across the street.

Soon Grant reminded him of his real mission in life, which was to feed him. Making a direct frontal assault, he began attacking the brown paper bag Tom had put on the counter. Grant always had been the more direct of the two, and he chewed at the paper with determination. Tom took the bag away from him and put the chicken scraps it contained in a bowl. Grant was black and white, with a white face and a black chin and neck that reminded Tom of a beard. Lee was Confederate gray with stripes of butternut brown and black. Her hair sprang out in a mane on either side of her neck, and she owned a beautiful fluffy striped tail that she liked to drape over her face when she slept.

Tom didn't think of himself as a cat lover. In his way, though, he supposed that he loved Grant and Lee. He supposed he had to considering all the litters of kittens he'd found homes for over the years. They certainly seemed to love him, or maybe they just loved the chicken scraps he brought them in the little brown bag. That was only part of it, he knew. They showed their affection for him in their own ways. Grant would never deign to curl up in Tom's bed at night the way Lee did. Tom imagined that he considered it beneath his dignity, but he seemed to love nothing more than draping himself across Tom's lap while he sat reading. Tom was catching up on the classics at the moment, feeling guilty about not reading enough of late. His library was modest but growing slowly. Dickens was his favorite, though he liked Mark Twain's stories a lot. He also had a growing collection of autobiographies and memoirs of key military figures from the war. Having served, it interested him to read the generals' views of the same events. It always astonished him how different those memories could be. Tonight, though, he was finishing up *A Tale of Two Cities*.

The big red chair by the front window was Grant's favorite. Tom hadn't so much as cracked his book when Grant was settling himself in. Lee, on the other hand, warmed his bed every night. She would push herself into the curve behind his knees, kneading him like a plumped pillow, and when she finally arranged him just to her liking, she would purr them both to sleep. Some of Tom's lady friends didn't like it. Oddly, Tom had to admit that those who didn't were usually not invited back.

Tom got up for a minute to fix himself a roast beef sandwich and get a bottle of Clausen's out of the icebox. He emptied the water tray from under the block of ice, which was getting small, he noticed. Then he settled back into the big red chair by the window, and Grant sauntered over, a little slower this time, probably annoyed at being upset so quickly. Tom patted his thigh.

"Come on up, fella." Grant jumped up, almost upsetting Tom's stout. "Get yourself settled, you old bastard. Spill one drop o' my stout and I'll skin your hide."

Grant slowly worked his claws on Tom's thigh in a shameless play for a neck rub, but the sandwich took two hands. Grant looked up with reproach. Once Tom had reduced the sandwich to one-hand size, he gave in and stroked Grant's neck. The cat closed his eyes, arched his head, and vibrated in contentment. Tom opened his book again and started over. He sipped his stout, which was none too cold. Mostly the pubs and saloons served it warm, but since Tom could afford an icebox and the daily deliveries of ice that went with it, he had been acquiring a taste for his Clausen's chilled.

He gazed out the front window. Dusk was falling, and he'd have to light a lamp soon, but for now he just enjoyed the gathering gloom. A line of carriages had filled the curb for half the block in front of the library.

"Big doings across the way, there, Grant. What do you make of it, old soldier? Some sort of trustee meeting, I suppose." Grant didn't answer. "Bunch of old farts plannin' a temperance meeting or some damned thing. Well, they'll never get my Clausen's, laddie. I'm defendin' the ramparts of drunkenness to my dyin' breath. 'Tis a far, far better thing I do than I have ever done . . ." Tom intoned, grinning at Grant. "Are ye with me? Sound off there, ye worthless flea bag. Are you goin' to let them top hats take our beer away?" Grant snoozed. "A little support here would be nice. It's a man's right to drink himself into oblivion if he so desires, and as long as he's not pissin' on their shoes, it's none o' their business." Tom chuckled as Grant half opened one eye. "A fine effort, old man. I knew I could count on you."

Night flowed softly through the tall window, painting the red chair black. After a while, when the words were blurring on the page, Tom got up, dumping Grant off his lap. He searched for a match and lit the oil lamp that hung from the ceiling. The room swam in yellows and reds. Tom sat thinking of potatoes and dirty, shoeless feet. Somehow, the image of Mike Bucklin, his beaming face smudged with dirt, stuck in his head . . . that and Mrs. Bucklin's plea. She had asked nothing for herself or her dying husband. She had asked for hope for her grandson. Hope was a rare commodity in her life. She was drowning in a black-water sea of troubles, but she held up the boy with the last of her strength. Tom had made a promise to her, a promise he half hoped he wouldn't have to keep. But he had given his word, so he thought idly of potatoes and a little boy's mischievous smile.

Tom roused himself from his reverie after a few minutes. Usually he didn't like to eat before he exercised, but he had been hungry. The beer and sandwich sat heavy, and he felt slow and unmotivated, but it was his ritual and he tried to keep to it. For about five minutes he stretched, back, shoulders, legs, and arms, until he felt warm and loose. Then came another five of calisthenics with a couple of quirts. By the time he was done, he had worked up a little sweat. The cats watched with lazy eyes. He envied them their ability to lie around all day, then burst into action at a moment's notice. For the next half hour, he worked his entire body, doing two exercises for each muscle group. For a time, Tom had gone to the Neue Turnhalle, on Fourth Street, to work out with some of the German cops in the precinct. He had liked the weights and had learned all he could about the muscles of the body and how to train them. A strict old German drill instructor used to put him through workouts that left him quivering. But he enjoyed the work and the feel of his muscles as they swelled. He had grown strong. He'd always had natural strength and as a boy had been able to do a man's work. Lifting weights with the Germans had added a new dimension, though. Within nine months of his first workout, he found he was one of the strongest men in the gym, stronger even than some who had been at it for years. When he moved out of the precinct, he bought his own set of dumbbells, keeping up his fitness regimen as best he could on his own. Between the workouts and the occasional training with Master Kwan, he was in pretty good shape. Tom had managed to talk the old man into letting him study with him many years before. He had gained much face in Chinatown for that. Most other cops would barely even speak to the Chinese; Tom was the only one to try to learn from them. It was a practical matter really. He was interested in anything that might give him an edge. He was a cop and being in good physical condition was part of the job. He enjoyed it, so he was in better shape than most.

Tom was slowly doing presses overhead, concentrating on the feel of the movement, when for some reason he started thinking about Mary. She had told him once how she liked to watch him work out. In fact, she liked it very much, and their exertions afterwards were memorable. Mary was an amazing woman, and he figured he liked her more than any he had known. It wasn't easy to know her mind sometimes. And there were puzzles to her that Tom had yet to figure, but when it came to feeling easy with a woman, Mary was it for him. Unlike many he had known, she didn't seem to have much in the way of inhibitions. If Mary liked you, you knew it. There weren't any ways Mary didn't like showing it either, at least not with him. He thought himself pretty lucky. Most of the men in the department agreed.

Tom pushed hard for one more repetition, feeling his deltoids and triceps burn. He put the weights down slowly. Mrs. Aurelio downstairs didn't like them banging on the ceiling. He looked at himself in the mirror. Not too good, he thought. Too many beers had put a handful of fat on his stomach. He could remember when he had ripples of muscle around his middle. At least his shoulders and arms were still taut, and he hadn't lost any strength. His chest was high and tight, with two sweeping slabs of pectorals that he flexed for the mirror.

"What do you say, Grant, old boy? Don't say it." He gave the cat a warning look. "I've looked better, I know." Grant lifted a sleepy eyelid in his direction. "You could disagree with me. It wouldn't kill you. Well, I guess Mary could do worse," he said, patting his middle, thinking he should cut back on the beer. Grant closed his eyes, cradling his chin in his paws. "All right. Suppose I could lose a few pounds," he told his mirror. "From now on, two's my limit. Hell of a sacrifice." He got no encouragement from Grant.

He was going to have to see Coffin tomorrow. He was really regretting having gotten mixed up with the captain, but he had been able to help with promotions. For a fee, he'd see that you got to the top of the list. Trouble was that his services came with a price beyond just the cost of the promotion. Tom started another exercise, his biceps bulging, feeling as big as baseballs. Fact was that he was hooked and there wasn't any way out of it. The reps were getting harder now, as he neared the limits of his strength. Sweat ran down his forehead, into his eyes. Feeling shaky but pleased with himself, Tom put the weights down and rested. The deal with Coffin was not perfect and had gotten more imperfect as time went on. Stops like the one he'd made earlier that day were far too common now. Even though he got a cut, there were some places they shouldn't offer protection to—some things that were so dirty they shouldn't be touched. Trouble was that the good captain didn't care to make such distinctions. Anyone willing to pay enough for protection got it. Maybe when he was captain of his own precinct, he'd change the rules, but more and more he wanted out of this particular game. Honestly, Tom couldn't complain about the money. That's what he had wanted, after all, fast promotions, more money, fatter assignments, and he'd gotten them. The price was high, though, and maybe it was time to stop paying.

❧ Chapter Five ☙

For night is turned into day and day into night in one of these bridge caissons, These submarine giants delve and dig and drill and ditch and blast. The work of the bridge-builder is like the onward flow of eternity; it does not cease for the sun at noonday or the silent stars at night.

—*THE HERALD*, MARCH 27, 1883

The area around Peck Slip and Water Street was almost deserted. The bustle of dock traffic, the noise and congestion of wagons, the shouting of stevedores, and the hawking of fish vendors was gone with the day. Few people walked the streets with late-night business. One man, tall and angular, with a loping stride, seemed to be in a hurry. His eyes moved constantly, scanning the street before and behind him. He hesitated for a moment at the front door to number 247 Water, looking back the way he had come, squinting through the shadows for anything out of the ordinary. Nothing put him on alert. He opened the door and slid through. He climbed to the second floor, where a pallid glow lit the glass door to the offices of Sangree & Co. He tapped lightly twice, then once hard and twice again soft. Footsteps approached, then the door opened cautiously.

"Sorry I'm late," he said, not appearing to mean it, as he slipped through. A metallic *click* brought him up short. To his right, flattened against the wall, a small clerkish man held a pistol aimed at his head.

"Evening, Earl," the man said in a voice like a knife on stone.

"Christ, Jacobs, put that thing away. Who the fuck you think it was gonna be?"

The pistol seemed to lower reluctantly, almost as if Jacobs wouldn't have minded an excuse to shoot him. Fact was, Bart Jacobs usually didn't need much excuse. Captain Thaddeus Sangree said nothing, just motioned for Earl to join the rest. They walked back to the meeting room and closed the door.

Captain Sangree wasn't real happy; Earl knew he wouldn't be. He'd done what he'd had to, gotten the job accomplished in his own way, and that was all there was to it. He didn't much give a damn what the captain said about it. What was done was done. He kept his mouth shut anyway, knowing it was best while the captain blew off some steam.

"You're a soldier, by God, and I expect you to act like one," the captain said after Earl had settled in, taking a chair beside the others already seated around the big table in the back room of Sangree & Co. He just started with no preamble. It was what they were all thinking anyway. Earl, though, wasn't quite sure if the captain was referring to his being late or his handling of the Bucklin matter.

"You may have jeopardized the mission. How can you be sure nobody saw you? You chased him through the streets, for Christ sake! After all these years, Earl . . ." he said slowly, emphasizing each word. The captain didn't have to finish the sentence. In fact, it was probably best he didn't. He might have said too much. Earl was far too valuable.

Instead Thaddeus said simply, "Do you take my meaning?" What concerned him most was the apparent breach of good procedure and planning. This was their first full meeting since Bucklin's murder, their first opportunity to asses the situation and control what damage may have occurred. The fact that Earl hadn't bothered to report until the captain saw him on the street earlier that day hadn't helped.

"Bucklin should have just been made to disappear, like McDonald before him, not cornered in an alley within a block of my office!"

" 'Suppose, Cap'n" was all Earl said, his head slumped a bit.

"Do you really?" the captain Sangree asked skeptically, raising an eyebrow. "I wonder, Earl. Pointing a finger at him, he said again for emphasis, "We've worked too long and hard to let any one of us ruin things, including me, I might add. Everything hinges on what we do over the next months. You do understand me, don't you, all of you?" he asked, scanning the eyes around the table. Nods and "yes, sirs" went around the room. "Good. I don't want to belabor the point, so let's move on. Earl, I want your full report on what happened with Bucklin. Everything, mind you, down to the last detail."

Earl Lebeau was not a big talker, as he would readily admit. Like most things about him, his speech was stripped down for the long march. He hadn't had much in the way of schooling past the fourth grade, and he could read and write and cipher just enough to get by. He was no fool, though, and had a natural, backwoods sort of cunning that had served him and "the cause" very well over the years. Thin as a pick handle and just as tough, his real skills ran in other directions.

"Well, sir, I've been keepin' an eye on Bucklin, jus' like you said. Followed him home 'out lettin' him see a bunch o' times. Looked for an opper . . . ah, you know, a chance to git him alone, on the sneak. Figured I'd cut his throat if the chance come," Earl said as if he was talking about planting vegetables. He went on to describe how he had followed Bucklin, hunted him actually. He'd tracked him home after each day's work, watched his tenement from a safe distance, even gone up to his door and lingered in the hallways in hopes of surprising Terrence in the one place he felt relatively safe. But Bucklin was either being very careful or he was very lucky. Earl wasn't a big believer in luck.

"Truth to tell, Cap'n, he was scared. Seemed he was bein' mighty careful." A fact Earl Lebeau had a grudging admiration for. "I got to thinkin' he was usin' the boy for cover when he had to go out for food an' such. He was keepin' to the crowds when he was out the last week, with the boy, or without." Lebeau had worked hard, even using disguises when he slipped into the tenement. "Camped in them shitty hallways, disguised like a beggar. Place is a rabbit hole. Folks in an' out o' there all hours, an' every kind o' goddamned foreigner ye can think of. Thought o' doin' him in the crapper once, but damned if even that didn't have a crowd." Grim laughter followed that observation.

The captain shook his head slowly, the disdain and disgust for the capital city of Yankee greed visibly sickening him. "People live like animals in this godforsaken city. Half of these pigsties don't have toilets. Streets full of beggars and orphans. Horse shit and garbage ankle deep." He shuddered visibly as he said this, disgusted by the filth of the center of the Yankee universe.

"God, how I miss the South. The smell of hay in the mornings, the redbuds, the cotton blowing like snow, a church choir on Sunday. That's the way God meant for man to live, not like this," he said, waving a dismissive hand toward the window. "Wallowing in filth, grubbing for the almighty dollar." The captain's eyes didn't see the little room anymore. They looked away to a land he remembered as in a dream. The years had colored the South of his dreams in increasingly rosy hues.

"The Almighty may not have seen fit to bless our armies with victory on the field of battle, but we have been called to do His bidding," the captain said, his voice ringing off the walls. "Just as Booth was called to bring down the serpent Lincoln, we too have been called." Like a good preacher, he swept the room with his eyes, driving them to his will and purpose. "We'll turn the dreams of that bastard Roebling to dust." He held up an open hand and closed it slowly as if crushing stone in his bare hand. "We owe him a debt of pain, boys. We were that close at Little Round Top." The captain held his fingers up, less than an inch apart. "And he snatched it away. He dares to dream of bridges." The captain sneered and shook his head as if this were the height of insult. "Oh, it's easy to dream and build when you've everything to build upon." Thaddeus took a deep breath, a slow grim smile creasing his features and a light growing in his eyes. "We're going to show Colonel Roebling what it means to lose everything." The men watched the captain's arms and hands as they seemed to show Roebling's downfall. "This bridge is his life. What else does he have left except a crippled body? Destroy the dream and we destroy the man." A bony fist smacked into his palm with a sound like a minié ball striking bone. "He will know then what it is to lose everything." He raised his hands up, his fingers spread wide, and said in a solemn tone, "So help me God!"

The captain's eyes were black holes, his mouth a thin line of barbed wire. Nobody spoke. When the captain was like this, it was best to keep still. They had all seen him this way before, and there wasn't one of them who'd ever gone against him at such a time. Others had in years past but it had proven to be a particularly risky undertaking.

Despite his zeal and lust for vengeance, there was still a man of the South inside, or at least the remains of one. "My one regret is that Mrs. Roebling will be hurt in this. She seems a decent woman." He gazed out the window into the deepening night and with a small shake of the head whispered, "Sometimes the decent reap what the wicked have sown." Like flipping a switch, he focused on Lebeau, his eyes bright in the dim light of the room.

"Uh . . . yes sir, amen to that, Cap'n." Earl went on to describe how he finally saw his chance, figuring to keep going before the captain went off on another one of his speeches. Earl tried to emphasize how careful Bucklin had been and how very few opportunities he'd had.

"He did seem to be a careful man, unlike our Private Watkins here." Too many beers, not enough brains. You should be more careful. The captain's words dripped sarcasm. Simon Watkins's Adam's apple bobbed in his skinny neck as all eyes turned to him. It was a cool night, but he looked like it was hot in his corner of the room. He was lucky to be alive, he knew. His loose tongue in front of Bucklin had nearly wrecked everything. The captain had a way of dealing with men who failed him. He'd seen it done—had done it himself on the captain's orders. Back in '76 when Jack Cummins managed to put another of their missions in jeopardy, the captain had dealt with him viciously. When it was over, he and Earl had been ordered to dump the body in the Ohio. It had been cold. Watkins could still recall how Cummins crashed through the ice when they'd thrown him off the train trestle. He was cold inside but his forehead beaded with sweat. Watkins started to think that if he managed to leave this room alive, maybe there was something he could do, maybe some way he could get out of the mess he was in. The possibilities swirled in his sweating head.

"Right," Earl said, trying to keep the heat off his friend. "So when Bucklin went off to Brooklyn to visit the cemetery, I figured I had a chance. Caught him on the way home. Had a gun to his back. Figured to take 'im up on the bridge where nobody could see, give 'im a little shove . . . look like suicide. He was quick, though, I'll give 'im that. Knocked my gun away. Threw a god-damn pipe at me—near took my head off. Then he took off runnin' like a scalded cat. Bastard could run too. Chased 'im across an' down the stairs. Didn't catch up with 'im till he tried to jump the gate of the alley. Missed his footin'. That's when I got 'im. Nobody saw. Hell, it was maybe three in the mornin'. He fell over the gate after I swatted 'im, so I went over too to finish up. That's about it, I guess."

"I would have liked the suicide. That was good thinking," the captain said dryly. There were chuckles around the table, even from Watkins, who was wiping the sweat from his forehead.

Earl glanced around with a question on his face. "You wouldn' be makin' sport of me, Cap'n? Ah don' take to bein' made sport of." There was the hint of trouble in Earl's tone. The others tensed.

"No, Earl, I wasn't making sport of you," the captain said evenly, looking him in the eye. "Please continue."

Earl seemed to take that at face value and went on. "Heard his head go pop, like I says. After, I threw a couple of crates over 'im, checked over the gate to make sure nobody was on the street, then I jumped it and walked away. Simple as that. Nothin' more to tell."

The captain probed for more details, digging for anything that might be of use or anyone who might possibly have seen or even suspected what Earl had done.

"Nothing else?" the captain asked one final time.

"No, sir."

The captain nodded thoughtfully, pacing the room for a minute. He stopped suddenly and said, "Earl, I want you to do a little follow-up work on the Bucklins. We'll talk after the meeting. There's something I have in mind." Earl nodded. "I suppose you did as well as could be hoped for under the circumstances," Thaddeus conceded. "Still, I can't help but wish that you were able to get rid of him like you did with that fool McDonald. Now, that was a thing as neatly done as ever there was."

Matt Emmons sat at the table with Earl, the captain, and the others, but he wasn't listening. The captain's mention of McDonald reminded him of the day he first started work on the bridge. They had all had plenty of experience with bridges during the war. They'd blown dozens. They'd even blown three after the war. The train trestle at Ashtabula in '76 had been a simple job by comparison. They got eighty Yankees when the trestle buckled under a passenger train. They had watched as eleven cars tumbled into the icy river over seventy feet below. Matt could still hear the screams sometimes.

When they first came to New York, after reading in the Richmond papers that the bridge would be built, the captain argued that working on the thing was the only way to fully understand it. It was like nothing they'd ever attempted before, and it made sense to know it inside and out.

"We'll have unlimited access. Nobody will question our comings and goings. It's perfect," he'd said. One by one they had all applied for jobs. Some were hired on the spot, some had to keep at it till a job on a particular work crew opened up, but after a while they all were in. Matt and Earl had started in the Brooklyn caisson in September of '70. That first day was one of the worst days of his life, maybe *the* worst. Nothing could have prepared him for the caisson.

"It's like being a miner," the captain had told them with some impatience. A wry grin crept across Matt's face at the thought. He caught himself when he noticed the captain looking. He made a show of paying attention but when the captain went on, Matt drifted back into his daydream. Although it had been years ago, the caisson was still fresh in his mind. After the first few days, he had sort of gotten used to the conditions. As for Earl, he didn't say much one way or the other, and hardly ever complained, except on the first day.

Caissons were essentially diving bells, they were huge inverted boxes designed so that gangs of men could work within in relative safety below the level of the river. Sunk on the river bottom at first, the caissons would partially fill with water, like a glass inverted in water, until the water pressure equaled the air pressure within. In order to force the water out, the air pressure had to rise. The deeper a caisson sank into the river bottom, the higher the air pressure had to be. Compressed air was the answer, pumped in constantly to maintain proper pressure and keep the river out.

The caissons were essential to the bridge, for upon them the stone towers would rise. They needed to go deep enough to rest on a completely solid footing, preferably rock. To do that, the workers slowly excavated the dirt and stone within each caisson, effectively undermining it and lowering it as they went. All the while, stone was piled on top. Caissons may have been big diving bells but they felt like tombs.

Matt recalled climbing down into the air lock the first day, through a hatch in the top. Once inside, he and Earl had looked up through the thick glass ports in the ceiling, the ghostly light their last connection with the outside world. The other men shifted on their feet nervously. The clang of the hatch reverberated through the walls of their cast-iron tomb.

"New fellas, ain't ye?" the air lock operator had said with a gap-toothed grin while turning a large valve. Compressed air shrieked, driving white-hot nails into their ears, which popped painfully as the pressure increased. Matt's breath came fast and labored. He and the others drowned in the crushing air as the pressure built to equal that of the caisson below. One of the others, a man named Mike Lynch, was the first to go down into the Brooklyn caisson. When the foundation was completed in March of '71, and the caisson filled with concrete, he had been the last man up. As quick as it started, the air pressure leveled off, and the hatch in the floor dropped open. A gaping black hole awaited them. As Matt looked down into the caisson, an unnatural light danced and flickered. He could still feel his guts twist as he looked down that hole at the bottom of the river.

Captain Sangree was droning on about some small details, which didn't interest Matt or even concern him that much. They'd gone over the damned plans so many times he could recite them in his sleep. He drifted off again, while trying to appear to pay attention.

One in three didn't come back after the first day in the caisson. He began to know why as they started down the ladder. The humidity rose to meet them, lapping in waves until it engulfed them completely. The heat was intense. Men took off their shirts immediately. Their voices had changed in the unnatural air pressure, becoming high-pitched and tinny. Matt grinned at the memory, hiding his smile from the captain behind a concealing hand.

"Matt, I say we get the hell outa here," Earl had said abruptly. He had a hand on the ladder leading up to the air lock, when a muffled clang from up above made them both crane their necks. The heavy, cast-iron hatch shut over their heads.

"Where do you two choir boys think you're going?" Matt could remember those words like they were spoken yesterday. It was their introduction to Charles Young. They turned to look at a big man. His wide shoulders and thick neck gave him an impressive presence that didn't match his reedy voice.

"We're new," Earl had said, shifting his feet like an errant schoolboy.

"Well, shit, I can see that," Young said, laughing. "You two look like a couple o' canaries in a cellar full o' cats. Thinkin' of going up the ladder? Can't say I blame you. By the way, your voice will be just as manly as ever once you get topside. It's the air, does strange things. Can't even blow out a candle down here. I've seen dozens try, but none as done it. Once a flame gets goin' there's no stoppin' it, so be damned careful with fire. That's rule one. You'll have a big appetite too and not just from the work, so pack a big lunch or you'll regret it."

Captain Sangree said something to bring Matt out of his daydream again and he nodded with the rest of them, as if he knew what was being said, then slipped back into his own thoughts. Working in the caissons had been a once-in-a-lifetime experience for him and Earl. He found himself thinking about it more often now that the end was in sight.

Oddly, the thing Matt recalled most was his growling stomach. It gurgled like a clogged drainpipe, twisting and cramping from nervousness or the air pressure or both. As Young showed them what to do, his gut growled and tumbled. They started by hauling dirt to the dredge pool. Two dredges were contained in large square shafts. These shafts, which were filled with water, extended down through the caisson roof into a pool of standing water in the caisson floor. The weight of the water in the shafts was counterbalanced by the air pressure in the caisson.

"Inside these shafts are clamshell dredges," Young said. "You boys dump the dirt and rocks into the pool and the dredge scoops it out and drops it topside. Fuckin' things get stuck all the time. We spend half our time fixing 'em."

There were gangs of men in the chamber, working at excavating under the edges of the caisson wall. The wall was only eight inches thick at the bottom edge, shod with cast iron that was called the "shoe." Matt remembered watching the men working at a boulder wedged under the shoe, going at it with steel bars and sledgehammers. It was still clear in Matt's mind, the pounding, ringing hammers, sweat glistening and running on shining backs, mud smeared on haggard faces, the heavy smell of creosote and tar that sealed the wood of the caisson walls, the cursing in high-pitched voices, the ghastly light and oppressive heat. Sometimes boulders broke quickly, sometimes they didn't. There were plenty of boulders. One hundred twelve men to a shift, in two daily shifts, managed to sink the caisson about two inches. Matt recalled how the heavy timbers groaned, creaked, and squealed around them as the 3,000-ton caisson was lowered, its load of granite above growing with every passing day. The Brooklyn caisson hit bedrock at forty-four feet six inches below the high-water mark. The New York caisson had gone much deeper.

Thinking back on it now, Matt could hardly believe he had gone through with it.

"Dear God, what have I got myself into?" he had mumbled as he picked up his shovel. So, they dug and sweated and wondered if any small part of their labor was worth the price. After about twenty minutes of hauling rocks and dirt, the cramps in his gut had gotten harder to ignore. Matt had searched desperately for an outhouse, going from chamber to chamber, until he ran into the foreman.

"You gotta go, you go in one of the chambers we're not working in. No shitters down here. I hear the engineers are working on one, though," he said with a laugh. Matt had found a chamber that was empty of any activity. It was without light and about as black as an executioner's heart.

He had felt his way down the wall, running his hands over the rough tarred timbers. He didn't go far till he stopped and dropped his trousers. Feeling like he was going to die, he started to pray. He prayed long and hard. It seemed an eternity at the time, alternately praying and shitting. But after a bit it began to pass, and he got to thinking that his prayers were answered. Then the horrible truth struck him. He had no paper.

Matt had to hide his smile again, and Earl kicked him under the table to get him to pay attention as the captain droned on, his back to them as he went over a diagram on the wall. Earl gave him a quizzical frown as Matt chuckled at his shitty memory.

Maybe this was a sign, he remembered thinking. Maybe God was punishing him. The captain could talk all he wanted about God's will, but maybe the captain didn't know God's will from a stump. Maybe this indignity meant that the stain on his soul could never be wiped away. Maybe he had sold his soul to the devil himself and that devil was the captain. He imagined himself in hell, and it didn't seem much different from that pitch-black caisson, twenty-five feet below the bottom of the East River. But then a copy of *Harper's* sailed out of the inky blackness, landing at his feet. His eyes couldn't pierce the dark. He was about to call out when a voice spoke from the dark.

"First day?" The voice startled him with its closeness. "You'll get used to it." The barest glimpse of a shadow flitted across the doorway to the chamber beyond. Matt couldn't be sure he had even seen it. He called out his thanks, but there had been no answer. Matt was pretty sure that it wasn't God that tossed him a copy of *Harper's,* but he couldn't shake the possibility.

He and Earl had survived their first day in purgatory, and a few months later, they lit a fire that nearly brought the bridge down and came close to killing Washington Roebling in the process. McDonald was the man they framed for it. His body still lay where they'd buried him, somewhere in the lonely marshlands of Brooklyn.

Matt was lost in his memories when he heard the captain say in a low voice, "Emmons! We're not keeping you from anything important, are we?"

"Duh . . . I mean, no, sir," Matt stumbled.

"Good. Now that we have everyone's attention, I was saying that we have nearly all the information we need, thanks to Corporal Jacobs, who has been good enough to liberate plans, specifications, order forms, letterhead stationery, et cetera, et cetera."

Jacobs smiled thinly and gave a small nod, gazing over the tops of glasses that clung to the bridge of his nose. They seemed about to fall in his lap, but that was nothing new. They gave the little man a schoolmarmish look. Behind his glasses, his bow tie, and clerk's demeanor was a most vicious little man. Jacob's slight build and medium height belied his real gifts. His eyes, small, black, and unblinking, were the only window to the real man. Usually they were taken to be the eyes of a bureaucrat. In reality, they more closely resembled the eyes of the razorback pigs he hunted as a boy in east Texas.

Throughout the war he never took a prisoner. Earl had asked him about it once, at the end of a day when he saw Jacobs run his bayonet through the throat of a wounded Union sergeant.

"Waste of time," Jacobs had said. "Takes men to guard 'em, wagons and trains to haul them to camps, and food to keep them alive, things the Confederacy has precious little of. It's just economics."

Bart had been a bank clerk before the war. Despite that, most men he had served with knew him to be bloodthirsty beyond all logic and reason. "Cold as the grave," someone had once said, out of Jacobs's earshot, of course. Earl was the closest thing to him in their little group, but where Earl was callous, he wasn't inhuman, and that was a word that fit Bart Jacobs like a coffin. The rest of the men called him Weasel, part because of his size and his pinched, tight-lipped expression, part because he had the unsettling habit of going for the throat. Of course, nobody called him Weasel to his face, leastways not if they didn't want a second windpipe.

Being an unremarkable little man, Weasel blended into a crowd better than anyone. He was a good clerk too and was much valued by the bosses in the bridge offices. He worked hard, stayed late, and over the years he had slowly stolen or made precise copies of most of the plans he thought they'd need and a bunch more that they'd never use. Weasel was very thorough.

"As you know," the captain said, looking at Weasel, "we have been ordering copies of various components from the very manufacturers that are contracted to make them for the bridge. Some steel, for example, has come from Roebling's own mills in Trenton. I take particular satisfaction from that. The idea that Roebling's own company would contribute to our plans is sweet irony indeed." There were chuckles around the table.

"Our brothers in Richmond have been very supportive over the years. They have been busy testing the components we send them." Glances were exchanged around the table. They all knew that the captain had shadowy backers in the South, but who they were was known only to him. Most figured it was the Klan. Nathan Bedford Forrest had testified in '71, before a congressional committee, that he had disbanded the Klan, which nobody really believed. Forrest, the original Grand Wizard, was a legend by any standards. During the war he had thirty horses shot from under him and killed thirty-one men in hand-to-hand combat. His battles were becoming required study in military colleges around the world. When he died, a few years before, 20,000 mourners attended his funeral.

"Their backing and assistance, combined with the proceeds from my cotton business, have helped fund our operations as well. The purchase, shipment, and testing have been expensive. By Jacobs's reckoning we have spent somewhere over $110,000 to date." A low whistle and a few raised eyebrows marked the reaction to that number. When most of them earned no more than $14 a week, $110,000 was an astronomical figure. "Would you put a price on justice?" Thaddeus asked, outraged that any of them would balk at such an expenditure. "Speak up. Who among you would sell your brother for less? Emmons? Watkins?"

"Just a heap o' money, Cap'n. That's all," Watkins said, trying to shrug it away. He was immediately sorry he opened his mouth.

"That's where you're wrong, Watkins. It's nothing. It's less than nothing. Measure it against a life . . . your life, for example. What's your life worth? Surely for you, Watkins, it's worth infinitely more, immeasurably more. Isn't that so?" The captain's eyes were hard again, and they bored in on Watkins who seemed to shrink before the heat of his gaze. The rest looked at their hands, or they looked at the grain in the oak of the tabletop, but they didn't look at the captain's eyes. "Isn't that so, Watkins?" Thaddeus pressed his point. He would spend anything to accomplish his mission. Money was nothing against that.

"A man can't put a price on his own life," Watkins said defensively. He almost thought the captain might shoot him right there in front of the others from the look on his face. At that thought, an idea occurred to him. Watkins started to think it through.

"But you find it easier to put a price on others?" the captain shot back. Silence. They waited for the storm to pass.

"We lost five hundred ninety-seven men, killed, wounded, and missing, at Gettysburg alone. They were our friends. They had families and children. Who among us doesn't mourn them, and all the hundreds of others fallen on so many other fields? So don't speak to me of money," he boomed at Watkins. "It's money and the lust for it that has infected the Yankees. Let it twist us . . . pervert us from our goals, and we'll be no better than they. We have a higher calling, a noble cause. Greenbacks have no part in it."

The captain was no fool, though. He knew that even though his small group was as dedicated as any men could be, there was a limit to how long men would work for a cause that didn't put any money in their pockets. They were not fighting for their homeland, after all. The war was over and they were in the North, where prosperity blossomed all around them. Commerce boomed and bustled. Great buildings and great fortunes were built up seemingly overnight. Although there was poverty to spare, there was glittering progress as well. Money coursed through the veins of the city in great pulses of green.

"But there will be reward, make no mistake," Thaddeus said, softening his tone. "There are those in the South who will shower us with gold when our mission is done. Rest assured, men, there will be ample reward. I personally know this to be true. We are not the only ones who wish to see a reckoning with the North. Riches beyond imagining will flow to us when this is over. Besides that, our investment in the ferry company will, no doubt, pay handsomely too." The captain smiled conspiratorially. Grins ringed the table as visions of riches swam through their heads. There was one smile, though, that was a grim twist of the lips. There was no light of anticipation in those eyes. Nobody seemed to notice.

Justice K. Lincoln had known the captain for longer than anyone else at the table. He knew the captain well enough to see when he was shoveling it thick—maybe so thick he believed it himself. Hell, they'd be lucky to get out alive. He guessed his best chance would be to book a steamer to Europe. Germany seemed a likely place for a soldier of fortune. A fine military tradition, friction between the many German states and principalities, the ever-present troubles with Poland and France seemed a perfect formula for an enterprising military man. If that didn't pan out, there were the English. They were always fighting somewhere. The one thing he wouldn't and couldn't do was go south. Any fool knew that.

Lincoln; that name had been a burden to him. Family legend had it that he was even related somewhere way back to the great man himself, not that Justice considered him a great man. He had been the butt of so many jokes and so much abuse during the years in the regiment that he ended up fighting just about every man who mocked him, regardless of size, rank, or station. For a while it became a sport in the regiment. But in the end, Justice K. Lincoln had earned their respect—not for his skill as a boxer, but for his courage and determination. For the regiment, the name of Lincoln was an odd mixture of curse and praise, and for Justice, with his flattened nose and battered face, that seemed just about right.

He had enlisted the same day as the captain and his brother. Of course, Thaddeus hadn't been the captain then. It wasn't till later, just before Chancellorsville, he had become the Captain of Company B of the Fifth Texas volunteers, of Robertson's Brigade, Hood's Division. Lincoln knew him best, of course, from their early years together, when they sat around campfires at night, drying their socks, telling yarns, or boiling coffee. That was in the days when they still had coffee. They had a lot of things then that they were to lose later.

They spoke of a few more things that night: about the detective who'd been seen at the murder scene—what he knew, whether he should be eliminated. It was decided to wait a bit, see what he had learned, if anything. They agreed there was no need yet to kill him, not at least until they knew more. They could deal with him at any time, if need be.

It was getting late, though, and there was work in the morning. The others had gone out the office door, when the captain had a last, whispered word with Lebeau.

"Find the boy, Earl," he said forcefully. "We need to know what he knows." Earl frowned his agreement. "Scare him, cut him if you have to, but get the truth." The captain added something else in a whisper. Earl smiled after a moment, then he simply nodded and followed the others out.

The captain watched from his office window. He was wondering about the sergeant. Sullivan hadn't said much that night. Probably just in a mood, he thought. Patrick could be like that sometimes. They were all tired too, as the ache behind his eyes reminded him. He watched as the six of them walked up Water Street, moving in and out of the halo of the gas lamps. Like ghost men, their footfalls echoed on the cobbles, falling dead in the heavy, March night air. There was just a bit of a mist crawling in from the river, snaking its way down alleys and side streets. They passed from the light of a streetlamp, and the mist sucked them into the darkness.

Mike Bucklin was struggling down the blackened stairway of his building. It was real late. Even though he felt like lying down and dying, he was doing what his grandma had asked. The bucket that Gramps used was full. Gramps was far too weak to make it down to the outhouse, back of the building, so the bucket was the only choice. Mike had forgotten about it in all the commotion of hearing about his da. He had forgotten about most everything. He was numb. His family was gone . . . all of them. As he lugged the sloshing pail down the coal-black stairs and out through the hallway on the first floor, he wondered if things could possibly get worse. He didn't think so.

The moon was a yellow slash cut in the blue-black sky. It peered over the top of the building behind as he went out to the outhouses. As soon as he stepped out the door he could smell them. They'd have to emptied soon. The night-soilers would come and haul it all away. That was about the worst job in the world, Mike figured, even worse than rag-picking. It helped a little to think that someone had it worse than he. He opened one of the creaking wooden doors in the row of outhouses, holding his breath so the stink didn't knock him over. As fast as he could, he emptied the bucket, trying not to splash too much but knowing he did. He hurried to finish before he had to take another breath and knocked the bucket against the side of the gaping black hole to get out the last of it. Then Mike turned and got out as fast as he could, slamming the door behind him. Before he'd taken another step, an arm came out of the blackness and clamped around his neck with terrifying force. Mike was pulled off balance and dragged between a gap in the outhouses. The foul air of the jakes seemed suddenly precious as he struggled to fill his lungs. Panic gripped him so hard he couldn't think. The arm held him like a vise.

"Quit yer strugglin', ya little bastard," a voice above him said. That was about the last thing Mike figured he'd do. Instead, he slammed his foot down as hard as he could, and was rewarded with a curse as he hit a big foot. The arm didn't let go though, so he tried it again. This time he missed, but was slammed into the wall of the outhouse for his attempt.

"One more trick out o' you, an' you'll be whistling 'Dixie' with your daddy," the voice said, low and menacing. The moon shone dully off a long, sharpened line of steel as it flashed before his eyes. The arm had him pinned against the wall, an immovable weight pressing against his throat. Mike stood still, frozen with fear. He almost couldn't breathe he was so scared.

"That's better. Just wanted to have a little talk, is all." The voice sounded conversational, but the pressure on his throat didn't let up. "You know what happened to your daddy." This was not a question. "He made a mistake, your dad. I'm here to see if he made any others we don't know about. You get me?" The steel swayed before Mike's eyes. He nodded. "Good. You know what mistake your dad made, Mike?" It horrified Mike to know that they knew his name. "Your dad ever say anything to you about it?"

"No, sir." Mike's voice quavered, and he was ashamed for the fear in it.

"Well, there's a good lad. Y'all help me and this'll be over in two shakes," the voice said. Mike looked up into the blackened face. He couldn't see enough to make out the features. "Don't look at me, squirt. Y'all don't want to be knowin' who I am. Now, your daddy never mentioned anything about the bridge?" Mike just shook his head and kept his eyes down, and tried not to sob. His da had talked about the job a lot over the years, but that wasn't what this man was after, he knew. This was one of the bad men his da had warned him about. Trouble was, he didn't know why. His da hadn't told him anything.

"Don't know if I can trust you, Mikey. You sure you never heard anything about funny goings-on at the bridge?" The steel was at his throat now. Mike could feel it cold and sharp against his skin. "Y'all would tell me if he did, right? Y'all might have told that cop too, the one was here today?"

A muffled cough sounded from the hallway at the back of the building, and an instant later a form was briefly silhouetted against the building's faint light. The arm tightened against Mike's throat.

"Quiet now," the voice said in a menacing whisper. The face was so close Mike could smell each stinking breath. The steel still pressed his throat. A door slammed, and they could clearly hear the man doing his business just a few feet away. They waited silent as the grave. Mike didn't even think about calling out or trying to run. He was too scared to think much of anything. After what seemed like an eternity, a door slammed again and the man went back inside.

"Good. Now, I'm not so sure you're telling me the truth, Mikey. You're scared, ain't you, boy? Question is, are you scared enough?"

Mike nodded his head and said, "I'm sc-scared mister. Please don't hurt me."

"Well, I believe you, Mike, but my friend here ain't so sure." The knife waved before him again, coming so close to his eyes that Mike had to close them.

"Please" was all could say.

"Open your eyes," the voice commanded. "I'm gonna ask you once more. What d'ya know about the bridge?" Mike started to say something, when, quick as a snake, he saw the blade slice past his head. He felt the needle-sharp tip catch on the edge of his ear and hang there for an instant.

"I—" Mike started. He felt the knife slice through his ear. He gasped but was surprised it didn't hurt more. A warm trickle ran down his neck.

"Now I got your attention, you'll answer me straight, right, boy? So what you know?"

Almost too scared to speak, Mike croaked out, "I swear, mister, my da didn't say nothin'. I don't know nothin'. Really, I swear!"

The knife came up against Mike's throat, the tip pushing up under his chin, so he had to stand on tiptoe to keep it from sticking him.

"I'm inclined to believe you, boy," the voice said as the knife eased off a bit. "But there's somethin' else I need."

"What? Anything," Mike said, trying not to beg but unable to stop.

"Y'all got to keep quiet about us. This'll be our little secret, right?" Mike just nodded. "Say it!" The point of the knife prodded him again. "And you better be tellin' the truth or we'll be meetin' again."

"I won't tell nobody, mister. I promise. I ain't seen your face. Who can I tell who'd believe me anyway?" Mike tried to reason with him.

"Good. That's good. You're a smart boy, Mikey," the voice soothed. "Smart, 'cause if I hear you tellin' anyone, it'll be your whole family that'll pay: your grandma, your granddaddy, and, most of all, you!" Mike was too petrified to say anything. "I guess you got my point." The voice chuckled. "Sleep tight, now," it whispered and was gone. A shadow passed through the back door. It banged shut, echoing down the stinking canyon between the tenements. Mike tried to run but his feet wouldn't do it. His knees buckled and he slid down the wall to sit in the mud.

❊ Chapter Six ❊

Caisson of the East River bridge was severely damaged by fire yesterday. I don't believe any man now living will cross that bridge.

—GEORGE TEMPLETON STRONG

Mike crept up the blackened stairs, feeling his way up the walls, along the wainscoting. The only light was the occasional glow from under a door. There never had been any lights in the halls or stairways, but that wasn't unusual for buildings in his neighborhood. He knew the stairs well though and managed only a couple of missteps before he finally reached his door. It was very late. He didn't have a watch, but the streets were deserted and that was about as good a timepiece as he'd ever known. He didn't want to wake his grandma, so he tiptoed through the front door, which was hardly ever locked. Mike stood there for a moment, listening to the snores of his grandparents. He knew he'd catch hell in the morning. It wouldn't be the first time. He had run for what seemed like hours, once he'd gotten his legs under him. He hadn't known or cared where he was going. All he could think of was getting away from that man by the jakes. His hands still shook when he thought about him. All night he kept seeing the dull reflection of that knife as it waved before his eyes. It made him weak in the knees just thinking about it. He thought about it a lot.

Mike knew he couldn't tell anyone about the shadow-man. He was sure that the man would know. Somehow the bad men seemed to know everything. Mike imagined them as having eyes and ears everywhere, watching him constantly. He didn't know how many times he'd looked over his shoulder that night—more times than he could count. The night had echoed with following footsteps. Shadow-men shambled after him, always just out of sight. Mike figured he couldn't go home. Though he knew that if they could find him out by the jakes, they could just as easily find his apartment, he didn't want to lead them to it.

Grandma could beat him all she wanted for staying out all night. He didn't much care. But he was so tired now he could hardly keep his eyes open, and this was the only place he felt safe to sleep. Bad things could happen to kids who slept on the streets. He shrugged grimly in the dark. How much worse could it get than tonight? He didn't know, but he could imagine. He rolled into bed. It felt familiar, comforting, like when his da gave him a hug. His throat got tight at the thought. He had been out all night thinking thoughts like that. His grandma and gramps were still alive, but they weren't the same as Mom or Da or Sis. They were old. They'd be gone into the ground sometime soon. Then what? He didn't know. Orphanages were full of boys like him. The streets were too, assuming he lived long enough to see an orphanage. Mike wasn't sure which was worse.

His da had said to watch for bad men. He had watched, but it hadn't been enough. There wasn't anywhere he was safe. His only safety was silence. The man hadn't killed him, after all, though he certainly could have. So if he kept quiet like he'd said, they'd be sure to leave him alone, not that he had anything to tell. Mike hadn't lied about the bridge. He reached a hand to feel his ear. Blood had soaked the handkerchief he'd wrapped around it. It was hard and crusty now. A noise out in the hall, a slow shuffling he barely made out set his nerves on edge and a cold sweat beaded almost immediately on his neck. He got up quietly to check the door. The lock was old and he doubted it could even keep him out if he tried hard enough. He locked it anyway, then, as quietly as he could, wedged a chair under the knob. It was the only way he figured to get any sleep.

He hadn't felt as if sleep was even a possibility, but he was out within minutes of his head hitting the pillow. Mike woke with a start, to the sound of his grandfather's coughing. He lay there half awake for some time hoping to drift off again, but he was unable to. Though he was still tired, the things that started swirling around his head wouldn't let him rest. He tossed for a while, trying to shake off men with long knives lurking around corners. After a while he gave it up. His grandmother was up by then, clattering pans in the kitchen. There seemed to be more banging than usual. He knew it was Grandma's way of showing her disapproval. He pulled his thin sheet over his head to block out the noise. It didn't work.

Grandma was giving him far worse than a beating. It was the silent treatment. And for Grandma, that was as harsh a punishment as ever there was. She hadn't said a word when he got up and went into the kitchen. She just looked at him with her big sad eyes. A little shake of her head as she turned away said more than a whole Sunday sermon. Mike wondered if it wouldn't be better to just go back to hide under the sheet. He noticed the chair was gone from the front door. It worried him. He tried to figure a way to convince her that they needed a better lock but knew this wasn't the time. The silence hung in the room so heavy he could feel the weight of it. The kettle on the stove suddenly started to shriek, startling him like a sudden slap in the face. Mike sat at the kitchen table wondering what would become of them. Grandma was supposed to go and claim his da's body later. It was just him and Gramps and Grandma now, and pretty soon Gramps would be gone too, no matter what his grandmother said. She turned back to him with a cup of tea, steaming and fragrant. He took it with careful hands, feeling the warmth through the porcelain.

"I'm sorry, Grandma," Mike said in a small voice.

Patricia Bucklin stood looking down at him for a moment. Suddenly she saw the blood-crusted handkerchief on Mike's ear. "What happened to you? What did you do to yourself?"

Mike hesitated for an instant. "I ran into the door out back, Grandma. It's all right."

Patricia Bucklin shook her head slowly, clucking something about clumsiness. A deep wracking cough came from the corner, behind the curtain. It seemed to startle them both and turned her around.

"Do you want some tea, Pa?" she said. The coughing wasn't done, though; it went on in deep, whooping gusts. "I'll take that as a yes." She poured a cup, and sliced the last of a small loaf of bread on the table. One slice she silently gave to Mike, one to Gramps. She sat at the table across from Mike. He watched as she peeled an orange for herself. His da used to bring him oranges. A fine spray of juice sprang from the fruit as she tore at its skin, shimmering briefly in the morning light. It was their last orange. He knew. He had stolen it. Mike drank his tea slowly, making it last as long as he could. He did the same with the bread. He had learned to savor every morsel in the last year or so. He looked up at the tintype on the dresser, the one of his father during the war. It was hard to imagine he wouldn't see him again. He realized that yesterday was the last time he'd wait for his da to come walking home from work. There would be no more oranges, pulled like magic from his da's pockets, no more roughhouse before bedtime. The eyes in the tintype looked sadder now. Maybe it was the light.

At least his da had given him the box. He fingered the small brass key in his pocket. It was a special box, just for his most treasured things. His da had given him two photographs to put in it. Why his father had told him to hide it, he wasn't sure. He just figured his da wanted it to be special just for him and nobody else. It was special. Later, when Grandma went out to the funeral parlor, he'd take it out. He'd look at the pictures his da had given him, and he'd remember.

The early morning sun peered over the parapet of the Astor Library. Tom's window faced east, and at this time of year the sun was his alarm clock. It crested the top of the library at about seven, from this angle, and lanced through his unshaded window with a persistent glare that rarely failed to wake him. Only Lee seemed to pay the sun no mind. If anything the cat welcomed the heat, her fur hot as a flatiron.

Plenty to do today too. He needed to see Coffin and bring him his payoff. He had a few people in the tenements to check out, names Patricia Bucklin had given as Terrence's friends. He wanted to get down to the bridge too and see what could be learned from some of the men Bucklin had worked with. "Somethin' not right with the bridge," old man Bucklin had said. What the hell that could be Tom wouldn't guess just yet. More than likely Bucklin owed someone money. Tom had seen men killed for less, and he didn't expect anything much beyond the usual motives. It bothered him that Terrence's money was still in his pocket, but you never could tell about such things. Bashing someone's head in can make a man skittish.

He figured he'd start at the tenements. The list was short, and unlike the construction site, he knew who he was looking for and where they were. After that, he'd get down to the bridge. With a bit of luck, that part of his day would be short and productive. It would be nice to solve this one. So many cases weren't solved in this city. It was that and the Bucklins too. He felt the need to ease their pain, if he could, and maybe feel that he did something for Mikey in the balance. That would be good. Perhaps in a few days he'd go and see how they were getting on. He had a fistful of other cases, though no other murders, so this one went to the top of the list. He'd have to get over to Bellevue Hospital sometime today too. The city morgue was there, down in the basement. Bodies were kept in a cold, thick-walled room, a fine spray of water directed on the corpses to keep them fresh. The city would advertise for any relatives if none turned up immediately. If no one came forward they'd keep the clothes hanging by the body for identification. Around a third of the bodies went unclaimed.

When he got off tonight, he was planning to see Mary. Tom remembered when he first met her. Perhaps that was the wrong word, he thought. Arrested was actually the word. He and Sam and a half-dozen patrolmen had been assigned to one of the regular busts of houses of ill repute. It had been Mary who opened the door. She had her hair down, and it gave her a wild, sensual look that was emphasized by the thin, low-cut cotton shift she wore. It was plain to every man on her front stoop that morning that Mary was quite naked under that wonderful cotton. The light in the hall behind her framed her in a soft halo.

"I suppose you must come in, gentlemen," she had said evenly. "Do you have time for coffee?"

Tom and Sam sometimes still shared a laugh over how the eight of them had stood staring as Mary turned and walked back into the front hall, her hips doing a mesmerizing dance. "Do wipe your feet, gentlemen, won't you?" she had said over her shoulder. They drank coffee in her parlor. By the time second cups were poured, they were chatting like old friends. She actually had them laughing at her stories of famous but unnamed clients. Mary was discreet, after all. Tom recalled how he sat in her parlor, sipping her in along with her coffee. Odd, how after they had exchanged glances for the second or third time, she seemed to avoid his gaze, and she pulled a shawl down from the back of the chair and covered her shoulders. He could still remember the sidelong look she gave him as she did it. The men had been disappointed.

They had to take her in but she and her girls were out in a day. Three evenings later he found himself knocking at her big oak door. A young woman had answered, and led him into the parlor. He would never forget what Mary said a moment later when she padded into the parlor, soft as snow. "You're late. But then I thought you might be."

That was nearly two years ago, before she moved her business uptown to Twenty-sixth Street. From the first she had treated him like a beau, not a customer. Tom had always treated her like a lady. She must have had the same sorts of fears he did, but it didn't show. It was as if her business was just business. She may as well have owned a hat store. Her business still disturbed him sometimes, though less now than it had at first. Actually, it wasn't the business . . . it was her part in it. He knew she still entertained clients with special needs. They were few but, almost without exception, either wealthy or influential. These longtime patrons of her arts paid handsomely for her discreet attentions and had the side benefit of offering connections to the powerful that could be beneficial in her line of work. At times when Mary had been with one of her clients, their need for each other seemed almost frantic. Tom tried hard not to analyze it too much, just accept it. But there were other times when the bad feelings would come. There were her sadnesses too that spoke to him in an unknown language. Being with Mary was the most difficult thing Tom had ever done . . . and the most wonderful. Things with Mary were getting complicated. Emotions tended to do that. He supposed that was where they were in their relationship: getting complicated.

. . .

Well, Lee, old girl, time to start the day. You've got mice to catch, naps to take, and my furniture to scratch, so you'd better get at it." Lee didn't move. When Tom got out of bed, she raised her head and watched him with blinking eyes as he stood in the light of the widow. He looked down at the front portico of the library and wondered about the woman he saw there last night. She dressed well, carried herself with confidence. Not too flashy, but speaking of taste and an understated elegance. She was obviously a woman of breeding, and some wealth as well, judging by her carriage—an attractive combination for an ambitious man such as himself. It surprised him that he would be worthy of notice to a woman like that. She had noticed, though. She had indeed. He gazed absently at the trees lining Lafayette Place as he thought of her smile.

"Don't know, Lee," he said to the snoozing cat. "Can't spread myself too thin. Does no good to be sniffing after a woman I'll never have either. Just gets a man distracted. Got Mary to keep me happy. That's enough for any man," he went on with a satisfied grin. "Most men would call me a lucky son of a bitch. They'd be right, I reckon."

Tom went into the bathroom and poured some water into a basin to wash and shave. He stropped his razor and worked up a lather with his shaving brush on a cake of soap. Rubbing the brush around his face like he was waxing a floor, he had himself lathered in short order. He pulled at an ear to tighten the skin and drew the razor from ear to chin. Mary liked watching him shave. She would sometimes lean loosely against the doorframe to the bathroom and watch with a wistful smile on her face like the Mona Lisa. He had asked her about that once. At first she had gone quiet on him, shutting him out with a long silence. Tom was getting to know those silences. He bided his time. He let her have her thoughts to herself, knowing they'd flower better if left unwatered by him.

"About the only happy memory I have of my father," she said at last, "was watching him shave when I was little." She'd told him she thought it was icing, until she'd decided to taste it. She had grimaced like a little girl and stuck out her tongue.

"I cut myself with his razor," she had told him. She had come close behind him and peered into the mirror around his shoulder, to show him the scar. "See this little scar on my chin?" She pointed to the left side of her chin. "I was maybe ten. I didn't think it could cut me so fast." Mary had paused, her hand held up to her face. "I remember how red it was, the blood, I mean. Funny how things stick in your head; the red blood . . . white shaving cream." Tom rinsed the soap off his own razor and splashed some water on his face. He rubbed himself hard and came up looking into the mirror, remembering.

"So that's how I got my little scar," Mary had said in a small voice. She hadn't been smiling when she finished. Tom remembered the way she had held onto him from behind, her head on his shoulder. There was a well of sadness in Mary.

Tom wanted to heal her. That was part of it, part of Mary and him. She could be so smart and sexy, so loving. But the sadness crept through now and again to remind her of what had been. It was his sworn enemy and Tom battled it regularly, though it mocked him sometimes when all else seemed right. Tom lived for the day when he would see her sadness for the last time. For now he'd take it a day at a time and measure his victories in smiles.

Tom locked the front door as he went out. Even on Lafayette Place you couldn't be too careful. Of course, cops lock doors like accountants watch decimal points. It was just something they did. Tom walked north up Lafayette to the corner, then east by the little park in front of Cooper Union. Old Abe gave his "Right Makes Might" speech there back in '60. It was the start of him being taken seriously as presidential timber. They say he had gone to McSorley's afterward, but none could say for certain if he drank a pint of ale or not. How it was possible to go to McSorley's and not drink a pint or two, Tom had never been able to prove personally.

He climbed the steps to the Astor Place station on the Third Avenue El. He got on the El when it rumbled in, heading south with the rest of the morning crush. Riding the El could be a little nerve-wracking. The whole structure seemed too insubstantial to be supporting trains or the masses of passengers they carried. In fact, the whole thing shook rather alarmingly when a train went by. The little engines chugged and belched black soot back on the cars behind. On a fine spring day like this, with the windows open, the smoke and soot could make catching a breeze an iffy thing. Tom saw one woman dabbing and wiping at her dress in a foolish attempt at getting the black off. It was far better to fan it off, as everyone knew. The noise made conversation a shouting affair.

Tom figured he could usually tell which conductor was at the controls from how far the train leaned on the bend at Cooper Square. Today he thought it was the short fat one, with the smudged derby pushed back on his head. When he got off downtown he looked ahead at the engine, but it looked like he had missed his guess when a thin face with a mouthful of chaw popped out of the engineer's window and spat on the platform. He hoped it was not an omen.

In a few minutes Tom was walking up the steps to 300 Mulberry Street, Police Headquarters. The building was showing signs of overcrowding. It had been built in '63 and was showing its age. Tom took the stairs two at a time up to the second-floor headquarters of the Detective Bureau.

"Morning, gentlemen," Tom said to the room full of milling sergeant detectives. They were an interesting bunch. The bureau was new just this year and had been filled with as diverse an assortment of policemen as the city had to offer. For the most part they were men who had shown a particular aptitude for solving cases. Persistence, and a strong sense of the street, especially for its informants, was a common attribute. More often than not they got their man simply because they would not give up. They were experienced men. They knew their way around the five points, or a barroom brawl, or a riot on the docks. And to a man, they were corrupt.

There wasn't a man in the room who hadn't bought his way onto the force. Interesting that in order to start a career in law enforcement, the first requirement was to break the law. The going bribe for a new recruit was about $300, give or take. Most had paid for promotions as well. The man who didn't pay for advancement simply wasn't advanced, promotion list be damned. Every one of them had paid at least $1,000 to get his sergeant's stripes, about a year's pay for most patrolmen. To reach captain, the tab was at least ten times that. The only way to get that kind of money was off the streets. Graft, protection money, "gifts," tribute, tithes, extortion, payoffs, and a host of more unsavory practices were common. That was not to say that there weren't honest cops. It was just that an honest cop, however well intentioned at the start, had to live on between $800 to $1,200 a year and watch while those around him pocketed many times that, eventually buying a higher rank where the money flowed like melted butter. It was not an atmosphere for growing virtue. In fact, Tom thought of the department as a kind of hothouse, where the plants grew to extraordinary size, their roots deep in the loam of corruption. The smell in the hothouse sometimes sickened him, but he was rooted in it like all the rest.

They were not bad men. They were good men doing bad things. That's how they looked at it, and in fact that's mostly how it was. Of course, there were some bad men, some who had let the hothouse atmosphere seep into their bones. Those were the ones for whom the law ceased to exist, at least in the traditional sense. They didn't serve the law, they *were* the law. And when you are the law, it becomes very hard to serve anyone other than yourself. Tom figured Coffin for one of those. He certainly had enough of that sort around him, doing his dirty work.

It had been almost two years now since he made his deal with Captain August J. Coffin. It had looked good at the time. The captain was all compliments and support, telling Tom what a fine sergeant he'd make and how he'd be proud to help him achieve the rank he deserved. Coffin could break through the corrupted promotion process by lining the right pockets. He'd assured Tom at the time that this was really a simple matter. Tom wouldn't have to put up a dime. All he'd need to do would be to pay Coffin back over the next couple of years, at a nominal rate of interest. He'd have his promotion and be guaranteed a slot at a lucrative precinct. If from time to time August needed a discreet favor, or a reliable man to handle a delicate situation, why, then he hoped he could rely on Tom. Tom remembered how good it sounded, and in fact it *had* been good in a lot of ways.

The trouble was that he was now deep in the netherworld between the law and the criminal, where morality had more to do with circumstances and situations than with the law.

Tom walked to his desk, exchanging "good mornings" with the men as he passed. Most sat at their desks, nursing coffee and looking like shit. It seemed to be part of the job to look like shit, at least judging by the group in this room. Tom was fairly sure he didn't look like shit this morning, but had to admit that the job would do it to you more often than not. He got a coffee off the little stove in the back, which had a habit of belching black smoke in the winter when it was fed too much coal. He had just turned, hot coffee in hand, when a loud call came from the other side of the room.

"Tom! Top o' the mornin', boy-o," came the gruff hail.

"Morning, Chowder. What's the news?" Tom asked, knowing he was giving Chowder an opening for one of his patented homilies on the department, the city, or life in general. Chowder considered himself something of a philosopher, though admittedly of the rough-and-ready sort, and Tom almost always enjoyed his observations. He had a way with words, and, when he wished, his lilting brogue adorned them with a charm beyond their meaning.

"Och, same, Tom, same. The captains're wanderin' around unable to find their arses wi' both hands, while we, the very backbone of the force, protect our finer citizens from the criminal classes, for Delmonico's greater good," Chowder intoned seriously.

"Another ordinary day at 300," Tom said, grinning.

"Exactly, Tommy," Chowder replied seriously. "Heard you've found yourself another case down on Peck Slip. Wouldn't be anyone I'd be happy to see dead, now?" An anticipatory light sparkled in his eye.

"Don't think so, Chowder. Looks like a worker off the bridge. Got himself into some scrape or other and found himself with one hell of a headache."

"Bullet?"

"Blunt object. Pipe, or blackjack, maybe. Left the back of his head soft as an old melon."

"That'd be a shame, now. Can't have our decent workin' folk fallin' to the forces of evil right before our noses, can we? Got a plan?"

"Going down to the bridge later, see what I can see. Gotta go over to the East Side for a bit first to check on acquaintances, that sort of thing. You know, dig around a bit, maybe see if I can scare something up."

"Tom, I know you'll strike a blow for the side of righteousness. There's still a bit of the believer in you that the job hasn't scoured away, unlike the jaded old sod you see before you. Take my advice, Tommy, you hold onto that. Help you keep your sense o' direction," Chowder said, all foolishness gone from his voice.

Chowder Kelly was indeed an "old sod." He had joined the force in '58. Even back then Chowder had to pay to get on the force. He claimed to have seen it all in his years as a cop—everything the city had to offer in the way of criminal activity. Nobody doubted Chowder Kelly. He had earned his name in '63 during the draft riots, by a heroic, single-handed defense of an oyster and chowder house on Pine Street. Chowder was in the habit of eating lunch there nearly every day, gratis, of course. He had developed an intimate relationship with the chowder, knowing its every nuance, spice, and texture. So when the rioting mobs threatened, he felt it his duty to defend the place. Chowder's financial interest in the less savory aspects of the chowder house's business may have influenced him. A small stable of four girls, catering to the dock trade, kept the rooms upstairs occupied steadily. Bedsprings creaked so often over the heads of the diners that nobody noticed.

On the first night, a mob took a notion to tear into the place. Chowder had been standing out front—probably all it took to set them off. A uniform could do that during the riots. The story went that he stood right by the front door as the mob came boiling down the street. They waved pick handles, cleavers, swords, knives, and clubs. A hundred red eyes in the torchlight marched down on him, shouting, confident, and defiant. He had held his ground, leaning against the door frame, looking like he was waiting for the Broadway stage. As the lead man in the crowd got within fifteen feet, Chowder brought up his twelve gauge and, without a word, blew the man's head off.

"You shoulda seen 'em scatter, Tommy." Chowder had laughed in his beer at the memory when he had told the story to Tom years before. "Nothin' like a shotgun fer crowd control. Splattered that poor bastard's head over half the crowd. Never bothered the place again after that. Went after easier pickings, I suppose. Anyway I just went inside and sat it out. Spent three days eatin' chowder till the troops arrived."

"What'd you do with the body?" Tom had felt stupid for asking as soon as it came out.

"Left it there, of course. Sort of like advertising. Very effective. That advertising's a real lifesaver."

"Sensible," Tom had observed.

Tom chatted with Chowder for a few more minutes, sipping coffee and going over the day's news in the department: who was arrested the day before, what detective was drinking too much and nearly got caught by the chief, Thomas Byrnes . . . that sort of thing. It sometimes amazed Tom that he could have those sorts of conversations nearly every morning. That's one of the things he liked about the job: It always changed, inside the department and especially on the street. This morning it was he who had the most news. Murders were always good for lively conversation. They were interrupted by chief of detectives Byrnes, as he marched out of his office and called the men to order with a big "harrumph." They lined up, chins out, stomachs in, doing their best to appear disciplined.

After roll call, they went to what Byrnes called morning parade. Down by the holding cells, they'd trot out everyone who had been arrested the day before. The idea was that it would help the detectives remember the faces of thieves, pickpockets, rowdies, and the like. It was one of Byrnes's innovations. Most thought it pretty useful. Once morning parade was over, they were all treated to a briefing from the chief. Byrnes, his high starched collar taking flight on either side of his chin, gave a rousing call to action to the detectives in the room. His mustache bristled as he reminded the men of their mission in life. The Detective Bureau was new, and the city had made a big commitment to it. It was their duty to show results. Arrests and convictions were the order of the day. They were an elite unit and they had to live up to a higher standard. Reassignment was waiting for those who could not toe the line. This was the worst threat of all. It meant not only humiliation and a big setback to the career, but a vast decrease in income too. Anyone reassigned by Byrnes would end up sucking hind tit on that gravy train for years to come.

Tom went to his desk feeling as if his cats had died. Byrnes was turning up the heat. The pressure was on to produce results. Not everyone was paying the cops for protection, after all. Those who didn't needed catching. Mostly it was the violent crimes they concentrated on, those and the minor criminals who couldn't afford to pay. The irony of the situation had not escaped Tom. It took money to break the law. So long as the money flowed, finding its way into the right pockets, the lawless didn't have too much to worry about. He spent an hour or so finishing up his initial report on the Bucklin case, made a new file, and placed it at the top of his stack.

Heading out of 300 Mulberry, he ran into Sam coming up the front steps.

"Sam, good to see you. What brings you to the sanctum sanctorum?" Tom asked, shaking his hand.

"The what?" Sam asked, perplexed. "Is that what they're calling this place now?"

"Nah, just me showing off my eighth-grade education. It means holiest of holies, or something like that."

"Hmph. Sort of fits. You always were a kidder. Only thing holy in this place is the shitter."

Tom laughed hard but cast a glance around his shoulder. "Best to keep that talk low around here though," he said softly. "Ears around every corner."

"Good advice. But I've got some advice for you. That's why I came up here. You planning to see Coffin today?" Sam asked hopefully.

"Why?" Tom already knew the answer.

"He was asking about you. Said he hadn't seen you much lately."

Tom just nodded, his lips pursed in thought.

"You'd be smart to keep in touch more. As long as you're one of his boys, you've got to play by the rules."

"We shouldn't be having this conversation here, Sam," Tom said, looking around. The two of them started south down Mulberry, the hustle and noise of the street making their conversation impossible to hear for anyone more than a few feet away. "I got myself in with the wrong man, Sam. I don't like it. I don't like some of the things I hear, and I don't like some of the things I have to do. He's got into things, taking money from some people who we shouldn't be protecting. I know you know what I'm talking about," Tom said as they passed one of the old-law tenements on the block. It reeked, just like his deal with Coffin.

"Listen, Tom, you don't have to like it, just play the game," Sam said, sounding reasonable. "Pay the bastard off and go your own way. You'll be rid of him. Listen, he was askin' for you yesterday afternoon. He sounded like he . . . Well, I think you should see him, is all."

"I understand, Sam. I was planning to pay him a call today anyway," Tom said as they passed the old St. Patrick's.

"Good. No point pissing him off. No time at all and he'll be off your back." Sam was trying to be reassuring.

"Don't think so, Sam. Coffin's a fucking tar baby . . . and I'm stuck."

The two men parted company a block farther on. Tom split off toward the east and Sam went to finish his morning rounds. Tom was in no hurry to get there, though, and walked the ten blocks or so to Suffolk deep in thought.

Tom found himself rationalizing the contradictions of his life more and more. He was a good man, a good cop, and he served the law well. His reputation as a solid sergeant detective and his record before that was well earned. He was proud of it. The fact was that he also did bad things. But the bad things he did were to bad people . . . people who made their money on the edges of the law—at least that's what he told himself. The numbers were against them. Too many homeless, hopeless, and penniless souls willing to do anything for their next crust of bread. Twenty thousand orphans running wild in the streets, selling newspapers, if they were lucky, or themselves if they weren't. Some said as many as 100,000 homeless lived in the city, in shanties, squatting on the evaporating vacant land, dying of disease in the summer, frostbite in winter. And seemingly as numerous were the ones who preyed on them, in a sort of urban Darwinian cycle. Criminals should be made to pay, though. They did pay . . . more often in dollars than in time behind bars. But for every dollar that found its way into Tom's pocket, he lost a little piece of himself in the transaction. He wondered if a Daniel Webster would come back and get him off this deal with the devil. He thought not.

For the next couple of hours, Tom canvassed the short list of Terrence Bucklin's friends. The story was pretty much the same. It was remarkable, really. His pastor, a sickly looking man named Father O'Brien, summed it up well.

"Detective, Terrence Bucklin was a man with nothing to confess." Tom had run into him as O'Brien was leaving the Bucklin apartment, where he had come to comfort the family and make final arrangements.

"I'm hearing that all over, Father. Nobody I've come across has had a bad thing to say about him. I've spoken to a number of people who knew him, and it's all the same lyrics, different tunes. I'm headed upstairs to the Loftus family now. That's my last stop. How're the Bucklins holding up and the boy, Mikey?" Tom asked, looking toward their door.

"As well as can be hoped, Detective. They've seen more than their share of sorrows," he said, his head hanging. "There's a toughness that God sometimes gives those in need, and the Lord has seen fit to bestow it on them, I think," the priest said slowly. "Mike is a worry to me, though. Children are so easily lost."

"I know what you mean, Father," Tom said. "It's hard."

"Indeed it is, Detective. I'll be keeping an eye out for him."

"Me too," Tom said. "Well, it was good to meet you, Father. I've got to get upstairs to talk to the Loftuses, see if they can tell me anything new."

"You'll hear the same from them too, Detective," Father O'Brien said. "A good man by all accounts, and not an enemy in the world."

Tom shook his head, his mouth pursed. "That's where you're wrong, Father. He had at least one, and I mean to find him."

❋ Chapter Seven ❋

*Probably no great work was ever conducted by a
man who worked under so many disadvantages.*

—EMILY ROEBLING

The Third Precinct was pretty quiet by the time Tom got there later that morning. Sam was out; Jaffey too. The desk sergeant nodded Tom upstairs to Coffin's office without breaking stride on his paperwork. Tom took the steps two at a time. He hadn't been looking forward to his meeting, especially not after his stop yesterday, but now that he was here, he figured to get it over as soon as possible. He knocked on Coffin's door, letting himself in before the captain even called, "Who is it?"

"Morning, Captain," Tom said evenly. He called him captain only in public. Behind closed doors it was August, mainly because he knew how much the captain disliked it, or Augie if he really wanted to piss him off. Coffin got up from his desk, half in surprise, half in anger at the interruption.

"Tom! How good it is to see you. I didn't expect you this morning," he said for the sake of anyone in earshot. "What brings you to our fair precinct?" They shook hands like old friends—a small show for those outside Coffin's office. Tom gripped his hand hard, grinding the bones. He could see the color come up over August's collar as he tried to pull back. All the while Coffin smiled and mouthed platitudes.

"Come on in to my office, Detective. Sergeant Halpern told me you're working on that body his man found on Peck Slip yesterday." The door closed behind Tom hard enough to rattle the big glass panel.

"Let's cut through the shit, Braddock," Coffin snapped as he sat at his desk. "You have something for me?" Tom didn't say a word, just passed two envelopes to him. Only half a dozen more payments, Tom thought.

"You're late," Coffin said. "And what's this?" Coffin fingered the second envelope, measuring its thickness.

"Made a stop at Madame LeFarge's yesterday," Tom said. "Had some trouble with that little pervert Grafton. You know the one?"

" 'Fraid so. Beat up one of Kate's girls. Put her in the hospital."

"The same." Tom put his hands flat on Coffin's desk, leaning over it, so he loomed over the captain. "Had to impress on him the need to stay out of LeFarge's, which brings me to my second point."

"Which is?" Coffin said with an innocent stare.

"Which is that we shouldn't be taking her money, August." Braddock growled. "You know the kinds of things that go on down there." Tom felt somehow naïve before Coffin's even stare. Coffin knew very well the kind of things that went on down there. Rumor had it that he'd been taking part in some of them himself.

"Let me set you straight on a couple of points," Coffin said with a raised hand, interrupting Tom in a low but powerful tone. "First thing is that I'm in charge here. I say who we protect and who we don't. Understand?" He didn't wait for an answer. "Second, what you like and what you don't is your affair, not mine. I value your opinions, Tom." He went on, trying to temper the hard edge of his voice. "But you must respect the fact that there are others involved in certain matters, and I am in a better position than you to judge what I do and don't do." August waited a moment. "We clear on that?"

"As crystal, Captain," Tom said flatly. What he thought was another matter.

"Good. Let's not dwell on these things, Tommy. Leave the decisions to me. It's my responsibility, which brings me to *your* responsibilities." He paused, tilting his head in an inquisitive stare. "Where have you been of late?"

"Been busy. Besides, we have a business arrangement, and you know very well I honor my obligations."

Coffin seemed to ponder that for a moment while he put his feet up on his desk and squeezed the envelopes once again. Tom took the chair across from him. August said nothing, just took up a pencil and commenced flipping it in the air. It was perhaps his most annoying habit. Tom sat silent, watching the little display.

Finally Coffin said, "Good man, Tommy. I knew my concerns were groundless. I won't even count it." He waved a hand at the envelopes. Tom wondered how it would sound when Coffin's neck snapped in his hands. He pictured his fingers digging into the flesh, the color draining, eyes bulging, the tongue lolling stupidly. He smiled inside.

"You're a bit of a rebellious spirit, I suppose, but that can be a strength as well as a failing. It's one of the reasons I decided to help you advance in the department," Coffin said as if all was forgiven. Tom figured that was the least of August's reasons. "How are things up at the bureau?" he asked, changing the subject.

"Pretty much as you'd expect. Byrnes is feeling the pressure from the brass. We got another one of his homilies this morning," Tom said with a raised eyebrow.

"Hmph. Tough job he's got forming a new department. A great opportunity though. Stick close to him and you'll go far, Tommy. The Detective Bureau will be a success, of that you may be assured. Byrnes won't have it any other way."

"Was a little rough at first," Tom observed. "Some of the boys in the precincts don't understand how we're supposed to operate. Think we're stepping out of bounds, sticking our noses in their cases. Makes for some awkward encounters."

Coffin twirled his pencil. "But you're doing well, I take it? You've prospered since your promotion, haven't you?" He stopped twirling his pencil in expectation. "Didn't I tell you it would be worth the investment?"

"That you did, August," Tom admitted with a shrug. "And I have done well, no denying it."

"Indeed. And I'm gratified to see you moving up, I truly am. It's very satisfying to me to know of all the very deserving gentlemen whose careers I've helped advance," Coffin said with a look that was smug and disingenuous at the same time. "They're a credit to the department, most of them. But, you know, Tommy, some have disappointed me . . . from time to time. And disappointments, even if they seem small . . . well, they add up, you know. I put a great deal of faith and confidence in my boys, and I don't expect to be disappointed. Makes me doubt. I hate doubts . . . really I do. Complicates things. Don't you agree?"

"No question, August," Tom said in an even tone. He knew where Coffin was going with this.

"Now I'm sure I can rely on *you*, Tommy. Isn't that correct? I can rely on you despite an occasional small *disappointment*?" Coffin pointed his pencil at Tom's chest.

"You can, August. We are bound, you and I. Sort of like a marriage, you could say," Tom said, praying marriage would never be like this.

"Just the point, Tommy, that's exactly it. And a marriage brings people together . . . joins them in the common enterprise of life, does it not? A marriage requires trust and confidence. That's the very glue of a marriage, don't you agree?"

"Love would come first in my book, August, but I see your point."

"You know, in a way I'm married to all my men and them to me. We have that trust and confidence for the most part. And I'm thinking now that perhaps a small disappointment here and there is nothing to end a marriage over. No need for that. A marriage is sacred, after all, and not to be broken lightly. Of course you wouldn't know about that, Tommy, you not being in that state of bliss, you old dog." Coffin forced a chuckle.

"Oh, I believe I know something on the subject, August," Tom said evenly.

"Indeed. Indeed, I'm sure you do. No, no need to break up a marriage over a trivial matter, like I was saying. But you know, Tommy, if one partner betrays the other's trust and confidence, then I feel that union should be broken. Don't you agree—broken swiftly and permanently, for the good of both parties?" Coffin flipped his pencil idly, tossing it by the end, setting it spinning a couple of times before he caught it.

"I suppose that would be best. No point prolonging a union that cannot possibly work," Tom said, playing along. He crossed his legs with a casualness he didn't feel and stared at the captain.

"I'm glad you see my point, Tommy. But I want you to know that I have complete confidence in you. No breakups going on here, oh no. We're a team, you and I. We're like a pitcher and a catcher; giving the signs, throwing curves or fastballs, watching for the steal and ready for the bunt." August smiled widely, pleased at his analogy. He caught his pencil in midspin, pointing it at Tom. "If I thought otherwise, Thomas, you'd be out of the game."

August no sooner threatened Tom than he asked a favor of him, knowing that he couldn't refuse. It was a trivial matter really, according to Coffin. "A small annoyance."

"I have a problem with the operator of a gaming parlor, and I was hoping you could do me a small favor." Tom said nothing, just sat in anticipation of the dirty work. "You see, this man Finney thinks he can carry on his activities without making the proper arrangements. He doesn't seem to understand how business is done in this town." Coffin wore a concerned frown.

A bored grin oozed across Tom's face. "I see. You'd like me to give him a lesson in economics."

"Precisely," Coffin agreed, smiling at Tom's euphemism. "Nothing extreme, mind you. Just a reasonable appeal to his better business instincts."

"So, he should not be inconvenienced by ill health or a sudden misfortune, I take it?"

"No, no. Not necessary at this point. I believe he'll see that we have his best interests at heart. Finney just needs a reminder of how those interests might best be served." Coffin twirled his pencil pensively. "Don't want Finney to go sprouting any false hopes about prospects, so the sooner the better, Thomas."

"All right, Augie," Tom said. He relished the frown the nickname brought to Coffin's face. "So where's this Finney character?" The captain told Tom how much he was expected to get from Finney. It was higher than usual— something Finney had brought on himself by not playing ball sooner, August had smugly assured him.

"Here's the address. When can I expect you to get back to me, Tommy?"

"Give me two days," Tom said over his shoulder as he opened Coffin's door to go. He didn't want to stay a moment longer than he had to. Coffin's feet were still up on his desk, but there were thunderheads hovering around his brow as he watched Tom walk away.

Tom was boiling as he walked out of the precinct. This was a new low for Coffin. It was the first time he had actually been threatened. While Tom didn't think much of August, he had to take his threat seriously. Not that he feared Coffin himself. Coffin didn't have the stomach for his own dirty work. If Coffin came after him, it would be with the corps. That's what he called it. It had taken time to build it up, man by man, with men just like him. In many ways it was a private army, men he had bought, corrupted, and manipulated over the years. No one knew how many there were. Tom knew of some but always figured there were others he hadn't heard of. Coffin had made quite a career of advancing "deserving" individuals. Once the hook was set, and the new sergeant, or wardsman, or captain, or detective started paying off the loan, he found that Coffin's interest wasn't the only price to pay.

Tom had every intention of getting the Finney problem out of the way as soon as possible. No point putting it off. It would only mean trouble for him, and for Finney too, not that he cared much on that account. The fact was that he was a lot closer to the bridge than he was to Finney's at the moment, which was a few blocks north near the corner of Baxter and Centre streets. So, Tom set his sights on the bridge, and crossed Park Row to the bridge approach. There was still a great deal of work going on on the Manhattan side. The approaches were elevated roadways that connected the bridge with the streets. They extended inland for blocks. Whole neighborhoods had been leveled to accommodate them. Tom paid closer attention to the details of the bridge as he walked alongside the approach beside the new train terminal. The roadway was supported by a series of stone arches, growing from about two to five stories high down closer to the river. The one at Franklin Square had the El running through it on its way uptown. The granite and sandstone contrasted with the small shabby-looking brick-and-frame buildings that surrounded the bridge, their fronts covered with signage on nearly every floor. As Tom went further he slowly rose above the surrounding rooftops. Tom had walked about two hundred yards up the approach before anyone bothered to ask what his business was there.

"Say, fella, what're you up to there? We don't allow no sightseers. You can just turn around and go back the way you come."

"I'm Detective Sergeant Braddock," Tom said, sliding aside his jacket to show the badge pinned to his vest. "I'm making inquiries about a man who worked on the bridge, maybe you know him, name of Bucklin, Terrence Bucklin?"

"Ya need ta go to the bridge office," the man said, waving his hand vaguely in the direction of Brooklyn.

"All right," Tom said, seeing he'd get no help from this one. "And where would that be?"

"Fulton and Front streets," the laborer said, not looking at Braddock. "The Brooklyn *Union* Building."

Tom started off across the bridge on foot.

"Ain't allowed to cross the bridge," the man called after him. "Hey, you hear? It ain't allowed."

Tom kept walking. It took him twenty minutes to walk over to the building that housed the bridge offices. Tom reminded himself to take the ferry back. He didn't much care for walking the wooden planking where the roadway wasn't finished. The river looked a bit too far down.

It took another twenty to get a fix on what construction crew Bucklin had worked on and where they were supposed to be this morning.

"We got hundreds of men on this job, Detective," a clerk had told him once he'd identified himself and explained his need to check on Bucklin. "I'll have to go over the payroll to make sure he's with us, first off."

"I'd appreciate it. I'll wait," Tom said.

It was some time later when the clerk asked, "Bucklin, eh? Got a Buckland, a Bucklin, and two Buckmans. You sure how it's spelled?" Tom spelled it for him. "Okay. Give me a minute, maybe I can tell you where he's assigned today."

Tom sat in the small lobby, reading a copy of the *Union* while he waited. The clerk buried his head in the day's work assignment sheets, rustling papers as he flipped through.

"Got it!" he said at last, holding up a slip of paper. "He's supposed to be working masonry on the New York side, doing brickwork on the vaults. His foreman's a fellow by the name of Hightower."

Tom got up, tucked the *Union* under his arm, and walked to the big desk that served as the office reception area. The clerk spread the sheet out for him.

"Does it say where exactly: north side, south side, which cross-street, anything? I saw a lot of men over there a little while ago," Tom said as he peered at the paperwork.

"Doesn't say," The clerk frowned. "Lots of times it don't," the man said apologetically.

Tom thanked him and headed for the Fulton Ferry Terminal. He'd had enough walking. He didn't notice that one of the other clerks who had been standing nearby watched him with special interest as he left.

A half hour later, after a delay on the ferry due to river traffic, Tom was staring up at the anchorage on the New York side. He looked left and spotted some men up on a scaffold under the Franklin Street overpass. He walked over and shouted to get their attention. "Any of you men know Terrence Bucklin?"

"Wha'?" someone shouted back.

"Terrence Bucklin," Tom called again.

"He ain't here" came the reply from somewhere up in the scaffolding.

"Any idea where I can find Hightower?" Tom tried next. The clerk had mentioned that Bucklin had been assigned to that foreman's crew.

"Thought you said Bucklin?" a voice came back. "Make up yer fuckin' mind." Tom started to explain but thought better of it and waited.

A minute later a head popped over the edge of the scaffold. "So, what is it?" the head asked.

"I need to find his crew, Bucklin's and Hightower's that is."

The head cleared its throat and spit down in Tom's general direction. "Supposed to be brickin' up the vaults. Up a ways," it said. An arm appeared and waved in the direction of City Hall.

Tom waved back, grunting an acknowledgment.

When Tom got "up a ways" he came upon another crew doing brickwork. He walked up to the man who appeared to be in charge.

"Hightower?"

"Who wants 'im?" the man shot back, standing with his hands on his hips.

"Detective Braddock. I'm investigating a murder. You know Terrence Bucklin?" Tom showed his shield.

"Don't know him. Heard his name, though," the man said, taking his

hands off his hips. "Works with Hightower's crew, all right. They was supposed to be with us today but we got bricks enough for just one crew, so they
moved on up to the roadway." The foreman pointed back to where Tom had
started about an hour before. "Think they're doing some damn thing up
there."

"What's he look like, this Hightower?"

"Round sort of fella. Suspenders, an' a bowler," the foreman said over his
shoulder as he looked up at his men laying bricks.

Tom took the three-block walk back to where he had started, feeling as if he
had wasted a lot more time than he really had. He checked into the train terminal first as long as he was there. The ringing of hammers echoed from the
cavernous roof of the half-finished building. Once again he was given a wave
of an arm and the general direction where Hightower could be found. Tom
figured he had found his man at last when he spotted a bowler perched on a
big head and an even bigger body.

"You Hightower?"

"What can I do for you, mister?" the fat man said. Tom identified himself
and asked if he knew Bucklin.

"I would say I do. Worked with him for three years past. James Hightower," he said, extending a thick hand. "What's this about Bucklin? Been
wonderin' where he took himself off to." Hightower tilted back his bowler to
scratch his head. "Hain't seen 'im for a coupla days."

"Bucklin's dead. Found yesterday in the alley behind Paddy's."

"Jaysus! The hell you say." Hightower almost shouted. "I tell you, this
city'll just eat you up and spit you out. No fit place for humanity. I'm a
Brooklyn man myself," he said, seeming anxious to make the distinction.
"What happened to 'im?"

Tom told him without giving too many details. "Tell me, how many men
on this job?"

"Well, I got twenty-odd on this crew, but there's dozens more workin' steel
and cable. Then there's those what's workin' on the train tracks and stations.
All told, maybe three hundred, give or take. That's both sides, mind you."

"Anyone else besides Bucklin been out of work the last day or so?" Tom
asked, looking around.

"Nope, not on my crew. Can't speak for the rest, o'course."

Tom spent maybe fifteen minutes talking with Hightower, asking a lot but
not getting much of use. The foreman hadn't been aware of anything going on
with Bucklin; no troubles to his way of knowing, no fights or disagreements,
just a good hard worker. He was aware of Bucklin's misfortunes and had gone

to the wake of his wife and little girl last year but couldn't claim to be really close with him, he said.

"Must be a big job making sure everything goes right on a project like this," Tom observed casually. "Got to be a million ways to screw things the wrong way."

"Maybe, mister, but I run a tight ship. Can't speak fer others but my crew's tiptop."

"Fine-looking bunch of men," Tom observed, looking around at the group. "You ever come across any shenanigans on the job? You know—work not done right, maybe shoddy materials, that sort of thing?"

Hightower gave him a stony look. "Not on my crew, mister. They had the cable fraud back years ago, but that was none of my affair."

"You ever hear Bucklin say anything about something not being right about the bridge?"

"What're you getting at, Detective?" Hightower asked defensively. "You think we're in on some fraud or somethin'? You're wrong if you do." He hooked his thumbs behind his suspenders. "Nothin' but honest work goin' on here. And to answer your question, Bucklin didn' say nothin' to me about any such shenanigans."

Tom raised a hand. "Not implying anything. Just a theory. It doesn't seem as though Bucklin had any enemies, but someone sure did seem to want him dead." He pointed a finger at Hightower's ample gut. "You figure it out. By the way," he said, looking around at the men, "how many men would you say chew tobacco on your crew?"

"What's that got to do with anything?" When Tom didn't answer, he just said, "I don't know, maybe half or more. Pretty common habit, ya know."

Braddock spent two long hours questioning everyone on the crew, including the German, Rolf Mentzer, Matt Emmons, and Earl Lebeau.

"You from down south?" Tom had asked Matt.

"Yup. Thought we'd come north after the war. Not much money to be had back home, and with the niggers takin' jobs it's harder than ever."

Tom just nodded. "What unit you serve with?" he asked casually, taking notes as they talked.

"Robertson's Brigade. Company B, Fifth Texas," Matt answered, unable to hide the pride or the tinge of a challenge in his voice. He'd never been able to mask his pride in his service, not even after years in the North. It had always been a badge of honor for him, always would be, and be damned to anyone who thought otherwise.

"You were at Gettysburg, then." Tom said, looking up from his notes. "Might be we saw each other. I was with the Twentieth New York."

"Uh-huh," Matt said appraisingly. "We weren't in it till the second day really. With Hood."

"Then you're the boys that almost took Little Round Top! Say, did you know that Roebling was a Lieutenant then and helped save that position? You know, Roebling . . . the chief engineer for the bridge?" Tom waved vaguely toward Brooklyn. "How's that for a coincidence?" Matt tried to look surprised. "Is that a fact? Small world, ain't it? If they hadn't reinforced, we might just have won that one."

"I'll not argue with you. You boys fought like the devil. Close thing." They both knew what an understatement that was. "The Twentieth was near the center on the third day," Tom said, knowing what it would mean to Emmons.

Matt put down his cement trowel. "You get in the thick of it?"

"Oh, yeah. We were at the southern edge of the rock wall, and by the time Pickett's line got across, it had concentrated on that little grove of trees a couple hundred yards north. That ain't to say we had it easy. We moved up to reinforce the center. Got into it pretty heavy."

"Never should have made that charge," Matt said sadly.

This was the first time Tom had actually talked at any length to someone who fought for the Confederacy. There was a kinship there, a shared experience too awful to voice. Tom figured it was somehow the dead that bound them. The sorrow for those who did not come home knew no side. A soldier became just a man again in death, an enemy no longer humanized and dehumanized at one stroke.

"Come July, it'll be twenty years." Earl shook his head slowly, as if this was the first time he had thought about it. He had sidled over as Tom and Matt spoke. Earl's brow wrinkled at the effort, and he chewed his tobacco contemplatively. Matt introduced Earl and told him Tom was investigating Bucklin's murder.

"Damn! Murder, you say? Well, you can count on us to help any way we can," Earl said with a sincerity that almost had Matt believing him. "How'd it get done, an' who done it?"

"Rather not say just yet," Tom said. "And as to who did it, well I have my suspects." Tom lied.

"Oh, I get it," Matt said. "Smart to keep quiet on the details till you nail yer man."

Tom just smiled knowingly, wishing he really did know anything of value. He continued to ask them both the usual series of questions, checking on Bucklin's friends, enemies, debts, quarrels, girlfriends, if any, and anything else that might seem productive. Matt and Earl appeared helpful but ultimately gave him very little except vague notions about Bucklin's finances. Earl spat tobacco with precision, Tom noticed. Braddock kept up this line of questioning, asking about the job, the pay, and anything he could find out about labor problems, shoddy contractors, and the like. He felt that he was going in circles, though, so he branched into another area.

"How many came north from your unit?"

"Three; us and Simon Watkins yonder," Earl lied easily, pointing to Watkins on the other side of the roadway. "Mr. Long-shanks over there by the train tracks."

Braddock sized Watkins up. "He *is* a lanky one. Watkins, you said?"

"Yep. Served with us most of the war, 'cept when he got wounded."

Watkins glanced over at them, then looked away quickly.

"Oh ... ah, you boys ever socialized with Terrence ... you know, go drinking, that sort of thing?"

"Sure did," Matt said.

"He was out with us at Paddy's two weeks ago, Friday. First time in a dog's age he even went out for a pint," Earl added.

Tom remembered Mrs. Bucklin saying Terrence was drinking more lately. He wondered who with.

"Couple Fridays ago, you say?" Tom perked up at the information. "You didn't mention that before," he said casually. He couldn't help but wonder why.

"Didn't ask," Earl said with a squirt of tobacco for emphasis. "Besides, there was a few of us. Mentzer was there, me and Bucklin, an' maybe three or four more."

"Notice anything strange?"

"Strange? No. Bucklin went home early, but nothin' strange about that. Mentzer had about two pints too many, but nothin' strange about that neither," Earl said.

"He went home early, huh? You see him leave?" Tom asked, scribbling notes on his pad.

"Not 'zactly. I recall him sayin' he had to go, then I think he went to the jakes, but I can't be sure. Sure I didn't see him after that, though." Tom watched them both closely, noticing how Earl fidgeted with the hammer that hung at his belt.

"You didn't see anything? Think back. Did he argue with anyone? Maybe even a little fracas could have gone bad."

"Nothin' to pernt to. Terrence was not the kind of fella to get into a fracas. Hell, I just thought he went home early. Who found 'im?" Earl asked, hoping to divert the questioning.

"Can't say." Tom gave back a blank stare.

"Wish we could help ya, Detective, we really do," Matt said sincerely. "Hate to see that sort of thing happen. Damn shame ya ask me." Matt shook his head. "Dangerous town, New York."

"Well, I thank you men for your time. Oh . . . here's my card. If you think of anything, you can contact me at 300 Mulberry."

"Sure will," Earl said, extending his hand with a politician's smile. "Hope you find your man."

Tom walked slowly toward Watkins. He could see the man watching him out of the corner of his eye.

"Simon Watkins?"

"Yeah. Who's askin'?" Watkins answered defensively, casting a wary eye over Braddock's shoulder at his friends.

"Detective Tom Braddock," Tom said, showing the shield. He didn't extend his hand as he had with Earl and Matt. "I'm looking into the murder of Terrence Bucklin. I'm told you knew him."

Watkins cast a quick glance up at the cables to his left, as if imagining what to say, Tom thought. "I knew him; knew him well enough to drink with now and again. Nothin' wrong with that."

"Didn't say there was. You don't seem particularly surprised to hear about Bucklin. Now, why would that be, I wonder?" Tom readied himself for whatever might follow. Something about Watkins had his ears at attention. Watkins's Adam's apple bobbed.

Simon thought fast for once in his life, saying, "Overheard you talkin' to Hightower. Dead, huh? How'd it happen?" He said this as matter-of-factly as he was able, rather proud of himself for carrying it off.

Tom eyed him closely. "Yeah, dead. Body found behind Paddy's yesterday. Your friend Earl says he sometimes went drinking with Bucklin there Friday nights, which reminds me, can you account for your whereabouts this past Friday?"

"I wasn't nowhere near Paddy's Friday night. I was up on fourteenth Street, at Bryant's theatre with a lady friend."

"I see. Who was playing that night? I hear they have some good acts. Might want to take in a show."

"Let's see . . . there was a singer name of Lynn McCloughic. Great little voice. There was juggling and tumbling Italians, name of The Rotinis, or Rot.'lis . . . something like that. They were somethin'. And a few others doin' comedy and such."

"Uh-huh . . . what'd you do afterward?" Tom asked, not trying to hide his skepticism.

"Went for a late dinner at the Monument Restaurant, right across from the statue . . . you know, the one of Washington? Then me and her, we went and had a little fun." Watkins spat a fat stream of tobacco juice over the edge of the approach and winked lewdly.

Tom just nodded. "Uh-huh. Well, I suppose I can rule you out as a suspect, can't I? You having such a busy social calendar and all. And when did this golden evening end for you two?"

"Stayed the night," Watkins said, grinning. A chipped tooth did nothing to improve his smile.

"I suppose you can give me the name and address of this lady friend?" Tom said with his pencil perched over his pad.

"That's right, it's Miss Clora Devine. She lives on Hester, number 340, but you can find her easier at Watley's dance hall on the Bowery."

"I'll pay her a call if you don't mind," Tom said, looking Watkins in the eye, but not for permission.

"Suit yourself. She'll tell ya the same thing, 'cause it's the truth." Watkins spat again for emphasis. "Listen, Bucklin was all right to my way of thinkin', and I sure as hell wouldn't want to go bash his head in or nothin', so . . ."

"What'd you say?" Braddock asked, looking off distractedly. "Say . . . Watkins, who's that woman over there by the north side of the tower?" Tom had seen her an instant before, recognizing her from the Astor library. Even from this distance it was plainly her. It was her carriage, he decided, the way she held her head, the way she walked. It was the same woman.

Watkins turned to look. "Oh, that's Mrs. Roebling. She's always around the job, mostly over in Brooklyn by the office though. Don't see her over this side much."

"Hm, thanks Watkins," Tom said over his shoulder as he walked away. "I'll contact you if I need any further information."

Watkins just snorted and watched him go. Last night he'd thought that maybe Braddock was the answer to his situation with Captain Sangree. But as he watched the detective walk up the bridge toward Mrs. Roebling, that idea took a different twist.

"Maybe I don't have to say a damn word to that fuckin' Braddock," he muttered under his breath. "Hadn't thought o' the Roeblings. Don't have to be Braddock that finds out what Cap'n Sangree's up to." Watkins stood stroking his chin in thought. Matt and Earl watched too, but they weren't watching Braddock, they were watching him.

Emily was with Charles C. Martin, checking on the roadwork. Wash had been very specific about the materials and methods of construction, and she had thought it necessary to go up personally to check. Reporting back to him that she had seen to such details herself always set his mind at ease.

"What will you do when the bridge is done, Charles?" she asked the assistant engineer as they walked together.

"I've had offers from three different railroads that I'm considering," Martin said. "But I'm not sure whether I'll be taking any of those positions. Not challenging enough, I suppose."

Emily gave a knowing shrug. "I know what you mean. After this, everything else will seem trite by comparison. Whatever you do, you'll be measuring it against this bridge. That's a measure that's sure to come up short, Charles. There will be no more Brooklyn Bridges," Emily said, looking up at the cables. "Regardless of what comes after, your name and Wash's and the others will always be known for it. Anything else you do will seem an afterthought."

Martin nodded slowly. "True. I've thought a lot about what to do after, but I can't seem to see an 'after.' It's as if I can't really accept that it will be over. It's been everything for me for the last thirteen years almost, and I can't seem to get my head around the notion that it will end." They both stopped and looked out over the Manhattan skyline. "And then what can I possibly do that will come near this?" Charles C. Martin turned back toward Brooklyn, taking in the sweep of the bridge. "It soars!" he said with a tinge of wonder in his voice. "We've built a cathedral, Emily. What can compare with that?"

Tom wasn't sure how to approach Mrs. Roebling. He hesitated, not sure if he should go over to her directly. Then he thought of Hightower.

"Mr. Hightower?" Tom said as he approached the foreman. "I wonder if I could trouble you to do me the favor of an introduction?"

"An introduction?" Hightower asked with a grin. "I don't think you need be so formal with the roughnecks on this job."

"Oh, no, that's not what I'm after. I'm talking about that woman over by the tower." Tom pointed her out.

"Had me goin' there for a moment. Thought another sightseer was wanderin' around the job. Have a dickens of a time with them. Nothin' but trouble . . . but that there's Mrs. Roebling. Come on, I'll do the honors."

They walked together toward Emily and Charles C. Martin, who were so deep in conversation that neither of them noticed their approach.

"Mrs. Roebling? Good morning, ma'am. I have someone here who would like to meet you. May I present Detective Braddock, of our New York City Police Department. Detective, Mrs. Emily Roebling." Tom had the advantage of her, he knew. He watched closely as the surprise, then recognition, washed over her features.

"Mr. Braddock. A pleasure, sir," she said with perfect composure. Her voice was like honey. It ran off her tongue thick and sweet. Tom could almost taste it.

"And this is Charles C. Martin, the assistant engineer," Emily said gracefully.

"Honored, I'm sure, Detective," Martin said.

"I'm delighted to meet you both, and grateful for the introduction, Mr. Hightower," Tom said, turning to the foreman.

"Think nothing of it, Braddock. You do me the favor of findin' Bucklin's murderer and I'll call us more than even."

"I'll do my best. Thanks."

As Hightower excused himself and walked back to his crew, Emily looked Tom over with an appraising eye. He was a bit taller than she had estimated from across Lafayette Place. Older too, but the laugh lines around his eyes and the thin line of a scar on his right temple lent him an air that was more compelling than youth. There was a small streak of gray in his hair, near the scar. She guessed him to be maybe thirty-five. He had an anxious, almost boyish air about him that she found charming, flattering even. She liked him immediately.

"So, Mr. Braddock, what's this about murder? Has there been foul play on the bridge?" Martin asked.

"No, no. But one of your workers has been murdered, I'm afraid; a Mr. Bucklin, Terrence Bucklin?" They both looked blankly at him. "At any rate, I was just questioning the men he worked with. I'm afraid I haven't found out much."

"You'll find, I fear, that not all the men we hire are Harvard graduates. Lack of breeding, refinement, and education have rendered some of them slaves to their baser instincts," Martin said with a shrug.

"I must ask one question of you, Mr. Martin, if I may," Tom said.

Martin raised a questioning eyebrow.

"Do you recall anything odd going on during the construction process?" Tom asked, knowing it was far too vague a question, but before he could rephrase it, the assistant engineer replied.

" 'Odd,' you say? Sir, there have been any number of things both odd and unbelievable on this job. I wouldn't know where to start."

"The fact that a woman is here on a construction site, let alone helping to oversee the work, is about as odd as things get these days, Charles." Emily said this with a twinkle in her eye that was both pride and humor too.

"Well, I'm thinking of something more sinister, I'm afraid," Braddock said. "You see, Mr. Bucklin was reported to have said to his father that there was something odd going on at the bridge, something dangerous perhaps. His murder only seems to put an exclamation point to that."

"You have no idea of just how sinister it appears in some circles for a mere woman to be in the position I am, Mr. Braddock." Emily looked at Tom evenly. "It undermines the notion, held dear by most men, I'm afraid, that women are made for child rearing and social ornamentation. Oh, I am sinister indeed and proud of it. But I realize, of course, that's not what you were referring to."

"It would appear that you have much to be proud of, ma'am." Tom's gaze followed the cables and stays up to their apex at the top of the towers. When his eye came back to earth it locked with hers. "If all women were as sinister, Mrs. Roebling, what a world we would live in."

Martin cleared his throat. "The sinister Mrs. Roebling aside, I'm sure I don't know what you're talking about, Detective." He twisted his mouth. "There have been no incidents aside from those well documented in the press that could be considered a threat to the bridge. I refer of course to things such as the wire scandal and the caisson fire. Do you have nothing more concrete to go on than that? An old man's rumor of something suspicious is hardly cause for alarm," Martin said smugly.

"I'd agree, not by itself, but the coincidence of Bucklin's murder lends the story more weight. It has to be checked out, no matter how wide of the mark it may be."

"Of course you must, Detective. You strike me as a man not given to dereliction of duty, and I urge you to investigate to the fullest extent you find necessary," Martin said brusquely. "Now, if you'll excuse me for a moment, I must see to some minor details down by the terminal. Emily, I'll be back in a few minutes. Do you mind being left in the care of the dashing detective?"

Tom blushed. It had been a while since he had been called dashing, and longer still since he felt it.

"Not at all, Charles. I'm sure I'm in good hands with the dashing Detective Braddock." They both blushed at that.

"I should never have smiled at you yesterday, Mr. Braddock. I'm not usually a forward woman," Emily said once Martin was out of earshot.

"A smile once given can never be taken back, ma'am. Besides, I don't recall hearing you say you didn't mean it," Tom said with a grin.

Emily looked at him a long minute, her eyes so frank and open, they made the color rise up over his collar. Tom met her eye for eye.

"First of all, Tom, call me Emily. Second . . . it was meant," she said at last. "But meant as nothing more than what it was, a smile at a handsome stranger whom I never thought to see again."

"Ah, but you have seen him again, and he has seen you. I would not give you back your smile if I could, but I can give you one of mine." Tom smiled his best boyish smile, full of mischief and more. Emily couldn't help returning it.

Chapter Eight

*I feel perfectly competent to take care of
the East River Bridge.*

—WASHINGTON ROEBLING

Mike listened to his grandfather's watery snoring. Gramps slept a lot, even in the afternoon. The wheezing gusts sounded shallow and labored, not at all like the healthy snoring his da used to do. Mike could still remember his father's snores. He used to think that a lion had found its way into their house. He'd cover himself with his blanket, hoping if the lion didn't see him, he wouldn't be eaten. For hours he had lain awake, listening to the lion snoring, almost too frightened to breathe till sleep finally took him. In the morning he'd told his mom and da and they'd laughed. They told him it was only his da's snoring and he needn't be afraid. He'd been a little afraid just the same.

Mike's grandmother was out, down to the police station to claim his da's things. There wasn't much to claim. Slowly he got off his small cast-iron bed and went to the corner of the room, beside the fireplace. He had discovered this secret place almost the first week they had been in the tenement. He had been playing by the fireplace when he first noticed that a board was loose. If the small piece of baseboard beside the hearth was pulled out just so, it was possible to take up two of the pine floorboards, which at that point were quite short. The space in the floor between the floor joists was perfect for the box.

His da had given it to him just a few days before he died, and though there wasn't much in it, he had taken to hiding it right from the start. His da had told him to, but he didn't really know why. There was nothing in it when he gave it to Mike, just a beautiful box with a curved top. The box had carvings like he had never seen before. His da had said they were Celtic, and they seemed to interlock and wriggle around the outside like some charm against prying hands. It was a beautiful box, and his da had told him that it had been in the family since the time when Ireland was free, which he knew was a long, long time. Inside, it was all done in green velvet, but most of it was threadbare now, except the bottom. Mike had told his da that he would always treasure it and keep only his most valuable things inside. The only things in the box now were two pictures, one of his mom and sis, one of his da. There were some coins too, but the pictures were the real treasures. He took them out one at a time. He held them up to the watery light that filtered down between the buildings and through their dirty window. His mom and sis had already begun to fade in his mind. Without their pictures he didn't know but they'd disappear altogether. Mike sat long in the midday gloom of their bedroom. Sometimes if he looked at the pictures long enough it almost seemed they could move. They weren't moving now, though, so he put them away. The box closed with a solid sound and Mike locked it with the little brass key his da had given him. His da had the only other, and even he hadn't known where Mike had hidden the box. It was strange, but that's the way da had wanted it.

Tom and Emily had gone to find Charles C. Martin, locating him finally, near the terminal, discussing some alterations with a foreman. Martin had suggested to Emily that they go for a quick bite. The lack of an invitation to Tom was of no particular concern to Braddock. He hadn't expected one. The engineer reluctantly included Tom after Emily's none-too-subtle reproof. Martin accepted it in the fashion of a true gentleman, though, asking Tom to join them as if he'd meant to from the first. The three of them managed to get across Park Row dodging wagons, horsecars, stages, and carriages. Drivers had no inclination to stop for pedestrians. Once across, they strolled down along City Hall Park, enjoying the trees and the grass, which were starting to become scarce in New York. Tom liked this area. The addition of the bridge, which would terminate just opposite City Hall, made this small part of the city seem like the hub of the universe.

The traffic was incredible. In spite of the general movement of business uptown, the intersection of Park Place and Broadway was still the busiest in the city. A number of horsecar lines terminated there, and at certain times of the day the crush of stages, wagons, horsecars, carriages, and pedestrians made the streets seem to boil. There were times when traffic was so tangled, it came to a complete halt. Tom nodded in the direction of the Western Union building. Its clock tower poked above everything though it was some blocks south on Broadway and Dey. The ball on the flagpole atop the tower was lowered every day at noon, keeping time for half the city and all the ships in the harbor.

"Seems every time I look at that building there's another ten wires sprouting out of it," Tom said in an effort to make conversation.

Emily looked in that direction with a skeptically arched eyebrow. "I can't help but wonder what the telephone will do to the telegraph business. They may not be sprouting wires for too much longer."

"Do you think so? I don't know. From what I hear the sound isn't that good. Can't misunderstand a well-written telegram," Tom said with a certain grin.

"I think people will always want to talk to each other," Emily said as they walked. "This is just the very beginning. They'll clear up the sound and wire the whole country eventually." Tom just listened. He had never heard a woman talk like this before. "Electricity is taking over," she went on. "It's the steam power of tomorrow, and there's no stopping it. Did you know we'll be putting electric lights on the bridge?" Emily said proudly. "It will be the first bridge in the country to be lit with electricity."

"Really? That's marvelous. Electric lights?" Tom actually didn't know what to say. This was a bit out of his frame of reference.

"Seventy, to be precise," Martin said. "The United States Illuminating Company won the contract. Underbid Edison by about three thousand dollars."

"We'll generate our own electricity too." Emily was obviously excited about the whole idea.

"Shocking!" Tom said with a straight face. They all shared a chuckle, and Tom started to feel almost as if he fit in.

They had crossed Broadway opposite the Astor House, at the south side of the park, an act of some bravery in that traffic. The Greek Revival hotel built by John Jacob Astor many years before had been the finest hotel in the city. Its style and grandeur had long since been surpassed by others such as the Fifth Avenue Hotel, on Madison Square, but it still held its cachet as the downtown meeting place of the powerful. Famous for its indoor plumbing on every floor, it had been a sensation when it was built. The interior courtyard and fountain presented a tranquil contrast to the hurly-burly of Broadway.

"Have you dined here before, Mr. Braddock?" Martin asked, appearing to know the answer before he asked. Tom figured he was just making a point.

"Haven't had the pleasure, sir." His flinty smile at Martin showed the engineer that the slight snub hadn't gone over his head. "But I am looking forward to it. Have you, Mrs. Roebling?"

"Oh, yes, but infrequently. My husband and the bridge keep me entirely too busy to be able to enjoy a luncheon very often."

Martin turned to Tom and said pretentiously, "They have the very finest continental cuisine here. I think they're a shade behind Delmonico's but that's just to my taste. As for the clientele, I think you'll find it the equal of the best the city has to offer."

Tom must have looked nervous, although he didn't think it showed.

When Martin turned to lead them through the lobby into the restaurant, Emily gave him a reassuring squeeze of the arm, whispering, "Just follow my lead."

They were seated at a table with a window on the garden courtyard. Its fountain gurgled and splashed in a calming counterpoint to the large dining room, bustling with lunch for the powerful. Tom noted Mayor Edson at one table with a gaggle of toadies. An assortment of people at other tables were doing their best to be seen. As he glanced around the room, he noticed Thomas Nast in a far corner. Nast, whose cutting cartoons for *Harper's* had hounded Boss Tweed into a jail cell, was regaling his table with glories past. For his part, Tom felt rather out of place and insignificant, a condition he wasn't used to. In his world, people took notice when he entered a room. Nobody cared a damn what he wore. The badge was the important thing. In his world power ruled. In many ways it was the only thing that the criminal types respected. The name of Braddock was known and perhaps even feared on the streets but not here.

A waiter arrived, in starched magnificence. After regaling them with a list of the chef's specialities, most of which Tom had never heard of, he took their drink orders, handing them each a menu. Tom had wanted to order a cold beer but contented himself with an iced tea. He was glad to see that the menu was in English. Most of the finer Broadway hotels did up their menus in French, but the Astor House refused to bow to the trend. Tom ordered a steak, with mashed potatoes and string beans. Not terribly creative, he knew, but what he wanted. No point putting on airs, when he'd probably never see either one of these fine people again. Martin ordered oysters to start, pheasant for his main course. Emily had a salad and the squab, which, when it came, hardly looked big enough to feed Tom's cats. She claimed to be pleased with it though. Tom's steak was big enough to feed a family in the tenements.

"So, Mr. Braddock, ah . . . may I call you Tom?" Emily said, playing to Martin's sense of propriety.

"Sure. I mean . . . you may indeed. I'd be . . . honored." Tom grinned while kicking himself for stumbling.

"And you must call me Emily." Tom played along. Martin, he noticed, didn't ask Tom to call him anything. "Tell me, what were the circumstances of this man Bucklin's death?"

"Well, Emily, I'd prefer not to go into too many details over lunch. Don't want to spoil your meal . . . but I can tell you that it appears he was struck in the back of the head with a blunt object. He was found in an alley behind Paddy's. It's a saloon on Peck Slip. No one saw it happen that we know of, and there doesn't seem to be any motive either, at least not any of the usual ones."

"Such as?" Martin asked with a raised eyebrow, clearly not conversant in the usual motives for murder.

"Well, robbery, for one. Bucklin's money was still in his wallet. It doesn't appear to be revenge or a chance fracas either. From what everyone has told me so far, this Bucklin was a pretty quiet sort. No troubles with anyone that I could find, not yet anyway."

"How puzzling," Martin said dryly.

"I was thinking," Tom said slowly, fork poised over his steak. "You know . . . being that there's none of the usual motives and all . . . that the bridge might be a target in some radical's mind. I mean, maybe this Bucklin was killed for something he knew or found out. Just a thought. After all, it represents a lot, if you follow me. Nothing could have greater . . . how should I put it . . . recognition, and . . . symbolism too." He halted for a moment to judge Martin's and Emily's reactions.

Martin nodded and cleared his throat as if about to reveal a great truth. "In many ways the bridge represents the triumph of the industrial age over the agrarian, the factory over the farm. It embodies all the greatest efforts of man to harness and tame the world around him. Maybe most significant, it bridges a great divide. There's powerful symbolism in that, don't you think?"

Tom wished he were able to use words like Martin. The assistant engineer went on. "If one were to draw that symbolism even further, it represents the industrial and political triumph of the North resulting from our recent civil war. It is not only in the North, it is in the heart of the greatest city of the North, a city which to some of our southern countrymen represents the very worst of industrialism, commercialism, greed, and corruption." Martin gave Tom a satisfied look, obviously pleased with himself for summing up Tom's awkward attempt.

Tom wasn't deterred. He admired the engineer's ease with ideas and language, but those gifts weren't everything. It was Tom, after all, who'd come up with the idea first. He sallied back as best he could. "I don't think that the importance of the bridge as a symbol is well appreciated, but I think that to some it may be a tempting target."

"Quite perceptive, Detective," Martin said, wiping his mouth. "An interesting theory, but somewhat outlandish, don't you think?" Martin's slight smirk said it all.

"Outlandish, sure," said Tom. "But as Booth proved, an anarchist who's willing to risk everything can do outlandish things. Lincoln was a symbol too as I recall."

"Point well taken, Mr. Braddock." Martin's voice had just a touch more respect. He seemed to have lost interest in his food. "It would be wise to keep the possibility in mind, however outlandish."

"What sad and gruesome work, Tom," Emily said as she dissected her squab. "What kind of special desperation must take hold to make one a murderer? I can't imagine it myself, the actual deed: the pulling of the trigger, the plunging of the knife. I know there are dangerous men out there. But it seems to me almost as if the taker of another life is not really human, not really one of us."

"Oh, I don't know about that, Emily. The depressing thing is how ordinary they are. Most murders are committed by someone the victim knows. Most are done in the heat of the moment and mostly for the stupidest reasons. Some people are just not able to control their impulses or emotions." Tom was cutting his steak as he talked. The knife sliced smoothly through the tender meat, which swam in a bloody pool on his plate. The knife's sharp edge ground the china with small screams.

"There are doctors who think it has something to do with the shape of the skull, the bumps on the head." Tom went on.

"Phrenology, I think it's called," Martin said.

"Yes, I think that's it. Some think it has more to do with family background, your parents and grandparents . . . the family tree, that sort of thing. Others think it has more to do with how a person was raised, and whether they had a stable home life, religion, and such things. I don't think it's any one of those things. It's all of those things . . . and more. The fact is that if it were any one of those things, then we'd have a pretty easy time of it. Why, we'd just have to lock up all the people with certain kinds of bumps in their noggins and murders would drop to zero." Emily chuckled at that. "You see my point? I've seen lots of murderers and all sorts of circumstances. What's sad is how normal they are."

"Yes, but aren't there those whose entire life has gone over to crime and wickedness, for whom the taking of a life is as nothing at all?" Emily asked. "Don't tell me you see them as decent if misguided human beings."

"You're right," Tom admitted. "There are men, and some women I've come across too, who use violence like a coachman uses a whip. Murder is a tool for them." Tom realized he was pointing with his knife for emphasis. He put it on his plate. "Life for them isn't worth very much. That includes their own. Not too many men like that, thank God. I've run up against that sort. I don't like it. Anyone who doesn't value life scares me."

"You surprise me, Detective. You don't appear to be a man of many fears." Martin was eyeing him with a look of open appraisal.

Tom looked at him as if he'd said something remarkably foolish. "Fear is a healthy thing, Mr. Martin. You're confusing it with fortitude."

Martin reddened just a bit but otherwise ignored the rebuke. "I see, so you're saying that the truly brave man is the one who conquers his fears." He turned to Emily, saying, "I count your husband as such, Emily. I would believe you to be such a man as well, Mr. Braddock, unless I miss my guess."

Tom flushed a bit, searching for something to say. Finally he raised his glass, saying, "A toast to Washington Roebling." Emily smiled at him over the rim of her glass. "Whose bravery is well documented."

"You know, it was very nice of you to ask me to lunch. The food here is good too. Do you like your squab, Emily?" Tom asked.

"Oh, yes it's delicious. The Astor House still has an excellent kitchen, although the hotel is a bit passé. Nobody builds Greek Revival anymore. I do love the interior courtyard though. There's nothing quite like it."

Tom looked slowly around the courtyard. The slanting sun slashed across it from the roofline to just past the fountain, painting it by halves in shade and light. A couple strolled its paths, and an old gentleman, who looked to be rooted to a bench in the sun, soaked in what warmth he could from it while he read his *Times*. Shrubs and scattered splashes of flowers softened and perfumed the little oasis. The fountain splashed and gurgled in a most civilized manner.

"It really is. I had heard it was nice, but didn't think it would be quite this beautiful. But I'm no judge of these things."

"But I think you are, Tom." Emily caught herself. She didn't want to be flirtatious, but somehow she ended up sounding so. "What I mean is that it doesn't take an extraordinary judge of beauty to appreciate a courtyard, or a garden, or a great work of art for that matter. Such things are very subjective after all, not bound by rigid interpretations, don't you agree?" she said, looking at Martin, who appeared puzzled.

"Subjective? I'm not sure how you mean that, Emily," he said, his eyebrows knitting. "Do you mean to say that a Michelangelo, for example, is not always to be admired as a great work of art?"

"No, not that at all. What I'm trying to say is that every one of us brings something different to their view of art and beauty. You'll agree that no two people see things precisely in the same way?"

Tom wasn't sure where this conversation was going, but somehow Emily made it seem interesting to him.

"That's perhaps the wrong question to ask an engineer," Martin said. "The currency of my work is precision. Calculations, mechanical drawings, measurements, and specifications are my stock-in-trade, easily translatable one to the other." The engineer's voice had taken on a touch of sarcasm.

"I know that, Martin. But the end result, the thing itself has a different impact on each person who sees it. It's as if all the prior experiences of our lives color how we see things . . . how we react to them." She looked to Tom for support, but he wasn't sure what to say just yet. "I can guarantee, for example, that my reaction to viewing the Brooklyn Bridge would be quite different from Mr. Braddock's here. Wouldn't you agree with that, Tom?"

Tom figured he had better start thinking of something to say, though this was a subject he had no experience with. Then it came to him. "You know, you bring to mind a conversation I had yesterday with a friend of mine. He had a very different impression of the bridge than I had."

"Oh, how so?"

"Well, honestly, I haven't given the bridge much thought one way or the other. After all these years, it's like it's part of the landscape; sort of like a tree, growing so slow you hardly notice the changes year to year, then before you know it, it's towering over the house."

Emily and Martin looked just a shade disappointed. "And how did that friend of yours see it, Tom?" Emily prompted.

"Well, that was the interesting part. Now, I have to tell you that Sam, my friend, is not a man of letters, not having got much past the sixth grade. Nor is he one to be going to art galleries and museums on his days off. Sam's a good man, who I'm proud to call my friend, but he's generally on the plain side, if you know what I mean,"

"Uh-huh." Martin was obviously bored with Tom's preamble.

"Well, he surprised me yesterday with his views on your bridge," Tom said. "He told me things about it I never took the time to know, like the miles of wire in the main cables, their strength, things like that. He even knew how much each of the anchorages weighed."

"Really, how remarkable," Emily said. "I doubt that Charles here knows that."

Martin looked as if he were about to quote specifications, when Tom went on.

"He remarked on its grace and the way it seems to fly across the river." He hesitated just a second before going on, not quite sure how to say what he wanted to. "He told me, Emily, that your husband was a sort of personal hero to him."

"Really? Well, then, would you do me the honor of conveying to your friend our appreciation? He's more than kind to think so."

"I will. He'll be jealous to know I've met you. But that wasn't all he said. There was one other thing that really stuck." Tom hesitated a moment, wanting to make sure he got the words right. "It is his opinion," he said slowly, "that to build a bridge like that was to achieve in a way . . . well, immortality." He could see from the looks on their faces that they were both skeptical yet pleased at the same time. He went on quickly. "Well, 'immortal' was the word he used. I think he meant that to be known for something that's so important and so permanent, that's a kind of immortality." Tom stopped to look from Emily to Martin, judging their reactions. "Your name lives on, forever tied to the thing you created. He got quite poetic about your bridge. It was a side of Sam I haven't seen before."

"How very flattering," Emily said, obviously meaning it. "You see, Charles? This proves my point. Here we have two contemporaries—two men of similar backgrounds. Sam is on the police force, I assume?"

"Yes. He's a sergeant."

"There, and both see the bridge quite differently. The fact is that their interpretations do vary, and quite markedly," Emily said triumphantly.

"I've got to tell you, Emily, that after talking with him I have started to at least appreciate the bridge more deeply," Tom said, perhaps a bit too anxiously.

"Bravo, Detective." Tom thought that Martin's tone was just a tad dry.

It had been an interesting lunch. In some ways, Tom supposed it had changed his life. If change could be measured in a man's regard for a woman, then his life had changed indeed. Tom was still humming barroom ditties on his way uptown. He felt elevated. He searched for another word, but that one kept popping back into his head. Elevated was the word for it. He knew that he wasn't of her class, but she had accepted him all the same. Charles C. Martin had too, though certainly to a lesser degree. She had asked his opinions and was interested in the answers. She had given him the feeling that what he thought mattered. In police work, of course, he was used to being listened to. Outside his world, though, he was as much subject to the rules of class and society as anyone else. In fact, in some circles, being on the force was rather looked down upon, and definitely not a social advantage. But that hadn't seemed to matter to Emily. To Tom, her not mattering mattered a great deal.

. . .

Emmons, Lebeau, and Watkins sat together on the edge of the Brooklyn approach, their legs dangling four stories above the street. As they ate lunch, they talked about Braddock.

"I don't know, he seemed all right to me. I think we had him goin'," Matt said. "What do you reckon, Earl?"

"I imagine. Didn't seem too interested in us. I don't think he knows shit." Earl took a big bite from his sandwich, appearing unconcerned.

"See how he got all excited to meet Mrs. Roebling?" Watkins chuckled. "He was like a hound on the scent. What the hell he would want with her I don't know."

"I guess he was just pleased to meet her is all," Matt said. "She *is* sort of famous." Looking around to see if anyone was in hearing distance, he said, "You know, she's one thing I'm gonna be sorry about when we . . . you know. What I mean to say is we're not out to hurt her, and it's kind of a shame that—" Emmons lapsed into silence. He sat with the others, looking out over downtown New York. There were no answers in sight. "She's put more into the work than her husband did as far as I can see. Hell, she's on the site all the time. When's the last time any of you saw Roebling?"

"Never seen him, except once in the papers," Earl mused.

"So, what are you saying, Matt? You feelin' like we shouldn't do this? We all swore, you know. We swore to go through with it no matter what." Watkins looked at Matt closely. He hoped Matt didn't want to go through with it. Maybe it would get him off the hook with the captain—sink the whole show if both he and Matt went against it. On the other hand, Matt's reservations gave Watkins a chance to appear as if he were still with them all the way. Watkins had to be careful, he knew. "You ain't backin' out now?" He was unable to keep the hint of hope in his voice.

"No, Watkins, I'm not sayin' that. I'm with you boys all the way through, whatever comes. I'm just sayin' it's kind of sad to see such a nice lady get hurt. That's all."

Lebeau, who had been pretty quiet finally said, "Gonna be a bunch o' folks hurt, Matthew." He threw some trash over the edge. "We hurt folks before. Ought to be used to it."

Earl had a point. This was hardly the first time they would be hurting the innocent. It hadn't been that way during the war. But after—when they started on their campaign of terror, there were plenty of innocent victims.

"Remember the trains we wrecked?" Earl said softly. "How many folks you figure we killed or hurt in them wrecks? Hundreds, I reckon." They all remembered them clearly. "There was Angola in '67, Prospect, I think it was, in '72, and Ashtabula in '76." Matt and Watkins nodded. "We killed a passel of Yankees with them wrecks, an' nobody the wiser neither. Ashtabula was my favorite, I reckon."

"If favorite is a word that can fit a thing like that," Matt muttered. Neither Earl nor Watkins seemed to notice.

"Me too, Earl," Watkins exclaimed. "Remember how them coaches just all toppled into that ravine, one after t'other? That was somethin'. Kilt 'round eighty, as I recall," he said proudly, looking over his shoulder as he did. "Thing o' beauty the way we done it too. Damn near froze my pecker off in that blasted snowstorm though."

"Up in the trestle sawin' for hours. Shit, I was so damn cold, I couldn't move my hands for days."

"Yeah," Matt said. "Snow covered for us though. Once the train went off, they couldn't figure what made the trestle let go." He had to admire the way the thing was done, if not the effect. "The captain had that one figured. Just some cutting in the right places and down she went with the next train."

They all sat quiet for a while, hearing the screams of the survivors as the fires swept through the passenger cars. The potbelly stoves at either end of the coaches had dumped hot coals, starting the cars blazing almost immediately. Most of the bodies were burned beyond recognition.

"Listen," Matt said. "I know we're gonna do damage to a lot o' folks with this, and like I said . . . I'm with you boys to the bitter end. I think you know that." He looked at both Earl and Watkins, who nodded silently. "Just gotta be ready for the hurt of it."

Tom stopped at 300 Mulberry to check in. No one was looking for him, and nothing particularly important was going on, so he told the desk sergeant he was off to Bellevue and headed out. He doubted the coroner could tell him much about Bucklin that he didn't already know, but it was wise to check. He took the El back uptown, resisting the urge to get off at Astor Place. He stood all the way, hanging on to one of the straps that hung from the ceiling. He couldn't help thinking about Emily. She was a married woman. He had no right to think that she might be interested in him. She had education, that was obvious, and a quick, inquisitive mind. She had wealth and social standing. The more he looked at the logic of it, the more illogical it looked. But then there was the way she had smiled at him when they said good-bye—not just with her mouth, but with her eyes. And there was that little tilt of her head and a lingering pressure from her small, warm hand in his. These things had nothing to do with logic. Did they?

After walking across town from the El, Tom plunged into the echoing gloom of the corridors of Bellevue. Tom never liked the place. Its hard tile surfaces; its smells and sounds; its perpetual gloom always left him feeling depressed and anxious. He dreaded the thought of waking up one day in this place. It was a tomb for the living, big, hard, and impersonal. As he neared the coroner's operating room, he thought he heard music. The sound of a string quartet drifted and echoed down the corridors. He heard the violins swell and it gave him a chill. They sounded too heavenly for this cold-tiled basement.

Tom walked down to the morgue and pushed the door open. He thought he heard the sound of a saw just as he entered. Dr. Thomas looked up from his work.

"Oh . . . Tom, c'mon in. I'm right in the middle of something, but if you'll bear with me for a moment I'll—" The doctor continued to saw. His apron was smeared with red, and there was a red blotch on his glasses. He seemed to be humming to himself. A gramophone was playing in the far corner of the operating room. It sounded like opera. Tom's landlady sometimes sang opera and this sounded similar, but he didn't know the tune. "So, Detective, what brings you to my, ah . . . my, ah . . ." Doc Thomas hooked a finger in the skull he was sectioning, pulling the top of the head open a bit more to keep the saw from binding. "Ah, where was I? Yes, what brings you to my dissectorium? As you can see, I have an interesting case . . . ah . . . here." The doctor had a habit of almost never finishing a sentence. He was famous for it, in fact. Most everyone in the department called him Dangling Thomas.

He went back to the job at hand, squinting through his blood-smeared glasses. He sawed slowly, taking his time not to cut too deep. Tom looked on in morbid fascination. The sound of a saw on bone was a chilling reminder to him. During the war he had been in many field hospitals. Thinking of it now, the word "hospital" was a vast overstatement. Most often it was a barn, or the nearest farmhouse. Usually the cutting went on in the kitchens.

As he listened to the coroner's saw, its rhythmic, muffled grinding took him back to a field hospital near Spotsylvania. His old head wound ached at the memory. He had followed the hospital wagons filled with wounded to check on a couple of men in his squad. The wagons snaked on rutted roads for about two miles back of the lines. The men bounced and moaned and dripped crimson on the red Virginia mud. It was easy to find the hospital. What he wished he could forget was the pile by the back door. Maybe four feet high, tangled in a grisly embrace was a collection of severed human limbs. Hands, feet, legs, arms, and unidentifiable bits drained into the dirt. As he walked up, a large pig rooting nearby dashed in and snatched an arm. The lifeless hand flopped and waved in the pig's jaws. Tom couldn't remember drawing his pistol, but he remembered the satisfaction of shooting the pig. He'd looked at the grisly pile for what seemed like an age. An odd notion about it had haunted him down the years. Did a limb mourn a body, as a body will mourn a limb? Did this pile of inert parts pine for the whole? Did a leg, on some biological level, cry out for its body, its blood, its energizing brain? Did these limbs long to run in a field, caress a lover's breast, or feel a newborn baby's tender weight? He could almost feel their searching loss.

"So, Detective, what brings you to, ah . . . Bellevue?" Dr. Thomas brought Tom out of his macabre reverie. He stood over the cadaver whose skull he had just sectioned, his saw dripping absently.

"A man brought in yesterday, about noon. Bucklin, Terrence Bucklin?" Tom stared at the top of the cadaver's brain.

"Oh, yes. The one with the, ah, cranial . . ." The coroner waved vaguely at the back of his head.

"Yeah, that would be him. Have a chance to give him a look?"

"Yes, this morning." Doc Thomas looked around distractedly. He put down his saw, shuffled over to a desk on the far side of the room, and pulled a report from the small pile atop the desk.

"Hm. Nasty bump on the head. Blunt trauma, extensive bleeding into the parietal and occipital lobes, extending also into the cerebellum, medulla oblongata, and spinal column. Ah, let's see . . . second cervical vertebra fractured at the vertebral arch, impacting and partially severing the ah, spinal column, transverse process detached, um . . ."

"Uh-huh. So what does that mean exactly, Doc?" Braddock asked, shaking his head. "Explain it to this simple old detective, if you would."

"It means someone didn't like him much," the doctor said, grinning over the tops of his glasses.

"Yeah, I guess not," Tom agreed with a little chuckle. "Anything you can tell me about what hit him?"

"Oh, yes, yes, here it is. I, ah, peeled back the scalp to get a look at the pattern of the fracture. Sometimes can tell from the way the bones break." The doctor stopped again, lost in his thoughts. Tom waited. He wondered if he was going to have to finish every thought for the coroner.

"Did a nasty job," he went on finally. "Crushed part of the brain itself. Massive internal bleeding . . ." The doctor paused, fingering the day's growth of stubble on his chin.

"So what caused it? What's your best guess?" Tom asked, hoping to hurry

- 117 -

him along. Doc Thomas looked up as if startled out of his thoughts. "By the pattern of the bone fracture, it's my opinion that it was something about one to maybe one point two five inches in . . . ah . . . diameter."

"Pretty small," Tom observed, holding his thumb and forefinger in a small circle that he guessed to be about that size.

"Yes, but heavy enough, or driven with enough force to, ah . . . crush the skull and . . . drive a section of bone into the . . ." Thomas paused again, peering over his glasses at his notes.

"So, I'm guessing a hammer, or the end of a pipe, or something."

"Hammer's more likely, Tom. A pipe, unless it had a cap on the end, would tend to leave a circular ah . . . cut."

Tom grunted agreement. "Looked like he was hit more than once, right?"

"Twice, you're right. Second time actually from a slightly different . . . angle. Hit at the base of the skull and into the second cervical vertebra, just at the top of the neck. A glancing blow, but still powerful enough to break the, ah . . . neck. Cause of death was massive cranial and brain damage, accompanied by, ah . . . intracranial bleeding, paralysis, and cessation of respiratory—"

"Okay, I got it. Did you have a chance to look at the stain on his vest?" Tom asked just a bit impatiently, anxious to move along.

The doctor didn't seem to notice, or if he did, didn't care. This was his world and it moved to his own sense of time and no one else's.

"The tobacco juice? Yes, your nice young patrolman, ah . . ." Thomas said, flipping through his papers.

"Jaffey."

"Yes, quite. Jaffey passed along your concern about that. It would appear as though someone spat on your victim."

"That's what I thought. Fresh enough to have taken place at the same time as the murder?" Tom asked.

"Yes. Definitely tobacco. Hard to be precise about the time, but ah . . . yes, I think they would coincide."

"Yeah, that's what I thought. Spat on him while he was on his back?"

"That would be my, ah . . . opinion," Thomas said, looking pointedly at Tom over his glasses. He obviously didn't approve of such things.

They spent another half hour or so discussing the condition of the body, approximate time of death, and contents of digestive tract, when Doc Thomas said rather suddenly, "Curious thing." Tom cocked an interested eyebrow. "The curious thing is what I found in your man's, ah . . . stomach. A key, to be precise."

"In his *stomach*?"

"Interesting, eh?" Doc Thomas paused for effect. "Curious place for a key, wouldn't you say?" He turned and rummaged through a drawer in his desk, which seemed to be brimming with oddities. "Now, where did I put that damn thing? Quite small, you know. Not hard to swallow at all. Ah . . . here it is!" He held the little key aloft.

Braddock stood, his big hand held out. "In his stomach, you said." The doctor placed the key in his palm. It was small, less than an inch long, with a tubular design, like a key for a pocket watch. Tom doubted that's what it was for. He had examined Bucklin's pocket watch. There was nothing hidden there, and the winding mechanism was in the stem. Tom stood gazing at it in his open palm. "How long would it take for something like this to get down into the stomach, Doc?"

"Depends," the coroner said with a shrug. "Not long."

"Yeah, I guess. But could Bucklin have swallowed this key before he was killed? Would it have had time to reach the stomach?"

"Possibly," the doctor admitted. "As to why your man might want to swallow a key, Detective . . . well, that's your job I suppose."

Tom stood silent, bouncing the little key in his hand, feeling its weight but weighing the possibilities as well.

After going over everything else he could think of, Tom was about to leave when the coroner said, "Oh, by the way, your killer was right-handed." He went on to explain how he'd arrived at the conclusion, while Tom kicked himself mentally for not thinking to ask. The key had him preoccupied, he figured. Minutes later he was heading back to headquarters. As he closed the door to the morgue behind him he heard Thomas say, "Now, ah . . . where were we?"

Back at Mulberry, Tom spent the next hour and a half filling out his folder on Bucklin. He included his notes on the interviews of Bucklin's coworkers as well as the general impressions he had of them. He had long ago gotten into the habit of writing down his observations of people he thought could have some bearing on a case. There were no established police procedures for such things, the men all had their own ways of doing things. From time to time those offhand observations proved more useful than expected. Those times were relatively rare, but Tom told himself that it was worth the extra time. Besides, Byrnes liked his men to be thorough. One thing he didn't want to do was disappoint Thomas Byrnes.

It wasn't until around 6:00 P.M. that Tom left 300. He wanted to see Mary. They hadn't been together since Saturday, and he was beginning to feel the tug of missing her. But he had Coffin and his veiled threats on his mind too. Tom started thinking that maybe he should just get the Finney thing over, and the sooner the better. If he could get that unpleasant "favor" out of the way, it would keep Coffin off his back, give him a little breathing room. Then he'd be free to concentrate on Mary. She was worth concentrating on. Tom hailed a cab.

"Corner of Baxter and Centre streets," he told the cabbie.

Tom settled into the back of the cab. It had been another warm day for March, but it was cooling off with the lowering of the sun. The streets were in the shade of early evening, and there was a chill in the air. Tom reached under his jacket and took out his pistol. He had carried it since the war. It showed. The old Colt was nicked and scratched, worn shiny. The engraving on the cylinder was nearly smooth, even though he had replaced it when the Colt was converted to cartridges. The walnut grips were the original, though, and glowed like an old saddle. The pistol and he had seen a lot of miles together. It had seen him through some tight spots. He couldn't begin to imagine how many times he had fired it in practice or necessity. He would never be certain either of how many men had felt its bite. Since the war he had used it only twice and felt himself fortunate not to have taken a life either time. The war was another matter.

As a safety measure Tom carried the Colt with its hammer on an empty cylinder. Although he had no intention of using the thing tonight, it was foolish to go where he was going and not be certain of his weapon. Slowly he spun the cylinder, listening to the measured, metallic certainty of the piece as each chamber indexed. He added a sixth bullet in the empty chamber, lowering the hammer on it gently, then pulling it back to the half-cock safety. No sense taking chances. He hoped he wouldn't need the gun, but if he did, he knew there would be no substitute. The old piece was getting just slightly loose in the frame. It hadn't been shooting as well in practice lately, and the frame was probably why. But practice was practice. In his experience, if he shot someone, it would probably be from no more than six feet away. Tom figured the Colt was still good at that distance. The department hadn't standardized sidearms, and as long as there had been a police force the men carried their own weapons. The word was that soon there would be a regular police-issue pistol for everyone, but until then he was satisfied with the Colt. It slipped back into the shoulder holster under his jacket like an old friend. Its familiar weight was a comfort. Won't be needing you tonight, partner, he thought.

The cab pulled up at the corner where a streetlamp had just been lit. Its light was watery and insubstantial in the early evening gloom. The cab rolled away accompanied by the dying echoes of hooves on cobbles. Tom felt very alone on the nearly deserted street. He searched for a moment for the number of Finney's gaming parlor, but after walking first one way then the next, decided that a plain unnumbered door, two houses down from the corner, had to be it. There didn't seem to be any lights on, and no sound came from within. It was early for the gambling crowd. Tom tried the door, and it swung open on well-oiled hinges. It reminded him that he should oil his own when he got home, though he knew he'd likely never do it.

The door opened on nothing but a blackened stairway leading up to the second floor. He took the stairs with caution. An unpleasant experience on a similar darkened stair some years ago had taught him well. Tom kept one hand on the wall as he went up, the other on the butt of the Colt. The stairs, unlike the hinges, creaked like the jaws of hell, and he was sure it could be heard all through the building. As his head cleared the level of the landing, he saw a light slash out from under the single door, bathing the floor before it in a bloodred wash.

"Somebody's home," Tom said to himself. He rapped on the door and listened. Heavy footfalls told him he had gotten someone's attention. The door swung open fast, and the light from the room was blinding in contrast to the stairway. A huge silhouette filled the door.

"What the fuck you want, Braddock?" a heavily accented German voice rumbled, sounding more like "Vat da fuck you vant, Braddock?"

It took a second for Tom to connect the voice and that massive outline in the door. "Ole, what a pleasant surprise. Haven't seen you in a dog's age," Tom's tone put the lie to the words.

"Not long enough, du sheis-esser. What you want? Why you come here?"

"Came to see Finney on business. He in?" Braddock said flatly, ignoring the insult. He wasn't here to get into it with Venkman.

"What business?"

Braddock wasn't about to discuss his business with the giant Dutchman, but since he was filling the door so effectively, he said, "Well, Ole, that's for me and Finney to discuss, but since you ask, Captain Coffin has a proposition for him and asked me to act as his emissary." He looked speculatively at Ole, not sure if he had any idea what an emissary was.

"What de fuck's that? You got business mitt Finney for Coffin, that bastard?"

"Just tell your boss I need to see him, Ole," Tom said with finality.

Ole Venkman stood silent for a long moment, blocking the door while his limited intellect worked overtime. With some reluctance, he stepped aside, saying, "Wait here."

Tom stepped into the room. It was well furnished, better than he would have expected. The ceiling was high, with broad moldings of cast plaster, and the walls were covered in a rich but tasteless damask wallpaper. A fire burned in a small marble fireplace. The chairs were of mahogany, in the high Victorian style, with expensive upholstery, that looked as if they came from a Fifth Avenue mansion's drawing room. A brass and crystal chandelier, so massive it looked out of place, lit the room. Venkman closed the door and rumbled toward the back of the building. Two young swells sat in one corner of the room, smoking cigars. They hardly looked up at Tom, and seemed more intent on their heated yet hushed discussion. Tom guessed they were waiting for a game. It was early for the regular crowd, he knew. Places like these usually didn't heat up for at least another hour or so. That was one of the reasons Tom had come when he did.

Ole was an old acquaintance. Tom watched his back as he stumped away. The Dutchman had been arrested a number of times for various offenses, from gambling, to loan sharking and assault. His mental capacities were in inverse proportion to his size, which was considerable. Tom was a big man by most standards, but Ole seemed almost half again as large. He stood at least six four, and Tom knew he weighed two eighty the last time he was brought in. It looked like he had put on some weight since then. Because of his size, he mostly worked as a bouncer and bodyguard, but Tom had heard rumors of him taking on more deadly work. As he waited, Tom slipped his left hand into the brass knuckles he carried in his pants pocket. Ole became just a little smaller.

Venkman rumbled back down the hall.

"Come mit mir," he said, almost spitting the words at Braddock. Tom followed Ole to the back of the building and up another flight of stairs to the third floor. The Dutchman pointed to a door without saying a word. Tom walked in, while Venkman loitered in the hall. Finney's office was large and stylish. He sat before a big oak rolltop set against one wall, his back to the door. He didn't look up as Tom came in.

"So, what brings one o' Coffin's errand boys to me, I'm wonderin'?" Finney asked in a conversational tone.

"Nice to meet you too, Finney. I'm Tom Braddock, and I'm here to do you a favor."

"A favor, is it? It's not every day one o' the Police Department's finest walks in my door, lookin' to do me favors. I'm all ears, Braddock." Finney still hadn't looked up at Tom.

"I'll get right to it then, Finney."

"Now you're doin' me a favor," Finney interrupted. "Got no time to waste on this crap."

"Humph. No point mincing it too fine for you. Coffin's willing to let you stay open and let you run your business undisturbed."

Finney finally turned to face Tom. He looked Tom up and down, an ill-concealed smirk on his thin lips. "Don't need that prick's permission to wipe me arse, let alone stay open. Who the fuck he thinks he is I don't know."

Seeing that this was not starting off well, Tom tried a more diplomatic tack. "Listen, Finney, Coffin doesn't want to shut you down. He wants you to make money. There's profit enough here for everybody, and Coffin doesn't want to get in the way of profits." Finney seemed to consider this, so Tom went on. "There's no need for any unpleasantness after all, and I'm not here to cause any. This is only business, and we all know how it's done, don't we?" Tom said in a reasonable tone.

"Sure, I know how it's done, Braddock. I've been shaken down by the best. But you know what bothers me is the gall of the man. Coffin knows damn well I'm already payin' that bunch in the Fourth Precinct. He knows it, by God, but he still keeps sendin' his lapdogs down here to bite out another piece o' me hide. You're the fourth, and I'm gettin' real tired o' your ugly faces poppin' up an' tellin' me to do business." Finney's voice raised as he said this, getting up a head of steam as he went. Tom did his best to hide his surprise. He didn't take to being called a lapdog, but that wasn't what got his attention. It just wasn't customary to be paying two precincts. Coffin should have worked it out with Coogan, in the Fourth, if he wanted a piece of Finney. There was no reason for him to be here, no reason except for Coffin's greed. He couldn't let Finney know that, though.

"What's gone on before or who you're paying is no concern of mine Finney. I sympathize with your problems, but you are, after all, running an illegal enterprise here." Tom didn't want to show any cracks in the façade.

"Oh, sure, I appreciate your sympathy, Braddock. I'm touched, really. But just what the fuck do you call what you're doin'? Answer me that? So don't be lecturin' me about legalities. You and that bastard Coffin are worse than me by a mile. Fuckin' cops're just bag men and extortionists, you ask me." He spat.

"Nobody's asking you, Finney. Fact is, we're telling you." Tom tried to maintain his calming tone. "There's room to make money if you play ball. You're a man of business. You know the risks, the costs of running a gaming parlor like you have here. It's a nice establishment, and Coffin wants you to keep it nice. You just have to be reasonable and play by the rules."

"Yeah, Coffin's rules. I already paid, like I said. You don't believe me, ask Coogan. I ain't payin' twice. I can't do it, an' I won't do it. It ain't right, an' you know it."

Tom was getting tired of this. He was getting nowhere, and now that he knew the score he'd lost whatever taste he had for this "little favor" of Coffin's.

"Finney, don't presume to be telling me what I know," Braddock said, pointing a finger at the wiry Irishman. "I'm telling you, you don't want to get on the wrong side of Captain Coffin. You don't know what you're dealing with. What you're doing isn't good business, and I'm warning you, the next visit you get will not be this civilized. Don't buck Coffin. I'm telling you for your own good, it isn't healthy." That actually was good advice.

"You fuckin' son of a bitch! You come in here an' shake me down, you fuckin' arrogant shit, an' then you threaten me?" Finney said, bouncing to his feet, his face getting red.

"Look, I—" Tom started.

"No, *you* look. You want an answer fer your master Coffin? Well, I'll give you one. Get this. Nobody fucks wi' Finney." Tom saw Finney's eyes flicker to his left, and he cursed himself for an arrogant fool. Like a rookie, he had left his back to the door. Those kinds of mistakes could end badly. Tom turned and ducked at the same time he pulled his brass-knuckled fist out of his pocket. Venkman's immense bulk loomed past his shoulder. How the giant had positioned himself there without his noticing, Tom would never know. Of more concern at the moment was the baseball bat whistling toward his head. Tom knew there was no way it was going to miss, so he did his best to limit the impact by twisting his head and stepping into the blow. If he could survive, he thought, then he'd see what could be done.

The bat glanced off Tom's brass knuckles, knocking them back into his forehead an instant before the bat exploded off his skull. He was staggered by the blow but amazed to find himself still on his feet. More amazing still was how little it hurt. The shock was too great to let the pain in just yet. He knew the bat must have done some damage, because things seemed so slow and fuzzy now. Venkman's follow-through sent the bat crashing into a picture hanging on the wall. The frame and glass bursting like Fourth of July fireworks. Tom was off balance, but he lashed out with his left foot at Ole's knee. He hit him a pretty good lick, but Venkman's legs were like trees, and all it did was drive him back a step with a grunt of pain. Venkman swung again, but this time it was he who was off balance. Tom stepped in and caught Ole's fists on his shoulder. The shoulder lit up in a bright circle of pain, and the force of it knocked him sideways. He heard a dull crack and saw Ole grit his teeth. Tom hoped he broke something important.

With a quick left, Tom clipped the big Dutchman's jaw, the brass knuckles opening a small gash. Venkman tried to step back and get some swinging room, but he bounced off the door jamb and managed a weak off-balance swing that accomplished nothing. It was time to put the Dutchman down before he got himself together. With a quick hard snap-kick, Tom connected with Venkman's groin. A gasping moan flew from the big O that was Ole's mouth. Tom expected him to crumple, but he just gritted his teeth, turning first white then red, and he stayed on his feet. Tom waded in with a right to the gut and a left to the side of Ole's jaw. The brass made a sickening crunch, and a spray of red flew in a flock of polka dots. Ole howled but managed a strong backhanded blow with the butt of the bat to Tom's temple. Tom's vision shrank down to a tunnel of twinkling lights, and he fought for consciousness, his brain flailing. Almost blind, he swung hard and wild, not sure of what he was hitting. The Dutchman backed into the hall, spitting red froth and covering up. Tom was breathing hard, but his vision was clearing. He knew he couldn't give the Dutchman a break. The bastard had already taken enough punishment to bring down two men, but there he was braced on those tree trunks. Tom was about to charge in again when he heard the unmistakable metallic click of a pistol behind his head.

"That's it for you, Braddock."

Tom ducked and spun, knocking Finney's pistol aside. As he came around, though, Tom wrapped his arm about Finney's. He either had to control the gun or get it out of Finney's grasp; anything else was death. The pistol was hard against Tom's side, smothered in his jacket, and Finney was wrenching hard to pull it away. They struggled in a staggering stiff-legged dance. Finney struck again and again at Tom's face and side. Tom just grinned at the wiry Irishman and wrapped his other arm under Finney's. Pushing up from the balls of his feet, throwing his legs and his back into it, he pulled up on that arm. Finney screamed, his arm tore and cracked, the pistol barked. The report startled Tom so much, he almost let go. He couldn't tell if he was shot or not. His side felt numb, but as long as he was on his feet, he was determined to hold on. Another wrench on Finney's arm, though, and the pistol clattered to the floor.

Tom pushed Finney back, and he crumpled against his desk, down on one knee. He was white and sweating, holding the arm that now had an unnatural bend to it. But Tom was more concerned with Venkman, and he spun about, expecting the huge Dutchman to splatter him with his bat, surprised he hadn't already. What Tom saw made him stop for a heartbeat. Ole Venkman stood braced against the wall in the hallway. The bat had fallen to the floor. The Dutchman looked at first as if he had donned a red apron. It was Finney's bullet. The soft lead had caught Venkman just above the lower rib. Ole had torn his shirt open, and he gaped at himself in a stupor as the little hole fountained dark blood. His lower torso and those tree-trunk legs were already covered in it. The red pool at his feet widened as the life rained out of him in arterial rushes. Ole looked up, helpless and scared, his huge, red hands trying hard to hold his life in. The red tide went out, and Ole slipped down the wall, to swim in the pool on the floor.

"You're a dead man, Braddock. You hear me?" Finney gasped through clenched teeth.

Tom was breathing hard, his hands on his knees. "You brought this on yourself, Finney. You stupid son of a bitch, this could have gone down easy. It didn't have to happen this way."

"Easy, my arse. Only thing goin' down is you." Finney pulled a nasty looking six-inch stiletto from his boot. He rose to a crouch, his useless arm swinging like a dead thing.

Tom straightened. "Jesus, Finney, haven't you had enough?"

"Not till I see your bleedin' corpse, Braddock. I'm gonna carve you like a Christmas goose." Finney made a quick charge, the stiletto licking out, sharp and venomous. His shattered arm swung loose and low, like an ape. Finney's eyes shone red. Tom reacted slower than he thought he would, or maybe Finney was faster; but the Irishman came near to fleshing his bright steel fang. Tom brushed the blade aside, but it dug a searing furrow along his rib. Tom's right chopped down hard on Finney's neck as he pivoted to one side. The knife came around, flashing silver and red, but aimless. Tom struck again, this time with his left. Finney's cheek and nose caved in from the force of Tom's brass-knuckled fist. The Irishman toppled back like fresh-cut timber. His head bounced doll-like against the desk on its way to the floor. Tom bent over again, his hands on his knees, trying to catch his breath like a miler after a hard race; sucking in great restoring lungsful. Finney, however, didn't seem to be breathing at all.

Tom would never really remember how he got out of Finney's. He stumbled down a back stair, he thought, but things were starting to haze over and he couldn't be sure. He would recall bits of it later; how he staggered through garbage and bounced off things unseen in the blackness between the buildings. Mostly he remembered the cold in the pit of his stomach and the retching. He tripped and went down in an alley, his head filled with spinning sparks of light and his stomach tossing about inside him. On his hands and knees, he emptied himself out. He remembered thinking that maybe if he tried hard enough, he could spit up the taste of the deaths he had caused. It was as if his body were trying to reject what he had done. He knew that if he had not done it, it would have been him lying cold on Finney's floor, but logic couldn't undo the guilt. He had killed—not for honor, not for country, not for high purpose, but for money. There was no washing it away, not even from the inside.

⚘ Chapter Nine ⚘

*If I get well, there is lots of big work in
the world to do yet.*

—WASHINGTON ROEBLING

The first thing Tom noticed was the cold. He groped for consciousness as if stumbling through a blizzard. His left hand felt like ice. It throbbed, in spite of being nearly numb, and the fingers felt thick as sausages. He moved the hand slowly, bringing it up close to his face. The hand went in and out of focus. It reminded him of a fun-house mirror at Barnum's, the way it blurred and changed shape. His shifting hand solidified before him, its images coming together. It didn't look like his hand, and he almost wondered whose it might be. If it was his, he reasoned, then it would move when he wanted, so he closed the fattened fingers down into a ham-size fist. Cracking fissures of pain ran down the fingers, setting his hand on fire. It coursed up his arm, and he could feel the pain coming like an express train on a foggy night. Someone groaned in the room. It was he.

"Miss Mary, Miss Mary! He's awake again," Chelsea called. Mary had stationed her in Tom's room for the last day and a half, watching for signs of improvement. Hard heels on polished wood clicked and pounded in Tom's head. "He moved his arm, miss," Chelsea said with a hopeful note in her voice. Chelsea had worked for Mary for three years, not as one of the working girls but as her maid. In reality she was the eyes and ears of the house. Mary often thought she couldn't run the place without her.

"Thank you, Chelsea," Mary said quickly as she entered the room. "Would you leave us alone for a minute? Oh, and would you ask Cookie to make some tea? Strong and sweet, if you please." Mary frowned down at Tom.

"Yes, miss." Chelsea was already half out the door.

A door closed out of his sight. The sound echoed through his head and rippled like a stone thrown into a pond.

"Tom, Tom, Tom. Tom, Tom, Tom? Tom? Tommy?"

"Yersch," Tom said through dry lips. He coughed to clear his throat. It now seemed to be home to a bird's nest. The cough sent planets of pain bouncing around inside his head, into his temples, and behind his eyes.

"Here, Tommy, have some water. Can you sit up a bit?" Mary asked, lifting his head. Tom did, but his body protested in every part. Something in his side felt like it was tearing. The pain made him catch his breath. "Oh, your stitches, they must hurt. What a fool I am. Let me help you." He drank half a glass of cool water and flopped his head back on the pillow for a rest. The water had an odd taste, he thought.

"What's in the water?"

"Just some willow powder. It'll help."

"How'd I . . . what am I doin' here? My hand's cold. Why's my hand so cold?"

"The doctor told me to put it in ice. We had to get the brass knuckles off, they were cutting off the blood."

"Oh . . ." he said slowly, rummaging about in his foggy head to make sense of that, remembering as if in slow motion how Venkman's bat had bounced off them. "How'd I get here?"

"Tommy, I really don't know. Two nights ago, about eight o'clock, a cabby was pounding on our door. I sent Chelsea down to see to it, and the cabby tells her he's got a man unconscious and bleeding all over the back of his cab. Chelsea came up and got me, and when I heard the story, I, well, I nearly sent the man away."

"I don't remember a damn thing. Must have been out," Tom mumbled.

"You were out, all right. Like I said, I almost turned the cabby away, but then he gave me your description," Mary explained feeling guilty. "I went down to check and I had you brought up. You've been here ever since."

"Ever since? Ever since when?" Tom asked, thinking it might have been earlier that night.

"I told you, it was two nights ago, Tommy. We've been worried sick, and—"

"Jesus!" Tom interrupted. "So this is what, the first of April?"

"Uh-huh. It's about five-thirty in the morning." Tom's mouth twisted into an ironic grin. "April Fool's Day."

"Tommy, what happened? Who did this to you? Sam wouldn't say a thing.

I'm not sure he knows." This was a subject Tom didn't want to get into, not yet at least, and especially not when the room was still going in and out of focus. His silence told Mary more than he could have imagined. They sat together on the rumpled sheets as the first glow of morning crept into the room on stealthy feet. Their breathing was the only sound; sometimes together, sometimes apart. Mary held his hand in hers, felt its strength and pulse. She never wanted to let this hand go.

They sat like that for some time, until there was a rap on the door, and Chelsea came in with a tray of tea and toast. Mary turned to get up but Tom held her hand tight, and she turned back to fall into his eyes.

"Uh . . . Mary . . . I . . ." he said, searching for the right words. "I . . ."

Mary understood perfectly. "Tom, the only thing that matters to me is that you're here with me now, having tea, eating toast, and feeling better. Anything else can wait."

"I—" He tried to continue.

"Shush. Have some tea. It'll do you good." Mary didn't notice the tear that dampened his cheek.

He wiped it with his swollen hand and winced. "I'm a lucky man, Mary."

She pushed a piece of toast in his mouth, with a wry smile. "And don't you forget it, Tom Braddock."

It was six-thirty and the city was just starting to come to life outside the office of Sangree & Co. Peck Slip and Water Street echoed with the sound of individual wagons, their horses clopping the cobbles on early-morning trips to the Fulton market. Later in the day the din from the streets would grow into a sort of clattering cauldron of sound, blending the noise of dozens of wagons, horses, stevedores, sailors, shopkeepers, and vendors. But now, an hour and a half before most businesses opened, there was a calm, almost villagelike feel to the place.

They were meeting over an early breakfast this morning. Matt had gotten some fresh muffins from the bakery around the corner from his flat. The captain had made coffee on the small stove in the meeting room. They all sat around the big table, appraising the situation.

"We're going to have to keep an eye on him," the captain said thoughtfully. "If he comes back again and gets too inquisitive, well, then, we'll have to see what can be done. He gave you no reason to suspect he knew anything, you say?"

"Naw, Cap'n," Lebeau said through a mouthful of muffin. "Seemed to me like he was just goin' through the motions. Leastwise he di'n show no interest in me or Matt. Can't speak for Watkins."

Watkins cleared his throat. "Same here. Told 'im I was out with Miss Devine. She knows what to say if he comes around."

"Hmm." The captain stole a glance at Weasel Jacobs. Something seemed to pass between them . . . an understanding.

"We didn't talk all that much really," Watkins went on. "Got interrupted 'cause he went sniffin' after the Roebling woman. Can't say I liked his manner much."

"What do you mean about Mrs. Roebling?" the captain asked sharply.

"We was talkin' about Bucklin, when he sees her a ways up by the tower, an' he just ups and skeedadles over to her like a cock rooster. Seen them an' Martin head off toward City Hall a bit later."

"Interesting." The captain seemed to ponder this information. "You say they went off together?"

Watkins assured him they had. Matt and Earl confirmed it.

"Hm. Well, probably nothing to it. It does bother me somewhat that he has made the acquaintance of Mrs. Roebling. I suspect we'll be seeing more of the detective." The captain stared with unseeing eyes up at the ceiling as his fingers drummed the table. "As I said before," the captain said almost to himself, "we may have to do something about this detective."

Sullivan's head went up. This whole business with Watkins and Bucklin was getting out of hand—*had* gotten out of hand already, he corrected himself. Now they were talking about killing cops. The shit was getting deeper and they didn't even seem to notice.

"You mean get rid of him? A little risky to be killing off the cops, don't you think?" This was the first comment Sergeant Sullivan had made on the subject, but it was on all their minds.

"No question, Patrick, but at this point we must not let anything stand in our way," the captain said, stabbing a finger at the table. "Of course, I'm open to other solutions. We do have time to plan, should Braddock come too close to the mark."

"Right, Captain," Sullivan said. He'd feel a lot better knowing they had a plan to deal with Braddock. "If we could take a few minutes to lay our cards out, I think it would be time well spent. Don't want to be in a spot where we're the ones reacting to him."

They spent the next half hour on this, touching on every contingency they could think of and a few that were nearly unimaginable. Jacobs in his usual pedantic way, kept a detailed list. He preferred the direct approach.

"A simple thing, really. I pass our Detective Baddock on the street one night and suddenly put a knife in his throat." Jacobs flinty smile said almost as much as his words. He showed no more emotion than if he was reading from a ledger. "I'm gone in seconds. He dies. Nothing could be easier."

A glance or two was exchanged around the room. The men went on, and in the end they narrowed their choices down to three, none of which involved knives in the throat, at least not yet. It was also agreed that nothing should be done until they knew more about the directions Braddock's investigation might be heading. They had expected his visit, after all, and his mere appearance was no reason to take action. That part of their meeting came to a close with all in agreement to bide their time. Weasel looked disappointed. They would never know how close Venkman and Finney had come to ending their problems with Braddock.

"Earl, you'll be going to the Bucklins' later, right?" the captain asked before they broke up.

"Yessir." Earl had reported privately to the captain. Earl believed that Mike didn't know anything. Even if he did, he'd thrown such a scare into the boy that he'd be too frightened to even think about what he might know, let alone tell anyone. Nevertheless, they had decided on one more step, just to be sure. Earl knew the plan.

"Next item on the agenda," said Jacobs.

"Hold on there, Bart," Lincoln broke in. "We need to get to work. Can't we take the next items up at the regular meeting?"

"This isn't a job like the Prospect wreck," Jacobs retorted. "We need to have precise, detailed plans. Time's running short." Weasel loved nothing better than a good plan.

"We know that, Bart, but we do have jobs to go to and so do you," Lincoln reminded him. "No point throwing a light on us."

The captain checked his watch. "I think we can spare maybe twenty minutes but no more. We can pick up from there this evening."

Weasel took a deep breath. "Well, like I was saying, we have issues of transport, timing, and stealth to deal with." He ticked off the items on his fingers. "We all knew this was not going to be simple." They had established a basic plan months before, but like any plan, it kept evolving, getting more and more refined the closer it got to completion.

"No lie!" Earl laughed. "Took near on to thirteen years ta build the goddamned thing. Should take some doin' ta bring it down."

At first they had thought to blow the towers—that is, once they decided there was no way for them to be undermined. Earl and Matt's stint in the caissons had proved that. Yet blowing the immense towers would take hours of drilling and tons of explosives. Eventually they had given that idea up. "You could fire a parrot gun at those towers all day long and not make a dent," the captain had said. The roadway was another matter.

"That's six thousand six hundred and twenty tons, not including the weight of the cables," Sullivan had reminded them. "We just need to cause a weakness. All that weight will do the rest. Remember Ashtabula." There they'd cut critical points in the trestle, letting the weight of a passing train do the rest. But from their calculations, even just weakening the roadway would take over seven tons of dynamite and days to set and wire charges. There simply was no way to transport, set, and wire that amount of explosives without detection.

They'd considered blowing the main cables too. Each of the four cables was fifteen and three quarter inches thick, containing over fifty-four hundred wires, bundled in a virtually solid steel mass. Many times stronger than needed to withstand the weight of the span, they would be nearly impervious to explosives, except where they crossed the towers. But transporting the explosives to the tops of the towers would take hours, and no one knew for sure whether enough explosives could be packed around the cables in that tight spot. After weeks of consideration, that idea too had been rejected.

The plan they had finally agreed upon was as elegant as it was efficient. It called for just a few hundred pounds of explosives and no more than an hour and a half to set the charges. It was not without risk, but risk was an old bedfellow.

The captain nodded but seemed to be thinking of something as he examined the plans laid out on the table.

"I think," he started slowly, "that Jacobs has an important point in principle." The captain had the look they had often seen during the war, when he was sitting with the colonel late at night, planning for the next day's action. He had never lost the habit of putting things in military terms. Sullivan though saw it as a crutch. Like a security blanket, it cloaked him in a mantle of command. The cloak was frayed now, but he wore it with pride and a dogged desperation. "Jacobs, will you please start a list of issues and tactics still needing to be finalized, the advantages and disadvantages of each?" Sangree said with a glance at his watch. "Do it like this." The captain drew two lines down a sheet of paper, making three columns. "Tactics down one column, and so forth. We'll lay out our options, eliminate those that seem impractical, and concentrate on the ones that offer the best chance of success." Once again they refined their plans, Jacob taking down the points in his elegant hand. It sometimes seemed that the final issues would take forever to iron out. They all knew the devil was in the details.

· · ·

Tom slept again, while a mile away the seven men planned. It was an uneasy rest. Venkman stalked through his dreams, rumbling like an avalanche, about to bury him. Finney was there too. He was the coroner now, with a white lab coat smeared with blood, a crooked grin on his ratlike face. Music played in the background. Tom stared up in horror as Finney's face leered down at him, his shattered arm hanging loose, head twisted at an impossible angle. Finney's six-inch scalpel started at his ribs, cutting deep, reaching in.

Tom's own cry woke him. After a moment's panic, he realized it was just his stitches pulling. He felt foolish, but he was sweating just the same. The next time he woke it was much later. The sun stealing in through the blinds slanted across the room at a more acute angle, painting the floor in zebralike blacks and whites. He thought he heard a commotion somewhere in the house, voices raised and tense. A door slammed, echoing through the house and his head. He drifted off in a haze that was not sleep, but near enough. Tom tried not to think about things but they kept swimming to the surface for his inspection, like floaters in the East River, bobbing on the waves, full of gas. What would Coffin say about Tom's handiwork? The possibilities seemed mostly bad. Venkman and Finney floated by. Tom wouldn't talk to them. He was afraid they'd answer back. Bucklin put in an appearance too, but his head was half gone, and he asked Tom what Doc Thomas had done with it. Tom asked Terrence who killed him, but he spat tobacco juice and faded away. Then Sam came. He looked down from a great height, his chin disappearing into his collar. He spoke to Tom, and it was so clear he could swear Sam was in the room, right there with him. But then he spoke again, and he could feel Sam's hand on his arm.

"Tommy? Tommy, it's Sam, c'mon, fella, give us a nod if you can hear me."

Tom looked up at him and wondered what he was standing on to make him seem so tall. Maybe he had grown. "You're taller, Sam," Tom mumbled, looking up at him appraisingly.

"Taller? You're a funny one. That's all you can think to say?"

Tom screwed his eyes shut and rubbed his temples. "Give me a minute, I'll do better."

"I hope so. You've given everyone a scare, Thomas," Sam said, sitting on the side of the bed.

"Didn't mean to."

"I suppose not, but what the hell were you thinking goin' up against Finney and Venkman alone?"

Tom's eyes jacked open in a hurry. "Don't worry, the papers are callin' it like they killed each other," Sam said, laying a hand on Tom's shoulder.

"The papers! Oh, Christ." Tom rolled his eyes up to the ceiling. His head was pounding.

"It's all over today's papers, sure. And wouldn't you know it, they're quoting Coffin on the need to clean up the gaming parlors. Let's see if I can remember the exact quote. It went something like, "The vilest elements of society are sucking the life blood from the heart of this city. Together we will stamp out this scourge and make the streets safe for our women and children," or something like that. Very high minded, very noble, very Coffin. You'll get a chuckle out of it. The *Trib* carried the whole thing. Him and Coogan are doing their best to keep a lid on and keep the press from gettin' too inquisitive. Very inspiring."

"But, Sam, why do you think I had—"

Sam held up a hand, giving Tom a stern look that said he wasn't buying a word. "Stop right there, Tommy. This is your old pal. Don't be shovelin' shit on my shoes," he said gruffly. "Just shut your yap. I'm on your side, remember?"

"Sorry, Sam. Not thinkin' straight."

"I'll say. It's not Byrnes you're talkin' to. By the way, you look like shit, so I forgive ya." Sam patted Tom's shoulder.

"Damn! My cats. I got to feed 'em. It's been two days." Tom started to throw a leg over the side of the bed and raise himself up.

"Hold on there, cowboy. Relax, I fed 'em this morning. Mrs. Aurelio let me in. Seemed real happy to see me, I can tell you. They're fine, the furballs."

Tom seemed genuinely relieved. Sam almost laughed out loud; here Tom was, all busted up, in a world of hurt, and he's worried about his cats.

"Thanks, Sam," Tom said gratefully. "Seems I'm doin' that a lot lately."

"What?"

"Saying thanks." Tom was quiet for a moment. He looked at his swollen hand; turning it this way and that, like a piece of evidence. "Sam, does Mary know?"

"If yer askin' me if I told her, the answer is no. Not my place to get between you on something like this. She's no fool, Tom. She'll put it together if she hasn't already." Tom seemed to chew on that, so Sam ventured on.

"Tom, I know you didn't ask . . . but if you *was* to ask my advice, I'd say to be straight with her. She's too good a woman to risk tellin' tales to."

"Yeah. I know . . . but I'm worried about her. If it gets ugly with Coffin, I don't want anything to blow back on her," Tom said with a frown. This was a real concern. Coffin wouldn't hesitate to strike at Mary if he thought it would serve his purposes.

"Tom, what Coffin does or don't do is his affair. Not much you can do about it. But bein' straight with Mary . . . well, that's all you."

"I suppose. Hell, I know you're right. Mary deserves the truth."

"Tommy, ah . . . I got to tell you, Coffin ain't happy."

Tom laughed with a sarcastic twist to his mouth, his stitches pulling. Tom could imagine just how unhappy Coffin was.

"No shit? What'd he say?"

"Just wanted to know where you was." Sam shrugged. "Told him I didn't know. Held him for a while, but not long. He turned up here an hour or so ago. Mary wouldn't let him see you."

Tom nodded, putting the pieces together. "That was the commotion downstairs."

"Yeah. I was here, but I hid out till he was gone. I gotta tell you, Tom, that Mary's somethin'." Sam's voice was full of admiration. "Stood up to Coffin like he was no more'n a night-soiler. Told him you weren't well enough and that's that."

"That's Mary. She's hard when she has to be . . . soft when she wants to be," Tom said with his eyes closed, but there was a big grin on his face. "Damndest woman I ever knew. She's got her own mind and a tongue like a rasp when she's crossed, but . . . she can be as sweet as new butter."

"Well, she let him have it." Sam gave a low whistle. "Don't think he liked it much."

"I've seen her get her back up," Tom said with a knowing smile.

Sam looked at Tom appraisingly. "He'll be back, you know."

Tom just nodded, the smile leaving his lips.

"Oh, ah . . . did you cover for me with Byrnes?" Tom asked hopefully, realizing suddenly that he'd have some awkward explaining to do if Sam hadn't.

"Yeah. Told him you was sick. Had the doctor write up a note that said you're dyin'."

Tom nodded his thanks. He knew he could always count on Sam. "Great. I'll be back in a week, good as new. Got to deal with Coffin first. Put a lid on that situation."

Sam grinned. "You're gonna keep a lid on Coffin. You're a funny one."

"Like to close the goddamn lid on him." Tom growled. "You know Finney and Venkman were crazy bastards, but I don't think they would've come at me unless . . . well . . ."

"Unless they had Coffin's blessing." Sam finished the sentence for him. "Thought crossed my mind."

"They were already paying Coogan," Tom said, watching Sam closely for his reaction. Sam knew as well as anyone how the system worked.

The surprise was clear on Sam's face. "No shit? Don't like the sound of that. That don't add up. You think Coffin would really set you up? Didn't think things were *that* bad between you and him."

"I didn't either. He was laying it on a bit heavy that morning, but I didn't think . . . Hell, I don't know." Tom thought for a moment, but his brain still felt fuzzy, and his brain felt like it was slopping around inside his skull when he moved. "He put me in that situation . . . I know that. He knew damn well what the score was, and he must have known the Dutchman would be there. Maybe Coffin wanted me to get taught a little lesson. Let the Dutchman do the dirty work. Maybe it just got out of hand, and they went farther than Coffin wanted. I'd like to believe that, but . . ."

"Any light you shine on it puts Coffin in the shadows, Tommy," Sam said with an appraising twist of his mouth.

Tom sighed. He was starting to tire and his stomach needed something in it more substantial than tea and toast.

"Gonna be more trouble. Coffin won't let it lie."

Sam nodded. "I'll back you as far as I can. You might need some backin' if this gets out of hand."

The door opened, and Mary came in with a tray.

"Praise God. You must have read my mind," Tom said.

Mary looked at him straight and serious. "Of course, Tom, that's what I do. In fact, I know your every thought. I can peer around inside that banged-up head of yours anytime I please and read what's in there like chalk on slate." A little smile started at the corners of her mouth. "Of course, there's usually not much to read."

Tom groaned but couldn't hide the grin sneaking around the corners of his mouth. "You just wait. Makin' fun of an injured man, staring at death's door . . . you should be ashamed of yourself. When my head stops pounding, I'll get you."

"And I intend to be got, Tom Braddock." Mary's smile lit the room.

God, she was beautiful, Tom thought.

Sam got up. "Well, got to get going. I'll stop in tomorrow." He stuck out his hand and they shook. "Glad to see you're doin' better, Tommy."

"Sam . . . thanks and . . . thanks for taking care of Grant and Lee."

"No trouble. You saved my bacon once or twice. Least I can do is feed your cats. Grant and Lee." Sam shook his head. "You are a pip, Tommy. I'll see ya." He gave them an awkward little wave, kissed Mary a quick good-bye, and said something to her that Tom didn't catch.

"He's a good friend," Mary said as Sam clumped down the stairs. She was getting to like Sam almost as much as Tom did, especially during the last two days.

"Yeah. Like brothers sometimes. It's a little strange, not another man in the city I can count on more."

Mary set the tray down on a table near the bed and lifted the cover from a soup bowl. The steam rose, filling the room with a wonderful air of rich broth, chicken, vegetables, and spices. Tom's stomach growled, but his mind wasn't on his stomach.

"Mary, you know I killed those two men," he said abruptly.

Mary looked at him with soft, sad eyes, eyes that had seen more than their share of sadness. "I know, Tommy."

Tom rushed on trying to explain where no explanation was necessary. His temples throbbed. He tried to tell he didn't have a choice, that it was their lives or his.

Mary hung her head, her long raven hair covering her face. After a time she raised her face to him, her sad eyes shining. "Tommy, don't." It was almost as if his words had hurt her. "You don't need to explain, not to me."

"But you deserve to know I'm not—"

"Tommy, don't you understand? You don't have to explain to me. I know what you are and what you're not. You're not a man that could take a life without cause." She paused, looking into his eyes. "It hurts me to think you don't know that."

Tom was about as puzzled as he had ever been. Mary had a way of doing that to him.

"Tommy, I've watched you when you don't know I'm watching. I've seen you sitting in the moonlight with Grant on your lap. I know how you are with your friends. I know how you are with women. Remember that squirrel you nursed when it fell from its nest in front of your house?"

Tom nodded with a small childish kind of smile.

"A squirrel, for God's sake. You're a gentle man . . . a man that wouldn't hurt anyone if it could be helped. I know you're no saint, and I know you can be hard when you have to be, but you're not a bad man. You're not a murderer. You aren't capable of that. I may as well ask you to live at the bottom of the ocean and breathe like the fishes. You couldn't do it."

Tom was surprised that in some ways she knew him better than he knew himself.

"I just wanted to be sure you knew," Tom said softly. "I needed to tell you . . . how it happened, so you didn't hear it from someone else. And how I felt . . . you know . . . about what happened."

Looking at his hand held in hers, Mary said simply, "I know."

❧ Chapter Ten ❧

Ah, how skillful is the hand,
That obeyeth Love's command!
It is the heart, and not the brain,
That to the highest doth attain,
And he who followeth Love's behest
Far excelleth all the rest

—HENRY WADSWORTH
LONGFELLOW

Washington Roebling's study was cluttered. Piles of documents, plans, and correspondence littered his desk. Emily was starting to pack things away. Most of it wasn't needed, now that the work was nearing completion. She was sorting through the correspondence, when she suddenly remembered.

"Oh, I forgot to tell you, Wash, I met the most interesting man the other day on the bridge."

"Huh? Ah . . . what was that, darling?" Washington had been bent low over the plans for the Brooklyn train terminal. Even though he had not designed it, he still insisted on an intimate knowledge of everything connected with his bridge. His poor eyesight made it difficult to make anything out of the plans before him. For years Emily had done all his reading for him. Though it seemed he could hardly breathe without her, that didn't stop him from trying to do things on his own.

"I said I met an interesting man on the bridge, a New York City detective by the name of Braddock."

"What was a detective doing on our bridge?" Wash asked, looking up from his plans with a frown.

"Well . . . it seems that one of the laborers was murdered," Emily said with the hint of an apology for not having remembered to tell him sooner.

"Oh? Wouldn't think there was anything extraordinary about that," Wash said, turning back to his work. "Thousands of men have worked on the bridge over the years. Most have been from poorer circumstances, from neighborhoods where crime is epidemic. This can't be the first time one of our men has met with foul play."

"I'm sure you're right, dear, but this had a peculiar aspect to it. It seems the family of this man claims that there's something not right with the bridge."

That got her husband's attention, and his head snapped up to stare at Emily. "Something not right?" His brows knit. "Whatever can he mean by that? The bridge is as sound as the U.S. Treasury."

"Well, he really wasn't sure himself," Emily said with a deprecating gesture. "It's just that this man died under somewhat unusual circumstances. With the father of the dead man telling him there was something untoward going on at the bridge, he felt he should investigate."

More dubious than ever, Roebling scratched his head with the end of his pencil. "This detective, you mean. That's it? On the strength of some rumor? Seems a little thin. He wasn't disrupting things, was he?" Wash was more concerned with keeping to his schedule than with some far-fetched rumors of anything not being right about the bridge. He was the chief engineer. If anything wasn't right with the bridge, he'd know it, and what he knew was that the East River Bridge was perfection itself.

"Not that I could see," she lied. Of course Braddock had disrupted things, but not in the way her husband meant. "Charles invited him to lunch with us at the Astor House. We had a lively discussion of the criminal mind. He seemed quite capable."

"Hm. So you were rather taken with him then," Washington said with a knowing look. Emily started to protest, but her husband stopped her. "Em. It's all right. You're a beautiful woman. It's only natural."

"Wash, it's not like that," she said, blushing slightly. "You know I'm totally devoted to you."

Her husband smiled warmly. "Oh, I know that Em." His tone told her she was being silly. He came to her and wrapped her in his arms. "I'm a believer in you, you see, a truster as well," he murmured. "I know I haven't been a husband to you in the . . . well . . . in the way we'd like. It's just that I can understand if you were attracted to this man, that's all. It's natural, all things considered, and I'm stunned it hasn't happened sooner."

Emily opened her mouth to say something, but shut it again without a word. Color rose in her cheeks.

"Don't worry about it, Em. Not another word on the subject. And as to his investigation, I don't think he'll find anything going on here except bridge-building." With that Wash turned back to his work.

Emily wanted to say more. A part of her felt very guilty for finding Tom attractive. She knew it was bad to think that way. Even thinking that way was a betrayal, and she felt the dirt of it on her like sand in her shoes. No matter how she tried to shake the sand out, it seemed to stick, a gritty reminder of her innermost desires.

"If you see this detective again," Wash said, looking up, "tell him we'll cooperate in any way we can, but if he has any information of malfeasance or fraud, or anything unsavory for that matter, he's to come to you first." Wash shook a finger at her. "I don't want to hear about it in the papers, or from the board."

Emily rolled her eyes in agreement.

"That bunch of political vultures have been circling my corpse for years. If anything is going on, I want to know about it before them. No point getting them in another dither at this late date."

"Couldn't agree more, darling." Emily knew very well the politics of the board. It was only because of her work and influence that her husband was still the chief engineer. "Even now I think some of them would grasp at any straw to erase the name of Roebling from the bridge. Don't worry, I'll be sure to tell him if I see him."

Matt Emmons and Jus Lincoln were walking together up South Street. It was getting late. They had just left their meeting and thought they'd get an ale before going home. The bridge loomed in front of them, just three blocks north.

"Ah dunno, Jus. You think we're on the right track with this plan?"

"Hell, Matt, I dunno. 'Sides, we still got some other angles we all need to talk over. Nobody said nothin' yet about how we're supposed to git out of the city."

"I heard the sergeant say we'd work that out later," Matt said hopefully. "Not to worry; there won't be anything undone." He paused for a bit. "You ever notice how it looks at night, Jus?" Matt was looking up at the looming presence of the bridge.

"What d'ya mean? Looks like a bridge I guess." Justice shrugged. He had a feeling he knew what Matt was getting at. He'd come to admire the bridge himself over the years, perhaps more deeply than he'd admired anything before. It troubled him, though, and he'd been careful not to say what he felt to the others.

"No, it's kind of like it looks like something else in the dark," Matt said, holding out his hands as if to frame it. "Like it changes with the light. As if it turns into a ghost ship or somethin'."

"Ghost ship! That's a good one, Matthew." Justice chuckled. "Where you come up with that?"

Matt shrugged, a little abashed at letting that notion spill out. "Don't know. Just thinkin' is all."

The bridge towered over the ships, masts, and rigging of the waterfront. Little waves slapped unseen against hulls and docks in the moonlight. Rigging creaked, and a small chorus of squeaks and groans sang like wooden bullfrogs as hulls rubbed against pilings and bumpers. The moon was sliced by the masts and struck a shimmer off the arc of the bridge's main cables, glimmering ghostly down the stays. The granite of the towers, solid as the mountains they came from, was gray and black—immovable. But the bridge did seem to move in the dark. It swung across the blue-black waves that the moon had brushed with silver. It scudded across the heavens, sailing the clouds as the stars wheeled overhead. Matt recalled seeing an eagle once, perched at the top of a tree, stately in its potential, ready to row the air with massive wings and leave the earth behind. The bridge seemed like that to him now. For a moment, they both stopped and looked at the thing they had helped create.

"You know, sometimes I can't believe I helped build it," Matt whispered almost reverently. A breeze blew in off the harbor, carrying the smell of salt and fish and tar. A piano tinkled somewhere back in the city. "It's been a long haul. Lotta water's run with the tides since we started. Just look what we done."

"Gonna make one hell of a splash," Jus said with a tone that Matt couldn't really identify. Was there some regret in it?

Matt Emmons glanced at his friend. The moon behind him made his face seem a black hole in the night. "Suppose it will."

"That's gonna be a day to tell the grandkids about," Lincoln said with a studied neutrality to his voice. "How we paid the Yankees back so's they'll never forget."

"Ain't gonna be just the Yanks not forgetting, Justice," Matt said with a touch of worry. "Gonna be the whole damn world. It'll be in the papers in Europe inside of a couple days. Hell, I bet it'd be in Chinese papers inside a week."

"We're gonna be famous, Matthew. The world's gonna know who we are and what we did." Lincoln sounded more pleased with the prospect than he really was.

"That's what scares me, Jus. No place to hide for the likes of us. They find out who we are, and we'll be runnin' our lives away. Ain't gonna be any rest for us after this."

"Oh, I don' know, Matt. Could still go down South America. Got some countries down there, so lost, you can't find yourself." Lincoln didn't relish the thought. "Got some hellacious señoritas, boy . . . make you forget the day you was born." He dug an elbow into Matt's ribs. They both laughed but it was an uncertain, hollow laugh, from the mouth and not the heart.

"Wouldn't mind forgetting some," Matt said. He thought for a moment, scratching his head. "You know, we need to say something when we do this, Jus."

"Say somethin'? What do ya mean?"

"The world, the North." Matt spread his arms wide. "You know, tell why." Their motives were so well known to them, almost a religion, that the notion of explaining why they blew the bridge hadn't even been considered. They had all just assumed that it would be as clear to the rest of the nation as it was to them, all except Matt.

"You mean ya don't think they'd know?" To Lincoln, who had lived with their motives all these years, it was crystal clear.

"Justice . . . think about it. The war's been gone for eighteen years, an' Gettysburg was near twenty years ago. There's lots of folks that never knew what we know. You think they teach in schools up here what a tyrant Lincoln was? You think they care that our rights were spat on by the federals? You think they teach how our rights to property and liberty was ground under heel? Hell no! You figure they teach their kids how they stole our slaves an' turned 'em against us, stole our property, burned our farms, killed our stock, and fired our crops?" Matt looked at his friend. He could see the understanding in his crooked face. "I don't think so. No, they've been busy rewriting the past. The victors write the history, Jus, an' we're on the short end of that stick. We got to say somehow why we did it. They need to understand. Ain't gonna do any good without the world knowing. Sure it'll hurt Roebling, but it ain't enough."

Lincoln and Emmons walked on in silence for a moment, Jus chewing over the idea as they walked. Finally he said, "You talk to any of the others about this, Matt? 'Cause I think maybe you should."

"I guess. Won't nothin' come out of it. All that work and risk, an' everything, and the world will just think we're crazy is all. And you know something? If I was them, that's what I'd think too. I'll bring it up at the next meeting, see what everybody thinks. You with me, Justice?"

They had turned from South Street, up Peck Slip, but by word unspoken hadn't gone toward Paddy's. Instead they went right at Water and up the short block lined with small warehouses to the clapboard building at the next corner. The Dover Street Bar, as everyone called it, was near a hundred years old, and the building was showing its age. Years of settling had canted the windows this way and that, and the clapboards waved and buckled, their dark red paint flaking with the salt air. The ale and porter were good here, though, and the liquor wasn't watered too much. It did a pretty brisk business. They were just about to go in the front door when Matt hesitated. From this angle, the bridge soared almost over their heads, and the towers stood tall in the river like dominoes in the darkness.

"I'm gonna be a little sad when she goes, Jus."

"Know what ya mean. Ain't gonna be another."

They stood at the corner, looking up. The noise from inside the bar suddenly washed over them as someone came out the door, releasing a welcoming blast of smoke, laughter, and stale hops. Justice looked over at Matt and with a grim grin said, "Hell, let's go have a beer."

Mary ran a discreet but active business. Through the small hours of the morning, Tom would wake to the sounds of sex. Giggles, moans, grunts, and rhythmic noises filtered up from the rooms below on an hourly basis. Sleep was difficult. Tom had slept and dozed on and off for two days and pretty much had his fill of sleep anyway, but sleeping while hearing the things he did was next to impossible. His imagination was working overtime. Tom found himself trying to picture Mary's girls and guess which one it was who made that little-girl squeal, or the quiet whimper, or the sultry moan. His thoughts turned to Mary and when he finally fell asleep at 4:00 A.M., it was she who slipped into his dreams, languid and yielding.

When Tom woke, he couldn't be quite sure where the dream ended and the reality began. His first sensation was the smell of Mary's long black hair as it fanned out on the pillow beside him. The scent was faint but unmistakable. She always wore a scent that was part musk, part spice, part honeysuckle. Some smells register with the nose, but hers always seemed to run right down his middle, with little ripples north and south. He moved closer and breathed her in. In a way he thought he quite literally had, as if he had internalized some part of her, made it his. The notion intoxicated him, and he nuzzled her hair again as she slept. Mary must have felt him move, for she rolled in her sleep to face him. Tom studied her face in the morning light, his face just inches from hers. His eyes traced the lines of her cheeks, the bridge of her nose, and the curve of her lips. They lingered and caressed her with long slow sweeps, drinking in her form and scent, storing them in that part of his brain reserved for all things wondrous.

She was not a beauty in the popular sense. Her skin was too dark, her cheekbones too prominent, her forehead a bit too sloping. But to him, she was the name of beauty. Mary had what could be called exotic looks that she inherited from her mother and father. She was mostly Irish but her mother was part Cherokee, and the races mixed in her in intriguing ways. She had her mother's coloring, she had told him once: the midnight hair, the dark eyes, the skin that always looked tanned. But the Irish showed through in the waves in her hair and the shine of copper when the sun struck it just so. Her nose was a mixture of both as well. It ran almost straight and thin from her forehead, with just a bit of a bridge, and it had a hint of an upturned Irish tilt at the tip. The nostrils flared, in a very Indian way, reminding him of a Thoroughbred mare's, although he never told her that. He wasn't sure how she might take it, but to him it would have been a compliment. It was an altogether intriguing nose, and he had yet to see its like. Her face swooped down to a wide, full-lipped mouth, framed by delicate laugh lines. Her chin was from Ireland, with the hint of a dimple and a bit of a point. Altogether, she had a chiseled, elemental look that her bronze coloring only emphasized. Mostly Tom didn't care for the idealized version of female perfection so popular then. To him there was much more of interest in imperfection. Mary was, for him, perfectly imperfect.

Tom leaned closer and kissed her nose lightly as a butterfly. A little smile played on her mouth, but she didn't wake. He got up to go to the bathroom. Mary had full baths installed on every floor when she bought the building. It was a necessary investment in the trade. The girls were all required to wash after each visit, something the cheaper establishments didn't do. Even rarer, she required all gentlemen to wash beforehand too. The result was healthier girls, lower doctor bills, and a better class of clientele—altogether a sound arrangement. This was the first time Tom had tried to actually use the toilet, having contented himself with the chamber pot, because he felt too dizzy to do more than lean against the side of the bed. When he got up at first he had a strange rushing feeling, like the tide was draining out of his head. It left him feeling as he had when he smoked his first cigar, not too good. He made it across the room all right, but held his hand on the wall as he went down the hall to the bathroom. He wondered if this was what old age felt like: dizzy, tottering, having to hold the wall to keep from keeling over. If it was, he wanted none of it.

Mary was still sleeping when he got back. He joined her, and they dreamed together. It was perhaps 11 o'clock when Tom woke to hear Coffin's voice downstairs. A minute later Chelsea gave a quick rap on the door and came in.

"Sorry to disturb you, miss, but Captain Coffin's downstairs waiting to see Mr. Tom."

Mary shot Tom a questioning look. Tom just nodded.

"Tell the captain that I'll be down directly, Chelsea, and offer him some tea or coffee, will you?"

When Chelsea left, Mary turned to Tom. "You really up to seeing him?"

"Yeah, I think so. May as well get it over with." Tom shrugged.

"Do you want me to send for Sam?" Mary asked. She was afraid of Coffin, and rightly so.

"No, no, won't be necessary. It's okay." Tom knew he sounded more sure of the situation than he really was. But there was no need to send up distress signals just yet. Tom had been ready for this visit since last night, when he first learned Coffin had come looking for him. He'd be ready for the captain. Mary threw a robe on and went out with a last glance over her shoulder. As soon as the door was closed, Tom got out of bed. He did it a bit too quickly, though, and reeled his way over to the chair where his clothes sat. His holster hung over the back, the Colt nestled inside.

Earl Lebeau sat in the offices of Sangree & Co., his feet up on a windowsill. He rocked back and looked out the window as he and the captain talked.

"Waited till the three of them went out," Earl said. "Stood across the street and watched 'em go. The boy saw me, I think, 'cause he started cryin'." Earl grinned. "Told ya he had a scare in him."

"You did fine, Earl. You found nothing, then?" Thaddeus asked.

"Nothin'. They don't got much, but what they got I searched." Earl shrugged. "Nothin' there to be found, Cap'n. I was real neat too. They ain't likely to notice anything out of place. Put everything back just like I found it. I don't think we have anything to worry about from them."

The captain put his feet up too, crossing them atop his desk. The Bucklin matter seemed to be resolving itself nicely. So long as that damned detective kept his nose out of it, things should settle down.

"That's good, Earl. You did just fine." Thaddeus pulled out his pocket watch. "Shouldn't you be getting back to work? Lunchtime's near over."

Earl heaved a sigh. "Suppose so. Don't want them to dock me." He smiled grimly. "See you tonight, Cap'n."

Coffin hadn't decided how to handle Tom until he started up the stairs. Mary had been civil with him, and maybe that had put him in a better frame of mind. Whatever it was, Coffin set his mind to it as he set his foot on the steps. After all, Tom was a likable sort and a valuable man. It would be a shame to lose him, and there might be repercussions if it were not done right. Tom had plenty of friends in the department. Perhaps it was just as well he hadn't seen Tom yesterday. He was thinking more clearly now. Braddock was too valuable to lose just yet. Still, as he took the stairs, his hand stole into his coat pocket. The little .32 Smith & Wesson rested there, its ivory grips warmed against his middle. He flipped the safety off.

"Tommy, good to see you're doing better! You had us worried, sport." Coffin had rushed in after a quick knock, sweeping across the room with his hand out, like Tom was a long-lost brother. They shook.

"Good to see you too, August. Good to see anyone, for that matter," Tom said, nearly choking on the greeting.

"I can imagine. Listen, Tom, I had no idea that Finney would go after you like that. He was a wild one, I'll admit, but to go and try to kill a detective . . . he must have been out of his goddamn mind. It was self-defense, wasn't it?" he asked as if he didn't know the answer.

"What the fuck do you think, August?" Tom growled. "You see me killin' fellas for sport?" August really could get under his skin, not that it took much right now. "Goddamn Dutchman tried to knock my head out of the park. Nearly did too. I didn't shoot him, though. It was Finney did that. Gun went off when I tried to get it away."

"Sure, sure," Coffin said solicitously. "He catch you with the bat?" He pointed to the bandage around Tom's head.

"Coupla times."

Coffin gave an inward smirk. At least Tom hadn't had it all his way, and he did look poorly at that.

"Jesus, Tom, what the hell made 'em go after you?" Coffin asked as if he had no idea in the world.

"You should know, August."

Coffin did his best to look taken aback. "What do you mean? Finney wasn't happy about payin' up, but I never thought he'd do something like this." August held his hands up in innocence. He was the master of the half-truth.

Tom had to give it just a second of thought, and Coffin the benefit of the doubt, before he said, "I know he was paying Coogan." Tom tightened his grip on the Colt under the blanket.

Coffin was amazing. It was no surprise he had come so far in the department. The bastard barely blinked an eye or missed a beat. "You mean to say you didn't know? You know we discussed this, Tommy." Coffin used his best serious voice. "I thought I made it clear what the arrangement was. It's not like you to forget things."

"That's because you never bothered to tell me. And you know, I can't help but wonder why." Sarcasm dripped from Tom's words. The son of a bitch not only lied to him, now he was rearranging the truth right before his eyes.

"Tom, you've had a bad head injury," Coffin said soothingly. "Mary tells me that the doctor says you had a serious concussion. It does things to you. You'll be all right soon, and maybe some of these details will start coming back. You really just need rest, you—"

"Nothing wrong with my memory, August." Tom had to interrupt him before it started sounding plausible even to him. Coffin had the gift, sure enough. "You sent me down there alone, to collect from a fucking lunatic and his goddamn executioner. What was it, August? Want to have them teach me a little lesson, 'cause I was late with a payment or two?" Coffin didn't answer, so Tom went on. "Or maybe you figured I needed a dose of humility, just on general principles."

Coffin had slipped his hands into his pockets as Tom talked. The ivory grips of the Smith & Wesson felt smooth as an undertaker's condolence. "Thomas, you're upset—"

"You're damn right, I'm upset. It was too close to being me on a steel table in Bellevue, and that's upsetting, very goddamn upsetting, August." Tom was almost shouting now.

"Tom, listen, there's no way I ever meant for you to come to harm. We're a team, remember? You're one of my boys, and I take care of my boys, right? Hey . . . when you feel better we'll have a nice long talk and see what can be done for you. Meanwhile I'll put the whole Finney affair on the shelf. Close the case, and have my friends in the press keep it off the front pages. You'll see, this'll all blow over, and we can get on with things the way they were." August stopped for a moment before he went off on another tack. "There's plenty of money to be made. I know you like the sound of that. Get yourself a new place in a little while, farther uptown, closer to Mary. Not a bad thing. Let's not let this unfortunate incident ruin our chances."

Tom sat there thinking. Goddamn Coffin. He could give you that wide-open, innocent look, swear that up was down, and have you believing it all in the same sentence. Maybe he hadn't meant to get Tom killed, and maybe he didn't even want to see Tom hurt. But he sure as hell left out the part about Finney paying Coogan, and he sure as hell lied about it to his face. Sure . . . it would be easier to just go along like nothing happened, take the money, and work on getting free of Coffin eventually, but that was the logical thing, the safe thing. He had done that before, had been doing it all along, and the fact was it was killing him, especially after the child prostitute murders a few months ago. It was gnawing at him like a three-foot tapeworm. Maybe it wasn't smart, maybe there was a better way . . . but finally Tom said, "Fuck you, Augie."

It really didn't take a detective to see that Coffin had a pistol in his pocket. Tom had it figured for the .32 Smith & Wesson. Handy little gun, small enough for a pocket without too much of a bulge, but packing enough punch for close work. Not a real stopper, but a good compromise. Now Tom could see the twitch of the hand in Coffin's pocket. Not wanting to get into a shooting match in Mary's bedroom, Tom continued, "Listen, August, I'll pay you what I owe you. I'm not backing out on that. You have my word, but no more of your favors and errands. No more extortion, and no more rackets. I'm through with that, and I'm through with you and your corps. No, don't say anything. I'm not finished. This has been eating at me for months so let me get it out." All the while Tom watched the hand in the coat pocket. "You know I used to like the money. I used to think that as long as I was getting mine and it was coming from criminals, then it was all right. Who the hell cares if some illegal bars pay us off to keep their back doors open on Sundays? Who gives a goddamn if pimps and gamblers and gangs get squeezed? Nobody . . . and for a long time I didn't either. But I'm tired of the kind of things I've been getting into with you, the kinds of money we've been taking. It's dirty, August. It's dirtier than most money to be found on the streets, and the things we have to do—" Tom hesitated a moment, remembering. "The times we have to look away . . . they take something out of you," he said sadly. "It's getting so that I see that stuff in the mirror. You *know* what I mean. I can see it on your face. It takes a toll. I feel it like a wet overcoat dragging my shoulders down."

August, to his credit, seemed to listen. Tom knew there must be some small part of Coffin that knew the truth of what he was saying.

August, his tone pragmatic, said, "What the hell, you haven't been blaming yourself have you? This is the way things are, Tom. You can't go beating yourself about the head because you took some money from some fucking criminals. Shit, they know damn well they'll have to pay someone to stay in business, so why not pay us?"

"You're right, they're gonna pay someone. But, August, for God's sake, there's some of them that money shouldn't be able to help. There's limits, you know, or should be. That Madame LeFarge, for example. We should have thrown away the key on her. But we didn't. We took her fucking money, and we looked the other way." Tom was referring not just to what he had collected the other day but events going back months. Young girls out of her place had gone missing more than once.

"Oh, Christ, Tom, that was months ago. There wasn't anything we could have done. How are we supposed to keep things like that from happening?" Coffin said, exasperated. He threw up his hands and stalked around the room. "Shit like that happens. It just happens, that's all. You know how things are in this city. If we had shut her down, LeFarge would have been open again in a couple of weeks. Jesus, look at the streets. There's parents who'd sell their children for a few dollars, for God's sake. Go down to Rag Picker's Court, or

Bottle Alley, they'll sell you more little street Arabs than you can shake a stick at. We can't stop it, Tom," August said with finality.

"Yeah, but we shouldn't be helping it." Braddock looked Coffin in the eye but wasn't getting a straight look back. "We're supposed to do good, August. We're supposed to keep vampires like her from sucking the life out of kids." A tousle-headed Mikey Bucklin, his dirty face and shoeless feet looking far too small under the grime, dashed into his head as he said this. He knew with sudden recognition why this had weighed heavier on him lately, and he wondered why he hadn't seen it sooner.

They were quiet for a long time, fingering the pistols at their sides. Coffin paced the room like a pallbearer. In his heart he knew Tom was right, and in fact the incidents at LeFarge's had bothered him too. But he had a broader perspective than Tom, a bigger view of things. That was Braddock's weakness. He saw things on a human scale. He sometimes missed the big picture because he let the small things get in his way. Not like him. He could see the forest, and he didn't let individual trees get in his way. He had a higher perspective, a bigger plan, and if some trees got cut down . . . what was that to the forest? Coffin stopped his pacing, the ivory grips of the Smith & Wesson tempting his hand like a stiff cock. He figured he'd try this without bullets, see how far a little blackmail went. Coffin turned to Tom. The muzzle of Braddock's Colt gaped round and black, like looking down a well.

"I'm getting a little tired of watching you fiddle with that Smith & Wesson, August. You weren't thinking of shooting me, were you, Captain?" Tom asked with a flinty grin.

For once, Coffin looked flustered, but he regained his composure in typical Coffin fashion. "Put that thing away. I'm a captain, for Christ sake, I'm supposed to have a gun in my pocket. And let me remind you of who you're pointing that pistol at, Detective. I'll forget this happened if you put that down now." The muzzle still gaped, unwavering. "I'm willing to see this as just the stress of your injuries. Put the gun down now, and nothing will come of this," Coffin said, trying for a tone of command, but missing the mark. He figured that the first thing he was going to do when Tom dropped the Colt was to see how many bullets he could put into Tom's head at this range.

"Well, let's just be on the safe side, shall we?" Tom said in a reasonable tone. "Why don't you just take that .32 out of your pocket. With your left hand, if you don't mind. Two fingers. Nice and slow." The pistol came out of Coffin's pocket as Tom instructed. "Good. Now empty the cylinder and put the bullets on the bed."

"Tom, this is ridiculous. I'm losing my patience, sport. Think what the fuck you're doing."

"Oh, I am, old buddy," Tom said, mimicking Coffin's tone. "Empty the gun, August." The bullets formed a harmless little pile of brass and lead on the blanket.

"Now let me tell you how things are going to be. First, I'm going to pay you what I owe you. Second, I'm out of your little operation. We go our separate ways, and that's that. I can't make up my mind whether you wanted me to take a beating, Finney and Venkman just got carried away, or . . . you wanted me dead."

"Tommy, it was just those two crazy bastards, I swear. Jesus, Tom, I wouldn't have you killed. What kind of man do you think I am?" Coffin held up his hands in feigned exasperation.

Tom figured Coffin didn't want to hear the answer to that question. "I think you sent me down there without full knowledge of the situation, and that's not something a good captain does to one of *his boys*. Beyond that . . . I don't know. I can tell you this: If I had proof that you planned to get me killed, you'd have been dead already." Coffin knew Tom meant his words. "So that's it. Oh . . . and by the bye, nobody's going to be telling any tales out of school, and I expect the same from you. Deal?"

Coffin looked at Tom's outstretched hand. What a schoolboy he was to think he could tell August Coffin what to do. Did he really imagine that he'd keep his end of this bargain, or was there something more to it? After a moment's consideration, he figured it was Tom's naïve view of the world showing through. He must be crazy, or maybe that knock on the head really did shake his brain loose. Whichever it was, Coffin had no problem agreeing to a deal he wouldn't keep.

"All right, Tommy, not a word on any of it, and no other repercussions. You pay me what you owe me, and we part ways. No hard feelings, sport, it just didn't work out." Coffin started to plan immediately, thinking of how he could control the situation. They shook on the deal. Tom felt like washing his hand.

The weather had turned chilly again, and a gusty wind huffed and puffed across the harbor. Whitecaps danced on the aqua-green waves. Sailboats leapt and dashed like porpoises on the crests. It was the kind of day when words were snatched away on the wind and clouds raced each other across the watery blue sky. Sergeant Patrick Sullivan watched a coastal steamer pass below him, its funnel belching black. The smoke swept back and was gone in an instant. The knife-edge bow cut the whitecaps with exuberant fountains of spray.

Sullivan had learned to like these days in the cables. It hadn't always been so. It had taken him hours to get used to the wind the first day he had been up in a real guster. Up on the cables, higher than the tallest ship, looking down on the tallest buildings of a tall city, he had come to know winds as he never had before. In '76 the captain had assigned him to work the cables, and there he had been ever since.

He sat on the seat he had lashed to the suspender cable, his feet dangling over two hundred feet above the chop of the river. It wasn't much of a seat really, just a board, maybe ten inches wide and about eighteen inches long. It had ropes through either end that came together above his head, and he had secured their ends to the cable. Safety ropes were optional, and most of the workers spurned them as unmanly. Sullivan's little seat twisted in the wind, and he had to hold the suspender in the crook of his arm to keep from swinging too wildly. He had wrapped his left leg around the cable too, so in spite of the wind, he was pretty secure. The men around him, mostly former sailors, worked much the same way. "One hand for yourself and one hand for the ship" was the saying. Most of them seemed little bothered by the wind. To him it was a one-arm, one-leg kind of day. They were doing some of the last lashing of the vertical suspenders to the diagonal stays. Each of the stays—cables that formed the hypotenuse of a right triangle, between the towers and the roadway—radiated down from central points on each tower at nearly the same point where the main cables crossed. At every point where a stay intersected a suspender, they were lashed. Each "rigger," as the men were called, had a bucket of marlin, or tarred line, used for the tying. With each of these intersections of stays and suspenders joined, the weight of the bridge would be equalized over the weblike, crossing cables. The only way to do those lashings, was to literally do a highwire act above the river, with riggers climbing, shinnying, and swinging from the cables like so many monkeys. Why none of them had fallen, Sullivan couldn't guess. He had come close a few times. After a good scare it had taken all the courage he could muster to go up again, his fear foul and metallic, like a penny on his tongue. He reckoned that going up was about the bravest thing he'd ever done. When it was just him looking up at the cables in the morning, wondering if this was the day he'd take his dive to the river, it had a lot of scare to it.

Sullivan had been in the crowd on the Brooklyn docks when the first cable had been strung across the river. They called it a rope actually but it was braided wire, just like the cables he worked on now but not as thick. He had wondered how they were going to string wires above the river. There were maybe five or six thousand folks on either shore wondering the same thing. Though the process wasn't easy, it was basically simple. The idea was to string a continuous wire rope, about three-quarters of an inch in diameter, from the Brooklyn anchorage to the Manhattan anchorage and back. Once it was spliced together, it would form what was really just a big clothesline across the river. All that would be needed was to attach the wires that were to form the main cables to that "traveler" and pull them across like laundry. A thirty-horsepower steam engine had been set up in Brooklyn to do the hauling. Using a system of cogs and drums, the cable could be reversed without stopping the engine. The drums were huge, twelve-foot-diameter oak affairs, set atop each anchorage, and the traveler ran around them. Of course Patrick hadn't known any of this as he watched with the others from the Brooklyn docks. In fact, he had no idea at all how the job would be done.

It had taken hours to get that first cable across. Two huge spools of wire had been positioned on the river side of the Brooklyn tower. The cables, one from each spool, were towed up and over the tower, then spliced and wound around the system of drums and, finally, the big oak drive wheel. Once all was set, they loaded one spool onto a barge for its trip across the river. When a break in the river traffic had come, the barge, towed by two tugs, started chugging across. The odd thing was, as the cable wound out, it disappeared under the gunmetal gray waters of the river. Sullivan somehow hadn't expected that.

It was pretty close, that day on the docks, a typical August day in New York, but the heat didn't seem to wilt the spirits of the crowds watching the spectacle. The cable was hauled over the Manhattan tower and all the way back to the anchorage, where it was wound on another big drum and secured. It was still slack, though. Most of it sat in the mud of the river bottom. Patrick recalled vividly when they started up the engine and began hauling the cable taut. Slow at first, then faster and faster, the cable emerged from the waves and the two ends seemed to race each other toward the middle of the river. At about the same speed, the notion formed in his head of the cable as a symbol of the ties between the North and South, submerged beneath the waves of war. Covered with the muck of the river bottom, soiled, dripping, the ties that bound the country emerged . . . unbreakable, never really broken.

As the cable sprang free from the river, a shower of water fell from it, glistening for a moment in the summer sun, like a waterfall across the waves. The cheers of the crowds and the bells and whistles of the steamers in the river were like a dirge for him. He knew then, beyond all words and expression, the ultimate futility of what he was about to do. That was August 14, 1876— nearly seven years ago, yet here he was, swinging in the cables. It was his duty.

Patrick had sat on a bulkhead, looking at the bridge, for a long time, on that day, seven years before. The sun had been an orange blaze west of the city before he stirred. It had taken him a long time to come to terms with what he had sworn to do. He wasn't happy about it then and still wasn't. But he remembered the reasons he was here in the first place. Those reasons were like cable too. They had sworn together, with God as their witness. Their oaths never wavered. Through all these years they had supported each other. But things had been clearer during the war. The road before them had been straight and true. Now it was just their oaths that held them. Sometimes he thought, in his most honest moments, that they were so scarred by the war that they could do nothing else. Like the captain, their shared experience had become a crutch, a shield from the bitterness of life after defeat. He didn't like to think that way.

It was an irony not lost on Sullivan that a bridge had become a symbol for them. It spoke of divides unbridged, of the end of the society they knew. It was the triumph of the industrial age, an age that placed products above people and money above all else. The bridge stood in the North, a tribute to industrial might and the self-righteous Yankee race. It stood for their subjugation, the death of a social order they held dear. It spoke to them of factories, railroads, commerce, and empire building. It was the dominance of machine over man, factory over farm, industry over society, and a turning away from the gentle seasons of the earth. The idea that such a system had prevailed was repulsive. The bridge, as a symbol of that system, was no less repulsive. So, for Sullivan and the rest, it wasn't a bridge they worked to destroy, it was a symbol.

Sullivan swayed in the cables as a gust caught him daydreaming. He tied a length of marlin about the junction of two cables, snugging it down after each turn. They'd be back up here soon, replacing these temporary knots with steel U-bolts, but that was after they "let down" the bridge. There was no way to be certain of the precise length each cable needed to be to account for the loads, grade of roadway, and elasticity of the wire. Roebling had designed a system to adjust each one of the cable suspenders individually, by attaching the end of each suspender to a cast-iron yolk that held two long bolts. The bolts were attached to the roadway beams. By turning the bolts the roadway grade and cable tension could be adjusted. That probably would be the last work he'd have as a rigger.

Another gust grabbed at his bowler, nearly snatching it off his head. If he hadn't wrapped his scarf over it and under his chin, it'd be floating down the river by now. Sullivan remembered how Farrington had doffed his hat and waved it to the crowd, back in '76. That was a man who had balls of solid brass. To take the ride Farrington had, it was a positive requirement. Once the traveler had been strung, it had been planned, as a public relations gesture, to have someone cross on it. Master Mechanic Farrington was an obvious choice, but at nearly sixty, everyone would have understood if he had declined the honor. But that wasn't Farrington. On August 25 a boatswain's chair had been attached to the traveler and preparations made for the historic journey. The wire looked mighty thin, Sullivan recalled. It didn't seem strong enough to hold much more than a flock of pigeons. Looking out over the river, it disappeared in the distance. With nothing below but air and water, it took an extra helping of courage to consider trusting your life to it. Farrington knew the wire could support many times his weight, but this was still the first go at a crossing, and it was his ass on the line.

Patrick had watched, craning with the others, as Farrington swung out from the Brooklyn anchorage and started to slowly make the ascent to the top of the tower. The crowds cheered as the master mechanic rode his little seat, much like the seat Sullivan used now. If he had been afraid, it didn't show. In fact, he actually had the nerve to loose his safety ropes and stand up on the swinging board, like some sort of highwire act. It was the hat waving that Sullivan remembered. The crowds cheered themselves hoarse. Farrington became an instant celebrity.

Sullivan hadn't really appreciated just how brave an act it was until he got his job in the cables about two weeks later. At first, just being up on the anchorage made him nervous, and he didn't like to go too near the edge. The anchorage was taller than any of the buildings in Brooklyn. Looking down chimneys was something that took a little getting used to. He had seen Farrington up close that first day, and he stopped his work to look at him. He remembered thinking that maybe there was something about the man that marked him for his courage, the set of his jaw or the tone of his voice. He couldn't be sure he saw any evidence of it, but he had gone over to the master mechanic and shook his hand, saying "Hell of a ride you took, sir. My hat's off to you."

Farrington had smiled with almost an aw-shucks kind of shrug. "Made me kind of famous in a little way. Never thought to see my picture in *Harper's*. Wasn't that grand a thing," he said modestly.

"Not to my way of thinking. Anyway, just wanted to say I shook with you. You're a man's got sand, and I respect that. How'd it look from up there, anyhow?"

"Well, if you're working cable, you'll see soon enough, ah . . . ?"

Patrick had introduced himself shyly.

"Well, you'll see, Sullivan. It's a sight. From Coney Island to Jersey, it's all at your feet from the top. Nothing like it on the continent," Farrington had said with great satisfaction. As Patrick Sullivan sat in his boson's chair high above the city, he had to admit it was a sight indeed. A gull lighted on the main cable, just a few feet away, its feathers ruffled with the wind. It turned a glassy, black eye at him, head canted to one side.

"Didn't think to see me up here, did ya?" he asked the bird. The bird said nothing, just shifted from one foot to the other, all the while regarding him with a shining pitiless eye. "If I was you, I'd stay clear of here in a couple of months. Just one bird to another, ya understand. Might not be healthy." Patrick looked down to his work for a moment. When he looked back the gull was gone.

Broadway was crowded with carriages. Their fine teams and fancy equipage dueled for the attention of the shoppers on the Ladies Mile. The day, though a little blustery, had turned brilliant, with a sun that Tom could feel on his face and the backs of his hands. It was Mary's idea to get him out for a stroll. Though he didn't care for shopping as recreation, he enjoyed the crowds, carriages, and life of this part of Broadway. Gentlemen in top hats, starched collars, and cravats with gold and diamond pins escorted ladies in full bloom. Tight-cinched waists and wide-brimmed hats in white, peach, rose, and lavender reminded Tom of a movable garden, its flowers having slipped their roots to parade down the avenue. The sidewalks, especially on the slightly more fashionable west side of the street, were alive with strollers. They stopped to look in the windows of Lord & Taylor, Arnold Constable, J & C Johnston, and at the southern end of the Ladies Mile, A. T. Stewarts on Tenth Street. From there to Twenty-third Street was gathered the very finest collection of retail establishments in the city. With Union Square anchoring one end, Madison Square park and the incomparable Fifth Avenue Hotel the other, this was the most pleasant and fashionable place in the city to shop, stroll, and be seen.

Tom, still a bit unsteady, enjoyed the show, but mostly he enjoyed being with Mary. Their relationship had been an almost unnatural nocturnal affair. Between Tom's unpredictable hours and Mary's virtual round-the-clock business, they usually only found time for each other in the evenings. They had gone out, of course, to the theater and dinner. Being out in the day, with the sun and the wind and beautiful people, was a thing almost unknown to them. Tom felt as if they were somehow coming out of seclusion. Having Mary on his arm, in public, on the most fashionable street in the city, taking the air like any other couple was an unexpected joy. Though his head still had a small bandage and he favored his left side, he was surprised at how good he felt. Maybe it was just being with Mary.

He noticed how people looked at her. The women, at least those who didn't know who she was, could sometimes be caught casting an appraising eye. Tom could see the curiosity. She was beautiful. She dressed well, she obviously had money. Who might she be? Others who seemed to know exactly who she was, did their best to look right through her. Some even made a small show of turning at strategic moments or sniffing as they passed. Tom figured their husbands were clients. He wrote them off for hypocrites, scorning the woman who provides what their husbands can't get at home. Tom didn't give it much thought, he just held Mary's arm a little tighter and smiled to the world.

They were almost down to Union Square when Tom started to feel a little tired and more than a little dizzy.

"I think maybe it's time to turn back home," he said with a tinge of uncertainty in his voice, as if maybe they'd come too far already. It scared him some that he was still wobbly. His old wound throbbed, setting his temple to aching dully.

"You all right? Do you need to sit for a minute?" Mary asked with a small frown.

"I'll be fine. Let's just stop, take in a store window. The head's a bit wobbly is all." As it turned out, they had stopped in front of a children's store. The window was full of clothes on one side, toys on the other. There was an army of tiny lead soldiers, parading off to bloodless nursery battles, their uniforms shiny with new paint, their rifles not yet bent by careless little hands. Tom thought he wouldn't mind having a set of those himself, they were that beautiful. He thought for a moment of all the parading he had done during the war. Every time some general or congressman took a notion of visiting the corps, they all trotted out for a review. The bands would play, the battle flags would wave, thousands of feet would tramp together, pounding the earth with measured tread, and afterward the bigwigs would retire to brandy and cigars, feeling very pleased indeed. Tom didn't have many fond memories of parading, except at the very beginning and the very end of the war. Those parades were different; like bookends, they bracketed the experience for him, brash exuberance on one end, tearful accomplishment at the other. Real marching was like neither.

He focused again on the store window. There was a hobbyhorse, with a real horsehair mane and tail, there were cast-iron wagons, fire engines, banks, and carriages with prancing teams. There were even a few clockwork toys from Germany. Tom forgot his woozy head and marveled at the display. The child in him stole across his face, lighting his eyes and painting a grin under his broad mustache.

"Never had anything this fine when I was a kid," Tom said wistfully. "Hell, I thought I was lucky to have an India-rubber ball."

"I had a doll for a while," Mary said. "She had real glass eyes, real hair too. It was red. She used to sleep with me every night." The memory softened her words. "Even after my father started . . . well . . . she always slept with me.

Her name was Amanda. Wish I still had her." Tom saw his old enemy flit across Mary's face: He tried to think of something to say.

A family appeared behind them, reflected in the glass of the window. They were a beautiful family, a perfect family, with a boy of maybe eight or ten and a girl of perhaps six. The parents beamed patiently as the children charged the window, pointing and laughing. Small noses pressed the glass. They giggled about some whispered secret and debated on which toy they each would have if they could have only one. Tom watched them from the corner of his eye. A smile crept across his face. He thought of dirty-faced Mike Bucklin.

"You know, we've never talked about children, Mary. Do you like children?" Tom asked brightly. The question seemed to catch her off guard for a moment. She had been staring into the glass at the parents behind them. Now she looked at Tom as if just hearing what he'd asked. Small wrinkles creased her forehead and were around her eyes. It was a strange look, one Tom hadn't seen before.

"Haven't given it much thought," she said too quickly. "I don't have the luxury. I mean, with the house and all, I haven't . . ." She paused for a moment. "There's that . . . and then . . . well, then there's what I am."

"What do you mean, 'what I am'?" Tom asked, knowing what she meant but challenging her notions.

"You know very well. My . . . profession," Mary said, as if any fool would know, and he was a fool for asking.

"What's that got to do with liking children? I mean, you either like them or you don't," Tom said, not giving it up, part out of stubbornness, part from the resentment of her tone. He never did care for anyone using that tone with him, not even Mary.

"Tommy, for a smart fella, sometimes you can be so thick," she said, shaking her head at him, exasperation clear in her tone. "You sure that knock on the head didn't shake something loose?"

"Pretty sure. Still don't see what your . . . job has to do with liking kids or not," Tom said, not realizing how deep this was cutting.

"Tommy, I'm a whore and a madame," Mary said, too loudly. "I sell sex for money. That's why I can't even think about children. It's not that I . . . well I'm just *not* . . ."

Tom looked at her, surprised at the sudden play of emotion, swirling and eddying about her eyes and mouth.

"Jesus, Tommy, I *want* to but I *can't*," she said, her words part exasperation, part plea. It was a hopeless, sorrowful tone that sank into him, fanning out like a shot of cheap whiskey, except it wasn't warm, not warm at all. The family, he noticed, was suddenly gone.

Tom looked at the glass, seeing nothing, not even their reflections. He knew this was a turning point, a fork in the road. But these sorts of things never came when he was ready. He wanted to shout at whatever fates had conspired to bring them to this. It wasn't time. His head hurt. The sidewalk moved when he walked. What was he supposed to do? He needed time but there was none. He had to do something, and he knew that what he did right now, right this instant, would ripple through his life in sunlight or darkness.

"Mary," Tom said, reaching for her hand. He turned to face her. The crowds on the sidewalks, the clatter of the carriages on Broadway, the sunny, blustery world around them, faded, growing quiet as if the world listened.

"Mary." He saw the dampness on her cheek, the sadness around her eyes, his old enemy. He reckoned then that he wouldn't mind whipping that old ghost through all the years that would be.

"Mary?" He pulled her to him, and for an awful instant he thought she would resist. But she came to his arms on Broadway, on a sunny guster of a day, this April of '83. People stared. It wasn't proper to embrace so close, nor so long in public, not even in the park at Madison Square.

"Mary," he whispered in her hair. "I'd make a life with you, for the rest of my days, if I thought you'd have me." She tensed and pulled back from him. He was afraid to let her go, afraid of her eyes. But when he looked in them, he was afraid no longer.

"You *mean* that, don't you?" she said with almost a touch of wonder in her voice. "Don't say it if you don't mean it, Tom. You don't have to—" She stopped herself, shaking her head. "But you know that," she said almost to herself. Mary looked hard at his face—the little crinkles around the eyes, the mustache, the scar at the temple, the small shock of white hair there. It was a strong face, a good face, a face she loved and trusted.

"I have my dreams, Tommy," she said, looking into his eyes. "I've locked them away. Doing what I do, I can't afford dreams of a normal life. Family and children; they've been just dreams to me. I can't let myself be dreaming like that but once." There was a powerful, desperate seriousness in her words. Tom knew the risk she was willing to take with him.

"If I take those dreams out again, it'll kill me if—" She paused for a long moment, looking off as if seeing something far off. "It would just kill me," she finished.

Tom believed it was so. "I just want to make you happy, is all. We'll take it slow but I'm thinking we're dreaming the same dream, you and I." He smiled a tentative, hopeful smile that said as much as his words. Mary hugged him with a ferocity that almost startled him. He knew he had taken the right turn.

Funny how the choice unmade is so uncertain but, once done, looks like no choice at all. Mary's hand was in his as they walked back up Broadway. The sun was warmer now. The wind had died to a whisper. They walked in silence down the road they had chosen.

Chapter Eleven

But when it comes to planning, one mind can in a few hours think out enough work to keep a thousand men employed for years.

—WASHINGTON ROEBLING

Captain Peter Coogan, commander of the Fourth Precinct, sat with the rest of the "corps" in Coffin's office watching as he stalked back and forth like a caged animal. Coogan and Coffin had been near-equal partners in the corps for three years. Coffin most always took the lead in things, though. August carried a cigar in his right hand that he was using to stab the air as he made a point. In between, he'd suck on it, so it glowed like a little furnace.

"I'm going to ruin that son of a bitch, then I'll see if he don't whistle a different tune."

"What're you going to do, August?" Coogan asked, almost amused by the show Coffin was putting on.

"Well, we've got a pretty good idea where Tom is getting his money, right? We know the bars, the whorehouses, the gambling dens as well as he does. It don't take an Edison to figure who's paying him off, does it?" Coffin almost shouted.

Coogan put his feet up, enjoying Coffin's tirade. He locked his fingers over his middle, twirling his thumbs in silent satisfaction. He'd warned Coffin against taking action against Braddock, and he was enjoying his little gloat.

"One by one we shut them down. It's got to look right: standard procedure, all that bullshit. Make it look official. Cracking down on the criminal element following the Venkman and Finney thing," Coffin said, waving his cigar. "That's the story. The fact that it's actually true is merely convenient. Hell, we arrest enough of them, we can hurt Braddock bad. Maybe then he'll knuckle under. What do you say, team?" he asked, challenging the others of the "corps" grouped around the room.

Coogan spoke first. "Never thought Braddock was a solid member of the corps, but he's a solid man. A good cop too. Can't say I want to make an enemy of him." A couple of the others seemed to nod in agreement.

"Not scared of him, are you, Pat?" Coffin asked sarcastically.

"Not scared," he said evenly, choosing to ignore the slur, "just not *stupid*. Ain't saying I'm not in, mind. Just saying let's be careful."

"And the rest of you?" Coffin peered around the office, his wide-open stare a challenge to each. "Good. We do this right, and he'll get the message in double-time. He's no fool. He'll see which side his bread is buttered on." There followed a general discussion of who they'd hit first. Once that was decided, Coffin dismissed the men. There were an even dozen. Coogan stayed behind.

"Why want him back in so bad, August? We can do fine without him."

"Well, I tell you, Pat, sometimes it's a puzzle to me too," Coffin said. "He's a burr under my saddle, but he's solid. He can be counted on to do what he says. That's more than I can say about some of the rest." Coffin knew that for an understatement. "And it's a whole lot better having him on the inside. We've got more control that way. Out of the corps, we can't be sure who the hell he's talking to." Tom knew a great deal about Coffin's extracurricular activities, enough to put him away forever. "Third thing, it's dangerous to kill the man, though I've been tempted. Don't know what went wrong with Venkman and Finney, but you saw what those two looked like. For God's sake, Finney's head looked like it got run over by a freight wagon, and his arm . . . how Braddock did that, I don't know." Coffin didn't bother to mention how Tom had disarmed him earlier, but it echoed in the back of his head, like a schoolyard taunt.

"Well, August, it might surprise you to know that I agree with you. Surprised you took the chance of riling him in the first place."

"Hmph. Plan went a bit overboard." He shrugged. "Figured Tom could be taught a little humility. Was getting on his high horse lately, complaining about who we're taking protection from and the like. Figured I'd put the screws to Finney for the beating. I'd have Tom in my debt and a bigger percentage from Finney in the bargain. It would have been pretty."

Coogan chuckled. "August, only *you* would call that deal pretty."

"Would have been," Coffin said defensively, "except those boys got carried away. I didn't want him dead, just 'rearranged' a little. That Dutchman didn't have the intelligence of a stump. Should have made allowances for that, but what the hell; what's done is done." Coffin never was one to dwell on his failures. He was always ready to get on to the next plan. It was one of his real strengths.

"Humph. But now we gotta be puttin' the squeeze on Tommy's payoff. Don't want to be doing that for long. Some of that money trickles into our pockets too, ya know," Coogan said, ever the more practical of the pair.

"Don't have to tell me. This won't take a lot of doing." Coffin sat back in his swivel chair. The spring in it gave out a long screech that Coogan could feel in the fillings of his teeth. "Gotta have somebody oil this goddamn chair," he said absently. "Hell, maybe I'll just put in a requisition for a new one." He put his feet up on the desk and smiled. He was more than willing to sacrifice a few dollars in the short run for a greater profit in the long. August twirled a pencil in his fingers like a bandleader's baton as he struck a reflective pose. He flipped it by one end, and it spun in the air at least three times before he caught it without seeming to try. Coogan sipped his coffee and watched the little show: the feet up, the pencil spinning, the pensive look. He knew something was coming.

"Nope, Tom won't take long getting the message. Of course, I have a contingency plan in case he proves hard of hearing. Tommy does have his weak spots, after all." Coffin smiled wickedly.

Captain Thaddeus Sangree sat at his desk, writing a note to his contacts in Richmond. The meeting the night before had been productive. Sullivan had suggested an idea that showed great promise. He said it had occurred to him while he was up in the cables, tying off the suspenders and stays. Basically it was just a refinement of their original plan, but it could turn out to be a critical piece in the puzzle of demolition. The simplicity and economy of the idea coupled with its enormous potential had great appeal. In truth, they wouldn't need to actually sever all the cable and roadway beam connections. All that was necessary was to sever some, and weaken the others enough so that the weight of the bridge would do the rest. Based on the tests they had already conducted, Thaddeus was sure this was the plan that would bring down the bridge.

Early on, when the towers were still under construction, Emmons had come up with the idea of planting dynamite in the hollow base of each tower. An explosion within the enclosed tower would be devastating and, with enough explosive, could have literally brought down the bridge like a house of cards. As attractive as the notion was, eventually they had rejected it. To do so before the bridge was finished wasted the symbolism of the act. It would also have meant that any dynamite planted in the hollow towers would have to sit there for years, until the bridge was finished. There was no way they could be certain that dampness and age wouldn't result in a big fizzle.

The plan they had agreed upon had its pluses and minuses too. No plan was perfect. But it had a certain economy and simplicity to it that seemed to bode well for its success. The captain chuckled when he thought of Roebling's reaction.

"I wouldn't be you for all the gold in California," he said to the window. Though Thaddeus couldn't actually see Roebling's big brownstone from his office, he knew the direction in which it lay. He often found himself talking to Roebling. He would face out his window, imagining him there in Brooklyn, a broken cripple, barely able to feed himself or move about the house. It amused the captain to think of him so. "I wish I could be there to see your face: the horror, the disbelief. It will be too much for the mind to grasp, too enormous, too awful. Will you cry out? I wonder. Will the shock alone kill? You *are* frail. Any shock might be fatal. Been known to happen and to healthier men than you." He chuckled at the thought of Roebling's death—the despair and defeat. "Will you bring yourself to watch? Will you watch the bodies as they splash, or will your eyes see only the bridge? Guess I'll never know," Thaddeus mused. He could imagine, though, and he gloated in his conjured images.

The captain tried to go back to his writing, but his pen stayed poised an inch above the paper. He tried to think of what he had to say, but it wouldn't come. There was just one thing that he could think of. It kept repeating in his head, and before he thought of what he was doing his hand had written it out. "I live for the day" was scrawled across the page.

"Damn!" the captain cursed, crumpling the paper and starting over.

Tom had gotten out of bed late. It was ten-thirty by the time he'd had a snuggle with Mary, got himself dressed and ready to head out. Mary's cook, known simply as "Cookie," had fixed him some eggs and bacon, which he wolfed down. He was feeling guilty. Despite the fact that he had plenty of good reasons for lying in bed, like a concussion, stitches, and a still-swollen hand, he felt the need to get moving on the Bucklin case. It gnawed at the back of his mind constantly, particularly now that his head was spinning a bit less. He remembered old man Bucklin's words, and as he left Mary's place, he jangled the little key in his pocket. He'd find out what the hell was going on with the bridge and who had killed Terrence for that matter too, but there was one place he needed to stop first.

He hadn't been home in four days, and he worried about Grant and Lee. Even though Sam had said he'd look after them, he knew how they could get when he left them alone for too long. It would be guerilla warfare with the two of them waging a relentless campaign of furniture scratching, carpet soiling, and general mischief. He was outnumbered and outflanked. He'd stop by just for a minute, just to see that they were okay, he told himself, then it would be back to business.

He hailed a cab and headed downtown. It was going to be a longish ride; the midmorning traffic was heavy. In some places they moved at not much better than a walking pace. Tom sat back and tried to enjoy the ride. Considering what his last cab ride had been like, that wasn't too difficult. He remembered suddenly that it was already April 3 and he hadn't made his collections. Cursing to himself, he figured that he had at least a dozen stops to make. It wouldn't do to have the criminal element thinking he was getting lax. Those types would start pushing back real quick if they saw a weakness. He made a mental list of the three or four most difficult of his clientele, figuring to visit those first. He didn't want to waste too much time even on this, not with the Bucklin business still hanging above his head. If he kept the hard cases in line, the word would get out that he wasn't getting slack. Being slack with that crowd was like blood in the water to sharks; he'd get eaten alive.

Tom tried to figure the most efficient route to make his collections. He wanted to end up on the Lower East Side, because he planned on paying a visit to the Bucklins, to ask them a few more questions. Tom jingled the key again, rolling it about along with his change. Would the key yield any secrets? There had to be something, some other bit of information they had but perhaps weren't even aware of. What was going on with the bridge he couldn't figure, but as Martin had said, there had been plenty of strange things happening during the construction, from payoffs, to fire, to fraud and death. It could be anything.

The cab pulled to a creaking, rattling stop on the cobbles in front of Colonnade Row. Tom got out, paid the driver, and went in. In the hall he passed Mrs. Aurelio's door. He could hear his downstairs neighbor singing Italian opera to the accompaniment of her gramophone. He was no judge of opera, but he figured the old lady was about as bad as he'd heard and louder than most. She was nearly deaf, and when she took a notion to start singing, the whole building knew it. Of course, in Italian, he couldn't really tell how badly she was butchering what she sang. Her late husband had been a butcher, and it seemed that she, in her own way, carried on the tradition.

Tom went up the wide staircase to the second floor, propelled by Mrs. Aurelio's operatics. He was so distracted by the music and her singing that he almost didn't notice that his front door was unlatched. The open door was like an alarm bell clanging in his head. He drew back the key like a burned finger from a hot stove. The key went back in his pocket. The Colt came out of his holster. Tom noticed his palm was already wet. He stood aside, afraid he might be shot through the door. With his left hand he reached slowly for the knob. But, as he touched it, he pulled back a second time.

"Son of a bitch, now what am I gonna do?" he grumbled under his breath. He remembered the squeaky hinge. What once seemed like a minor annoyance, or a sort of homey welcome, now took on the aspect of a death knell.

Tom stood outside the door for what seemed like a long time, though it was barely a minute. He could already hear that damn hinge like a siren for anyone waiting inside. He considered just waiting in the hall, but that wasn't something he had the temperament to do. It could be that Sam had just forgotten to close the door all the way, or maybe Mrs. Aurelio, when she let the iceman in. Tom knew he'd be healthier not to assume those sorts of causes. "Well, Tommy boy, you're a cop, you've got a gun, you can't stand out here forever," he whispered to himself. Tom crouched low, Colt in his right hand, left on the doorknob. His heart was pounding in his chest, galloping at full tilt. As gently as he knew how, he pushed the door in. It swung open, silent as a snake. Nothing. On careful cat's-paws Tom crept into his front hall, Colt held in both hands close in front of him. He had once seen a cop have his gun knocked from a one-handed grip. It had almost cost that man his life. Tom had learned from the mistake. He heard a voice in the front room.

Shit! There must be two of them, he thought. His best guess was a couple of Coffin's goons, come to pay him a little visit. But Tom didn't care who it was. If they were in his place, they were where they shouldn't be, and that was going to cost them. Two did present a problem, though.

Grant must have heard him come in despite his pretensions at catlike stealth. The big cat came out of the door to the kitchen, and when he saw who it was, sneaking in his front door, he trotted over. With uncharacteristic abandon, Grant purred and rubbed himself against Tom's legs, twining around his feet in delight. Beyond all caution and reason, Tom found himself reaching down to rub his head in a silent greeting. Another snatch of conversation from the front parlor brought him back to the job at hand, but he still couldn't make it out over the bad opera from downstairs. He crept down the short hall, almost to the kitchen door. From there he could see a corner of the front room. He waited, crouched low, straining to detect any sound or movement. Movement caught his eye, and he realized there was a huge shadow on one wall, outlined by the light from his front windows. As he watched, a shadow arm rose with something in its hand, lifting it up over its head. It looked like a club, or a hammer. Images of Terrence Bucklin's broken head danced through Tom's brain.

He slipped through the kitchen to his right, then around through his bedroom on the other side. Every step he took an agony of tension. At any instant he expected a desperate, brief struggle: life or death on the kitchen floor. At last he was in position, his back against the wall beside the door to the parlor. Grant had followed, indignant at the lack of a proper greeting. Tom's heart was still racing. Sweat ran down his back in icy tentacles. He tried to calm his nerves, taking big gulps of air. He figured he'd go for the shadow-man first. The one he was talking to was probably in the red chair. That would be the second target.

With a final draft of air, Tom whirled into the open doorway, the Colt held out like a talisman.

"Police! Drop it!" he shouted. The form before him was backlit by the glow from the windows behind. Tom couldn't see precisely who it was, but there was something familiar about him. "Drop it, I said!" A tremendous, explosive bang shook the room. Tom could feel it through the floor. Like a lightning bolt, a sheet of flame erupted from the barrel of the Colt. The explosion in the room had Tom's ears ringing instantly. Lee screeched, jumping straight up from the red chair. She streaked through the parlor, headed for the kitchen, her back and tail stiff as a bottle brush.

The shadow-man still stood, then he gave a strangled shout. "Jesus, don't shoot me! Sam just sent me to feed your cats."

"Jaffey! Christ . . . if I hadn't recognized you!" Tom gasped. "What the hell was that in your hand?"

"Dumbbells. I was trying them out," Jaffey said with a nervous laugh.

"It's a good thing I pulled my shot," Tom said.

"It's my fault. I should have . . . But you were so fast. When you told me to drop it, I—I did," Eli said quickly.

"Shit!" Tom said, taking a deep breath. "I thought you were laying for me. Saw the shadow of the dumbbell . . . thought . . ."

"Oh, yeah," Jaffey said, nodding.

Tom was looking around the room with a frown. "Who were you talking to. The cat?"

"We're pals," Jaffey said sheepishly.

Tom gave a strangled chuckle. He felt light-headed, giddy. A door slammed down below, followed by feet pounding up the stairs.

"Whata-you do uppa-there? You knock-a my ceiling all over my flaw. Whata-you do? Wait-a till Mr. Tommy come-a home."

"Don't go anywhere," Tom said. "Have a seat. You look like you might fall down anyway." Jaffey was feeling faint. It wasn't every day he got shot at. He didn't much care for the experience. He plopped himself into the big red chair that Lee had so recently vacated as Tom went to talk to Mrs. Aurelio. He heard them out in the hall—her yelling about her ceiling, Tom shouting to her that everything was all right and that he'd see to having her ceiling fixed. Conversations with her were always loud, he had learned. She couldn't hear much otherwise. But this one was rattling the windows. Jaffey spent most of the time staring at the bullet hole in the wall near where he had been standing. His hands started to shake on the arms of the chair. After another minute of loud conversation the front door closed.

From the hallway, Tom called, "Care for a beer, Jaffey? Don't know about you, but I could use one."

Jaffey didn't give the regulations a second thought this time. "Sure."

"Stout okay? It's all I've got. I'm not sure it's cold, though."

"Stout's fine. There was fresh ice yesterday. It's cold," Jaffey called back.

Tom came back a moment later, handing Jaffey a bottle. He looked at the hole in the wall and the litter of plaster dust on the floor. "Looks like I've got a little weekend project, don't it?" He levered the porcelain top off the bottle and held it out to Jaffey. "Here's to not blowing your head off." A grim chuckle escaped them both.

"I *will* drink to that, Detective," Jaffey said, noticing that Tom's hand had a bit of a tremor to it too. He began to feel better as the smooth, bitter stout slid down his throat.

They sat there in Tom's parlor for quite a while. In fact, it was a two-stout conversation. After a bit, Jaffey asked, "Remember when you knocked me out in the back of Paddy's place? I asked you how you did it, but you said that was another story? Care to tell me now?"

Tom grinned, remembering how he'd come to know about the ancient art of kung fu, and the beating he'd taken to learn the lesson.

"Why not? A few years ago I was a roundsman in the Irish neighborhood around Chatham Square. Back then the Chinese were settling on Mott, Doyers, and Pell, and there probably weren't more than oh, say, a thousand or so. Very tight-knit group too, mostly laborers from the Union Pacific and such. Called themselves the Tung people. Ninety-nine percent men. Very few women came over. Well, one day I broke up a fight on Doyers. This one fella was using some very fancy moves on this other Chinaman and generally giving him a good thrashing. When I stepped in . . . he starts in on me," Tom said, slapping a hand to his chest. "Let me tell you, this little bastard was tough! Almost had me more than once. Quick as a cat, and comin' at me from every angle. Hands, fists, feet, everything. Gave me a good beatin' and I'm not ashamed to say it." Tom paused to take a sip of his Clausen's. "Drew a crowd too. I think some of the Chinese liked to see a white-devil get his ass kicked.

Finally got lucky, laid him out with a left to the gut and a right to the jaw." He swung his fists at the air. "The thing of it was, I found out later this fella was the scariest man in Chinatown. He did collection work for the tong. Got a lot of respect after that but I was curious . . . like you, about what kind of fighting he was doing. I figured if he could give me hell at his size—he was maybe five-six, one-twenty—then this was something worth knowing. To make a long story short, I joined up with a group of Chinese who were teaching and studying this stuff. They call it kung fu." Tom remembered the first time he heard the words. "It's not just a style of self-defense, it's a whole philosophy. Not really Chinese originally. I think it was started in India. Anyway, the more advanced you get, the more mental it becomes. Master Kwan, the instructor, says it's about channeling energy along the path of least resistance. When you do it right, that's what it feels like, sort of a flowing feeling, smooth but powerful." Tom seemed to gaze inward. "At first it's all hard work, lots of stretching and exercises, learning new punches, blocks, kicks, and forms. But after a while, when all the elements start to come together, you stop thinking about what to do next and start to feel the flow. That's when you'll begin to be a dangerous person," Tom said, looking at Eli over his bottle of stout. "I was the only white man in the society, and the only cop that ever took an interest. Took a ton of grief about it once they found out at the precinct." Tom shook his head. "When my captain found out, he told me to drop it. Said we shouldn't fraternize with the coolies. I went on the sly anyway. My captain wasn't a bad guy really, but he had the usual dislike for the race."

"I can imagine. Not a lot of love for the Chinese around the department, though I'm not sure exactly why," Jaffey said with a shrug.

"True, but I learned a lot from them. Still got some good friends down there. I stop in for a workout every so often, just to keep the skills up."

"You think you could take me along next time you go?" Jaffey asked almost like an anxious boy.

Tom seemed to consider this, and sipped his beer before answering. "We'll see. I have to ask. They don't let just anybody in. You have to know somebody, get the blessing of the teacher, or one of the head men from the tong. We'll see." Braddock was impressed with Jaffey for asking.

"Thanks. I'd appreciate it. I'd be a real attentive student." Jaffey said, eager to learn and willing to do whatever it took to be as tough as Braddock. He had a growing admiration for the man. The more he came to know him and the more he heard about him from Sam and others in the precinct, the more he realized that this was a cop to model himself after, a man whose footsteps he'd gladly follow. Jaffey had been in need of a hero, someone to take him under his wing and bring him along, teach him, toughen him, show him the ropes. He figured Braddock was about as good a model as he'd ever find.

Tom would have been amused and maybe a little embarrassed to know how Jaffey felt. He sure didn't think of himself in heroic terms, but he had an inkling of how Jaffey saw him and supposed that maybe there might be a few things he could help the lad with. He hadn't really taken an interest in bringing anyone along in the years he'd been on the force. He'd always been too busy looking out for his own hide and career. He supposed it wasn't a bad thing to do, taking someone like Jaffey under his wing though, and maybe something he should have been doing more of. In a larger sense it was good for the department, which with all its imperfections was an institution he deeply respected. In a way it would be like he was giving something back by bringing Jaffey along, building the next generation, so to speak. These thoughts flitted through Braddock's head all in an instant before he said, "I suppose you would at that."

Later, as Jaffey was leaving, he said, "Oh, your hinge was squeaking, so I oiled it."

"Thanks, I guess. I've been meaning to do that one of these days. Never thought I'd nearly kill somebody 'cause of it. Funny how a little thing like that can get so big," Tom said as he swung the door back and forth on its hinges.

Later Tom set out to make the rounds of his pickups. A number were bars. They would pay to keep their back doors open on Sundays, or run a few girls in the upstairs rooms or a bit of gambling in the basement. A twenty for Tom every month helped ensure they were left to do business undisturbed. It was accepted too that if a crackdown was in the offing, an effort would be made to give advance notice. That was a risk for Tom, but he'd managed to get the word out once or twice when it was necessary. Most precinct captains were very understanding in that regard and gave at least a day's notice of upcoming raids except in the most politically sensitive cases. All things considered, the system worked well. The money flowed with a wink and a nod.

Tom had a middling list of businesses that he attended to personally. Most detectives did, but there was another, larger group who paid off at the precinct level. A percentage of that money found its way into Tom's pocket as well. In return he'd send notice whenever possible of any major crackdowns. It was a fairly efficient system so long as nothing went wrong. Of course something always did, but those were the risks. After about two hours of running about, Tom had over a hundred dollars in his pocket and a splitting headache. As usual, pickups from the bars included a ritual pulling of the beer. It was considered bad form to leave without a taste. All the activity was probably not good for his head either. The doctor had left instructions to take it slow for at least a week. "Slow" wasn't how Tom would have described his day so far. It didn't take a doctor to tell that the mushy ache in his head and the blur at the edge of his vision was due to more than a few sips of beer.

It was when he was coming out from one of his stops that Tom realized that he was very close to Watley's dance hall. He figured he might as well follow up on Watkins's alibi as long as he was in the neighborhood. It made him feel a little better to get something done on the case. The collections hadn't helped to stop the guilty voice at the back of his head. A few minutes later he was standing on the Bowery in front of the place. It had the garish, shabby look of so many of the dance halls. Huge billboards flanked the door. More signage covered the building up above. Down the street a pair of eyes watched from under the brim of a rumpled hat. Tom went in and took a stool at the bar, asking the bartender for Miss Devine. The man checked the time when Tom disappeared. He settled against a doorway to wait.

"Ain't been 'ere for days now. Plenty other girls 'ere to tickle the fancy of a man such as yerself," the bartender said with a knowing wink.

Tom showed his badge and asked again for Clora. "It's official business," he said firmly.

"Better see the manager." The bartender shrugged his shoulder toward the back of the big room. "Door on the left."

Tom's visit with the manager wasn't much more helpful. Miss Devine had not come in for three days, and it was apparently a source of some annoyance to the man who ran the place. He was a German, named Haupt, who reminded Tom of an officious burgomeister.

"That girl, she went off und we've not seen her again," Haupt told Tom, hooking his thumbs behind suspenders that appeared about to snap.

"Was she seen leaving with anyone?"

"Ach, she vas a popular girl." Haupt smiled. "Lots of gentlemen wanted to dance mit her. Some of these gentlemen would take her out sometimes. I couldn't keep track of all the girls und what they do after work."

"You ever recall seeing someone with her by the name of Watkins? Tall, skinny fella, with a southern accent?" Tom held a hand up to indicate Watkins's height.

"Got the pox marks on his face?" Haupt asked. When Tom nodded, he said, "Ya, I remember him. Clora vas seeing him sometimes."

"Got an address for her?" Tom asked, more than half expecting he wouldn't.

"Sure, sure. I look it up for you." Haupt was efficient about his records apparently, for within a short time he had Miss Devine's address. He handed it to Braddock, saying "Clora's not in trouble? She's a goot girl, und I'd hate to lose her."

"No, no trouble. Just need her to confirm something for me. Mind if I ask around, see if anyone might know who she was seen with last?"

Haupt didn't have any objections. He suggested Tom start with the bartender, whom he said knew the goings-on in the place better than anyone.

The bartender wasn't able to help much except to say that he did remember Watkins, though he couldn't say he recalled seeing him on the previous Saturday night.

"Too many men in here on a Saturday to remember 'em all," he said. He looked toward the front door, saying, "Oh, there's Patty. She was pretty close with Clora." The bartender waved to a girl who had just walked in. "Patty, c'mere a minute. This 'ere detective is lookin' for Clora."

"Well, ain't we all," the woman said. "Ain't been in since Tuesday."

Tom got her name, and asked the usual questions about Clora, whom she was seen with and whether Watkins was one of those. Patty confirmed that Watkins was a regular, but she couldn't be sure if he'd been there last Saturday. "Was pretty busy myself last Saturday, ya understand."

"You said Clora was last seen on Tuesday?" Tom asked. "Did she leave with anyone? Or was there anybody she was spending a lot of time with?"

After a moment's thought, Patty said, "Well, there was this one fella. Sort of a clerk, you know, bow tie, glasses . . . little guy, maybe five six, five seven. I think he left with Clora. Seemed harmless. Had kind of a mousy look to 'im." Patty scrunched up her nose, exposing her front teeth in a ratty parody.

Ten minutes later Tom was at the address that Haupt had given him, a reasonably clean-looking four-story tenement on Broome Street. A few minutes later, after finding nobody home, he was being let into her apartment by the landlord. There was no sign of Miss Devine. The apartment looked as if it had just been left for an hour. Tom looked into the armoire in the bedroom. It was full of clothes, especially the kind of flashy dresses a dance hall girl might wear. Tom took his time, looking through her things for any sign of a connection to Watkins, the bridge, or Bucklin for that matter. He was keeping an open mind on the possibilities. As it turned out, the only thing of any significance Tom discovered was that Miss Devine was not there. She appeared to have left suddenly.

Taking a hack to Suffolk Street gave him a little time to relax. By the time he reached the Bucklins' place, his head was pounding to a less insistent drum. Tom got out and stood in the crowded street for a moment. He had a notion that Mikey might be out there somewhere. It was nearly four, so he'd be out of school, if he even went. If Mike had been near, it would have been tough to spot him among all the kids running about. Tom turned and trudged up the dark stairs.

Watkins had almost made up his mind. In fact, he would have stopped Braddock on the street before he went up to the Bucklin apartment, but he was more than a block behind. "Don't matter," he muttered. He got himself a *Tribune* and sat on a stoop about half a block away. He spread the paper out on his knees, pretending to read, while casting a frequent eye toward the Bucklin place. Watkins never had been much of a reader, but he was so nervous he doubted he could have read a word anyway. He kept telling himself this was the only way. Even though Thaddeus hadn't shot him outright, it didn't mean he wouldn't. The captain was just biding his time till he was off his guard. He knew how the captain operated after all these years, had seen how he handled men who'd done him wrong. He was living on borrowed time by his reckoning. His palms started sweating just thinking about it.

This was the way it had to be, the only way he could see himself clear of the mess he was in. He'd give up the captain. He had to. Just running wouldn't be enough. That maniac would find him wherever he went. No . . . he'd have to turn him over, Earl and Weasel too, come to think of it. They'd kill him sure if the captain got pinched. Matt and Patrick, they'd see the right of it. They weren't cold like the others. They might not like it much, but they'd be so busy covering their own tracks they wouldn't waste time on him. Watkins wasn't that sure about Earl or Weasel. Those two were as crazy as the captain, maybe more. They'd find him if they weren't locked up. He was sure of *that*. "Kill a man for havin' too many beers," Watkins mumbled to himself. He glanced toward the front door again, looking over the top of his newspaper. "Still . . . it ain't easy." When it came right down to doing it, he wasn't sure he could. It would mean jails and courts and testifyin' and lookin' the captain in the eye when he told the Yankees what they were planning to do. That part of the plan was almost as bitter as getting shot. He didn't know how he'd stand up to that. Turning traitor like that just wasn't in him, nor his family. "Thank God my daddy won't see it," he said to himself. If his father had still been living, he'd never even think about this.

Tom's visit with the Bucklins was nearly as depressing as before. They had buried Terrence next to Julia and the baby in Brooklyn, Patricia told Tom. It had taken their last dollars and some credit too, but they felt they had to do whatever it took so Terrence could sleep with his wife and child.

"One odd thing," Patricia said. "When we got back from the funeral, I could have sworn that Terrence's picture had moved." Tom had raised his eyebrows at that, and she could see the skepticism on his face. "It's true," she insisted. "It was as if our Terry had given us a sign." She looked longingly at his tintype on the bureau.

Tom looked at it too. "Nothing else moved while you were out?"

"Not a thing. It's a sign. He's with the angels now. It's a comfort to know he's at peace."

Tom nodded silently. He wasn't much of a believer in signs.

Mike hadn't taken it well, Patricia told him. He'd been out nearly all night the day they broke the news to him. He seemed wilder now . . . distrustful, like a dog that's been beat too much. He cried, they said, but then Patricia and Eamon did too. To make whatever she could, she had taken in some seamstress work and was making lace as well. She had learned lace making in Ireland and had done it on and off ever since. Now it would at least keep some food on the table. Eamon was a little thinner and grayer, a step closer to the end. He didn't have anything to add to what he'd told Tom already, and not much breath to do it with. Mikey was out with his mates most of the time. Patricia worried and sewed. Tom reached into his pocket and took out the small brass key that had rested there since his visit with Doc Thomas.

"Have you ever seen this key before, Mrs. Bucklin?"

Patricia took it, turning it over in her hands. "Can't say so, Tom. Looks something like a key to an old box that Terry had once. I think it was lost in the fire, though. Haven't seen it in years."

Tom took it from her. He thought for a moment about how to ask his next question, and finally said, "Do you have any notion why this key might have been found in Terrence's stomach?"

The shock was clear on her face. "His stomach? My God, no! What would a key be doin' in Terry's stomach?"

Tom frowned down at the small brass key in his hand. "That's exactly what I'd like to know."

It was around five-thirty when Tom trudged down the steps to the street. He had an urge for a back table at McSorley's. A couple of ales, some crackers with onion and mustard, and some convivial solitude sounded just about right. Watkins got up from his seat on the stoop when Braddock came into sight. His hands shook as they folded the paper and tucked it under his arm. He stood for a moment, rooted to the spot. Tom turned south down Suffolk, walking slow and thinking slower. The sounds of the street bubbled around him into an inaudible froth. Snatches of conversation in accented English, or Gaelic, Italian, and a handful of others he couldn't place went by like shooting stars and were gone. He didn't know how many times he heard the name Mikey before it registered, but he turned to the sound of the boy calling the name from across the narrow street.

"C'mon, Mikey. Move yer arse, ye'll miss the fun."

"I'm comin', Smokes. Keep yer knickers on."

Tom turned and saw Mike dart across the street, dodging wagons. He stepped off across the cobbles after him.

"Mike! Hey, Mike!"

The boy turned, his eyes narrowing. His friends, three or four of them, stopped a little way ahead.

"Mike, hi. Remember me?"

Mike had the look of a rabbit smelling a fox, and he appeared ready to dash off. He took two steps back.

Tom let him have his space. "Mike, I'm Detective Braddock. I came to see your grandparents last week?" There was a flicker around the eyes—recognition but still the wariness.

"Whadya want with me? I ain't done nothin'." Mike cast a quick glance at his friends.

"I know. Just came by to see how you're getting on."

Mike actually liked this Detective Braddock but he couldn't let his friends see him be too friendly with a cop. He wasn't sure if he could trust him either, and lately he felt he needed proof of everything. He'd been nice when he was here before, but that wasn't enough now. "What do you care how we're getting on? You don't know me family."

Tom was caught off guard and searched for something to say. He unconsciously reached into his pocket, fingering the small key. "Well . . . that's true, Mike. I don't know them but . . ." How could he explain to this boy what it was like to sit in his grandma's dark kitchen, thinking that but for the grace of God, it might as well be him whose life's candle guttered low. Terrence's picture stared at him from the bureau, calling to him to do right by a fallen comrade. Would this kid understand that? He doubted it. Still, he needed to say something. "Well . . . for one thing, Mike, your dad and I were in the same army back in the war. I didn't . . . well, I didn't know him then, but I knew his unit and I knew some of the men," Tom started lamely. He rubbed the key in his pocket as if doing so would give him luck. He took it out.

"That don't mean nothin'."

The kid was right. It didn't mean nothin'.

What did he want to tell this boy? He wasn't really sure. Feelings were hard to put into words. Most often when he did find words, they didn't seem to be the right ones. Tom looked at the eyes, full of hurt and loss. There was the wary squint that hadn't been there just a week ago. This wasn't the same little boy.

"Maybe it's like you say. Maybe it's nothing to you, but it's something to me. If you had been in the war like me and your dad, you might understand." That wasn't all of it by a long shot, but it was what Mike might understand. There was a flicker in the wary eyes.

"You might just be sayin' that. How do I know you're not lying?"

Tom was taken aback but acknowledged the truth of it. "You're right. You don't know for sure. I guess you either trust me or you don't. Up to you," Tom said, tossing the key in his hand the way he sometimes would do with a coin. It was an unconscious act, a way to relieve tension, keep his hands busy.

"C'mon, Mike," one of his friends said. "We got no need o' cops. Lot o' good he did yer da."

Mike's face darkened. "You go away now, Mr. Braddock. We don't want you here. You couldn't stop me da gettin' his head bashed in, an' you can't help me." Mike turned and ran with his mates. Tom watched the boys disappear. A great sadness fell over him. He thought of his brother, Billy, who had died of a fever when Tom was thirteen. It was Billy he saw in Mike, and it hurt more than he imagined it could to see the boy run from him. He tried to think of something to say, something to bring Mike back. He knew the boy didn't mean it. He heard the torment in his voice. For an instant he thought to run after them, but he stopped himself. That would do more harm than good. He stood like a post, rooted to the spot, while the tide of the street washed around him. He started to walk again, going slow . . . thinking. Mike had said things that seemed to echo in his head. There was something there, something important. Someone else had used words very similar, but he couldn't place what or who. He cursed his fuzzy head, still throbbing and a little unsteady. He felt he should know. Tom rubbed the smooth brass of the key, turning it over and over in his fingers. It would come to him.

Watkins watched him walk away from inside a dry goods store, peering out between pots and pans hanging in the window. He'd ducked in there when Braddock came out. It was the boy who made him stop, he told himself. The boy had been in the way. He'd just have to wait for another chance. When Braddock turned the next corner, Watkins went out of the shop. "Give me

✻ Chapter Twelve ✻

"I was a Rebel, if you please,
A reckless fighter to the last,
Nor do I fall upon my knees,
And ask forgiveness for the past."

—MAURICE THOMPSON

Mike hadn't wanted to run with the rest of the gang. Smokes was right, though. If Detective Braddock was so concerned, why wasn't his father still alive today? He didn't really believe that, but he wasn't sure what to believe right now. Mike wanted to trust Mr. Braddock. He seemed nice. But since he watched his father's casket lowered into that dark hole in Brooklyn, he didn't trust anyone. Well, that wasn't all the way true. He did trust Grandma and Gramps. Harlan, the cop who walked the beat through his neighborhood, was the closest thing to a trustable adult outside of home. The problem was that Harlan the cop didn't trust him. Harlan didn't trust anyone, as far as he knew. He spent too much time chasing kids, knocking heads, and collecting little envelopes. He guessed he could go to the police building, where all the cops came out of early in the morning. He didn't know anyone there. They'd laugh at him if he went there. They'd look down over their mustaches, their cheeks all puffed out and important, and they'd laugh. He was a kid, after all. He didn't trust cops and they didn't trust kids like him. He could try but if the bad men had ears in the neighborhood, maybe they had ears in the police building too. He couldn't tell Grandma. What could she do? She couldn't fight bad men like he'd met by the outhouses. She was old and got out of breath just going up the stairs. If some bad men had killed his da, they'd have no trouble with her. He didn't want to see her go into the dark hole in Brooklyn too. Besides, she had Gramps to take care of. That left Mr. Braddock. He seemed all right, and was nice enough when he came the first time. He hadn't told about the potatoes, and he'd even shown him his gun.

Still, it was hard to believe that he really gave a cracker about him or his family. But why did he come back? Was it really that stuff about his da and the war and all, or something else? He was a little sorry he'd been bad with Mr. Braddock, but he couldn't let his gang see him go easy on a cop. He'd have to ask Grandma. She might know. Maybe that's all he had to do, talk to Grandma. She could tell him if Braddock was trustable. He had to be careful, though. He couldn't let Grandma know his secret. He didn't want to see himself go into the dark hole in Brooklyn either.

Grandma?" he said later that evening, "I saw that cop on the street today. He tried to talk to me. Is it okay to talk to him?"

"You mean Detective Braddock, the man who was here about your da?" his grandma said, looking up from her sewing. "Sure, Mike. The detective is a fine man, far as I can tell. He's just tryin' ta help. Did you talk to him?"

"No, ma'am, not much. I was with me mates, an' . . ." Mike hesitated.

"Oh, I understand. Couldn't be seen gettin' too cozy with the law, eh?" Patricia said, smiling.

"Yes, ma'am, somethin' like that."

"Well, Braddock's all right to talk to. You go ahead if you want, and don't let yer mates decide for ya."

"Uh-huh, I'll try. Do you think he might find who killed Da?" Mike asked hopefully. He'd like to see what the big detective might do to a black-faced bad man.

"I can't say, Mikey. But I think he'll do his best, and that's all we can ask."

"I hope he does. I been scared those men might kill me." Mike said it before he realized it.

"Lord, Mike. What'd make you think that? Nobody's goin' ta hurt you, not while I've got breath in me body."

Mike wasn't reassured.

Tom surveyed the wet plaster. When it dried, it would shrink, leaving a dimple where the bullet hole had been. He'd have to give it another coat, but the plaster had to be dry before he did. It would wait till tomorrow. As he put his tools away and cleaned up, he thought about the Bucklins. It didn't take a crystal ball to see there'd be another funeral there soon. Eamon was near gone. It was as if the death of his son had aged him by years within the last week. With no income aside from what Patricia could make with her lace making and sewing, he wondered how long they could last. She couldn't make more than a dollar a day or so. Tom wondered how much Mike understood of their predicament. The boy probably knew better than he imagined. He was depending more on his little gang. Tom had seen what happened to children who lived on the streets: sleeping in doorways, scavenging, rag-picking, selling themselves when they could. Mike was headed down that road. He'd have to see if he could talk to the boy—away from the influence of his friends. Maybe then he could make some progress with the kid.

He stopped himself for a second. What was he thinking about Mikey like this for? He seemed like a nice kid, but he wasn't his responsibility, after all. He had promised Mrs. Bucklin to help if they needed it, but nothing beyond that. Maybe the best thing would be to see that Mike got into a proper orphanage if it came to that. Tom didn't know exactly what he'd do now that he thought about it. That was the thing; he had said he'd help without thinking. But as he washed the wet plaster from his trowel, he looked into himself and saw the feeling he had for the boy. Maybe feeling was too strong a word, but there was something there beyond just a promise given to a grieving mother. Billy had been just about Mike's age when the scarlet fever took him. They'd been out playing in early spring when it had suddenly turned cold and a drenching rain had fallen like nails from the sky. He and Billy had been soaked. They hadn't bothered to run for cover. When they'd finally gone home, shivering and blue from the cold, their mother had scolded them, saying "You'll catch your death, you two!" Billy had caught his death and Tom had never stopped blaming himself. He had been the elder. He should have gotten them to shelter. His adult self knew the lie of that notion, but the part that was still the child remembered. Was that it? he asked himself. He tried to get hold of the feeling, tie it down, put it in a Mason jar so he could see it from all angles. But feelings are skittish things, and his swam away like a fish in an icy-clear stream. He could see it, but getting his hands on it was something else. He knew this fish, though, and began to understand it for what it was. Tom stood still, the trowel dripping water on his kitchen floor.

He put his tools back in the bucket. Tom had always been an indifferent handyman, and the bucket served as well as any fancy carpenter's box could. He put the bucket in the back of the hall closet, with the winter boots and the flag that he brought out for the Fourth. Closing the door, his eye was caught by the hammer that stuck out from the tangle in the bucket. A shaft of light pierced the inky confines of the closet, striking its head. The light turned the rusty blue-gray steel the color of summer wheat. Tom stopped, staring, the doorknob gripped tight in his hand. "Son of a bitch. Watkins!"

He knew it would come to him. All evening through the hour at McSorley's and then at home, while fixing the wall, he'd thought on and off about it.

How many times tonight had he seen the hammer? It sat in the bucket for hours right out in plain sight, but he hadn't seen it. He shook his head. He remembered it clearly now—Watkins saying something like, "Ah didn't have no reason to bash his head in or nothing." But Tom had been distracted. He had seen Emily on the bridge, and everything else had gone out of his head. His mind had wandered; otherwise he surely would have realized that he'd never told Watkins how Bucklin was killed.

"Son of a bitch!" he said again softly. He felt like such an idiot for not seeing it sooner. "Let that be a lesson to you, Grant." The cat watched him with yellow, saucer eyes. "Think with your dick, and your brain gets fucked." Grant sauntered over and wrapped himself around Tom's legs. "Maybe you don't have to worry, come to think of it. Not much brain in your head anyway." Tom rubbed Grant's head absently. "Gonna have to pay Mr. Watkins a call tomorrow. Could be an interesting day. Say, Grant, old man, what were the names of those other two who were from Watkins's unit in the war? Edmons, or Ebins, something like that, right, and Lebeau, I think. Gotta check my notes in the morning. Quite a coincidence, them being from the same unit."

Emily never liked the little clerk in the bridge offices. He'd been there so long now she couldn't recall when he had started. Whenever it was, she hadn't liked him from the first. She couldn't put her finger on why, really. On the few occasions they had spoken he had been polite, courtly even. His southern accent and manners, coupled with a fine vocabulary and obvious education, made him an interesting conversationalist. But there was something else about him. Like an open window on a January night, he could pebble her spine with goosebumps. It was a chill that his warm southern manners couldn't thaw. Maybe it was the eyes, she thought. If the eyes were the window to the soul, then the little clerk was as soulless as a machine. She didn't like to look in those eyes. She could feel Bartholomew Jacobs's unblinking black orbs on her now, from across the room, as she talked with Martin and Hildenbrand, the chief draftsman for the bridge. They bored into her over the tops of his wire-rimmed glasses. Emily suppressed a shiver.

"And by the way, Charles," she said to Martin, "if you see that detective again, please give him every cooperation. I spoke with Washington about it, and he agrees that his fears seem far-fetched but he should have all the latitude we can afford him."

The assistant engineer nodded his acquiescence with a wry smile. "Ah, yes, the good Detective Braddock. I haven't seen him since last week, but if I do, I'll be sure to be accommodating."

Hildenbrand gave a quizzical look. "Who's Braddock? What's this about the bridge? Shouldn't I have been informed?"

Martin filled Hildenbrand in about Braddock and his suspicions, but added that they didn't put much stock in them.

"In fact, I think it best to keep such talk to a minimum. You know how rumors can get out of control."

"Wash was concerned about rumors too, and he's anxious to avoid any hint of scandal," Emily added, her voice lowered.

"Understandable considering all of both we've had over the years," Martin said.

"Exactly. So if you see the detective again, you are to ask him to inform us *first* of anything he uncovers." Emily wagged a finger at Martin for emphasis. "Wash was emphatic on that. He's rightfully concerned that we *not* learn of anything in the morning papers."

"You may rely on me, Emily."

"I know I can count on you both, gentlemen." Emily said her good-byes, leaving Hildenbrand standing in the office. She and Charles went down to the power plant to see about preparations for the lighting. Weasel's eyes followed her as she left. Perhaps it was best she didn't see them.

A few minutes later Emily stood beside the door to the power plant. It was amazing how the U.S. Illuminating Company had planned to supply electricity for the lights on the bridge. Just a couple of years ago she hadn't known enough about electricity to fill a thimble, let alone power plants, turbines, and such. But she had learned. She had needed to. Still, the huge wheels, belts, and ozone-charged atmosphere of the power plant were rather intimidating. Looking out over the river, she noticed one of the ferries puffing across, throwing up a froth of East River water from its blunt bow. She had a sudden, flashing image of old John Roebling, intent on his surveying for the bridge site. He had been out on the pilings of the Fulton Ferry slip as a ferry approached. His foot had been crushed between the beams and pilings of the dock as the ferry nudged its way in. The stubborn old German, his boot full of blood and shattered bones, had continued giving orders and calling out measurements till he passed out. It was the same stubbornness in insisting on treating himself with hydrotherapy that cost him his life. Lockjaw was not an easy death. Why she was suddenly thinking about John Roebling's death here by the power plant she couldn't say. Even now she could see the ghastly, smiling grimace that gripped his face in a premature death mask. The muscles of his face and, slowly, the rest of his body had gone through horrible convulsions, becoming rigid as stone as the infection worked its deadly magic. The doctors could do nothing. Emily had been there, yet she knew she could only begin to imagine the torment. Wash had taken over for his father at the age of thirty-two.

As suddenly as it came, the vision of her father-in-law's death passed away. A small chill passed through her, and she shook herself mentally to rid herself of the ghost. It was gone. Afraid the vision would return, she thought of Braddock again. Emily hadn't seen the detective for at least four days, and couldn't help but wonder at what he was doing. Emily had been down to the bridge at least once or twice a day and had kept a casual lookout for him. In truth, she had been spending more time at the site lately. She lied to herself that Wash hadn't noticed, and had to admit to being just a little disappointed at not seeing Tom. She thought that he had been as smitten with her as she was with him, and his absence rather dashed her daydreams. It was just that it was so pleasant to have someone notice her as he had and talk to her as he had. Emily liked that and wanted more of it, regardless of how pointless. She wanted to at least call him her friend. Emily walked to her carriage feeling tired. Arrangements for opening day ceremonies would have to be finalized soon. With just two months left, there were a thousand things left to do. But she was tired now. The arrangements could wait just a bit longer.

Later that night, sitting at the big table at Sangree & Co., Jacobs related what he'd overheard at the office.

"So, your impression was that this detective had suspicions that he shared with Mrs. Roebling and C. C. Martin?" the captain asked.

"Definitely. I distinctly heard them discussing it and use the words 'sinister,' 'scandal,' and 'controversy.' "

"Could mean most anything. It doesn't mean they got any idea what we're up to," Lincoln noted.

"No," Jacobs admitted, "at least not that I heard. But we'd be wise to assume the worst. We know Braddock met with Roebling and Martin. We know what brought him to the bridge." He said this looking from Watkins to Lebeau. Watkins's Adam's apple bobbed on cue. Lebeau wore his usual dead-man's stare.

"Whatever roused his suspicions, he obviously thought it serious enough to pass on to them." The captain looked at Lebeau. "Any reason why this cop should think that Bucklin's death was connected to a deeper conspiracy?"

"Cap'n, we don't know that's what he thinks," Sullivan broke in. "Don't think we should assume too much. There's no way for him to know, right, Earl?" Pat said, looking to Lebeau for confirmation.

"If you're askin' if I done him clean, the answer's yes. I sure as hell didn't leave nothin' that was gonna connect us. Think if I had, he'd-a been after me from the git-go."

"Yeah," Lincoln said. "All this cop's got is suspicions. We'd have heard from him before now if he really knew anything."

"He don't know shit! No way! Hell, even Bucklin didn't know all that much. My tongue may have wagged a bit with the beer and all, but he never got no particulars," Watkins lied loudly. In truth, he wasn't sure exactly how much he'd spilled of their plans. He had lost count after the eighth pint. He remembered bragging about some of the trains they'd wrecked, but what he'd said about the bridge was a blur.

"Watkins, you'll forgive me if I'm not reassured," the captain said with a dry rattle at the back of his throat and a twist of his mouth.

Watkins noticed the tone. He figured he didn't have much time. He'd need to act soon if he wanted to stay alive.

The discussion turned to Braddock, how much he knew and how he knew it. Earl was certain that it wasn't Mike who had told anything.

"If he knowed, he'da squawked," Earl said with certainty. "Kid practically pissed his pants he was so scared."

Either way, whatever Braddock had was not enough to act on. The question became what to do about it.

"Kill the son of a bitch," said Watkins, looking to the others for support.

Jacobs cleared his throat in that officious way of his and drawled, "You'll recall I was in favor o' that two meetings back.

"No problem, Cap'n. This Braddock's no harder to kill than the next man. Done it before. Ain't scared to do it again." Lebeau had a killer's confidence in his abilities, and saw Braddock as simply a bull's-eye to hit.

"The point," Sullivan said, "isn't just killing the man. We thought that getting rid of Bucklin would solve our problems, but it only created more. I say we need to think this all the way through . . . do it right, or not at all."

"I second that," Matt said. "This is a New York City police detective we're talkin' about boys. Don't think they'll take kindly to someone killing one of their own. Raise a hornet's nest for sure." Some of the others nodded agreement. "We're not even sure that killing the man would do any good. He reports to a captain, or police chief, or something, right? Who knows who he might have told about his suspicions? Killing this man might blow back in our faces. All he had to do was tell one other cop about his investigation. If Braddock was to turn up dead somewhere, we'd have cops down here thicker than flies on a dead dog's eye."

The captain looked up from the table, his face weary. "Gentlemen! We've got plenty to discuss beyond what we might do about this damned detective. I'm not against killing the man, but we must know that he is closing in on us before we act. Nothing must be done before that," the captain said emphatically.

"And *we* can't do the killing," Thaddeus said, smiling grimly.

Jacobs and Lebeau looked disappointed. Weasel took his glasses off, making a show of cleaning the lenses with a pocket handkerchief. Lebeau gave an almost imperceptible shrug.

"We get someone else to do it."

Jacobs looked up at that then perched the glasses on the bridge of his nose. His small black eyes peered over the tops of the half-lenses. A predatory smile curled his thin lips. "I have someone who can help with that if need be," Thaddeus said with a satisfied grin. There were nods around the table.

"Someone needs to be there," Jacobs observed coldly. "Beyond needing to be sure the bastard is fed to these wolves, we should be ready to step in and finish it if the outcome appears uncertain." Weasel, of course, had himself in mind. He wouldn't mind sliding his blade into that damned detective if need arose. Might be more of a challenge than what he'd done to that whimpering Clora Devine.

The captain rubbed his chin in thought. "I'm not against it," he said slowly. "Has to be one of us he's not seen before. Wouldn't do to have him recognize one of us before the trap is sprung."

Jacobs nodded in apparent agreement. He didn't give a shit about being recognized. He could be as inconspicuous as a priest in a confessional when he needed to be. He'd take his chances with that, so long as there was a chance for blood.

"I'll rely on you to carry out that task, Bart . . . assuming, of course, that Braddock hasn't seen you before we set this in motion."

Jacobs just grinned.

"Okay, Captain, so what's the plan? How're we gonna make sure of the whys and wheres and whatnots? I mean, this has to be arranged just so," Matt said.

Thaddeus steepled his fingers under his chin, a wisp of a smile creasing his face. "Some little arranging, Earl, but nothing we can't see to. Here's how I see it." The captain laid it out for them, what to do if Braddock came by again, what to say, what not to, and how to handle the situation if it appeared he was showing particular interest in any of them.

Thaddeus said. "We'll have no more than an hour's lead on him, so there's not much room for error. Matt, you and Lebeau will be the point men tomorrow. Braddock showed the most interest in you, so Watkins, you take tomorrow off. Any questions?"

Thaddeus looked around the room. He looked back to Watkins. "And, Watkins, listen to me well. Stay out of your place tomorrow, and keep the hell away from your usual haunts. You hear me, Private?" Thaddeus waved a finger for emphasis.

Watkins nodded. Maybe with some luck he'd be able to find Braddock himself and settle the whole affair, he thought. Tomorrow would be the day to do it.

Captain Sangree looked at Watkins hard. Watkins had had his uses over the years, but in truth he wasn't more than a twelve-year-old in a man's body. The captain figured he'd stuck to the work as much because he had no idea what else to do as out of any conviction in what they were doing. He was lazy, stupid, and dangerous, as his drunken exposé to Bucklin had demonstrated. Though he'd been loyal to the cause in his way, and a good man in a fight, his uses in the present circumstances were very limited. Watkins was expendable. He was the kind of man the captain wouldn't mind losing, the kind he'd gladly sacrifice for an objective—not like his brother at all. Franklin was a diamond to Watkins's clay. Holes in the line ought to be filled with clay, after all. Save the diamonds for the important things, the cutting of things uncutable. But that wasn't how things had gone so long ago at Gettysburg. The diamond was under the sod. The clay sat before him, dull-eyed and needing a shave. Captain Sangree sighed. "Let's move on then. We're running late, and I have arrangements to make."

Tom noticed the Black Maria on the side of police headquarters as he walked up to the building. The wagon—a black box on wheels, with a single door in back—was used to transport prisoners. Every morning the wagons would make the rounds of the precincts, picking up those arrested the day before. Prisoners would be brought to the Tombs, for processing and to await arraignment. Before the prisoners were hauled to the Tombs, they'd be paraded in Byrnes's rogues' gallery during morning parade. The fact that none of these men and women had been convicted of anything yet didn't seem to bother anyone.

Tom went in and waved to the desk sergeant, who sat at a raised oak desk, with heavy railings on either side. He bounded up the broad staircase to the second floor. He turned down the paneled hallway, past the offices of various superintendents and departments, their high oak doors reeking of importance. At the end of the hall, he made a left to the front of the building where the new detective bureau offices were. Tom got a warm reception when he strode into the squad room. Slaps on the back, robust handshakes, and lots of "atta boy, Tommy," "Good to see you back," and "You've got sand, Tommy" almost overwhelmed him. It seemed there were no secrets here. Any thought he might have harbored of pretending to have been sick vanished. Chowder Kelly pushed into the small crowd, clapping a thick hand on Tom's shoulder.

"Good to see you back, Thomas. The streets of the city 'ave been runnin' riot without your calmin' influence. Barely able to see above the flood of crime and lawlessness this past week."

Tom laughed doubtfully. "Is that so? Thought you boys had a better lid on things."

"Oh, we're tryin', Tommy, but the floodgates're open, an' the criminal classes are taxin' our poor abilities to hold back the tide, they are. Why, no more'n a week ago we found Venkman—you remember Venkman, Tommy? Well, we found the Dutchman all busted up and shot through the middle by some fella name o' Finney. And would you guess—Finney was stone cold too! Oh, you missed all the fun, you did." Chowder aped a broad wink. "You bein' sick and all."

"Sounds like it. I remember Venkman; big stupid German with a long sheet?" Tom said, playing along.

"Very stupid and very long. That would be him. Nobody here mourns his passing; Finney neither." There were similar comments around the group.

"Finney I don't know." Tom scratched his head and looked at the ceiling. "Course I read about it in the papers while I was laid up."

There was a twinkle in Chowder's eye. "I suppose you did at that."

"Detective Braddock!" Chief of Detectives Byrnes's voice boomed above their heads.

"Yessir!" Tom called back immediately.

"May I see you in my office?" the chief boomed back.

The little crowd melted faster than snow in April. Tom exchanged a look and a shrug with Chowder.

"Good to see you back, Thomas," Byrnes said as he closed the office door behind Tom. The chief of detectives had a large office, with high ceilings and a big door with his name and rank stenciled on the frosted glass. "How're you feeling?" Byrnes asked, looking closely at Tom.

"Very good, sir. Ready to get back at it." Which wasn't precisely the truth, but close enough. His stitches still pulled and oozed, and his hand hadn't gone back entirely to normal size. He'd even get a little dizzy if he got up from a chair too quickly, but he could get by.

"Excellent, excellent," Byrnes said as he strolled around to the other side of his desk. The room smelled of the cigars that Byrnes smoked constantly. The walls were hung with an endless array of photographs of Byrnes with politicians, officials, business and civic leaders, even one with J. P. Morgan himself, all of whom seemed to be very pleased to be in the company of the great detective chief.

"We have to watch our health, you know. Fresh air, good solid food, vigorous exercise, those are my prescriptions for a sound constitution. Don't you agree?" Byrnes asked, pounding his chest.

"That's the truth, sir. But I'm near to tiptop now," Tom said without feeling it.

"Well, that's fine, that's fine." Byrnes put his hands behind his back and rocked back on his heels. "You know, there's a couple of men who came in on the Black Maria this morning who you might know."

Tom became instantly wary. "Really?"

"Yes, I believe so. Haven't seen these boys through the system in a while. Don't really belong here from what I hear." Byrnes's neck challenged his stiff starched collar as he glanced down at some papers on his desk. He was a big florid walrus in a tight suit that barely buttoned across his middle, but he was a man of some vigor when it came to enforcing the law as he saw it. He also knew the score as well as any in the department.

"I'll be interested to see them," Tom said flatly.

"Coogan brought them in, you know. Good man, Coogan, a bit zealous at times, and overly jealous of what he sees as his, if you take my meaning." Byrnes peered at Tom from under overgrown brows, his mustache balanced on a pursed lip. "You might want to see to this personally, Detective. I'll not have friction between departments." Byrnes turned and looked out his window at Mulberry Street, his hands still clasped behind his broad back. "Got plenty of other problems to deal with in this city, Thomas. Don't need Coogan mucking up the works. I imagine he's overreacting to this Finney thing." Byrnes words ricocheted off the glass, hitting Tom in the guts like the sharp twist of a knife. His stitches began to ache.

"I'll see to it, sir."

"Good man, Braddock," Byrnes said encouragingly. "Dismissed," he added without turning, then watched Tom in the glass as he left.

Tom closed the door to Byrnes's office behind him. He walked through the rows of desks that filled the squad room, his eyes down, looking at the worn maple floorboards. He wanted to go down to the holding cells but felt it was better to wait. He'd see who they were in good time, but curiosity gnawed at him like a maggot. Tom must have looked the way he felt. Chowder came over to his desk.

"What's going on, Tommy? You look down. Byrnes giving you a hard time?"

"Nah. Byrnes is okay. He gave me a tip. Just not sure exactly what to do about it."

"Ah, well, then, all will be revealed in time, don't you know. The priests 'ave been sayin' that for centuries. Any time they can't figure why God's doin what he's doin, they say that sort of rubbish: 'It's God's will, or the Lord works in mysterious ways' and such. My favorite is 'God has a bigger plan.' " Chowder chuckled with an ironic, almost bitter set to his mouth. "It's just their way of sayin' they don't know what the fuck is goin' on whilst appearin' to know the mind o' God. So, don't worry about not knowin' what to do, Tommy. When it comes right down to it, nobody does."

"Very deep, Chowder. We really have to talk philosophy some time," Braddock said sarcastically.

Just then Byrnes came out of his office, and the squad assembled for roll call and briefing. A half hour later they were all headed down to the cells for the rogues' gallery. It would have been the right thing for Coogan to have alerted Tom before arresting some of his own, but he supposed that was payback for Venkman and Finney. He'd have a talk with Coogan later and try to smooth things over.

Sure enough, when the "rogues" were trotted out, there were two of Tom's boys. One ran a small brothel. The other owned a bar, with the usual vices on the side. Hardly big fish. This was going to set Tom back maybe thirty to forty dollars a month each, about as much as the average man made in two weeks' time. It wasn't a big dent in Tom's collections but it was hurtful nonetheless.

"Fuckin' Coogan," Tom muttered under his breath. At least he could offer some discreet assistance in getting them out a bit sooner, depending on which judge they went before. The two of them stared daggers at Tom. He couldn't blame them. Just yesterday afternoon he was drinking their beer and taking their money.

"Fuckin' Coffin too, that son of a bitch!"

Chowder nudged him. "Kettle on the boil, Tommy boy?" he whispered, while Byrnes droned on about crimes and criminals.

"Hmph. Was I that loud?" Tom asked sheepishly, looking around at the other detectives.

"Just a tad, laddy. What set you off?"

"Och, nothin', Chowder. Just an annoyance. I'll set it right by the end of the day."

Chowder turned to appear to pay attention to the Chief, saying out of the corner of his mouth, "I'd expect nothin' less, Thomas."

Lebeau saw him first. Braddock was walking fast with the look of a predator. Tom's head swiveled side to side; his eyes were bright, even from this distance. Earl gave a whistle, and Matt turned to see Braddock striding up the bridge approach, just past the terminal.

"He's got up a head of steam, Earl. Lookin' for somebody, seems like," Matt observed, trying not to be too obvious. "Keep to the work, Earl. Let him come to us." He put his head down. Earl just grunted and bent to his work. Matt moved within supporting distance. Out of the corner of his eye he watched as Braddock loomed closer. He could feel those eyes fix on him. The head stopped swiveling, and he barreled straight for them. When Braddock blotted City Hall from his sight, Matt stood and glanced in his direction.

"Morning, boys," Braddock said, but this time it sounded none too friendly.

"Mornin'."

"Looking for that fella Watkins. Where can I find him?" Braddock asked brusquely.

"You're outta luck this mornin', Detective," Earl said laconically. "Watkins di'n show today. What're you takin' an interest in him for?"

Braddock ignored Earl's question. "Where I can find him?" he asked with forced patience.

"You'd have to check at the bridge office," Matt answered, shrugging. "Watkins moved lately. I ain't certain of the address. Might have it on file. Ask for Jacobs, he'll help."

"Right. I'll need to talk to both of you later. Don't make me come looking for you," Tom said in a tone that said he wasn't about to trifled with. He had no reason to suspect these two of anything, but they were friends of Watkins's, and Tom sure as hell suspected him.

"You know where to find us," Matt said, matching Braddock's tone.

Braddock stared back hard at Emmons, weighing his answer and tone. "That I do," he said finally. "By the way, you boys right- or left-handed?"

Matt and Earl stood watching as Tom walked up the span toward Brooklyn.

"Couldn't have gone better if we'd wanted. Wonder why he's fixin' on

Watkins?" Earl said, scratching his head. They'd been lucky that it was Watkins that Braddock was after. The captain's plan was looking better and better. The timing of keeping Watkins out of work today seemed more than just luck.

"And what the hell was that bout bein' right-handed?" Matt shrugged. They were both right-handed.

"Don't matter. We won't be seeing him again." The satisfaction was clear in Matt's voice. They both grinned.

As Braddock rounded the New York tower, Earl said, "Best be goin'. Cover me with Hightower." Earl trotted off to set the wheels in motion.

Tom could see the row of town houses on Columbia Heights. He'd have thought it ironic that in many ways his reaction to this walk out on the bridge was very much like Emily's. Moments before, striding away from Earl and Matt, he had been focused, intent on finding Watkins. Being out on the approach already, it seemed best to take the direct route straight across. Doubling back to the Fulton Ferry would have wasted twenty minutes, time Tom was in no mood to waste. Yet, as the span soared up and over the river, Tom found himself transported. As he looked back, the teeming city seemed suddenly small, inconsequential. Everything was small, everything except the looming towers. Their gothic arches left him craning and open-mouthed. He had a sudden urge to put his hand on the stones. They were only stones, but he wanted to feel them all the same. He sensed the weight, the tension, the harmony of the bridge. He grasped a suspender cable, surprised at its size. They looked so weblike and thin from down below, but it filled his hand, rigid, braided, and tense. The twisted steel rope vibrated almost imperceptibly, as if a harmonic thrummed through it, a sort of metallic, vibrating life-blood. Tom imagined he felt the pulse of the bridge. A broad grin spread across his face.

With a conscious effort, Tom shook off the spell. He had a job to do, and sightseeing had no part in it. Still, he let his eye be drawn up the cables. He watched some riggers wrapping marlin around suspenders and stays. He never fully appreciated how brave a thing it was to work in the cables. Sullivan glanced down at the stranger below. Patrick chuckled to himself and gave a little wave. Braddock smiled and waved back.

Tom's thoughts turned to Emily; he was amazed that the woman had seen this marvel through to completion. He didn't think he could have done what she had—in fact, he knew it. He tried to imagine what it would be like to learn engineering from scratch, the math, the measurements, the mechanical drawings. What would it take to learn what she had and work side by side with the engineers? Picturing her, at lunch at the Astor House, he couldn't imagine she had done such a thing. He had heard it said that she was the real engineer of the Brooklyn Bridge. Walking the span, the reality of that notion was hard to get his head around.

By the time Tom walked into the bridge office, his mood had mellowed, but he was no less determined. He found Jacobs and, after a brief introduction, asked if he had a record of Watkins's address.

Bart Jacobs peered over his glasses, fixing his small, dark eyes on Braddock. "Has this Watkins fellow been involved in a police matter, Detective Braddock?" Weasel was doing his clerkish best and succeeding admirably.

"He's wanted for questioning" was all Tom said.

"He's a suspect, then, I take it? What was the crime, if I might ask?" Jacobs persisted, wanting to get all he could before sending Braddock to his fate.

"Murder, Mr. Jacobs. You may recall that one of your workers, a Terrence Bucklin, hasn't reported for work for a week past?"

"In fact I do," Jacobs pointed a pencil at Braddock. "Used to be common when the caissons were being sunk. Could hardly keep track of them. Different story now. But yes, Bucklin was missed."

Tom just nodded. "He was found murdered. Watkins may know something about it."

"How ghastly!" Jacobs said, putting a hand over his mouth in shock. "Well, sir, we'll be happy to render what assistance we can. Let me look up that address for you. Watkins moved recently, as I recall," Jacobs said while he thumbed through a record book.

A repulsive little man, Tom thought, though he couldn't say precisely why.

"Yes, here it is, 39 Cherry Street. A somewhat unsavory address. An appropriate domicile for an unsavory character, if I might be so bold," Weasel said, smiling at Tom over the tops of his glasses.

"Yeah. Listen . . . if you see Watkins, you are not to tell him I've been here. Got it? Don't try to detain him yourself, he may be armed. Just send for me. Here's my card." Tom handed it over.

"You may rely on me, Detective." Jacobs squinted at the card for a second and placed it in his vest pocket. "I certainly have no intention of trying to stop a murderer, heavens no! I know my limitations. I'm afraid that a pencil is my weapon of choice, Detective. Not a man of violence, you see."

Braddock nodded, giving Jacobs a patronizing smile. Though the clerk didn't look to be a "man of violence," as he put it, there was still something about those eyes. Braddock dismissed the thought and extended his hand to shake with the man. His hand gripped Tom's like a bundle of steel wire. Tom was surprised at its strength.

"Good-bye, Mr. Braddock." An obsequious smile lifted Jacobs's lip. His teeth were none too good, Tom noticed.

The address Jacobs had given him was unsavory to say the least. In fact, it was one of the most notorious tenements in the city. Most called the place Gotham Court. Erected in 1850 as a model tenement, it soon became one of the worst examples of its kind. Two rows of back-to-back houses, five stories high, 234 feet deep and 34 feet wide, formed number 37–39 Cherry Street. Narrow alleys running the length of the buildings served as entryways. Somewhere near 500 people lived in those buildings, with no running water, no lighting, little ventilation, no toilets, no sewers, and only occasional garbage disposal. The infant mortality rate was one of the highest in the city. Cops made a point of not going there alone. Doing so could be very unhealthy.

Though he hated the loss of time, Tom made a detour once he was off the bridge. He hadn't even stopped to talk to Matt and Earl, wanting to make up for his earlier dawdle. He headed for the Second Precinct. Even though he knew that Cherry Street was out of their territory, he didn't want to go to the Fourth for backup. That was Coogan's precinct, and there was no one there he trusted enough for that. It didn't take long to find Sam. The desk sergeant told Tom he was making his rounds and gave Tom a good guess where he'd be. Tom could smell the chowder from half a block away, and sure enough, when he went in the door to Chowder's place, Sam was at a small table facing the door. He saw Tom come in, in midslurp.

"Hey, Sam, how's it goin'?" Tom said, flopping into a creaking chair.

"Mmph. Hot chowder. Join me?"

Tom checked his pocket watch. "Sure, I guess. Won't have another chance to eat for a while."

"What's up? You're lookin' better," Sam said, eyeing him over his soup spoon.

"Yeah, feeling okay. Listen, I've got to go up to Gotham Court. Need some backup."

Sam looked up, interested. "Who're you after?"

"Man I think killed Bucklin."

Sam's spoon stopped midway between bowl and lip.

"Really? Wouldn't mind taggin' along." He sighed. "Got some horseshit to take care of, though. Captain's on top o' me. Reports and all. You know how it is."

Tom shrugged. "What about Jaffey?"

Sam laughed. "Not enough you takin' a shot at him? Now you've got to give him some action too?"

"Something like that," Tom said sheepishly. "You heard about our little misunderstanding. He takes getting shot at better than most. Besides, it was you told me he was all right, as I recall."

"Reckon he might do," Sam said, appearing to think about it. "Sure, take him along. Be good experience for the kid. We'll go find him after lunch. He's on rounds."

After a steaming bowl of chowder, some bread and conversation, they set off to find Jaffey. Freight wagons were lined up at warehouses and wharves, huge draft horses stomped shaggy hooves on rounded cobbles, teamsters swore, and the constant clatter and clamor of commerce bubbled around them as they walked toward Jaffey's beat.

"So you got it settled with Coffin?" Sam asked offhandedly.

Tom didn't answer him directly. Instead he said, "Coogan brought in two of my boys yesterday. Saw 'em in the rogues' gallery this morning." He looked at Sam. "Caught Byrnes's attention. Wants me to have a talk with Coogan . . . iron things out."

"And you think Coffin's behind it," Sam said. It was not a question. "Could be they're getting carried away with this crackdown horseshit. Could be they're puttin' the squeeze to you. Knowing Coffin, I'd go with the squeeze."

"Told you it wasn't over," Tom said grimly. He thought of his handshake with Coffin.

"I don't recall disagreeing," Sam said.

They found Jaffey, who seemed eager to go with Tom if it meant something more interesting than directing traffic. Sam said he'd cover, so they set off uptown, catching the El at the Franklin Square station. It was only a couple of stops to where they were going, and in ten minutes they were within a couple blocks of Cherry Street.

"Hold up a minute." Tom raised a hand to make sure Jaffey was paying attention. "Around here, you've got to worry about your back. That's where I want you . . . watching my back," Tom said, signing with his thumb. "Not too close. Give me some room, say half a block or so. When we go in, close up. Got it? And keep an eye to your own back too."

Jaffey just nodded and Tom could see him swallow. He seemed nervous. Tom figured that wasn't a bad thing.

"Right. Stay alert. This neighborhood is hard even in the daytime. Watkins could be our man, and he might not be alone, so don't give him an inch. Anybody tries to interfere, use the club and don't back up."

Tom was about to start off again when he remembered one more thing. "Oh . . . and if a crowd forms, we get the hell out of Dodge. Riots can start quick, so don't dawdle if it starts lookin' ugly."

Jaffey was looking more serious, just what Tom wanted.

Gotham Court was a dismal place. An airless, fetid alley, paved with uneven flagstones and slick with sewage, ran between the two buildings. Faded laundry hung from lines strung between, out of reach of anyone on the ground. The clothes hung limp in the dead air, dripping gray water. Filthy blank windows, like empty sockets in a death head, looked out on streets so thick with horse droppings it nearly covered the cobbles. The gutters ran black.

"Stay here for a minute," Tom said to Jaffey. "I want to check around back."

Jaffey leaned in a doorway as Tom crossed the street and disappeared down the alley. It was like diving into a sewer, and at first he held his breath for fear of sucking in the heavy air. When Tom finally took a breath, he didn't want to hold it. He spat out each shallow lungful, afraid of what the air might carry. His head swam, feeling just slightly dizzy just from the stink of the place.

The alley was long but seemed even longer. The light there was tentative, as if the stench of the place alone could dim the sun. Tom doubted if the flagstones ever dried. He passed people in the alley. Their vacant, glazed eyes did not meet his. They slumped and shuffled as if laboring under invisible bonds. Tom suppressed a shudder. As he neared the rear of the building, the garbage grew thicker, the human detritus more jumbled, the air heavier. In an instant, the alley was blocked. Three men seemed to materialize out of the shadows, the trash, and the filth of the place. They stood silent, broken-toothed grins splitting predatory faces. It was as if the atmosphere of the Gotham Court had taken flesh. The three leered at him. A quick glance over his shoulder revealed a black silhouette against the gray light at the end of the alley. He was cut off.

They advanced slowly, sure in their advantage. Tom didn't like the odds. He wondered where the hell Jaffey was.

Tom tried diplomacy while he figured what to do. "Don't want trouble, boys. It ain't any of yours I'm after." The three were obviously Plug Uglies, a particularly vicious Five Points gang identified by their headgear, usually a crumpled top hat, although one of these wore a bowler. Tom played for time, taking slow steps back. Appearing weak had its uses.

"Don't give me trouble and I won't give you any. Here on official police business," Tom said, showing his badge. "Got no quarrel with you boys." Tom thought about the Colt, but they were sticking so close, he doubted he'd have time to get it out before they were on him. All three had cudgels and he had to assume knives too, at the least. He figured he'd rather risk a fight than a gun battle. Tom had skills these three would never know, and their numbers in this narrow space could work to his advantage. He flexed his bruised hand, wishing he had his brass knuckles.

"Cain't let ye go," said the one with the bowler. "Cops're dead men what comes down 'ere. Makes you a dead man." The bowler-man stepped out just a little in front of the other two.

Tom saw he had to act. Putting his hands up, he stepped toward them. Keep your eyes on the hands, he thought. He took on a more pleading tone.

"Now, please, fellas, no need for this."

They grinned, more sure of themselves than ever.

Close enough, he thought as he waved his hands meekly. *Now!* Tom's right foot lashed out, catching the bowler-man high in the gut. It was a beautiful kick. Master Kwan would have been proud. Bowler-man was propelled back like a balloon with the air rushing out. His feet came off the ground, and he crashed into one of the others, bouncing him into the rough brick wall of the alley. The third swung his club almost straight down, as if he were chopping wood. Fortunately, Tom saw it coming. Braddock half stepped to one side, ducking forward, taking a glancing blow with his upraised left. The stitches in his side tore in a bright slash of pain. His right still came up with all the force of his legs and arm, catching the man under the chin. The heel of his hand drove up, snapping the open jaw shut, wrenching the head back. In morbid slow motion, Braddock saw a piece of tongue as it flew in a pink parabola past him. There was a tooth too, white and jagged. The force of the blow almost upended the man, and he landed with a flaccid crunch on the flagstones.

The third Plug Ugly had recovered himself, and his swing was almost too quick to block. The club came at Tom in an arc, from his left. Braddock caught it as best he could, but it hit his stitches in a burst of pain that took his breath away. He held on, though, trapping the club with his left arm. Using his attacker's momentum against him, he pivoted to his left, whirling the man about. With his right, he propelled the man past him. A foot caught on Tom's outstretched leg, and the man flew headfirst into the bricks of Gotham Court with a sickening impact. Dizzy now and off balance, Tom slipped on the sewage-slick flagstones. He hit hard, cursing and gulping for the stinking, dizzying air. Feet pounded down the alley toward him—the backup man. Tom rolled to his knees as fast as he could, but the feet were almost on top of him. He wouldn't make it. Fuck! his brain screamed. From behind he heard a thud and a grunt of pain. A tremendous impact knocked him flat, pinning him to the ground. Arms and legs flailed and kicked on top of him. Tom could hear the crack of a club on bone. He felt the impacts through the body. He was pinned, facedown. He couldn't see who it was but he heard the pain in the man's voice. He hoped it wasn't Jaffey. Another cracking impact and the man was silent. Tom waited.

"Braddock! You all right?"

Tom felt the body being pulled off his back.

"You took your sweet time getting here." He grunted into the flagstones and heard a relieved exhale above him.

"Thank God you're all right."

"Suppose I am. Don't think this suit'll be the same, though," Tom said as he got to his knees. "Christ, I smell like shit!"

"I'm sorry, Detective," Jaffey said, almost wringing his hands. "I came as soon as I saw that fella at the head of the alley move in."

Tom stood. The grin on his face stopped Jaffey in midexplanation. "Jesus, you're bleeding!" Jaffey said, pointing at Tom's side. His shirt was stained a blotchy red.

"First off, call me Tom. Second, you did just fine." He looked down at his side. "This does smart a bit though, I'll admit." He winced as he peered inside his shirt to get a look at the wound. "I'll be okay," he said without much conviction. He looked down at the motionless body that had been on top of him. He booted the man in the gut getting a low moan in response. "He'll live."

Tom looked over at the bowler-man, who had rolled to his knees and was making a wheezing attempt to stand. Stepping over to him, Tom said, "Somebody put you up to this, or this all your idea?"

The man turned a pained face up toward Braddock, gasping. "Bugger off, copper."

"Ah! Bugger off, is it?" Tom stepped back and kicked bowler-man's buttocks so hard it lifted him off his knees, sending him rolling into a pile of garbage, where he lay still. "He'll be shitting standing up for a while." Tom grunted.

"These two are none too good either," Jaffey said. One lay sprawled on his back, a bloody froth bubbling from his mouth at each breath. The other lay slumped against the wall, one arm over his head. He looked young, not much more than sixteen, Braddock guessed, and very pale beneath the dirt.

Noise and movement at the head of the alley caught their attention.

"Oh, shit!" Tom spat, exasperation, fear, and resignation mixing in his voice. "Time's up. We gotta go! Stick close, don't stop, and don't slow down. Just follow my lead." Half a dozen men and women filled the head of the alley. From the look and sound of them, they were not happy to see the police.

"Goddamn coppers come 'ere ta bust heads o' decent folk," someone said.

"Fookin' bastards carn't leave us be."

"Oughta give 'em some o' their own medicine, I says," a woman's voice barked, rough and gravelly.

"Stick close," Tom said over his shoulder to Jaffey. He tried to focus. He was still dizzy, and blood was running slowly now in a warm stream into his pants and down his leg. Braddock gritted his teeth.

"Get the fookin' cops!" someone yelled.

"Yeah, let's get 'em!" came the chorus.

As they neared the crowd, which was growing every second, Tom quickened his pace. So fast, Jaffey almost didn't believe he'd seen it at first, Tom's hand licked out at the first in the crowd. The man went down as if he were a bag of rags. Tom's pace didn't slow, nor did his hands or feet. With a terrible silence, he cut a path through the crowd, which suddenly seemed to melt before them. Jaffey looked at the men on the ground as he went by, almost as amazed as they were.

"C'mon, Jaffey! No time to dawdle," Braddock shouted over the noise of the crowd. "We'll come back for Watkins another day." Tom broke into a trot once they hit the street. He headed toward the Fourth, on Oak Street. Jaffey ran, looking over his shoulder for pursuit. All he saw was astonished, angry faces. Some followed, bellowing their frustration. None got too close.

When Braddock and the patrolman came boiling out of the alley, Jacobs was waiting a few doors down the street. He lounged against the doorway to a particularly fetid grog shop. At the first hint of a fracas, drunks had started shambling out, bleary and stinking, blinking in the light for the source of the noise. Despite his amazement at seeing Braddock not only alive but laying people out like tenpins, Jacobs barely raised an eyebrow. He simply stared hard at Braddock's disappearing back and swallowed his anger. This was business, he reminded himself. There would be other opportunities to skin this troublesome detective. Of more immediate concern was the fate of the four Plug Uglies. There wasn't much he could do about Braddock, but they might be another matter. Quickly he crossed the street, hustling through the confused crowd, most of whom had gathered after the cops had gotten away. There was much cursing of cops, shouting, shoving, and not a few calls for a march on the nearest station house, which few seemed inclined to heed. Small knots of people concentrated around three men who were still down, and there were calls for water and shouts to stand back so the fallen could breathe. Jacobs slipped through the confusion easily, his fist wrapped tightly on the hilt of the elegant stiletto in his pocket. He turned the corner into the alley, walking fast, knowing there would not be much time to do what he hoped he had to. His heels clicked on the greasy flagstones, blending with the echoes of the angry mob on the street. In the dim light of the alley he could see a slowly moving mass near the other end, black shapes groaning and writhing. The mass resolved itself into four prostrate forms as he drew near.

He needed to be efficient about this, he knew. None of these carrion could be allowed to be caught and questioned. The cops could be back at any minute, and in the condition they were in they might say things without using what little brains they had. The stiletto slithered out of Bart's pocket, a long, cold fang of softly glinting steel. He'd worked its planes patiently, sharpening and stropping in the sunless hours, caressing them to an edge that would shame a razor. He loved the weapon. It was such a wonderfully unambiguous tool, so efficient, so . . . beautiful.

As he stepped closer, one man slowly rose to his hands and knees. Jacobs reached down, grabbing the unwashed hair, pulling the head back. The stiletto slid across the soft skin of the throat so quickly Jacobs almost couldn't feel the tug of resistance as the flesh parted. He pushed the head from him before the arterial spurts could ruin his suit. He looked down dispassionately at the second, a pale boy who lay crumpled against the wall, his head at an odd angle and his breathing shallow. The knife flashed in a backhanded arc, ending what Braddock had begun. The third lay on his back, blood bubbling in his open mouth at each breath. Jacobs cut his throat as quickly as the last. He had to admit to a grudging admiration for Braddock as his blade parted the flesh. He had done quite well. They'd need to be more careful the next time. Jacobs turned to the last of them and was gladdened to see that the man had hauled himself up, propping himself against the wall. His eyes were wide in horror as all three bodies around him pumped blood in crimson fountains onto the slimy flagstones. Jacobs didn't hesitate. He stepped close, ignoring the hands held up in fear and supplication. He swung as if swatting a fly, cutting through one palm, fascinated to note how the fingers flopped when the tendons were severed. The howl was cut short a moment later. Jacobs wiped his blade on the man's vest while craning to watch the crowd out on the street. He stood then, turning to disappear out the other end of the alley. It had taken no more than thirty seconds. He smiled to a ratty-looking woman as he turned into the street, his hand going to tip his hat and cover his face. He was rather pleased with himself.

⚘ Chapter Thirteen ⚘

Let us cross over the river, and rest under
the shade of the trees.

—STONEWALL JACKSON

The orange ball of the sun had just been extinguished below the sooty horizon. The west still glowed red, framing the skyline of Manhattan, and setting the treetops of the Palisades on fire. The last of the sunset was reflected in the mirror surface of the reservoir. Like an immense pool of blood, the crimson bled slowly into the west as the night approached, surrendering the city to the deepening gloom. Hard leather soles crunched on the gravel of the walkway, seeming to echo across the water. The crowds were thinner now. It was a good place to meet. They couldn't be seen meeting too often at Coffin's office, after all, nor at their town houses either. Suspicions could be raised.

"He came to see me yesterday—late, about six o'clock," Coogan said with a sly grin. He stuck his hands in his pockets against the evening chill.

"And?"

"Sent word I couldn't see him. Too busy . . . make an appointment." They both smiled at that.

"Good. Keep him guessing. Who's next on the list?" Coffin asked, enjoying their little conspiracy.

Coogan squinted at the sheet of paper on his desk. "Those places down on Pearl, near Beekman."

"Yeah," Coffin said with apparent relish. "I'll make arrangements in the morning. He'll really start feeling the pinch." Coffin actually rubbed his hands together, delighted at the prospect.

Coogan was not quite as sanguine. "We'll see if he squeals, but it might be Byrnes he goes yelling to. You ready for that?"

"That's all right," Coffin said, kicking gravel into the water just to watch the splash. "I'll see there's no interference."

Byrnes wouldn't be all that easy to keep out of the picture, especially not where Braddock was concerned. Still, Coffin was hopeful.

"Really?" Coogan was impressed. Byrnes was not an easy man to manipulate.

"Byrnes and I have an understanding. We go way back," Coffin said evenly.

"Oh . . . one odd thing I forgot to mention," Coogan said. "After Tom left, my desk sergeant sticks his head in the office. He says to me, did I get a whiff of Braddock? So I says I didn't see him, 'cause of being too busy, and he says Braddock looked like he'd been rolling in a sewer. Smelled to high heaven."

"Interesting," Coffin observed. "What *has* our prodigal son been getting himself into, I wonder?"

Jum-bo the el-e-phant! Hey, Mouse, did you see this?" Mike asked, pointing to the fantastic, colorful poster pasted to a wall.

"Yeah, they're all over," said Mouse, feeling superior for knowing before Mike. "A man come down the block yesterday, pastin' em up. Where you been?"

"Smokes," Mike said, turning to the eldest of the gang. "You can read real good. What does the rest of it say?" Mike knew better than to ask Mouse. Mouse couldn't read any better than he could even though Mouse was nearly a year older.

"Says he's a packy-derm, whatever that is. But this Jumbo is the biggest packy-thing in the whole world, at least accordin' to this. Says he's appearin' ex-clu-sive-ly at the P.T. Bar-num circus."

"Where's that, Smokes?" Mike asked. The picture of the huge elephant had captured his imagination.

"Uh, let's see. A place called Mad-is-on Square Gar-den." Smokes read, sounding skeptical.

"A garden? What they want to let this packy-derm run around in a garden for?" asked Mike, shaking his head.

"It's an elephant! I don't know what a packy-derm is, but that's a picture of an elephant, like from darkest Africa." Mouse always had to get his two cents in.

"Well, it could be an elephant and a packy-derm too . . . maybe. Could be that's what they call it in African, you know, like the Jewish people on Hester and Delancey. They got different words for everything and letters too." Smokes and Mouse seemed impressed with Mike's reasoning. "Could be that's what they call an elephant where this Jumbo comes from."

"Still, don't see why it's gonna be in a garden," Mouse said. "Don't make sense. I ain't payin' money to see no elephant in a garden."

"You don't have no money anyways, Mouse," Smokes pointed out, which was quite true. None of them had any money.

"Well, I wouldn't pay it if I did," Mouse said indignantly, at least as indignantly as he could muster. "What do they want to see this elephant?"

"Uh . . . looks like fifty dollars," said Smokes, giving a low incredulous whistle.

"Fifty dollars! You could buy the whole elephant for fifty dollars. You sure?"

Smokes looked again, shifting the cigarette he always hung on his left ear into his mouth. He didn't light it though, he never did. "Maybe that's fifty cents. I always get confused. The cents sign is the one looks like a C with a line through it, right?" he asked, knowing his mistake. "Well, then, it's fifty cents."

Mouse whistled. "That's a lot of money to see a packy-thing in somebody's garden."

"Yeah, but they got other stuff too," Smokes said, trying to read the rest of the poster. "Death de-fy-ing tra-tra-peeze ar-tists from you-rope, clowns, dancing bears, all sorts of stuff."

Mike's face glowed a little brighter with each act Smokes read off.

"Dancing bears?" Mouse and Mike chorused.

"That's what it says. See, right here." Smokes pointed at the place where there was a picture of three bears. "Dan-cing bears," he read again with more certainty this time.

"Wow!" was all Mike could say. "Smokes . . . what's you-rope?" he finally asked with a frown. He'd heard it somewhere before but couldn't place it.

"That's a city, I guess. I think it's far away . . . real important too. Any time a sign wants to say somethin's important, they say it's from you-rope," Smokes said knowingly.

The three of them stood examining the poster with its huge rendering of Jumbo, the world's largest elephant.

"Do you think it's really that big, Mouse?" Mike wondered out loud. "I mean, look at them horses in the picture. Look like mice next to that Jumbo."

Mouse and Smokes squinted appraising eyes at the poster.

"Naw. Nothin's that big," said Mouse. He waved a dismissive hand. "No way!"

Mike studied the picture still. "I wonder how much it eats. A packy-derm that big must eat whole big wagon-loads of stuff. What do packy-derms eat anyway?"

Smokes shrugged. "Shit, I don' know. Most anything it wants, I'd guess," he said, laughing.

"Shit!" Mouse giggled, doubling over at the thought. "I bet he shits a ton. Now, *that* I would pay to see. Bet he shits houses!" They all laughed hysterically, doubled over and red-faced. Smokes's cigarette fell out of his mouth.

"Shits houses." Smokes chuckled, after they'd laughed themselves out. "It probably eats straw and mud and shits bricks." That broke them up again.

"Say, how we gonna get the money?" Mike asked. "I sure would like to see the circus. I never seen one." The notion of giant packy-derms, dancing bears, and who-knows-what kind of other amazing attractions had got him going like nothing ever had before.

"Me neither," Mouse and Smokes admitted. They glanced around as if money could be picked up off the street if they only looked. They didn't see any.

"Gotta be a way ta get that money," Smokes said with a stronger-than-usual resolve.

"We could lift some fruit an' sell it ourselves," Mouse said, as if this were a new idea.

"What if we got caught? Ain't gonna see no packy-derms in the jail, Mouse," Mike warned.

"I'll take my chances. I been in the jail over on Essex Street. It ain't so scary." Mouse was trying to sound tough, like the older boys in the neighborhood, but Mike knew he wasn't.

"We . . . could get jobs," Mike said tentatively. "We could sweep out stores and such. Old man Brower let me do that a couple of times for hard candy. Maybe he'd pay me."

Smokes looked at him as if he was seeing packy-derms and dancing bears di-rect from you-rope. "You crazy? I ain't doin' that. Besides, who'd hire me and Mouse? Nobody's hirin' the likes of us. May's well steal fruit."

Mike and Mouse slumped. Unless they were willing to work in a place like the furniture factory on Broome, for ten or twelve hours a day, there weren't many prospects.

Mike's head came up, a bright grin on his face. "We could steal coal. There's that big coal yard up on Rivington. Everybody needs coal," he said. They had never tried that before because the coal yard was in another gang's territory.

"I think I'd like stealin' fruit better. Don't get dirty stealing fruit. Coal's heavy." Mouse didn't like anything that sounded like work.

"Yeah, but we can steal coal by the *bucket*," Mike said, using his best persuasive tone. "Fruit we can only get maybe one or two at a time."

Lights went on in Mouse's and Smokes's eyes.

"Your grandma got a bucket?" Smokes asked Mike.

"I got one," Mouse piped up.

"My grandma's got one," Mike said, confident he could get his grandma to part with it for a while. "I can get it."

"I wonder how much we can get for a bucket of coal? Whadya think . . . maybe ten, twenty cents?" Smokes speculated. "Could be. We gotta see. Won't take long ta get to the circus that way." Visions of giant packy-derms thundered in their heads.

Captain Sangree woke early. He hadn't had the dream during the night. He counted that as a blessing. His dread of it often kept his eyes open long after his head pressed his pillow. It was always real, no matter how many times it came. It was only lately that he'd been able to control the dream at all. He could still not alter his brother's death, nothing could change that, but sometimes at the end, when he was firing at Roebling, he thought he had hit him. He couldn't be sure. It gave Thaddeus a hope he never thought he'd have, but it still couldn't change history. Franklin's voice still came to him, the voice of a boy hurt beyond all healing. At times it would stay with him for hours after he'd woken. Often he'd have to rise when the dream jolted him off his pillow, his brother's blood covering his arms to the elbow. Half awake, he'd scrub his hands on the sheets, but it would linger, cool and sticky between his fingers. The only way to reclaim his sleep was to wash it away, wash the blood only he could see. Thaddeus was grateful it wasn't the dream that kept him up.

It was Watkins he was worried about. He hadn't reported in yesterday evening. After seeing Watkins outside the Bucklin tenement yesterday afternoon, he wasn't sure what to think. Although his first reaction was to think that he was planning to kill Braddock himself, he was starting to think differently now. After so many years of trusting Watkins the possibility of betrayal hadn't crossed his mind. But it had done so now. Thaddeus was worried. After Jacobs's news that the ambush had failed, it was imperative that he find Watkins before Braddock did. He had underestimated Braddock—that was obvious. How he had escaped unharmed was a mystery. Four of those Plug Uglies should have been more than enough, even with a backup man, as Bart said he had. He'd had to dress down Jacobs for going to observe, when he'd been told not to, but he was grateful for the information. Perhaps he should have let Earl or Bart hunt him. It was too late for that now, though. Braddock had seen their faces, had talked with them. For them to stalk him now would be nearly impossible. Better to throw him off the trail somehow, give him a different scent or perhaps no scent at all. The captain thought of Watkins again as he lay staring at the ceiling. One by one he counted his options: the frontal assault, the flank attack, the feint and maneuver, the strategic retreat. He calculated outcomes, based on what he knew of his men and his adversary. He examined the terrain, seeking the high ground. He weighed each man, his strengths, weaknesses, and value to the mission. All of this kept him staring at the ceiling for hours in the blackness of his monkish room. In the end, he decided.

It was a heavy decision, one he didn't like to make. But the decision was his. He had lost men before to gain an objective. His memory couldn't hold the names of all those he had sacrificed one way or another. If he had done it during the war without hesitation, how could he hesitate now? The men whose lives were traded for uncertain goals in those years called out for it. Could this sacrifice be any greater than theirs? Thaddeus thought not. It was a decision best made alone, though. The men would understand and accept it once it was done. The captain took that as a matter of faith. They were soldiers, after all. They would understand.

As he thought this through he recalled an ode by Whitman, written for the death of the tyrant, Lincoln. Though he hated the tyrant, he admired the poet. As they sometimes would, parts of poems came to him, seemingly of their own accord, bringing light to his darkness. But the lines that shone brightest in his brain brought no light or comfort:

> Then with the knowledge of death as walking one side of me,
> And the thought of death close-walking the other side of me,
> And I in the middle as with companions, and as holding the hands of
>   companions,
> I fled forth to the hiding receiving night that talks not,
> Down to the shores of the water

Tom hadn't been surprised when Coogan wouldn't see him. The captain of the Fourth was playing hardball, as he'd expected. Coffin was probably behind the assault on his payoffs. Coogan wouldn't be so bold without Coffin's backing. It would be Coffin he'd have to see if he was to make any progress. He worried about Byrnes's reaction, though, if any more of his boys found their way into the rogues' gallery. On the other hand, maybe that might not be a bad thing. Byrnes could be very persuasive, and having the chief of detectives as a mediator could have its advantages.

As he dressed in the hopeful light of morning, Tom imagined he'd have no more trouble with Coffin and Coogan if Byrnes got involved. In fact, he thought it might be best to go to the chief and report that Coogan had been uncooperative. Even if no more of Tom's boys found themselves in a lineup, he'd be on record as playing by the rules. That would put the onus on Coffin and Coogan. At least that's what he'd imagined, but later that morning, after roll call and briefing, Tom found himself trading stares with another one of his own in the lineup. This time there was a significant difference. This time Byrnes didn't say a word. He didn't even look at Tom. The chief just went through the names and offenses as routinely as if it were a grocery list. Either he didn't know that one of the rogues was Tom's, or Byrnes had been taken out of the game. Tom didn't like to think it was the latter. Tom was one of Byrnes's men. He was due a certain amount of backup. If Byrnes was cutting him loose, things could get much worse than he'd imagined.

After the usual morning paperwork, Tom set out for the Tombs. With luck he might be able to get the two Coogan had brought in yesterday a reprieve. It all depended on which judge they were to go before. Bribing judges was something Tom didn't care to do. It wasn't because of the ethics or morality of the thing. Judges could be as pliant as anyone else if the right lubrication was applied. But it was the danger. Judges being political animals, you could never be certain that one wouldn't turn on you. If one of them got his balls in a wringer, he might find it expedient to give up a detective. For that reason Tom was not a regular contributor to judicial reelection funds, though he had on occasion done what was necessary. He was in luck this morning. After checking with the clerk, who was the real power in the place, he found that one of the more cooperative judges was sitting today. Tom got himself a quick audience with the man, and not more than ten minutes later, his problems were over. He hated spending the money, but the wheels of justice did have to be greased from time to time—the cost of doing business. The trouble was the cost kept rising. He'd have to deal with Coffin and Coogan too, but the bridge came first. Not wanting to go back to Gotham Court for a couple days, Tom figured his next best bet was to check on Watkins's known hangouts and his last address before the Cherry Street move. He didn't have any better ideas at the moment, so he headed for the bridge.

On the way he weighed what was going on with Coffin and Coogan. Coffin's fear of letting him go his own way was the problem. It was Coffin's ego, Tom figured. The man did not take well to challenges to his authority or judgment. Coffin needed to be in control. With Tom broken away from the corps, his control was weakened, his authority in doubt. Coffin had to be worried about the rest. Tom's leaving could be the snowflake that starts an avalanche. Next thing August might be just another precinct captain—no fancy house, no fancy rig for Sunday gallops up First Avenue. Without the corps, his power and income would be crippled. If the rest of the men saw that Tom could just walk away, what would hold them? He doubted that Coffin commanded any real loyalty. He needed fear to keep the men in line. August liked to be feared. He worked hard at keeping his men off balance, apprehensive. He used his authority as a weapon, a club in the velvet cover of the hale fellow well met. His convivial, clubby sort of charm was a thin veil for a man who fed on fear and respect in generous helpings. The problem was that Braddock feared no man, and Coffin knew it.

Matt saw Braddock coming first. He and Earl were on the New York approach again, finishing the curbing. Earl was mixing cement in a big steel trough. Matt troweled it into the gaps, setting the stones in place with the help of two other men. It was hard work.

"Say, Earl, here he comes," Matt said, looking up. The other two men were out of earshot, fetching another stone.

"Yeah, I seen 'im. Relax, he ain't after us." Earl turned his back to the approaching detective and spit out the wad of tobacco he was chewing. He put a bucket of bricks over the splattered brown stain.

"Morning, *boys*," Tom said like flint on steel.

"Hey," Earl said. Matt just nodded.

Tom stood for a moment, eyeing them both. "Still looking for your friend Watkins. Seen him this morning?" he finally asked.

Earl stood, straightening his back with a grunt. Mixing cement was rough on the back. "Nope. We was wonderin' where he got himself off to ourselves. Ain't showed fer two days now."

Matt looked Braddock over. For a man who'd been attacked by four Plug Uglies, he didn't show any signs of wear. Nobody could believe it when Jacobs had announced at last night's meeting that Braddock had come away unhurt. Once when he had first come to the city back around '69, Matt had wandered into the Five Points alone. He was rewarded with a sound beating by three of the most desperate, stinking savages he'd ever seen. Even at Andersonville, there'd been no worse. With empty pockets, he'd staggered out of the neighborhood, poorer and wiser. Matt figured Braddock for one tough bastard to best four thugs.

"Any idea where he might be found, other than home, I mean? He drink in any particular bars, grog shops, dance halls, that sort of thing?" Tom held little illusion about these two being of much help, but it had to be asked.

Matt and Earl exchanged a quick glance. "Aside from Paddy's, don't know anyplace he went regular. That right, Earl?"

Earl didn't even look up from his cement, which he had commenced hoeing again. "Yup" was all he said.

"What about Watley's and that girl, Clora Devine?" Braddock figured he'd throw in a little of what he knew, see if it raised a reaction. He didn't get what he'd hoped for.

"Well, you know . . . Watkins sorta went his own way, if you take my meanin'," Earl said, as deadpan as the best poker player. "Didn' see her but once with 'im. Cain't say more'n that." The two of them stood there doing their best blank-faced innocent stares.

Braddock looked them over, not saying anything for a second, a half grin on his face. "How long you figure you've known Watkins?" he asked offhandedly.

Earl scratched his chin. Matt ventured, "Since about '61, I reckon."

Earl wagged a finger in agreement. "Yeah, that's about it. He didn't join up with the first of us."

"And you've stuck together for all these years. What is it, twenty-two years, right?" Tom looked from one to the other. "You expect me to believe you don't know shit about him? What the fuck you take me for?" he almost shouted. Some of the other men turned to look. "I know you want to protect a friend. I respect that, I do. But I'm gonna get some answers from you boys." Tom held a thick finger up under Earl's nose. "And if I got to haul you in to do it, I will." He looked from one to the other with a glare that could split rocks. "Now, we can have a nice friendly goddamn chat up here on the bridge, or I can throw you boys in a cell, maybe round up some rebel-hating blackies to bunk with you a few days. Am I getting through?" Braddock was tired of playing games.

They were damn cool, he thought, looking into their eyes for a reaction. Neither Matt or Earl feared anything Braddock could do to them physically. But they did fear what he could do to their plans. They looked at each other, deciding they had held out just long enough. They didn't want to make it look too easy, after all.

About five minutes later, Braddock was on his way across the bridge to the office once again. Matt and Earl smirked as they watched his back. They had given Braddock enough dead-end leads and sleazy Bowery dance halls to stake out to keep him off their backs.

"That dog's gonna be chasin' his tail for a while," Earl said, chuckling, though he didn't look amused.

"Reckon so. Can't help but wonder where in hell Watkins got himself off to. By rights he shoulda been at the meeting," Matt said with a small frown. "Worked out for the best, though, him not showing up this morning."

"Got that right. Braddock'd have him in a cell by now. That boy'd wring Watkins like a pair of wet socks." Earl shook his head. "Well . . . one thing about Watkins. He might be stupid but he was always lucky."

Thaddeus had set out early to find Watkins too. Knowing his habits in drink and women, Thad didn't bother to go to his rooms. He waited opposite the Fulton Ferry Terminal in Brooklyn. Thaddeus was there with time to spare, so he ducked under the awning of Ethier's Hotel. He sat for a while in the front parlor, drinking coffee and watching the street. As the traffic from the ferry grew with the day he finished his cup and walked to the corner opposite the terminal to wait by the Annex Cigar Factory. He stood with his coat folded over one arm, drinking in the smell of the leaf. It reminded him of the South.

The Captain recognized Watkins's slouching form before he picked out the face.

"Watkins!" he called a bit too urgently. "I'm glad I found you. Where in God's name have you been, man?"

"You tol' me to get lost, Cap'n," Watkins said defensively, holding up innocent hands.

"I didn't tell you to get so lost nobody could find you," Thaddeus said angrily. "Now listen, things have changed. You'd better come with me, I'll explain." The captain turned Watkins around, and they went back into the terminal. They stood in a corner, backs to the wall as he told Watkins the news.

"So, Braddock's on your trail now, that's certain," the captain said while watching the crowd. "If he catches up with you, he'll have your ass in a cell."

Watkins look was appropriately concerned. "So what're you sayin, I gotta skeedadle?" Watkins tried to keep the hopeful note out of his voice. This, he figured, might be his way out, but he couldn't appear too anxious to take it, not in front of the captain.

The captain just nodded. He seemed distracted. Watkins guessed it was just Braddock he was worried about.

"I've booked passage on the Old Dominion line for Richmond tomorrow. It leaves at three P.M., pier twenty-six, North River." Watkins looked at him, blank as a blackboard on a Monday morning. "Ya really mean it, don't ya, Cap'n?" The surprise was clear in his voice. He was glad now he hadn't turned traitor, though he'd come close. The captain was letting him off the hook, giving him a way out. He began to feel extra guilty for even considering going to Braddock.

"It's for the best, Private," Thaddeus said, throwing in his rank to remind him of his duty. "You'll be best off out of this city. Don't want to tangle with that cop, do you?"

"Hell, ah'd skin that bastard in two shakes, you let me." Watkins bared his teeth with a low snarl. He meant it too. He'd nearly turned traitor to save his own skin, not for any love of Braddock. The *Montauk* docked, and they boarded with the rest of the crowd. Neither looked up at the bridge.

The *Montauk* had just pulled in to the Brooklyn Ferry Terminal. Tom had noticed it as it left the terminal on the New York side. It had chugged by him as he crossed the span, its tall funnel belching black. It made good time, certainly faster than he could walk. The *Montauk* seemed to be nearly full despite the fact that the "rush hour" was long gone. By the time Tom reached the Brooklyn tower, the ferry had emptied. He stopped for a moment looking down at the crowd as they pushed on. With the terminal and docks right beside the bridge tower, on the downstream side, he was able to clearly see the press of carriages, people, and wagons.

But as Tom stopped for that moment in an idle sort of way to see the ferry board its passengers, he saw a tall lean form in the crowd. Thinking back on it later, it amazed him that he should have picked the man out among all those people. In fact, he really couldn't account for it. But like an insect under a microscope, Watkins appeared to Tom with crystal clarity. Braddock turned instantly, running down the span toward the approach, his stitches, which had been repaired the night before, pulling sharply at the sudden movement. But he hadn't gone more than three or four steps before he realized he'd never make it. It was nearly a quarter of a mile before he'd reach street level, then he'd have to double back to the terminal. He'd miss it for sure. But if he raced back to the New York side, he might have a chance. The *Montauk* was still two or three minutes from departure. That much lead time might be enough for him to catch it on the other side. So he turned and pounded back up the span, workers staring and pointing after him.

In his haste to beat the *Montauk,* Tom had started much too fast. Though he was in good shape, he was no runner. Within two hundred yards he knew he'd have to slow his pace. He was sucking great gulps of air and his lungs felt like the bellows at the blacksmith's shop in Kingston. The thought of Kingston settled him as he thought of the running he'd done as a boy, the ease of it, the long loping strides, the spring of his legs and the bottomless depth of his lungs. He was a boy no longer but he remembered what it was like. He ran on remembrance.

The captain steered Watkins toward a bench in the back of the boat. The crowd always shoved forward when the ferry docked. Thaddeus counted on that.

"Look on the bright side," he said, giving Watkins's arm a familiar squeeze. "You'll be going home, while the rest of us have to live here." He cast a hand about, waving at the city of the enemy. The ferry cast off and the side wheeler turned the river to foam as its captain gave it full throttle.

Watkins looked glum. "Yeah, but you're gonna get the glory when"—he glanced around at the passengers nearest them—"when the job's done."

Thaddeus took a deep breath. "Private, I swear to you, you'll be remembered for your sacrifice." He had meant to say something like "work" or "contribution" but "sacrifice" came out all on its own.

Watkins seemed pleased at that, though. After some minutes of silence, as he picked absently at his fingernails, he murmured, "Would be nice to see Richmond again. Last time I was there, it didn' look so good. Bet it's changed plenty since then."

Thaddeus nodded distractedly. "It has indeed. You'll hardly recognize it."

"Wonder if there's still them whorehouses down by the river? Ain't been whorin' with proper southern women in a dog's age," Watkins said wistfully. He was starting to look forward to this. A slow grin started to split his pocked face. "Reckon I might enjoy this trip some at that."

"That's the spirit," Thaddeus said, patting Watkins on the leg. He draped the arm with the coat over it on the back of their bench.

Tom had passed midspan and was halfway to the New York tower when he heard the *Montauk*'s whistle. A glance over his shoulder showed him the smoking iron monster churning the river in its wake as it left the dock. Tom still had a ways to go to reach street level all the way back by Park Row. He'd have to head south and double back to the ferry terminal, which on the New York side was four blocks south of the bridge. He started to doubt whether he'd make it until he thought of the stairs. A temporary spiral staircase had been erected on the north face of the New York tower. If he could reach that, he'd cut the distance in half. The problem was that he was on the south roadway. Tom swerved to his right and ducked through the trusses that enclosed the train tracks. In three steps he was across the tracks, sliding through the diagonal trusses on the other side. Suddenly he looked down and froze. A gaping, dizzying emptiness yawned under him. He grabbed for one of the cables as if it were a lifeline as one foot slipped from a beam and dangled over the river.

"Shit!" He was unable to pull his eyes from the gap below him.

Unlike the promenade, which ran above his head, there was no flooring here, just steel beams and endless drops between. Tom hesitated, glued to the spot. He thought of clambering up the truswork and over the promenade. It might be safer, but it would cost time he didn't have. Taking a shuddering breath, he set his foot firmly on the beam before him. He never had liked heights. The beam was about ten inches wide but seemed slender as a tightrope to him. The only thing he could think of was to do it fast and do it before he lost his nerve. Looking down made his head spin, so he focused on the other end of the beam and prayed this was not a huge mistake. His feet carried him across, shuffling and scraping little bits of debris off to fall to the river. With a trembling hand he grasped a suspending cable on the other side. It was only twelve feet, to the other side but it felt like twelve hundred. He slipped through the trusses on wobbly legs and headed for the spiral stairs. Tom hit them at a run, his hard shoes hammering on the echoing iron. He went as fast as he could, but after a few flights he had to slow. His head still hadn't recovered fully from the concussion, and the constant spiral had started his head spinning. He gripped the thin handrail hard to keep from falling over. Twice his feet slipped, sending his heart up into his throat. He slowed some more. The thought of a fall terrified him, but as he neared the bottom he sped up again, surer of himself and anxious to make up time. Tom bounded down the last steps, trying to hit the ground running, but his spinning head betrayed him. It sent him crashing into the granite of the tower. He went to his knees, momentarily stunned, but staggered up again, holding on to the rough stone. Shaking the dizziness out of his head he started off at a shuffling pace, fighting the urge to spiral to his left. Soon he was able to break into an exhausted run. His shirt on the left side was speckled red again. Looking off to his left at the *Montauk* as it approached the dock downriver, he knew it was going to be close. It was about three hundred yards out but slowing. He'd have to be fast.

The *Montauk* had cut its engines. The passengers started to press forward, leaving the two men almost alone in the back of the boat. Thaddeus knew the routine. The ferry would drift in at an alarming rate until the signal to reverse engines. A large bronze bell would sound and the engines would then be thrown into reverse. The bellowing of the steam engines and the thrashing of the side wheels as they churned the river was a thing to behold . . . and very loud. Thad put his arm, draped in his old overcoat, around the back of Watkins's shoulders. He bent close, lowering his voice.

"I'm going to miss you, Watkins." For an instant he faltered, doubting his will, his right to do this thing. The big bronze bell suddenly clanged three times. Thad jumped as if a spark had been put to him. He settled, saying "Good-bye, Watkins," almost tenderly, leaning close. The steam engines churned to life, their noise and fury sending a powerful shudder through the boat. They throbbed and bellowed; steam hissed. The gray waters churned a frothy green as the side wheels spun in reverse.

Tom pounded down South Street, dodging horses, wagons, stevedores, and pedestrians. He was tired and the difficulty of running in traffic exhausted him. Two blocks to go and he heard the whistle of the ferry as it docked. Desperate, Tom poured on a final sprint, running hard for the terminal's arched portal. A moment after he got there, winded, flushed, and sweating, the gate opened. Tom tried to catch his breath while he craned to see every passing face. Watkins was here, he knew, but it would be easy to lose him. Faces, forms, horses, wagons, and carriages blended, merged, and flowed. Tom loosened the Colt in his shoulder holster. Watkins was near. He could feel it.

In a minute or less, the crowd started to thin. Tom slowly worked his way through the stragglers as they left the boat. As he neared the *Montauk*, just a handful were left. Watkins wasn't one of them.

"Son of a bitch!" Tom spat. He dashed onto the boat, running down one side, checking every bench, every corner, all the time scanning ahead and behind. He went out the back doors, crossed over the wide vehicle deck, and burst through the doors to the passenger area on the other side. He stopped short, panting. Watkins sat on the last bench, his legs stretched out comfortably before him, his hat down low over his face. Tom grinned like a hungry wolf. He held the Colt low but ready as he padded over to the sleeping man. Watkins's head was slumped on his chest. One hand lay on his middle, the other hung loose at his side. Something about that hand bothered him. Watkins must be a heavy sleeper. Tom pointed the Colt at Watkins's middle as he kicked a foot. It flopped loosely to one side. He booted the foot again. Watkins didn't stir.

"C'mon, Watkins. No good playing possum. You and me gonna have a little talk," Tom said loudly. "Get up, man! I'm warning you. You do *not* want to make me mad!" Watkins still didn't budge. Watching the hands for sudden movement, Tom crouched low. He peered under the brim of Watkins's hat. The man's features were as still and smooth as the surface of a pond before a summer rain. It was then Tom saw them, two small strands of red, one from the nose and one from the corner of the mouth creasing the chin with crimson. They ran down into the collar of Watkins's shirt and spread out, merging into a widening red stain.

❄ Chapter Fourteen ❄

Stealing coal was a pretty good idea. Mike and Mouse and Smokes had managed to each get a bucket, and they marched off together like a junior fire brigade toward the coal yard in the back of the Talbott Manufacturing Company. At first they went to the front gate on Rivington to see if they could sneak in that way. They gave up the notion, though. Too many people went in and out of the place. And they stood a good chance of being seen by one of the other gangs. They might get away with it once, but they counted on having to make at least three trips to earn enough for the circus. Nosing around the borders of the coal yard, they found their way down a narrow alley behind the wooden fence that ran along one side. After a bit of searching, they found their spot, behind a pile of coal at least seven or eight feet high. With just a little effort, they pried up a loose board so one of them could slip through. They could get all they wanted without being seen. Smokes went through first. When he gave the signal, Mouse went through too. Mike handed in the buckets and stood guard. In no more than a minute, a blackened little hand poked through the fence with a brimming black bucket in its grip. Two minutes later, all three were lugging their buckets down the alley. A quick check at the street for any cops or coal yard workers and they were gone.

At first they tried selling on the street. They sat on a stoop, the three of them taking turns yelling, "Coal for sale!" That didn't work as well as they had hoped. Most people didn't carry buckets around with them, and they couldn't sell theirs. This was something they hadn't counted on. After only two sales of a few lumps, Smokes was getting restless. "We gotta do somethin' different. Gonna take a year like this."

They kicked around their problem for a while. Mike suggested they sell it door to door. The lack of something to carry the coal was what was holding them back, he reasoned, so why not bring the coal to the customer, just like the iceman brought his ice?

"I don't know. Sounds like a lot of work, draggin' buckets upstairs, and all," said Smokes.

"Well, I'll try anything," Mouse said. "Two more minutes of this shit an' I'm done with the whole thing."

The idea worked like a charm. It didn't take more than fifteen minutes in just one building and their buckets were empty.

"Wow, that was great!" Smokes exclaimed. "We even got a little more than we figured."

Mouse was suddenly enthusiastic too. "Ya wanna go back fer some more, fellas?"

Smokes was more in favor of savoring their riches first. "I say we go to Browers an' get some candy. Who's wit' me?"

Mike liked the sound of that. "We could get some of them long hard, twisty candies. I love those." So they walked to Browers, arguing which was better, licorice, hard candy, toffees, or chocolate. It ended up two to one for hard candy. Later, sitting on the curb in front of the store, they licked the last of their treats from coal-blackened fingers.

"Yeuch! That last little bit tasted like coal," Mike said, his mouth twisted up in disgust.

"Yeah, mine too, but most of it was . . . real good," Mouse said in between licking his fingers. "So, what do we do now? Go back for more?"

The second trip went much as the first. By the end of the second load, they were black to the elbows. Sweaty black streaks and smudges painted their faces, anthracite Indians in black war paint. But they had money in their pockets and a new found ambition, so they went back again.

Perhaps success made them careless. Maybe they were unlucky. Whichever it was, the third coal run didn't go quite as smoothly. They had loaded their buckets as they had before. Nobody saw them slipping in or out of the fence. A day at the circus, with all the excitement of dancing bears, giant packyderms, clowns, and lion tamers was just in sight. But as they rounded the corner of the alley onto Rivington Street, a big blue arm reached out and grabbed Mike. Mike jumped, dropping his bucket, the coal spilling at his feet. Mouse and Smokes, just behind him, were brought up short. Mouse stopped so quick, Smokes bounced off him.

"So, it's stealing coal you are, eh?" It sounded like Harlan the cop.

Mouse and Smokes started to back up as the big blue arm grabbed Mike by the scruff of the neck and yanked him from view. Mike's bucket lay on its side, the coal fanning out, black as their luck. Smokes's bucket knocked against the fence, sounding loud as a cannon in the narrow alley.

"Who's down there? Come outta there, whoever you be. Don't make me come in after ye."

They turned and ran as fast as their buckets would allow. Coal sprayed this way and that like big black hail.

"Run if you like, boys. Your friend 'ere is gonna tell me all I need to know," the cop called confidently.

They kept running, tossing the buckets aside for greater speed. Mouse thought he heard Mike cry out. It had a hurt sound to it—at least from down the alley and around a corner.

The raised voice of the cop followed them:

"I'll be comin' for you, boys. Ya can't hide from Harlan."

The boys from the coroner's office were just about to put Watkins on a stretcher. It had been nearly two hours since Braddock found him, and the captain of the *Montauk* was in a sour mood for having been held up for so long. The dumpy little man with a rumpled captain's hat and faded gold braid on his sleeve paced the deck mumbling about schedules and dithering cops. Tom and Sam paid him little mind. A couple hours of fruitless investigation had left them in no better mood. The body had been picked clean. If Tom hadn't already known who Watkins was, he'd have had a tough time finding out.

"Someone's going to great lengths to cover his tracks," Tom said with a wry scowl. "Every time I turn around there's another dead end."

He looked toward the other end of the boat and saw Coffin heading their way.

"Well, well, Detective Braddock. I should have guessed. Seems that your friend here, Sam, is the police equivalent of a week of rain."

Sam gave Coffin a perplexed frown. "Oh ... and how's that, Captain?" Sam asked, the slight sarcasm seeming to slide right by Coffin. "I'm not following you."

Coffin didn't look at Sam when he answered. His eyes bored into Braddock instead. "Because bodies seem to sprout like mushrooms wherever he goes," Coffin said as if it were a joke.

They knew there was no fun in it, though.

"Hmph." Sam snorted.

"There's some that say an officer much like our Detective Braddock was seen yesterday when those Plug Uglies were killed," Coffin said offhandedly, but both Sam and Tom knew there was nothing offhanded about it.

Tom noticed August's quick glance at the bloody spots on his shirt that his jacket didn't hide. Tom couldn't help the sudden drop of his jaw. Still, he said nothing.

Sam wasn't so circumspect. "Killed, you say? And where'd this happen?" Coffin looked at Sam disapprovingly. "I see you haven't read this morning's papers, gentlemen. You know I can't stress enough the importance of our police being well informed on the goings-on in this city. You should be reading the papers, Sergeant. It's a duty not to be taken lightly."

Sam rolled his eyes. He hated it when Coffin got preachy. "Right, sir. I'll do that." He smirked. "Just happened to miss it this morning. So, where did they find these bodies then?"

"Gotham Court. An appropriate place for finding bodies, I'm sure." Coffin sniffed.

Tom couldn't contain himself any longer. "How'd they die, Augie?"

Coffin treated Tom to one of his patented stares. He hated being called Augie, especially in front of his men. He cleared his throat. "Throats were cut."

"Jesus H. Christ!" Sam exclaimed. He whistled and rolled his eyes at Tom when Coffin wasn't looking. "Now, who the hell could do a thing like that? You don't just sneak up on four men and cut their throats."

"Quite. Perhaps whoever did it asked their permission." Coffin gave a wry chuckle. "Or perhaps they cut their own throats. The odd thing is that police were reportedly seen leaving the scene before the bodies were found. Quite a crowd you know. Nearly a riot, from what I heard. Some described a cop quite like you, Tommy." Coffin emphasized the name. "I'm sure they're wrong." His dismissive tone wasn't meant to fool either of them. "That's not your style, is it, old man? More of a bone breaker, right?"

Tom didn't answer. Instead he said, "It didn't come up at morning parade. When'd you find out?"

"Papers got it first, apparently. Went out on the telegraph to the precincts late this morning. That's Coogan's problem, always a bit slow on follow-through. Not quite so much attention to detail as he should have."

The implication wasn't lost on Tom.

The coroner's team picked up Watkins's body and it was carried out without a word.

"Grisly business," Coffin said.

Tom and Sam just looked at Coffin, saying nothing.

"Like to have a word if I can, Captain," Tom said as they started off the boat.

"Certainly, Tom, let's walk," Coffin replied affably enough.

"I'll come by tomorrow to pay you what I owe." Tom took a deep breath of fresh salt air. "Get my obligations settled, make a clean break." He exhaled. Coffin didn't say a word. "Said I'd pay you. No point stringing it out." He looked to Coffin for any reaction.

"That's fine" was all Coffin said.

"That's not what I wanted to talk to you about, though," Tom continued.

"Oh?" Coffin asked innocently. He knew damn well why Tom wanted to have this little conversation. Tom was feeling the pinch, just as he'd planned. The question was whether the pinch hurt enough just yet. Coffin figured Braddock's pain threshold was a bit higher. It was too soon for him to give in, to his way of thinking. Tom was too proud, too stiff-necked to knuckle under so soon.

"No, it's not. It's Coogan," Tom said, pausing to gauge any reaction. There was none, so he went on. "You know he's pulled some of my guys and I'd like it to stop . . . well, at least I'd like notice like before. I think I'm due the courtesy."

"Are you?" Coffin stopped in his tracks to stare at Tom—a long, skeptical look full of feigned surprise. "Tom, we are charged with upholding the laws and preserving the peace of this great city. It's a heavy responsibility which we, you and I and every officer of the law, are sworn to carry out."

Tom had to bite his lip. Being lectured to by the likes of Coffin was almost more than he could bear.

"You know as well as I, Tommy, that arrests must be made. Those who break the laws are subject to arrest at any time. You also know that in the current climate, it is politically imperative, shall we say, to show that we in the department are tough on crime." Coffin slapped a theatrical fist into his palm. "Now, if some of your little fish happen to get caught up in that, well that's a shame, but they are, after all, criminals, Tom. Times like these we all feel the pinch." Coffin's facility with lies never ceased to amaze Tom. When he thought that Augie could be nothing but straight with the facts, the man would blandly tell him that the moon was made of blue cheese.

"August," Tom said, "why do you have to feed me this horseshit? I know how things run. I know we're going to have to take a pinch now and again. This is looking like a lot more than that."

Coffin glared at Braddock, his fists clenched at his sides. "This *horseshit*, as you put it, is the reality of *your* situation, Detective. In your circumstances, it's something you're going to have to live with."

Tom thought about the implications of what Coffin was saying. Things were *not* going to get any better. In fact, they'd get worse. The bastard was going to try to put him out of business, and he could do it too. That was the stick. Tom waited for the carrot.

"Of course, if you were on the inside, things like this could be avoided. You would be due a certain additional consideration, similar to what you enjoyed in the past. It might even be that additional rewards could be forthcoming."

"So, that's the carrot, eh, Augie?" Tom said.

Coffin sighed. "You have such a need for unambiguous speech, Tommy. But in fact that is the carrot, as you so aptly put it. We can do a great deal together," he said, thinking longingly of his plans. "As long as you continue to be stubborn, you'll have to do without the . . . advantages of our association."

Tom walked on in silence. He was tempted to go back. Somehow he hadn't believed that Coffin would squeeze him this way. He kicked himself for not realizing the lengths that Coffin would go to, to hold his little empire together. Coffin could hurt him. Even if he knew only half of the places Tom took protection money from, the other half would learn soon enough. The thought of all the money he stood to lose was staggering. He took in more than twice his salary in protection money every month. Coffin could virtually eliminate that if he closed down those bars, brothels, fences, and rackets long enough. Even though some of that money funneled up to Coffin through Tom's kickbacks at the precinct level, Coffin could afford it. What effect it might have on Tom's future with Mary he could only guess. Being a poor cop had not been his plan. He wondered if marrying one was Mary's. Tom wished he either had less scruples or more greed. It would hurt a lot less either way.

"Can't do it, August," he said almost reluctantly. Coffin didn't say a word, and Tom couldn't bring himself to say more. Those four words were hard enough, considering what it was costing him. "You knew what I'd say, didn't you? You really thought I'd say something different?"

"I'd hoped you might see the sense of it, Tom." Coffin exhaled slowly, almost in resignation. "I'm offering quite a lot, you know. It could go very easy if you let it." Coffin's tone was almost melancholy. Tom was reminded not of how easy it might be but of how hard it would be. There was a threat behind Coffin's sad refrain.

Tom briefly considered a threat of his own, one not so veiled with regret. He thought to throw Coffin up against a wall and tell him exactly what he'd do to him if he had any more trouble. He wanted to kick him in the balls, leave him gasping on his knees in the street. But he did none of that. It would only make things worse. Coffin had the power of rank and connections and his corps behind him. Tom couldn't hope to prevail against that kind of power. It was going to take more than threats. There had to be some way to get Coffin off his back, but he had to have time to figure it.

"I'll bring you the rest of your money tomorrow, August." Tom had cleaned out his account at the Dry Dock and borrowed some from Mary to make up the difference. It didn't feel good to be broke. Tom turned, walking away quickly, pounding the pavement for blocks before he blew off enough steam to think of anything else. With an effort he turned his mind to Watkins, deciding to check out that address on Cherry Street again. This time he went without backup. It was a risk but being in plain clothes had its advantages.

Justice Lincoln and Patrick Sullivan straddled the main cable on the south side of the bridge as they ate lunch.

"You notice the ferry stopped?" Lincoln pointed down at the *Montauk*.

"Yeah. Bet that's got folks hopping. Everybody's in such a damn hurry in this town. Never have gotten used to it." Pat looked down at the ferry, which seemed to be about to leave the dock.

"Bet they can't wait till this bridge is done."

"Damn, but there's gonna be a lot of disappointed folks in this city." They laughed, feeling like gods sharing a joke at the expense of the unsuspecting ants below. Silently they ate their sandwiches, drank their beer, and dangled their feet on either side of the cable.

"You recall when Harry Supple died?" Pat brought up something they hadn't spoken of in some time. All the riggers knew Harry Supple, the most famous rigger of them all. His reputation had only grown with the years, and to some in the cables his memory had taken on an almost mythic status.

"Sure. What made you think of that?"

"Don't know." Pat shrugged. "Just thinking about all the men gone . . . you know, building this thing."

"Plenty. Must be twenty at least." Lincoln's brow furrowed in thought. "Don't know how many are cripples from the caisson disease too. There's Roebling for one."

Pat snorted. "Yeah, well, I don't give a rat's ass for Roebling, but there's some good men under the ground 'cause of this bridge. Supple was the best of 'em."

"Had balls of brass. Nobody was as sure of himself in the cables as Harry.

Remember when he went out hand over hand to cut that fella loose?" Justice swallowed a gulp of beer.

"Sure . . . what the hell was his name?"

"Carroll, I think. Big fella."

"Yeah, that's him. Got himself hung up cutting the lashings on the second wire. Rig on his boatswain's chair jammed."

"Couldn't go back, nor forward . . . dangling a hundred feet out from the tower," Justice added. "Yup . . . Harry just swung out like a damn monkey, cut Carroll free . . . cool as you please." They smiled at the memory.

The *World*, in its headline the next day, called it a "Stupendous Tight-Rope Performance." Supple seemed to have as many lives as a cat. He had survived the collapse of a boom derrick during the construction of the Brooklyn tower. Men around him had been crushed or thrown from the tower.

"Gotta admit, Harry had sand," Jus muttered. "Course, didn't get to know him till a little later, but I remember watching him that first day. Remember the cheerin'? Hell, I cheered too and I ain't ashamed to admit it."

Pat smiled. It had been a great day. "Shame the way he went, though. Least it was quick."

Harry Supple died spectacularly, as befits a legend. It was June 14, 1878, and Farrington, Supple, a man named Blake, and two others were easing off one of the strands. Each strand was composed of 278 wires and was strung above the level of the main cable and then lowered, or "eased," into place. Farrington ordered the engine to lower the strand, when suddenly the cable attached to the engine snapped. The strand and its cast-iron shoe crashed into Supple, tearing open his chest and throwing him off the anchorage to the street below, breaking his back, arms, and legs. Incredibly, Supple clung to life for nearly another day, though he never regained consciousness. Blake was killed instantly and the other two men were badly injured. Farrington had only a scratch on his hand.

You know, Jus, I wonder about Harry sometimes. I mean, if anybody was sure to live through the wire rigging it was him. That man was born in a tree, I swear," Pat marveled. "Wasn't none of us could keep up with him."

"Damn near killed myself trying," said Justice. "Gave it up. Couldn't out-supple old Harry."

"Yeah, but he's the one that's gone. Don't make sense." Pat looked out over the harbor toward Staten Island. "I mean here we are, planning to do . . . well, you know, and we're still breathing, whilst a good man like Harry is in the ground. Makes you wonder about things."

Justice could see now where Pat was heading with this. He kept silent, listening.

"Like God's will, sort of. You know what I'm saying?" Pat asked.

"Well, I don't claim to know about those things, Pat. Any notions I had on them subjects got bleached out by the war, I guess. Tried to see some sense in it back then . . . but I gave up trying." Jus was silent for a moment, then said, "Want a pickle? I got an extra."

Pat took it. For the next minute all that passed between them was the crunching of the big dills.

"I know what you mean," Pat said at last. "I used to lie awake nights, wondering why I was still alive. Like the captain and his brother. Why was Frank the one to go like that? Thaddeus always said Frank was the better of them. But there he was, his guts spilled out and the captain couldn't catch a ball if he'd a-paid for it."

They both sat thinking, watching the river traffic.

"I don't know, Jus, maybe the Lord's been saving us for this. Maybe all our lives have meant to lead us here. Ever think about that? What if this is the only real thing we been put on this earth to do?"

Justice had been thinking the same thing, especially lately. It wasn't something he talked about, not even with Pat. He wasn't sure just how far he should go, so he answered warily. "Thought . . . occurred to me." "Reckon if that's so, then there ain't much I can do about it. God's gonna do with me what he will, I guess." It felt better to think that way.

"But we got a will of our own, Justice. God gave us that too." Pat looked straight down toward the river, something he didn't do much of. "I could jump off this cable right now, and God can't stop me."

"Yeah," Jus admitted slowly "but it was God's will, put you here," he pointed out. "You gonna go against God?"

That sort of talk got under Sullivan's collar. "How the hell you know what God wants? How can anybody? That's just a blind so's you don't have to think the hard things for yourself." The exasperation was clear in Pat's voice. His tone didn't seem to bother Jus. He had always been more of a believer than Pat, more willing to let his faith do the thinking for him.

"Don't take a crystal ball, Pat. Gotta see inside yourself . . . like. It's like God's in your head sometimes and all you gotta do is look for him," Jus said softly. He'd been looking more himself lately.

"What if I do and he tells me things I don't want to hear, Jus? Suppose he says what I'm doing is wrong?" Pat said, voicing both their fears.

"Can't decide such things for you, nor you for me," Jus answered. "I think that if a man goes searching for the Lord's truth, he'll find it. I mean . . . if it's inside his own self . . . or out there somewheres"—he waved vaguely out at the river and harbor below them—"if you look for God, you'll find him."

They both sat there for a while, Patrick munching a pickle and Justice nursing the last of his warm beer. Pat wasn't so sure about finding God's will. To know the will of God would be to know certainty, like knowing the winning numbers in the Kentucky lottery before you bought a policy. He just didn't believe things were that certain.

"We doing God's will, you figure?" Pat asked, hoping for . . . what? he asked himself. He felt as if he were groping in the dark.

"Fact is, I don't know. I think so . . . but." Jus veered off to a familiar refrain, the anchor they all clung to. "We got a score to settle with Roebling. I know that much. The captain's got a debt too. Makes me see red sometimes, when I think what the Yankees done to us."

"I know. I used to feel that way a lot," Patrick said, seeing into himself. Those feelings had been slowly fading for years. "Takes longer to get there now, like I got to try to bring it out."

Justice knew exactly what Pat was getting at. It scared him though to let go. "We got our oaths, Patrick. We all swore to do this thing."

Pat could hear the warning in his voice. "I know. I swore too . . . but it's hard. Things aren't as clear . . . now." Pat was trying to make it clear for himself and Lincoln too. "This job—the bridge, I mean—guess I didn't expect to like it so much. Didn't expect to lose my hate neither."

"I don't hate like I done in bygone years," Jus admitted. "But that don't mean I don't know what it feels like, nor why I'm here." Lincoln sounded as if he were trying to convince himself.

"Reckon. Be honest with me now, Jus. Aren't you going to feel just a little bad to see her go down?" Pat slapped the cable he sat on, then slapped it again, softer this time, almost a caress. "It'll be like losing a piece of myself."

Justice was quite for a long time, so long that Pat almost wondered if he'd heard him.

Finally Justice turned, his battered face wearing a sadness Pat had rarely seen.

"I don't like to think about that," Jus said, his eyes saying more than his words. Here was the one thing that stood in the way, the thing that was in danger of cutting across faith and mission and vengeance: the bridge itself. Its hold on him had grown to the point where he could not speak of it with the others, hardly even with Pat. But he had just then, in more than words. The horse was out of the barn now. Jus waited to hear what Pat would do with it.

"Me neither, Jus" was all Pat said. It was enough.

"Funny. After blowing all them bridges in the war, it's kind of odd getting attached to one," Justice mused with a softness in his voice that he didn't mean to be there. It crept in anyway. Finally he decided to voice something he had only thought before. "Listen, I never said this to nobody, Pat, and you got to promise me that you won't tell . . . the others." Jus twisted back toward Pat.

"Sure. It's just us talking," Patrick said with a shrug.

"Well . . . sometimes, like times when we're up in the cables and the sun is just right, I swear I see the Lord's work here. And . . . damned if I don't feel proud. Shit, Patrick, I ain't never felt like I was doing the Lord's work—never except maybe at the start of the war." The strain was clear in his voice. "That's why I try to see what we're doing here in the right light . . . see my duty." He squinted back at Sullivan, the conflict clear in his face.

Sullivan knew the feeling, but had been scared to even think it in light of what they'd all sworn to do. Still, he confessed.

"I know, Jus. It's as close to a thing of beauty as these hands ever made." Pat held his hands up as if looking at them for the first time. Justice grunted his agreement. Patrick mumbled, half to himself, half to the winds in the cables, "This will be a trial for us all."

Mike wasn't going to cry. He sat in a small cell in the basement of 178 Delancey Street. The Thirteenth Precinct station house was old. It still stood much as it had in the 1840s when it was first built. The cell Mike was in was windowless. The stone walls were cold. Water beaded and dripped on their irregular surfaces. The iron bars of his cell were damp too. Rust blossomed on the old iron like fungus. When he put his hands on them, they came away brown. The homeless the city sheltered in police stations every night had gone their way at first light. There had been maybe a dozen of them, all ages and sizes. But they had left. Their doors weren't locked. For the first time, Mike envied them.

There was a cot and a small washstand, with a metal bowl and pitcher. The water in the pitcher smelled funny, so Mike didn't drink it. He did use some to wash the blood off though. Harlan the cop had not been easy on him. The backs of his legs were so sore he could hardly sit. Long welts from the cop's nightstick ran across them in hot, angry streaks. Harlan had whacked him all the way to the station house. It hadn't helped that he wouldn't rat on his friends. Harlan seemed to have no respect for Mike's silence. Each time he got no answer to his questions, he whacked a little harder. His butt had taken a few too, and he felt like he'd been kicked by a mule. His "accident" on the stairs hadn't helped either. He'd taken no more than two uncertain steps down, the musty putrid air pushing back at him, when a shove came from behind, and he was launched into space. The next thing he knew he was in a cell, on a cot ... alone. Bedbugs already crawled in his hair and on his clothes. A swipe at his sore head left his hand streaked with crusty brownish blood. The funny-smelling water stung when he washed the cut by his hairline. He whimpered a bit but it wasn't the bruises and cuts that hurt most. He'd had his share of fights on the street. He'd taken his share of lumps. When his ma and sis died, he'd tried to be strong for his da. But at least then his da was there, and he had someone to be strong for. He was alone now. Though he loved his grandma and gramps, they were not his da. In the gloom of his small, damp cell, he felt the loss down to his bones. It hurt in a way no physical pain could.

The only thing Mike could think, when they asked him whom to contact, was "Detective Braddock."

The desk sergeant had looked at him with a raised eyebrow, and asked, "Detective Braddock, you say? And what would your relations be with him?"

Mike didn't want to explain how he came to know Braddock nor that he knew him barely at all. All he could think to say was "He knew my father." He wouldn't say more.

"The nerve of this kid, eh, Theron?" said Harlan. "Wants us to think 'e's got big connections. Well, we'll see about your friend Mr. Braddock, but for now you'll be spending some time as our guest. And ... if by and by we find out you've been tellin' tales about this detective, it'll go that much harder for you. Come along, boy."

Mike figured that maybe his naming of Braddock had earned him his "accident" on the stairs.

Mike sat with his head in his hands. He thought of the coins he had put in a small pile on the sergeant's desk. Would he ever see those nickels and dimes again? He thought about Mouse and Smokes. If he knew them, they were staying away from home, watching for cops from down the block. He wondered if they'd go to the circus. He mourned the circus already. There was no way he'd get there now. Bragging to the other boys in the neighborhood had been something he had relished in advance. But there would be no bragging, no Jumbo the giant packy-derm, no nothing. He'd be lucky not to be sent to the Juvenile House of Detention. Even if he got off, his grandma would punish him forever. The future did not look bright from the basement of the Thirteenth.

Mike thought about his da too. Small rivulets ran down his cheeks, carving lines through the coal dust and dried blood. He tried to cry quietly. He didn't want to give Harlan the satisfaction, but his chest heaved and his throat felt chokey. As he cried, he suddenly thought of the black-faced man by the outhouse. He hadn't thought about that for days, but now it wormed its way back to the surface of his mind. Even though he was in a police precinct house, he knew it would be useless now to tell anyone. They'd just see it as a wild story, a kid's way of trying to get off lightly. They'd laugh at him. Maybe they'd do worse than push him down the stairs. Some of the older boys from the neighborhood had to go to the hospital after a visit to the Thirteenth. Besides, even Braddock's name had been met with sneers. This wasn't the time to tell what he knew about men behind outhouses. He'd have to wait. Maybe if the detective came, he'd see if he could tell him. Right now, though, that was not at the top of his list of worries.

After his talk with Coffin and a predictably unproductive and uneventful visit to Gotham Court, Tom had gone back to get Sam and a roundsman who happened to be with him.

"Nobody ever heard of Watkins in Gotham Court," Tom told Sam as they marched to the bridge. "Fuckin' dead end. No record of him ever being there, far as I can tell."

Sam shook his head. "Smells bad. You figure someone set you up or just sent you where you'd be likely to find trouble?"

Tom shrugged. Either way it stunk. The three of them went back to the bridge approach and brought Matt Emmons and Earl Lebeau in for questioning. Tom was certain they hadn't killed Watkins themselves. That would have been impossible. But it was equally improbable that these two knew nothing of who might have done it. They had to know what was going on. But two hours of grilling didn't reveal a damn thing. In fact, their stories were too tight. It was rare to get the same story from different people. In his experience it was more common to get differing accounts from witnesses to the same event, let alone the same relationship. But Matt and Earl's accounts left hardly enough room to pass a knife between them. It could mean nothing, or it could mean a great deal. There was no way to know.

One thing that was significant in his eyes was that they both seemed surprised by the news of Watkins's death. They were hostile at first, thinking maybe that Tom had killed him. But when they were told of how Watkins was found shot in the back of the head, they couldn't hide their shock. From that point on though, nothing seemed to fluster either of them. Most people brought in for questioning showed some raw nerves, sweaty palms, dry throats. Even the innocent ones had a right to be nervous. With the exception of some fidgeting, they were both as cool as lemonade on a hot afternoon. They didn't appear to hold anything back. It was just the same story in different voices, of their years together serving the Confederacy, the drifting back to their homes after the war, the despair at finding little to go back to and the eventual journey north. The three of them had been working on the bridge on and off since 1870. They liked the work, they said. They had to, to stay on that long, Tom figured. "Any other boys from your unit come up here with you?" he asked both of them. He got virtually the same answer: Just the three of them. Tom didn't think much of it. One thing he thought a little odd was that none of the three had married. Of course, neither had he, but he didn't consider that. What he did consider was that the odds of three young men coming north, living and working here for thirteen years, without at least one of them finding a wife were pretty long.

Something was sure as hell going on. Two men were dead. There had been an attempt on his life. Though it could have been just bad luck to meet up with those four at Gotham Court, Tom didn't believe luck had much to do with it. There was a connection to these men from the South, but what that was, he couldn't establish . . . not yet. Tom figured to take a different road with them. The War Department might have their records, and Tom hoped there'd be something in them to give him a clue. So much was lost in the closing days of the war, especially in the frantic retreat from Petersburg and Richmond. But if records existed, the War Department would have them or at least know where else he might look. Tom didn't know what he was looking for, but he had to start somewhere. He sat at his desk once they'd released Emmons and Lebeau. With his feet up and hands behind his head, he stared off into space, trying to make the pieces fit. He reached absently into his pocket fingering the little key. Taking it out, he turned it over in his hand, examining it for the hundredth time. He frowned. Trouble was he was missing half the puzzle . . . at least.

Braddock! Detective, I need a word with you in my office."

Tom was startled for a second, but tried not to show it. He knew what Byrnes had on his mind. In a way he was surprised the chief hadn't summoned him sooner. Tom closed Byrnes's door behind him, knowing this would be a closed-door talk.

"Yes, sir?"

"Tell me about Gotham Court, Detective." Byrnes stood with his back to Tom. He looked out the windows behind his desk and appeared to be watching the ebbing activity on Mulberry Street as the day faded into night. Tom could see the light of his eyes though. They watched him in the glass of the dirty windows. His cigar glowed like a little furnace in the dim light of the office.

"I heard about the Plug Uglies, sir. Maybe I should start off by saying that they were alive when I left them, though none too healthy."

Byrnes grunted and let the smoke drift from his mouth as he spoke. Tom had the odd thought that Byrnes was on fire inside, like a potbelly stove.

"If I believed otherwise, Thomas, we'd be having a very different sort of conversation."

"Yes, sir, I suppose we would. Well, first off . . . I was at Gotham Court to apprehend a suspect in the Bucklin murder. Name of Watkins."

That brought Byrnes around, his cigar poised, ash drooping. "Watkins, you say? Isn't that the man you pursued this morning and found shot on the ferry?"

"The same," Tom said evenly, a slight grin on his face. He knew what Byrnes's reaction would be.

"Interesting." Byrnes looked pointedly at Tom. "Go on."

Braddock proceeded to fill Byrnes in on the Bucklin case. The chief seemed fascinated. His cigar ash dropped to the floor unnoticed. By the time Tom finished his report, the cigar had nearly gone out and Byrnes puffed on it in haste, making little sucking pops with his lips as he tried to get it going again.

"So, you have two men dead . . . executed, to be precise. You have an apparent attempt on your life, and you have a man's word that his son was afraid of something in connection with the bridge. It would seem, as well, that these former Confederates are involved. Whether that's just coincidence or part of the bigger picture, we don't know." Byrnes pointed his cigar butt at Tom with raised eyebrows.

"That about sums it up, sir. And that dance hall girl, the one who was supposedly Watkins's alibi. She just plain disappeared. I telegraphed all the precincts to keep a watch for her, but she hasn't been seen." Tom was having the increasing feeling she wouldn't be seen by anyone . . . ever. "As for Emmons and Lebeau, I was just writing to the War Department to try to retrieve their service records. Don't know what I'll find but . . . worth a try. Lots of men served the Confederacy. I'm not sure that means anything."

"Good, get a warrant, search their places. I want those two to feel the pressure. Might turn something up."

"Already done. It occurs to me too, sir—" Tom paused, then went on with his idea. "Well . . . that it might pay to investigate records, look for contractors who may be dissatisfied, workers who've been laid off under unusual circumstances, that sort of thing. I'll need some help though." He was doing his best to lead Byrnes to water.

"Of course, Thomas. I'll assign Dolan and Heidelberg to you. Assist you in any way you see fit. Probably nothing more than your garden-variety fraud case"—Byrnes puffed—"but those two will be a big help in digging through records. They've done that sort of investigating before, had some success, so they'll come in handy."

Tom couldn't suppress a smile. "Very good, sir." He was amazed it had gone so easily. Dolan and Heidelberg were old-timers and one of the best detective teams in the city.

Byrnes turned to look out the window again, puffing and thoughtful. He said to the glass, "You suppose the four who attacked you at Gotham Court were killed because they failed?"

"Can't ignore the possibility," Tom said. "The attack could have been random. Down there it's always a risk, but if it was planned, and that's the way I'm leaning, then could be you're right."

"That makes six men dead because of this and maybe a woman as well. Someone's awful anxious to keep their activities quiet," Byrnes said almost to himself, obviously deep in thought.

"Yes, sir, quiet as the grave."

They wrapped up, and Tom promised to report developments to Byrnes at least every other day. He was about to leave when Byrnes said, "I expect you to get backup, if needed, from the precinct whose boundaries you're within, Thomas. Can you tell me why that didn't happen yesterday?"

Tom hesitated. Byrnes, who was watching him closely, broke in, saying "No. Don't tell me. You've not resolved your differences with Coogan, right? You didn't trust him to back you, so you rounded up someone you could count on."

Byrnes nodded thoughtfully. "Better to keep still, I suppose. Wise man, Tom. I told you to get your misunderstandings behind you. You see now how these things ripple through the system?"

Braddock gave an almost audible sigh. "Yes, sir, I suppose I do."

"Mmm. This appears to be a dangerous investigation you're into, Thomas. If you could have a man, a roundsman, say, to watch your back, who would it be?"

Tom knew plenty of good stout men who he'd be glad to have in a tight spot, and it looked like Byrnes was letting him have his pick. But almost before he realized what he was doing, he said, "Jaffey, sir." Tom winced once he'd said the name, mentally kicking himself for speaking too quickly.

"Really?" Byrnes turned to stare at Tom, the surprise clear on his face. "Don't know him. A rookie, right? Why?"

Tom wished he had a real good answer to that, but he'd opened his mouth and he wasn't going back on it, not in front of Byrnes. "Call it a feeling, sir. Jaffey's new but he shows promise. Unlike some of the more experienced men, he'll listen and take orders. He also behaved very well in our fracas at Gotham Court. Saved my skin, is more like it. So—"

"I don't know, Tom. I've never met your man Jaffey, but I would hesitate to have a new man behind me on a case like this. He's only been on the force a short time I take it?"

Tom shrugged. "Six months, give or take."

Byrnes took a last pull at the stub of his cigar, then crushed it in the ashtray on his desk. "Well, that's a decision I can't make for you. I suppose you know best who you'd like to watch your back. Sometimes it's best to go with your instincts, even if it doesn't seem quite right at the time." Byrnes hesitated an instant before saying somewhat reluctantly "I'll request Jaffey's detachment to you for the duration of the case."

Tom went back to his desk, hoping he'd made the right decision. He got back to his unfinished letter and read it through once more to get his train of thought back. He decided to add that he was interested in the records of all the men in the regiment, especially their company, date of enlistment, deaths, date of discharge, and parole. He figured he'd get Byrnes to sign it too. It might get a little quicker response coming from him.

"May as well cast a wide net," Tom muttered. "You never know what you might catch."

Mary let herself in. Her key was pretty new, and it caught in the lock. For a moment she thought it wouldn't turn, but a jiggle and a twist did the trick. Grant and Lee waited like library lions at the end of the hall, eyes bright and ears pricked forward.

"Well, hello, you two," she said sweetly. "You going to sit there, or do I get a proper greeting?" They slowly got up and meandered toward her, dignified and aloof. "That's a fine welcome. I don't suppose I ought to give you the chicken scraps I have in this bag." She held it up as if they'd know what she was talking about. "I'm not at all sure you deserve them." Grant rubbed her leg, arching his back and rubbing his ear on her calf. "That's more like it, soldier. You always were a ladies man, just like your master. You may just earn a treat, after all." Mary fed the cats her scraps. They jostled each other to get their heads into the bowl, and Lee bit at Grant when he got too rough. "You show him who's boss, Lee. Got to keep your man in line. They need to be shown their place every so often, and it's up to us ladies to show it to them." A smile stole across Mary's face.

She went into the bedroom and started to unpack a few things from the small bag she carried. As she did, she began to imagine herself unpacking all her things some day. It hadn't been that long ago when thoughts like that were beyond her imagination. She was a whore and a madame. Marriage had no part in either of those occupations. Over the years she had built her walls high, the better to protect her heart . . . and her dreams. It had taken discipline to deny herself what she wanted most. She had denied herself but not her dreams. Those dreams were modest, really. She didn't want the fancy Fifth Avenue mansion, like Madame Restell. She did not crave fame or harbor ambitions for the stage. She liked money and the things it would buy, but she didn't dream of having more of it than would keep her comfortably. Her ambitions were much more commonplace and ordinary than most would have imagined. The love of a good, honest man was at the core of it. He wouldn't care what she did for money. He'd be able to see beyond that, and he would love her for herself. They would reveal themselves to each other in the quiet hours and share life's joys and sorrows. There would be children and the miracle of birth would be her miracle. They would build a family.

Ordinary dreams. But they called for an extraordinary man. Thinking back, she supposed she knew that the first day when she saw him on her doorstep, ready to arrest her. He hadn't lusted like the other men, though the lust was there. He hadn't ogled her body, though it was there for the ogling. He had looked her in the eye, as if trying to see the person behind the madame. Though they hadn't said much to each other, there were volumes sent and received.

She was loosing the reins on her dreams now. It was dangerous, she knew. She risked everything when she risked her heart. She had suffered many a cut to that vital organ over the years, and there wasn't much left unscarred. What there was she was willing to give to Tom. He knew what she gave. And he knew in his awkward way what a delicate gift it was. Mary smiled to herself as she started a bath. She had another gift in mind when Tom got home.

Matt and Earl had split up when they left police headquarters. For the next half hour, they watched their backs for detectives, doubling back, stopping to watch the street in store windows, and popping into shops to check for anyone following. Neither was followed. They met up again at Paddy's. It was still an hour before their regular meeting, so they took a table in the corner, where they could watch the street without being surprised or overheard.

"Who the hell done it, ya think?" Earl wondered once they had settled with their beers.

"Shit, I don't know. Nobody knows what we're up to but us seven . . . well, six now," Matt corrected himself.

"Only thing I can figure is that fuckin' Braddock done it, or had it done."

"Nah! I don't think he did it. It don't make sense," Matt said, shaking his head. "Watkins would be worth a lot more to him alive than dead. You see how anxious he was to get something out of us?" Earl nodded agreement. "He needs information, not dead men. He's in a hog wallow, looking for clover," Earl said into his beer.

Matt looked back with a puzzled expression but there was the start of something else. "So, who done it?"

Paddy's was filling with the evening crowd. Bob held court in his corner table by the window, telling two others how Hooker lost his nerve to Bobby Lee at Chancellorsville.

"Only good thing come o' that was Jackson gettin' shot by his own men. Some say that was worth losing the battle for. Cost the rebs more than most anything else that fool Hooker could have done."

"Damned if I wouldn't like to put a ball in that man's head, talkin' about Stonewall like that," Earl said under his breath.

Matt shrugged. "Hell, he's right, Earl. We woulda been better off losing the battle than Jackson. Besides, he's a cripple already. Putting a ball in his head might be doing him a favor."

Bob was warming to his subject. The beer was talking, and it was loud enough to be heard anywhere in Paddy's.

"Damn Jackson flanked the whole fuckin' army. First thing we knew was when the skirmishers drove the deer out of the woods into our lines. Hell, deer, rabbits, coons; they led the fuckin' assault. Jackson just brought up the rear." Everyone at Bob's table laughed.

"I swear one more word, and I'm gonna take off his other damned leg."

Matt put a hand on Earl's arm. "No good doin' that, Earl. Let's go. We can get a beer somewhere else."

Earl grumbled, but he got up and walked through the sawdust and out the door, all the while glaring at Bob.

Matt looked at his watch. "Don't really have time for another beer anyway. May's well go over to the office." They walked down the stone sidewalks of Peck Slip and headed for the offices of Sangree & Co.

Tom was stamping his letter to the War Department, when he thought of another he should send. It wouldn't be proper to just show up at the Roeblings' door like some traveling salesman. Such things had to conform to the social graces. Social grace was an area not fully developed in Tom. It was a matter of thought, not instinct. Still, he did his best at writing a note to the chief engineer, asking if he could call in two days' time. He checked it over after he had finished. Aside from one careless blob of ink and some doubtful phrasing, it would do. He sent it off with the other.

His purpose was not to interrogate Roebling. Rather, he hoped that the man could shed some light on some things. It was clear that somebody was very concerned about keeping their activities quiet. Tom had to treat every possibility seriously. Thinking of the possibilities, the list he came up with was short. The most likely cause was fraud. As J. Lloyd Haigh had proven when he supplied defective wire for the main cables, there was a lot of money to be made from promising one thing and delivering another. Haigh had been able to commit fraud, supply substandard wire, and still keep his contract after being caught. It wasn't such a stretch to assume some other group was trying something similar. When the layers were peeled back, murder was usually about money. Where a project like the great East River Bridge was concerned, the money came in buckets. All sorts get drawn to the trough. Even small leaks in a few of those buckets could mean big profits to anyone willing to drill the holes. Tom walked out of police headquarters trying to imagine how he'd go about defrauding the bridge project. The possibilities seemed endless.

He kept turning what he knew over and over in his mind while the El chugged uptown toward home. He liked taking the El after dark. Lighted windows flashed by, like moving photographs. It reminded him of a moving picture book he had seen once. He had flipped the pages and watched, fascinated, as a horse and rider seemed to gallop across the pages. He stared out the windows, a mobile urban voyeur, peeping into living rooms on the fly. Pieces of people's lives flitted by. Tom thought of the million and more inmates of New York. What were they doing now, at this instant? Eating, drinking, rolling a sucker on the Bowery, making love, driving a hack, patrolling the streets; a million things in a million different ways went on at any instant in time. But out of all the human hustle and bustle, all the infinite variety of activity, there were some whose minds were focused on the bridge. He knew they were out there somewhere. They had left their calling cards. They knew who he was and what he was about. Though they might include Matt Emmons and Earl Lebeau, he couldn't prove it, at least not yet. There might be some on this train with him now. Let them come, Braddock thought, looking over his shoulder. He'd welcome an end to the mystery.

Tom was still thinking of conspirators as he walked up the stairs of his place. He opened the door tentatively, almost expecting black hands to reach for him from his darkened hall. He closed the door with a soft click of the latch behind him. Something registered in his mind, raising the beginnings of alarm. He sniffed like a hound testing the air. With careful steps, he prowled the hall. As he neared the bedroom door, he recognized the scent of candles and the faint hint of honeysuckle. A dim warm glow crept from under his door. The beginnings of a smile teased the corner of his mouth. With a slow hand, Tom pushed in the door. It swung lazily, revealing a different room from the one he'd left that morning. Candles bathed the walls in fluid yellow light. It seemed as if he'd stepped into a chapel, each candle a prayer and a devotion. He hardly recognized the place. Mary lay on his bed. The light rippled on her golden skin, as if she swam in a veil of fire. Her smile was slow and teasing. Tom stood rooted in the doorway.

"Oh, Mary," he said like a whispered prayer.

"Welcome home, Tommy. I've been waiting for you." Her hands stole to her breasts in a soft insistent caress, her taut belly rolling in supple waves. Tom drew a long ragged breath. She purred to him softly. "You were so long in coming, I started without you. You don't mind, do you, Tom?"

He just smiled and started to unbutton his shirt.

"Mmm, yes," she whispered. "I want to see you."

"Oooh, you wicked, wicked girl." He groaned. Tom's clothes came off without his eyes leaving hers. Mary watched, her hands moving over her body as Tom bared himself to her. It was Mary's turn to draw a ragged breath. She watched, fascinated. This was a game they hadn't played before.

"I want you so much, Tommy," Mary said in a whisper.

A mischievous grin split Tom's face. "Show me."

❧ Chapter Fifteen ❧

Continuing to work has been with me a
matter of pride and honor!

—WASHINGTON ROEBLING

When the meeting had convened without Watkins, there was a buzz of speculation around the table. Matt and Earl started to tell how Braddock had taken them in for questioning when the captain stood, serious and erect, as if on parade. With an officer's dignity he called for silence in a tone that stilled the room instantly.

"Watkins is dead," the captain said clearly. "I killed him." The words fell like sword strokes. Thaddeus let the silence reign for what seemed minutes. "As captain, I have the dual responsibility of the welfare of my men and the success of the mission. As you know, I have tried to balance the two . . . but we know too it's the mission that has to come first." The men listened. Thaddeus couldn't tell if they were with him or not. They gave no sign of what they felt. "We knew that in '61 . . . and nothing has changed with the years. It is the one constant in military life." He gave a small internal shudder the men didn't see. "The burden I swore to bear. Our mission . . . was in jeopardy, put at risk by one of our own. Faced with that situation, a sacrifice had to be made."

He had wanted to end it there but almost before he realized it, he went on to tell them his heart. "I swear to you, I would just have readily sacrificed my own life if it could accomplish the same end." He tried hard to maintain his air of command, his military demeanor. The men deserved that. It was hard, though, when he spoke of Watkins. "I pray you all understand how very seriously I approached this. It was something I was loath to do, and I prayed that the Almighty might assist me and show me the true and righteous path." He paused for a moment, needing a second to collect himself.

"You must know—I mean, I want you all to understand that—this—was an agony for me. I did not make it lightly, and though I know in my heart it was the right thing to do, it will forever be a burden of . . . of regret to me, that I had—was forced to do it." He had no intention of telling the others of his suspicion of Watkins. Some things were best left unsaid. He looked at the men one by one, seeing each truly. "I know I will have to answer to my maker some day, just as I answer to you all now." By the time he finished his head hung to his chest. He hadn't wanted to let his emotions show, but it couldn't be helped. Maybe that was the thing that made it easier for the rest to accept. They could see the beast he'd wrestled. He was the captain, but he was just a man.

It was done and it could not be undone. None of them liked it but they all seemed to accept it. Even Sullivan, who could be more sensitive to the human issues of their little group, took it well. The fact that Watkins was the least valued member of the team was an advantage. There was a feeling too that Watkins had brought this on himself. His wagging tongue had killed him, as sure as any bullet. Jacobs, in his clerk's voice, said it first.

"It wasn't you who killed him, Captain. You just finished the job started by his big mouth. He was dead already. Just didn't know it." A couple of them nodded agreement.

"Reckon it's true," Earl said. "Don't like one of us goin' down, but when I think on it, he did kinda have it comin'." He looked around the table for agreement, then went on. "Watkins coulda paid that price weeks ago fer blabbin' to Bucklin. You just done what you had to, Cap'n, and you could have done it sooner, 'ceptin' you not wantin' to put down one of yer own."

One by one they voiced their support. Each was sad to lose a comrade, but they had lost so many over the years that one more didn't hit them the way it might other men. They would stick by the captain till the end. Let the bodies pile where they may. At the last, when they drank to their success, they'd toast the dead. They'd drink in silent remembrance to those who fell by the side of their long, long road. The captain had his absolution.

The conversation turned to Matt and Earl next to report on their treatment by Braddock. They were all encouraged to hear how little the detective seemed to know. It appeared too that the death of Watkins came none too soon. It was noted how quick the police were to appear on the scene. A sleeping man, as Watkins appeared to be, might have ridden back and forth across the river for hours before being discovered. The police had been watching the ferry, they decided. It had been a closer thing than they would ever know.

The captain, taking control as usual, turned to Sullivan and with an encouraging smile said, "Now, Patrick, can you move on with the plans as you outlined them to us a few days ago? You've had time to work out some of the details, right?"

Sullivan stood. "Pretty much, sir." He didn't feel much like talking, not after just hearing that the captain shot one of their own. He felt like death. The doubts he'd talked about with Lincoln seemed to have mushroomed in the last few minutes. He couldn't stow them in the back of his mind any longer. Looking at Justice, he could see the same in his eyes. Still, he went on outlining his plan.

They'd done this before, on a smaller scale with the many bridges they blew during the war and the three train wrecks they'd engineered after. The methods were similar. The scale and complexity of this job was altogether different though.

"As you know," he began, "we're going to blow just enough so it will tear itself apart. Thanks to Bart we have the plans, and he and I have gone over them carefully for the last two weeks."

Bart rolled out some plans on the big table and they all craned to get a good look. It was a work of art really, an incredibly precise scale drawing of the bridge as seen from the side. All the major components were shown: caissons, towers, anchorages, approaches, roadway, main cables, suspenders, and stays.

"Now, gentlemen, here's how I see us bringing down the Eighth Wonder of the World," Pat said.

He could have a flair for the dramatic when he got warmed up, the captain thought, smiling.

Sullivan recapped the basics of the plan, which they had decided on some time before. He wanted to be certain everybody was following.

"The trick is to make the span unstable. The stiffness of the roadway is the key. That's why Roebling put this bracing in." Jacobs did the pointing for Pat. Even if by some miracle the bridge held together and didn't drop into the river, the carnage from the explosions would be devastating. Hundreds would die, certainly. Sullivan had a mental image of it as he spoke. He could hear the explosions like dull thunder, the sharp metallic twang as the stays snapped and whipped down on the crowded roadway.

"You see, by cutting the stays here and here," Pat said absently, lost in his vision of destruction, "and the suspenders from just two of the main cables, we can drop one side of the roadway."

Within twenty minutes Sullivan had laid it out for them, at least the parts he'd worked on. The vision had faded. Timing was as critical as placement of the charges, he told them. "First the suspenders, trusses, and beams, then the stays, say about five seconds apart." Ideally that's how it should work, but there would be problems coordinating that. They went over the obstacles for a minute till the captain finally said to move on. He wasn't at all sure they'd be able to time it that closely. The last thing Pat touched on was the number of charges and his estimate of how long it would take to set them—not more than an hour and a half. Charges would be placed on a total of twenty-six suspenders where they connected with the support beams, thirteen charges each for the upstream main cable suspenders. Additional charges would be placed to cut the stays and the trusses over the tracks. They needed to work at saving time, and preparation was the key. Sullivan had ideas for practice drills, some of which could be carried out on the bridge itself. They didn't anticipate any police patrols on the bridge, but there would be police at each end, and traffic to watch out for even at three in the morning. They needed to expect the unexpected.

"Very good, men," the captain said when Pat and Bart had finished. "One other thing we should work on is the running of the detonator wire." The detonator wire and the positioning of the portable dynamo they'd need to generate their charge were real sticking points. So far they had only sketched out plans in this area. "It occurs to me that the wiring for the lamps will be commencing soon. Suppose we were to have Earl and Matt assigned to the crew. Might be possible to run our wire along with the wiring for the lamps."

"The wires to the charges on the stays will have to be run along with the explosives. Those charges will be up on the towers. Nothing to be done about that," Pat pointed out. "But if we could get our wire out to midspan beforehand, it would save a bunch of time and risk. I been working on how we might do that, but truth be told, I don't like what I've come up with. I do like the sound of your idea, though."

Thaddeus agreed but looked off as if calculating odds. "If we can get our wire to midspan under their noses it would be sublime," he said, relishing the thought.

The meeting broke up shortly after that, with a plan for Bart to get Matt and Earl assigned to the lighting crew immediately.

"Anything to add?" Thaddeus asked, looking around the room.

Earl spoke up in his laconic drawl. "Yeah, Cap'n. I don't think Roebling's gonna like it much."

When Tom got to his desk for the dog watch at 6:00 A.M., the first thing he noticed was the telegram. It lay in the top of his in box, small, white, and harmless. Like most people, Tom figured that unexpected telegrams were not good news. He picked it up as if it might bite. It was from the desk sergeant at the Thirteenth. It read: boy in custody on thievery charge stop claims to know you stop holding him for arraignment at Essex Market Police Court at noon stop boy claims to be Michael Bucklin stop advise stop Tom read it again. After their last meeting, he would have bet he'd never see the boy again. It sounded like he was in trouble, though, and Tom didn't think Mike's grandparents needed any more of that. He went to the telegrapher's office in the basement.

The telegraph office was in rooms 1 and 2 of the basement of Police Headquarters. From there, headquarters was in touch with every station house, hospital, railway station, including the Els and fire house, in the city. Wallace Wylie was on duty when Tom went in.

"Morning, Wally."

Wylie looked up from his desk. His head had been very nearly touching it.

"Shouldn't you be heading home? Where's Brennan?" Tom asked.

"Not in, I'm covering."

"Ain't life grand? How've you been, Wally? Haven't seen much of you lately."

"Oh, fine, Tom, fine," Wally said through a yawn. "Nothing new. Kids are growing like weeds. Wife's getting big with our third." Tom almost envied him. "That's great. Nice to hear some things are normal. Got a message for the Thirteenth." Tom held out a slip of paper.

"You've been busy lately, Tom," Wally said as he started to finger the telegraph key. "I hear things even down here in the catacombs."

"I bet you do." Tom knew that Wylie was probably the best-informed man in the building. "Things have been interesting. What was that old Chinese curse? Something like: 'May you live in interesting times.' Last couple of weeks, I'm thinking maybe things have been a little too interesting. Anyway, I gotta run. Thanks for the help."

Tom ran into Chowder on the way upstairs.

"So, I hear you got Dolan and Heidelberg assigned to you now," Chowder said. "What's up? You into something big?"

"Bucklin case. Looks like it may lead to other things." Chowder just raised his eyebrows. "Like the East River Bridge." Tom answered his unasked question.

Chowder whistled. "You wouldn't be shovelin' shit on my shoes, now, would you, Thomas? What's the bridge go to do with that Bucklin case?"

"Pretty strong whiff of something like fraud or conspiracy. Byrnes smells a big case, wants to keep his hand in. You know how that goes." Chowder understood completely.

"I don't give a damn," Tom said honestly. "Let him grab the headlines, if it comes to that. At least I got some extra help and I'm still in charge of the show."

Chowder slapped him on the shoulder. "Could be a big career move for you, boy-o. Keep you out from under Coffin's thumb. How's it look? Any suspects?"

Tom turned suddenly glum. "That's sort of a problem. My main suspect turned up with a .32 caliber headache yesterday."

"The fella on the ferry? Heard about that," Chowder said, putting the pieces together. "The plot thickens, eh, Tommy?"

"Got Byrnes's attention," Braddock said in an obvious understatement.

Chowder gave an exaggerated nod of his big head. "Now I got it, laddie. Crystal clear, it is. Well, listen, I got to get movin'. You be careful, y'hear? Sounds like that could be an unhealthy case."

"Sure thing. We gotta have a beer sometime, catch up, you know?"

Chowder looked pleased. "Right-o, Tommy. Let's do it soon."

By the time Tom got back to his desk and filed his reports for the prior day, it was seven-thirty. He talked to Pat Dolan and Charlie Heidelberg just long enough to arrange to meet at eleven to talk over the case and decide where they would start. Then he went out the back way on Mott, heading for the El. In ten minutes he was chugging uptown behind a particularly smoky engine. He thought about Mike as the El swayed and rattled. The boy must have been arrested yesterday. The telegram had been put on his desk late, so he'd been in custody now for probably about eighteen hours. His grandparents must be worried sick. They'd be getting frantic in another couple of hours, if they weren't already.

It wasn't more than fifteen minutes before Tom was standing at the front desk at the Thirteenth.

"Morning. You Sergeant Thompson?"

"Nope," the desk sergeant said without looking up.

Tom waited. That seemed to be all the man had to say. "All right, then. I got this telegraph from him. You got a kid by the name of Bucklin in custody. I'd like to see him."

"And who might you be?"

Tom didn't answer. He waited until the sergeant finally lifted an inquiring eye from his desk, then pulled open his jacket. He kept his shield pinned to his vest, so it couldn't be easily seen. Most detectives did.

"Sergeant Detective Thomas Braddock, Central Detective Bureau," Tom said distinctly. "And you are?"

"Sergeant Roodman. What's your business with the prisoner?" the sergeant asked, his demeanor only slightly improved by the sight of Tom's badge. Braddock asked for the arresting officer and Roodman replied, "He's off duty, in reserve. I'll check if he's in the building." That was the first civil thing Roodman had said so far. There might be hope for him yet, Tom thought.

"Thanks. Where are you holding Bucklin?"

The sergeant handed Tom a key ring and said, "Basement holding cells. Third one on the left."

Mike was asleep when Tom found him. It was cool and damp in the basement. A threadbare blanket in a dirty shade of gray was pulled up to his chin. His feet stuck out the other end. Tom opened the cell door. The rusted iron hinges screeched and groaned as the door swung open. Mike jumped awake, sitting upright on the small cot.

Tom looked at him closely. "Hey, Mike, how're you doing?"

"Okay, I guess. You scared me. I thought it was Harlan the cop, come to ask me questions again. I don't like him much," Mike said in a small voice.

Tom gave him a careful look, squinting slightly in the gloom. "Got a nasty bump on the head there. Anybody take a look at that?" Tom sat on the cot. Looking at the boy close, he didn't like what he saw.

"I washed up a little," Mike said, nodding at the pitcher and basin.

"Come on. We're going to get you cleaned up a bit. Can't have your grandma and gramps see you like this, right?" Tom noticed how Mike winced when he got up. He didn't say anything. When they got to the front desk, Tom asked where the bathroom was as he tossed the keys to Roodman. Braddock was washing the swollen cut on Mike's head when Harlan Connolly came in.

"This how they treat little thieves down at the Detective Bureau?" Connolly asked loudly. Tom turned at the sound of Connolly's voice. He smiled broadly for the patrolman.

"Patrolman Connolly, I presume." Tom extended his hand. "I'm Detective Braddock. Thanks for the telegraph. I owe you for that."

Harlan took Tom's hand. Tom couldn't help but notice how Mike sort of sidled around behind him when the cop came in.

"Yeah, sure. This kid said he knew you . . . so." Harlan tried to pull his hand away but Tom held on, pumping it as if he'd met an old friend.

"I want to thank you, Harlan, for the good treatment you've given the young Master Bucklin here."

Connolly was getting just a little red in the face. His knuckles were white in Tom's grip. "Yeah . . . well, the kid did take a nasty spill but he bounced back. You know how the little street Arabs are: tough little buggers."

Tom's grip tightened. "I'd take it as a personal favor if you were to release this boy to me, Harlan. I'd *really* appreciate it."

Connolly actually seemed to be pulling now to free his hand from the vise it was in.

Tom just smiled his warmest, most sincere smile. Mike watched, fascinated.

"Sure, sure, Braddock. You can have 'im. Just held him as a courtesy to you . . . you know . . . anyway . . . that is, once we heard you had an interest."

"Ah, that's real nice of you, Harlan. Can't thank you enough."

Connolly was a lovely shade of crimson now, his fingertips squirming like maggots in Tom's fist.

"Could you do me a favor, Harlan?" Tom asked as if he'd just thought of it. "Would you mind sort of keeping a special watch out for my little friend here? Keep an eye out for him, so to speak? The streets are rough on kids, and it would be grand to know he's got someone keeping a lookout."

Connolly was almost hopping now, shifting from one foot to the other. Little beads of sweat were popping out on his forehead.

"Was gonna suggest it meself, Detective. Be . . . happy to keep an eye on the tyke. No problem."

"Ah, that's just grand, then. You have no idea what a comfort this'll be to his grandma and me too for that matter. Thanks a lot." Tom gave the hand a final crushing squeeze, grinding bone beneath his fingers.

A small strangled yelp escaped from the cop. He tried to cover it with a cough. He gave a vengeful look at Mike, once Tom released his hand. No sooner had he done that than Tom laid a heavy hand on Connolly's shoulder.

"Now, I don't want you to think that Bucklin here is getting off scot-free." Tom clamped his hand on the muscle at the side of Connolly's neck. He squeezed hard. "No, he's going to pay, I can assure you. So don't worry about him getting what he deserves. I'll see to that."

Connolly twisted in Tom's grip but couldn't shake off the hand without losing the remains of his dignity in front of the kid.

"That's good, Braddock. Don't want the kids goin' bad on us from bein' too lenient," Connolly said through gritted teeth.

"No, sir, no, we don't, Harlan. So remember," Tom said. "I'd appreciate it if you kept a special watch. Make sure nothing happens to him. Sort of like a guardian angel. Can you do that for me?"

Mikey couldn't see the tips of Tom's fingers they were buried so far in Connolly's neck.

"Sure, Tom, sure. You can count on me," Harlan choked out.

Braddock released the cop, all the while thanking him and patting him on the back.

. . .

Tom and Mike were walking down Delancey a few minutes later. Mike's hands were in his pockets, fingering the little pile of dimes and nickels that rested there along with the little key to his secret box. The coins seemed even more valuable now, and his fingers caressed them one by one. He and Tom walked in silence for quite a way. Mike limped a little. The bruises on the backs of his legs had lost their sting, but a heavy ache had taken up residence where the sting had been. Tom saw out of the corner of his eye that the boy was having trouble keeping up. He wasn't quite sure what to say to him. He just walked beside him, figuring it would come on its own.

Mike's head was so full of stuff he thought it'd bust. He was mostly relieved at being free and out of that cold, buggy cell. He worried though at what Braddock might do to him and what his grandma surely would. He was going to be punished that was certain. But he was overjoyed at having his money back, and it was so fantastic to see Harlan the cop, the ogre of the neighborhood, get run over by Braddock that he could hardly contain his glee. All of that tumbled and swam in his head like a stream tripping over boulders in its path. He couldn't think what to say first to a man like Braddock. The stream of his thoughts kept bouncing off boulders. So he walked beside Tom, all running and tripping inside, but still as a millpond on the surface.

It was Tom who finally broke the silence. He saw Mike wince as he stepped around someone in his way. "That cop; he hit you with his stick, didn't he?"

"Yeah," Mike said with his head down.

"He whacked the backs of your legs, right? You fall down the stairs or something too?"

"I suppose," Mike said, not knowing how much to tell the detective.

"That cop do things like that to other kids?" Braddock asked, looking down at Mike as they walked.

"Maybe. Maybe some had it comin'. I don't know."

Tom nodded at the wisdom of that. "Well, I don't think he'll bother you anymore, but keep clear of him anyway, just to be sure."

Mike turned a beaming face up to Tom. "I think you busted his hand, Mr. Braddock." There was glee and triumph and wonder in his voice, all mixed in a boy-soup of admiration.

"You think so?" Tom asked with a smile. "I hope to hell I did." He grinned at the boy, and Mike smiled back.

"What were you doing to get on the wrong side of that bastard?" Tom asked as they walked.

"Stealin' coal."

"Coal, huh?" Tom said appraisingly. "No vegetables this time?"

Mike shook his head, but his chest puffed up as he said, "We got good money for it."

Tom seemed impressed. "You buy anything with your money?"

"Just some candy at Brower's. We didn't want to spend it all. We were planning on the circus. Ever hear of Jumbo?" Mike looked up at Tom brightly.

"He's that big elephant, right . . . with Barnum's?"

"That's him. He's a packy-derm," Mike said knowingly. "And we want to go see him." His enthusiasm was just about bubbling.

"Who's we, the fellas I saw you with the other day?"

"Yeah, but I can't tell their names, sir." Mike hung his head again.

Tom held up a hand. "That's okay, I understand," he said, and he did. "You going to school, Mike?"

"Sure, I go to Grammar School 75, on Norfolk."

"Yeah? Who's your teacher? I know some teachers in that school," asked Tom, testing the boy.

"Well, they sorta change a lot, you know . . . but I guess it's . . . Mrs. Doyle." He stole a glance at Tom to see if he was buying the story. "Yeah, it's Mrs. Doyle," Mike said as surely as he could.

They were nearing Mike's block. The narrow streets were teeming with the morning's activity. The smell of a thousand breakfasts floated down the cobbles.

"They give you anything to eat, Mike?" Tom asked, stopping to appraise him. His hand was in his pocket, fingering the small key. Mike just shook his head. "You've got to be hungry, then."

"I guess," Mike said. Though his belly felt like it had a hole he could put his fist through, he was sort of used to the feel of being hungry.

"Me too. Let's go eat." Tom put his hand around Mike's shoulders and steered him around a corner.

"Oh, yeah! Can I have pancakes with butter and syrup?"

"Sure, anything you want. And don't worry about your grandparents. I sent them a message before. They know you're with me."

"Could we maybe bring them some food too, do you think?" Mike asked hopefully, not knowing how far he could go. "My grandma, sometimes she doesn't eat too much. She gives hers to me, 'cause she says I'm growing."

Later, as Tom sat watching Mike swab up maple syrup with his pancakes, he asked, "How's your gramps, Mike?"

Mike swallowed quickly before he answered. "He coughs a lot now, Mr. Braddock. Grandma says he'll go to God soon. He'll be with my da, and ma, and sis though, so he won't be lonely." Mike played with the food on his plate, swirling the syrup in patterns around the pancakes. "It makes me sad, Mr. Braddock. I wish I could see them too and I don't want Gramps to go."

Tom wasn't quite sure what to say, or how to make it better. He took the key out of his pocket, turning it over and over in his fingers.

"Your grandma getting on all right?" he asked.

"I guess. She's up late a lot. Sewing all the time now. She makes real pretty lace and stuff too."

"I bet she does." There was a long silence and they both sat staring out the window.

"So, you wanted to go see Jumbo, huh?" Tom asked finally.

"Oh, yeah, more'n anything. He's so big he shits houses." Mike broke up, laughing so hard that Tom got carried along with him. The kid did have an infectious laugh. "That's what Smokes said. He's my friend."

"Uh-huh. Shits houses, huh?" Tom asked with a broad grin. "That's worth seeing, I guess. Never did see an elephant shit a house. Seen some houses that look like shit though." This time they both roared. Mike laughed so hard that the milk he was drinking came out his nose.

"I tell you what, Mike. I've got a proposition for you," Tom said, pointing his fork at the boy once they had stopped the last of the giggles. "You know what a proposition is?"

"Sure, it's a deal."

"Exactly. So, here's the deal. You've got to start going to school. I don't mean once in a while either. I mean every day."

Mike looked glum. He started fiddling with the remains of his pancakes, his head hanging so his hair fell over his face.

"What's so bad about that?" Tom asked innocently.

"I dunno. Nothin', I guess," Mike mumbled.

"You have to go to school, you know. You're only going to get into trouble again on the streets."

Mike's hair nearly brushed his plate.

"You don't want to take up residence in the basement of the Thirteenth, do you?"

"No, sir," Mike said to his plate.

Tom sat looking at the top of the boy's head. He tried to remember what it was like to be ten. It didn't come back easy and it didn't come back whole. He tried to put on the clothes of his youth, the shoes, the pants, the shirt with the plaid checks. They didn't fit, but he remembered when they had. He began to think of himself in them and as he did he recalled how he felt in the clothes of a ten-year-old.

"How long's it been since you were in school, Mike?"

"I don't know."

"How do you feel about seeing the other kids? You have friends there?"

"Sort of." Mike took a nibble at a pancake.

"Most of your friends are on the streets, right?" Tom asked, knowing the answer. "You know, Mike, I never said you'd have to stop seeing your friends. You can see them after school."

Mike shrugged. "Yeah, I know."

Tom still fished for the real problem. "So, what is it . . . your friends don't like kids who go to school?"

"Maybe." Mike's tone made Tom feel he was getting closer to the mark.

"You think they'll be your friends even if you go to school? Or kick you out of the gang, or something?"

Mike still didn't look at Tom. "Something like that . . . maybe."

"Probably don't have many friends in school either, right?"

Mike just shook his head, the tips of his hair brushing the syrupy plate.

"That's pretty rough," Tom said gently. "Can I tell you something?" Mike didn't say anything. "You can't control what other kids do, Mike. You can never do that. All you can do is be yourself." Tom started off, not sure exactly where he was headed but feeling it was the right direction. "You can be a friend to them and you can be a friend to the kids in school. The important thing is to be yourself no matter what." Mike seemed to look up at that. "The ones who like you," Tom went on, "and are your friends when you're your-self . . . those are your real friends." There was a glimmer of understanding in Mike's eye, the one he could see through his hanging hair. "Real friends don't try to make you into something else. They like you for yourself." He thought of some of his friends in the department, wondering just how many were real. "Sometimes it's not easy finding out who your real friends are. Worth know-ing though."

"I know who my real friends are, Mr. Braddock," Mike said defensively.

"I'm glad," Tom said, not really believing him. He paused in thought for a moment before saying "Going back to school might test your friends . . . you too. I'm thinking that if you stay in school you're going to need a special reward." Tom began to grin as Mike's head came up. "When did you say the circus was in town?"

Mike's head shot up. "I'm not sure, Mr. Braddock. But I can find out."

"You do that. And if you're still in school a month from now then you're going to the circus, Jumbo and all."

"Wow, you'd take me?" Mike asked, not believing his luck.

"Sure would," Tom said, happy to see the boy perked up. "I want to see that Jumbo too. We got a deal?"

Mike hesitated only an instant. "Deal!"

Tom flipped the small key in the air for emphasis. It glittered as it spun. Mike watched, suddenly distracted. Tom caught the key, and with a small flourish of his hands, it disappeared. Mike smiled, but it was a puzzled sort of look. Tom reached over to him. "What's it doing behind your ear?" And when he pulled his hand away, there was the key again. Mike didn't smile at all this time. In fact, he frowned as his hand went into his own pocket.

"What are you doing with my da's key?" he asked as he held a hand out to Tom. A small brass key rested there. Tom looked at Mike in a piercing sort of way that made him nervous. He thought for sure he'd done something wrong.

"This was your dad's key?" Tom asked, holding it up.

"Sure. He had the only other one. When he gave me the box, he told me to keep it hid. He didn't even want to know where it was, but he wanted to keep a key. I don't know why."

"You have the box this key goes to?"

"Sure. My da said not to tell anybody, but I guess I can trust you, Mr. Braddock."

"I'm glad you feel that way, Mike. I hope you *can* trust me." As Tom said this, he had a sudden fleeting image of Finney lying sprawled on his office floor.

"I do," Mike said instantly.

"So, what did your da tell you, Mike?" Tom asked shaking off Finney's ghost.

"He told me there were bad men, and there are, I know. I guess they were the ones killed my da. One of them came after me when I was emptying the chamber pot."

Tom shook his head, not sure what to believe. This was starting to get real strange.

"Mike," he said. "I want you to tell me all about this, but you have to do it on the way to your house. I need to see that box, partner, and I have to see it right away." Tom rose, rummaging in a pocket for some money. He slapped it on the table without counting it and started to go.

"All right, I guess. Nothing in it, just a couple of pictures and some hard money," Mike said sulkily.

Tom made himself slow down for a moment, noticing the change that had come over the boy.

"Listen, Mike . . . this is real important. It might give me a clue to who killed your da." Mike said not a word. "And don't worry. I promise we'll see the circus . . . *absolutely promise*. We made a deal and I'm not going back on it, partner." Mike gave him a doubtful look. Tom crouched down so he was face to face with the boy. "Mike, I wouldn't do this if I didn't have to. I've got to see that box right away, okay?"

Mike shrugged his shoulders and mumbled, "Nothin' in it anyway."

Tom just stood there, puzzled at Mike's reluctance. He figured that the sudden interest in the box had Mike thinking he'd forget about the circus.

"You swear we'll go see Jumbo?"

Tom gave him a steady stare. "Mike, so long as I'm alive, I've got a debt to you that only the circus can pay," he said as they walked out to the street. "We'll see Jumbo . . . and all the rest. Count on it."

Mike nodded a bit more willingly but said again, "Still nothin' in it."

"That's okay. Now tell me everything about this bad man and the chamber pot," Tom said, trying to sound as if he believed the tale. He would come to believe shortly.

They walked to Suffolk Street as fast as their legs would take them, Mike occasionally running to catch up with Tom. Tom listened to Mike's story of the dark man by the outhouses, he fingering the two keys as they went. There had to be something in that box no matter what the boy said. There *had* to be. They were at the Bucklin place in fifteen minutes. Once Mike was able to extricate himself from the relieved hug his grandma immediately had him in, he removed the baseboard by the fireplace and brought out the box from its hiding place. All the while Patricia Bucklin was thanking Tom in a steady stream. She stopped when Mike produced the box.

"Well, I'll be!" she exclaimed, as surprised as Tom to see it.

"Mind if I take a look, Mike?" Tom asked, barely able to keep himself from reaching to it. The boy handed the box over. Tom took Terrence's key and, after a moment's hesitation, put it in the keyhole. It opened the little lock with a small click. Mike was right. All that was in the box was a couple of photographs and three coins, which Tom emptied out on a bed.

"See, I told you there's nothing in there," Mike said, the resentment showing a little.

"Looks like you're right, partner," Tom said, turning the box this way and that. His shoulders slumped, belying the optimistic tone he tried to keep. "That's all right, Mike."

Mrs. Bucklin offered him tea.

"As long as you're here, Tom, sit and have a drop o' tea with us."

He did, sitting at the small table in the kitchen, sipping the hot tea. Patricia brought a cup to Eamon, who rarely left his bed now. Mike told his grandma of the deal he'd made with Tom, when she sat with them, the excitement lighting his face.

Tom nodded and said, "That's our deal. You've got to hold up your end of the bargain though," he warned Mike. "No slackin' off. 'Cause I'll be checking on you."

He idly turned the carved oak box over and over in his hands. It was a beautiful thing, obviously quite old. The carving had worn smooth in places, and there were some nicks and scratches on its surfaces. Looking inside again, he noticed that the green velvet that lined the bottom wasn't as old as that on the sides. It was a minor difference, barely noticeable, in fact. His fingers reached in and ran across the fuzzy material, which should have been threadbare if it was as old as the box. More interested now, he tapped at the bottom. It made a sound like an empty coconut. With a sudden rush of excitement, Tom said, "Mike, would you mind if I tried something with your box here?"

Mike looked at him with a small frown.

"I won't hurt it," Tom promised.

Mike nodded but watched intently. Tom fished in his pocket for his penknife, unfolding it in his hand. Carefully he wedged the tip of the blade in along the edge of the velvet, twisting and prying as he moved it around the seam. He felt it give, then suddenly the bottom of the box was in his hand. But it wasn't the bottom really. It was a false bottom, creating a slim compartment on the bottom of the box. Fluttering to the floor were photographs and some papers that had been hidden there. The three of them stared open-mouthed.

The first photograph that Tom picked up was of four men. One was Terrence Bucklin. Standing with him somewhere on the bridge was Earl Lebeau, Matt Emmons, and Simon Watkins. Mike and Mrs. Bucklin crowded close to see. The other shot was just of Matt and Watkins. They were smiling. Tom turned to the papers that had fallen out of the box. One was a newspaper clipping from the *Times*, about the fire in the Brooklyn caisson. Dated December of 1870, it was yellowed and frayed around the edges. Bucklin must have either saved it, or gotten it from the *Times*. It was an odd thing to hide. Odder still was the second clipping. This one was from the *Trib,* and seemed to have been torn out in a hurry. The papers seemed to be bits and pieces of articles, but none whole. The one that stood out was a story about the trains that would soon be running on the East River Bridge. Tom scanned it quickly and turned the sheet over to check the other side. There again, nothing seemed whole. There were ads and an article on the Manhattan social scene as well as something about Memorial Day festivities, but nothing that stood out and no notations. Turning the page over again, it seemed obvious to Tom that the key had to do with the trains. It was the only thing with a direct link to the bridge. If Terrence had discovered something about the trains, some fraud, or maybe something more, then perhaps—Tom stopped himself in midthought.

"Awful lot of maybes," he muttered, wishing for more to go on. He was disturbed too by the old clipping about the caisson fire. Obviously there was a connection, but what the one could possibly have to do with the other he couldn't fathom. The fire had been nearly thirteen years before. The only connection seemed to be that the two stories both concerned the bridge. Aside from that they appeared unrelated, at least on the surface. Tom knew there had to be more. Bucklin hadn't taken the time to collect this stuff for no reason. He knew too that Watkins had been involved in some way. With Watkins gone, that left Lebeau and Emmons, and he sure as hell hadn't gotten anything out of them yet.

Tom met with Dolan and Heidelberg when he stopped back at headquarters about an hour later. They spent some time going over the case from the beginning, taking a step back, trying to get a clear picture. Tom had the idea of charting out everything they knew so far, laying it out on a blackboard at the back of the squad room. It wasn't standard procedure, but it helped get things in perspective. He drew boxes and lines connecting them. Inside each box was the name of some person connected with the case. Bucklin, Watkins, the four Plug Uglies, Bucklin's family, Earl Lebeau, and Matt Emmons each had a box, as did Clora Devine. Others they left empty for persons unknown. One fact at a time, they went over what they knew. As the facts were ticked off, any connections between the boxes were drawn in solid lines. Suspected connections they drew with dotted lines. It didn't take long to get a graphic picture of the case as they knew it so far: what they knew, what they guessed, and what they needed to know to complete the picture. Dotted lines outnumbered solids by about three to one.

Once done, they set about listing the information they needed in order of importance. First on that list was more on Lebeau and Emmons. Their connection with Watkins pointed to something, and it was one of the few solid lines on the chart. Tom had taken the first step in writing the War Department. Dolan and Heidelberg would take the second step, getting a warrant as Byrnes ordered. Next was to dig into the details on the trains: the manufacturer, the company that made the steam engines, the bidding on track, and a half dozen other things. How Earl and Matt could be involved with any of that they didn't know. Neither had worked on the tracks or trains. They considered tailing the two but figured it could wait till they had more solid evidence. Even with Pat and Charlie they didn't have men to spare on tails. There was little hard evidence against the two anyway, just the fact that they knew Watkins. Braddock couldn't even be certain it was Watkins that killed Bucklin, just that he knew how Bucklin had died. That coupled with Watkins's murder left a bunch of dotted lines on their chart, all leading to an empty box.

With the two other men, Tom kicked around the kinds of questions he should ask the Roeblings later that afternoon. Information on the trains topped the list, but Charlie was quick to remind Tom of other issues.

"See what he knows about any disgruntled employees or contractors—anyone who might have a grudge," Heidelberg said. "They've been at this for, what, fourteen years? There's got to be some unhappy people in all that time—a contractor who thinks himself poorly used, a laborer fired without cause."

"Yeah, we'll need access to records too: accounting, payroll, orders, those sorts of things," Pat said, opening a can of worms Tom would have just as soon left closed. He hated tedious records-search sorts of cases.

Just then Jaffey walked in, nervous and owl-eyed.

Tom called to him from across the room. "Hey, Jaffey, glad you're here."

"Yeah, got the word I'm assigned to you for the rest of the case." Jaffey did his best to hide his enthusiasm, but it leaked out around the edges.

"Right. This is Pat Dolan and Charlie Heidelberg. Boys, Eli Jaffey. You don't mind me calling you Eli, do you?" Tom asked, doubting there'd be an objection.

"No, no. Pleased to meet you both. You two are legends. Best detective team in the city, they said in the papers." Jaffey caught hold of his hero worship before it got completely out of the barn. "Well, ah . . . guess you don't need me to tell you."

"That's okay," said Pat. "It's just Pat and Charlie from here out."

Tom noticed there was just a little lack of enthusiasm in their voices. To be expected, he figured. Eli was an unknown to them, and it was always wise to be a little wary. The handshakes were quick and tentative.

"Eli's my backup. He's here to save my ass when I hang it out too far."

Pat did his best to hide his skepticism, Charlie wasn't as successful. "You should be very busy then, Eli."

The four split up shortly after, arranging to meet at the end of the day to compare notes. Pat and Charlie set off to get a warrant on the Emmons and Lebeau search. The two shared a tenement apartment on Henry Street. Tom knew they'd give the place a thorough going-over. If there was anything to be found, they'd find it. He and Eli set off toward the ferry. They figured they'd catch a bite in Brooklyn somewhere, then head over to the Roeblings'.

"Want to stop in the bridge offices on our way," Tom said. "Talk to a clerk I know there. He might be able to help. Besides, I want us seen more often around the bridge. I want whoever's involved to know we're around . . . feel the pressure. If they think we're on to something, they may get nervous, sloppy, who knows." He threw up his hands. Any angle was worth a play.

When they got off the ferry in Brooklyn, they walked the few blocks to the bridge offices. It was eleven-forty-five when they asked to see Bart Jacobs.

"Detective," Jacobs exclaimed, hustling out from a back storeroom. "How good to see you again. I read of your exploits just yesterday. Quite an exciting business." He was bright-eyed with enthusiasm. "I dare say that's the first police chase across the great bridge." The papers had picked up the story. It made for exciting copy. The *Trib* featured a fanciful etching of Braddock sprinting across the span.

Braddock shrugged but couldn't hide a small grin. "Didn't end quite as I had hoped."

"No, I imagine not," the clerk said with mock disappointment.

Tom introduced Jaffey, then got down to business. "One small thing. When we went to the address you gave me, we found it was occupied."

Jacobs tried to look surprised, adjusting his glasses with a doubting frown. "Really? Not by that Watkins fellow, I take it?"

"Precisely. A wretched little Italian clan. They didn't speak much English and they had no idea in hell who Watkins was. That was about all I could learn without having someone who spoke their gibberish."

Jacobs gave his best concerned look. "I'm not sure how I can help, Detective. It's apparent Watkins was less than truthful. I'd be happy to check again, though," he offered.

"Thanks, I'd like to see the record myself if you don't mind."

There was only a moment's hesitation. "Of course, let me get it." Jacobs was back after no more than two minutes of rummaging in a tall records cabinet at the back of the office. "Look for yourself." There in perfectly formed letters and numbers was Watkins's address, in pencil on the green, lined page.

Looking closely, Tom noticed the ghost of something under the fresh writing. "This was his new address, right? What about the old one, where he lived before this?"

"When he moved, we simply erased the old one." Jacobs shrugged. "That's why they're done in pencil. They change all the time."

Braddock nodded his understanding. "I want this page."

"I'm not sure you can have this one. It's our only copy." Jacobs stalled.

"Well . . . I'm going to have this page one way or another. Tell you what. Why don't you have someone copy it on a new sheet and I'll be back for the original in, say, two hours. Hate to bother you, after you being so helpful," Tom said with a grateful but firm smile.

Jacobs was none too happy. "I suppose, Detective."

Tom gave him a satisfied wink. "Appreciate it. Be back around two."

Tom and Eli Jaffey went to find some lunch.

"Oh, I almost forgot," Tom said suddenly. "I went to see Wei Kwan the other day."

Eli gave him a baffled look. "Who?"

"The Chinese Master I train with," Tom explained. "Wasn't too willing to take another white-devil pupil, but I convinced him to let you attend a work-out or two, then we'll see."

Jaffey brightened. "Great, appreciate it."

"This time around, you can just get a taste of it, but if you want to learn . . . get all you can out of it, you've got to be dedicated. It's my face you'll lose if you quit or don't show enough sand."

Eli was nodding but frowning at the same time. "What's face?"

"Oh, God, don't get me going on that," Tom said, knowing it was a subject that could take years to explore fully. "It's the Oriental equivalent of honor. Taken very seriously. So, you want to learn, you will honor me as your sponsor with your seriousness and dedication. Of course, you'll gain honor yourself too," Tom said patiently.

Jaffey agreed with an appropriately serious look. "I'll give it my best. I sure don't want to be a bad reflection on you."

Tom nodded his approval. "Good. Let's eat."

Emily caught herself looking at the old clock again. She had lost count of the times she had glanced at it today. In the week or so since she'd met Tom Brad-dock, she never imagined he'd come to her door. But now that the old clock had struck one, she paced from room to room, straightening pictures, plumping pillows in the parlor, and peeking out the wooden Venetian blinds. Wash had dressed comfortably as was his custom. He was up in his study, working as always. He didn't give a damn if the detective came or not.

"He'll just ask a lot of fool questions that I don't have answers to. He'll leave with nothing, and I'll be exhausted," Wash had said. "Suppose I did offer to help, so it's my own fault," he grumbled.

Emily had gone back to ask Martha to make tea and set out some pastries, when the big brass knocker on the front door boomed through the house. She almost went to answer it herself but stopped as soon as the thought crossed her mind. She could hear the door being opened and Hughes's measured tones as he ushered the visitors in. A minute later Hughes poked his head in the kitchen.

"Ah . . . ma'am? A Detective Braddock is here to see you and the colonel. He has a patrolman with him as well, a Mr. Jaffey."

"Very well, Hughes. I'll be there directly. Would you ask them to have a seat in the parlor?" She gave Martha some needless instructions, and when she felt a sufficient amount of time had passed she sailed out of the safe harbor of the kitchen to greet her guests. Martha smiled when she'd left.

Emily wasn't sure what she'd feel when she saw Tom again. It wasn't supposed to have been in her parlor, nor in her house at all, for that matter. She felt too constrained here, unable to say or do what she might have out on the bridge. On the bridge, things were different. There she felt a freedom that existed nowhere else in the world for her. Up over the water, free from the attachments of earth, she could let her words go where only her thoughts had gone before. She didn't understand how that could be; it just was. The bridge would always be a magical place for her. She wished as she entered her parlor that she was there now.

"Detective! How good it is to see you again," she said a little more formally than she intended, holding out her hand. He'd changed, she thought. He looked tired. There were lines at the eyes she hadn't noticed before.

"The pleasure is mine, Mrs. Roebling. Allow me to introduce Patrolman Jaffey." Emily greeted Jaffey a shade absently before offering tea and pastries. Jaffey accepted, but Tom asked if he could just have a cup of tea while he met with the colonel.

"Eli, if you don't mind, could you wait here? I don't want to overburden the chief engineer with too many visitors," Tom said, remembering the reports of Roebling's limited tolerance of visitors. Jaffey didn't mind sipping tea and eating pastries much. He figured he could put up with this sort of duty for some time.

Emily showed Tom up to Wash's study. As they went up the graceful curving stair, she said softly to Tom, "This is quite a surprise, you coming like this." She hesitated a moment and asked, "I wonder . . . if you could do me a favor."

Tom would have gladly done anything in his power for her. "Certainly, anything."

Emily hadn't expected exactly that word. It made her pause, thinking that Tom had anticipated something other than what she had planned to ask.

"If you see Mr. Roebling is becoming irritable," she explained patiently, "or if it seems his attention is wandering, I must ask you not to overtax his constitution and end the interview."

Tom seemed let down but was instantly understanding. "Of course, Emily, I mean Mrs. Roebling. I was going to ask you how I should come at this, and I'm happy you brought it up."

Emily smiled gratefully. "I appreciate your sensitivity, Tom. Washington is frail, though he is improving. He never has visitors, can't stand crowds at all, and conversation taxes him terribly. He rarely goes out, so he doesn't get much exercise, not that he could stand it. He can't walk about much, you know."

"Thanks for telling me. I have to say I'm a little nervous meeting him," Tom admitted. That wasn't true very often, but it was today.

"Oh, you mustn't be. He's just a man, Detective." Emily turned to Tom, smiling brightly.

She tapped lightly on a mahogany door then, not waiting for a response, turned the knob and went in. Tom wasn't sure what to expect. The papers had been painting Washington Roebling as an incurable invalid for years. He was by all accounts a mystery, a suffering hermit-engineer locked away in his monkish room in Brooklyn Heights, his existence defined by the bridge he built and its toll in misery. Tom expected the smells of a sickroom! the faint whiffs of ammonia, the medicinal odors that always made him vaguely uneasy, the bottles of viscous dark liquids with vague curative powers, pills . . . crutches. What he saw when that mahogany door swung open was quite different.

Washington Roebling stood by his desk. His eyes were clear and piercing, his physique seemed solid, even robust. He stood erect before his window. The Brooklyn tower and a portion of the sweep of the cables could be seen over his shoulder. Tom had the instant impression of a great and active mind, fully in command. In fact, the first impression was more mental than physical. The power of intellect and will radiated from the chief engineer like a measurable thing. The only weakness Tom saw at first was a slight squint of the eyes as they tried to focus on him. Maybe it was the air of command, maybe it was the respect he had for the man; whatever it was, Tom found himself standing at loose attention, his hand to his forehead in a salute.

"My compliments, Colonel. It's a pleasure to meet you."

Roebling seemed a little taken aback at first, then his features softened into a wistful smile. "And I you, Detective." Roebling returned the salute. They stood awkwardly for a moment, both surprised that an old habit came back so effortlessly. Roebling broke the silence first. "Well, that was strange. Can't remember the last time I saluted anyone," he said, still grinning.

"To be honest, sir," Tom said, a little embarrassed, "I can't either." They shared a private laugh as they shook hands. Emily watched with her mouth open.

"So, what unit were you with, Detective?"

"The Twentieth New York State Militia. Well, the Eightieth, actually. It was redesignated the Eightieth when we volunteered."

"I remember the Eightieth; the Ulster Guard, right?"

"That's right," Braddock said, pleased the colonel remembered.

"Colonel Gates, as I recall. I knew him slightly. A very good man . . . commanded one of the best regiments in the corps. You came through all right?"

Tom touched his temple where the small shock of white hair shone. "A bit of a crease in my skull to show for my efforts, but no permanent damage. That's a lot more than I can say for most of the rest. Out of 375 engaged at Gettysburg alone, there were 170 killed, wounded, or missing," Tom said, surprised that he remembered the numbers and even more amazed that he felt the need to tell Roebling. It was almost as if he'd stepped back in time.

"You were with Reynolds on the first, right?" Roebling said, knowing the answer. "That must have been a hot fight. I didn't come up till the second, so I missed it. Shame about Reynolds."

Braddock shook his head slowly. He hadn't thought about Reynolds in ages, but he remembered clearly enough. "Yes, sir, it was. Gave 'em hell till we got flanked. You had a close shave there too."

Roebling smiled. "Gouverneur always had a wonderful sense of timing."

"General Warren?"

"Yes. He had a knack for sending me places where nothing seemed to be happening, but once I got there all hell would break loose."

Tom knew exactly what he was referring to. "Like Little Round Top."

Wash sat slowly, exhaling with a sigh. "Among others. We had closer calls, but none that meant so much."

"Suppose not. It's not every day you save the flank of the Army of the Potomac," Tom said, the admiration clear in his voice.

"Oh, we didn't save the flank, Detective, far from it. The boys of the Twentieth Maine, the One Fortieth New York, Hazlett's battery, and all the rest did the saving. Gouverneur and I—we were just directing traffic."

Tom chewed on that for a moment. "That's not what the papers said, as I recall."

"Can't believe everything you read in the papers, Tom. Can I call you Tom?"

Braddock smiled. "Sure. Funny thing, though . . . once it's in the papers, it's real. You can feel like you were a traffic cop till your dying day, but my guess is you'll always be counted a hero of that battle." He saw the colonel start to shake his head but he went on. "Sometimes the papers get it right, you know." They grinned at each other with the knowledge of a shared understanding.

Roebling folded his arms across his chest, leaned back in his chair, and said, "So, what can I tell you about our bridge?"

Emily sat with Tom and Wash for nearly two hours as Tom asked his questions. The list was long. With a construction project the size and length of the Brooklyn Bridge, there had been ample opportunity for fraud, chicanery, rigged bids, disgruntled employees, and the like. Roebling did his best to shed light on any possibilities, but aside from the wire fraud and some other well-publicized shenanigans, there wasn't much else to point to. He gave Tom all the details on the trains, the engineering, the bidders, suppliers, everything. There had been nothing odd in the bidding or construction of the tracks or terminals, at least nothing that would point to fraud or thievery. There were some employees who had left under a cloud as might be expected.

"That McDonald fellow, for example . . . though the Brooklyn fire marshall ruled he accidentally set the caisson fire in '70. We never did find out what happened to him. He simply disappeared. Maybe he bore some grudge . . . we don't know. We always assumed the fire had been an accident, but what if it wasn't?"

"Quite! Can you think of any possible connection between that fire and the trains . . . some common thread, anything could be of use?"

"Nothing, Tom, except that they are both related to the bridge. They're completely separate events, separated by many years. I'm sorry, I just don't see any commonality."

"That brings up another question. Is there anything tying together the men who've died on the job?"

Emily and Wash discussed that for some time, but aside from the obvious fact that they had all worked together, there were few threads linking the various deaths during construction. The single most common cause of death was the caisson disease, or, more commonly, "the bends" which had nearly killed Roebling as well. Though in many ways the caisson disease was a mystery, resulting from exposure to the compressed air atmosphere of the caissons there was nothing like a conspiracy about it.

Finally, after all the other possibilities had been covered, Tom asked, "Suppose I were a saboteur. How would I go about blowing the bridge?"

The colonel frowned in disbelief. "You can't be serious. Could anyone be that mad?"

"Hope not, Colonel, but I'm paid to look at the possibilities, especially in cases like this. Right now we have only the secondhand word of a dead man that there was something going on with the bridge. Someone or some group felt that what that man knew was serious enough to kill him for it. The clipping about the caisson fire disturbs me too. You said it was ruled an accident, but you never did find the man who set it."

Roebling seemed to think that over as he turned to look out the window toward the bridge. "Not much of a connection, really," he said at last. It was obvious from his tone that he thought the idea of sabotage to be a leap of logic. The technical difficulties aside, he simply could not imagine what might motivate men even to think of such a thing.

Tom shrugged. "True, but it's all I've got, so the question stands. How would I blow the bridge if I were crazy enough to attempt it?"

Roebling seemed suddenly tired. His shoulders sagged.

Emily, who had been sitting quietly across from Wash, shot Tom a small frown.

"Well, Tom," Roebling said at last. "The key to the bridge is really very simple." For the next fifteen minutes, he outlined a plan to blow the span. He would have been shocked to know how much it resembled the plan Patrick Sullivan laid out just the night before.

Emily had to make a stop at the bridge after they were through. She offered to drive Tom and Eli. Washington looked played out and his handshake was weak, his fingers trembling. His eyes, though, were still bright, alert, and vital. Tom had thanked him, told him it had been an honor to meet him and meant it.

"Perhaps we can visit again when things calm down a bit, Tom," the colonel said. He appeared to mean it too.

"I'd like that very much. I will, of course, keep you informed of anything that develops, at least as far as the bridge is concerned."

"He liked you," Emily said after they got in the carriage.

Tom smiled warmly, surprisingly pleased at that. "I liked him too. He's stronger than I had—well, you know how the papers picture him."

Emily smiled. "He was putting on a show for you. He doesn't go much beyond an hour or so in situations like that. He'll have to rest for hours, otherwise he won't be able to do much the rest of the day. That's why I say he likes you. Anyone else, he would have asked to leave long before."

They bumped to a stop on the rough cobbles by the bridge office. Tom got out first and helped Emily down. Emily was about to say her good-byes when Tom said that he had business inside with Jacobs. Emily grimaced.

"Yes, charming fellow, I know." Tom chuckled.

They all went in, Emily looking for Hildenbrand and Tom for Jacobs. Eli brought up the rear. As it turned out, Hildenbrand was out on the span, seeing to some detail with the promenade.

Once Tom had gotten the copy of the page he wanted from Jacobs, Emily asked, "Would you walk with me, Tom, and you as well, Mr. Jaffey?"

They couldn't refuse, of course. When they were up on the approach, Tom told Emily how he had spotted Watkins from the roadway near the Brooklyn tower.

"Must have looked like a damn fool, running across the bridge like that. It was in the papers . . . the chase and all," he said as if to legitimize his story.

"Really?" she said, impressed. "I confess I hadn't had time to read them today."

"All for nothing," Tom said disparagingly. "Whoever these men are, they're always one step ahead. One of the reasons I have Jaffey here to watch my back."

Eli smiled and nodded, doing his best to look confident.

Chapter Sixteen

Cheap steel insures a weak bridge.

—*The Herald*

Coffin cursed under his breath. He should have taken the El. It would have been faster than this by a long shot. He hated the goddamn Els, though, with their smoke and noise and crowds. They made him nervous, careening about the city nearly three stories up, driven by engineers whose qualifications seemed to be that they were both Irish and drunks—at least that's how Coffin saw it. Not that stages were exactly safe either. Just getting on and off the things was a challenge, what with traffic barreling by, not stopping even for women. But right now there was no barreling going on at all. Broadway was jammed, and he probably could make better time walking if he had a mind to.

That he didn't have a mind to was due in great part to Tom Braddock. Coffin was on a little pilgrimage to visit Captain Parker of the Sixteenth Precinct. He had some business to attend to with the man. The squeeze on Braddock hadn't panned out yet; in fact Braddock showed even less inclination to rejoin the fold than he had just days before. Coffin needed to put a stop to it. He and Coogan had agreed finally just an hour before.

"The right amount of force, the right amount of pain, the right spot," Coffin had said. Coogan had nodded his agreement, though August could see he didn't care much for the method.

"If he's got a weak spot, that's it. But it's got to be handled just so," Coogan warned. "It goes too far and we'll be dealing with this problem on a whole 'nother level."

"Don't worry. I'll have a talk with Parker," Coffin said confidently. "I'm meeting Byrnes for dinner tonight too. There'll be no interference."

"You be careful how you put this to Byrnes. You say you go way back, but Braddock's on a big case. Byrnes assigned Dolan and Heidelberg to him, so he's taking it seriously. This mucks up the case he'll be looking for someone's head," Coogan had warned.

Coffin smiled coldly as the stage rumbled up Broadway. Coogan was always the more cautious, he the more daring of the team. If, after this final bit of pressure, Braddock could be bent to their will, they'd be unstoppable. Braddock held the key, though he wasn't aware of it. He just hadn't been shown the possibilities. It took vision, after all, and vision was something Coffin had in abundance. If Braddock had to feel a bit of pain first, so be it. The pain would pass. The wounds would heal with proper care, then he'd show him the future. Coogan was right in one respect, though. It was a delicate spot they aimed for, this chink in Braddock's armor. They would do well to be cautious.

Sullivan and Lincoln stood looking glumly at the cluttered room.

"This might take a skosh longer than we thought," Sullivan said. The place looked like the cavalry had camped there.

"Not really surprised, are ye, Pat?" Lincoln shot back. "Watkins never was one to keep his camp in order. I shared a shelter-half tent with him for about three months in '62, until he lost his half." Lincoln stood, looking about the place.

"Maybe we can just take the important stuff. Looks to be a lot of trash mixed in." Pat shook his head. He didn't like this job any more than Lincoln, but he knew the captain was right.

"Captain said to empty the place. We could miss something important in all this shit," Justice said.

"Feel like a goddamn grave robber," Pat grumbled. "Let's get at it. The sooner started, the sooner done."

The two of them set about emptying the room. Watkins had rented it from a couple of Germans. Their lack of English was an advantage. For a couple of dollars a month he had this one room to himself, while the Germans had the rest of the tenement flat. It was cramped, windowless, smelling like a long-unwashed body. Watkins hadn't been much of a housekeeper. The floors, aside from the space occupied by the single dresser and bed, were piled high. It looked like Watkins was in the habit of picking up things he thought might have some value. Food tins, broken coffee grinders, enamelware in various stages of rust and chips, at least a dozen oil lamps, and countless other items clogged the place. It was a pack rat's dream.

"What the hell did he think he was going to do with all this stuff?" Justice wondered out loud after the third trip to their wagon on the street.

Sullivan shrugged. "Who's to say?" he mused. "Not much to show for the life he's lived."

"I don't have all that much more," Justice said. "Less shit anyways. Never was good at keepin' a grip on my shin plasters. Course they wasn't worth holding for long. Started me on bad money habits, I guess." He shook his head.

"I haven't done much better," Pat admitted. "Got a little stashed in case we have to decamp in a hurry, but that's about it."

"Maybe when it's over we can cash in some of that stock in the Union Ferry Company. Should be worth a mint once the bridge is gone."

Lincoln always was a dreamer, Pat thought. "Don't go spending it just yet," he muttered.

They worked at cleaning Watkins's place out for over an hour. He had a prodigious collection of newspapers and periodicals. Moving them was heavy work. Patrick Sullivan had just picked up a pile of boxes, when one toppled over on the floor. A small blizzard of miscellaneous junk spread out on the worn floorboards, but one item caught Pat's eye immediately.

"Damn," he said as he picked it up. "Will you look at this? Ain't seen this picture in maybe twenty years."

Lincoln craned to look over Sullivan's shoulder. "Were we ever that young? Look at you, all decked out in that new uniform. Had to be '61 or '62. Sure as hell nobody had a good uniform much after that, at least not a whole one."

Sullivan chuckled. He did look young. They all did, even the captain. They were all there, along with some others who didn't survive the war.

"Had fire then too," Justice observed. "Damn, we were going to roast up Yankees for dinner, remember?" He elbowed Sullivan.

"Yeah, 'cept it was us got roasted in the end," Pat observed glumly. There wasn't much fire in his words.

"Get a load of Watkins," Justice said, trying to change the subject. "Remember that Bowie knife? He used to say he was gonna stick it up Lincoln's ass." They both laughed at that, but their laugh had a hollow ring in the grubby little tenement room.

"I want to keep this," Sullivan said. "We should, don't you think?"

Justice just nodded, turning away. He cleared his throat before he picked up another box. "Be good for everyone to see that," he said as he walked out with the last of Watkins's effects.

. . .

As they had all expected, nothing much came of Dolan and Heidelberg's search. There were a couple of letters to Lebeau from a sister in Louisiana, some old tintypes of him and Emmons, looking fierce in their best Confederate getup, knives and guns at the ready. Almost every soldier who ever served had one of those. There were no weapons to speak of, nothing more sinister than a couple of sheath knives. In fact, it was the lack of anything suspicious that had Pat Dolan wondering.

"I could toss just about any apartment in this city—any *man*'s place, I mean—and turn up at least one gun. Even if it's just a boot pistol, or one of those little gambler guns, most everybody's got a gun at home," he reasoned. Heidelberg agreed.

"Here we got two men and not a gun between them. Meanwhile there's their pictures with them armed to the teeth. Seems odd."

"No laws against it, Charlie," Tom said. "Maybe they had their fill of shooting in the war," he added, playing devil's advocate. "Wish you had turned something up but I'm not surprised you didn't. Those two are just too clean."

Tom outlined the interview he'd had with the Roeblings, the few suggestions they had, and Washington's outline of how the bridge could be blown.

"First thing," Tom said, "is to go over the records of materials ordered for the bridge! the stone, steel, iron, wood, wire, everything. We need to know who those contractors are. Next comes the train contracts. Anything that has to do with those trains has to be combed finer than a prize angora. Tracks, cars, steam engines, terminals, everything, including the contractors that got the jobs and the ones that didn't too. All the bids were well conducted, according to Roebling, except for the wire. The Roeblings got squeezed out of the contract by some pretty sly maneuvering." Tom told them the tale of political corruption and greed regarding the bidding for the wire contract.

"You boys recall Abrahm Hewitt?" Tom asked. "Anyway he was vice president of the board of trustees, congressman, and manager of Tilden's campaign for president." The detectives still looked at Tom blankly. "Does this sound at all familiar to any of you? You're looking at me like a bunch of cigar store Indians." He went on. "Well . . . the upstanding Mr. Hewitt held a mortgage on J. Lloyd Haigh's wireworks, and made a deal with Haigh not to foreclose, provided Haigh turned over ten percent of what he made on the contract. Hewitt apparently made it his business to see that Haigh got the contract. First he got a resolution passed by the board that no one connected to the bridge should be allowed to bid for the wire. Figured he'd squeeze the Roeblings out of the bidding."

Pat chuckled. "Pretty slick."

Tom held up a hand. "Wait . . . it gets better. Classic political bullshit."

"Sounds like he took a page out of 'Slippery Dick' Connolly's book," Charlie said dryly.

"Yeah, well, Hewitt was a lot more slippery than anyone gave him credit for. Roebling was so insulted that he and Emily wrote his resignation. Delivered it to Henry Murphy, the president of the board." Murphy wouldn't accept it; said it had to be voted on by the entire board. Never brought it to a vote, though. So Roebling did the only other thing he could: sold his stock. It was the only way for his company to bid."

Charlie shook his head. "That took guts! How'd Hewitt get around that?"

Tom smiled wickedly, admiring Hewitt's ruthlessness on some level. "He wasn't about to let Roebling outmaneuver him out of his ten percent," Tom explained, "so he tried a different tack. All bids had to be in by early December '76. The Roeblings had submitted the lowest bid for Bessemer steel. Haigh submitted the lowest bid for Crucible steel. The plans didn't specify Bessemer or Crucible," Tom said slowly so they'd follow him. "With me so far? By some incredible coincidence, which Roebling didn't believe for a second, the *Herald* ran an interview with an unknown engineer named Albert Hill who questioned the specifications for the wire."

"Oh, yeah, I remember that article. Caused all sorts of shit if I'm thinking of the same one. Course that was years ago," Charlie said.

"I didn't remember it myself," Tom admitted. "So, Hill claimed that Roebling's specs were poorly written, too complex, vague, that sort of thing. He also questioned Roebling's having final say on the tests, in spite of the fact that he was not told which manufacturer had submitted each batch of wire for testing. Even worse, he said Roebling wasn't the man for the job due to his injuries."

Jaffey, who had been listening intently, said, "Basically just an outright smear campaign. How was the colonel supposed to defend himself? Anything he said would look like excuses."

Tom slapped Eli on the back. "Exactly, Eli. That's why it was pure genius. Now, Hill had never built a suspension bridge himself. God knows where the *Herald* found him, but once it was all over the press, people started believing him. Bessemer steel was suddenly not good enough."

Tom took a sip of his coffee before going on. He felt that this was a great example of the kind of fraud, maneuvering, and chicanery they should be on the lookout for.

"Roebling was mad as hell. Even now I could see how much it bothered him and his wife. His honor and reputation were dragged through the mud. When Kinsella, the publisher of the *Brooklyn Eagle,* backed Hill, it put the last nail in the coffin."

"We know how that turned out," Pat mused.

"Yeah. Haigh got the contract. Hewitt got his ten percent, I guess too. Nobody ever questioned *his* motives or integrity." Tom shook his head in disbelief. "Not even after Haigh got caught in the wire fraud. Hell, Haigh even kept the contract!"

"Unbelievable! Pays to have powerful friends. Same old story," Dolan said.

"The point of this tale, gentlemen, is that there could be more than one Haigh or Hewitt out there, one that's willing to kill to keep his secret and his profits."

Dolan and Heidelberg agreed immediately.

"We'll start with the big ones," Charlie said, "then we'll work our way down."

"Might pay to have a look at some of the contractors' order books too. Get an idea of whether they match up with the bridge contracts," Pat added.

"Right. May as well start there," Tom replied. This sort of work didn't thrill him but at the moment it seemed the only avenue.

They left it there for the evening. Pat and Charlie stayed to finish up some paperwork from another case while Tom and Eli headed off for Pell Street and Master Kwan's class. Jaffey didn't know what to expect. He'd never had any organized exercise, except for calisthenics at the police school. He thought he was in pretty good shape, but, in truth, he had no way to measure that. He was nervous about the Chinese too, especially the head man, whom Tom told him to call "Master Kwan" or just "Master." He felt strange about calling any Chinese "Master." To be Chinese in New York was to be even lower than the blacks. The Chinese exclusion acts were proof of that. Jaffey had never heard of any race being excluded from the country before. He didn't know enough about the Chinese to know the reasons why either. They were a mysterious, quiet people, about as different from him as a human could be. That was part of the problem, he suspected—they were so different from the majority of the population. Maybe it was the opium trade that seemed to follow them wherever they went. He had learned a little about the opium problem during training, but it didn't seem to be taken too seriously. There were said to be scores of opium dens in the city, but even though a law had been passed making it a misdemeanor to smoke or eat opium, there had been only twelve arrests in '82 and not many more in '83.

"Say, Tom, do you know any opium dens?" Jaffey asked.

"Sure, plenty to choose from down here. Why, you want to hit the pipe?" Tom said with a sarcastic grin.

"Don't think so. Just thinking about the Chinese and what they told me about the opium trade in police school."

"Well, if you'd like some firsthand knowledge on the subject, we can take a detour after the workout," Tom offered in the same tone he'd have used if he was suggesting they stop for a beer. Jaffey agreed immediately. As they neared Pell Street, Jaffey could see the change in the neighborhood. The smells were different. The air bore the tang of spices and foods he could only guess at. The talk on the street melted from Italian into Chinese—Cantonese, actually, but Eli didn't know the difference. The signs were unreadable, the alphabet a jumble of lines and slashes. It didn't feel like New York at all. One thing was the same though: the bustle of the street, the pushcart vendors, the produce stands, the traffic, the pedestrians.

As they drew deeper into the few blocks near Chatham Square that were considered Chinatown, he began to notice that he and Tom were the subject of some attention. They were outsiders here. But Jaffey noticed that Tom was exchanging an occasional subtle greeting with Chinese on the street. At first he wasn't sure what it meant—the short bob of the head and the smile that wasn't; then he noticed Tom doing it too.

"You know some of these people?"

"Sure, you don't walk patrol for three years without getting to know people," Tom said. "Things have changed since then, but I still know a lot of them. Good, hardworking people, mostly. They've got two vices though: They gamble like fiends and they love their opium." Tom motioned with his head as they turned a corner. "Before we go to class, I want to stop off at a little place I know."

"I thought we were going to an opium den *after* training," Jaffey said, confused.

"Oh, we'll do that, but first I wanted to see if the master is through with work. We're a little early, see."

"Oh. Where's he work?" Jaffey looked around.

"Someplace more addictive than the opium dens," Tom answered with a mysterious grin.

I'm a few minutes they stood before a red-brick four-story tenement. Its basement was only partly below street level. Through the large window in front, Jaffey could see a table with two Chinese seated over steaming bowls. They were going at the contents with what appeared to Jaffey to be a pair of pencils. Tom went down the four steps to the front door.

"It's not a restaurant officially or legally, but down here the rules get bent in unusual ways." Tom said. "I always liked it because it's close to headquarters but still out of the way."

Eli kind of turned up his nose. "The master works here?" His skepticism was clear. What he expected, even he couldn't have told, but it wasn't this.

"Listen," Tom said, stopping before they went in. "Lesson number one, don't judge a man by the job he does. Jobs aren't exactly open to Chinese, in case you haven't noticed. It's near impossible for men to find work, and when they do, they earn much less than whites. As for Master Kwan, he's part cook, part waiter, part owner. Take your pick." Tom opened the door and a wave of hot aromas washed over them. "See what I mean?" Tom half turned with a big grin. "Better than opium." He turned to go in but wasn't more than two steps inside when he pulled up short, like a ship run aground. Jaffey almost bumped into him. Tom turned with a quick, silent gesture and got Eli going back out the door.

"What's wrong? Why'd we turn around?"

Tom hustled Jaffey away down Mott, toward the square. Once they were a couple of doors away, Tom turned to look back.

"It was Coffin and Byrnes having dinner. I don't think they saw us." Tom craned to see if anyone followed. "Master Kwan saw me coming and gave me a sign."

"Damn, I didn't see any of that. Where were they?"

"Off in a corner. The master covered for us. Did you see the man folding the tablecloth?"

Jaffey gave Tom a confused squint. "What are they both doing down here together?"

Tom was no less puzzled. "That, my lad, is what's worrying me."

They went on to 16 Pell Street, where Tom turned in at an unmarked door that led them upstairs.

"This is the headquarters of the Hip Sing Tong," Tom said softly. "Don't ask questions. Don't say anything, in fact. Just follow my lead. Without Master Kwan here, there might be some who don't appreciate our company."

"I'm right behind you." Jaffey couldn't hide the doubt in his voice. He was the foreigner here, and help was a long way off if it was needed. Tom didn't seem to hesitate, though.

Fortunately, there were three men in the room at the top of the stairs who knew Tom. Some of the rest didn't seem too friendly. He introduced Jaffey to the three, each of whom bowed slightly at the introduction, then shook hands. Eli did his best to ape their bows, but his reception was stiff and as understated as only a Chinaman could make it. The five men went into a large room at the back of the building. It was empty, save for some straw mats on the floor, some bamboo poles leaning in one corner, and a couple of heavy padded poles that Eli guessed were for punching practice. Tom and the Chinese stripped down to just a pair of shorts and started stretching. Eli tried to match their movements and quickly found he couldn't.

"Just try to relax the muscles. Don't force it," Tom warned him. "Slow and easy." They all worked silently, the Chinese bending their bodies in ways Jaffey could not imagine himself doing. Even Tom could not match the three of them, their supple limbs stretching as if they had no joints.

After about fifteen minutes, Master Kwan came bustling in. He didn't look much like a master of anything to Jaffey. He was small and slight, not weighing more than 130 pounds, he guessed. He wasn't young either. Eli figured him for at least fifty, maybe more. To his eye, Chinese didn't age the way Americans did. Old and skinny or not, Tom and the other three stopped what they were doing and bowed deeply, much more deeply, Eli noticed, than the bows he had received. He did his best imitation as Tom watched from the corner of his eye.

Master Kwan summoned Tom with a lifted finger and a twitch of the head. They went to one corner of the room and spoke softly for a few minutes. At one point, Eli noticed them watching him as he stretched. Tom came back to Eli with a grin on his face.

"Master Kwan hates Coffin more than average, maybe more than me. He says he pays the Chinese no respect, treats them like dirt under his heel. He says the cook spits in his soup," Tom said with an ear-to-ear grin, "but Coffin keeps coming back."

"He doesn't hate the Chinese," Jaffey said. "That's the way he treats everybody."

Tom laughed. "That's exactly what *I* told him. Anyway, the master says anyone who hates Coffin is a friend of his and can study here."

Jaffey turned to look at Master Kwan and bowed deeply. "Very good," Tom said under his breath. "You're learning."

The three Chinese took turns sparring in one corner, while Tom and Master Kwan worked with Eli. They took it slow, showing him the basics of punching and a couple of simple kicks. Once he had them down, Master Kwan said, "Practice! You do one hundred each, now!"

Jaffey did as he was told. Tom worked with the master, their movements fluid and effortless. They flowed like water from one movement to another in a stylized dance. Sometimes slow, sometimes with speed and ferocity, they moved together. Eli was struck by how alike they were and how different. Like mirror images, strangely altered, they flowed to the rhythms of the art. Eli kept at his practice well past one hundred repetitions.

"You did good. The master was pleased," Tom said later as they were leaving. "He said that for a clumsy white devil, you show promise. You honored me before him, so you gained face all around. Now I'm taking you to the best opium den in Chinatown."

Eli didn't know quite what to make of that and it must have shown. "Don't worry, Eli, we won't be hitting the pipe tonight."

"Tom, if you don't mind my asking, you sound like you know a lot about opium. Ah—what I mean is . . ."

Braddock looked at Jaffey closely, then gave a little shrug. "Yeah, I've tried it . . . more than once, if you gotta know," Tom admitted easily. "Let me get something clear, first off. It's good . . . really good . . . how can I describe it?" Tom mused, trying to put words to what could not be translated. "Ever read Coleridge . . . the poem about Kublai Khan?"

Eli shook his head.

"Well, Coleridge smoked a lot of opium, and if you read the poem you can get a glimpse of what it's like. It's like floating on a cloud . . . being master of the cosmos." Tom smiled in dreamy remembrance. "Like spending . . . except it goes on and on in the mind. Not as messy, of course," he said with a laugh, elbowing Eli in the side.

Jaffey seemed embarrassed. Tom guessed his experience with sex was limited to a squeeze and a grope on some Staten Island porch.

"But that's the problem, Eli," Tom said, his voice growing hard. "If you do it enough, you won't want to do anything else, and I mean *anything*." Tom said this as if he knew what he was talking about. "One by one the things you hold dear will go up in smoke: money, career, family, girlfriend, everything. The pipe will take it all and demand more. So do it once if you want, but leave it at that, or you risk everything."

"C'mon, Tom, it's really that strong? I mean, a strong will, moral fiber, and—"

"Don't mean a damn thing!" Tom interrupted. "Nobody does it for long and comes out a winner. Here we are."

They stood before another tenement, just like every other one on Mott Street. The one difference was the pair of Chinese lounging on the front stoop. They had watched Tom and Eli from the time they turned the corner. Up close they were a vicious-looking pair. Pockmarked faces, one very round, one thin and angular, were home to black expressionless eyes. Like razor slits in a bag of coal, they took in light but gave nothing back.

"Hello, boys," Tom said to the two of them. "You're out again, huh, Lee? How are things on Blackwell's Island?" he said to the round-faced one. "Well, don't worry, I'm not here for you or anyone else. Just want to show my friend here the way of the *heen cheong*."

Without saying a word or changing expression, Lee nodded toward the steps leading to the basement.

Tom took Jaffey by the arm. "Down we go, lad."

They opened the basement door to a different world. An ancient Chinaman with a face like an old sack sat behind a small desk in a lavishly decorated vestibule. Silk wall hangings with painted dragons writhed and breathed fire across their shimmering length. Tassled curtains hung from the door opposite the one they had entered. A carved three-panel screen in dark, exotic wood glowed from hand-rubbed polish in one corner. Another young tough was with the old man. He was instantly on guard when the cops walked through the door. Eli saw a hand go into a pocket. Without thinking he reached under his jacket for the butt of his pistol. Tom put a restraining hand on Jaffey's arm and lifted one finger to the young man.

"How've you been, Sung Chow?" he said genially to old sack-face. The man said something in Chinese. Whatever it was, it was quick, sharp, and had the effect of calling off his guard dog. The tough relaxed and the hand came out of his pocket. "How's business, old friend?"

"Ah, Tommy. Not see you on Mott Street long time," he said, springing up from behind his desk with more energy than Jaffey would have imagined. He bowed and shook Braddock's hand like a long-lost uncle. "Hard to get good product. Long way to China. Cost lotta dolla. Gotta go up price all time. Still not make profit."

Tom gave him a conspiratorial grin. "Yeah, but you're gonna stick it out for a bit longer, eh, Sung?" They exchanged pleasantries and gossip for a few minutes. It was obvious that Tom knew old sack-face well. "Listen, I just want to give my friend here a little tour. Told him you have the finest place in all New York."

"That right, Tommy. Finest place, numba-one opium, very fine. You go in, but no scare customa, okay?"

"Sure, sure. We're not here to arrest anyone," Tom said, holding up his hands innocently.

They went through the curtained door into a room lit only by a few flickering candles.

"That old bastard owns half a dozen places like this," Tom whispered. "Got more goddamn money than the Vanderbilts. They're gold mines."

As Jaffey's eyes became accustomed to the gloom, he could see the room was bare except for bunks set up against the walls. There was room for eight in this one room, and he could see another just like it behind. There were four men in various bunks. They had no mattresses. The bunks were really just wooden frames where the smokers could recline. Jaffey noticed with some surprise that two were not Chinese. Tom noticed too.

"Some uptown swells out for an evening of slumming," Tom said, motioning toward them. "More than half the opium smokers aren't Chinese. Getting pretty popular with the uptown types."

They watched as one of the Chinese began the ritual.

"Now watch," Tom whispered, motioning with his head. "He takes a little from the *hop toy*."

"That little box?" Jaffey asked. "That's a *hop toy*?"

"Right. What he's going to do is to cook it a little first before he actually smokes it, get it soft and sticky, like tar. See . . . he sticks the little ball with that needle. Then he'll—"

"Looks like my ma's darning needle," Jaffey said, the image of his mother smoking opium bringing a grin to his lips.

"That's the *yen hauk*. Watch what he does with it." The Chinese had speared the tarry opium ball on one end of the needle. "Now he'll cook it a bit and roll the needle in his fingers like a pig on a spit . . . cook it all around evenly. It's called chying the mass."

"Smells nice," said Jaffey, breathing it in tentatively. "Sort of a musky, fruity smell to it. It's almost as if I can taste it."

The Chinese slowly rolled the needle in his fingers over a small oil lamp, not letting the flame lick any spot too long. The ball of opium smoked and expanded as it heated. Tom seemed to relish the aroma. Jaffey saw him breathing deep but said nothing.

"Okay, now it goes into the *heen cheong* and he'll smoke it down to a cinder . . . but slow, nice and slow."

The man carefully smeared the small tarry mass around the bowl of the pipe, his fingers rolling the needle. The man wore a look of such concentration, it was like watching a fine craftsman at work or a priest preparing the host.

"Why do they smoke lying down like that Tom?" Jaffey asked when the Chinese had finished inhaling the smoke from the heated opium. It seemed as if he'd taken in the whole thing in one huge lung-ful, holding it for an eternity before finally letting it out in a rapturous gasp.

"Well . . . depending on how much you smoke, you might just fall down anyway. Saves getting a nasty knock on the head."

"It doesn't look all that great," Jaffey said after the man had finished. "He's just lying there." Eli waved a dismissive hand at the man.

Tom said patiently, "Trust me, he's somewhere else entirely right now. While you're seeing his body looking like a dead man, on the inside he's flying in the best damn dream you can imagine."

Later, back out in the cool evening air of Mott Street, Jaffey wondered at the experience. It had a strange attraction, and just breathing the smoke in the room left him feeling unsteady but remarkably pleased with himself, almost euphoric. It was at once a peaceful yet powerful feeling, and all was right with the world for him.

"Feeling a little strange?" Tom asked, grinning. "You can imagine a little what it's like to smoke it, then. Take my advice, though, don't do it."

Jaffey shook his head slowly. "Wasn't thinking I'd like to. The idea of coming to that depressing cave like a mole person and sucking on a pipe in the dark really doesn't appeal to me. It's all turned inward. There's no fun to it. At least if you go to a bar, there's friends and laughing, and people to share a song or a joke with."

Braddock grinned. "Quite right, lad. I'll take a good loud bar any day over that tomb. Sort of like a crypt too, now that I think of it. They just don't know it yet. Still, it's a sight you should see if you're a cop."

They parted then, at the el, saying their good-byes and going their separate ways.

It was probably around 1:00 A.M. when Tom heard the pounding on his door. He'd been dreaming of Mary. It was her body, and it felt like her in the dream, not the physical feel, but the emotional one. He didn't need to see her face to know it was her. It wasn't her face he was concentrating on anyway. But the pounding rippled in his sleep and he looked up at Mary, but it wasn't her. It was Emily in his arms. It shocked and fascinated him at the same time. What surprised him more than anything was how much he liked the idea. Not so surprising was the wave of guilt that cascaded over him like a cold shower. Emily disappeared. The pounding came again and he imagined it as shots being fired, *boom, boom, boom!* Bullets bounced around his sleeping brain. He imagined it was Mary shooting at him for being such a cheating bastard. He didn't doubt for a minute that she'd do it. He dove for cover, rolling over on his belly, covering his head. *Boom, boom, boom* again. But this time it wasn't gunfire. His waking brain couldn't make it out as he drifted somewhere between sleep and consciousness. *Boom, boom, boom!*

"Tommy, wake up, man!" someone called from the hall. His eyes snapped open and he jackknifed up in bed, awake but groggy. *Boom, boom, boom, boom.*

"C'mon, Tommy. Open up!" That got him going finally. He came near to tripping over both Grant and Lee, who were milling nervously in the hall.

"Out of the way, fleabags!"

It was Sam. Tom knew immediately from the look on his friend's face that it was not good news.

"Sam, what the fuck time . . . ?"

Sam's look stopped the words in Tom's throat.

"It's Mary, Tom. Get dressed, and let's go." Tom hadn't heard anything beyond "It's Mary." He lived in dread of this sort of thing, knowing it would happen in the course of a business like hers. He didn't say a word, just turned and ran back to his bedroom. His dream lingered and the guilt of it left him with a gnawing hole in his gut, as if he really had been with Emily. He cursed himself as he dressed. Sam stood in the hall outside his door for a second, then came in. Tom had a dozen questions he wanted answered but he knew it would just slow him down to ask them of Sam. Mary was alive, that was all that was important. Sam would have told him right away if she wasn't. He never dressed so fast in his life, at least not since the war.

He was back out in two minutes, tucking the Colt under his arm.

"Let's go. You can tell me on the way." There was a hack waiting on the blackened cobbles of Lafayette Place. They got in and Sam barked, "New York Hospital."

"How bad is it, Sam? No sugar-coating."

Sam took a deep breath. "First off, she's not gonna die or anything. She's pretty busted up, though. Left arm's broke, maybe a rib or two. Hurts when she breathes," he explained. "She's got a hell of a shiner . . . face is swole up. Aside from that, bruises and such." Tom listened grim and stony-faced, his mouth set like a straight razor.

"A client? I want to know, so I can kill the bastard." Braddock growled. The clatter of hooves and wheels on cobbles couldn't mask the tone. Knowing Tom, it was no idle threat. A chill went through Sam as he hoped he could contain Braddock before things got completely out of hand. He took a deep breath.

"It was a raid. You'll not be killin' anyone, partner."

Braddock almost jumped out of his seat and the cab rocked as he slammed his fist against the door.

"Christ! What the fuck is going on? The Sixteenth's never given her any trouble, not like this. She pays who she has to." Tom almost shouted, the confusion clear on his face as he looked to Sam for answers.

"I know. I can't make it out either." Sam watched Tom from the corner of his eye as he said this.

"Besides, they know who some of her clients are so they leave her alone," Tom said. "I don't get it. It's not like Parker," he said, referring to the Sixteenth Precinct's commander. "Sure it was them?" Tom couldn't see Sam's face clearly in the darkened cab but something wasn't right.

"We're almost there," Sam said, looking out the window. "Mary'll tell you what happened. Don't know it all myself."

Tom gave him a short, hard look. "Not like you to hold out on me, Sam."

Sam hesitated, opening his mouth for an instant before he stopped himself. "Just my guess is all, so I'll keep it to myself," Sam said carefully. "We're here anyway. I'll pay the cabbie, you go on up. Room 214."

Tom bounded up the stairs to the second floor and blew down a broad corridor. His shoes clacked and echoed on the tile floors. After a wrong turn and a quick about-face he found the room. He turned the knob quietly, as if he were housebreaking, and eased the door open. There was no light in the room. The dark and the sickroom smells hung inside, solid as a wall. There were two beds. Tom couldn't make out which Mary was in. Then he saw Chelsea crumpled in a chair beside the far bed. The window near the bed let in a soft gray light from the gas lamps on the street. Tom stole across the room, to Mary's bedside, not wanting to wake them. The lamplight cast long thin shadows across her bed like prison bars. Even in the night's indistinct caress Mary's face looked swollen and dark. Her head rested on the pillow, the uninjured side down. Her hair was matted and wild. One arm lay on the blanket. It was swathed in a white sling. Her breathing seemed swift, shallow, birdlike. Tom heard footsteps in the hall. A moment later Sam crept in.

"Sleeping," Tom whispered.

Sam nodded. "Maybe I better go. You're staying." It was not a question.

"Yeah," Tom said more to Mary than his friend. "And, Sam . . . thanks."

Sam put a hand on Tom's shoulder. "No problem. I was on duty anyway." Sam said good-bye softly and went out, closing the door behind him.

"Tommy . . . that you?" The door didn't close hard, but it must have been enough to wake Mary.

"It's me, sweetheart." He bent low to kiss her damp forehead. Her hand found his. "How're you feeling?"

"Bout as good as I look, maybe worse," she said with a weak grin. "How . . . I look?"

Tom didn't answer. "Who did this? Sam said it was a raid."

Mary fixed worried eyes on Tom. "It was," she said slowly. "Couldn't understand . . . at first," she said, shaking her head a little. "Haven't had . . . trouble from them. Then I saw the others."

Tom stiffened. "What others? Who was with them?" he probed a little too roughly.

Mary hesitated. "Only knew one or two by sight," she said cautiously, seeming to want to hold it back. "Tommy, I don't want to get you upset. What happened was partly my own fault," she tried to explain, but he could see she was trying to gloss it over. "I got so mad. You know how I can get." Tom nodded. He knew. "Well, I got so mad . . . was screaming at them and hitting and one of them hit me back. I fell over a chair," she said with a rueful chuckle that drew a grimace of pain across her face. "That's what hurt my arm. Hurts to breathe too but that was *my* fault," she was too quick to add. The real story was much worse than that. It hadn't been just one fall that caused her injuries, and not just one officer who'd hit her. There had been other things too, things she'd never tell Tom. Those things she could withstand; she wasn't so sure about him. It wasn't for herself she wasn't telling it all, it was for Tom. She looked into his eyes seeing the doubt and the anger, knowing he suspected more. "Nobody to blame but me," she said quietly but as firmly as she could.

Tom was silent, his face half in soft, gray light, half in tar-black shadow.

"You haven't told me who the others were," he reminded her in a voice soft yet hard.

"Tommy, promise me you won't do anything," Mary said, pleading.

Tom looked at her, his face dark and purposeful. He was not to be denied. "Tell me," he said flatly. "I won't have you busted up like this and do nothing. What kind of man would I be?" he asked, knowing the answer. "They busted up your place too, right?" He'd seen those kinds of raids before.

Mary tried to reason with him. "This isn't about you, Tom." Though she knew with perfect clarity that it was. "It's not about whether you can defend me or not. And my place . . . ?" Mary was quiet for a moment, thinking of herself more than her place. "There's nothing broken that can't be fixed."

Tom was getting tired of her trying to protect him. She didn't really have to say the name. He knew.

"It was Coffin's boys, wasn't it? He's behind this. Should've seen it right away." He could see the confirmation in her eyes. "That son of a bitch!"

Mary clutched at his arm with her good hand. "I think so," she said in a small voice. "I heard them talking."

"*Fuck*! That son of a bitch!" Tom almost shouted. He got up, a huge black silhouette looming against the flannel-gray light outside. His black hands looked like sledgehammers clenched at his sides.

Mary had feared this more than anything. He'd kill Coffin if she wasn't able to control him.

"*Tommy, no!* You can't solve anything that way," she pleaded. "They'll be waiting for you too." She tried to appeal to his logical side. "There's other ways to handle this."

"Not for me, not this. That bastard won't face me himself, so he hits at you!" Tom said in a low, almost incredulous growl. "He's gonna find out what it means to be hit. I *guarantee* he won't like it." Tom started for the door, a shadow blacker than the night. He was in a rage that took him out of himself, a blinding state of limited thought and unlimited action. How much of it was a residual guilt from his dream of Emily he couldn't know, but it clung to him like cheap perfume. Nothing Mary could say was going to stop him, so she said the only thing left to say.

"I love you, Tommy."

He stopped at that, his hand on the doorknob. In two heartbeats he was back at her side, holding her so close it made her ribs ache. "I love you too, Mary. Always."

She felt the tension in him as he said that, the rage below the words, the frustration. She held him tighter despite her ribs.

"But I have to go."

"Tommy, don't." She tried again. "Even if you kill him . . . and his men don't kill you . . . they'll hang you for it. There's no winning." She could see that none of this was working. Tom wasn't thinking. He was acting on some instinctive level. His eyes just glazed over when she talked of the consequences.

"I'm going." He kissed her one last time. This time he rose and left quickly, afraid she might stop him again.

Mary wished she could cry. She wished she could slap some sense into him. Tom was running out to throw away his life and their future with it. But when she cried her ribs hurt so badly it took her breath away. So the tears ran down her cheeks in silent little rivers. The stabbing pain in her side was to her the death of hope and of heart.

Striking at Mary made it not just business anymore. This was *personal*. Coffin had made the mistake of his life if he thought that something like this could put the reins back on him, Tom thought. Coffin would pay and to hell with the consequences. The fact that Coffin was a captain of police meant nothing. The fact that his little corps of men were probably ready for him meant nothing. Tom's rage was like some force of nature, swirling blowing and crashing inside his head, obliterating everything in its path, blotting out all reason, logic, and caution. Right now it focused on blotting out Coffin. Tom's shoes echoed down the tiled corridor like a metronome. They fell fast and heavy.

Tom knew where Coffin lived, over on Thirty-sixth Street, near Lexington. There were no cabs in sight, so he set off on foot. It was the walk that saved him. The streets were deserted. Nothing moved, no horsecars were in sight, no carriages or pedestrians. Tom walked the streets alone, in an alternating dream of blackness and light. The gas lamps cast pools of artificial day and reason somehow seemed stronger in their bright circles, but there were black gulfs between, gulfs where rage and madness ruled. As he strode from one pool of light to the next on those blackened sleeping streets, the light slowly started to seep in and the light was Mary.

He thought of the things she'd said, felt the things she hadn't. For perhaps the first time since the war, he started to think of someone else before himself. It was something he hadn't had much practice doing. But now, with his future and hers in the balance, he was compelled to. At first, he cursed in the darkness between the gas amps. Coffin had earned his death. He would deliver it. Terribly, swiftly, Coffin would finally reap what he had sown. That was a promise and a commitment that he'd not go back on. But as he thought of *his* Mary, for that was how he thought of her, his temper cooled. On that long echoing walk, his brain slowly started to take control. He needed a plan. He couldn't just knock on Coffin's door and shoot him in his pajamas, no matter how appealing that might be. He wanted to be with Mary for the rest of his life. The only way that could happen was if he was very smart about what he did in the next few minutes. His mind was working feverishly when he heard footsteps behind him.

It didn't really surprise him that he had been tailed. In the state he was in when he left the hospital, he wouldn't have noticed an army behind him. It only made sense for one of the corps to keep watch at the hospital. Tom was surprised it had taken him this long to wake up to it. He had just come to Thirty-fourth and Fifth. A. T. Stewart's marble mansion loomed on the opposite corner, a monument to the merchant prince. It was said that the place cost over $3 million. Stewart had razed Sarsaparilla Townsend's brownstone mansion just so he could build a bigger one of marble on the same spot. "Money to burn," Tom thought absently. A quick glance over his shoulder showed his tail had stopped half a block back to loiter in a doorway. He didn't like being tailed. He didn't care who it was, whether he knew him or not, whether they had gotten drunk together or not. He'd have to put a stop to it. Nobody was going to tail him and get away with it.

Tom crossed Thirty-fourth and walked up Fifth past Stewart's mansion, then trotted quickly across Fifth on Thirty-fifth, and out of sight of his pursuer. He heard the footsteps before he saw his man hurrying to catch up. From the blackness on the side of a brownstone's front stairs, he waited as his quarry hustled past. Tom didn't recognize him. It didn't matter. Tom sprang out behind the man with his best speed and stealth. The cop was alert, though, and the scrape of Tom's shoe brought him around in a backhanded swipe as Tom closed in. A heavy sap whistled over Tom's head as he ducked. An instant later Tom's right drove into the cop's side. It landed just below the ribs, and Tom was rewarded with a sickening *whoof* of pain as his man doubled over. He caught a halfhearted swing of the sap with his left, then chopped down on the exposed neck with his right. It felt good to watch the man go down. For all he knew this might have been the one who hit Mary.

The cop was down, but a hand fumbled for his pistol as he lay on the sidewalk. Thinking of Mary, Tom kicked the cop in the ribs. He thought he heard something break. Tom bent over, reached under the man's jacket, and took his pistol.

"No hard feelings, sport," Tom said without meaning it. In another five minutes, Braddock stood before Coffin's town house. He looked up at the double doors with their heavy brass knobs and knocker. He was going to enjoy this, he decided. A grim smile creased his lips but he wiped it away. It wouldn't do to smile right now, not with what he planned to do. The big brass knocker boomed through the house, shaking the front doors in their hinges.

☆ Chapter Seventeen ☆

And it is our own city which is to be forever famous for possessing this greatest architectural and engineering work of the continent and of the age.

—THOMAS KINSELLA

M ary slept fitfully. Though her body yearned for it, her mind gave her no peace. Silent tears carved her cheeks. In the course of just a few hours she had lost nearly everything of value to her. Her business was in shambles. Her girls, whom she cared for like family, were in Jefferson Market jail cells. Her clients would probably not return anytime soon, if ever. And far, far worse was Tom. He had gone to throw his life away and their future with it. She had longed for that future. Its pull was irresistible. But he was sacrificing it for his pride and his stupid, manly honor. She thought she had loved him for those things. She wept in the dark, mourning the life they might have had.

It wasn't that she didn't want Coffin to pay for what he'd done. He deserved a savage beating at the very least. But as much as Mary might have wanted Coffin to suffer, she knew it was useless to try. If his private army didn't get Tom, the law surely would. Mary didn't imagine there was any clause in police regulations permitting the beating of captains. If Tom was lucky enough to live, he'd be spending the next few years on Blackwell's Island. He might not survive that either. Mary had no doubt about Coffin's reach extending into that place. Tom had put plenty of men there over the years. He'd be living among a crowd who'd like nothing better than to see him dead.

It wasn't worth it, none of it. Coffin could go on living a long and happy life for all Mary cared. He could become police commissioner, or mayor. It didn't matter. He could feel he'd won, take pride in punishing her and Tom and bringing him to heel. What did it matter, so long as Tom and she were together. They could go anywhere, San Francisco or Chicago, anywhere they could rebuild their lives. That didn't seem possible now. Chelsea held her hand through her mourning night. Mary must have fallen asleep like that, surrendering at last to exhaustion. She woke with a little start. The hand in hers stroked her fingers, a soothing, healing caress. Her right eye opened halfway. The left one, swollen shut, didn't open at all. Through the sand of her sleep, the half awake world took on a bleary cast. Her room was gray. The black of night had fled to the corners and behind the bed. Chelsea stroked her hand, caressing her back to a painless sleep. Chelsea's big strong fingers seemed to cradle her little hand like a broken bird, calming, soothing. In her half sleep Mary imagined the hand was much bigger than Chelsea's. It seemed half again too big. A lazy eye opened to resolve the disparity and put her maid back into proper perspective.

The gray-lit room swam, blurry and colorless. Chelsea loomed large, her outline a massive, darker gray. A small frown sent a stab of pain through her swollen eye.

Mary stirred and focused. "Chelsea?"

"It's me, sweetheart. I'm here," a voice said. Chelsea had never called her sweetheart before. She was so big in the dark. She'd never noticed how big Chelsea was. Mary began to imagine it wasn't her maid who held her hand. But that wasn't possible.

"Tommy?" she heard herself say. "Tommy?" His hand tightened on hers in a reassuring squeeze.

"Yeah, it's me," Tom said softly, almost sheepishly. "Didn't expect to see me, did you?"

Mary jolted awake. For an instant she thought she might have dreamed the whole thing. Maybe he'd never gone to kill Coffin. Maybe he'd been here all along, holding her hand in the dark. But that was only for an instant.

"Tommy! You came back!" she croaked through dry lips. Though her voice was gravelly, the wonder and the relief were clear. It was a sweet reward to Tom, who knew then how right his choice had been.

"Where else would I go?" he replied softly.

"Don't play with me, you bastard," she said with an anger she didn't feel. "What happened? You didn't . . . ?"

Tom shook his head slowly in answer. "Coffin is safe in bed. He won't be doing any dying just yet." Tom's voice had an edge that didn't sound like kidding.

"What do you mean, 'just yet?' " she asked with a confused frown.

"Funny thing . . ." Tom said, seemingly half in thought. "I'd be dead or in jail by now if it wasn't for you. I left here with nothing in my thick skull but killing that bastard. A roaring fire in the furnace and a full head of steam . . . Coffin has you to thank he's still alive. Kind of ironic, actually," Tom said with a twist to his mouth.

Mary still frowned. "What are you trying to tell me?"

"I'm telling you I love you. As if I ever had a doubt."

"I'm not getting this. . . . You're killing Coffin, you're not killing him yet. You love me. What are you . . . ?" She stumbled, putting a hand to her eyes. "I'm confused. I mean . . . I love you too, you idiot, but I'm not following you at all."

He gave her a patient smile, knowing he wasn't being as clear as he'd like. "It was you that stopped me," he said. "I was gonna kill him. When I left, that was the only thing I could think to do. You stopped me, though."

Mary shook her head again. "You keep saying that. How?"

"Mary . . . it was for the love of you I held off killing Coffin. You were right. I was throwing away everything. I was just too . . . fired up to see it. What we have together is too precious," he whispered. "Worth so much more to me. . . ."

"Oh, Tommy!" She hugged him till her ribs sent jolting icicles of pain through her side and her tears soaked through his shirt. "God, I'm so happy, I can't believe it. I've been thinking all sorts of terrible things tonight."

They sat in silence, her hand in his.

At last he said quietly, "I'm not really all that good. I'm gonna make him pay, you know. He can't do what he did and get away with it." His voice held a quiet intensity. "It's kind of funny actually. I asked him to loan me some money to help you out, fix up the place and things."

Mary looked at him in shock. "I don't need his money. Why would I . . ."

"It's okay," he interrupted. "I know. Besides, I'll never have to repay it. I know that much."

Mary heard the hard edge in his voice but she asked anyway. "You sure about this? This is dangerous. You're talking about . . . you're talking mur-der?" Mary didn't even like to use the word. She didn't like to think of Tom doing it either, not even to Coffin.

"Yeah, I guess that's what it's called," Tom said evenly. "Not sure that's what's in the cards for the captain, though I gotta admit I'd enjoy it." He smiled grimly. The sight sent a chill through Mary to see it. "Murder or not, Coffin's not gonna like it one little bit."

. . .

Later that morning, as he climbed the steps to the Marble Palace, Tom thought about what he had told Mary. Maybe it would have been better if she didn't know. If anything went wrong the cops would be sure to question her. He could have just said he was going to do it and leave it at that. But he felt the need to be honest with her, to tell her everything. His risk was hers and hers his. One boat, two captains.

"Mornin', boys." Tom dragged himself over to a chair. Pat, Charlie, and Eli said nothing until he collapsed into it.

"You're late. Not like you," Pat said.

"And you look like shit, if you don't mind me saying so," Charlie added. "You see a bed at all last night?"

Tom shrugged and ran a hand through his hair. "Oh . . . had a little excitement, is all. Don't make me tell you . . . rather not. Just lost a little sleep."

They took his words at face value. They trusted Tom enough to know that he'd tell them if it was something that was going to affect the case. Anything else wasn't worth worrying about.

They decided on what was to be done first, mainly which bridge and contractor record books they wanted to take a look at. It would be tedious work, like looking for a screw in a bucket of bolts. Pat and Charlie would go over to the bridge office first and get the process going. The first thing they'd do would be to find some record of what areas of the bridge Bucklin and Watkins had worked on. Tom reasoned that maybe he could tie them to some part of the train construction process: tracks, steam engines, terminals . . . anything could be significant. It seemed a likely place to start, and it would narrow the search down to a smaller group of contractors.

They all knew this could be a huge waste of time. It could lead nowhere and, worse, it could lead them even further from the real conspiracy if it turned out they'd guessed wrong. But they had to make choices. They had to narrow their options and bring the case into focus. Without anything else to go on, all they could do was look for connections. Requesting service records was one route to that end. There was a definite connection there, tying Watkins to Lebeau and Emmons. Whether that would pay off or not, Tom didn't know. It all looked like wasted effort and always did in investigations like this, until they turned up those one or two kernels that broke it open. Those kernels were out there. They just needed to do some scratching in the chicken yard to find them. Besides, they needed to show Byrnes they were doing something.

Thinking of Byrnes, Tom said, "I'll catch up with you boys later. Got to report our . . . progress." The way Tom said "progress" there was little doubt of how much he thought there had been. He wasn't looking forward to the briefing.

Good morning, Chief, Tom said as he entered Byrnes's office a few minutes later. Byrnes's cigar smoke already hung still as morning mist. It swirled around Tom as he entered the room.

"Morning, Tom. How are you?" Tom could tell from his tone that it wasn't just a pleasantry.

"Fine, sir. Lost a little sleep, is all," Tom said, hoping Byrnes didn't already know what had gone on last night. That hope was dashed a second later.

"I got the morning reports from the precincts. How's Mary?"

Tom took a deep breath and gave it to him straight. "She's pretty badly hurt, sir. Arm's broken . . . maybe some ribs too. Her eye and face on one side are all swollen. She's tough, though, she'll be looking to get out of the hospital soon."

Byrnes sighed, puffing his cigar as if it held the answer to his troubles. He looked at Tom in that very direct way of his, the waxed mustache bristling. "I want you to know, Tom, that I don't approve of such tactics. Sent a telegram to Parker expressing my . . . disapproval." Byrnes seemed about to say something else, so Tom waited. "I've asked that any charges against Mary be dropped. She's had it quite hard enough, I think."

Tom was shocked. "Thank you, sir. Mary will be very grateful." It was rare to see Byrnes interfere with the precinct captains. "And . . . you have my thanks too. I appreciate it."

Byrnes made a disparaging gesture with his cigar and a walruslike "Harumph." "Let me know if there's anything else I can do. Don't think Mary will have any more trouble, though." Coming from Byrnes, that was like a guarantee.

Tom thanked him again and went on to give his report. It wasn't much as reports went but Byrnes seemed happy with the direction they were headed. Tom showed him the clippings from Bucklin's box. Byrnes examined them closely, flipping the sheets over more than once, looking at everything on both sides. At last he murmured, "Something to do with the trains, eh?"

Tom agreed. "That was my best guess. It's the only way this points."

"Don't like the feeling I get from this," Byrnes said. "Caisson fire was ruled an accident, as I recall." He rubbed his chin thoughtfully. "This seems to be implying something else. Got nothing concrete on any of the others. Fucking picture of some smiling workers don't mean a damn thing. The devil's in the

details, Tom . . . Looks like you'll have to do some digging on this one."
Byrnes handed the papers back to Tom.

"Yes, sir. Starting to look like a paper case for now."

"Start with the trains, Tom. Sure as hell something going on. I want to
know what." He pointed his cigar stub at Tom. "And, Tom, take a half day, go
see Mary. You should do that. Send flowers too," he said with a smile. "Flowers lift the female spirit." Tom was amazed for the second time. The chief
wasn't one to dispense time off, nor advice on flowers.

"Thanks, sir, I'll do that."

"And, Tom . . ." Byrnes said, turning to shuffle papers on his desk. "Get
some sleep. You look like hell."

Tom grinned. "Happy to follow that order, Chief."

Byrnes looked up, fixing a serious eye on Braddock. "One more thing . . .
Get things straight with Coffin. Got to be resolved—no more dawdling on it,
okay?"

"Already done," Tom said in as positive a tone as he could muster.

"Good." Byrnes slapped a fist into his palm. "Good, glad to hear it.
Now . . . out of here and get that case solved. Got my own work to do."

Tom was closing Byrnes's door behind him when the chief called after him,
"Say, Tom, do you know a cop named Zimmer?" Braddock stopped for an
instant, wondering about the cop he left in a heap on Thirty-sixth Street.

"Zimmer? No, don't think so. Why?"

Byrnes let the ghost of a smile pass across his face. Tom didn't catch it.
"Oh, nothing. Not important."

Matt and Earl didn't know a damn thing about electricity. They didn't
really need to. Workers from the U.S. Illuminating Company did the actual
wiring. Matt and Earl had been assigned to mount the pipe that the wires
would run through. They knew enough about pipe fitting to pass muster and
watched the other pipe fitters for the stuff they didn't know. On the first day
they spent a lot of time looking for ways to run their wire without the foremen or electricians seeing it. They realized quickly that simply having jobs
on the lighting crew didn't help much. The plan, at least in principle, was
simple. The wiring for the lamps on the bridge ran back to the dynamo room
under the Brooklyn approach. If they could figure a way to run their wire
along with the wire for the lights, they could set up in the big vaulted room
under the roadway in Brooklyn. The bridge could be blown safely from
there. They would be completely concealed, secure from prying eyes or curious cops. As part of the wiring crew, Matt and Earl had complete access to

the power station, which was next to the approach and the engine room itself. Nobody would question their presence, and they'd have access to the keys, so they could come and go as they pleased. The trains wouldn't run until September. The only thing the power plant was needed for at this time of year was the lighting. In late May, it stayed light until at least seven even on a cloudy day, so the men who worked in the power plant didn't come in until five. They would fire up the boilers and, after they had a head of steam, they'd engage the dynamos. The captain's plan was to blow the bridge at no later than four.

But running the wire was going to be tricky. Electricians from the contractor were overseeing the work. They watched everything, every joint in the conduit, every connection and fitting. Where the main lines split off to the individual lamps, they paid special attention to the wire connections, which they made themselves. Matt and Earl were just doing the grunt work. They had been prepared for that. Once they knew they'd be assigned to the work, they spent a lot of time planning how best to run their wire, but planning was one thing and doing was another.

Earl had told the captain his worries after their first day. "It just can't be done, Cap'n. We make one wrong move an' they'll be down on us like fleas on a hound's back."

Thaddeus had turned to Matt for his opinion, and he'd echoed Earl. "He's right, Captain. Earl and I've been studying the plans Bart copied for us. Havin' a hard time figuring how we can run detonator wire under their noses without someone seeing."

"Yeah. I think they might get a little curious, they see us stringin' some extra wire," Earl drawled sarcastically.

Thaddeus didn't want to hear it. "All right, all right. I know all that. It's got to be done, though. Running our wire this way will save hours. You want to be exposed out on the bridge for any longer than absolutely necessary?"

Earl shook his head, already dreading the time they'd have to spend setting charges. "No, but this way's right in front of 'em. Ye talk about bein' exposed. Hell, that's as exposed as it gets." The captain wouldn't accept that there was no way this would work. He stooped over the plans, his sleeves rolled up to the elbows, frowning down at the drawings intensely.

"Let's go over it again. There's something here we're not seeing, some detail we've overlooked," Thaddeus said, almost as if he was talking to himself.

"I don't know, Cap'n," Earl said, scratching his head. "Might sound crazy, but the thing comes to mind is when I used to go 'tween the lines, huntin' Yankee skirmishers."

The captain looked at him as if he'd lost his mind.

"How's that help?" he asked with a skeptical twist to his mouth.

"Ah don' know exactly," Earl said. The words for things didn't always come easy for him. "It's just that sometimes it was best to hide in plain sight. Like they see ya, but they don' see ya. If we could maybe think about *not* tryin' to hide what we're doin' so much, maybe we'd come onto somethin'."

It was another hour or more before they decided on it. It was Sullivan who finally came up with the plan.

"We'll need to talk to the electrical foreman first, but what if they were going to add more lights a couple of years from now? They'd have to run more wire, right? Well, suppose we suggest that they run two more wires in the conduit? Makes sense. Suggest they can be used for some future project without having to run more pipe. We gotta put it to them like it would save them thousands of dollars, which I guess it would if we didn't blow up their damn bridge," Pat said with a shrug.

"Are you suggesting that we tell them about *our* wire?" Thad asked. He was having trouble with the concept.

"But it doesn't have to be *our* wire. It's *their* wire. Let them run it for us," Pat said, clearly convinced this was the way to go. "Hell, we just came up with an idea that'll save thousands in the long run. Ought to thank us."

Lincoln was the one to voice what they all feared. "Suppose they don't like the idea?"

Sullivan threw up his hands. "No worse shape than we are now, Jus. Besides, I've got another idea in case this one don't work."

The captain smiled slowly. Sullivan never disappointed. The sergeant had been like a rock for all of them down the years. He always came through in a pinch. Steady, smart, resourceful, daring, Sullivan was in a lot of ways the best of them.

"And your contingency plan . . . ?" Thaddeus asked.

"Well, if they don't want to run extra wire, we leave a snake in the conduit. When we set charges, we just open the nearest junction and pull our wire through from the dynamo room," Pat explained. "It'll take more time, but not more than say fifteen, twenty minutes when the time comes." They all liked the sound of that, though there was more of a problem of secrecy if they had to do it that way. Jacobs had his doubts. He didn't see how Matt and Earl would be able to leave a thin wire snake in the conduit without a foreman catching it.

"Suppose neither idea works, what then?" he posited, looking over his glasses at the rest.

"I'll let you boys come up with that. I'm fresh out for tonight," said Sullivan. "Guess we could always just string wire the night we set the charges, but that don't have much goin' for it," he said, shaking his head. "They're gonna have cops just for the bridge and right now we've got no way of knowing what their patrol schedule will be. Hell, they might not patrol at all after midnight. I just don't want to be running wire out there and have some cop tappin' me on the shoulder."

Nobody disagreed with that. For now they basically just needed to plant the seed with the lighting company, probably with a foreman. They'd just have to hope the idea took off.

"If they don't get the idea, maybe nudge a bit," Matt said. They didn't want to appear to be pushing too hard, though, fearing to raise suspicions.

"I like it, Matt," Thaddeus said. "If it works, they'll be doing the work for us, making our jobs a whole lot safer in the bargain. Approved, gentlemen. Matt, you take the lead on this with the contractor. Look for an opportunity to engage the foreman tomorrow, and let's get it moving before too much wiring gets done."

"Right," Matt said, smiling.

Thaddeus moved on.

"I've got some news on the explosives," he said brightly.

Earl grunted. "Can't use a couple of sticks like we did at Prospect. Gonna need a wagonload, right?"

Thaddeus nodded. "You're right, but it's not as bad as we thought it might be. Richmond sent an estimate of both the individual charges we'll need to blow components and for the total. So . . . for example, the places where the main cables meet the roadway support beams, we'll need to pack eight sticks around each. Here's how it should be laid out, three on either side of the cable on top of the beam and one on either end."

"We're gonna make some noise!" Earl observed sarcastically.

The captain's eyes glowed. A smile flitted across his face, touching the edges of the mouth and setting the eyes alight. He sat like that, lost in some private world of retribution for some seconds. The rest could only imagine the things he saw. Snapping back, he looked around the room, blinking like an owl, almost as if he were surprised to see them.

"Ah . . . yes, so there's eight each and, what, twenty-six cable connections we want to blow? So that's a little over two hundred sticks. Now, that is not including the charges for the stays."

"What do they say it'll take to blow them, Captain?"

"Pat, the estimate is for twenty at each one of the pivot connections. That's another forty total at each tower."

"What about the stays that run over the tower? They reach out farthest," Sullivan asked.

"Right," the captain said, checking his notes. "Here it is. Ah . . . sixteen packed around them where they cross the saddle. Says we'll need less there because the blast will be more contained." Thad was grateful beyond measure to his backers in Richmond. Without them they'd be guessing at the charges.

"We'll need a light wagon, or a carriage, something like that," Sullivan said, breaking into his thoughts.

Thad had considered this already. "I'm thinking we should split up. Be less conspicuous. Use a carriage *and* a wagon. Drive onto the bridge from either side. Six men in one wagon at two in the morning might draw attention."

"Got a point, Cap'n," Earl muttered.

It was agreed that the captain and Jacobs would be the drivers. Neither had any experience working on the structure, and their presence would only be a hindrance.

"So you'll keep watch on either side for patrols?" Sullivan paused, thinking about this arrangement. "Won't give us much of a warning if you have to high-tail it back to center span. You'll need to keep a sharp eye. Still and all, I think it's a better use of a man than setting charges." The discussion went on like that for some time. Any device to save time was examined closely. Everything from shoes with India-rubber soles, to how they might bundle charges beforehand, to color-coding and premeasurement of wire was discussed. Jacobs made up lists of what they'd need to buy over the next few weeks. It would take time to collect everything. They didn't want to buy it all from one supplier.

One idea that seemed to hold promise was something Earl came up with.

"Y'all recall when we blew that trestle in—what was it, June '64? Didn't have nothin' to tie the charges in place. Used clay from the riverbank. Remember that one?"

"Sure. Blew that son of a bitch right out from under them! Worked damn good in a pinch."

Thaddeus remembered the incident too. He turned to Jacobs, saying, "Find out where we can get some clay in a color just like the paint on the bridge."

Jacobs grinned while he scribbled. They went on like that well into the night.

The next morning Matt sidled up to the foreman on the electrical crew and tried planting the seed. It didn't go quite as they had planned.

Mike couldn't remember when he had been quite so miserable. Even when he was in the basement of the Thirteenth Precinct, he didn't think he felt so low. School was torture. His teacher, Mrs. Greable, was working him like a farmer whose mules had died. He was so far behind the rest of the class that he spent most of his time feeling stupid and red-faced. Mrs. Greable was not one to hold back when it came to the flat of a ruler either. The pain he could take. He'd had worse. But the teacher didn't spare him a cutting word either. "Nincompoop" seemed to be her favorite for him. It was a word the rest of the class took a real liking to. The giggles and snickers cut Mike worse than the silly word itself. He wasn't even sure it was a word. Whatever it was, it was his, and he wore it like the ancient mariner wore his albatross. The girls in class had taken to calling him "Ninny." The boys just called him "Poop."

Mike knew he wasn't stupid. He knew he was smarter than most of the kids in class in lots of ways. The trouble was that a lot of what he knew had nothing to do with ciphering or reading and writing. One of his biggest fears and humiliations was to read in front of the class. He *sounded* stupid. He *felt* stupid. He *was* stupid as far as the other kids could see. He really regretted making his deal with Mr. Braddock. He couldn't imagine the circus was worth what he'd endured the last few days. As he sat on a stool in the corner, a dunce cap on his head, he tried to imagine just how big Jumbo the elephant was. He pictured the giant packy-derm wrapping its leathery trunk around Mrs. Greable's nunnish body. He imagined what her screams would sound like. Would she scream real loud, or just sort of gurgle as Jumbo's trunk squeezed the air out of her? He tried to picture one of Jumbo's massive feet on her head and wondered what a head like hers would sound like getting crushed. The thought of Mrs. Greable's head squashed like a grape made him feel a little better.

"Do I see a smile on your face, Master Bucklin?" Mrs. Greable's voice cut through Mike's daydream like vinegar in tea. "Do you have something to smile about?"

Mike was too horrified to speak. He thought for an instant that she had somehow read his mind.

"I should think not. Why don't you share your private little joke with the rest of the class, you nincompoop? This way we'll all have a good laugh."

Mike stuck to his silence like a life preserver.

"No? Nothing to share?" she asked sarcastically. "Well, you'll be staying after class then for a little extra work, Master Bucklin. Now get back to your seat and not another peep out of you. Do you understand?"

"Yes, Mrs. Greable," he said as glumly as only a ten-year-old can. Extra work usually meant writing something on the blackboard fifty times. It was a chore he was getting used to.

Mike sat at his desk. It had an ink pot in one corner with a brass lid that he liked to play with. He didn't do that now. Some of the other kids looked at him and whispered to each other. He heard a whispered "poop" from one of the boys. Maybe if he busted a head or two they'd leave him alone. That's how Smokes would handle a situation like this. Smokes did more talking with his knuckles than any other kid he knew. Sometimes he solved things that way, sometimes he didn't. Smokes had told him to knock a few teeth in, and that would be the end of anyone calling him Poop. As much as he wanted to whip the tar out of one or two of the other boys, Mike figured that would only make things worse and it sure wasn't the way to get to the circus.

Mike was glad that Smokes, Mouse, and some of the other kids had been easy on him for going back to school. So long as he ran with them in the afternoons, he was still okay. He was feeling different, though, and it wasn't just the miserableness. He couldn't put a finger on it just as yet. He just felt different somehow from the kids on the street. The last few days had been tough, and he hated the way the teacher and the kids made him feel, but some of the stuff they were doing was fun. Even though he was behind the others, he drank things up like a dog on a hot day. He thought about Gramps and Grandma as one of the other kids wrote spelling words on the blackboard. The chalk squeaked like the brakes on the El. Gramps wasn't doing too well now. He wasn't getting out of bed anymore. It was sometime last week since he'd seen Gramps walk. He would be going to see Da real soon, he guessed. Mike wished he could see his da too.

Coffin and Coogan sat at a back table in a dimly lit bar just two blocks from the Third Precinct. August was triumphant. He drained his beer, calling for another round a second later. When the barmaid had delivered them and left them alone, Coffin lifted his dripping mug in a mocking toast, saying, "I told you it would work! Braddock was pounding on my door yesterday morning like a whipped dog." Coffin's smile lit up the room. "The man was almost in tears on my doorstep, all weepy over his whore. I knew it would hit him where it hurts. He sat in my goddamn study and practically begged me to take him back in and to help Mary out with Parker. I told you that was his goddamn weak spot, didn't I?" Coffin exulted, barely able to contain his triumph.

"No denying it, August. You have his Achilles' heel. So . . . what did he say?" Coogan asked, leaning forward in schoolboy anticipation.

"Well, like I said, he looked like shit when I answered the door. He comes into my parlor and just flat out tells me he needs my help. He must have had to swallow pretty hard to get all his pride down, but he managed it."

"Really? Did he suspect it was us behind the raid on Mary's?"

"I don't think so. He was playing it like it was all out of the Sixteenth. Told me the whole story, said he needed to get Mary fixed up, her place back in business, and help getting Parker off her back. Sounded sincere enough. Gave no apologies for his earlier bullshit but, being in a magnanimous mood, I let it slide by."

"That's it?" Coogan asked, knowing there had to be more. He'd known for weeks that Coffin had to be up to something to want Braddock back so badly. He was a patient man, though. He could wait.

"He says the place was busted up, which I hope it was," August went on. "He wanted to get some money to help Mary set herself up again. I gave him a few hundred to cement the deal," he said nonchalantly. A few hundred was more than the average cop could make in four months.

"Sounds almost too easy. You think he was straight with you? I mean, I doubt that Mary was short on funds."

Coffin seemed to consider this. "He was upset and worried, like he really did need my help, which of course he did. If he hadn't come, it would have just gone worse for Mary."

Coogan made no comment at first, then said suspiciously, "Reason I asked if he was straight was my man Zimmer, the one that was watching the hospital?"

Coffin looked up, one eyebrow raised in a question.

"He followed Braddock on his way to your place. Got jumped. He thinks it was Braddock, though he couldn't be certain. Short story is Zimmer's in New York Hospital now. Kind of funny actually. He's just a floor above Mary," Coogan said with a wry grin.

"He going to be okay?" August asked with no real concern.

"Pissing blood. Some bruises and scrapes. He'll live, but he's not ready to do the steeplechase either."

"Probably his own fault. Braddock had no way of knowing who it was. He doesn't know Zimmer, does he?" August asked, twirling his pencil as he thought this over.

"Not as far as I know." Coogan shrugged.

August grunted in response. "Braddock's nobody to take chances with. He wasn't in the mood for any shenanigans last night either. He was plenty mad under all that repentant stuff. But he wanted to help Mary and he knew damn well I was the one could do it for him."

Coogan sipped his beer and stared idly at the photographs lining the walls of the bar. "So what's the plan for our prodigal son? Does everything go back to normal—all is forgiven—or are you planning something else?" Coogan asked finally, impatient to hear what Coffin had in mind. There had to be a plan.

"Well, actually, I rather like the prodigal son analogy," Coffin smiled contentedly. Did Coogan guess his real motives? Coogan was no dummy, and they'd been working closely for years, so August figured he'd have suspicions. He decided to play it out a bit longer, keep Coogan guessing.

"Braddock's had some hard times, but now that he's seen which side of the street the sun's shining on, he deserves a break. No, that's not accurate," he corrected himself. "He needs to be treated like a *real* prodigal son. You know, show him there's no hard feelings, turn on the money tap so he'll have to carry it home in buckets. I want to make him see he's done the right thing. Let him know how good things can be," Coffin said grandly.

"So . . . no grudge, August?" Coogan asked, knowing that Coffin could hold a grudge longer than most when it suited him.

"It might surprise you to hear . . . but I wouldn't call it that. I know Tommy, you see. He's got principles, and that's what he acts on." He gave a small shrug. "It's his little curse, his . . . cross to bear. He's pretty predictable, really, so nothing he did surprised me. Just his nature." Coffin turned even more philosophical, staring into his glass. "Do you hold a grudge against a dog that barks or a fish that swims? It's in their nature to do those things. I might want the dog to stop barking but I can't begrudge him doing it. See what I mean?"

"Well, I don't know about dogs and fish, August, but what I think you've got is a big old bear. If I were you, I'd be careful for a while . . . be sure he's house-broke. Might have a notion to take your head off," Coogan warned, the caution plain. "Who could blame him? It's a bear's nature."

Coffin gave a strained laugh, trying to show a confidence he didn't feel.

Coogan watched, growing tired of dancing around. "So . . . what's the play, August?"

Coffin eyed his partner over the top of his mug. He figured Coogan had just about enough suspense, so he put the beer down with a satisfied sigh. "Well, the play, as you put it, is really kind of simple. I think you'll like it, though." For the next ten minutes, August went over the bare bones. It really was simple, elegant too. It would make them rich beyond anything they had known before and vault them into positions of real power. The possibilities seemed endless as Coffin painted his picture of their future. The palette was all glowing pastels. Once he was finished he could see Coogan was as entranced as he was.

"Holy shit!" was all Coogan said, before he took an oversized gulp from his dripping mug.

"So you see, from here on out, Braddock gets treated like a fatted calf," Coffin concluded. "The slaughter can wait," he added, grinning.

❧ Chapter Eighteen ❧

The bridge is a marvel of beauty viewed from the level of the river. In looking at its vast stretch, not only over the river between the towers, but over the inhabited, busy city shore, it appears to have a character of its own far above the drudgeries and exactions of the lower business levels.

—*Scientific American*

Tom was amazed at how fast the last few weeks had gone. Mary had gotten out of the hospital in three days, and by the end of the next week her place was back together and her girls satisfying almost as many customers as before. Mary, of course, had to cancel her regular appointments for a while, which put a sizable dent in her income, but she wasn't complaining. In fact, she seemed happier than she'd ever been. Still, she had reminders of the beating. Her eye was still dark around the edges, though the swelling had disappeared. Her ribs ached and her arm sent off pulsing balls of pain whenever she had it out of the sling for more than a few minutes. But those were just physical things. They would pass. Tom thought that in some way he couldn't really define, Mary had never looked better. It almost made him have second thoughts about Coffin.

As Tom went with Jaffey for another workout with Master Kwan, he wondered about that. The last few weeks had been good with Coffin too. In fact, things hadn't ever been better. His payoffs were back on schedule. August had even cut him in on a couple of new deals, giving him a percentage on some policy games Coffin was protecting. The dirty work that usually went with being a member of the corps had been almost nonexistent. Coffin had been going easy on him, he knew. The hard edge to the man was back in hiding during their "all's forgiven" honeymoon. Things were so good now, the money flowing, the work easy, the pressure lighter than air, it was almost hard to think about retribution—almost. Tom had to keep reminding himself not to be taken in. He knew the man. He was being wooed, fattened for something. He was sure of it. Things were too good, the money too easy. Something was coming and though Coffin gave him no reason to be uneasy, that was the very reason he was.

It was the workouts that kept him focused. Master Kwan even commented on how his dedication had improved. Jaffey too was doing well and seemed to genuinely enjoy the work.

"Never felt better in my life, Tom. I'm sore half the time but it's a good kind of sore. Feel like I can handle myself better too," he'd commented after yesterday's workout.

Tom had other reasons for going to Chinatown. While working, stretching, and sparring had kept his mind clear and his body sharp, it also gave him a physical outlet for the anger that still boiled deep in his gut. Every time Coffin smiled or slapped him on the back or gave him a fat envelope full of greenbacks, Tom reminded himself of what the man really was and what he'd so easily arranged for the woman he loved. The workouts were a focus for his anger and an outlet. He had to restrain himself sometimes when he sparred. He'd hurt a couple of the other students by putting Coffin's head on their bodies. Master Kwan had admonished him more than once for it.

But there was another reason for Tom's dedication. He'd had talks with Wei Kwan, lasting long after their workouts were over. Master Kwan knew who had to be seen if certain things needed to get done. He was respected, even revered in that part of the city. The master could be very helpful in Chinatown. Tom had told him all there was to tell about his problems with Coffin. The master was a good listener, only occasionally asking a question. But the questions were always probing, seeking the whys and hows of a problem. Tom always felt like an onion after a talk with Wei Kwan. They would sit for hours, the master peeling back layers. Yes and no were rarely used and not respected.

"There is no love for your Captain Coffin among the Tung people, Tommy," Wei Kwan had assured Braddock.

Tom wasn't sure of a lot of things but he was certain when he said, pointing to his chest, "There is no love for him here either, Master. Perhaps there is a solution here to both our problems."

Wei Kwan simply nodded, revealing nothing. Tom didn't push. He knew better than that. He was taken seriously. Words were said into the right ears.

The last of the invitations had been sent, nearly all the arrangements made. The invitations were beautifully engraved by Tiffany's. The list included the president, the governor, the mayors of Brooklyn and New York, congressmen, trustees, and nearly a thousand more. Emily took a hand in everything. At one point Wash had considered going to the opening ceremonies, but he was afraid he wouldn't be able to last through all the speeches that were planned. It would be bad form for the chief engineer to have to leave during the ceremonies. Emily instead brought the celebration to him. It was to be the grandest reception ever held in Brooklyn. The house would be festooned with bunting, filled with flowers, music, fine foods, and the most powerful and influential people in the land. Emily, with the help of some of her closest friends, saw to it all.

She thought back to the day, a couple of weeks ago, when she had made the first official crossing of the bridge in a vehicle. Once the roadway was complete, she had ridden in their brand-new Victoria to test the bridge. Again the honor had gone to her to be first—first for her and first for her husband. It had not been President Arthur, or Governor Cleveland, or any other of the high and mighty, it had been Emily. Countless millions of others would pass over the river in the years to come, but only one was first. For as long as the bridge would stand, the name of Roebling would always be first. She had carried a rooster as a symbol of victory. It sat calmly in her lap as she crossed, its black eyes giving no clue to what it might have felt. It had been a landmark day for her and though there was still much to do at that point, the main work of the bridge was behind them. Tom's friend Sam had been right, Emily thought to herself. This was a kind of immortality. She had always had a sense of the importance of what she and Wash were doing, but she hadn't thought of it quite that way before. Now that the end was near and the final reality of what they had accomplished was seeping in, she began to see it that way too.

In a way it was better than being president of the United States. Presidents were elected and unelected. Rarely did they last more than four years. The bridge would still be there spanning the river when fifty presidents had passed into history. Only one name would ever be tied to it, one name but three people: one dead, one disabled, one triumphant, Roeblings all.

It had been their first major setback—that is, if they didn't count the whole Bucklin affair a setback. Nothing Matt had said to his foreman, no argument he'd used, had shown even the slightest chance of bending the U.S. Illuminating Company or anyone on the engineering staff to their plan.

"Just get back to work, Emmons," his foreman had told him roughly after his third try at convincing him of the need for extra wire. "Keep your fool ideas to yourself. Got a contract here. Ain't no altering it. Just do what you're told an' keep your pie-hole shut."

"What the hell we gonna do?" he'd whispered to Earl when he'd gone back to work. "Can't even get the man to hear me out."

Earl shrugged. "Best get crackin'." He nodded in the foreman's direction "He's watchin'."

Other attempts at catching the ear of anyone in authority had proven no more fruitful. The captain had shouted, slamming his fist onto his desk, ranting for a good ten minutes when he learned of the stone wall they'd run into. The next meeting had been taken up with nothing else. Ideas flew like snow in February, most of them with little more substance than a snowflake. Different methods, different arguments, different people to approach had been agreed upon, but to no avail. Everyone they talked to rejected the idea. Matt and Earl knew they'd have to give it up or risk drawing too much attention. It wouldn't do to have their motives questioned, especially when there appeared no chance of success. The roadblock had set off a virtual panic in the group. No one wanted to take the risk of running hundreds of yards of wire at night once the bridge was open for traffic. What they finally agreed upon pleased none of them and was risky as hell. But none of them could come up with anything better. No one was about to volunteer to detonate the charges from out on the bridge either. Suicide was not in anyone's plan.

While the wiring crisis had thrown them an unexpected curve, other elements were proceeding exactly as hoped. The Rendrock Powder Company, of 240 Broadway, had delivered the crates this morning. They sat in the small warehouse that the captain rented for Dunn & Scrivner's use. Everything they needed was there: Rackarock blasting powder, basically dynamite with some small variations in ingredients, packed into foot-long red tubes about an inch in diameter; detonator caps; wire; the plunger-style dynamo that supplied the electrical charge; and various other necessary items. The captain was pleased that they had been able to find an explosives manufacturer close by. It simplified matters and reduced expenses. A stack of smaller boxes held slabs of artist's clay: big, moldable, sticky bricks of it perfect for forming around odd-shaped surfaces. Over the next week, the team would work at packaging individual charges, measuring and cutting wire and color-coding it to correspond to various points on the span. Last, they would allot a certain amount of clay to each.

They had already done three dry runs on the bridge. With a stopwatch they'd gone from one cable connection to the next, allowing twenty seconds at each to plant the charges. Of course, during the workday they couldn't do much more than walk from one spot to the next with a watch in their hands, but it gave them focus and a sense of timing. One part they couldn't practice without drawing too much attention was the actual running of the wires to the individual charges. They had to be strung out of sight. The wires running to the charges on the upstream cable had to run under the roadway as well. Stringing them over the roadway would make them far too obvious. Earl had volunteered to be the one to cross beneath the roadway, the most dangerous task in the whole affair. Over the last couple of weeks he had taken every opportunity he could to hang from precarious positions while on the job.

"Gets my hands strong fer hangin' off that beam," he said, "and it gets my head used to the idea . . . stomach too. That's the hard part," he admitted. "It's a long ways down. Real soberin'." "Even when the head's willin' sometimes things start to flyin' around in my gut, so's I can barely set one foot before t'other. Gittin' used to it, though. I'll be all right come demolition time."

Matt sensed there was another reason why Earl had stepped forward for that duty. Earl knew that Matt didn't have the stomach for it. Whether it was Earl's way of sparing his old friend a real hardship, or whether it was just because he knew he could perform the task quicker, Matt wasn't sure. He was grateful Earl had volunteered either way.

Sullivan and Lincoln hadn't been idle either. Careful measurements had been taken to estimate the amount of wire they'd need. They'd climbed the main cables, pacing off the distances while doing their jobs. They'd practiced clambering up the big cables as fast as they could go. They even made a race of it, amusing the others as they ran up the cables to the top and back down again. To the riggers it was a big game. To Pat and Jus it was valuable practice and deadly serious. They even practiced carrying packs loaded with a weight equal to the charges and wire they'd carry. They tried not to give much thought to what they were about to do.

Tom, Eli, Pat, and Charlie sat glumly in the back of the squad room. The chart they had started weeks before was not much more complete than when they'd begun. With the exception of Watkins's box, with a big line now drawn through it, not much had changed. The box with the word "key" in it had lines extending to Bucklin, Watkins, and a box marked "trains." Pat and Charlie had come up empty when they searched Lebeau's and Emmons's rooms. There was nothing concrete to tie the two to whatever was going on. There was no solid lines to those boxes.

Tom looked at the clipping with the article about the trains once more, skimming it again for anything he might have missed. He almost had it memorized. He knew all about the steam engines, the cable cars and tracks, their schedule, everything. It was badly frayed around the edges. A large coffee stain colored one corner. There had been hardly a day gone by over the last few weeks that he hadn't thought of it. He kept it in his pocket, a constant reminder. More like a burr under his saddle, he thought.

"Been weeks now, boys, and I'm getting damn tired of reporting nothing to the chief," Tom grumbled. "He hasn't put much pressure on me but you know Byrnes. A wave of his cigar can say more than the Gettysburg Address. His patience has limits. We need to turn up something or we're gonna find out where that limit is."

Pat Dolan pulled at the corners of his mustache. "I don't know. We've been staring at ledgers and contracts, invoices, bills of lading, accounts payable records, canceled checks, and a slew of other shit till the numbers are swimming on the page. Can't put our fingers on a damn thing," he said with a dispirited shrug.

"What about the contractors these men might have come in contact with?" Tom asked, grasping for anything new to tell Byrnes.

"Mostly the three of them—Emmons, Lebeau, and Watkins—worked on the masonry. Never was any involvement with the trains. Lebeau and Emmons did work in the caissons years ago, but it didn't seem to be worth the effort to go that far back. Whatever is going on is current, we figure," Pat Dolan said.

"Could be. They were working in the caisson when the fire happened, though. That's too damn coincidental for my taste," Tom muttered as if talking to himself.

"Couple dozen others worked in the caisson at the time too. We'd have to track 'em all down. Besides, the fire marshal ruled it an accident."

Tom gave a grudging grunt.

"Probably not worth the effort," Jaffey added. Nobody disagreed.

"Things match up on the masonry contracts too," Charlie said. "We went over the paperwork on the stone, brick, concrete, and paving, both at the bridge office and at the contractors. Nothing." He threw up his hands. "It all looks legitimate."

"We might be missing something," Dolan said slowly, shaking his head, "but I don't think so. Ain't too many stones we left unturned."

"Goddammit, there's something missing." Tom growled in the back of his throat. He was getting as frustrated as the rest. "We're not looking in the right places . . . or asking the right questions," he said for what seemed the hundredth time.

"I know," Jaffey said. "Got the feeling it's right in front of us but we just can't see it."

"Should've turned up something before this," Charlie said with resignation. "I'm with you, Tom. Whatever's going on has nothing to do with the things we've been checking." His tone sounded as if he were closing the book on this phase. "Would have found it by now."

Tom paced back and forth before his desk, hands stuffed in pockets, shoulders hunched. "People are dead because of whatever the fuck is going on! *Got* to be something..." Tom almost pleaded as he crumpled some paper and tossed it in the general direction of the already overflowing wastebasket.

"There's one thing, Tom," Charlie said. It was clear from his tone that he hardly thought it worth bringing up.

"Well...hell, Charlie, spit it out so the whole class can hear it."

"It's nothing, really," Charlie started slowly. "It's just that when I was at Haigh's, checking on their paperwork, I noticed that there was one other customer for a small batch of Crucible steel wire, just like they're using on the bridge."

"That's it?" Tom asked.

"Well...I know it don't sound like much, but Pat came up with the same name on an invoice at the Edgemoor Iron Works." Charlie's voice had the slightest inflection of hope.

Tom's mouth twisted in an ironic grin. "That's real exciting, Charlie." There was silence in the little group around the desk. Heidelberg stared at Tom evenly, careful not to let his feelings get the better of him. Jaffey too gave Tom a small frown.

"Listen, Tom. Spare me the sarcasm, okay. We're all frustrated here. Me and Pat been goin' blind looking at fucking records. Not fun, in case you were wondering, and you're not makin' it any easier." His voice rose as he went on.

Tom held up a hand. "Sorry, Charlie," he said, patting the man's shoulder in a silent peace offering. "You're right. I owe you a beer."

Charlie gave Braddock a sideways look and a small smile. "A big one, you bastard."

Tom took away his hand like it had been on a hot stove but grinned his agreement.

"Okay," Charlie went on. "The interesting thing is that in both cases the invoices were for the exact same kinds of items being used on the bridge. Difference is that the quantities were small."

Jaffey broke in. "Somebody else building another bridge or something? I mean, this isn't the only suspension bridge in the country, is it?"

"Don't know. But even if it isn't, the orders are way too small. It's just a couple of spools of wire, cable, and one or two each of a bunch of other things, like roadway beams, brackets, flanges, couplings, all sorts of shit."

Braddock grunted, deep in thought. "Probably nothing, but it should be checked," he rumbled almost absently. "Nothing connected to the trains?" he asked, looking up hopefully.

"Sort of . . . in a way. One or two components were to the trusses running over the tracks," Pat said, looking at his notes. "Going to Trenton tomorrow to check order books at the Roebling works. There's another two or three suppliers we thought we'd check with too. Probably nothin'." He shrugged.

Tom nodded. It probably was but it was the only "nothing" they had. "So who's been placing orders for this stuff?"

"An outfit called Sangree & Co.," Pat said, looking at his notes again. "Funny thing is that the invoices are going to an address on Water Street, but the delivery address is in Richmond, Virginia."

Tom stopped his pacing and turned in his tracks, folding massive arms across his chest. "Now that *is* a curious fact, gentlemen."

Mike knew what had happened as soon as he saw the wagon waiting at the curb in front of his building. Gramps had gone to see his da. He didn't need the long faces of his neighbors to tell him. A small, curious band had gathered to watch the ambulance wagon and its tired horse as it dropped steaming turds on the cobbles. They watched the motionless wagon and horse as if they'd never seen the like before. As he pushed past, his school books tucked under one arm, there was much sad shaking of heads and clucking of tongues. A mournful murmur passed over like a cloud at his appearance. Mike wasn't quite sure what they shook and clucked and murmured for. Though he'd miss his gramps, he knew that he was with the angels now. Being with the angels was probably a sight better than coughing up bits of your lungs day by day. Though he'd never seen an angel, he'd seen his gramps when he was sick. Being with the angels had to be better. In fact, it was bound to be better than anything on Suffolk Street. He'd trade the whole place to be able to see his da too. So Mike didn't cry or carry on. He didn't put on a show of tears for the morbid neighbors. They just wanted to see Gramps come out covered with a sheet. They wanted a reminder that no matter how shitty their lives were, someone else had it worse. Mike trudged up the dark stairs. He'd save his tears for Grandma.

The day had limped by like a three-legged dog. It was late now. Tom's shift had been over for hours. He and Coffin sat in the library of August's town house. The smell of leather-bound volumes and waxed mahogany gave the room a clubby, manly sort of warmth. It even seeped into Tom as he swirled a crystal glass of port. It had been a good day in one respect, with another fat envelope filling both their pockets. Tom had to force himself to say what he did next though.

"You know, August, I want to thank you for helping Mary. She's doing pretty well now, and she's had not a peep of trouble from Parker or anyone else at the Sixteenth." Tom almost chocked saying it but in a way it was true.

"Oh, think nothing of it, Tom," Coffin said, waving a dismissive hand with a smile that seemed genuine enough. "Happy to be of assistance. Always liked Mary myself, so full of life and fire. You're a lucky man." At times August could be disarmingly charming, thoughtful even. Braddock tried to keep that in mind.

"I know it, August. I've got to take better care of her, though, if I want to keep her."

"Can't blame yourself, Tommy," Coffin said, shaking his head. "You can't be there every minute. She's in a business that's prone to certain risks. She knows that. I think she's tougher than you give her credit for."

"She's hard when she has to be, I'll give her that, practical too," Tom said truthfully. "Doesn't hold a grudge. Doesn't believe in it. Just gets on with business. She's not one to worry much on things she can't change."

"A very practical outlook, Tom. It would seem lately that you've taken a page from her book." Coffin pointed a finger across his desk at Tom. "It's a more productive way of looking at things."

Tom smiled inside. Let Coffin think what he wanted about his acceptance of the new order, he figured. "I've got to admit, the last couple of weeks have gone a long way toward convincing me of that. Frees more time to work on the things you can change too," Tom said without inflection, wondering as soon as he'd said it if he'd hinted at too much. He reminded himself to be more careful.

Coffin sat back in his tufted leather chair with a self-satisfied grin. If he'd caught the double meaning in Tom's words, it didn't show. He smiled warmly across his desk. It was a genuine smile, as genuine as he was capable of.

"We're going to do very well together, Tom," Coffin said at last. "The money's been good, right?"

"Very good," Tom admitted.

Coffin beamed, like a magician about to pull off an impossible trick. "It can be better," he said, leaning forward.

Tom's eyebrows arched in interest but his jaw tensed all the same. "I was never against making money, August. One of my favorite things," he said honestly. Still, he felt the need to add, "You know how I feel about some things, though, August. That hasn't changed. There's some money we shouldn't take, some people we shouldn't protect."

They grinned at each other across the desk, each putting his own gloss on their recent troubles. Coffin's smile had a waxy quality, as if it had been painted there. The look passed quickly, a rogue thunderhead on a sunny day.

"This is nothing I think you'd object to, Tommy. Just some areas I'd like to explore," Coffin said tentatively. "Might open up whole new sources of revenue. Bigger than anything else we've been into." A suggestively raised eyebrow tested the waters between them.

"Really? I thought you were already into more pies than you had fingers for." Tom laughed.

"That's a good one. I like that. But I think I might find an extra finger for this particular pie."

Tom tried to imagine what Coffin had on his mind. There weren't too many opportunities Coffin had missed over the years. If he didn't have a percentage, it probably wasn't worth taking. Of course, his corps was spread through a number of precincts, increasing the opportunities tremendously.

Tom was curious. "So what's so good that you're not already into?"

Coffin seemed to hesitate just an instant, as if weighing whether he should reveal his plans just yet.

"Well, that's something you might be able to lend valuable assistance with," he said finally, twirling a pencil deftly.

"Oh?" Now Coffin really had Tom's attention.

"Uh-huh." Coffin seemed to be musing over his next move. "You patrolled for some time in Chinatown, right?"

Braddock's whole body came to attention. Fire engine bells clanged in his head. "You know I did. Three years, give or take." Tom could not believe the direction this conversation was taking.

"You know some important Chinamen down there still, I believe." August tapped his pencil lightly on his desk.

"Some," Tom admitted, not wanting to volunteer anything too soon. Better to let Coffin show his hand.

"You know about their societies, the tongs as they call them?"

Tom took a deep breath, as much to give himself time to think as anything else. He paused to take a long, contemplative drag on his cigar, letting the smoke drift slowly out of his mouth toward the ceiling.

"The tongs are tough," he said at last. "They're supposed to be business and social organizations but they go way beyond that." Tom wasn't telling Coffin much he didn't already know. An expectant ghost of a smile painted August's lips. "The controlling powers are not always clear, especially not to outsiders. Too many barriers. Language, culture, customs, that kind of thing. Not talked about by many Chinese, at least not to us whites."

"But you would know who to talk to," Coffin prompted. It was not a question.

Again Tom took his time to answer. He thought of his long talks with Master Kwan, seeing the beginnings of a plan in the drifting smoke. He took a sip of his port as his mind raced ahead.

"I'd know where to start, sure," Tom allowed guardedly. Figuring to limit the captain's expectations, he added, "Can't say how far I'd get, but . . ."

"Farther than most, I'd venture," Coffin broke in.

Tom took another long pull on his cigar, eyeing the captain through the smoke, thinking to the next move. "Maybe," he admitted with a shrug. "So what're you after?" He had a damn good idea what it was, but he wanted Coffin to be the one to lay it out. It hadn't taken Tom long to figure what Coffin's plan had to be in Chinatown, or at least what it centered on. There were rackets, gambling, whoring, and the like going on there, just like anywhere else, but the only thing that set the place apart, made it truly unique as an opportunity for the likes of Coffin, was the tarry, black gold: opium.

"What I'm thinking about, Tom, would have to be handled just right." Coffin opened his humidor and offered Tom another cigar.

"We're talking opium here aren't we, August?" Tom said, kicking himself immediately for letting himself slip. He gave the cigar a long sniff, grinning in outward contentment. Coffin did have good taste in cigars. Inside he was on edge, like a cat in a junkyard full of dogs.

"Ah . . . always the detective, eh, Tommy? We are indeed talking about opium." August lit up another cigar. "It's been a frustration to me, the opium trade. The opium trade and the dens have been expanding over the last few years," he said, leaning forward and putting his elbows on his desk. "There are perhaps five thousand users in this city alone. The average opium smoker uses about a dollar's worth a day. Five thousand a day, going up in smoke." August almost cooed, his eyes lighting at the thought. Coffin, of course, wasn't getting a dime of it . . . yet. A huge frustration, no doubt. "Even a toehold could be worth a couple thousand a month, Tommy. The damn Chinamen are so secretive, so closed off from the rest of the city. Almost impossible to get hard information on who is actually running things. You know how it is: We shut down an opium den, haul them all in, and it's always the same story. Nobody knows anything. Nobody speaks English. Nobody knows who runs the show. A week later they open up somewhere else."

"Been through that more than once," Tom said, remembering his early days on patrol in the neighborhood. He'd never made any progress till he started to know the real lay of the land. "They're a tough bunch to break into." No one had been able to break open the iron grip of the tongs or even put a dent in their trade.

"But you have, haven't you, or at least you know how you could," Coffin said, smiling an insider's smile.

The thought that somehow Coffin knew of his late-night conversations with Wei Kwan, that he knew his inner thoughts and could read him like an open book, sent a sickening chill through Tom. That's all this might be, a clever subterfuge, a way to trap him into showing his hand. Tom sipped his port slowly, swishing it about in the glass, watching the bloodred liquid cling to the sides. That knife could cut both ways, Braddock figured as he looked at Coffin's expectant pose. The only way to find out was to play it through, see what developed. The possibilities swirled about in Tom's head, plans and outcomes bobbing to the surface in confusion. Where there's confusion, there's opportunity, he figured.

"There would be a couple of people I'd have to see," Tom said slowly, appearing to contemplate the next move, though he knew very well what he'd need to do. "I'd have to go alone at first. They wouldn't open up to a stranger, especially not you, I mean, you being a captain of police. You'd be playing fan-tan with them all day, get nowhere."

"That's why we're having this conversation, partner," Coffin said with a broad smile.

Tom took note of the word "partner." "You're going to have to offer them something, you know," he said, puffing his cigar thoughtfully. "Can't just walk in there and demand a percentage. I'd lose face and we'd be worse off than we are now. They know damn well that we can't really stop the trade. Threats won't be taken seriously. They're businessmen. They want to make money like everyone else. That's the way to go at them."

Coffin seemed disappointed. "Can't play the usual squeeze, huh? What if we get rough?"

Braddock shook his head vigorously, as if the notion were the height of stupidity. "Forget it, August. You might be able to hurt them—put a dent in the business—but you can't shut them down altogether. You'll *never* get a piece that way either." He stabbed the cigar at Coffin for emphasis. "They can be very patient. They'll take their losses and wait you out rather than share the trade."

The captain just nodded. He preferred the strong-arm approach. It worked just fine with the Irish, Italians, Germans . . . most Europeans, for that matter. But the Chinese were another story. This opportunity was too important to let his usual methods get in the way. Nothing else had worked in Chinatown. It was time for a different approach, and Braddock was going to be his key, his passport to the Far East.

"You've got an idea, Tom. I can see it on your face."

"Not really," he lied, wondering if he'd been too obvious. He'd had an idea, had one weeks ago when Mary got hurt. Tom played the game, wanting to lead Coffin on a bit more. "All I'm thinking is you have to offer them something. Go to them with a proposition. You know, offer something they don't have already."

"Yeah, well, I'd like to offer them some broken legs if they don't kowtow."

Braddock smiled wryly. "I'd advise against it, August. Might play well with the chief, but it won't get you what you want."

"I know, I know. It just galls me that these damn little Chinamen can come to America, set up shop in our own backyard, and we can't squeeze a dime out of them."

Braddock gave a little grunt of understanding. "It's simple, August. They've got three advantages." He held up three fingers and ticked them off one by one. "Language, customs, and, above all, supply. The first two are like a wall of silence. The third is our real weak point. Combined, it makes for a fucking tough nut. You want my advice? Do business with them." It was good advice, at least in principle.

Coffin seemed to ponder that for a few minutes. His feet went up on his desk. He twirled his pencil, tossing and catching the spinning stick absently. He seemed to be looking right through Tom, his agile mind casting about for angles and advantages in the cigar smoke.

"I suppose you'd agree that their weakness is their inability to expand much beyond Chinatown. I mean, once they get into other neighborhoods, they have to do business with us . . . Americans, I mean."

"Pretty much. There's some they've worked with, I think, outside of their own areas. Small stuff, though . . . or so I've heard."

"Suppose I could offer them wider distribution, get them into other markets outside their little area? Suppose we went to them and said we could double their business in a year or two?" August said speculatively. "We could, you know. It wouldn't present too many difficulties. I have the network to do it. Just takes a bit of arranging."

"Now you're talking." Tom nodded his approval. "They won't accept our first offer, you know," he cautioned. "Not a chance. They wouldn't want to appear too confident. Don't matter how good the deal is."

Coffin frowned, sticking out his jaw. "Goddamn it, Tom! Tell 'em who runs this town. Remind them of that! Who the fuck do they think they are?"

"It's just business," Tom said soothingly. "That's the way they do it. To their way of thinking, only a fool would accept the first offer. You any different?" Tom said, knowing he wasn't.

Coffin smiled for an instant before the frown took over once more. "No. But I'm not a goddamn yellow bastard in a white man's world!" he exclaimed, slamming his fist on his desk.

Tom understood why Wei Kwan's cook spit in Coffin's soup. "August, you don't have to like them but if you want to do business, you've got to show respect. You want my help in this, you're going to have to play ball the way I tell you." Tom felt good about having his hands on the reins. He took another pull at his cigar, his thoughts ranging far ahead. He thought he saw the solution. He needed time, though, and room to play the game.

"Now let's get down to what our negotiating positions are. I'll make some contacts and we'll see if they want to talk."

It wasn't exactly the sort of contact Coffin had in mind. About two hours later, Tom and Wei Kwan went to have a long talk with Sung Chow. The sack-faced old man sat silent through most of what Tom had to say, his leathery features immobile while he listened. Aside from an occasional nod, the old man could have been taken for an ancient woodcut. Wei Kwan spoke only occasionally for emphasis. When Tom was finished, Sung Chow said, "And for this service, what will you do in return?"

They had gone over this before. It was part of the ritual, Tom knew. Each time a party to a deal was made to repeat his part of the bargain, there was a natural tendency to embellish and offer more than first intended.

"You do this service for yourself as much as for me," Tom said slowly. "You have said that Captain Coffin is a hated man in Chinatown. This is well known. It is also well known that he has disrupted the trade and arrested many of your people. I tell you now that he wants more. He wants a percentage of your trade." Tom paused to let his words sink in. "He will not stop there. If you allow it, within a short time he will take it all and leave you only as the supplier." Tom didn't know that for a fact but he knew Coffin. "In addition, I will give you warning of any raids that I know of on your business. I have eyes and ears in the department. You know I can do this, and I do this freely. If you agree, there will be people I need to speak with inside the department, people in positions of authority on whom I can rely. They will be grateful to you for this service and in turn will protect your business so long as it stays in Chinatown." Tom was not certain of this, but he was sure enough to at least set the parameters of the deal. The details could be ironed out later.

Sung Chow just nodded. "You ask much, Tom Braddock. You give not so much."

Tom started to say something, but the old man held up his hand.

"You have always been good friend to Tung people. You have done many kindnesses without reward over many years. Master Kwan, my very esteemed brother, speaks of you with praise. He says you are a white man to trust. He says you have . . . heart of tiger. He is proud to call you friend. I believe these things are true. These things are worth much . . . and must be weighed." Tom bowed silently. Sung Chow continued, "I will talk with my brothers in business. I believe what you say of Coffin. He is an evil man who will take what he can and leave us with little in return. To do business with such a man is to put the knife to my own throat. We talk again soon."

There was a pleasant hum of activity in McSorley's the following evening. Most of the tables were full. Occasional ripples of loud talk and laughter washed through the smoky haze of the back room. The smell of smoke and ale were like a tonic for Tom and made him feel more at ease than he had in weeks. He and Chowder had finally arranged to have that beer they'd been talking about, and Tom was intent on enjoying it. After the events of the day before, he needed to relax a bit.

Chowder must have sensed it, for not long after they'd settled themselves into a table, he said offhandedly, "You've got the look of a man with a load on his mind. Worried about somethin'?"

Braddock was on guard immediately, a condition he was far too used to lately, and he made a mental note to try to ease up.

"Just this case, Chowder," Tom grumbled. Half a truth was better than none. "Got nothing to show for weeks of work. Chief's getting impatient too."

"Byrnes ain't a man known for his patience, Thomas." Chowder took a long pull at his glass of ale, smacking his lips and licking the foam from his mustache when he came up for air. "You know, this is my favorite spot in the whole damn city. A foin ale, a warm stove keepin' the night chill at bay, good company, and a healthy corned beef sandwich, wi' plenty o' hot mustard. Life don't get better'n that, boy-o."

Tom raised his glass. "To McSorley's!"

"To McSorley's, lad. The foinest pub in the whole of New York." They drank and whistled up another round.

Chowder let Tom's explanation lay for a while as they downed their second round. But whether it was just curiosity or something more, he came back at it again later.

"You sure that case is all that's botherin' ya? Not like you ta worry over much. Not still thinkin' about Captain Parker an' the Sixteenth, are ya?"

Tom went on alert. Though Chowder was a friend, Tom wasn't so close to him that he felt free to talk about everything that was going on. The truth was that he was becoming overly wary, not trusting anyone he wasn't absolutely sure of. Tom hated that, hated the necessity of it. Still, he was on guard when he answered.

"Why d'ya say that? What's done is done," he said. Could Chowder detect the edge to his voice? "Mary's not one to hold a grudge. Don't see why I'm any more entitled to a grudge than her."

Chowder gave him a quick glance. There may have been a flash of doubt. Tom couldn't be sure, but Chowder went on. "Ach, that's sound thinkin', it is. Nothin' but grief would come of it. What could you do anyway? He's a goddamn captain, an' we're lowly sergeant detectives."

"Yup. Couldn't do a damn thing if I wanted to," Tom said over the lip of his glass.

"Exactly. And what would you do if ya could?" Chowder asked rhetorically.

"Can't kill the man. If he were any other fella than a captain of police, I might give it a thought. Can't say I like having Mary busted up like that by any man, but when a cop's involved and a captain no less . . . well ye've got to step back a bit."

Chowder sipped his beer slowly, as if it might hold some immutable truth in its amber depths. There was truth in ale, he thought. It was a truth peculiar to itself. Though there were times when it seemed that no truer truth could be found, oftener the truths in ale were all fizz. Like a fine thick head, it tickled and delighted the senses, delivering promise but no substance. Such was usually the truth of ale, but not this night.

"There's always ways, Tommy. A man who's a captain of police is just a man, after all. He's not above the law, boy-o. If he's a law to himself, why, then I say he's accountable to whoever can bring him to account. It's the law of the better man, I say."

"That's just the beer talkin', Chowder. I don't see you off gunning for captains."

"There's powerful truth in beer, Tommy, and no doubt. The trick is knowin' when the truth is startin' ta blur . . . so to speak. Besides, I don't have no captains ta gun for. There might be one or two needs killing," he said with a sideways glance, "but none by me direct."

"And suppose I was to do that . . . kill a man like Parker . . . say," Tom said with an arched eyebrow at Chowder. "Is there ever a time when a killing is right except in self-defense?"

Chowder hesitated only an instant. "Oh . . . I'd say there's all kinds of self-defense. There's plenty of ways for someone to come at you, some not so direct, but deadly as a bullet in the head in the long run. So where d'you draw the line on defense? With someone like a captain, d'you have to wait till ye see the gun in his hand?" He didn't wait for Tom to answer. "I reckon not . . . no more than for any other man."

"You know the legal distinctions of self-defense, though, Chowder. Gotta be pretty clear cut. Can't go killing on a threat. That's where we're supposed to come in—the cops, I mean." Tom wasn't comfortable with confirming to anyone, even in a theoretical, beery sort of conversation, that he'd be willing to kill anyone for something less than self-defense.

"There's truth in that," Chowder agreed, "but it's the *legal* truth. Some things don't call for exactly legal solutions." Coming from Chowder, Tom knew exactly what he meant.

Chowder paused long enough to take a huge bite from his sandwich. The hot mustard oozed out the edges as he tore a chunk out of it.

"Damn, that's a good sandwich," he said after washing it down with another gulp of ale. "Seems to me that you're a man livin' under a cloud. Now, a man livin' under a cloud . . . he ought to get himself an umbrella, 'cause whether he likes it or not, it's sure as hell gonna rain."

Braddock couldn't restrain a wily grin. "We talkin' about Captain Parker here, Chowder?"

Chowder grinned back, his mouth full of sandwich. "I don't know Tommy, are we?"

It was late when they finally broke up. Tom walked back to his place, just a couple of blocks away, leaving Chowder at the steps of the El. They said their good-byes a little blearily, the ales having done their duty. Tom heard Chowder's heavy feet pounding up the iron stairs in the night as he strolled back to Colonnade Row. Tom whistled as he went over the events of the last days. He didn't think he could have planned it better if he'd plotted it all along. For weeks he'd played Coffin's game, looking for an angle, a way to pay him back for Mary. And now Augie had handed it to him—his greed finally supplying the hook he'd use to haul the big fish in. If this one got away, though . . . A chill went through Tom at the thought. If this one got away, it could be him that would end up floating in the river. Braddock knew he'd have to take his chances on that but he figured he could swim with the best of them.

Chowder's steps echoed through the iron stairway to the El. He looked back in the direction Tom had gone, puffing a bit on the top step, the beer making him tired. His pulse pounded in his ears and he made his usual promise to himself to cut back a bit and get more exercise. Tom had disappeared down Lafayette. Chowder grinned to himself. He liked Braddock, always had. He walked slowly out onto the platform, looking left and right. It was nearly empty. A chilling night wind whistled through the cast-iron railings. The couple of people waiting on the platform were hunched, as if they'd been waiting for some time. Chowder walked south, as agreed, trying to see the faces he passed. He recognized no one. He walked slowly on, past the last person on the platform, casting a quick glance at the man as he went. His heels knocked on the wood planking, a lonely sort of sound, a sound that went well with conspiracy and betrayal.

Chowder had just passed the far end of the waiting room, when a voice came out of the dark from around its corner.

"Took your time coming."

Chowder stopped short, turning to squint into the dark corner where no lamp cast a revealing beam. "Took as long as I had to. No more, no less," Chowder said without apology. The figure stood silent, a black outline against the city. Chowder matched him, silence for silence.

"So . . . how'd it go?" the shadow asked at last.

"Good. Ale was cold, sandwiches fantastic." Chowder knew very well this was not what the man wanted to know.

"Don't fuck with me, Detective. You know very well what I mean."

Chowder just chuckled. "Nothin' like a long wait to make a man testy," he said, shaking his head. "It went fine. Don't have to be worryin' about Braddock. There's nothin' up his sleeve." Chowder waved a hand dismissively.

"Glad to hear it. But as you know, Braddock is just recently back in the fold, so to speak, and what's planned is rather delicate and very important. He'll be relied upon more than I would perhaps prefer."

Chowder grunted an acknowledgment.

"So pleased you understand," the man said sarcastically. "What do you say we go over your evening in a bit more detail, shall we?"

Chowder heaved a sigh as the man lit a match. It flared briefly, illuminating Coffin in a ghastly sort of glow, a good cigar clamped in his white teeth. "One needs to be so careful these days, don't you agree?"

Potter's Field was a barren, hopeless place, with far too much fresh-turned earth. The grass was long and wild. Weeds groped for the fresh clods of clay thrown over plain pine boxes. Many of those boxes were very small, Tom knew. He had been there before and didn't want to go back. Nobody should end his days there, nobody who had any family or friends with a bit of money. Tom had some money. When he heard that Eamon Bucklin had passed away, he arranged to have him buried in Brooklyn, beside Terrence and his family. No grass had yet grown on that grave. He stood silently, a step behind Mike and his grandmother. Their hands were clutched as if each might slip away if not held tight. They'd seen too many funerals. The priest droned on, going through the ritual in Latin and English. There was mud on the bottom of his robes and an old wine stain near his collar. It seemed he too had seen too many funerals.

Later, as they walked from the grave, Tom talked to Mike a little. He didn't want to talk about his grandpa, for fear of making it worse, so he asked about school.

"Okay," Mike told him. It was hard, but he was starting to catch up. He'd even started to make one or two new friends. He had one question, though, and he hesitated asking it but finally let it out. "What's 'nincompoop' mean, Mr. Braddock? The teacher called me that a lot at first . . . not so much lately."

Tom frowned down at the boy, knowing in that moment how hard school must have been these last weeks.

"It just means someone who doesn't go to school, but that's not you now is it?" he asked gently.

"No, sir."

Tom put his hand on Mike's shoulder. "Good. You keep going. I'm going to get tickets to the circus tomorrow. You kept your part of the bargain, now I'm keeping mine."

"That's great! I can't wait to go!" Mike beamed through eyes glistening with graveside tears. He stole a guilty look at his grandma a second later. Tom noticed.

"Yeah, me too. Listen, I need to talk to your grandma for a minute, okay?" Mike watched from a distance as they spoke in hushed tones.

It was many hours later, long after Mike and his grandmother had gone back to their empty rooms on Suffolk Street.

Clocks in the city had just struck three, echoing out over the harbor and the darkened bridge. Nothing stirred, not even the ferries. The bridge was all in blackness. Not even a light was visible anywhere except at either end in the night watchmen's shacks. They rarely came out, though, and wouldn't be much of a problem. The watchmen were mainly there to protect against thievery of lumber and materials. They wouldn't be looking for anyone out on the bridge.

"Son of a bitch!" Earl grumbled for the tenth time in the last hour. "Still think we coulda come up with a better goddamn plan than this shit." He'd just skinned another knuckle in the dark and was in as foul a mood as Matt had ever seen.

"Just stow it and feed that wire through," Matt said, as anxious as Earl to get this job finished. "Went over this a million times. Wasn't none of us could come up with a better plan, so let's just get 'er done." Matt pulled the wire through the stretch of conduit while Earl fed it in, making sure it didn't tangle. It was hard work in the dark, which was why they were doing it. They knew the wiring better than any of the rest, so the job fell to them.

This was the third night in a row they were out on the bridge, the third night of little sleep, skinned knuckles, and nerves on edge. Once it became obvious that there was no way they could convince anyone to run extra wire, they had to come up with something. What they had decided on pleased nobody, especially not Emmons or Lebeau. As hard as it was, it was still better than running wire on the same night they set charges. The lights would be working by then, and the extra exposure out on the span just wasn't worth it. Each night for the last three, Matt and Earl had slipped past the watchmen and went to work undoing what they had done during the day just hours before. Each junction in the conduit was opened and their wire snaked through, up to one pipe-length away from where the crew would start in the morning. Working fast, they could snake a lot of wire each night. The first night had been touch and go. They'd had their only close call at about 3:30, while in the dynamo room, under the Brooklyn approach. They hadn't had any trouble getting in. Jacobs had supplied them with the key. But working inside in the dark was next to impossible. They couldn't risk lighting up the windows at night, so they'd devised a screen around their lantern, so it cast light in just one direction. Working in that light was a difficult, almost ghostly experience. They had been working quietly for almost an hour when Earl heard the crunch of feet on gravel outside. In an instant he doused the lamp, plunging them into total darkness. He and Matt stood frozen, listening as someone tried the lock. The door creaked and the bolt rattled in the frame, sounding deafeningly loud in the silence of the vaulted brick and stone room. Matt could feel Earl looking at him in the dark, wondering if he'd locked the door behind them. A long silence followed. At last the sound of retreating footsteps broke

❦ Chapter Nineteen ❧

Thought may the minds of men divide,
Love makes the heart of nations one,
And so, the soldier grave beside,
We honor thee Virginia's son.

—JULIA WARD HOWE

P at and Charlie were perched on either corner of Tom's desk. They had come back from Trenton the night before. The two of them had spent the better part of the day looking over books and interviewing foremen and engineers at the Roebling Works. It hadn't taken long to find what they were looking for. The orders all had the same delivery address.

"From what we can see, it's time to talk with someone at this Sangree & Co. outfit," Charlie said flatly. "Quantities are too small for bridge building. We questioned foremen, engineers too. According to them, someone's probably doing repairs. They don't see any other use for the stuff. Showed them the list we'd gathered from Haigh and the others. The only other possibility they could guess is that someone is trying to copy their designs. Either way we should check on it."

"Thanks, Charlie. Me and Jaffey'll go over there this afternoon. The part that interests me in all this is where that stuff is going."

"Yeah, we thought so too. Course your boys, Watkins, Lebeau, and Emmons, are from Texas originally. I know they're about a thousand miles apart but they're both in the South," Pat said a little too hopefully. "It's the only damn thing we've got, so what the hell."

Tom looked at his watch and sighed, "Gotta report to Byrnes. Me and Eli'll go to Sangree & Co. after."

"We'll keep digging but I can't say I'm too optimistic," Charlie said, brushing some lingering breakfast crumbs from his vest. "Gonna pay a visit to the contractor on the trains. Might turn something up."

Tom gave a hopeful but resigned shrug. He was getting used to dead ends.

"Wonder when those service records'll show up. It's been near three weeks ago I sent for them. Right about now, any new information would be welcome."

"Well, I'd be pleased to look at anything other than contracts and order books. I'm starting to see numbers in my sleep," Pat said, rolling his head in a dizzy pantomime.

"Keep it up for now, Pat. Who knows, you might have turned up something with this Sangree & Co. stuff," Tom said over his shoulder as he marched toward Byrnes's office.

Tom's report to the chief was short. He filled him in on the lead to Sangree & Co., and that was all. Byrnes looked preoccupied, barely raising his head from the paperwork piled on his desk. After only a few minutes, he waved his cigar at Tom mumbling something about keeping him informed. Tom took that as his cue to leave, which he wasn't unhappy to do.

Captain Sangree sat at his office desk jotting down some thoughts on arrangements for escaping South once the mission was accomplished. He reminded himself that he needed to put some more work into their manifesto. He and Sullivan had done an outline a few days before. It would be a grand document, and he was pleased with it so far. It would start with a preamble, just as the Declaration of Independence had, stating the rights of the South that had been denied. It would list their grievances—the rape of their land, the loss of life, the burning and pillage of farms, businesses, and homes. All these things must not be forgotten. They were open wounds in the South. Occupation and Reconstruction had been the crowning insults. The list had been long once they started in earnest to tote it all up, the evidence of Yankee tyranny undeniable. It would be a brilliant document. It couldn't set it all to rights, but it would tell the world the whole truth, not just the Yankee truth. That would be a victory in itself.

Thaddeus didn't plan to put anything in about Roebling. Even though the longing for revenge had driven him through the years, he knew that it wouldn't help their cause. It would be enough that Roebling would suffer. A loud knock on his office door startled him. He wasn't expecting anyone. Quickly he shoved his papers into the top drawer of his desk and locked them in.

"Just a moment," he called out gruffly. He rose and strode to the door, annoyed at the interruption. The captain threw the door open, intending to dismiss whoever it might be as quickly as possible. Braddock filled the doorway like a guilty conscience. Thaddeus did his best to control his voice, asking politely. "How can I help you gentlemen?" but he wasn't sure he'd succeeded. He tried to think what to do. His brain felt like it was squirming about inside his head. His pistol was in the desk, locked away. That wasn't an option. He measured the chances of getting by the big detective and the cop behind him. They didn't look good. There was nothing to do but carry on the charade.

"We're investigating some malfeasance, sir, and we wanted to ask you a few questions." Tom started off putting on his best official voice. Intimidation was a useful tool.

"Malfeasance, how so?" Thaddeus asked with a well-executed frown. He thought he carried it off rather well, the confused, innocent tone was almost perfect. He was glad they couldn't see his suddenly sweaty palms, which he wiped quickly on his trousers.

"May we come in, sir?" Braddock asked, looking over the captain's shoulder.

"Oh, yes of course. Forgive me. Would you gentlemen care for some coffee?"

"Sure," Tom said. "Black." Tom scanned the room with a practiced eye as they entered, filing things away for future reference. Jaffey declined the offer of coffee. Tom watched for any tremors as Thaddeus poured. It was his real reason for accepting the coffee. He didn't see any. Thaddeus was doing his best to appear indifferent, but his insides seemed populated by fleas on a hot stove. He handed Tom the coffee and took a seat behind his desk. Tom and Jaffey found chairs. "I'm Detective Braddock and this is Patrolman Jaffey," Tom said in a belated introduction.

"And I am Thaddeus Sangree, owner of this firm," Thad said, casting a hand around the room. "So what's this about malfeasance? I can assure you that this firm has a reputation for scrupulously fair business dealings."

"Yes, I'm sure." Tom's tone said he wasn't sure at all. He took out a pad, poising his pencil above it, before he raised his eyes to meet Sangree's. "Have you placed orders recently for Crucible steel wire?" he asked slowly.

The captain hesitated only an instant before answering. "Yes, of course. That was about six months ago, if I recall." Thad's mind was in turmoil. *"They know!"* a voice screamed inside his head. *"They know!"* How, he couldn't imagine.

"You also ordered some steel and cast-iron structural components similar to those being used on the new East River Bridge, is that correct?" Tom went on.

"Well, I can't say whether the steel and cast-iron parts I ordered matched anything on the East River Bridge, but yes, I did order such items." Thad felt the best thing to do was to admit as much of the truth as he could, the better to conceal it. "Have I broken some law?" he asked, sipping his coffee innocently.

If this Sangree fellow was guilty of anything, he sure didn't show it, Tom thought.

"Not that we know of, Mr. Sangree. Can you tell me why these orders were placed?" Tom would volunteer nothing more than he had to, and he had no intention of being the one answering questions.

"Not precisely, Detective," Thad said. "You see, I was simply an intermediary. Some men with whom I have not done business in the past had asked that I assist them in procuring and shipping these materials."

Tom seemed to weigh this, scribbling on his pad as he did. "And who would that be, sir?"

"A Mr. Lansdorf and a Mr. Limner. They are the principals in a firm by the name of Liberty Construction. As you probably already know, they're located in Richmond," the captain said, taking it as a matter of faith that if they knew of the shipments, they'd know where they were bound. "I haven't actually done business with them directly before, but they bore sound references from people whose word I trust." Sangree went on to give Tom the references. The story sounded perfectly plausible.

"And you say you acted as their intermediary?"

"Precisely. You see, I have been doing business in the North for some time—since before the war, actually. I've always kept business ties to the South, so I was in a unique position to help with procurements in this area."

Tom nodded, waiting longer than he needed to ask the next question. "I see. When did you come to New York, Mr. Sangree?" he asked offhandedly.

"Oh, back in '59, I suppose it was."

"You must have been a young man then."

Thaddeus smiled. "Yes, not quite eighteen at the time. Came with my parents who didn't agree with what was going on in the South," Thad said, swallowing the lie as easily as air. "They didn't own slaves, you see, and didn't aspire to. They . . . saw slavery as an issue that was . . . potentially destructive." He choose his words carefully. "Felt the North was a better place to live at the time. As we now know, they were quite right." He added a knowing smile at the end. He was getting better at this, more comfortable. He started to relax a bit, secure in his story.

"Did you serve in the army, Mr. Sangree?" Tom asked, scribbling still.

"No, I'm ashamed to say I didn't. My father wouldn't hear of me taking up arms against my native soil. Though we had moved North, we still had family in the South. My father paid the three hundred to hire a replacement for me. It's something I'm not proud of, Detective," Thad said with a slightly bowed head. He didn't want Braddock to see his eyes just then.

"Uh-huh, and how did you come to do business in the South?"

"Oh, I simply picked up where my father left off. He had maintained his contacts after the move. I continued them after his death, back in '73."

It seemed a reasonable story, and it was one he had thought to use for just such an occasion. Thaddeus knew they'd ask how to get in touch with Liberty Construction. He also knew that they never would be able to. When they found that out, they'd be back with questions that wouldn't be so easy to answer. He had no way of knowing what other sources of information or evidence they may have developed. He could delay them a few days perhaps, but that was all. This little visit, complete with coffee, had changed everything. He'd have to move up the timetable. The bridge would open in just a few days, but they'd need more than that to get ready. With a little luck, maybe they'd be able to finally kill this Yankee detective while they were at it, something that Thaddeus wanted more than ever as he smiled at Braddock over his coffee cup.

"Do you have any idea what Liberty Construction was going to do with these materials?" Tom continued in a voice devoid of inflection.

"I'm afraid not. I assumed they were working on a structure of some sort."

"The fact that the components you ordered were identical to components on the bridge didn't raise your curiosity?"

"Are they? I had no idea." Thaddeus said, all innocent ignorance. "I'm not an engineer, gentlemen. I received instructions to locate and purchase specified items. The order came from a legitimate firm, with good references, so that's exactly what I did," Thaddeus said, putting down his coffee and staring at Braddock. "There didn't seem to be anything wrong with the request. Certainly the Roebling Company, J. Lloyd Haigh, and the others I placed orders with didn't question them. Why would I? You see, I deal primarily in the factoring of cotton and in a variety of farm equipment, so my knowledge of what I was ordering was limited."

"Why would they have chosen your firm, then, do you think, Mr. Sangree?" Eli asked, jumping into the questioning for the first time. Tom looked at him with a caution in his eyes. The question was good, but he was supposed to be asking it.

"Well, I always assumed it was because of a referral—you know, mutual business acquaintances, that sort of thing."

"Hmm. And this is the address you had them shipped to, correct?" Tom said, holding out a small sheet of paper for Sangree.

Thaddeus looked at the address, pretending to read it carefully. "Quite right, Detective," he said, cursing to himself all the while. "I wish I could help you with something further, but I'm afraid there isn't much to add."

"Yes, I see. Well, you've been very helpful anyway, Mr. Sangree. I'll be in touch if there's any further questions you might be able to help us out with," Tom said as he rose.

"I have one question, Detective, if you don't mind. You spoke of malfeasance before. You never told me what exactly you were investigating."

Braddock turned back toward Sangree. "Murder, Mr. Sangree."

Thad gave them his best shocked reaction. "What could these purchases possibly have to do with a murder investigation? Murder is a serious charge, Mr. Braddock."

Braddock didn't answer, except to say "Murder is indeed a serious charge, sir. Thank you, and thanks for the coffee."

"My pleasure, gentlemen. Good day."

Suddenly and with calculated afterthought, Braddock turned in the doorway. Thaddeus, who had his hand already on the knob, was brought up short.

"Tell me," Braddock said, "do you happen to know any of these names? Let's see, ah . . . Matthew Emmons, Earl Lebeau, or Simon Watkins?" He gave Sangree an apologetic smile.

Their conversation had prepared Thaddeus for this possibility, but it still gave him a sudden knot in the pit of his stomach to hear those names from Braddock's lips. "I can't say that I do, Detective. Who are they? Oh wait, wasn't there a Watkins found on the ferry some time ago? I did read about that, but that's not the same man, I take it."

Braddock said nothing for a long moment before he spoke. "You don't know any of them, *you say*?" Braddock asked again.

"Of course not, Detective." Thaddeus sounded offended. "Why should I know these men?"

"Quite true, Mr. Sangree. Why indeed?" Then he asked one more question, his pencil poised once more. "Oh . . . your address, if you please, sir?"

A minute later the captain closed his door on their backs with a huge sigh of relief, which soon turned to anger. "Fuck!" he cursed through gritted teeth.

So, Eli, anything seem odd to you about that meeting?" Tom asked as they went out the front door of Sangree's building. Jaffey had a few ideas and Tom did too. They kicked them back and forth, weighing the possibilities as they walked to the El. One thing they both agreed on more or less was their suspicion of Sangree. It was nothing they could prove but more a collection of observations that bothered them. The train roared and clanked over their heads and almost drowned Jaffey out. He had to shout. "I thought that for a man of business he had damn few papers on his desk. Most offices I've seen have whole stacks of it. He seemed real uninterested in what he was ordering too. I think I would have been more curious in his shoes."

"Maybe he's just neat," Tom said doubtfully. "Seemed real surprised to see us at first but he calmed down pretty quick," he observed. "Could be nothing. Most anybody'd be nervous to find cops at the door. You noticed he was alone too. I thought that was a little curious—him running the show all by himself, no clerks or nothing. Notice that room in back of the office?"

"Seemed he had plenty of chairs," Eli said dryly.

Tom nodded his agreement. "One other thing. You notice how close that place was to Paddy's?"

Jaffey shrugged. "Could be just a coincidence. There's dozens of businesses close to Paddy's."

"Sure. Dozens," Tom said the doubt etched on word. "Let's go see Byrnes."

The meeting with the chief went on for some time, though the decision on whether to follow up on Liberty Construction took only minutes. It was Tom's other agenda that took some going over. Byrnes was very attentive, and, in the end, very cooperative.

"You ever been to Richmond before, Eli?" Tom asked as they headed for the Old Dominion Steamship Line.

"Never been much beyond New Jersey," Eli admitted a little sheepishly.

"Well, lad, it's time you saw the world. Last time I was in Richmond—well, let me rephrase that. I was never actually in Richmond. Closest I got was the other side of the James River. Anyway, the last time I saw it, it wasn't looking too prosperous. Mostly burned out buildings down by the waterfront. Couldn't stop to gawk much. Busy chasing Bobby Lee at the time."

"You were at Appomattox?" Eli asked, eager for a war story.

"Well, never actually saw that place either. Saw Lee though—the one and only time I ever did."

Jaffey's curiosity was fully piqued. "Really? What was he like?"

"Well, I don't remember all the details," Tom said slowly, though he remembered it very well indeed.

"He was riding back from the McLean house, where he surrendered. Riding that great white horse of his, Traveler," Tom said slowly. "Thing I recall most was . . . dignity. It's the only word comes to mind. I've seen generals strut and prance like peacocks, so full of themselves there was hardly air left in a room. Wasn't like that. Lee was dignity itself." Tom gave a soft smile. "Like it was something he grew into and wore like a . . . cloak, sort of. No prance or pomp to him. He was an old man by then. Not all that old in years, but the war had aged him. His beard was snowy white, but he rode that horse erect and strong as a grand old oak. All decked out in his best uniform: gold braid, white gloves, big polished boots," Tom said, holding himself erect and dignified. "He rode slow, almost like at a funeral. Didn't look left or right. And as he passed, I saw his eyes and they were swimming, so he had to blink back the tears. It was sad to see. As he passed, the boys—one by one—took their hats off. I did too. Got real quiet, just the sound of the horses' hooves, the squeak of leather, the jingle of harness and scabbard. Like a hush traveled with him. We all stood quiet and watched the old man pass."

The hack they were riding in bounced on the cobbles as they neared pier 26, North River, where the Old Dominion Line docked. Tom was quiet for a couple of blocks. Eli figured he was remembering his war years. He didn't ask Tom any more. Let him have his silence if he wanted it. They rolled to a stop and Tom snapped back to the present. As they walked toward the steamship office, Tom said, "That man was a god in the South. I could see why. He still is like a god down there," Tom said. He pointed a finger at Jaffey. "One piece of advice: Never speak poorly of Robert E. Lee south of the Potomac." He paused for a second and said, "Come to think of it, never do it in front of me either."

They booked passage to Richmond, leaving next day at 3:00 P.M. They shared a stateroom because Byrnes wanted them to keep expenses low.

"All right, we got that done. I've got to go to the Second and see Captain Coffin. You can come if you like, but—"

"Sure, I'll come. Haven't seen Sam and some of the boys in weeks now. Give me time to catch up." Neither of them noticed Earl as he lounged behind a wagon across the street, his hat pulled low over shining black eyes.

The precinct house was quiet when they got there at around twelve-forty-five. The squad room was nearly empty, and the desk sergeant was nibbling the remains of a sandwich while reading the *Tribune*. Tom was able to see Coffin right away.

"Got a few minutes, August? I've got some good news," he said as he poked his head inside the captain's door.

"Always got time for good news," Coffin said jovially. "Close the door behind you, okay? You have a conversation with our yellow brethren on Doyers?"

Tom hesitated a moment. "Yeah, our 'yellow friends' are willing to meet tonight." Coffin ignored the sarcasm in Tom's voice.

"Good, what time?"

"Around seven. Just you and me," Tom said, doubting that Coffin would go anywhere without some backup, however well hidden.

August was pleased but Tom felt the need for another caution. "Like I told you, this will take more than one meeting, so don't be surprised if nothing seems to get accomplished this time around."

"I understand. I don't like it, but I understand it. So we'll meet . . . say six-thirty?" Coffin said. Tom just nodded and was about to go. In fact, he had hold of the doorknob, when Coffin stopped him. "Oh, Tom?" he said casually. "You do understand the situation here, right?"

"How do you mean, August? I know what I have to do, if that's what you're asking."

The captain shook his head, his lips pursed as if he was considering something. "Not precisely. What I'm getting at is your understanding of who's running this deal," Coffin said flatly.

Tom had to make himself take a breath before he answered. "You're the captain, Captain," he said as matter-of-factly as he could.

"Good. I know these are your connections," Coffin conceded. "Don't worry, you'll be in for a big cut when this comes together."

"I live for my cut, Captain," Tom shot back. His conspiratorial grin felt so false he wondered if it showed.

Coffin just laughed. "See you at six-thirty then."

Tom closed the door behind him, cursing under his breath and more determined than ever.

Tom, Eli, and Sam had a late lunch together. It was three when they split up.

"Listen, boys, I'm going to pay a surprise visit to a certain address on Twenty-sixth Street. Anybody comes looking for me, you know what to say," Tom told them.

Sam grinned, giving Tom a broad wink. "Have fun. Give Mary my best," Sam said.

Jaffey stood, a little confused, as Tom and Sam started to walk their separate ways.

Tom looked over his shoulder at him, realizing the younger man's indecision. "Why don't you take a nice relaxing ride on the Staten Island Ferry, Eli? See you in the morning."

Jaffey grinned and waved, sauntering off a temporarily free man.

. . .

The afternoon was fading into evening. Shadows crept across the floor as the setting sun turned to gold. It was a golden afternoon in more ways than one.

"That was lovely, Mr. Braddock," Mary whispered. "You should surprise me more often."

"Glad to oblige. I didn't hurt you then, did I? I couldn't tell if that was a good moan or a bad moan."

Mary rubbed her side. "The ribs are still a little tender but it was mostly a good moan—a rather special moan I save just for you."

Tom cradled her in his arms. "I love it in the afternoon and that lazy, nothing-else-in-the-world-to-do feeling . . . after."

"Not bad work if you can get it." Mary grinned at him. "I know the feeling. It's a lot like work," she said playfully. They laughed hard, till Mary had to hold her side and whistle for air. Tom hit her with a pillow, then and giggled as she hit him back with her good arm. It was a losing battle though. She surrendered and was pinned. Sometimes you must surrender to win the war, she thought.

Later, as they lay on the rumpled covers, tiny beads of sweat glistening like stars in the afternoon sun, Mary waited for what Tom had come to tell her. She knew him well enough to know that this special afternoon had more than one purpose. She could be patient, though, and knew he'd reward her in his own time. She had a feeling that he needed to make love first, so that in the quiet time after, it would be easier to share what he had to.

"Our first meeting with the tong is tonight," he said to the ceiling at last.

He was so predictable, she thought. She would have grinned if what he told her wasn't so serious. Mary wondered if it was just her or if everyone saw it.

"Just you and Coffin?" she asked softly.

"Supposed to be," he answered.

"Don't trust him to come alone?" Mary asked. Not trusting Coffin seemed entirely sensible.

"Don't worry, I don't expect him to. We'll have a tail. Shouldn't be too hard to spot once we get close. No Chinese in the corps, you know."

She turned to him, so close she could count the tiny lines at the corners of his eyes. "Be careful, Tom, please." She squeezed his arm.

"It's Coffin needs to be careful. I've got everything sewn up tighter than a fat lady's corset," he said, grinning at the image. He wished he was really as confident as he sounded.

"What'll you do if you're followed?"

"Got a plan. There'll be a dozen eyes on the street. There's help if I need it."

"Nothing's happening tonight?" she asked, knowing where this was leading.

"No. It won't happen until I get back. Probably the Twenty-fourth."

"Getting back? Where are you going?" Mary asked, surprised. "And by the way, the twenty-fourth is the big fireworks display for the opening of the bridge. You promised we'd see it."

Tom had forgotten but acted as if he hadn't. "We will. I wouldn't miss that for anything."

"Yeah, but where are you going all of a sudden?"

"Part of the Bucklin case. Going to Richmond . . . check on some construction company that doesn't sound like it's on the up and up," Tom said, trying to minimize it. "Long story. We think maybe Bucklin was killed because he found out about some contract-rigging scheme. Not sure just yet but it's our best guess. Leaving tomorrow at three. Jaffey's going with me."

"So that's why you came calling this afternoon. You knew you wouldn't be seeing me for a couple of days so you . . ."

Tom held up a hand, a theatrical look full of hurt and indignance painting his face. "Oh, now, Mary, that's not fair. I was thinking of you," he said, all innocent concern. "You would have missed me terribly if I'd gone off without seeing to your intimate needs, now wouldn't you?" Tom nuzzled her breast playfully, a wicked grin on his face.

Mary fixed a mock frown on him, stern and demanding. "I have one more intimate need for you to satisfy, Detective, so long as you're so concerned for my welfare." Mary straddled him, throwing a golden thigh on either side of his chest. "Can you imagine what that might be, or do I have to draw you a picture?"

"Oh, I think I get the picture . . . dearest. I live to satisfy."

Earl sat with his feet up on the big table. He picked at his fingernails with a small knife as he talked.

"Watched 'em come out of the Old Dominion office. Checked with the ticket clerk. They're on the three o'clock steamer tomorrow."

The captain paced his office, his brow furrowed and his hands knotted behind his back. "That means we've got no more than two–three days at most before they're back here with more questions. I'll telegraph our friends in Richmond."

"You gonna arrange a special reception for 'em, Cap'n?" Earl pointed his pocket knife at his throat and grinned slyly.

"I'm open to suggestions. If it fails, though, they'll be back here with a vengeance," Thaddeus said. "Hell, even if we kill them, there's bound to be others who know where their investigation was heading. We'll have a fire under us either way. Still, it's better to eliminate them in Richmond. Might throw the cops off our trail for a few days till they sort it out." Thaddeus hesitated for a moment, thinking the matter through. The cops were closer than any of them had imagined. Though none of the options looked good in the long run, what they needed was a little more time. If they could buy themselves a few more days by killing off Braddock in Richmond, it might just be enough. "We need more time" was all he said as he paced.

"Why wait till they git to Richmond, Cap'n?" Earl drawled.

Thaddeus turned to him, cocking his head quizically. "Kill 'em on the steamer," Earl said as if it was a given.

Sullivan spoke up at that. "I don't see how that would really change anything. I mean, aside from giving you some sport, there's still others who'd follow up where they left off. Don't know how much time it might buy," Patrick said doubtfully.

Earl grinned. "Not if they go missin'. If they wuz to not show up here in a couple of days, the cops would waste buckets o' time lookin' for 'em. Buy us maybe a week or so, easy." It was a good point.

"You thinking you're going to be able to kill both of them, dump them over the side, and not be seen or heard?" Pat exclaimed, the disbelief so thick in his voice he could spread it on toast. "Might be possible if everything went perfect, but you know the odds of that. You've got no time to plan. Even if you did, I'd say it was too risky to try. No plan ever goes perfectly. There's always something unexpected. You know that. Look what happened when we set those Plug Uglies on them. Anybody at this table think that wasn't going to work?" Pat looked at each face around the room. There was no disagreement.

"Yeah, but this time"—Earl started.

"Forget it, Earl!" Thaddeus snapped. "I appreciate your zeal, soldier, but I think in this circumstance we need a different tactic. I'll make arrangements for them in Richmond," he said with finality.

"Meanwhile, there's another little problem I'm thinking we should deal with," Thaddeus said half to himself.

Everyone was still, listening intently. Even Earl had stopped his whittling to peer at the captain curiously.

"I've been thinking about how this goddamn detective got wind of the Richmond connection." Sangree looked around the room. "I mean, how in hell could he have known about that if he wasn't told? I suppose he could have stumbled on the orders from the Roebling Works and the others, but that would have taken a huge amount of digging. And what would he have been doing that kind of digging for in the first place? Made me wonder about why he was on to Watkins the way he was too. He sure as hell didn't get any clues from any of us." There were nods of agreement to that. "I'm thinking maybe somebody knows more than we thought he does," the captain said, turning to Earl.

Earl was shaking his head. "Don't know, Cap'n. If I'm followin' you, an' you're talkin' 'bout the Bucklin boy . . . well, I jus don' know. I tell ya this, I believed 'im when he said he din' know nothin'. Had him near to pissin' his pants. Hell, I even cut him an' he didn' say nothin'."

Thaddeus nodded, not convinced. The boy *had* to know something. Terrence had kept him close in his last days. Why? There had to be more there. Maybe the grandmother was the one, though he discounted that thought almost as soon as it occurred to him. If that had been the case, the cops would have been on them as soon as Terrence was gone. He would have told her everything he knew, in detail, but the boy . . . perhaps the boy had just heard some things, just part of the story, just enough to give Braddock the scent. Perhaps Terrence realized the boy knew more than was healthy. He turned to Earl, having paced the length of the office.

"I think another visit to young Master Bucklin is in order nonetheless. He may not know much, but it seems likely he knows more than he should." There was general agreement with that, he could see from the faces around the table. "When Braddock doesn't return from Richmond, and they start back-tracking his investigation, it'll lead right back to the kid, you know that."

Earl sighed. He didn't have much stomach for killing kids, though he hadn't minded throwing a scare into the boy. He supposed he would have killed him then if he'd spilled what he knew, but this was different. This wasn't the same. All they had were suspicions about the boy. Still, he wasn't one to leave a job undone. He knew his duty, and he'd do it the best he was able.

"So ya want me to do it?" Earl said, not really asking.

Thaddeus looked at him for a moment, thinking. "No Earl, I think not," he said slowly. Earl tried not to let the feeling of relief leak onto his face. "No, I have someone else in mind for this."

It was decided quickly. Braddock, in Richmond, and the Bucklin boy here in New York would be gone within a day of each other. Two more dead ends. Two less stumbling blocks in their path.

"Buy us a few days perhaps while they clean up the mess. Meanwhile, we retreat. Well, not retreat precisely; fade into the landscape would be more accurate," the captain explained. "Once we drop out of sight, it would take an act of God for them to find us again, especially with Braddock and the boy out of the picture."

"We're pitching tents somewhere else," Matt said, finishing the captain's thought. He was resigned to do whatever it took. At this point, disappearing didn't seem all that bad an idea.

"Not all of us, no . . . least not right away. But Earl, Matt, and I have to. Better not be here if they get back. Better not be here either way, for that matter."

"Okay by me, Cap'n," Earl said, resuming his whittling of fingernails.

"Sure," Matt said. "Our jobs are pretty much done on the wiring." He and Earl needed just one more night to finish snaking wire. Officially the wiring was done, but they were as planned, a step behind. "After the test last night, there isn't much more we need to do, at least not as far as the mission is concerned."

Last night, May 19, long after the red ball of the sun disappeared below the craggy skyline and its orange halo retreated after, the cities of New York and Brooklyn had been treated to a spectacle never before seen. The power plant in Brooklyn hissed and pounded with a full head of steam. Huge cast-iron wheels, with yard-wide belts attached, drove the dynamos, which spun with dangerous speed and irresistible power. The smell of ozone swirled on the restless currents of air as the dynamos hummed in deep-throated electric harmony. Switches were thrown, and at once there was light across the East River. Seventy lamps blinked on, bathing the bridge and the river below in the glow of a new age. One by one, ships on the waters below started to blow their whistles and ring their bells. People on shore cheered. Matt and Earl had been there too, watching from the approach above the power plant. Though neither one could have told the other why, they cheered as well. From a distance the lights looked like luminous pearls strung from city to city. They burned softly in the moonlight, miniature suns captured in glass. The triumph of the industrial age basked in the electric glow. Never before had the two come together so beautifully. It was hard not to cheer.

"You should've seen it, Cap'n. It was something!"

"Never saw the like in all my days," Earl said, shaking his head. "Sure was pretty."

The captain didn't share their enthusiasm. "I'm sure it was, boys, but let's get back to it, shall we? So . . . the three of us need to go to ground. You two"—he pointed to Earl and Matt—"put in your resignations tomorrow. You'll be done with the wire tonight, right?" He got nods in reply. "Good. Tell the clerk you're going back to Texas when you resign. That'll keep the cops guessing. I'll close up shop here. We all need to find new rooms too."

"Now, Pat and Jus and Bart, they don't got to move, right?" Matt asked, making sure he had it right.

"There's no suspicion on them that we know of but, Bart, you should quit anyway. No point taking chances."

Jacobs just shrugged. He didn't much care one way or another. Pat and Justice had been laid off the week before. With the cables finished, their jobs were at an end.

"There's no reason I can think of for you to stay on, is there?"

"I've done about everything I can in the office, Captain," Weasel admitted.

"All right then, we move tomorrow. It shouldn't be hard to find new rooms somewhere. Won't be for long. No hotels, though, Matt, and no correct names either. Got to be careful. From now on we'll meet at Bart's place, let's say tomorrow at seven?" The captain looked around the room for agreement. "Meanwhile I believe I'll set up a reception in Richmond. With any luck it'll be the last we see of them. And Bucklin, well . . . you know what has to be done there."

Thaddeus didn't expect an answer and got none.

Tom watched New York slip behind them from the fantail of the steamer *Norfolk*. It filled the island from shore to shore, spilling into its liquid boundaries in a confusion of funnels, masts, and rigging. The hard outlines of the buildings seemed to fade into the water at the edges.

"I wonder what it looked like before all this was here," Jaffey mused. "Ever wonder about that? Can you imagine sailing into this harbor for the first time? It must have been wonderful, like a paradise."

"Forests, I guess," Tom said. "Marshes and such around the edges in Brooklyn and Jersey. The air clear and clean, no garbage, no smell of sewage on the water. Must have been pretty."

"I think about it sometimes when I take the ferry. I think what it must have been like. Won't be that way ever again, I guess."

"Called progress, Eli. Hard to put a brake on it," Tom said. "For everything we build, something from nature is lost. That's the way of things, I guess. Like the bridge." He waved a hand at the fading structure. "Somewhere there's a mountain with a big hole in it from all the stone they quarried. That mountain won't ever be the same."

"Yeah . . . but look at it," Jaffey replied. "It's magnificent."

Tom gazed at the span, soaring across the river in the distance, dwarfing everything else on the skyline.

"You know, you might regret the loss of the natural things that were here before, but that's a piece of progress to rival anything in nature," Jaffey said.

The two men leaned on the aft rail. Tom's thoughts trailed away to the meeting he had had with Coffin and Sung Chow the night before. It had all gone according to plan. Old sack-face had sat silent and intimidating while Coffin talked. Tom had to give the devil his due. Coffin did a masterful job of putting his case to the old Chinaman. He was very convincing and spoke in broad, glowing terms of how they could expand the trade and blossom together, like an ever-expanding field of poppies. It was hard to refute his logic. With his kind of help, the opium trade would flourish as never before. Money would flow. They all would be rich beyond counting or spending. Things would be good for everybody. Old Sung Chow had nodded at the appropriate points but wore his best poker face when Coffin made his offer. The old man just said he'd have to think about it but doubted it was good enough offer to even consider. He played it well.

To Tom's amusement, Coffin was steaming by the time they hit the street. They came out fast and Tom's eye was caught by movement in the shadows near the end of the block. Coffin had a tail, though Tom hadn't noticed it before they had gone in. Somehow the shadow reminded him of Chowder, but he put it down to the light and the fleeting glimpse he had had.

"Damn Chinamen think they can squeeze me! Who the fuck do they take me for?" Coffin had fumed.

"I told you it would go that way, August. Don't let it get to you," Tom counseled. Despite Coffin's great skill at putting his deal before the old man, he simply couldn't hide his contempt for the old man. That attitude helped to seal his fate. Sung Chow had given Tom a cryptic smile as they had left last night. Coffin hadn't seen it.

Tom smiled grimly at the memory. He and Eli watched the Jersey shore slip by as the light faded and the second round of beers came. They turned in early after a satisfying meal. That suited Tom just fine. When they woke, the Chesapeake was slipping astern and the James lay wide before the bow. Breakfast was long gone when the outskirts of Richmond hove into view. The docks were bustling with barges, coastal steamers, fishing boats, freighters, and everything in between. Stevedores cursed and sweated. Teamsters maneuvered heavy wagons and heavier teams through the crowded streets.

"It's on Carey and Fifteenth." Tom pointed. "I think that's to the left," he said over the noise. They strode up Carey gawking like tourists. "Don't recognize anything. This was all burned out in '65. Nothing left but brick walls and chimneys." They walked farther, with Tom marveling at how the place had changed, when he stopped short at the corner of Carey and Nineteenth.

"What's the matter?" Jaffey asked, almost bumping into him.

Tom didn't respond right away. He stood silent, looking at the building on the corner. "You ever hear of Libby Prison?" he asked softly.

"No."

Tom turned to glare at Jaffey, the surprise clear on his face.

"What the hell did they teach you on Staten Island?"

"Plenty," Eli said defensively, "but nothing I can recall about Libby Prison. What was it?"

"Prisoner-of-war camp," Tom said shortly. "Was a warehouse or factory before the war, I think. Mostly held officers, but later in the war, it was pretty much everyone they had a square foot for." Tom stood silent for a moment just staring up at the place as the street traffic went by unheeded. "Remember this place, Eli. More good men came out of here feet first than from most battles. Disease, mostly. Bad food, and not enough of it, crowded conditions, not a whole lot of heat in the winter, and hot as hell in the summer. Men just gave up." Tom walked away at that. Jaffey thought he saw him shudder. He stared for a moment longer, then followed.

They found the address they were looking for on Fifteenth and Carey. The sign on the door said Broome Brothers Warehouse. They looked at each other silently. This was not a good start. It didn't take long to find that nobody there had ever heard of Liberty Construction. Nobody knew if the firm had ever occupied that address or one nearby. Tom and Jaffey questioned at least a dozen people, from the general manager down to a handful of men on the warehouse floor. The story was the same, remarkably the same. They spoke with the manager first, a man named Chester Wilsey. When Tom asked if he could see the books, the man gave him a cold stare and said in a slow drawl,

"I don't got to show you Yanks shit. You got no jurisdiction down here."

Tom stared right back. "I can get the cooperation of the local authorities if I need to, Mr. Wilsey," he said evenly, not at all sure that he could. "I don't want to do that, so I'd consider it a personal favor if you'd help me out with this." He even managed a smile for the man.

"Hmph. What the hell? Won't find nothin'. Go ahead . . . poke around all you like, jus don' waste my time, nor slow my workers. Them niggers're slow enough already." Wilsey grumped, waving at a few idlers who were watching them.

Wilsey was right. They found nothing.

For the next few hours they canvassed the neighborhood looking for anyone who knew of Liberty Construction. They went to City Hall and checked records for a company by that name or anything close. Again they came up empty. There were two Lansdorfs but no Limners on the records. They checked on both. One turned out to be an old woman, the other a haberdasher. Neither had ever heard of Liberty Construction. There were two other places of business with "Liberty" in their titles but one was a dry goods store, the other a securities trader. The closest thing they had to luck was when they talked to a frail-looking older man on the street opposite Broome Brothers. The man's nose was swollen and red like a ripe strawberry with veins. He reeked of drink and walked unsteadily on his one good leg.

"You boys lookin' fer Liberty, eh?" he asked in a cracked and boozy voice. "You won't find 'er. Won't never." He pointed a bony finger at them. "You want my advice, you'll stop lookin' too." The man cast a furtive look across the street as he spoke. In an instant his expression changed, like a dark cloud scudding across the sky of his weathered face. "That's all ah kin say." He started shaking his head and exclaimed, "Goddamn Yankees! Leave me be! Not enough ye took my leg at Chicamogy." The man waved his cane at them. "You git. Got nothin' to say to the likes a you."

Tom followed his eyes across to the warehouse. Two of the white foremen stood in an open doorway, arms folded. Tom thought he'd do the man a favor and called out to his retreating back. "Thanks for nothing."

The two by the doorway just stared.

It was getting late by the time they had finished checking records at City Hall, so Tom asked a clerk about the nearest hotel. They were told that the Powhatan was closest but the America, down the hill from the old capitol building, was cheaper and nearly as good. They were looking forward to a hot bath and an early bed. After all the running around they'd done, Eli and Tom were frustrated and dragging.

"The fellas at Broome were holding back on us," Jaffey said over dinner, his mouth full of steak.

"Oh, yeah," Tom agreed ruefully. "Not going to get anything from these folks. Whatever they were up to is well hid. Eli . . . we are into something here that's far bigger than we'd imagined."

"Got that feelin'. Can't say I'm comfortable here either." Eli looked around the dining room. "Had the feeling we've been watched all day. Can't shake it. Can't say I'm sure who's watching, but the feeling's there."

"Keep your voice down," Tom said, looking at the other tables to see if he'd been heard. "I thought the same thing. Noticed a couple faces on the streets more than once today."

They finished their meal and went up to the room. Tom took note of where the stairs were, walking to each end of the hall to peer up and down the staircases. He checked utility closets too, rattling the knobs to see if they were open or not. He and Eli went to the toilet together. Back in the room, Jaffey pushed a chair against the door.

"That ought to make enough noise if somebody tries sneaking in."

Tom nodded and went to check the windows. They were four floors up with no outside stairs. At least they wouldn't have to worry about someone getting in that way.

"Only one way in or out. Sleep light," he warned.

Tom wasn't aware of the time when he woke much later from a dreamless doze. He'd been catnapping for some time. It had to be late, maybe two or three, he guessed. Something had woken him and his senses were suddenly on alert. The creak of a floorboard out in the hall focused his attention on the door, his head snapping around like a bird dog on point. The dim light seeping under the door from the hall cast a moving shadow. Tom watched as it stopped. Quick as he could, he hit Eli with one hand and grabbed for his Colt with the other. Tom was rolling out of bed when the door burst open. The chair clattered across the room. There was a dresser near the bed and Tom dove for its cover. At almost the same instant, the doorway erupted in sound and flame. A shotgun lit the blackened room like lightning, leaving Tom's ears ringing. The bed exploded in a snowstorm of feathers. Jaffey's bed was next. Jaffey was dead if he hadn't moved, and there was no way to tell in the dark. No sooner had the shotgun shredded their beds than pistols took up the barrage. A second black form in the doorway cut loose with a pistol in either hand, emptying them at the beds blindly. Bullets ricocheted around the room as sheets of yellow flame leapt from the pistols. Splinters flew. Glass shattered. A big pitcher and the bowl it stood in disintegrated in a shower of porcelain and water. Tom did his best to make himself small behind the dresser. It was dark, and he doubted that the gunmen could see what they were shooting at, so he waited till the storm petered out.

As he expected, there was a momentary lull once the pistols had given up their bullets. The two gunmen stood silent for an instant—no more than a heartbeat, really. Tom could see the shotgun coming up again. The man had reloaded while the other had emptied his pistols. Tom wasn't sure if Jaffey was in any shape to return fire, but he figured this was his one chance. With the two backlit by the hall light his chances were pretty good. Tom brought the Colt up, aiming around the corner of the dresser. The one with the shotgun must have seen the movement, and he started to bring the gun to bear. Suddenly, from Tom's left, a pistol barked, lighting the room an instant before his Colt. Tom fired again to be sure, but it wasn't necessary. The man fell, crumpling backward in the hallway. The second man disappeared. Heavy feet pounded down the hall.

"Jaffey," he shouted through the smoke and floating feathers. "You all right?"

"Yeah." A voice from the other side of the room broke through the ringing in his ears. He sounded surprised.

"I'm going after him," Tom said. He was through the door, vaulting the sprawled body, and sprinting down the hall almost before he finished saying it. He heard feet pounding behind him but didn't look back.

Sleepy heads were poking out of doorways, and some even ventured into the hall, watching, groggy and open-mouthed, as Tom and Eli ran by. A door slammed up ahead and they both bolted for the stairs to follow. Tom was through first. He leapt down the stairs two at a time with Jaffey close behind. As they reached the next landing, shots exploded in the stairwell. Tom dove and rolled, coming up against the wall. Jaffey flattened himself against the other side. Neither returned fire. Tom took a moment to reload, as did Eli.

"You see him?" Eli called. The sound of running feet were his answer. As they took up the chase again, they heard another door slam at the bottom of the stairwell.

"He's outside." Tom panted. They burst through the door just in time to see a form rounding the corner onto Carey.

It was a long chase through the darkened streets of Richmond. Tom, dressed in his underwear and socks, and Eli in only his shorts, ran up Carey then followed their man down toward the canal, making a left on Seventh. He had nearly a block lead on them. Catching him was going to be tough with no shoes, but they kept on. It wasn't worth a shot from that distance, not with a pistol in the dark, so they saved their ammunition and ran as fast as they could. They caught glimpses of the man as he ran over the canal and turned toward the hulking form of the old Tredegar Iron Works. The buildings loomed in the night—massive forges, foundries, sheds, and chimneys formed a maze and a perfect refuge. Tom saw that there was no way they'd catch him before he got lost among the blackened buildings, so he puffed to Eli to try a last sprint to close the gap. He thought to try for a shot while their man was still in the open, but they needed to be closer to have any chance. Tom's feet were raw and bleeding and he was certain Jaffey's couldn't be any better, but he put on a last burst of speed and drew within about a hundred yards of the man.

It was too late. Tom could see that, but he pulled up short, steadying his aim with two hands. A hit at that distance would be nearly impossible, especially at night after a long run, but he had to try. Jaffey stopped beside him, taking aim too. Almost simultaneously their pistols lit up the night. Tom fired methodically, doing his best to steady his breathing and aim true. Jaffey just blazed away. Eight times their pistols barked, but the man kept running, seemingly untouched, then he disappeared in the shadow of a building at the edge of the canal.

"Did you see that?" Jaffey asked, breathing hard. "I think we hit him. I think I saw him stumble." Back in the city, they could hear cop's whistles and voices in the night. They seemed to be getting closer.

"I don't know, Eli. Let's move in, but be careful." Tom panted. "You have any bullets left?"

"One." Jaffey huffed.

Tom had saved one too and was glad Eli had kept his wits about him. "Okay," he said, wincing with each step. "Let's see."

It took an hour to find the body. It was floating facedown in the canal. One of the local police found him. There were three bullets in him, none of which would have been instantly fatal, but they were enough to stop him. Tom cursed their luck. Judging from the wounds, the man probably drowned. A dead man was little use to them. The man with the shotgun was in a similar condition back at the hotel, they learned.

"You boys been busy," one of the cops observed laconically, once they had identified themselves.

"Yeah," Tom replied glumly.

It took the rest of the night to explain to the local police exactly what they were doing shooting up the town. They sat in police headquarters, their guns temporarily confiscated, their bloody feet leaving sticky red smudges on the floor while a string of cops questioned them. Tom and Eli didn't tell them everything they suspected about the case, just enough to keep the cops satisfied. Early in the morning Tom and Eli were brought down to view the bodies. They lay on tables in the basement of the headquarters building. It was the first time they got a good look at them. The one who had been fished out of the canal looked to be asleep on the worn wooden table he was laid out on. There were three small red holes: one in his upper right arm, on in his left calf, and one in the lower left side of his back. The one they had shot in their room was in ghastly condition. One of the bullets had caught him in the face, ripping most of his lower jaw away, punching a big hole through the back of the skull. The local cops claimed there was nothing on either of them by way of identification. Tom accepted that with a grim nod. Jaffey wasn't quite as successful at concealing his suspicion.

They were released by about nine in the morning, when they hobbled out into the bright sunlight, blinking like a couple of raccoons. The local cops had retrieved some clothes from their hotel, and then gave them a ride to the hospital, where a doctor looked at their feet. Iodine and bandages swathed their feet when they left the hospital. Getting their shoes on when they got back to the hotel was a painful chore. They made arrangements to take the next steamer back to New York and, with the assistance of a telegram from Byrnes, got a promise of cooperation from the Richmond police.

"What's your guess on whether we ever find out who those guys were, Eli?" Tom asked while he changed his bandages later that day.

"Well," Jaffey said slowly, "my uncle used to say that you can't find gold in a coal mine."

Tom laughed grimly. "Your uncle sounds like a wise man. Five to one we never get anything of value on those two." He paused for a minute, thinking. "Now that Sangree, on the other hand, we need to squeeze him like a ripe melon." Tom hoped his follow-up telegram to Dolan and Heidelberg accomplished what he wanted.

"You figure they'll catch him?" Eli asked.

"Shit . . . I just don't know. He could have cleared out as soon as we left his office two days ago. Be long gone by now. We'll see tomorrow. Done everything we can for now."

Later, on the steamer back to New York, Eli grumbled, "Well, that was a big waste of time. Nearly got ourselves killed and didn't learn a damn thing."

Tom looked at him as if he'd grown a second head. "You think so, eh?" Jaffey would have caught the edge to his voice if he'd known Braddock better.

"Well, yeah. What the hell did we learn actually . . . I mean, hard facts?"

Tom shook his head slowly, like a teacher with a slow pupil. "Learned plenty. First, this is bigger than we expected. Second, it involves far more people at a variety of levels, especially in this town. Third, Sangree's probably in it up to his eyeballs, whatever it is. That's just off the top of my head. I think we did pretty well, all things considered. We're alive, for one thing, which beats hell out of the alternative. Didn't get much hard facts, I'll admit, but we know more than we did before. You notice the farewell committee at the dock?"

"The two across the street by the tobacco warehouse?" Eli asked. "I thought they were a little too interested in us."

"Yeah. This bunch has things buttoned up tighter than a flea's asshole. Wish I knew what the fuck was going on." Tom shook his head. "One thing's for damn sure, Eli; this has got to be more than some fucking contract fraud."

"Yeah, but what?" Jaffey winced as he shifted his weight from one foot to the other.

Tom just grunted. He didn't want to voice the word that came to mind. Instead he just muttered, "We're lucky to be leaving town standing up, my friend."

Mike's grandmother had left the apartment early to deliver the lace she'd
been working on to a store over on Hester. After that she was going to some
woman's house she was making a dress for, and stop somewhere to buy more
cloth and lace-making stuff. Mike hadn't paid much attention. It was clear
she'd be out for a while, and that's about as much as he was interested in
knowing. As usual, he kept a chair, their sturdiest, propped against the door.
Though he hadn't seen another threatening-looking man in the neighborhood
for weeks, he still felt it was a good idea to be careful. A scare like he'd had out
by the jakes had a way of sticking in the back of his head and coming back to
give him a chill now and again. It had scared him enough so that he'd gotten in
the habit of taking precautions. He'd double around the block before he went
in the front door, and sometimes he'd cut through from the back street, navi-
gating the maze of fences, outhouses, and litter-strewn lots behind his building. He was always careful on the stairs and at the landings, cautiously peering
around corners. He even had some special plans, just in case.

Mike had been counting the change he'd managed to hold onto from selling coal. There was less of it than there had been. The allure of the candies by
Brower's front counter had whittled his pile some. Still, he had shepherded
his little hoard carefully and had enough to buy some stuff when he and Tom
went to Barnum's. A light knock at the front door startled him, and he swept
the change off his bed and into a jar before he went to answer it. He didn't
expect it was any bad men, not in broad daylight, but still you couldn't be too
sure. He bent to peer through the small hole he'd drilled in the door. He'd
done it weeks before with his da's old drill . . . just in case. Before he even
said anything to answer whoever was knocking, he took a quick look. At first
all he could see was a dark coat, as if the wearer were listening at the door. It
was that close. But then the person stepped back and knocked again, rapping
right above Mike's head, and he could see the man. It was a little clerkish-
looking fellow, with small glasses and a neat bow tie. He looked harmless
enough.

"Wait a minute," Mike called through the door. He pulled the chair aside a
little, unlocked the lock, and opened the door about a foot. "Whadya want,
mister?"

The man gave him an insipid smile as Mike peered up at him, the kind of
smile that adults give to kids they don't want to be bothered with. Mike knew
it well.

"Is Mrs. Bucklkin at home, son?" the man asked solicitously. Mike hesitated. There was something he didn't like about this man. He didn't answer,

and the man went on. "I'm from the coroner's office. I have some things that belonged to Terrence Bucklin. This is the Bucklin residence, isn't it?"

"Yeah," Mike answered warily. He remembered his grandma going to get his da's things a long time ago, back when she got his body. "My grandma's not home," he said before he realized it, then tried to make it better by saying "She'll be home real soon."

"So, you're the man of the house for now?" the man said. "Mind if I come in and wait for your grandmother?" A foot was now over the threshold. Mike started to back up, then stopped. For the first time he noticed the man's hand was in his coat pocket. Something was in the pocket along with that hand, something long and pointy. It was pointy enough so that just the tip of it was poking out through the seam. It gleamed for an instant, then disappeared as, in slow motion, the hand came out. Mike's instincts were sharp for a boy of ten. He slammed his heel down as hard as he could on the foot and slammed the door in the man's face an instant later. A cursing grunt of pain came through the door and a hopping sound. Mike slid the lock into place and was bracing the chair under the knob when something crashed into the door. Splinters flew as a length of blade sliced through the old wood just near his face. Mike retreated, watching in frozen fascination as the door was hit again and again. He saw the door flex, the door jamb start to crack. It wouldn't hold long, he knew. He turned at last and ran to their bedroom at the back of the tenement, slamming the door behind him, pushing a chair against it and a small bureau against that. He needed time.

Bart Jacobs wasn't a big man. Though the door was old and loose on its hinges, it still took too much time before he felt it give way. All the while he cursed the kid and the throbbing pain in his foot where the boy had stomped him. With a final shove he sent the chair skittering across the room and the door slamming back against the wall. He rushed into the room, his knife held out, ready to skewer the little bastard. There was nothing to be seen, but a noise at the back of the apartment brought him around and running. He threw himself at the closed door which opened halfway with a crash of furniture behind. A second shove and he was through. He stood there panting, searching this way and that. There was nothing in the room but the chair and bureau and the single bed. He bent to look under it, sweeping his knife back and forth, not caring what he hit, so long as it was flesh. Nothing.

"What the fuck?" He stood bewildered for a moment. The apartment was empty. There was no place the kid could have hidden, no closets, no armoires, no bathroom. He did a slow pirouette, momentarily bewildered. A noise from outside the open bedroom window caught his attention. He dashed over, looking out just in time to see Mike drop the last two feet to the ground from the rope he'd tied to the bottom of the bedpost.

"Shit!" Jacobs hesitated for a moment, unsure whether he might go down the same way. He didn't. He watched Mike disappear in the labyrinth of fences, outhouses, sheds, and junk between the buildings, noting the direction, then turned and dashed out the way he'd come in.

Mike knew this labyrinth maybe better than anyone on the block. He'd played here countless times with his friends. He knew every corner, every turn, every dead end, every hiding place. He knew where he had to go. He was almost hoping the man would follow, even though he was so scared he shook all over. He ducked through a low hole in a wooden fence, not caring as he smeared himself with shitty mud. Brushing himself off, he stopped, listening for pursuit over the sound of his rapid breathing. Sounds of pursuit were coming from farther back, near his building. Mike waited. There was just one way in and one way out of where he was. Sure of his getaway, he set himself up to wait at the right spot. He'd done this before, at play. Mike wasn't playing now. There'd be just one chance, he knew. The fence was high, maybe eight feet. The man would have to come through the hole. Mike shivered in silence, more scared than he'd ever been. His knees actually shook—so much that he wondered if maybe the man could hear his bones rattling. His breathing sounded so loud it could be heard across town. Any attempt to slow it down only seemed to choke him. Still he waited. Another noise, closer this time, sent an icy jolt of fear through him. He listened as footsteps approached. He could see the man in his mind, feeling his way to this spot, maybe following his tracks in the dark soil that the weeds seemed to love so much. The fence moved as the man leaned against it. Fingertips appeared at the top as he tried to vault over it, feet scrabbled against the wood. Mike heard the man curse. A few seconds later a clerkish, bespectacled, bow-tied head popped through the hole.

Jacobs had his shoulders through and had planted both hands on the dirt to pull himself the rest of the way when he saw the foot. It appeared from behind some junk leaning against the fence to his left. He had the bastard, he thought, anxious to butcher the kid. His suit was smeared with shit, his foot hurt like hell, and this little fuck was going to get it. Then he looked up.

Mike brought the old chair leg down with all the force a scared ten-year-old could muster. It was maple, from the back of one of those old, straight, uncomfortable chairs from years ago. Sometimes he and his friends had used it to play ball. It broke over the back of bow-tie's head, cracking with such force it left his hands numb and knocking bow-tie's glasses into the mud. He had a fleeting image of the head and the glasses and the bow-tie lying still in the dirt before he took off. He ran hard and he ran long, and he didn't come back for a long, long time.

Coogan was washing down the last of his steak with a bottle of beer. Coffin sat across from him in the dining room at Nash & Fuller, on Park Row. The late-afternoon crowd was thinning, and there was nobody within two tables of them.

"How'd it go with Braddock and the Chinese?" Coogan asked with his mouth full.

"Well, I've got to give Tom credit; he knows how the bastards think. It went all right, I guess. Hard to tell. That Chinaman has the best poker face I've ever seen."

"So you think they'll go for it?"

"I think so, at least Braddock says they will. Tell you the truth, all we need is a toehold right now. Give us a couple of years and they'll be the ones coming to us to get things done," Coffin predicted. "We build it enough and we'll control more of the retail trade than the Chinese ever could. Let 'em have Chinatown and the import end. The rest of the pie is so much bigger that hardly even counts." Coffin almost sighed. He took a sip of his wine, savoring it, like a symbol of their wealth to be. "Once we've got supply and distribution secured, the money will flow, my friend."

"And Braddock?" Coogan asked, wiping a spot of beer off his shirt absently with the corner of his napkin.

"Well . . . by that time Tom will have outlived his, shall we say, usefulness," August said with a wicked grin. "I'll have to cut his career short. Not that I hold him a grudge, mind you." Coffin grinned at his bit of sarcasm. "It's just business. But we'll see. For now he's being very useful indeed."

"All in good time, eh, Augie?"

"Exactly. Let him enjoy life, spend big, fuck his whore, who cares? We're after bigger fish. We can fry him later."

Tom hadn't slept well on the voyage back. He was worried that another attempt on their lives would be made during the night. He hadn't shared his fear with Jaffey, who didn't seem to give the menacing atmosphere of Richmond another thought. The younger man had snored through the night while

Braddock sat wide awake in his bunk, his Colt on his lap. Every creak of the deck, every unidentified noise in the hall outside their door had him gripping the pistol with a sweaty palm. He'd drift off for just minutes before some noise had his eyes wide open and his heart racing. He got off the steamer rubbing his eyes and yawning, feeling foolish for being spooked. They headed to the Marble Palace first. Tom wanted to fill Byrnes in immediately. They found him just coming back from an afternoon court date. They met behind closed doors.

"So, Jaffey . . . Tom teaching you anything worth knowing?"

Eli hesitated a moment, startled by the question.

"Yes, sir. I'm learning a great deal."

Byrnes smiled pleasantly behind his mustache, nodding his approval. "Good. Name one thing."

Jaffey turned the color of one of the tomatoes in his mother's garden as he tried to think of something.

"Anything?" Byrnes prodded.

"Observation, sir," Jaffey said at last, letting it out as if he'd been holding his breath. "More than anything, I guess I'm starting to learn how to look beyond the surface, sometimes to trust my feelings more than the actual evidence."

Brynes smiled through the cigar smoke. "If you've learned that, son, you've learned a lot. Looks like you're learning to take care of yourself too. You boys did well to come out of that scrape."

"That's if you don't count our feet, Chief," Tom said, wincing.

Byrnes chuckled. "So what did you learn in Richmond?" he asked as he settled behind his desk and proffered them cigars. Braddock took one, handing the other to Eli.

"Nothing and everything," he said as he lit up.

Tom laid out their dead end in the former capital of the Confederacy with Eli's assistance. In spite of the lack of hard facts, there was a lot to tell and even more to speculate on. Tom finished up by saying, "I'm leaning away from the contract fraud theory. Still believe it has to do with the trains, though. Bucklin left us a map in his own way. It's got to lead to the trains somehow. Nothing else makes sense."

"Sabotage?" said Byrnes, finishing his thought, but with a note of skepticism and a small shake of his head.

"Could be," Tom said thoughtfully. He hated to even think it but there it was. "There was a great deal they were hiding from us and on a lot of levels too. Got the feeling the police weren't telling all they knew either. That's not the way of fraud. Fraud is like a magic trick; you watch one hand while the other does the real work. The magic trick down there was a disappearing act. We need to talk to this fellow Sangree. Turn over his business and house for anything we can find."

"Do it. You know where to go to get it done. Take Pat and Charlie with you. Bring this gentleman in and squeeze him till he bleeds. I want to know what the hell is going on, and I don't care if he gets bruised in the process," Byrnes said with an emphatic stab of his cigar. "Can't say I agree with you about sabotage, though. That's just plain crazy. Pretty goddamn ambitious too. Have to see more evidence to convince me of that one."

Tom shrugged. Byrnes wanted proof, he'd get the proof.

"I wired Pat and Charlie yesterday to pick Sangree up," Tom said.

Byrnes looked pleased yet perplexed. "That's good, but I haven't heard they brought anybody in."

Tom and Eli exchanged glances . . .

"We were afraid of that," Tom said.

Twenty minutes later the four of them stood outside the door to Sangree & Co. When they hooked up Pat told Tom that they'd been there yesterday but found nothing. Sangree's address proved the same, just an empty apartment. Braddock had insisted they go and check again. He needed to see it for himself. Charlie jimmied the door and swung it silently. The place was bare.

"Son of a bitch!" Tom's voice boomed on the empty office. "Shit! We had him, Eli. We had the bastard right here!" Braddock grabbed the back of a chair, tossing it across the room as if it were paper, sending it crashing and splintering against the wall. "*Shit!*" The rest of them were silent. They set about a quick search of the office, which turned up nothing of value.

About ten minutes later, Charlie said, "Let's go see if Lebeau and Emmons are still at work. Any odds on that?"

"Fool's bet, Charlie. We know the answer already," Tom said, frustration twisting his mouth into a sour grimace.

Nearly an hour after that, Tom and Eli stood before another door. This time they knew they'd find who they were looking for. The knurled brass knocker boomed on the imposing, varnished mahogany. They had only to wait a minute before Hughes pulled open one side of the portal with a deliberate dignity.

"Good morning, gentlemen. Do you have an appointment?" he inquired.

"No, I'm afraid we don't, Hughes," Tom said. "It is Hughes, isn't it?"

"Quite so, Detective."

"I would be very grateful if you would inquire if the colonel or Mrs. Roebling could spare a few minutes."

Hughes raised a disapproving eyebrow. It was obvious that there was a lot going on in the house today. Flowers were everywhere, bunting hung from the door frames and the windows at the front, and there was a constant bustle of people within the house.

"It's important," Braddock said apologetically.

Hughes eyed them both skeptically but said, "Certainly. Will you come in? If you'll wait in the parlor, I'll be back directly."

Hughes was as good as his word, returning to lead them back to the garden a few minutes later. Emily stood on a wide brick patio, the midmorning light making her seem to glow as they approached from the relative darkness of the house. She was supervising the setup of a couple of large tables while caterers saw to the details.

"Tom . . . what a pleasant surprise. I hadn't hoped to see you again." She extended a dove-white hand.

Tom took it as if it might fly. Their eyes met and held. "The pleasure is mine, Emily. It's good to see you again, but I'm afraid the reason for my visit isn't so good."

"Oh?" She took her hand back with an awkward hesitancy.

"Yes, but first, let me congratulate you and the colonel on the completion of the bridge . . . a magnificent accomplishment. You must be very proud," he said. He had rehearsed the words coming over on the ferry and thought they came off rather well. Emily thanked him graciously, blushing slightly, he thought. "Oh . . . I'm sorry, you remember Patrolman Jaffey, don't you?" Jaffey was looking at him strangely, Tom noticed. Jaffey shook Emily's hand with an awkward stiffness.

"So, Tom, what's this about?" she asked with a frown. "Something about bad news?"

"Is the colonel in? I'd like to tell him what I've found out . . . and . . . what I suspect. He may have some thoughts on this, which would be useful."

For the next hour or so, Tom went over what he knew with Emily and Washington. By the time Braddock had finished, a deep frown furrowed the colonel's brow. For the fifth time, Tom apologized for bringing this to them on the day before the opening, "But I thought you should know, Colonel. The events of the last few days . . . the attempt on our lives . . . the disappearance of Sangree and the others—"

Roebling interrupted Braddock. "Yes, I see, Tom. But what are we to do? You know my opinions about your sabotage theory. In spite of what you've told me, I still find the idea far-fetched."

Tom wasn't entirely sure what to do either, but there were two things that could be done. He stood in an instant of awkward silence before suggesting the obvious. "An inspection would be wise."

Roebling nodded quickly, almost dismissively. "I'll have a talk with Mr. Martin. We'll keep it very quiet, though. No need to alarm anyone at this point."

"An increase in the patrol schedule of the bridge police too, sir," Tom said. The bridge police were not under the jurisdiction of the New York City Police. The only thing Tom could do was suggest a stepped-up vigilance. "Beyond that, I'm not sure there's more we can do. The investigation is continuing, of course."

"Emily and I were to go to Newport after the opening," Wash said, looking at his wife. "I'm not so sure I can leave just yet in light of this. What do you think, Em?"

She sighed almost inaudibly. "We can't stay here past the thirty-first, Wash. It's rented as of June," she reminded him. "You see, Tom, we won't be returning, now that the bridge is finished. We'll be going back to Trenton."

Tom nodded. "It occurs to me," he said, thinking out loud, "that it might be best if these men think you've left the city. I don't want you to be targets. If you feel you have to stay, why not send Hughes and your maid in your place? I have a friend at the *Tribune* who could be persuaded to report that you've left. You'd have to confine yourselves to the house, though. It wouldn't do to be seen." He looked from one to the other. Washington was looking at Emily. They communicated without words, Tom saw.

The colonel turned back to him. "Just for the week, Tom. Then we'll see."

Emily walked them out. Eli had gone out the big front doors when Tom turned to say good-bye. As he did, he took something from his pocket and pressed it into her hand.

"What's this?" she asked, feeling its compact weight.

"You may need this," Tom said, quickly seeking to head off her refusal. "I pray you don't, but I'd feel a lot better if you took it."

"Tom, I don't—" she started to say, but he cut her off.

"Emily, these men are dangerous. Take it . . . please, for my sake if not your own. I'd feel better," he ended awkwardly, unable to say how worried he was for her.

Emily looked down at the double-barrel Remington derringer, its ivory grips shining in her delicate hand. She closed her fingers around it. "All right, Tom."

Braddock breathed a sigh of relief. He gave her hand a gentle squeeze. "Thank you."

"You don't think she'll really need that, do you?" Eli asked as they went down the front steps.

Tom turned at the last step to look back up at the bunting-festooned house. "I hope not, Eli."

Tom and August sat in the captain's office late that same day.

"No luck finding those three yet?" Coffin seemed just a little smug. Maybe it was the feet on the desk.

"Not yet," Tom said. "Cleared out. Disappeared! Quit their jobs, left the business, left their apartments bare. Everything that might point to who these men really are and what they were about is wiped clean." Tom shook his head. "These are professionals, August. They knew I'd be back from Richmond with a head of steam and they just melted away. Byrnes is madder than hell. He wants these men found no matter what it takes," Tom stated grimly, knowing how difficult that might be. "Needless to say, they didn't leave a forwarding address. Well, that's not exactly true. They told a clerk at the bridge office they were going back to Texas—Lebeau and Emmons, that is. Sangree we don't know about."

"And you believe that?" Coffin asked.

"It's something we followed up on but to me it's a waste of time. Tickets were bought in their names, but that doesn't fit with the rest of what they've done; too careless. They won't be found on any train to Texas."

"You wired ahead?"

"Got a marshal waiting at the next stop. Wired ahead to search the train. They won't be on it." Tom was certain. "Nobody that thorough could make a mistake like that. Just want us to chase our tails. They're still here . . . right here in New York. I can almost feel it."

"Interesting case, Tom, but that's not why you're here," Coffin said, twirling his pencil.

"Nope." Tom took a deep breath like a diver taking a plunge. "Had a talk with Sung Chow. The old man wants to meet tomorrow night."

"Shit. What time?" Coffin asked irritably. "I have to be down at the bridge. Most of the precinct is on duty for the opening, all day and through till ten o'clock, after the fireworks are over."

Tom nodded "Yeah, I thought so. Fireworks start at eight, right?" Tom knew very well when the fireworks started; in fact, he was counting on it.

"Yeah, but I'm there all day, from around eleven. Going to be a long day."

"Sung Chow wanted to meet at eight," Tom said. "I'm supposed to be on duty too. Byrnes has everyone working the crowds for pickpockets."

Coffin nodded. "He's right to. Sounds like a pickpocket's dream come true.

Supposed to be the biggest event this city has seen since the opening of the Erie Canal. I was looking forward to seeing it."

"Well, the Chinese like fireworks as much as anyone, but old sack-face doesn't seem to give a damn. I was thinking that among all those people, it might be pretty easy to slip away for a while," Tom said, knowing that timing was essential to what they were about. "I don't know, what do you think?" His casual tone hid his nervousness.

"I think I want a piece of the opium trade. That's what I think," Coffin said firmly. "I don't want to get off on the wrong foot either. Would it offend him if we didn't come?"

"It might," Tom warned. "Every move, everything we say, body language, tone of speech, everything is important. Nothing is insignificant to the Chinese."

"That's what I thought you'd say." Coffin sighed as he made up his mind. "I'll jump to his whistle for now. I can be patient. He'll be dancing to our tune in time anyway." Tom just grinned. "Let's say we meet at Chatham Square at about seven-forty-five," August said finally. "Who knows, Tommy, with a little luck we might still catch some of the fireworks."

There was nothing left to do. Emily lay awake listening to the old clock downstairs. Washington snored in the bed beside hers. For the last fourteen years there had always been something left to do. For fourteen years she had gone to sleep with a list of things undone and more to do come morning. Now the future beckoned and threatened at once. She yearned for the rest—for the summer sun of Newport, the sea air, the beach, the pure lazy indulgence of having nothing in the world to do, except be with the man she loved and admired. This would be their summer, a time like no other. She and Wash would rock on their dappled porch and watch the sun chase the moon across the sky. They would listen to the crickets in the evenings, the doves in the morning, and they would plan the rest of their lives together. Emily tried to sleep but sleep wouldn't come. Tomorrow would be the culmination of everything they had worked for. Tomorrow, though Wash couldn't come to the opening ceremonies, Emily would bring them to him. He deserved it, and she had made certain he'd receive the recognition he had earned. But then what? The arrangements were made, they'd stay while Martha and Hughes left, masquerading as them. But what could they really do, cooped up, hiding in the house? She couldn't imagine they'd be able to do much good, but Wash had looked so worried she'd had to give in. It was only a week, after all. Surely the rest of their lives could wait that long.

Mike had hidden for a while in the back of a dry goods store, pretending to shop while the owner watched him warily for things that might disappear into his pockets. Mike, in turn, watched the street through the front window. Once he had calmed down enough and gotten his confidence back a little, he'd gone in search of his friends. There was strength in numbers, even if the numbers were ten and twelve years old. It hadn't taken long. Smokes, Mouse, and another boy named Willie who sometimes hung with them were pitching pennies at a stoop just a block from Mike's place. They were laughing and talking excitedly about how they would go see the opening of the bridge tomorrow afternoon and the fireworks that night. There wasn't a kid in New York or Brooklyn who wouldn't want to see that.

Mike ran up as they were talking about their plans. His breathless account of what had happened not a half hour before put an end to that conversation.

"You say you laid 'im out with a chair leg?" Smokes asked incredulously.

"It's true, I swear. I caught him coming through the hole in the big fence, the one that's at the back of the green building on Norfolk," Mike said, his tone somewhere between a plea and a brag. "He had a big fuckin' knife, but he looked like a clerk. You'll see. C'mon an' look if ya don't believe me." Mike was actually more interested in backup than in proving he'd brained the clerk. If the bow-tie man was still there and still alive for that matter, it might be smart to have a few of the gang around. Besides, Mike reasoned, there might be more men. He couldn't be certain, but the man who'd waylaid him by the outhouses weeks before was taller than Mr. Bow-tie. What if he was waiting somewhere for him to return?

"That's next to my building," Willie said.

"Right," Mike agreed, as if this proved his tale somehow. "C'mon! Any you guys got knives?" he asked over his shoulder as they started off. He had left his pocket knife back in his bedroom in his hurry to get out the window. Mouse and Smokes had theirs and even Willie had a small one, so Mike started to feel like he had a small army behind him, equipped for any danger. They marched toward his tenement on Suffolk full of enthusiasm and grim boyish determination. It was probably well for Jacobs that they didn't find him.

The boys reconnoitered carefully, watching the outside of the building first and scanning the block for strange faces. They'd gone upstairs slowly, pocket knives held at the ready and eyes as big as saucers. The broken door convinced them, as did the rope hanging out Mike's window. They strained to get a look out at the maze in the back, trying to see if the clerk was still there. They couldn't see from there, though, and the only way was to go and check. They didn't find him. They did find the broken chair leg and some blood.

By the time Mike's grandma got home, he'd cleaned up and stowed the rope under his bed. He told her the door had been like that when he came back from playing with the boys. Break-ins were pretty common things, and nothing seemed to be missing anyway, so she said she'd get some wood to fix the frame with later, and that was that. Despite his worries about bow-tie men coming back again, he didn't want to worry his grandmother. Besides, he'd done pretty well with the last one to show up at his door. Why worry her? He could take care of himself, he figured. Mr. Bow-tie was likely to have one hell of a headache for a while anyway.

✣ Chapter Twenty ✣

Hardly had the last spark died out, when the moon
rose slowly over the further tower, and sent a broad
beam like a benediction across the river.

—THE TRIBUNE

May 24, 1883

The statue seemed to be a rallying point. By 10:00 A.M. the disembodied hand and torch of the Statue of Liberty, recently moved from the Centennial Exhibition at Philadelphia, had started to draw a crowd. It stood at the northwest corner of Madison Square Park and reached nearly as high as the trees around it. But the people weren't gathered there to see the hand of Liberty. They waited for a glimpse of the president of the United States. Chester A. Arthur was staying at the Fifth Avenue Hotel, just a block and a half south. He was to be the guest of honor at the opening ceremonies. There were hundreds milling about already but he wasn't scheduled to appear for another two hours.

The opening ceremonies were scheduled for 2:00 P.M. They were to be held in the big iron-and-glass Brooklyn train terminal. Only the important, the politically connected, or the wealthy had gotten the specially engraved invitations from Tiffany's for that event. Others had received a lesser class of invitation, which allowed them to stroll the bridge before the official opening. By nine o'clock the fence, which had blocked the roadway in New York, was taken down, and anyone with that class of invitation was allowed to walk the span for the first time. It would still be hours before the president, governor, and assorted dignitaries would make their pilgrimage across the bridge. The crowds were already packing the shore on either side of the river. Most businesses were closed by noon. Most of the city was a ghost town by one. It seemed as if at least half the population of the island was packed into the few blocks immediately surrounding the bridge. Up and down the river, and especially all the blocks around the bridge, the crowds pushed and jostled for position. Rooftops were standing room only. Many of the tallest buildings in lower New York hosted bridge parties for invited guests. Street vendors did a nonstop business in ice cream, popcorn, candy, ices, and dozens of different kinds of souvenirs, from buttons to folding fans, all with the image of the Eighth Wonder embossed, like some talisman for the second coming. Flags by the hundreds hung from windows and rooftops. Bunting in red, white, and blue draped and fluttered. It was a carnival, on a scale never before seen in New York. Street musicians and organ grinders added to the din as the thousands upon thousands swirled and eddied, lapping at the shoreline.

On the river and in the harbor, thousands of ships and pleasure craft plied the gray-green waters. It seemed as if everything that would float was dancing gaily on the waves. An agile man almost might walk across the harbor from deck to deck. Dozens of excursion steamers plowed foaming furrows in the harbor as onboard bands played jaunty airs. Some of the biggest carried nearly a thousand passengers. The North Atlantic fleet was there, six giant warships, with blue-jacketed sailors at attention lining the decks and spars. All the while the ferries shuttled through the floating melee, passengers packed so tight they could hardly move, but nobody getting off.

It was twelve-forty, Emily noticed, when the band began to play. The Twenty-third Regiment band in white helmets and blue coats, along with a detachment of artillerists from Fort Hamilton and marines from the Brooklyn Navy Yard, led the way from City Hall. They slowly headed off down Remsen Street, the procession stretching out like a giant accordion as it went. Mayor Low, Emily, and her son John who'd just returned from boarding school in her sparkling, lacquered Victoria, her entourage and about two hundred city officials, bridge trustees, and special guests followed. At precisely the same time, President Arthur stepped into the bright sunshine from the Fifth Avenue Hotel. A roar went up from the crowd. Minutes later the Seventh Regiment band struck up a marching tune and set off down Fifth Avenue. A mounted police escort and twenty-five carriages followed. They turned east on fourteenth, then south at Broadway to City Hall. Cheering crowds lined the route, then followed behind. It took almost an hour to reach City Hall, where the crush was nearly beyond control. Cops sweated and cursed, pushing at the solid mass of humanity to make way for the president. Within ten minutes, the whole entourage set off on foot, with the band playing hard and still leading the way.

The roadways of the bridge were jammed with thousands of special ticket holders. The trustees had issued about thirteen thousand in all. Seven thousand pale-blue tickets were good for admittance to the roadways, the rest were for the ceremonies at the Brooklyn terminal. It seemed that all seven thousand, and then some, lined the roadways as the president strode across on the promenade. The cheering was constant and rolled like a wave across the bridge with him. Mayor Low waited under the soaring arches of the Brooklyn tower and watched as the band crested the arch of the span, appearing to rise up slowly from the deck of the promenade, the brass of their instruments sparkling in the sun. At last, as the mayor of Brooklyn greeted the chief executive of the land, a signal flag was dropped. Within seconds the entire fleet commenced firing its guns, rattling windows for miles. Then every ferry, excursion steamer, tug, and anything with a bell or steam whistle started to bellow, scream, toot, and clang. A cheer went up from countless thousands of throats. The band rendered "Hail to the Chief" as loud as their instruments could be made to play and kept playing it over and over, while the citizens bellowed themselves hoarse.

Emily sat in the Brooklyn terminal with six thousand guests around her as the cheer went up. The huge flags hung from the tall glass roof seemed to sway with the rush of air from so many throats. The windows rattled, the very ground shook with the cannonade. Emily beamed as congratulations were heaped upon her. She accepted each graciously, but they blended and ran together until she heard them no longer. Her thoughts were only of Wash, and a chill ran through her as she whispered, "Look what we've done!"

She may as well have been alone for all the thought she gave the crowds around her. She could just as well have been back at home with her husband. Washington sat as he had so often, in his study, his field glasses scanning the bridge and river. He hadn't really been in favor of a big celebration for the opening. Though he'd spent a third of his life on this one bridge, and knew better than anyone its costs and significance, he was more inclined to just put up a sign saying THE BRIDGE IS OPEN. Regardless, he couldn't suppress the chills that ran down his spine at the spectacle laid out before him. It was amazing. Wash found himself wiping at tears as they rolled down his cheeks. He tried to hold them back, his throat tightening at the effort, but after a time gave it up. It seemed they would come regardless. It wouldn't have surprised him to know that the words he whispered in the empty room on Columbia Heights were nearly identical to Emily's.

The department had dropped everything else for the day. The search for Sangree, Emmons, and LeBeau was put off, and every other aspect of the investigation postponed. Every man was needed for the opening ceremonies. The crowds were expected to be the largest ever seen in New York, and Byrnes wanted every available man working the crowds for rowdies and pickpockets. Tom hadn't liked it, arguing with Byrnes that he should be working at finding the conspirators rather than catching pickpockets and drunks.

Byrnes understood, sympathized even, but finally said, "Look, Tom, the bridge has been inspected. Nothing has been found. Not so much as a bolt out of place. There are cops and soldiers everywhere. Everything that could be done has been done. Their descriptions have been circulated to every precinct. If these fools want to die attempting whatever, this would certainly be a good day for it."

Tom started to try one last time.

"But—"

Byrnes cut him off.

"Not another word, Detective," he said with a stern grin and a finger pointed out his office door. "Besides, the trains won't be running for months yet. If there's a time to worry, it'll be then. I'll see you later," he called to Tom's retreating back.

Tom arrested his third pickpocket by two o'clock. Byrnes's instructions to arrest known pickpockets on sight were carried out zealously. It didn't matter if a pocket actually had been picked. Fainting women, crushed by the press of people and too-tight corsets, kept the police busy too. Jaffey had spent the last two hours pulling gawkers from lampposts and a variety of other precarious roosts. He'd been vomited on once by a man he found trying to scale the El and hit with a parasol by a woman who demanded that he clear a path for her carriage right down to the river. It was a long hard day to be a cop. All things considered, though, it was a remarkably good-tempered mob, and an air of celebration was everywhere, as if it were the Fourth of July, New Year's Eve, and Christmas rolled into one.

In all the crush and with all the things he had to do, Tom's mind was constantly on his meeting tonight. He went over it again and again. He thought of every possible scenario, every improbable event that might occur, and weighed his response to each. Everything rested on it. He risked his future and maybe his life if things got ugly. It was a possibility he'd considered and accepted. It was also a possibility he'd done his best to avoid.

"All will go as planned," he told himself for the seventeenth time. "Just like clockwork." He wished he could believe that. He had battled his doubts through the day as he battled the crowds, wading through them one by one. Some he reasoned out of his way, others he merely pushed aside. This night would be a turning point for him, just as it was for the city. He'd be free after tonight, he and Mary. He'd cross over a river of doubt that flowed with the certain knowledge of right and wrong. That he planned to cross on a bridge of betrayal was a grim irony. The contradictions swirled and eddied. On the other side was freedom from Coffin and retribution for Mary, but his bridge stood on a foundation of quicksand. It was well he'd only need to use it once

Emily didn't wait until the long orations were over. Besides, the train shed was not the best place for speeches. The acoustics were terrible and only those closest to the podium could make out what was being said anyway. It was mostly in the same vein, and though the speeches ran for hours, the message was simple and clear. This was the finest example of man's capacity to change the face of nature the world had yet seen. It was a monument to the skill, fortitude, and genius of its creators, and a tribute to the cities it served. But there was something else. Most of the speakers couldn't really get hold of it either. It was a combination of the deceptively simple beauty of the thing and the almost spiritual delight of being on it. Emily thought that Brooklyn's mayor, Seth Low, said it best. "The impression upon the visitor is one of astonishment that grows with every visit. No one who has been upon it can ever forget it."

Emily needed to be home with Wash to greet her guests as they arrived. She was expecting a thousand people would come to pay their respects. As her Victoria turned the corner onto her street, she marveled again at how wonderful it looked. Most buildings were covered with streamers and bunting. The trees were hung with Chinese lanterns. Flags flew from almost every window. The front of their house was covered with flags, shields, flowers, and the coats of arms of Brooklyn and New York. One huge flag hung suspended above the street just high enough for carriages to pass beneath. Mayor Low's house, down the street, was graced with clusters of flags over windows and the flag of Brooklyn hung above the big front doors. The mayor's reception for President Arthur was to follow the Roeblings'.

Emily found Wash with his eyes closed and his hands folded across his middle, on his bed. He looked so peaceful she almost didn't want to disturb him. That he could sleep with all the bustle in the house was amazing. Caterers had been running in and out all day. The band, which Emily had positioned on the balcony in the drawing room on the river side of the house, was starting to arrive, and there was much clumping of feet up and down the stairs. She reached out a gentle hand to his shoulder.

"Wash? Darling?"

His eyes opened and a slow smile crept like a sunrise across his face. "I was thinking of you today. As I watched all the crowds and commotion, I . . . remembered," he said wistfully.

"Remembered?" Emily asked. "Remembered what, dear?"

"Do you recall the day when you first walked across the bridge?"

A smile crept across her face. "Of course," she said in a voice like melted butter.

"I thought of you as you were that day: the wind in your hair, the way you looked back at me, as if you could see into my heart of hearts. Everything else faded and I saw you . . . so beautiful, like a prayer come to life." He smiled up at her.

Emily sat on the side of his bed and took his hand in hers. "I know *my* prayers have been answered. We've done it Wash, and we've still got so much ahead of us. You're only forty-six, and you've been getting stronger every day. I can only imagine what the future will bring. But first, my knight in shining armor," she said with mock seriousness. "You must gird yourself for battle and prepare to accept the laurels which are your due."

"Do I have to?" he pleaded, playing a part, but half meaning it.

She pulled him by the hand, tugging him to his feet. She threw her arms around his shoulders then, kissing him lightly on the nose. "I intend to show you off to the highest in the land, O husband of mine. And they will know you for the brilliant, handsome hero of the age that you are. So go get dressed. You're not getting out of this one," she said, poking him in the ribs.

Washington Roebling put on his Prince Albert coat and a few minutes later went downstairs, arm in arm with Emily.

"God, what you've done with the place, Em!" he exclaimed. "It's wonderful, really." Roses in red and white, wisteria, lilacs, lilies, and a variety of cut flowers were distributed throughout the house in big baskets, with smaller arrangements in every room. The house literally swam in the sweet smell of success. They sat together on a sofa in the front parlor and waited for their guests. They were not long in coming. By the time President Arthur arrived at five-thirty, the crowd in the street was so heavy that the best the police could do was keep open a narrow path to the door. The president noticed Washington immediately. He strode over, his hand outstretched and a smile of genuine delight lighting his features.

"Sir, it is a very great pleasure indeed to make your acquaintance," he said, pumping Wash's hand.

"And I yours, Mr. President," Washington said, a wide grin splitting his bearded face from ear to ear. "You honor me, sir."

"Colonel, you have done a magnificent thing in that bridge of yours. It is simply stupendous!" the president said, waving his arms for emphasis. "You've done your country an invaluable service, sir, and created a lasting monument to the ingenuity and inventiveness of the American people. We are all in your debt."

"You are too kind, Mr. President," Wash said modestly. "All I did was build a bridge."

"Poppycock!" Arthur bellowed, thumping Wash on the back. "I'm not kind enough by half. I tell you, when I walked across this afternoon I was positively . . . giddy. I had seen pictures, of course, but being up there on the bridge itself . . . it was . . . how shall I say it? uplifting. That's the very thing. I congratulate you, sir. You have done what no man has done before. I envy you, Colonel, and I salute you."

Emily blushed with pride, and clutched Washington's hand tight in hers. Wash bowed his thanks. He could think of nothing to say.

"And you, Mrs. Roebling," the president said, turning to Emily. "If half the things I hear are true, then it is you who deserves half the credit."

Though she knew it was true, she blushed anyway.

"More than half to my way of thinking, Mr. President. More than half," Wash said, squeezing her hand tight.

The president gave Emily a piercing glance, seeming to appraise the truth of it in an instant. "I believe you, Colonel," he said firmly. "There's steel in those lovely eyes."

Wash laughed. "You have no idea how much, Mr. President."

They all laughed at that but the president took Emily's hand, bringing the white glove to his lips for a formal kiss.

"Again I envy you, Colonel. I am doubly honored to meet you both."

As more and more people kept pressing through the door, the president drifted back to the drawing room, surrounded by well-wishers, toadies, and politicians.

"The president envies you, Colonel," Emily whispered in Wash's ear.

"And I am the envy of every man here," he said with an air of complete confidence. "Not for me, but for you do they envy me. I am the luckiest man in all the world."

Mayor Low, Governor Cleveland, William Kingsley, the general contractor General Henry Slocum, all the trustees, many of whom would meet Washington for the first time this evening, pressed through his doors, filling the house to overflowing. The band played. Guests found food and refreshments in a great pavilion set up in the garden overlooking the river. Hamilton Fish, former Secretary of State, and family friend, the Reverend Henry Ward Beecher and his wife, Wash's brothers and their wives, his sister and her husband, former Mayor Grace, and hundreds of others showered the colonel with congratulations and undying admiration. After an hour or so, the president left for the mayor's reception. Wash was glad of it, for he felt he couldn't abandon the reception while the president was still there, but he was exhausted after nearly two and a half hours of being mobbed.

"Em, I have to go upstairs. I'm all washed out, dear. Can't take another minute."

She could see it in his face. "Go ahead, Wash. Lie down for a while. I'll come up when the guests have gone. Is there anything I can get you?"

"No, no. You've already done more than I deserve." As he slowly climbed the stairs back to his room, someone in the crowd started to clap. It was just one person at first, but before he had taken another two steps, the entire house seemed to have broken into a rolling burst of enthusiastic applause. For a moment it confused him. He almost didn't know how to react. He was embarrassed, in fact, blushing like a schoolgirl beneath his beard, but he continued his slow climb, humble, amazed, triumphant.

One more pickpocket, one unwary foot in the crowd crushed by a wagon, two drunks, and one assault later, Tom stood in front of the *Tribune* building. The crowds here were almost as thick as down by the river. The hotels and bars and restaurants were doing a record-breaking business too. Most of the bars were so full people overflowed onto the street. When one or two washed out, one or two more shouldered their way in. Tom watched the crowd with glazed eyes. The day had been hard enough, and his feet were so sore they seemed to be boiling out of his shoes, but the stress of what he was about to do weighed even heavier. Tom had arranged to meet Mary at the *Trib* at seven-thirty. She was late, but that didn't surprise him. The crowds and confusion were bound to slow her down. Suddenly she materialized before him just as he checked his watch again.

"God, there must be over a hundred thousand just around City Hall. It's lucky we arranged a place. I'd never have found you otherwise." Mary kissed him and looked up into his face. "You look tired, Tommy. Been hard, I guess."

"It's been lively," he admitted. "You want to go up?" Tom, who knew some reporters, had wheedled a couple of invitations to their bridge party, which was already well under way. It would be good to be seen there. In the confusion of the crowd he could slip away and back unnoticed.

"Sure, let's go. I could use something cold. You look like you could too."

Tom didn't stay long, just long enough to be seen by a few people he knew and to introduce Mary to some friends and acquaintances. He checked his watch for the last time and said, "I have to go."

She looked at him, her deep brown eyes wide and unflinching. "You be careful, Tommy. I'll see you later. I'll be right here." Tom started to say something but she stopped him. "You'd better get going. We'll talk later." Tom gave her a quick hug and she whispered, "I love you, Tommy. Come back to me."

A wistful but determined smile played on Tom's face.

"I will," he murmured.

The walk to Chatham Square was longer than he'd anticipated, at least the first part. The people slowed him down, and more than once he was less than civil with those who got in his way. It got his blood up, so that as the crowds started to thin out, he steamed along leaving a wide wake behind. He got to the corner of Park Row and Worth at exactly seven o'clock. Chatham Square was nearly deserted. Everyone was down near the bridge, and those who weren't were up on the rooftops. Tom crossed the intersection of Worth and Mott, continuing on to the corner of Doyers. He waited as the evening gloom settled over the square and the gas lamps were slowly lit by a trudging, top-hatted civil servant who appeared to be thoroughly in his cups. Tom would have enjoyed watching the man stumble through his job if he wasn't so anxious. Absently he pulled Bucklin's clipping from his pocket, scanning it again, looking for the things he couldn't see. He glanced at his watch again. It was three minutes after seven and Coffin was nowhere in sight. He leaned against the lamppost watching every person walk through the square from the intersecting streets. There weren't many. Doyers was the perfect place for this night's activities. Curving and dead-ended, it was hidden from view from everything except the few buildings around the bend. According to Sung Chow, no one in those buildings would be watching.

Coffin came trotting up St. James Place five minutes later. He was sweaty and rumpled when he arrived under the halo of the gas lamp.

"Was beginning to worry about you, August," Braddock said, the annoyance clear in his voice.

"Damn crowds made it harder to get here than I thought. It took me ten minutes to get from Dover to Pearl! Been a hell of a day too," he said, dusting off his jacket and smoothing the rumpled collar. "No mood for any of Sung Chow's Chinese horseshit. Let's get the deal done and get on with business."

"I'll do what I can, but I can't speak for them," Tom said, trying to keep his tone under control. "I think they're ready to do business, though, and if my guess is right, I think you're going to get more than you expected."

Coffin seemed to brighten a bit. "Think so?"

"Just a feeling," Tom said. "We'll see."

Coffin smoothed his rumpled shirt and jacket one last time. "Well, let's get moving. There's money to be made tonight."

As they walked up Doyers, their footsteps echoing on the deserted street, Coffin remarked, "Christ, this place is like a ghost town. Even the Chinamen are down by the bridge."

"Well, the Chinese like fireworks as much as anyone else, maybe more. After all, they were the ones who invented gunpowder." Tom knew that would bother Coffin.

"Hard to believe that coolies could invent something like that."

Tom looked at Coffin with a direct, level gaze. "Don't underestimate them, August," he warned. It would be his last warning to August, one he'd do well to heed, Tom thought with an ironic twist at the corner of his mouth.

"Yeah, sure." Coffin's tone showed his contempt. "This is it, right?"

Tom just nodded at the dark stairway to an unmarked basement door. "I'll go first." He went down the steps, which seemed the top steps to hell. They were black as the soul of night and he had to feel for them as he descended.

The meeting went well. Tom set the stage, doing and saying the right things, observing the rituals, paying proper respect, acting the honest broker. Coffin laid out his offers with the flair of a born salesman. He painted his picture in shades of green and gold. They'd all be rich, he stressed, if they could see beyond their differences and work together to expand the trade. The potential was enormous and the cash that flowed from it could buy cops, judges, aldermen, and Tammany Hall, for that matter. There was no end to the power and influence they could enjoy, if only they could cooperate. He could guarantee safe expansion into new uptown markets, tapping into the pockets of the wealthy, the jaded uptown thrill-seekers, the swells looking for new and different entertainments. In time, prostitution could be coupled with the trade, bringing the two businesses together under one roof. There were endless variations on these themes and endless money to be made. All they needed do was to shake hands. Just the word of two businessmen, seeing eye to eye, and the world could change for all of them.

Tom hardly heard a word. His thoughts were elsewhere. Soon the handshake was done, the vows exchanged, the wheels set in motion. Throughout the show Tom's face wore a painted smile.

At last Sung Chow and August Coffin bowed each other farewell, promising to meet again soon. Details needed to be ironed out, after all. Sung Chow bowed to Tom as well, but after they did so, old sack-face clasped Tom's hand, murmuring. "You have done well, Tom Braddock. We will not forget."

Tom went out into the night that was blacker than betrayal, his feelings surprisingly mixed. He didn't turn when he heard the scuffle of feet behind him. He almost didn't want to face a doomed man, even one such as Coffin.

"Hey! What's this? Tom! Tell 'em we're here to see Sung Chow," Coffin demanded. "Get your hands off me! Tom!"

Tom turned and took two steps back to Coffin's side.

"Tommy, tell 'em to get their goddamn hands off me." Coffin seemed more annoyed than worried. There were three Chinese, one man on each arm and one at Coffin's back. Where they had been hiding, even Tom couldn't have guessed.

"Goddamn it! I'm a captain of police," Coffin exclaimed, pulling at the men on his arms. "Let me loose, you fucking—"

Tom reached into Coffin's jacket and removed his pistol without a word.

"Tom?" That one word encompassed surprise, indignation, and defeat.

"Did you really think this could end some other way, August?" Tom said, the firmness of his voice tinged with regret. "You know me. Did you imagine I'd let what you did to Mary just slide by?"

Coffin didn't answer. The shock on his face said it all.

"You may as well have turned yourself in that night, Augie. You've been doomed ever since."

Coffin stopped struggling and looked at Tom as if he was just seeing him now. He said calmly, "This is not how I planned it, sport." His intentions for Tom clear in just those few words.

"Sorry, August," Tom said, meaning it. Tom nodded to the Chinese a particularly evil-looking trio, he noticed. They started to herd Coffin back down the stairs. The door at the bottom of the black stairs opened again. This time Byrnes stood outlined in the soft golden glow of the lamps within. Coffin saw him immediately. He stiffened for a moment, then blurted, "Chief! Christ, am I glad to see you! These—these—" he stammered as he saw the look on Byrnes's face.

"I heard everything, August. I was in the next fucking room!" Byrnes's voice sounded like the birth of an avalanche. "We need to have a *talk*, you and I." As he said this, Byrnes slowly pulled on a tight black glove over his huge fist, pulling at the fingers so it fit just so.

Coffin looked from Byrnes to Tom, desperation written large in his eyes. A small, defeated croak escaped his throat, and his mouth worked soundlessly.

He took another step down, seemingly held up now by the three Chinese. He was only two steps down when footsteps were heard pounding hard from around the curve of the street. With the echo, it was hard to tell if it was one or two coming at a run. They all froze. Tom still had Coffin's pistol in his hand. He checked to see the safety was off. In an instant, the echoing footsteps materialized from the gloom into a large black shape. There was something in its hand, thick, stubby and menacing. The black form slowed to a deliberate walk as the distance narrowed. There was something familiar about that walk. Tom brought the pistol up, pulling back the hammer as he did, his hand trembling slightly. He wasn't about to take any chances.

"Chowder, he's got my gun!" Coffin cried out. At that very instant, at the dot of eight o'clock, fifty rockets and another twenty huge aerial bombs went off on cue over the Brooklyn Bridge. Even from over a half-mile away, they could all feel the concussions and see the sky light up. Tom flinched and thought for an instant that Chowder had fired. He almost fired himself. Only the knowledge that it was Chowder Kelly out there in the dark kept him from doing so. Down in the stairwell, Byrnes had his pistol out too. It seemed almost an insignificant thing in that huge black-gloved hand. Chowder, a sawed-off shotgun gripped in his big paw, was lit in a flickering, eerie glow, a ghoulish, menacing thunderhead of a man with a gun that looked like a small cannon. He called to Tom over the noise of the explosions.

"Damn! Looks like we'll miss some o' the fireworks, eh, Tommy?"

"Chowder, look out!" Coffin cried, struggling now with his captors. "There's three of them here."

Chowder flinched a little at that, not sure what to expect. But in an instant he relaxed and said, "You can tuck that pistol away, Tommy. You won't need it."

"Chowder!" A despairing note in Coffin's voice now.

Tom didn't say a word, just stuffed the pistol back in his pocket.

"Chowder, help!" Coffin called again as Chowder stopped in front of him.

"Shut the fuck up, Augie." Tom grinned, amazed and relieved at the same time. He hadn't wanted to shoot Chowder Kelly.

"Looks like you've got yourself some fireworks right here, though, Tommy," Chowder said as the rockets continued to rumble and crash in the distance. "Yes, indeedy, you do!"

Coffin, with a violent effort, somehow wrenched free of his captors, one of whom tumbled down the stairs and into the door. He tried to make it to the street and had his foot on the top step when Chowder lashed out, kicking Coffin in the stomach. He would have fallen back down the stairs if the two Chinese hadn't caught him. Chowder grinned and said, "Damn, that felt good."

Coffin was doubled over, retching on the stairs. The three Chinese had him pinned again.

"Chowder . . . you . . . *Fuck!*" He retched and spit. "*Rot in hell . . . you . . . fucking . . . bastard.*"

Chowder, lit by the flickering colored fireworks, in a fun house–devil sort of glow, grinned and said softly, "After you, August."

Neither Braddock nor Byrnes said anything. Byrnes simply nodded to the Chinese, who pulled the captain off his feet and down the stairs. They dragged him down into the basement on Doyers, his heels bouncing as he went. To his credit he went silently, his accusing eyes the last Braddock would see of him . . . in this world.

Captain Sangree sat on the edge of a wharf a quarter mile upriver from the bridge. Jacobs, Lebeau, Lincoln, Emmons and Sullivan were all with him, though he hardly noticed them. It was as if the fireworks had transported him. Perhaps it was the explosions when the first salvo went up. They sounded like artillery. They *felt* like artillery, the way the sound and shock waves compressed the air about their heads. It brought him back to Gettysburg and the barrage on the third day. Lee's guns had opened the attack, focusing the whole of the cannonade on a single point in the Yankee line. The cannon roared and thundered. A tornado of howling shells, bright-orange explosions, whistling fragments, and fountains of earth seemed to settle on the Yankee line like an avenging hand. Too soon the smoke of the guns obscured everything, but they fired on blindly into the Union center. Thaddeus remembered thinking about what a shell had done to Franklin. He remembered wishing the same for the Yankees. A sudden salvo of bursting rockets snapped him out of his reverie. They rained red, white, and blue stars, floating and flickering over the river. The ships below were illuminated in a ghostly sort of way, all light on one side and blackness on the other. The black waters reflected the explosions and sparkling waterfalls so at times the ghost ships seemed to ride on waves of fire. Rolling billows of smoke started to settle over the river. Soon, he imagined, the artillery wouldn't be able to see their targets.

Sangree fingered the folded telegram in his pocket. It had come days ago from his backers in Richmond. The news had been worse than he'd expected:

reception for your friends did not go as planned stop coming back to NY tomorrow stop they'll want to visit you immediately stop strongly suggest you move up timetable stop waste no time stop do not fail stop

Thaddeus knew the words by heart. "Goddamn Braddock! God *damn* that *fucking* detective!" he said under his breath. He looked over at Jacobs, his head wrapped in a white bandage, looking pale. Even a child had beaten them, he thought. What was happening to them? Why had they been unable to eliminate the detective and that brat? He was beginning to hate Braddock almost as much as Roebling. The thought of Roebling turned his mind elsewhere. The possibility of failure started to congeal in his head. It was not to be accepted, not even the possibility. The threat was clear enough in the telegram. Not that he needed a threat to goad him on. If they did fail, what then? What if he survived the attempt? There would be no going south. His life would not be worth living. He'd be hunted, and if he were unlucky enough to be captured, he'd be hanged. No . . . surviving a failed attempt was not an option. But there would still be Roebling. If all else failed, there would always be Roebling.

Damn, that was pretty, Jus. Did you see the way those colors changed as they fell? How they do that?" Pat wondered out loud.

"Yeah. This is really somethin', Pat. Never seen the like."

"Haven't ever seen this many people in one spot before either. Looks like the whole damn city turned out. Just imagine how many are in those boats." Pat pointed out at the clogged river. "Must be twenty–thirty thousand at least."

"Sure, maybe more," Justice agreed. "There's probably three or four thousand on those navy ships alone." The men almost had to shout at each other over the explosions and the din of the cheering crowds.

"I never imagined anything like this, partner. I know it's a big thing, but somehow I just never thought they'd put on this kind of show."

"And ain't she beautiful, Pat?"

"Yup. Whatever happens, I got to say I'll always be proud I worked on her."

"Me too," Justice said honestly. "I'll do what I got to, you know, but . . ." His voice trailed off into silence as the rain of fire silhouetted the massive bridge in sparkling relief. The people around them "oohed" and "aahed" and cheered.

"Jus, you know, it don't have to go like the captain says," Pat said into his ear, keeping an eye on the captain. "I mean—oh, hell, I don't know what I mean. It's like when we were talking up in the cables, you remember?" Justice just nodded. "You said if I looked for answers they'd come, remember?" Justice looked at Pat knowing what he was getting to. "I've been looking, and—" Sullivan stopped, afraid to actually put his thoughts into words.

"Don't tell me, Pat. I don't want to know. That's something you got to do for yourself. I can't help you . . . can't ask me to neither." Jus was afraid of hearing what he knew could change their lives. There was near desperation in the way he spoke.

Pat could see Justice had been wrestling with his own demons. It was in his eyes, lit by the brilliant flashes of fireworks. It was almost as if his thoughts shone out in shifting patterns of fire and shadow. They warred across the craggy landscape of his face, at least that's how it looked to Pat.

It was a long time before Justice spoke again. The fireworks had been going now for nearly half an hour without a break. At last, Justice turned his battered face to Pat and said, "Whatever you decide is okay by me, Pat. I won't stop you nor stand in your way."

Pat didn't say anything. He extended his callused, scarred rigger's hand to his old friend. Justice took it and clasped it tight. The captain didn't seem to notice.

Alone in Wash's darkened room, Emily and Wash clasped hands in Brooklyn too. They didn't say much. Emily felt strangely detached. They were spectators now. They had done their work, had won their laurels, but now were no different from any of the thousands of others who watched the bridge tonight. The house was silent. The band had packed their instruments and left. The caterers would be back in the morning to clean up. It was just her and Wash. She suddenly felt very tired, even old. It was as if just now she began to let herself feel the weight of the last fourteen years.

"You're in the history books now, Colonel Roebling," she said as the bridge was bathed in the fitful light of exploding rockets.

"I'm not there alone, Em."

"Who knows what they'll remember a hundred years from now?" Emily sighed. "Things are easily forgotten."

Wash shook his head adamantly. "Em, the *bridge* will be here a hundred years from now. As long as it stands, your name and mine will always be linked to it. Some might forget. But something like that"—he waved his hand to the window—"something like that . . . people will always want to know more about. There will always be those who want to know, and we'll be discovered, over and over, from one generation to the next."

Emily smiled softly at the idea. "That's a lovely thought." She cradled against him. "Do you really think people in the future will be curious? Someone is bound to build a bigger bridge, you know. Besides, there'll be so many wonderful new things." She held up a hand, ticking them off. "Electricity, telephones, horseless carriages, and a thousand other things. It could be that man will fly before the century's out. Do you still think that, with all that, a bridge will spark anyone's curiosity?"

"I do," Wash answered slowly. "That bridge is more than just engineering or . . . science. It's not some . . . appliance to be used up and thrown away. It has substance and grace and timeless beauty. There's harmony and proportion to it that goes beyond mere function. Such things will always have value." Wash gazed out the window. "The bridge serves not only the body but the soul as well. You know what it's like to be up on the promenade. Can you imagine that the world will ever tire of that? I don't think so."

They watched the fireworks as they boomed and echoed over the bridge.

"I think that a hundred years from this day the world will know it for the treasure it is," he murmured.

"Who knows?" Emily beamed at her husband. "They may throw us another party."

Mary watched from the *Tribune* windows as the almost constant barrage lit the night sky. The windows rattled and the concussions of the bigger bombs could be felt right through the floor. The guests were jammed four deep by each window, and they clapped and cheered in unison. She had to admit it was the most spectacular display she'd ever seen. The papers said that fourteen tons of pyrotechnics were to be set off within an hour. She couldn't judge, but it seemed like more. It seemed like the rockets and bombs and mortars had been going off for hours. It seemed they'd never end, and each one jangled her nerves and pounded at her temples. Mary looked at her watch once again: ten to nine. If it took this long, it couldn't have gone as planned, could it? The longer Tom was away, the worse she felt. As the city celebrated, her spirits sank. She could see herself in a while, the only person left in the building, waiting for a man who would not return, while cleaning people took out the trash.

"You come back to me, Thomas Braddock," she said to herself as the people cheered.

It was just minutes to nine, and Mary had checked her watch twice more. The minutes crawled into the past like a tortoise on a hot day, stretching each plodding second. Her palms were sweaty and she actually started to flinch and twitch with each explosion. She tried hard not surrender to her nervousness. Even though she saw the most terrible things in her mind's eye, she clapped absently at the show. By nearly nine o'clock the fireworks were building to a shattering crescendo, with scores of big illuminated balloons raining sparkling icicles of fire down on the city and aerial bombs and rockets going off in thundering staccato. It numbed the senses. Suddenly she felt a heavy hand slip gently around hers. Her intake of breath was almost a gasp. She didn't need to see who it was to know, but she turned anyway and threw her arms around Tom's neck.

"Oh, Tom . . . oh, God, you're back," she whispered. "I've been so worried. Are you all right?" Her hands went over him, taking inventory.

"Of course I'm all right. I told you I'd come back, didn't I?" he said nonchalantly.

Mary hit him in the arm and he yelped in surprise.

"Don't you pull that with me, Tom Braddock," she said as angrily as she could. "I died ten times in the last hour waiting for you."

Tom's voice softened. "I'm sorry, Mary. I'm sorry I put you through this." The fireworks boomed, sparkled, and lit up the city in flashes of color. "Some fireworks display, huh?"

"Don't you change the subject, you bastard," Mary said fiercely. "You hold me right now, Tommy. You hold me, before you have to catch me."

The fireworks ended almost as suddenly as they'd started. In the deafening silence that followed, Tom held her close and whispered their future in her ear.

That silence lasted only a few short heartbeats. Before the smoke had settled on the black waters under the bridge, first one, then dozens, then hundreds of boats blew their steam whistles, rang their bells, and fired their cannons and guns. The noise was taken up on both shores. Church bells, factory whistles, horns, drums, and anything that would make noise added to the din. Hundreds of thousands of throats roared their approval. The bridge was open, the way clear to the other shore.

❧ Chapter Twenty-one ☙

To trust it loyally as he
Who, heedful of his high design,
Ne'er raised a seeking eye to thine,
But wrought thy will unconsciously.

—AMBROSE BIERCE

Jacobs lay on his bed, an ice pack on the back of his head. Icy rivulets ran down his neck and into the sheets. Despite the ice, his temper was boiling. Beaten by a boy! Beaten into unconsciousness! If he hadn't been hurt so bad, he'd never have let himself be seen like that by the others. As it was he barely made it back to Brooklyn. He'd thrown up over the side of the ferry, so dizzy and nauseous he was staggering like a drunk. He had a knot on his skull the size of an egg and a cut that hadn't stopped oozing in three days. The biggest blow was to his ego. He was a killer, a thoroughly dangerous person. He'd spent years cultivating that reputation. The other men feared him, he knew . . . at least they *did*. Yesterday they'd laughed at him! *Laughed!* He still couldn't believe it. It had been in fun, but still it hurt, maybe more than the lump on his head. *Beaten unconscious by a ten-year-old*, he thought for the hundredth time.

That little bastard was going to pay! Bart didn't care what Thaddeus said, didn't give a shit that killing the boy was no longer a priority. He would butcher that kid if it was the last goddamn thing he did on this earth! After the fiasco in Richmond, the boy was no longer important, the captain said. Braddock probably knew everything the boy knew anyway. With him still alive and on their trail, the boy was less than an annoyance—but not to him. He had something to prove. No kid was going to beat Bart Jacobs, *ever*. He'd gut the little fuck and hang him by his intestines . . . kill him as gruesomely as possible any way he could . . . set an example. He'd show the others he was still nobody to mess with. There'd be no laughter then!

He rolled out of bed, wincing and screwing his eyes shut as the room wobbled. Tomorrow he'd see. Tomorrow he'd hunt. For now he'd join the rest of the men, carry on with the plan, act as if nothing was going to happen. He'd keep his plans to himself. The less the captain knew, the better. Hell, maybe he'd just surprise them all and bring the kid's head back in a basket. He smiled at the thought.

The bridge had been open two days now. The captain had done all he could to throw the cops off the scent. With the police looking for them all over the city and their old apartments watched, there was great danger in every move they made. Even Sangree & Co had been staked out constantly over the last few days. It was fortunate that Sullivan and Lincoln didn't seem to be suspects. They were able to monitor the police with complete safety. Their reports were unsettling, though. Everyone's nerves were wearing thin. Tempers were short. Sleep was light.

Their manifesto was nearly done. Pat and Matt had agreed to read the captain's draft and suggest any final changes.

"Men, this is our word, our code. We'll be speaking for the whole South and all our martyred brothers with this one document," he said, pacing back and forth in Jacobs's small apartment. "It will be a fitting coda to the destruction of the bridge."

"Amen to that, Captain!" Earl exclaimed, not sure exactly what a coda was but liking the sound of it. He slammed a bony fist into his palm. "Make them Yankee pigs squeal!"

Over the days since the opening, they had been able to perfect their plans and get in some valuable practice. The night before, they had actually driven their wagon and carriage onto the bridge. One from New York, one from Brooklyn, they started at exactly the same time, met in the middle, and unloaded their boxes at center span, though they didn't use the actual dynamite crates. It was 2:15 A.M. when they tried it. Apart from a sole carriage crossing the bridge toward the Brooklyn shore, which threw their timing off some, it went according to plan. From the time they stopped at center span, they took only forty-six seconds to unload the boxes and pile them on the railroad tracks. Within two minutes they were packed again and on their way to the opposite shore. It was faster than any of them had hoped.

Not everything went more smoothly than planned. Jacobs had gone to the bridge offices the second day after the opening. He returned to report that the bridge police would patrol around the clock.

"Christ almighty," Earl had almost shouted. "That's gonna throw a wrench in the gears for damn sure!" He got no disagreement. They attacked the problem with their usual skill and determination.

Over the last couple days they'd studied the patrol patterns. It had meant some long hours, but it bought them what they needed. There was a problem though, and it became evident by the second night of observation. Starting on the twenty-fifth, two men watched the bridge, beginning at 2:00 A.M. They noted when a patrol left either side, and when one arrived. They'd watch until 3:30, then compare times in the morning. The patrols were supposed to be on the hour at that time of the night, and at first they were. By the second night, though, both the time the patrols set off and the time they took to cross the bridge had started to vary. The differences weren't great, no more than ten minutes one way or the other—of no great consequence at that time of the morning, at least not to the cops. But ten minutes could mean everything to them. It vastly increased the risks. And it only got worse. A couple of cops had a habit of loitering in their walks across, stopping for a smoke in the spectacular solitude of the promenade at night.

"We've got to keep timing 'em till the night before, Cap'n," Earl said.

"Precisely. It makes Jacobs's and my jobs that much more critical too. We've got to be ready to move with a warning if need be. Who's to say what kind of interval we might have? The way it looks right now, it could be anywhere from fifty minutes to an hour and ten."

"Those two detectives been nosing around the bridge office since Thursday," Bart said offhandedly.

"You keeping in touch with someone at the office?" Thaddeus asked. Jacobs nodded. The cops were busy everywhere, and their world had devolved to staying in hiding during the day, with practice at night, at least for Matt, Earl, and the captain. How long would it be before the rest of them were identified and hunted? Not long, Bart figured. He fingered his bandage and thought again of his plans for the Bucklin boy.

"You did well to stick in there as long as you did," Thaddeus said with a pat on Jacobs's shoulder.

"Thank you, sir. Just playing the good little clerk, which by the way allowed me to make some extra copies of the keys to the power house and the doors to the steam generators and dynamos." Jacobs chuckled, holding up the keys and jingling them for the group.

"Anyone care for coffee?" he offered genially.

There were two takers. Jacobs bustled about the stove. He measured the beans and ground them with deliberate twists of the little handle on his coffee grinder, getting into a rhythm, as if doing it to a metronome. He seemed to enjoy this, concentrating on each turn of the crank. Finally he poured the grinds into the pot. Even when he stopped for a moment to breathe the essence of the beans, it was apparent that this too was part of the coffee ritual. The others watched him, fascinated. It was like watching a machine, all efficiency and precision even in this small, pleasant task. Jacobs could be just as precise about his killing. Most of the others considered his recent misadventure with the Bucklin boy a fluke, something that happens once in a blue moon. None doubted his abilities, though they couldn't resist an occasional ribbing.

"Damn, you are the neatest fella I ever seen, Bart," Earl marveled sarcastically. "You'll make some lucky man a good wife one day." They all laughed, even Jacobs, who had his back to Earl. Suddenly, with alarming speed, Bart whirled about, his hand licking out like a snake. A bit of bright steel spun through the air and hit the wall above Earl's head with a *thunk*. A knife quivered there like a rattler's tail.

"And I'm handy with cutlery too," Jacobs said merrily. There was no merriment in his eyes, though. He'd had about enough from Earl over the last couple of days.

Earl half rose from his chair, but the others burst into raucous laughter and drove him back.

"Oh, that's rich, Bart!" Matt laughed. "Come near to givin' ol' Earl a trim. You are a conjurer with a blade."

Pat chuckled too, figuring it was the best way to defuse the situation. Earl sat silent, dark as a thunderstorm, while the rest of them had their chuckle. Finally after the room had quieted, he said in his best slow drawl, "Ah b'lieve ah git yer pernt."

"All right, gentlemen, now that we've had our little laugh, let's get back to business, shall we?" Thaddeus said. We've only got three days."

Sullivan was happy to take the spotlight off Jacobs and Lebeau. Those two never did get on real well, so it was best to keep them occupied with other matters. "We've got to be clear on our positions, timing, signals, everything."

Braddock's investigation had cut their practice time to the bone. They had planned on having more time to prepare. Everyone was under pressure and it was beginning to show, as Bart's little flare-up proved.

"Signals will be critical," the captain said, trying to keep them focused. "There will hopefully be thousands on the bridge. It's essential that the men on the span will be in proper position to see the signal. I don't want to blow you boys along with the bridge," he said with a grim smile. Sullivan knew the captain wouldn't hesitate if he had to. He'd blow the whole lot of them without a second thought. "Once you see the signal, you'll have exactly five minutes, no more." They all knew the captain meant it. "For you men on the span, that should be enough to make it beyond the towers at either side. Which way you go is up to you, depending on the number of people in your way. Once you're beyond the towers you'll be safe. The land spans may sag, but they will not collapse."

"That's a real comfort, Cap'n," Earl said, smiling. "We'll meet up later then, after . . . or what?"

The captain dropped his pencil with an exasperated sigh. "No, Earl! We went over this yesterday. We go our separate ways. We meet again only when the circumstances are right. If things are clear, the shade will be drawn in the room on the northwest corner, third floor, of the Powhattan Hotel. If you see that sign, check at the front desk for a message. Instructions will be waiting for you. Is everyone clear on that?" The captain cast a challenging eye around the room. "Good. Let's go over those positions and signals again then. We only get to do this once."

Headquarters was more of a beehive than usual, with detectives scurrying in and out at all hours of the day and night. Coffin's sudden resignation had left a void in the power structure, and perhaps more critical, it left others feeling vulnerable. Rumors had been running around the Marble Palace like a plague, leaving festering sores of doubt and suspicion. Tom felt an almost macabre sense of fascination at the workings of the rumor mill. He had no way of knowing how many were involved with Coffin's "corps," but if all the activity was an indicator, it was plenty. Some no doubt had plenty to worry about too. Byrnes wasn't a murderer, nor was he one to let Coffin get off with a resignation without some quid pro quo. Coffin had spilled everything. He'd had to. Tom knew how Byrnes could be when he got his temper on the boil. There would be more "resignations" to come, of that he was certain. Meanwhile, he noticed a steady stream of men filing in and out of Byrnes's office. Braddock found it fascinating to watch the faces "before" and "after" a meeting with the chief. It was most revealing. For the majority, though, the increased activity was simply a nervous reaction to the shakeup. It wasn't a good time to be seen doing nothing.

The other factor was opportunity. Any time a captaincy opened up, which wasn't all that often, dozens of men tripped over themselves to be noticed. The sudden increase in official preening was like watching some bizarre mating ritual. Blue-bellied, bowler-headed cop birds were strutting all over the building, brass polished to a blinding sheen, pants pressed to a knife edge. It was a fascinating, Darwinian display. Tom took it all in as he went about his job. He could afford to do the job as he'd always done it. It was the one thing he really cared about, the one constant in this frothy blue sea. He let the waves break around him, the foam and spray fall where they would. It couldn't touch him.

It was midmorning when he got a summons from Byrnes. They'd already had a couple of conversations over the last few days about Coffin, the corps, and Braddock's involvement in it all. Tom had come about as clean as he could without revealing things that Byrnes didn't need to know. The chief was understanding enough to keep Tom's revelations focused just on Coffin's operations, leaving the rest to Tom's better judgment. It wasn't Tom he was after. Byrnes couldn't help being annoyed at the whole episode, though. He'd literally beat everything he could out of Coffin, taking out his fury on the captain for putting him in this situation. Shakeups like this could be messy, brutal affairs. It was a job Byrnes was well suited for, but still he hated doing it.

"The papers are starting to get real curious about his finances," Byrnes said without preamble as Tom closed the door behind him. "Things are going to come out." Byrnes's tone was ominous, as was the look he gave Tom. "I hope you can spare Pat and Charlie for a while longer." Byrnes had "borrowed" them back from Tom to help with the Coffin affair.

"Of course, sir," Tom said, knowing Byrnes would keep them anyway. He couldn't be seen as standing in the way of investigating Coffin, regardless of what he thought was going on with his own case. Still, he found himself saying, "But, sir, I have to tell you, I still have a bad feeling about the Bucklin case." He fingered the tattered clipping in his pocket as he said this as if by rubbing it he could conjure a solution. "They're still out there. They've just gone underground. Scares me . . . to be honest."

Byrnes didn't say anything—not exactly an endorsement of Tom's position.

"It's not that I don't appreciate your need of the manpower, sir," Tom went on. "It's just that . . ." Byrnes was frowning now. "Well . . . just wanted you to know how I felt, that's all," Tom ended, seeing he wasn't going to get anywhere with this line of attack.

"Thanks," Byrnes muttered. He didn't see the urgency. If this was connected to the trains, as the evidence seemed to point, then they still had time. It would be months before they'd be running. The latest reports predicted it would be sometime in September. There'd be time to sweep the Coffin mess under the carpet and deal with the conspiracy too, he thought.

"I've got them checking into Coffin's finances. Don't like some of the things they've found," he continued.

Tom understood the chief's position. "I know, sir. Coffin's . . . finances were only part of it. It was his *business practices*, so to speak, that convinced me to come to you," he said, getting as close as he wanted to the truth of it.

"Mm . . . yet you didn't report anything for some time. Didn't occur to you to come to me sooner?" Byrnes asked. They'd gone over this before, but it was Byrnes's way of testing him.

Tom knew this and accepted it. "First off, sir, I figured you were aware of at least some of what Coffin was up to. I had no hard evidence." A lie, it was true, but one he figured he could get away with. "And . . . I'm not sure I would have told you if I had. Don't think it would have been my place. It was only when I saw that Coffin was getting out of control that . . ." Tom trailed off, wondering if Byrnes had caught the dual meaning of what he was saying.

Byrnes puffed out a small cumulous cloud of cigar smoke and seemed to examine the ceiling. "Suppose I agree, Tom. I'm a great respecter of the chain of command. No way to advance your career generally . . . going around a superior's back. But I understand about Coffin. He *was* out of control, beyond the pale so to speak. I understand about the incident with Mary too." Byrnes gave Tom a significant look through the cigar smoke.

Tom nodded with the ghost of a grin. "I'm relieved you understand, sir."

"You're not telling me everything." Byrnes blew smoke for effect. "I know that."

Fresh sweat blossomed on Tom's back, an icy trickle running down his spine.

"But that's all right. It's not you I'm looking at here. I know how things work. Came up through the ranks too, you know." Byrnes gave him a conspiratorial grin. "But Coffin has gone and got himself in the soup, and I have to separate the broth from the noodles. Now the superintendents and the commissioner, they don't need to know all we do, right?" Byrnes asked rhetorically.

Tom grinned his understanding. "Of course not, sir."

"They want this thing put to rest one way or another. The less waving of dirty laundry, the better."

"Probably wise," Tom agreed.

"Uh-huh. I'm going to give this thing just a little more time . . . but the papers start getting too close to what really went on, and I'll shut it down in a hurry."

Tom nodded. He was curious about one more thing, and he had to ask. "So . . . what's going to happen to Coffin?"

Byrnes looked at him with an appraising frown. "He leaves with nothing. If he hadn't spilled his guts, he'd have been prosecuted. Probably would have done a long stint in Sing Sing. At least he saved himself that." Byrnes waved his cigar. "Pretty good deal all the way around, actually. He doesn't do jail time, the department doesn't get dragged through another scandal, and you get out from under his thumb. We then have an opportunity to replace him with someone more"—he seemed to search for the right word— "cooperative, so to speak."

Tom grunted. "Suppose it worked out pretty well at that."

Tom ran into Chowder on his way out. Kelly was heading toward Byrnes's office.

"Hey, Tommy! How goes the war?"

"Okay, I guess."

Chowder lowered his voice a few octaves. "He give you a hard time?"

" 'Bout what I expected," Tom said with a shrug.

"Anything new on Coffin?" Chowder asked seriously.

"Nothing you don't already know, partner." Tom looked him in the eye. "Byrnes has found some skeletons in his closet, the sorts of things you'd expect. No surprises. He'll put a lid on if too much starts to get out."

"A wise move for the good of the department, laddie." Chowder chuckled. "Byrnes was always a practical man. Might be best for all concerned if Coffin just fades away," he said with a wink. "Well . . . it's my appointed hour for grilling, Tommy. Don't want to keep the chef waiting."

"Right," Tom said with a smile. "Let's get a beer sometime soon. I hear McSorley's calling."

"Damned if I don't too. 'Tis a siren's song, Tommy! the call o' the ale," Chowder said over his shoulder, grinning as he sauntered toward Byrnes's office.

Tom went back to his desk, throwing himself down onto his hard oak chair. His in box was full again but he had no interest in plowing through it. His talk with Byrnes had taken the wind out of his sails. He picked up some papers from his desk and shuffled them idly, not even seeing what was written on them. It was an old habit, formed of the fear of appearing to do nothing if his boss came by. He thought about losing Pat and Charlie and how that would slow the investigation. Between the opening of the bridge, which had cost them a day, and the Coffin debacle, which had thrown the department into chaos, they hadn't had time to do much. He and Jaffey had checked out Emmons's and Lebeau's rooms, of course, which were as empty as the offices of Sangree & Co had been. They'd staked the places out with help from the precinct. Sam had helped with that. Tom had sent out a telegram to the other precincts to be on the lookout for Lebeau, Emmons, and Sangree as well, and there were posters up in railway stations and post offices. Big block letters read WANTED FOR CONSPIRACY, and the names and descriptions of the three were included. It had turned out that Emmons and Lebeau had never been on any train to Texas, at least they hadn't been found.

Pat and Charlie had started to canvass explosives suppliers in and around the city just yesterday but hadn't turned up anything by the time Byrnes pulled them off. It was a long shot, Tom figured, but the violent reception he and Jaffey had gotten in Richmond got him thinking along more sinister lines. Besides, they'd checked nearly everything they could about the trains, with nothing to show for it. He pulled the clipping from his pocket once more, reading the lines he'd come to memorize. In awkward hyperbole it gushed about the wonderful convenience of being whisked across the river in only five minutes. The comfort of the cars was outlined in glowing terms. The brilliant technology of the cable system was described in detail and compared to the new cable cars in San Francisco. Tom knew it all by heart. He focused on the papers on his desk, putting the clipping aside.

Charlie had given him a list of the places they were checking—if he could find it. After going through the piles on his desktop, he'd finally looked in his top drawer, and there it was. Efficient as ever, Dolan and Heidelberg had checked off the ones they'd already stopped at. Little notes filled the margins concerning whom they'd talked to and what they'd found out, which apparently wasn't much. Braddock looked at it with glum resignation.

"What the hell," he mumbled. "Beats waiting for the next rumor on Coffin." He heaved himself to his feet and went to find Jaffey.

It was a long day of running about the city, checking on explosives distributors. Each stop meant slow hours of clerks going through order books and invoices. They searched for sales to any of the names known to Tom. He and Jaffey ate up the day scouring books for Sangree, Emmons, Lebeau, and Watkins, coming up with only one delivery to a Samuel Watkins in White Plains. It didn't look like a fit, but Tom made a note to telegram the local cops there to check the man out.

By the time they got back to 300 Mulberry, the afternoon editions were getting bolder about the reasons for Coffin's resignation, hinting at corruption in high places. Byrnes would have to put an end to it soon, or all hell would break loose. Tom had anticipated this sort of reaction from both the press and the department. He tried to put it to the back of his mind. With everything else that was going on, it worked for short intervals. But like a ghost rising from his haunted brain, Coffin came back to him many times during the day. Sometimes it was only as a feeling, a prickling of the hair on the back of his neck. Other times he could see Coffin's face, twisted with hate but frightened and hopeless too. Those eyes would look into his for the rest of his days. As hard as that was, he knew too that it would have been just a matter of time before Coffin did the same or worse to him—probably with less conscience.

Byrnes called Tom in to confirm that Pat and Charlie had officially been taken off the case and reassigned to Coffin's investigation for the next few days, or until they shut it down.

"Tom, that's got to come first for now. We'll talk later," Byrnes said dismissively, cutting Tom off before he could mount more objections.

Tom told Jaffey a few minutes later.

"Not surprising." Jaffey shrugged, though it would mean extra days of legwork for him and Tom. "Not every day something like that happens. Obviously there was something going on. The whole thing stinks, and the fact that Coffin isn't saying anything makes it smell even worse. I've heard he was into all kinds of things—extortion, prostitution, policy rackets, you name it."

"Yeah . . . I don't doubt it," Tom said softly. He started to count the lies, big and small. It would be a tower before it was over, heavy and unstable. He prayed it wouldn't topple.

Mike thought he'd seen the bow-tie clerk twice during the day. The first time he'd looked again and it clearly wasn't the same man. The second time he wasn't so sure. The man had dropped from sight an instant later, lost in the hurly-burly of the street. It had given him a chill. Still, he had hung out with his friends all afternoon after getting out of class. They'd made no effort to hide or keep special watch. This was their neighborhood, after all, their streets. They'd notice anything out of the ordinary.

Dusk had fallen, and the streetlamps were being lit by shuffling civil servants when Mike saw Bow-tie for real. He was just heading home for dinner. He'd told Smokes that maybe he'd be out after, and he'd started up Norfolk when the scary little clerk seemed to materialize out of the gloom in front of him. He'd never seen anyone look at him the way that man did. The eyes were black holes in his face, scary black wells, with a glint that chilled him like a winter gale. Mike stood frozen for an instant, like a jacked deer staring into the light, then he turned and bolted, yelling for his mates. He felt the air stir behind his neck as he took off. He didn't even see the blade. He didn't have to.

He ran fast, maybe faster than he ever had, hoping his gang had heard him but not turning to look. He knew instinctively that one hesitation, one wrong move, and he'd be dead. Like a rabbit, his one chance was to run from the fox. He prayed he was fast enough. Pounding footsteps followed so close he could almost mistake them for his own. He could hear the man's breath gusting behind. It sounded loud, but to his ears it didn't sound labored. The bow-tie clerk could run! Mike was fast for a boy of ten. Bow-tie was just as fast. Mike's lungs were beginning to burn when he darted sideways across the cobbles in front of a wagon, whose horse snorted and reared, kicking out at the air. It threw his pursuer off a bit, as he'd hoped, but it didn't stop him. Up Norfolk they ran, past Rivington and on toward Stanton. No one seemed to pay them any regard whatever. Adults chasing kids weren't all that uncommon here. There weren't that many people on the streets at this time anyway. The smells of dinner wafted around them as they ran.

With a sudden impulse, Mike ducked down an alley. It was actually a lot, but at twenty feet wide wasn't much different from an alley. There was a wall at the end that Mike hoped he could scale before Bow-tie got to him. Maybe then he'd be able to lose him in the lots between the buildings, as he had before. He vaulted over some bricks as he heard Bow-tie round the corner. He used a box near the wall to boost himself, shinnying up a drainpipe at the corner of the rough brick wall. He wasn't going fast enough! His hand slipped! He was only five feet off the ground as he heard Bow-tie vault the pile of bricks. Desperately he climbed as fast as he could, realizing it wasn't fast enough. He began to panic.

Jacobs was exultant! The little bastard was cornered. He saw it as soon as he rounded the corner. Trapped! Though the kid tried to shinny up a drainpipe, Jacobs saw right away it wasn't going to be enough. He had just jumped over some bricks when something hit him in the shoulder, and he went down hard. He wasn't sure what had happened at first. The impact and the fall were almost one. He rolled with the fall, bouncing up as best he could, looking behind him for what had caused it. As he did, a bottle flew by just inches from his head. He hadn't even seen it coming. He raised an arm to shield himself too late, and he saw five silhouettes at the end of the alley outlined by the streetlamps. Another bottle sailed out of the darkness, glancing off his forearm as a kid's voice said, "Leave our friend alone, mister!"

A barrage of bottles, rocks, and at least one brick followed. Jacobs was pummeled. He ducked and weaved, but in the dark he couldn't see the missiles coming. One or two hurt like hell.

"Fuckin' little bastards!" he cursed, holding up his arm as he charged them. He expected them to run, imagined they'd scatter at the sight of an adult charging them with a naked blade. He was mistaken. A second barrage came whistling in, bottles smashing, rocks bouncing. Jacobs was already cut or bruised in five or six places. "Kill you bastards!" he screamed with dogged determination, leaning into the blizzard of projectiles. He'd gut these kids once he got close enough. But when he got close, he found that three of them had trashcan covers in their hands, like knights with shields, and he saw the glint of steel in their hands too—pocket knives. Still he came at them, unafraid, slashing left and right, dodging catlike and striking out with deadly skill. His blade struck sparks off the steel of the trashcan covers, it cut thin air, it even found boy-flesh more than once. But the kids were circling, three to one, and the other two were standing off and hurling stuff when they could. They didn't run or give up. They fought.

Jacobs had forgotten about Mike Bucklin. He'd just caught one of the kids on the arm, cutting an instantly bloody furrow through his shirt sleeve. The kid yelped, not sounding like a knight at all now. Bottles were thrown but missed. The tide was turning, when suddenly he was hit from behind.

Mike had come down from the wall when he saw his friends attack Bow-tie. He advanced slowly to the pile of bricks, watching the battle as he grabbed one in each hand. The clerk didn't see him. He was too busy with Smokes and Mouse and the others. When Mouse got cut he saw his chance. Mike rushed at Bow-tie's back. He wasn't more than eight feet away when he let go with the first brick. Without looking to see if it hit, he threw the second. The two impacts took Jacobs off his feet in a heartbeat, his back feeling like he'd been hit with a cannon ball. Before he'd recovered or even fully realized what had happened, they were on him, kicking, stabbing, beating him with their trashcan shields and yelling like fiends. All he could do was cover up and flail with his knife. He hurt all over, he bled from a dozen small wounds, his back felt like the ribs had been caved in. A few more minutes of this and he'd be a dead man. Striking out, he saw his blade dig into a leg, heard the kid scream, saw them back off just for an instant, ready to swarm in again.

Jacobs rolled painfully to his feet, lunging at the boys to make a hole in their ranks. They parted as he slashed left and right. He made it to the street, where a few people watched from a distance. He ran staggering, bleeding, cursing. The boys didn't follow far. Bart Jacobs disappeared down Norfolk, bottles breaking on the cobbles behind him and the voices of the boyish victors taunting him in the night. He was almost too relieved to care.

An hour later, in a very different part of town, August Coffin sat staring with bloodshot eyes. He saw the trappings of success, the photographs with famous and influential people, the framed testaments to his virtue, his civic pride, his service to city and country. He had been an important man, a respected and powerful man. His word had meant something. His opinions had value. He was a leader. He looked about the room paneled in Honduran mahogany, noting the shelves of leather-bound volumes, some quite valuable, the silver writing set, with inkpot and blotter, the big oak desk he sat at, its quarter-sawn oak striped like a tiger. Oils by worthy artists hung from his walls. They were of the sea and ships, of billowing creamy-white sails against blue-green waters . . . paintings of self-reliance, of strength in the face of the overwhelming elements. He had loved those paintings, had seen something of himself in those images.

The room breathed power. An air of elegant taste and refinement, of under-stated assurance permeated the place, as it did the rest of his castle on Murray Hill. It was illusion. He had loved this room at the heart of the house, the heart of his power. He loved it still. He had reveled in the knowledge that his grasp on power and influence reached far beyond these paneled walls. He recalled his best days in this room, the fires in the marble-manteled fireplace and how they warmed the space on winter nights. He recalled the deals made here, the triumphs celebrated, the victories, the defeated enemies come to grovel. This one room embodied all these things. He recalled them all, and he remembered Braddock as he sat across from this very desk in the red-leather wing chair moaning about Mary, his whore of a girlfriend. How full of himself he had been, how sure of his victory over Tom. He'd been so certain. The great manipulator had triumphed, bringing his whipped dog to heal. Coffin grunted in the darkness, his blindness surprising even now. He took another long pull from a crystal tumbler, swirling with amber scotch. It burned as it went down.

None of it had meaning for him. There was numbness where his feelings should have been. Even his anger had gone numb and cold. There was empti-ness now, a great yawning void of it. The utter defeat of soul gripped him, a depression so deep it paralyzed him in a cold, penetrating embrace. He barely had energy to breathe, to move, to eat. He didn't even remember how many days it had been since Byrnes beat him into confessing everything, giving up everyone, even his corps. He couldn't feel his bruises. The numbness drowned even that ache. He looked down at the .32 Smith & Wesson, an elegant weapon. It glowed invitingly from the leather-bound blotter on his desktop.

August gripped the pistol deliberately, feeling how the curve of the grips fit his hand, the small chill of the steel frame, the warm checkered walnut under his fingers. His finger felt the sensuous curve of the trigger, the little ridges in its surface. The muzzle fit easily in his mouth, as if it were made to go there.

A promise made is a promise kept. Tom had always believed that. Though he was in no mood for the circus, he'd made his deal with Mike and he was bound to keep it. But as he walked up Suffolk Street on the evening of the twenty-ninth, he couldn't suppress the feeling that while he was going to see Jumbo, there were at least three men somewhere in the city who worked even now to sabotage the bridge. He carried the thought like a millstone. Since Richmond, he hadn't been eating right, nor sleeping well either. It was due partly to Coffin, but mostly it was the unshakable feeling that whatever Sangree was planning would happen soon. A sense of impending doom had hovered over him like a storm cloud for days, and no amount of investigation, distraction, or rationalization could dispel it. He'd been driving himself and Eli hard, working leads, staying in constant touch with the precincts and the detectives who were watching Sangree & Co. and the apartments of Sangree and the rest. There was nothing, no sign of them, no indication of anything wrong at the bridge either. The bridge police reported nothing but ordinary patrols. It was to Tom an ominous silence.

"Maybe I really do need to see Jumbo," he muttered. "Get my mind off this goddamn case for a couple hours."

He collected Mike, who was so excited he was almost jumping out of his skin. There was something odd about the boy, though. His grandmother was oddly silent too, as if there was something she was holding back. More than once he thought he saw looks exchanged between Mike and her but he couldn't place why. He put it down to some family argument or other. Mike chattered all the way to the El, seemingly so excited that all else had been purged from his brain. He went on about all the oddities that were on display at Barnum's. Everything from fat ladies to dog-faced boys and a hundred amazing creatures and people in between were there for the amusement of the crowds. Pygmies from Africa, giants from China, and midgets from who-knows-where were all part of the show. Mike's enthusiasm was contagious. By the time they reached their stop on the El, Tom was smiling along with the boy, forgetting for the moment the oppressive feelings that ruled him.

They were walking to Madison Square Garden and had just crossed Lexington Avenue. Mike was going on about how he wanted to buy some souvenirs and stuff to show his friends, when he said, "Is it all right if I keep my ticket, the stub, I mean? I want to save it so I'll remember today."

"Sure. That's a great idea. Why don't you take mine too once we get in," Tom offered.

"Thanks. That's great." Mike was quiet for a minute and Tom got the feeling he wanted to say something. He held his tongue and waited. Then Mike picked his head up, looking at Tom in a level, grown-up sort of way, and said, "Thank you, Mr. Braddock. I don't want to ever forget this day."

Something about the way Mike said it made Tom stop and look down at the boy. They stood like that for an awkward moment, staring at each other, until Tom held out one arm. He put it around Mike's shoulder and the boy leaned in against his side.

"Me neither, partner," Tom said, giving him a tentative hug. "So, what're you going to do with those tickets?" he asked, afraid of letting the scene get too mushy.

"Oh, I'm gonna put them in my box." Mike held up his small brass key and beamed up at Tom.

"Good place for 'em." Tom nodded his approval. He realized once he'd said it how important the circus was to Mike. That box was reserved for only his most precious things. "I'd feel real good about that," he added. Mike looked up at him with an open, appraising sort of look, as if he were weighing Tom's words. Tom just looked back evenly. Mike turned away with a little smile.

Tom cleared his throat, then asked, "You prefer peanuts or ice cream? Me, I kinda like 'em both."

The circus was everything Mike hoped it would be. Jumbo was even bigger than he or Tom imagined. The beast shuffled around the big arena with an almost jaunty air, as if he enjoyed strutting for the cheering crowds. A lumbering herd of lesser beasts, with colorful, tasseled rugs on their backs, followed the great pachyderm. Jumbo, it turned out, did not shit houses. But Mike seemed fascinated nonetheless by the clown whose job it was to follow the elephants with a shovel and wheelbarrow.

"You figure that's where they put the bad clowns?" Mike speculated.

Tom grinned. "Yup. That's what we do with them in the department. Plenty of clowns shoveling shit around the city. Department's full of 'em."

Mike seemed to take that at face value.

An amazing menagerie of bizarre animals and even more exotic humans followed the elephants. Ornately carved and garishly painted calliopes, pulled by snowy-white teams tooted, whistled and steamed. The band, all decked out in red uniforms with lots of gold braid and white gloves, banged out tunes at ear-splitting volume. Mike shoveled peanuts into his mouth as fast as he could chew. He was in heaven. Tom wasn't far behind. For a time he forgot his work and set his imagination free to run with the boy. They had needed the release, both of them.

It wasn't till much later, on the way home, that Mike told Tom about the bow-tie man. Tom didn't believe it at first. He thought maybe Mike's imagination was overheated, or maybe he'd had too much ice cream, which he had. But one look into Mike's face convinced him otherwise.

"Would have told you sooner but I was scared . . . you know, scared we . . ."

"We wouldn't go to the circus," Tom said, finishing the thought.

"Sort of."

"Suppose I can't blame you. So tell me about this bow-tie fella. I gotta know everything, Mike. It's real important."

Mike took a long time describing everything, from the first time Mr. Bow-tie had come after him, to the battle just hours before. Tom tried not to interrupt too much, letting Mike tell it his own way. He remembered a lot and had a good eye for details, Tom noticed. When Mike was finished, Tom gave a low whistle.

"I'll be damned if that doesn't sound like that fucking clerk! Mike, we're going back to your place just to pick up some clothes and stuff. You and your grandma will be spending some time someplace else till I get this sorted out. And thanks for telling me, partner. This might be worth more than you imagine."

An hour later, Mike and Patricia Bucklin were safe in one of Mary's spare bedrooms. Tom headed back to headquarters. He needed to work things out. Even though it was late and there was no hope of finding Jacobs till morning, he needed to do something. He had no address for the man, no idea how to find him. The bridge offices would be closed this time of night. He briefly considered going to the Roeblings but rejected the notion. That was too much of a stretch. It wasn't worth waking the colonel on a hunch. He decided to wait. Still, sleep was not an option. A while later, alone at the back of the squad room, Tom slowly drew new lines on his chart. When he was done, he stood back from the wall, his arms folded across his chest.

"Bastards!" he muttered to himself.

The midmorning heat was beginning to turn the warehouse into an oven. Sullivan and Lincoln were sweating. Lugging the crates of explosives and especially the heavy modeling clay was hard work. The warehouse on Canal Street was a dingy little affair, with windows covered by cast-iron shutters and one large sliding door off a battered loading dock. The place had seen better times and appeared half empty. With the exception of one myopic clerk and a sleepy laborer who doubled as a dispatcher for the small freight line that operated out of the place, there was nobody around. Pat and Jus had been hauling boxes for about ten minutes, trudging back and forth to the second floor, where their crates were stored in a far corner. They were anxious to get it done. As they did they talked about Jacobs.

"Never thought to see the day when Bart would get bested by some street Arabs," Jus said, amazement in his voice.

"You get a look at him? Took one hell of a beating. Think the captain would have finished the job if he wasn't so bad off already. Guess he took pity on him."

"Cap'n was pissin' mad. Told Bart not to go after the kid and there he goes anyway. Stupid, you ask me," Jus opined.

"Yeah. Wasn't much thought in it. Bart didn't take to getting brained by the brat," Pat said. "Jacobs never was one to forget a debt." Sullivan stretched his back, and said, "Best get going. Braddock probably knows about Jacobs by now. Who knows what else he might know?"

Even though their descriptions had yet to make it onto wanted posters, they figured it was just a matter of time. The captain had warned them when they'd left to fetch the explosives.

"There's no telling Braddock hasn't gotten a fix on the explosives," he'd said, cursing the detective. "Keep a sharp eye. Go round the block a couple times before you go for the pickup. The place may be watched." They thought the captain was being overcautious, but it was clear from the report that they'd had from Richmond that caution was wise if they wanted to stay healthy.

The traffic on Canal was heavy this time of day. It was nearly midday and it seemed as if the press of wagons were slowing to a crawl as they converged onto the wide roadway. Once Pat and Jus had the wagon loaded, they were to meet the rest of the men at Jacobs's place. He had the perfect setup. It was a small house in the "flats" of Brooklyn with a tight courtyard and tiny barn behind. Jacobs had the rooms at the back of the first floor. They'd be able to drive their small wagon in off the street and go to work on bundling and wiring charges unseen in the barn.

Sullivan, looking out over the traffic on Canal, turned to Jus and said, "Reckon it might take a bit longer than we thought."

Jus nodded. "Looks like folks're trying to get things done before the holiday."

Pat shrugged and turned to go back up and fetch the last of their load.

. . .

Tom and Eli were on Canal themselves. They had started early at the bridge office and had rushed to the address they'd gotten for Jacobs. Tom wasn't all that surprised when it turned out to be a dead end. Jacobs wasn't there, never had been as far as they could tell from the current occupants of the dingy little tenement on the Bowery. They left the place dragging their heels, even less excited about the drudge work before them. A couple hours later they left the Rendrock Powder Company at a run, feeling very different about their prospects. They hailed a cab immediately and set off as fast as the thing could be made to go. The cabbie whipped his sway-back mare, urging more speed than the poor animal had in her. Tom and Eli held on, leaning forward as they bounced over the cobbles. Rendrock had been their second stop after the fruitless trip to find Jacobs. Tom figured it would be another endless slog through more order books and ledgers. It was anything but. Once they'd introduced themselves to the clerk in the front office and told him about their investigation, they'd been given every assistance. The president of the firm, a man introducing himself as J. C. Rand, had come out of a back office to make sure Tom was given full access to their records.

"We make the finest blasting powder available, Detective, every bit the equal if not better than dynamite, I daresay. Do quite an active business too. With all the construction going on, our Rackarock blasting powder is more in demand than ever. New York island is mostly rock, you know."

Tom asked him if it could be used on steel and iron.

"For demolition purposes, yes . . . I suppose. We mostly supply construction firms, though." Rand was helpful, giving them his order books to pore over. Tom and Eli had settled themselves at a desk in the corner, Tom with an order book, Eli with a ledger.

"Nothing to do but work our way backward, I guess," Jaffey said with a deep breath. The clerk brought them coffee as they started.

The cups were nearly empty and the pages of the records turned back to orders placed weeks before when Braddock suddenly said, "Whoa! What's this?"

Eli craned over to look at what he was pointing to. "So?" Jaffey asked once he'd read the notation.

"So . . . Mr. Bow-tie!" Tom said triumphantly.

"Mr. Who?"

"The clerk, Jacobs. This bill's made out to him!"

"Oh, shit!" Jaffey cursed. "What's the number of that order? I'll find it in the ledger and we'll check the billing address." It took only moments to find that the bill had gone to Sangree & Co. Within minutes they were heading for the warehouse listed on the manifest. They had just passed Christie Street when Sullivan and Lincoln slammed shut the gate on their wagon, pulled the canvas tarp over the load, and headed out into the traffic on Canal.

Minutes later the myopic clerk at the warehouse was frowning at Braddock and Jaffey through thick glasses.

"Jacobs, you said? You mean Sullivan. He's the one signed for 'em." Tom looked puzzled. The cleck clucked. "Just missed 'em. Had a bunch of boxes up on the second floor. Moved them no more'n—"

"How long ago?" Tom almost shouted, interrupting the man in midsentence. "How long, dammit?"

The clerk, so startled his glasses almost fell off his nose, stammered out, "Just a—just a couple min—"

Braddock grabbed the front of the clerk's coat, lifting him so he was on his toes. His mouth formed a big O of surprise under his nose as his feet scrabbled for the floor.

"Which way?" Braddock shouted so close to his face his glasses fogged. A croaking sound from somewhere in the back of the throat was all the clerk managed, but he pointed out toward Canal. Tom said, "West?" The clerk, nodding vigorously, was tossed into a chair, and Braddock was out the door onto the loading dock in seconds. There was another wagon pulling in now and the dispatcher was watching as the driver backed the wagon in. Tom stopped on the loading dock, scanning west down Canal, craning this way and that.

"The wagon that was just here," he said to the dispatcher. "What'd it look like?"

The man looked up from his clipboard and grunted, "Smallish blue affair. One horse. Two men."

Braddock was jumping down from the loading dock before the man was finished, with Jaffey close behind. Tom cast around for a cab but gave it up almost immediately.

"Traffic's too heavy, Eli. Think we'll do better on foot." He didn't wait for a reply, just set off at a jog. Pat and Jus were about to make the turn south onto Centre Street and started to bull their way through the jam of wagons and carriages when a traffic cop held up a white-gloved hand and blew his whistle for them to stop. Sullivan pulled up with a curse under his breath but a smile and a nod to the cop. They were seven blocks ahead of Baddock, but the gap was closing. Tom and Eli were making good time on foot, doing their best to crane over traffic and get a look at the wagons on Canal and each street they passed. They were actually moving faster than traffic, which at most of the intersections was a tangle. As they neared Bowery, Tom spotted a man as he tied his horse to a rail in front of a shabby bar. The door had just closed behind the man as Tom ran up. After running about six blocks by that time, he was about ready for a ride. Looking over his shoulder, he could see that Jaffey looked to be fading too. Tom ran up to the horse, pulled the reins off the rail with a yank, and vaulted into the saddle. The big bay reared a bit at the feel of a strange rider and trumpeted his objection. People nearby turned to see what the commotion was.

"C'mon, Eli, jump up. We'll make better time," he called. Eli had just scrambled up behind Tom when the horse's owner burst out of the saloon, shouting like a madman. Tom tried to make himself heard. He yelled over his shoulder. "Police business! Need your horse! Police business!"

But the shouting man would have none of it. Maybe he was doing too much shouting to hear or maybe he simply didn't speak English, which was entirely possible. Either way, Tom wasn't about to stand around and negotiate. "I'll bring him back," he called as he and Eli rode off.

By then a small crowd had gathered outside the saloon, some of whom joined the din. Shouts of "Horse thieves!" and "Stop!" flew from a dozen throats as they galloped off. Some men from the bar followed on foot, others went for their own horses or wagons. Shouting seemed to follow Tom and Eli as they galloped down Canal.

Pat and Jus had sat impatiently waiting for the cop to let them by but the traffic down Centre Street was pretty heavy too and the cop seemed in no hurry to stop it. At last he did though and they turned left with a flick of the reins that got the light wagon moving smartly. Just as they completed the turn and were about to pass behind the buildings on the south side of Canal, Pat looked back. Whether the hurried movement of a horse and two riders had caught his eye or it was simply a random glance, he couldn't say. At over a block away there was no way he could know it was Braddock. But their speed and the way the man and the rider behind constantly scanned the crowded street convinced him he didn't want to find out. Sullivan turned, shouting to the horse and cracking the reins on his back. The wagon lurched and rumbled over the cobbles as they picked up speed.

"What the fuck're you doin' Pat?" Jus cursed over the noise of the rattling wagon.

Pat cast a worried look over his shoulder. "I think it's Braddock!" He cracked the reins again.

Jus cast an eye over his shoulder too, grabbing the seat with one hand and the butt of his pistol with the other.

Tom and Eli were moving faster but they still needed care to scan the street and intersections as they went. The cries of "Horse thieves!" seemed to follow them like a storm cloud, sometimes even moving ahead of them, so that teamsters and carriage drivers turned back to see them coming. One or two even tried to drive in their way. It was Eli who noticed the wagon turn onto Centre.

"I think I saw them!" he yelled in Tom's ear.

"Where?" Tom shouted back, turning this way and that.

"They made the left down Centre," Eli said, pointing.

Tom kicked the horse's side and urged him into a gallop. It was another block to Centre, and they covered it in no more than twenty seconds, but the cries of "Thieves" went faster, flowing around them. Eli glanced back to see dozens of angry twisted faces shouting in their wake, fists shaking in the air and more riders not far behind. As he turned back he saw the cop at the intersection turn their way, a surprised frown on his face. Tom saw it too.

"Careful" was all he said over his shoulder.

Calls to stop the thieves, the boil of angry pursuers, traffic coming south on Centre, and the lone traffic cop all converged at once on Tom and Eli. Slowing to ride around a wagon in their way driven by a man who had heard the commotion, they were nearly overtaken by the crowd behind. The cop in the intersection was rushing toward them, reaching into his coat as he came. The din was growing and Tom's call of "We're cops!" went unheeded. With both Tom and Eli in plain clothes it wasn't surprising. The pistol came up from the deep blue coat and the cop fired a warning shot that sent their horse rearing in fear, its hooves skidding on the cobbles. Pat and Jus heard the shot behind them, ducking instinctively as they sped away. They didn't look back. Tom and Eli almost went down, and it was all they could do to hold on to the frightened horse.

"Halt!" the cop shouted, bringing the pistol to bear.

Braddock put up his hands, saying with sour resignation "Put up your hands, Eli. No point getting shot." To the cop he said, "We're police, they're getting away!" and he motioned with his head down Centre.

"We'll just see about that," the cop shot back. "Get down off that horse and be quick about it!" Eli started to protest but the cop snarled, "Do it now or so help me I'll blow ye off that animal!"

Tom and Eli watched for an instant as the wagon disappeared down Centre, two hunched figures hanging on as it sped away. It was a long afternoon before things were sorted out. Pat and Jus were safe in Brooklyn by the time Braddock and Jaffey got themselves out of hot water.

It was hours more before Tom had a chance to get back to 300 Mulberry Street. He'd gone back to the bridge office yet again, this time to check out the man named Sullivan. He learned that Sullivan was a rigger, or at least had been. He learned too that he was most often seen in the company of a man named Lincoln.

"That's them, Eli," Tom said. "Knew all along there had to be more in on this."

"Yeah, and now they've got a wagonload of explosives."

"Yeah." Tom's shoulders sagged. The addresses they got for the two proved no more fruitful than the rest. Tom and Eli were beat by the time they got back to headquarters. When he got back to his desk he found a telegram had come from Charles C. Martin that outlined a second bridge inspection he'd carried out at Washington's orders. Not so much as one bolt was out of place. Martin and a small team of engineers and foremen had gone over the bridge from top to bottom just the day before. It was obvious from the tone of the note that the Roeblings were satisfied and would follow Hughes and Martha to Newport. At least that little ruse had gone well; the press had dutifully reported their departure the day after the bridge opened. They'd kept a low profile at the house. As far as anyone knew, they were sunning themselves in Rhode Island. But in two days they would be really leaving; as far as Tom could see, there was no reason to stay. The bridge had been inspected, the bridge police alerted, descriptions of the suspects posted. He'd had a talk with the captain in charge of the bridge police late in the day as well. Tom had tried to convince the man of the need to step up patrols. The captain's overconfident response did nothing for Tom's peace of mind.

"We've got things well in hand here, Detective," the captain had assured him rather smugly. "All due respect to your Chief Byrnes. Got his telegram a while ago," the man said, referring to the message Tom had urged the chief to send. "Don't need you city cops telling me how to run my show. *My* men're keeping a sharp watch. Don't you worry, Braddock. Nobody's blowin' up *my* bridge."

Tom had left, uncertain of how much good he'd done. The bridge wasn't his jurisdiction. The best he could do was make sure they were on alert. The rest was up to them.

It had been a long, long day, made longer by the constant, grinding unease in his gut. Tom kept replaying the chase in his mind, thinking if he'd only been quicker or had made it to the warehouse a few minutes sooner. . . . His thoughts churned into the evening. He ate a late meal with Mary, Mike, and Patricia, hardly hearing the conversation around him. Mike was still bubbling about the circus, and said he couldn't wait to tell his friends. He had brought his box with him when they came to Mary's, and he opened it before them all to show the ticket stubs inside. It reminded Tom of the clipping that still resided in his pocket, now so tattered it was hardly readable. He brought it out, opening it on the kitchen table while the others talked. Bending close, he read it again. The article gave him some small hope. The trains wouldn't be running for maybe two months yet. There was still time. But why then were Sullivan and Lincoln fetching explosives today?

Someone mentioned the bridge, and it brought Tom's attention back to the conversation.

"What?" he asked absently.

"I was saying," Mary said, "that I think it would be wonderful to go out on the bridge tomorrow. I haven't been yet, and I hear it's just fantastic. It will be open to everyone, even the roadways."

"Mmm, yeah, it's nice," Tom murmured.

"And since *you won't take me*," Mary huffed, trying to break through Tom's preoccupation, "I'll just have to go myself, me and Chelsea, that is."

Tom finally got the point. "Oh. . . . yeah. I'm sorry, Mary. You know I'd like to, but this case . . . you know how it's been. And with Pat and Charlie off the case, there's just—"

Mary stopped him with an upheld hand. "Tom. It's okay. I do understand, really. I was just trying to get your attention. You've been like a mad scientist lately, mumbling to yourself, shutting everyone out. You're preoccupied. But I understand, really. I know it's important." She cast a quick glance at Mike and Patricia. "We'll have plenty of time to stroll the bridge when this is all behind us."

Tom smiled, as if seeing the day already. "Have I been mumbling?" he asked with a concerned frown. "I haven't *mumbled*, have I?"

Much later, Tom lay listening to Mary snore lightly. He finally drifted into a fitful, exhausted sleep around 3:00 A.M. The border between the waking world and the dreaming was almost seamless. He was running up the promenade. Mary was there, at the center of the span. She held Mike's hand and they waved to him. It was a sparkling day, the sun pouring down like honey. Crowds jammed the promenade, human cattle. They jabbered and laughed.

He bounced off them and was not noticed. He pushed them and was not rebuked. They existed only to slow him. Mary waved in the golden sunlight. Mike held a flag and waved it too. An impossibly tall Uncle Sam on stilts, a fugitive from the circus, sprouted from the promenade, waving flags in both hands. Suddenly they all had flags, waving them in slow hands.

He needed to get to Mary. It was the most important thing he'd ever do. Her smile, so radiant it shamed the sun, washed over him. It somehow made his fear grow stronger. Looking to his left, he recoiled to see Terrence Bucklin beside him. Bucklin looked at him, his dead eyes imploring. He said nothing—he didn't have to. A flash and a rolling thud, like a drumroll, shook him, rattling the boards of the promenade. The cattle-people gaped. Flags drooped. The bridge dropped in a drunken, sickening swoop. The roadway twisted, the broad ribbon dropped on one side, as the wires snapped and sprang like whips. Mary and Mike were thrown from the bridge, disappearing before his eyes. The world erupted in screams. The cattle stampeded, suddenly swift and wild, clawing, trampling, crushing ... Tom woke, breathing hard, clutching the sheets to steady himself. He wiped the vision from his eyes, his hand coming away damp. It was 4:45 A.M., Memorial Day, 1883. The explosives had been set nearly an hour before.

Everything had gone well at the start. The wagon and carriage were loaded, the carriage taken across on the ferry with the captain, Matt, and Justice. The wagon with Jacobs, Sullivan, and Lebeau waited on Park Row, just across from the *Tribune*. They kept careful watch, but they knew well enough when to set off. They were set to go at two-thirty, or whenever the patrol was seen clearing the landward side of the tower. At two-twenty-four, the cop was spotted heading down the promenade back toward New York. Jacobs clicked to his team, snapping the reins on the horses' backs. After paying the dime toll, he urged his team into a trot up the gentle slope. They were the only vehicle on the bridge, and the cop glanced at them idly as they passed. The noise of the team's hooves on the wood-block roadbed echoed in the dark. One carriage was seen to go in the opposite direction, disappearing toward New York, but that was all. Within two minutes, they had reached center span. Forty seconds after that, after working like madmen, their cargo was sitting on the railroad tracks and Jacobs was clicking his team into motion. As he left, the carriage pulled to a stop on the opposite roadway. In an even shorter time, it was empty and on its way.

Like the well-trained soldiers they were, the four sprang to their assignments. Pat and Justice strapped on packs and climbed up the trusses onto the empty promenade. Within another two minutes they had climbed their assigned cables far enough so they were out of the lamps' glow. By the time Pat reached the top, he was breathing hard. He and Jus had trained for this, so he wasn't winded. Pat took off his pack, heavy with Rendrock explosives, blasting caps, and wire. After tying the pack to the main cable handrail, he went to work. In preparation for this part of the assignment, he and Justice had tied charges together, so they'd be easier to attach to the big bar where the stays were anchored. He pulled the explosives out of his pack in bundles of three, with coiled strands of wire hanging from each. One end of the wire had wrapped the charges, the hanging coil Pat would use to wrap around the bar, and tie the charges in place. Though Matt and Earl were using big slabs of clay to hold their charges in place, Pat and Jus didn't feel it was right for the stays. They worked with silent efficiency. Within fifteen minutes they had set their explosives in place, wrapping the extra wire around and around the bar, just where the stays were attached. Bundles of three sticks each were tied behind the bar, wedged between the stone of the tower and the ends of the stays. Others were fitted between the stays where they radiated out from the anchoring bar. Pat started on the upper stays without pausing. Lying on his belly on the big main cable, he packed his explosives in around the stay-cables, being sure to leave his leads hanging clear. Pat had thought it all through, doing the work as though his life depended on it. Every connection was tight and clean. He ran his lead wire down the main cable handrail, looping it as he went, to a point about eight feet above the promenade. From there he took the wire down one of the supports for the wire handrails and under the main cable. From that point, it traveled down one of the suspenders. They had taken the precaution of dipping their spools of wire in the paint used on the bridge. It had been easy to steal a half-used can. The wire was nearly invisible.

He ran back to center span, playing out wire as he went. Justice wasn't far behind. They met at the middle, sweating and out of breath.

"Everything set, partner?"

"Good as it's ever gonna get, Pat. Worry how it'll look in daylight though. You think someone might notice the charges?"

Pat glanced up. Even though he knew they were there, it was impossible to distinguish in the dark. "Don't think so, Jus." Pat played out a bit more wire, then snipped it clean. "Same color as the bridge. From this distance . . . don't think anyone could tell."

Lincoln shrugged. "Suppose. Can't do nothin' about it anyway," he said, taking a deep breath. "Ready to do the other stays?"

As the two had clambered down the trusses to the train tracks, they heard voices from off toward the New York tower. Dropping down, they called softly to Matt and Earl, who were about twenty feet to either side of them, setting charges on the roadway beams.

"Get back under the promenade, someone's comin'," Pat called in a hoarse whisper. Silently each man slipped like a ghost beneath the cover of the promenade. They balanced on the roadway beams, nine and five-eighths inches wide and with nothing but air to the river.

Voices approached above their heads. Footsteps rattled and squeaked the decking. They were drunk, whoever they were. The talk was loud and boisterous. The footsteps pounded in uneven staggers.

"You'd break yer neck, you fuckin' fool!" one voice said.

"That's for damn sure, Bob. You wouldn't be sayin' that if not for the pints. If the fall didn't kill ye, the water, an' the currents would."

"Ach! This fuckin' bridge ain't so high. Could be done, I tell yez. The man what does it's gonna be famous too . . . mark me words."

"Sure that's the beer talkin', Odlum. Ye're a crazy bastard, but not that crazy."

"Nah, Gil, here's how I'd do it . . ." the one called Odlum said as they passed out of earshot.

They all looked at Sullivan for the okay to get moving again.

"Ain't enough money in the whole damn city could make me jump off here," Jus said, looking down at the oily black water.

They'd lost valuable time and were behind schedule now by at least five minutes. After checking for traffic on the roadway and promenade, Pat and Justice sprinted across and scrambled up the upstream cables as far as they could. Again they swung down from the main cable, close to the granite of the tower and down the bar, where the stays were anchored. They worked steadily, the height and their precarious positions not hampering them as much as the darkness. Up there the lights from the promenade below cast only a feeble glow. It was like flying among the stars. Pat had to stop for a moment to savor the feeling. It would be his last time in the cables, just as it was his first time up there at night. The stars were bright in the blue-black sky. He craned his neck, scanning the heavens. The stars wheeled above his head. Could God somehow see what he was about? He believed it was so. The heavens seemed hopelessly cold and lonely without that small comfort. He hoped that God could see the choice he'd made.

Jacobs looked at his watch for the sixth or seventh time. It was almost three.

"Just about the halfway point," he whispered to his idle team. He stretched his shoulders to ease the muscles in his back, groaning in the process. "Little bastards," he cursed. He was so sore he could hardly move, and he had so many small cuts on him his shirt looked polka-dotted with blood. The bruise on his back was the size of a melon, and he'd been pissing blood since last night. He grumbled to himself once more, then glanced at the bridge and was astonished to see a cop, striding up the approach, heading toward New York.

"Christ!" He whipped his team, setting them off at almost a run. He slowed and flipped his toll to the sleepy-eyed collector, slapping the reins, urging the team on. He passed the cop just before the Brooklyn tower and tried to get as much speed as he could without being too conspicuous. "Shit! Not supposed to be a patrol for another thirty minutes!" Jacobs pulled into the left lane, closest to the trusses over the train tracks. They blocked the view from the promenade at that angle. As he neared the center, he slowed to nearly a stop. At first he couldn't see anyone, but he whistled and Matt's and Earl's hands popped up from behind the upstream main cable. Jacobs pointed back toward Brooklyn and called "Cop!" then drove off.

Matt Emmons and Earl Lebeau had been working faster than they had anticipated. Using clay to anchor the charges was working better than they had hoped. They had their charges set and wired on all thirteen beams on the upstream center cable before Pat and Jus were down from the stays. They moved over to the upstream cable after the drunks had passed but found that to be slower work. They had to work hanging on to the outside of the roadway railing, using whatever handholds they could find on the cable and beams. They started to fall behind immediately. Matt was more terrified than he'd ever been. Not even the caisson scared him so much as clinging like a fly to the edge of the bridge at night. A ship hissed by below him, its side wheels churning the black waters into a milky gray wake. He looked down at it and was almost sick. He reeled and clutched at the cable, holding on till his panic passed. He and Earl worked their way slowly toward the middle. They had to keep climbing back over the side to get more explosives and clay.

Earl and Matt had just run back with a third sackful when they heard the wagon coming at a run. Not knowing who it was, they ducked down behind the cable to wait. The whistled signal brought them up like gophers from their holes. They couldn't see the cop but there was no doubt he was coming. Earl saw Matt looking at him questioningly. To stay put, or risk a run across the roadway to the cover of the promenade? Earl figured it was better to stay put, as uncomfortable as it was. The main cable concealed them pretty well, and they could actually sit on the very end of the beams until the cop was gone. It seemed the better choice. He held his hand out, palm down motioning Matt to stay put.

The cop was taking his time. It was another couple of minutes till he reached center span. Instead of walking on, through, he stopped, leaning on the rail of the promenade. They could hear the striking of a match in the silence above the river. Maybe that's why the cop loitered there. The view at night was magical. Waiting for the cop to leave, Matt hung on, his fingers stiffening, muscles aching. While the cop smoked, Earl and Matt sat, feet swinging loose over the river. Not more than twenty feet separated them. Up in the tops of the main cables, cloaked in woolly blackness, Pat on one side, Justice on the other, lay flat on the cables, reducing their profile as much as possible. Neither of them moved a muscle. Even the mask of the night wouldn't hide movement, so they did their best to become part of the bridge.

Matt was almost afraid to breath at first, but the longer the cop smoked, the more at ease he became. The trouble was that his hands were cramping and his feet were going numb. The hard edges of the beam he sat on were cutting off circulation. The constant grip he had to maintain had his hands burning. His seat on the edge of the beam was so precarious that he had to lean back just a bit to stay on it. The minutes crawled by and his panic slowly increased as his grip weakened. To distract himself, Matt hummed old tunes, barely audible even to himself. Tunes from around the campfires of the war and from the long marches all chorused inside his head. He needed to do something to get his mind off his predicament. He hummed softly, desperate for relief. He hummed "Lorena."

It was another couple of minutes before the cop continued his stroll toward New York. He went so slowly though, that it was more tortuous minutes before he reached and passed the New York tower. Earl scrambled up first, shaking the blood back into his cramped muscles. He walked unsteadily down the roadway toward Matt's hiding place, wincing at each step on his pins-and-needles feet.

"Shit, Matthew—thought that bastard was gonna camp out all fuckin' night!"

"Ooh, Christ . . . I'm stiff." Matt groaned.

"Need a hand?" Earl offered.

"I guess. Not sure I can get up. I'm all cramped up in my hands . . . legs are numb too."

"Hold on," Earl said, hearing the scare in Matt's voice. "Wait till I get a grip on ye." Earl hung over the big cable and reached down for his hand. Matt put one foot on the lower lip of the beam and started to stand. His legs felt dead. He couldn't feel his feet at all. "Give me yer hand, partner." Matt reached but as he did, his sleeping foot slipped from the lip of the beam. He went down hard on the steel edge, then off, into space. The one hand he still had a grip with couldn't withstand the jolt. Earl stood frozen, transfixed by Matt's eyes. They stared, wide as they would go, black holes surrounded by white. It was only for an instant, but Matt's eyes spoke of an eternity of terror. His hands, thrown out to Earl as if throwing a lifeline, couldn't span the widening gap. Earl watched as, in a flash, terror turned to resignation. Falling back into the blackness above the East River, Matt Emmons disappeared. Earl stared in disbelief. Matt had not screamed, as another man might. He made no sound at all, save the distant splash of black Yankee waters. Pat and Jus came running a second later. They had scrambled down too when the cop passed out of sight.

"Oh, Christ! Oh sweet Jesus, Pat," Earl cried. "He was right here, he was right here. I had 'im, I was lookin' right at 'im, he was giving me his hand. Oh, Christ! We got to do somethin'." Earl moaned, hopping from one foot to the other. "We got to get 'im, oh sweet Lord!"

"Jesus! He went without a sound," Jus said, looking over the side. A slight grayish-white foam was all there was to see on the smooth black surface. "He's gone, boys. Just gone."

"Don't we got to find him?" Earl said, looking from Pat to Jus. "We got to, right? He might be alive, he might—" Earl put his head in his hands, his fingers spread out through his wild hair as if to hold his head on. "I almost had 'im too." Earl said, reaching his hands out with his fingers spread. "He was just reachin' up when he slipped. Oh, God, I saw 'im go! I saw his eyes." He covered his own to block out the vision. "I looked right at 'im."

"Earl, there isn't a damn thing we can do. He's gone," Pat said softly, putting his arm around Earl's shoulders. "Damned if he didn't go like a soldier too!" Pat was amazed.

"Fuckin' right!" Jus said, the admiration clear in his voice. "Kept his tongue for fear of giving us away. *Jesus, that took sand!*"

"He . . . set us an example," Pat said softly. "After what he did, we can't quit. Got to finish." With a last look over the side, Sullivan said softly, "Let's get moving."

"Time for grief later," Justice added solemnly, suppressing the chill that went through him.

Pat turned and headed back up the cable. He had almost been done when Matt fell. He needed to wire three more sticks then run his lead down the cable. That took another few minutes. They weren't good minutes. He found himself clinging tighter. There was a tremor in his hands that he could not command. Within ten minutes he and Justice were done and helping Earl finish the charges on the roadway beams. Once they had been wired, there was one task left. Earl took the spool of wire, which tied in to all the charges on the upriver side, and hooked it to a long, bent wire hook attached to his belt. It was designed so the spool could unwind by itself as Earl made his way across on one of the beams beneath the roadway.

"You ready?" Pat asked, looking closely at him.

Earl, who had been silent as the grave once he had gotten control of himself, took a couple of deep breaths and flexed his hands before saying "Yup."

Without another word, he went over the side, climbed down under the roadway, and disappeared. His feet were the last to go. He had them hooked on either side of the beam as he went across, hand over hand. Pat and Jus ran over to the other side, waiting by the beam, bent low, ready to grab Earl when he came back into sight. Carriages went by, but in the shadow of the promenade, the men weren't seen. A second later they heard Earl, grunting with the effort as he neared them.

"Give me a hand. I'm 'bout played out." He panted. They reached and grabbed him by his shirt, one on either side, holding on as he carefully pulled himself atop the exposed beam. He lay there hugging it, breathing hard and staring down at the river. "Christ!" He gasped. "Christ!"

They finished the final wiring about ten minutes later, tying their leads into the main wire coming from the dynamo room. Pat was to be the last to go. The plan was to simply walk off the bridge one by one once they were done. Earl had gone first. He disappeared toward New York, vanishing like a ghost in the gloom.

"Can't believe Matt's gone," Jus said as he and Pat waited for Earl to drop out of sight.

"In all the years in the cables . . . not one man fell," Pat said almost to himself. "Now here *we* are . . . and we lose a man within an hour." He shook his head slowly.

"He slipped," Justice said to the unasked question.

Pat didn't say anything. He looked at his watch. "Well . . . Earl's been gone five minutes. Guess you better get along."

Patrick Sullivan sat on the top of the truss that formed the railing of the promenade, watching his old confederate go marching down the slope to the city of the Yankees. This would be their last march. Watkins was gone. Now Emmons wouldn't walk away either. Pat wondered how many might die tomorrow. He looked up to the circle of stars, like a crown to the bridge. He had helped build this thing. Was this how God felt in creation? Did the Almighty somehow share his pride? He thought that maybe it was so. It was like a living thing, this bridge. He could feel its vibrating heart through the cables. He wouldn't have a hand in killing it.

He couldn't thwart the others, but he'd take no hand in it himself. Justice felt the same, he knew. He'd said as much. Pat checked to see that Jus had disappeared beyond the New York tower, then turned, his pocketknife in his hand. He'd have to be careful how he cut Jus's wires. It would be bad if it was discovered tomorrow. Maybe with the stays in place, the bridge wouldn't fall. Pat was leaning over the truss, reaching under to cut the wires, his knife poised when he heard the creaking of promenade boards behind him.

"Just what the *hell* are *you* about, if I might ask?" a voice boomed in the dark, startling him with its closeness. Pat didn't need to look around to see it was a cop. He'd been so intent on watching Jus walk off and then feeling for the wires, he hadn't checked to see if anyone was coming from the Brooklyn side. He stayed for an instant, doubled over the truss, his face fairly hidden as he slipped his knife up one sleeve and tried to think of what to do.

"*Speak up, man!* What were you doing there? You sick or something?" the cop demanded.

Pat's mind, which had been racing to find a way out, latched onto the phrase as if it were a life preserver. He groaned in the dark, hoping it sounded sick enough. The prod of a nightstick in the ribs was his reward.

"Eh . . . what's that?" the cop asked, clearly not satisfied. "You're not sick," he said skeptically. "What were you doing there?"

Obviously they were on alert, Pat thought. Playing sick wasn't going to be enough. He felt the knife in his sleeve but held that back as a last resort. A heavy hand slapped onto his shoulder, trying to spin him around. His panic doubled . . . tripled in the night. Turning away so his face wasn't seen, he rammed a finger down his throat as far as it would go. It was magic.

With a spasmodic heave his stomach emptied itself over the side of the trusswork, covering the wires underneath, where he'd tried to cut them. He turned toward the cop, vomiting on his shoes and himself too.

The cop jumped back as if scalded. "*For the love o'—*" he shouted as Pat staggered toward him, holding his gut with both hands. "Get the fuck—" the cop held out a hand to stop him from getting any closer. A second heave splattered on the promenade. "*Christ! Goddamn drunken bastard. Get the fuck off the bridge!*"

Pat waved his hands apologetically. "Sorry. *Really* . . . sorry, Officer," he said, holding back a third retch.

"Yeah, just get the hell out of here," the cop said, stamping the vomit off his shoes. "Go back to the Bowery where your kind belongs."

Pat staggered a little more, still holding his gut.

"Go on. *Git!*" the cop shouted, prodding him again with his nightstick from long distance.

Sullivan apologized again, then turned, weaving his way down the promenade to freedom.

✹ Chapter Twenty-two ✺

And I a missile steeped in hate,
Hurled forward like a cannon-ball,
By the resistless hand of fate,
Rushed wildly, madly through it all.

—MAURICE THOMPSON

May 31, 1883, 5:30 A.M.

Tom stood before the door to Sangree & Co. The dream still lingered, the horror still strong like a smell he couldn't get out of his clothes. He had gotten up, needing to do something, hoping that by activity he could put his demons to rest. He had to go over the office once more. Actually, he'd taken the El south at about 5:00 A.M. with little notion of what he would do, just an idea that he needed to do . . . something. He'd ended up going to Peck Slip first, where he stood for some time in front of Paddy's, while the street came to life. Perhaps by going back to the beginning he could raise old ghosts or come up with new ideas. He wasn't sure. It hadn't taken long to get himself moving in the direction of Sangree & Co. He'd see what there was to be seen once more, he thought as he looked at the frosted glass of the front door. Then he'd go to work over at the bridge offices. He had to be missing something. These men couldn't be that good. Pat and Charlie had gone over this place before, and they were as thorough as any men he knew . . . but.

"What the hell," Tom muttered, and kicked in the door with a tremendous crash of splintering wood and shattering glass. He didn't feel like going to fetch keys.

He stood in the doorway for a moment, surveying the place. There wasn't much to survey: A big roll-top desk in one corner, a couple of chairs, a coat rack, a shabby rug, and a couple of ordinary-looking framed prints hanging on the walls outfitted the front room. Everything was shrouded and indistinct in the early morning light, giving the place a dreamlike quality. He took a deep breath and stepped into the dream—or was it the nightmare? This place seemed home of the nightmare. Things were planned and done here that he could only imagine. If such plans left a residue, some lingering trace of negative energy, they'd be here. Sangree planned right in this room, a room that echoed with the crunch of Tom's feet on the door's broken glass. There had to be something left, some lingering trace of insanity from thoughts and plans like that. He started to search.

It was dawn when Tom quit his search of the office and started on the meeting room behind. The desk had yielded nothing but a few pencils and an ink bottle, half empty. He'd even take the prints from their frames, hoping for some hidden information. He'd been disappointed. The meeting room showed even less promise. Its only contents were a table, maybe six feet long, and eight mismatched chairs. The sun slanted through the dirty windows, throwing a bright slash of color across the dim, gray room. Tom went about moving chairs and checking under everything. A look under the table revealed that there was a drawer on both ends. Tom's hopes rose for an instant, but there was nothing in one drawer and only a blank pad in the other. He flipped through the empty pages. They seemed to laugh at him as they fluttered in his hand. He tossed it on the table in disgust, raising a golden dust storm in the yellow slanting light. Tom watched, momentarily fascinated, as the dust drifted and swirled on invisible currents of air. Interesting, he thought . . . how a thing sometimes doesn't have to be seen to know it's there.

Tom looked at the pad, shining with the reflected light of dawn. Perhaps it was the angle of the sun, perhaps he was just ready to see what had always been there, but he saw the writing now, or at least its ghost. He picked the pad up again, turning it this way and that, angling it to the light to highlight the faint impressions on the paper. There seemed to be multiple impressions, one overlaying the other. He thought he could make out a word or two but wasn't certain. Tom went back to the front office and looked for one of the pencils he'd pulled from the desk. Softly he lay the pencil on edge and drew it back and forth across the page, highlighting the words. There was a lot he couldn't make out but some that he could. Most of it was disjointed: a word here and there and a jumble in between. But the words that stood out were like gold to him nonetheless. One word seemed to shine brighter than the rest: "dynamos."

Within twenty minutes, Braddock was bounding up the front steps of police headquarters. He noticed the large yellow envelope on his desk from across the room. It must have been dropped there late yesterday.

"Hmm, could be your Uncle Sam finally came through with those service records, Tommy boy," he said softly to himself. He'd guessed right. They were copied in a fine hand, in neat columns, with headings for date of enlistment, deaths, missing in action, capture, wounds, release from service, and date of parole. There were a number of pages. The writing was small and tight. It looked like it might be a long read.

The first name to catch his eye was Thaddeus Sangree, which was no particular surprise.

"The goddamn captain of the whole bunch!" he exclaimed, realizing for the first time just how far in the past these men had been bound together. A minute later he burst out "Fuck! That little clerk too!" A couple of the men looked over as he pounded his fist on the desk. "Son of a bitch! Been with 'em since the beginning," he said to the papers. One thing was sure: He'd have to check these names against the list of bridge employees. There was no telling how many others there might be. He knew of six now, but there could easily be twice that.

By seven-thirty he'd rounded up Pat Dolan and Charlie Heidelberg, after telling Byrnes what he'd found. After his close call at capturing the two with the explosives, one of which was certainly Patrick Sullivan, Byrnes was taking the case more seriously. Tom told Byrnes too about the attempts on Mike Bucklin's life and the pad he'd found in Sangree & Co.

"Chief, what I'm afraid of is that maybe they've moved up their timetable."

Byrnes nodded, stroking his mustache.

"We've got them on the move, sir. They've had to pack up and clear out. They're in hiding. They wouldn't be acting that way if they were confident."

"Agree with you there," the chief muttered.

"Remember," Tom went on, "symbolism is extremely important to them. Why else choose the bridge?" He paused to let that sink in. "Chief, I think they're going to try and blow the bridge soon, regardless of what that clipping seems to indicate." Byrnes didn't say anything at first. Tom sat silent while the cigar smoke swirled from Byrnes's first of the day. The chief got up from his desk and paced by the windows, his hands behind his back.

He turned to Tom after a minute.

"Take Pat and Charlie. I'll send word to the bridge police to render whatever assistance you need. And take Jaffey with you too." Eli was chatting with Pat and Charlie when Tom came out of Byrnes' office. They could see right away that something was up.

"Let's go, gentlemen," Tom said. "Pat . . . Charlie, you're assigned to me again today. Any of you know anything about electricity?"

"Yeah," Charlie said. "Ben Franklin discovered it."

"Great," Tom said over his shoulder as they followed him out. "Ever consider vaudeville?"

The four set about skimming the employee list for matches with the service records of Company B, Fifth Texas. The lists of employees went on for pages. The clerk who'd let them in said he guessed over two thousand or more had worked on the bridge over the years.

"Christ," Jaffey grumbled, "we're going to go blind looking through all this."

"Don't have to really, Eli. We know that Matt and Earl were on the job until recently. Maybe there were others in the group that we never even guessed at. They could have just left, like Jacobs, for all we know. Any way to narrow this list down to the most recent employees?" he asked.

"As a matter of fact," the clerk said, "Maybe the best place to start would be the list of men who were paid off and let go earlier this week."

"Think we ought to take a peek at that, eh, Eli?"

Within two minutes the policeman had confirmed Patrick Sullivan and Justice Lincoln. Tom dispatched Pat and Charlie to check out their addresses. telling them to rendezvous later, out on the bridge. He had little hope of their finding anything, but it had to be done.

Tom was on edge. He needed to be out on the bridge, not cooped up in an office, looking over lists. They agreed to meet in a couple of hours. First Tom and Eli checked with the cop on duty in the New York terminal. He had only come on duty at six and said everything had been normal this morning. Looking at the night log, he said "Nothing much last night. Some drunk puked on Bob Brenner, but that's it." Tom made sure the cop had the sketches of Earl, Matt, the captain, and Jacobs. He knew the chance of him spotting any of them was slim, but it was worth a shot. They headed back toward Brooklyn then. The cop had said they'd find his sergeant in the terminal there, and he had the keys to the power plant, generator, and dynamo room.

It was well after nine by the time they found the sergeant and convinced him that he needed to give them the keys to the engine room and the power plant. Even though he'd seen the telegram from Byrnes, he hadn't been easy to convince.

"Listen 'ere," he said at one point. "Me men been patrolin' night an' day. We stepped up the schedule. Mr. Martin, 'e insisted on it. Nothin's goin' on 'ere me or me men' aven't seen nor won't see. Don' see why you boys snoopin' about is goin' to do any more'n we been doin' all along." Eventually the Sergeant gave them the keys but sent a patrolman along to keep an eye on things. The cop, Dan Monzet, was as new as all the rest of the bridge force, but he'd at least had some experience. He'd been a cop before, working way out on Coney Island, but it was too dull for him in the winter, he said.

"When I heard they were looking for men here on the bridge, I figured it would be a little more interesting than Coney Island in January. Well, here we are," he announced. They stood before one of the huge arches, under the Brooklyn approach, near Prospect Street. "This building here's the power plant. The boilers are in there." He pointed to the building beside the approach. "The engine room's through there." He motioned to a heavy door in the brick wall under one arch. "That's where the steam engines are." Monzet opened the door. "Nobody's here this time of day. They come in around four and get up steam in the boilers," he said over his shoulder.

Tom looked around the big, vaulted room. Ten-foot-tall cast-iron wheels, with yard-wide belts running round them, dominated one side. Wires, levers, and a dozen different contraptions gave the place the look of a mad scientist's lab. He could imagine Dr. Frankenstein feeling right at home. He suppressed a shiver; the feeling of menace seemed stronger here.

Tom didn't have a clue what he was looking at, let alone what exactly he was looking for. He turned to Jaffey. "Any guesses where we should start?"

"Not me, Tom. Electricity gives me the willies. I don't understand it, to tell the truth."

"Well, let's look around anyway. Obviously there's no goddamn anarchists in here, but let's see what we can see." Even if they had thought to look in the junction box on the wall, they never would have spotted the extra wires or known their real purpose. They checked through the engine room too. The two massive steam engines sat silent, their pistons seemingly caught in mid-stroke. Each was attached to a cast-iron wheel that Tom guessed had to be about twelve feet in diameter, with spokes as thick as his leg. They drove the cable that would pull the trains.

"Tom, this is all very interesting, but there's nobody here." Eli stated the obvious with a shrug.

"We don't know what the hell we're looking at anyway." Tom sighed his agreement. "There's one thing we can do though." He turned to the cop. When Tom and Eli trooped off, Officer Dan Monzet stood guard at the engine room door.

With Officer Monzet on guard, Tom felt a bit more secure. He didn't know how much use he'd be against the likes of these men, but at least he was a deterrent. They set out to go back over the bridge once again. Tom figured the more they were out on it, the better. They had walked slowly over to the New York side, where they carefully watched the strollers and sightseers parade by.

There were thousands, and after a while the faces started to blur as their concentration slipped.

"Sure would be a good day for sabotage," Eli observed. "As if there was ever a *good* day for such."

"Yeah," Tom agreed. "Memorial Day's a big enough holiday as it is, but this bridge is like a magnet. Looks like half the damn city's here." He wondered if he'd see Mary. He half hoped he would, half hoped he wouldn't. He didn't have a good feeling about this and preferred that she kept away. But he couldn't keep her from it on a hunch, not even a nightmare. He didn't tell her about that; he'd have felt silly for using that as a reason.

"How many died in the war, Tom?" Eli asked.

"What?" Tom replied, confused at the change of topic.

"That's what Memorial Day's all about, right, remembering the dead, I mean? So, I was just asking how many died."

"I've heard some numbers around maybe six hundred thousand, that's North *and South*, you under . . . —*Oh, Christ!*" Tom looked puzzled, then panic-stricken.

Jaffey watched, unable to understand what had come over Braddock. "What? What is it?"

Tom didn't answer. He fumbled in his pocket, his hand shaking in his haste to remove the clipping.

"Shit!" Tom cursed as the paper tore. "I hope to hell I'm wrong about this, Eli." He laid the pieces out on the railing to the promenade, the corners blowing in the wind.

"We've been thinking all along it was the trains they were after, but *look!*" Tom pointed to the page. It was the opposite side of the clipping, the side that had the article about Memorial Day festivities. "What if *this* was what Bucklin was trying to tell us?"

A strong chill went through Jaffey. He opened his mouth, but nothing came out. Finally he exclaimed, "The explosives!"

Tom's first thought was of Mary. She had to be stopped. He didn't want her anywhere near the bridge today. He thought to send a telegram, but on a holiday it might take hours to reach her. He couldn't go himself.

"Eli," he said, turning a worried countenance to Jaffey, "I need you to do me a favor."

Dolan and Heidelberg found Tom about an hour later. They'd come up empty, as Tom had expected. If they had ever lived at either of the listed addresses, they were long gone. Tom told Pat and Charlie what he suspected about Memorial Day. He had just finished when Jaffey came trotting up.

"She wasn't there," he said breathlessly. "The Bucklins said she'd left maybe an hour before. Chelsea's with her."

"Great! They've got to be out here somewhere," Tom said, looking around at the constantly changing crowd. "God, I hope I'm wrong about this!" Images of his nightmare flickered in Tom's head, sending jolts of fear through him in sickening waves.

The four of them started back across the bridge, Tom asking Pat and Charlie to check work assignments. There might be a clue in the kind of work Sangree's men were doing, especially Sullivan and Lincoln, about whom they knew very little. Grumbling about paper trails and going blind, Charlie and Pat set sail for the bridge offices.

"Me and Eli'll be on the span, fellas," Tom said, more worried about finding Mary than he was about the bridge. He kept his hands in his pockets, lest he show the others how they shook. "Let's try the downstream roadway this time, eh, Eli?"

The four parted ways, arranging to meet around three-thirty near the Brooklyn terminal. Tom and Eli sliced through the crowds like sharks, their senses on full alert. They came across two bridge cops and made sure they had descriptions of the conspirators and of Mary as well.

"Keep a sharp eye," Tom said. It was as much a plea as an order. At just about that time Mary was up on the promenade, enjoying the sunshine with Chelsea, and wishing it was Tom who was by her side.

The men were ready to go. This part of the operation was easy compared to last night. They would get into position, check to see that they were positioned where they could signal one another, while waiting for the assigned hour. The captain planned on 4:00 P.M. He estimated that late afternoon would be most crowded, and he hoped there might be as many as ten or fifteen thousand out enjoying the Eighth Wonder. Since it had opened the week before, it had already become quite an attraction. Just last Sunday there had been 163,500 strollers during the day. Ten or fifteen thousand at any one time was conservative by those standards.

It was two-thirty when they got to the New York side. It was a good thing they had been so careful with the wiring and explosives. From the roadway they'd be easier to spot, even though the inner cable was blocked partially from view by the train tracks and its trusses. Still, it appeared as if most people were on the promenade. As they approached the bridge, Pat said, "I think we ought to have a quick change of plans, Captain."

Thaddeus looked at him as if he'd lost his mind. "Why, what's wrong?" he said in a panicky voice.

Sullivan shrugged. "Look at those crowds," he said, pointing. "We need to allow more time for Jus and me to get off. Five minutes after the signal ain't gonna do it."

Thaddeus nodded thoughtfully. "What do you think? Ten?"

"That's safer. I don't know about Justice here, but I don't fancy being caught out there when it goes up." Pat prayed he'd be able to do today what he hadn't been able to accomplish last night, but he couldn't be sure.

"Done. Ten minutes then. You men get moving. Earl and Justice on the promenade, Pat on the roadway, just as we practiced. We'll coordinate signals at precisely three-thirty. Let's synchronize watches. I have exactly two-forty-seven . . . mark!" They all set their watches together. "Get moving and good luck, gentlemen." Thaddeus shook hands all around. "I'll see you in Richmond." There was an unreality to their parting as if there should be something more. Instead there was an awkward silence, as they blinked at each other in the Memorial Day sun. Sullivan, Sangree, and Jacobs set off up the roadway on the upriver side. Braddock and Jaffey, patrolling the downriver side, never saw them.

Officer Dan Monzet was about as bored as he'd ever been. At least when he'd patrolled on Coney Island, there had been summers filled with beautiful women to ogle. After guarding the doors for hours he was thinking that even in January, Coney Island weather was not so bad. He didn't think much of anything as the two men approached him. The short weaselly-looking fella was probably a clerk, he figured, though he wondered at his bruises and limping walk. Maybe they were from the U.S. Illuminating Company, here to run some inspection or other.

"Afternoon, gentlemen," Monzet said, friendlylike.

"Good afternoon, Officer," the bigger one said. He seemed surprised to see him, Monzet thought. If he'd been more alert, that might have put him on guard but he simply asked, "How can I help you?"

"We're from the U.S. Illuminating Company, Officer," Thaddeus said with a worried look. "Why are you guarding these doors? No guard has been placed on them before."

"Oh, some nonsense about saboteurs. Haven't seen one all day," Dan said, smiling.

Jacobs and the captain smiled with him.

Jacobs went on in his best official manner. "So, could you let us in then?

We've got instruments to check." Monzet turned toward the door, fumbling with the keys in his pocket. "I'll need to see some identification, gentlemen," he said as he put the key in the lock.

"Of course, Officer," Jacobs said. "I have it right here."

Dan Monzet threw open the heavy door and turned to check their credentials. As he faced them, though, a curious thing happened. The little man before him struck him in the throat. At first he thought it had to be some mistake, some accident. Monzet looked quizzically at the little man, confused more than hurt. Then, quick as a snake, the little bastard did it again. It wasn't till the second time that Monzet saw the blade in his hand, red with his own blood. He tried to cry out, but his voice just gurgled and whistled through the holes in his throat. There seemed to be a great deal of blood too, and it was making a hell of a mess of his new tunic. To Monzet's credit, he managed to get his pistol out of its holster. Brooklyn was starting to spin by then, though, and all he managed to do was shoot himself in the knee.

Oh, Christ! he thought as he fell. Now look what I've done.

Shut the door. Hurry," the captain rasped.

Jacobs kicked at Monzet's feet, then hit them with the door.

"Pull him in more, Captain."

Thaddeus did, dragging Monzet by the tunic collar. They slammed and locked the door a moment later, then went to the window, looking out for signs of alarm. There didn't seem to be any. The pistol hadn't made much noise. On this side of the bridge there were mostly warehouses, closed for the holiday.

"Excellent. No one seems to have noticed," Thaddeus said.

"Excepting him," Jacobs said with a jerk of his head toward Officer Monzet, whose breathing was getting shallower by the second.

"That worries me, Bart," the captain said, looking down at the officer.

"Exactly." Jacobs glared over his glasses at the body. "Whoever posted him here is bound to be back."

"We'll deal with that problem as it arises," Thaddeus said, getting moving. "Let's get set up. I want to be able to blow it at a moment's notice."

They set to work quickly, setting up their wiring and generator. Within five minutes they were wired in to the main lines to the charges, the wires screwed tight to the terminals of their portable dynamo.

"Ready, Captain!" Jacobs called out when he finished.

"Ready here too, Bart. What time you have?"

"Three-twenty-one, Captain. We check signals in nine."

"They can't stop us, Bart," the captain intoned solemnly. "Not now!"

Sullivan was amazed by the crowds. He'd never seen anything like it. They had waited about fifteen minutes after the captain and Bart had set off, not wanting to bunch up and attract attention. The promenade was packed shoulder to shoulder. He was happy to be down on the roadway. Traffic was light, consisting mainly of carriages. The holiday kept the freight traffic down to almost nothing. He looked at his watch again. They had time. He was keeping pace with Justice and Earl up on the promenade. He could see them occasionally through the top hats, parasols, bowlers, bonnets, and skimmers. It was a lively, happy crowd despite the crush. The beauty of the day only added to the general feeling of celebration. The novelty of the bridge hadn't worn off yet. It was truly the Eighth Wonder of the World. People wanted to see it, marvel at its monumental architecture, and most of all just be on it.

The thing that disturbed Patrick was the women and children. There were hundreds of children. Their parents, for the most part, held onto them tightly for fear of losing them. Still, some ran free, giggling and laughing. They pointed with delight at the boats, like so many toys in a bathtub, at the gulls that flew about them, at the people on shore, so small and antlike. Children were freest to express the wonder of being out on the bridge. In them Patrick could see the uninhibited joy, the exhilaration, and freedom of it. Somehow the reality of their plan hadn't fully struck home until now. Last night he'd tried to cut the wires for the love of the bridge, the thing he'd given more of his life to than anything before. That was all about him, though, him and Jus. He realized now that that was only part of it. It was about parasols in the sun and laughing, delighted children. It was about parents holding their children's hands and strolling out to see the city from a place no one had seen it from before. It was about rising above the teeming confines of the city and feeling for just a while like a king.

Sullivan looked over at Justice. He caught a glimpse of him through the crowds, moving slowly. He looked directly at Pat, as if seeking his eye. It was clear from that one glimpse of his old friend's face that he felt the same horror. Earl, however, seemed oddly pleased with himself. But they were at the center Sullivan realized. He stopped, almost bewildered, as he realized it. Unthinking, he went through his mental checklist. He checked out the charges without being too obvious. He could see Earl and Jus doing the same. They located their positions and settled in to wait. Sullivan lounged against the outer railing, seemingly a relaxed spectator to the parade of life strolling by. Inside he struggled, his mind wrestling with what he had sworn to do. It was worse than torture. At least under torture he could have given voice to his pain . . . and have someone else to blame for his suffering. The seconds ticked by slowly.

Tom and Eli waited for Pat and Charlie by the terminal. The two dogged detectives had been searching the files for over two hours. Matt and Earl, they knew, had been on masonry, like Watkins. They had no idea what Sullivan and Lincoln had worked on, nor what any of them may have done in past years. Tom felt stupid for not checking it out sooner. He told himself that he'd had no firm direction at all until just days ago. Still, he kicked himself. He was wondering how he could have figured it out sooner when Pat and Charlie jogged up.

"Tom! They were assigned to work on the lights." Charlie gasped.

"The lights?" Tom asked. "What the hell would that . . . oh, shit!"

"What?" It came like a chorus from Eli, Pat, and Charlie.

"Let's go."

"Go? I don't get it," Charlie said, bewildered.

"Charlie, whoever blows the bridge has to run wire," Tom exclaimed. "You can't just drive a wagonload of dynamite out there. It wouldn't work. Besides, how're you gonna get away?"

"Yeah, so?" Charlie asked.

"Listen, these guys are good." Tom explained quickly. "They've worked here undetected for years. We have to assume they're sophisticated enough to blow the bridge from a safe distance. They've had plenty of time to work this out."

"That's for sure," Eli said.

"Exactly. Remember, Jacobs worked in the office, Tom reminded them. He's probably the one had them assigned to the lighting job. Now, suppose they were to run their detonator wire along with the wiring for the lights?"

"Whoa, Nellie! Hold on there, Tommy," Pat said, stopping in his tracks.

"What?" Tom asked.

"Well, they got electricians, foremen, engineers, everybody lookin' over their shoulders, right? Inspecting everything, I'd imagine." Pat looked from Charlie to Tom. "How're they gonna run their wire without somebody catching it?"

"Hell, Pat, I don't fucking know! But you got a better theory?" Tom growled. They all stood for a moment, staring at each other. "I rest my case," Tom said. "Let's get going." They had almost left the terminal when Tom saw Sam Halpern ambling toward them.

"Sam! What the hell are you doing here?"

"Good to see you too, Tommy. Eli, Pat, Charlie, how's it going? You all look like you're headed somewhere."

"Yeah, it's going great," Tom said distractedly. "Want to come along? We need to get moving."

Sam didn't hesitate. "You lead, I'll follow."

Tom headed off toward New York at a brisk walk. "So, what're you doin' here, Sam?" he asked over his shoulder.

"I was up at the Marble Palace, taking care of some bullshit, and I heard you were in a lather this morning. I figured if Byrnes let you have Pat and Charlie back, then maybe this was important."

"Your instincts are impeccable, Samuel," Tom congratulated him. "These goddamn fanatics had jobs on the electrical work, and—"

"What? What fanatics?" Sam asked, bewildered. "How many we talkin' here?"

"Don't have time, Sam. They're gonna blow the bridge," Tom said quickly. "Could be today. I don't know exactly, but it could be."

"Say no more, I'm right behind you."

They got through the terminal as fast as they could, hindered by the crowds then made their way onto the promenade and up the stairs onto the bridge itself.

"Colonel Roebling told me how it might be done," Tom explained as they shoved through the packed strollers. "Of course, it all seemed pretty theoretical at the time, but the most efficient way is to set explosives at the center"—Tom pointed out toward the middle of the river—"cutting the connections between the main cables and roadway beams. Now, if you cut enough of those connections where they attach to the support beams, then the whole thing will start to come apart. He said . . . if it was him, he'd blow the stay-cables too."

"The diagonal ones?" Charlie asked from behind.

"Yeah, Charlie. We've got to check 'em. Climb up there if necessary. Whatever it takes."

"Great." Charlie didn't sound too enthusiastic. I'll let you do that stuff."

They had just passed the Brooklyn tower when Tom stopped, that nagging feeling strong in his gut. The others stopped too, questions on their faces. Mary was standing out of Tom's sight just on the other side of the tower, her creamy-white dress blowing in the gentle breeze. She had stopped to admire the view of the Heights. She didn't see Tom.

"What's the matter?"

Tom turned back, staring toward Brooklyn. "We should check the dynamo room," he muttered, looking back at the power house but thinking there was something else he couldn't put a finger on.

"Huh?" Sam looked at the others to see if they knew what Braddock was talking about.

"We left that cop there, Tom," Eli said. "It's covered."

"Just got a feeling. Remember what I found on that pad this morning? Think about it. Where better to set up their generator? Nice and quiet, out of sight . . . it's perfect." He looked at Sam, who nodded slowly.

"Yeah, but the charges would be at the center of the span, right?" Sam asked.

"Good point. We'll check there first, . . . dynamo room after." Tom turned on his heel and headed out over the river. It was three forty-five.

At three-thirty precisely, Partick Sullivan had flashed his small mirror at the Brooklyn shore. Almost instantly, there was an answering flash from a spot near the power house. Pat flashed "ready." Jacobs flashed back "set." Sullivan put the little mirror back in his pocket and gave a quick hand signal to Jus and Earl. They'd wait now for the traffic to build a bit more. One way or another, traffic or not, they'd blow it by 4:00 P.M. Patrick settled into his private hell again.

I wish I could see his face, Bart," Thaddeus said, his voice echoing in the dynamo room. "I wish I could see it when he hears the explosions. That was pretty work, by the way . . . finding out about them."

"Thank you, Thaddeus. Didn't take much digging really," Jacobs said modestly. "I know the grocer where they buy their food. Odd, them getting deliveries of milk, eggs, and such, while they're supposed to be in Newport."

"But you're sure it's him . . . Roebling and his wife?" Thaddeus asked, concern knitting his brows.

"The old bastard isn't the only man with a pair of field glasses, Thad. It's him, all right."

"I wonder why the ruse? You think they were afraid to leave? They must have been alerted by the good Detective Braddock." Thad chuckled. "So diligent, so dedicated, but always a step behind. Too bad we can't blow him along with the bridge. He's been a thorn in our side for months, that bastard. Who knows, maybe we'll get lucky and blow his Irish ass into the river." Bart and Thad had a good laugh at that.

"Well, I'm glad they stayed. I'll be thinking of him when I push this plunger down," the captain said, lightly tapping the handle. He paused for a moment, a look in his eyes that had Jacobs wondering. "If anything goes wrong, Bart . . . I mean, if somehow this"—he tapped the generator—"doesn't work, I'm going after him. He'll pay, one way or another."

"Roebling?" Jacobs asked, knowing very well who the captain meant.

Thaddeus shrugged. "Just in case . . ." he said, feeling sure the possibility was quite remote. "Everything will go as planned. It *has* to." He looked at his watch again. "I've got three-forty-eight, Bart," the captain said, the tension tightening his throat. "Better get into position."

Jacobs went outside and leaned against the wall of the power house, the small mirror in his hand once again.

"Looks like a hell of a crowd up there, Captain. Casualties will be high . . . better than we'd hoped," he called to Thaddeus, who waited inside the door, just feet from the detonator.

"This is a day the country will remember for centuries, Bart. It's even bigger than the Lincoln execution. We'll be in the history books, my friend," Thaddeus intoned. "Think about it, an act of such daring, such symbolism, that it burns our names forever into the national soul."

"Must be twenty thousand up there, Captain," Jacobs called. "This is going to be spectacular! Ashtabula was nothing compared to this. Gonna be falling like leaves on a windy day." He looked at his watch. "I've got ten of, Captain. Shall I give the signal?"

Thaddeus hesitated just a moment, more for dramatic effect than anything else. "Give the signal, Corporal. On my mark . . . Now!"

Jacobs flashed his mirror in the Memorial Day sun. "Done, sir!" It was 3:51 P.M.

Earl had seen them coming. The group of detectives and cops stood out in the holiday crowd like bulls at a horse show. The signal had been flashed just a moment before.

"Let 'em come," he figured. There wasn't much they were likely to do unless they knew what to look for and where. Earl turned his back to them, leaning his elbows on the trusswork railing. He felt them pass and turned to look at the backs of the dead men. That's what they'd be if they were still out there in ten minutes. But as he turned, Charlie looked over his shoulder. In his days going over to the bridge office, before Emmons and Lebeau dropped out of sight, Charlie had passed Earl once or twice as he worked on the roadway. Tom had shown them all the pictures just this morning too. It didn't click right away.

Charlie hadn't gone more than a half-dozen steps farther though when he said to Pat, "I think I saw Lebeau!"

They both turned, with Charlie pointing at Earl's retreating back.

"That's him, I think."

In an instant they called to Tom, who had gone on. "Spotted Lebeau! We're going after him." Then they took off in pursuit. Tom, Sam, and Eli stopped short to look, but after a moment's indecision decided to go on.

"They've got him covered," Tom barked. "Let's go." They picked up the pace, heading out over the river, Tom's gut feeling like it was tied in a knot. He scanned for Mary as sweat broke out on his brow.

Earl knew it was a mistake as soon as he did it. He could see the look in the big German's eyes. He slipped one hand under his jacket to the pistol he carried, tucked in an inside pocket. The detectives kept on though, going toward New York. Earl turned and stepped quickly toward Brooklyn, figuring he hadn't been recognized after all. He moved a lot faster than the rest of the strollers, cutting a swath through them. They were stupid, slow Yankee animals, lowing mindlessly to the slaughter. He had passed the Brooklyn tower when he ventured a look behind. The two detectives were back there, bowlers bobbing in unison, heading after him. The others were nowhere in sight.

"Shit!" Earl swore out loud. A matronly woman frowned her disapproval at such foul language in public. Earl picked up the pace, hoping to lose them in the crush, something his long legs both helped and hindered, for his head stuck up above the crowd. He hadn't gone more than five more steps, when he heard someone call out.

"Hold it, Lebeau!"

Earl didn't stop, or turn to look. He broke into a run, caroming off people like a cue ball on a hard break. The end of the promenade was just fifty feet away. He planned to vault down the stairs that led to the level of the approach.

"Halt!" he heard behind him. It seemed a little farther back. Earl felt his chances were good. As he neared the stairs, though, he had to dodge around a perambulator pushed by a beautiful woman in a striking white bonnet. He managed it well, actually throwing an apologetic look over his shoulder to her for his rudeness. His momentum carried him into a gentleman in a silk top hat, whom he jostled badly, bouncing off him toward the stairs. He hit the steps at a staggering run, definitely not in control of his balance and going far too fast. A woman was directly in front of him, just at the top step. He tried to avoid her but his momentum carried him into her back, propelling them both headlong down the stairs. Her scream seemed to carry above the crowd, cutting through the hubbub. Earl knew right off that it was going to be bad. He covered his head as best he could in the split second before he hit the steps. He hit hard, his side landing on the edges of the steps. The impact was blinding. The edge of one step caught his upper thigh, on the right side another hit a rib like an explosion. The next step he caught with his elbow and upper arm. The three impacts were so fast, it was like a Gatling gun of pain raking him from thigh to shoulder. He'd been shot before. This was not much better.

He wished that the damn woman would stop screaming. She was loud enough to be heard halfway across the bridge. They tumbled to the bottom, bouncing into others as they went. The next thing Earl was conscious of was the cold texture of concrete pressed against his face. He had no idea if any time had passed, if he had blacked out or not. He was numb and the concrete vibrated against his face as people came running. He tried to rise. The two detectives would be on him in no time. As he tried to push himself up, his side erupted in a brilliant bayonet point of pain. He fell back to the pavement, crying out breathlessly.

People came running to the screams. They could be heard all along the Brooklyn side of the bridge. Some in the crowd, alarmed at the growing stampede, cried that the bridge was collapsing. As the mass of humanity broke for the Brooklyn shore, the press became overwhelming. Mary and Chelsea were caught up in it immediately. People who a moment before stood at the top of the stairs, aghast at Earl and the screaming woman, were now thrown down by the press of the crowd behind. Earl tried to rise again, but someone had fallen across his legs. He struggled and kicked despite the pain, but he couldn't break free. The body on top of him wasn't moving. Someone else tumbled down on him. Arms, legs, and elbows knocked him flat again. He felt hard shoe leather on his back, as the maddened crowd trampled over the fallen, who were now all around him. His side felt like a stake had been driven through it. A broken rib, he recognized. He tried to move, to crawl, but the crushing weight of bodies piling up on him pinned him helplessly. Screams, shouts, crying and the moans of the injured filled his ears, drowning out all else.

People continued to fall as the panicked crowd behind poured off the promenade. Hundreds were pressed between the railings, thrown down the stairs, crushed and trampled by the weight of the thousands behind. With every body that was added to the pile on top of him, the jagged end of Earl's rib dug farther into his chest. Breathing was becoming difficult, movement impossible. He was entombed, crushed inexorably into Yankee soil . . . into the bridge itself. All around him was blackness. Earl opened his mouth to scream, as even more weight piled on. He felt something give with the stabbing pain in his side, as one lung collapsed. Earl's scream became a gurgle of blood. He gasped, drowning in it. He tried to spit but had no breath even for that. His fingers, ragged from clawing the ground left bloody streaks on the concrete.

Earl Lebeau's world had come down to a narrowing circle of light as his life slipped away. He stopped struggling, fascinated by its brilliance. His oxygen-starved brain saw it as the blinding flash of explosives and he imagined the captain had blown the bridge. Then it flickered and went out.

Pat Dolan and Charlie Heidelberg saw it happening but were powerless to stop it. Thousands came running down the promenade from behind them, pressing them forward no matter how they yelled or tried to hold the mob back. Everyone was in a panic. Incoherent with fear, the crowd had taken on a life of its own, rushing toward the stairs like lemmings in a massive rush of self-destruction. Most had no idea why they ran, they just bolted with the rest. The two detectives were very nearly swept under by the screaming, hysterical tidal wave. They had to climb up on top of the trusswork over the train tracks to save themselves. From there they pulled as many to safety as they could, helping them down to the roadway below. Women and children were sometimes passed over the heads of the boiling mob. Others were not so lucky.

Screams that the bridge was collapsing, screams that anarchists were dynamiting the span were heard. Both detectives heard the cries, but there were so many injured and dying before their eyes that it was impossible to turn away. People crushed in the mob bled from the nose and ears. Some walked on the backs of the writhing mass to escape. Clothes were torn and shredded. Some ran naked.

Beneath the bridge, a bizarre rain of shoes, handbags, hats, parasols, clothes, canes, toys, wallets, watches, and loose change sifted down on the roofs and cobblestones of Brooklyn. They fell between the railroad ties, disembodied evidence of the carnage above. Among them was a striking white bonnet and an infant's coverlet.

Justice hadn't seen Earl try to saunter away from the two detectives. It was three-fifty-six when he and Pat heard the screaming and saw the sudden surge toward Brooklyn. Why they were still there, neither could have said. By rights they should have been well on their way to New York. Instead they seemed rooted to the spot, almost as if they both were under some spell, doomed to die with the bridge they helped build. Oddly, it was Earl who broke it. Earl Lebeau, the diehard Yankee-hater had somehow managed to clear the center of the bridge. Within two minutes Lincoln and Sullivan were practically alone, while the promenade and roadway on the Brooklyn side appeared to actually boil.

"Jus, it's three-fifty-eight," Sullivan called in a panic, looking at his watch. "Either we run like hell, or—"

Justice didn't say a word. He reached into his back pocket, his hand coming out with a large folding knife. He flipped it open with a grin. Patrick climbed halfway up the trusses and was looking up at him. Justice reached down, feeling for the wires . . .

"*Hold it right there!*" a voice called behind him, freezing him in place for a split second. Jus's eyes locked with Pat's in that instant. He seemed to be saying good-bye as he handed him the knife.

Tom, Sam, and Eli had just broken through the fleeing mass of people when they saw Lincoln bending over the truss. It seemed that no sooner had Tom called out than Lincoln spun around, a pistol in his hand. Eli was slightly ahead. He saw it too.

"Gun!" Eli cried before Justice fired. They were so close that Tom could swear he felt the heat of the explosions. Jaffey crumpled but Tom was on Lincoln before he could fire again. He hadn't had time to pull his own pistol. Tom went at him with his bare hands, knocking the pistol away with a backhanded swipe that sent it clattering over the side of the promenade. Braddock struck out with his right with all the power he could muster, feeling as if the blow came right from the floor. Braddock's fist landed with a sickening impact, knocking Lincoln, arms flailing, clear across the promenade, where he came up hard against the trusses. Amazingly, Lincoln didn't go down. Braddock didn't wait for him to recover. Roaring his anger, he grabbed Lincoln, lifting him overhead and throwing him off the promenade to the train tracks eighteen feet below. Justice Lincoln's life ended abruptly.

"Eli!" Tom called as he whirled around. Sam was stooping over the patrolman. The look on his face was grave, though Eli held up a shaky hand to prove he was all right. Movement in the corner of his eye brought Braddock around, his Colt appearing in his hand almost before he thought of it.

"*Halt!*" he shouted at Sullivan, who had clung there transfixed by the sudden, terrible action before him. Sullivan was at the main wire where it emerged from the junction box for the bridge lighting. He yanked at the connection but it wouldn't come loose. "*Halt I said! Don't move!*" Braddock's pistol was suddenly inches from Pat's head, the barrel looking big enough to swallow him whole.

Sullivan took a deep breath and, looking straight at Braddock, said, *"For the love o' God, Braddock, I got to cut these wires or we're all dead."*

The shock on Tom's face must have been clear, but the pistol didn't budge. He knew instinctively that Sullivan was telling him the truth but to act on it, he needed to trust . . . the enemy! He stood for eternal seconds. His heartbeat thundered in his ears as the time ticked by.

Braddock suddenly tucked the pistol in his belt and said, "Give me the knife."

Pat hesitated now himself.

"Give it to me!" Tom commanded. The knife was handed over giving trust for trust. "Where do I cut? *C'mon, show me!"* Braddock shouted. Suddenly Sullivan seemed to come to himself and said, "There. Cut those wires there, where they come out of the junction box!"

Tom had to bend almost double over the trusses to see what he was doing. He located the wires and started sawing. An instant later he was through and started yanking at them, pulling them apart to be sure there was no contact. When he looked down to the train tracks for Sullivan, all he saw was his back as he raced out of sight toward New York. Tom, his hand still on the naked end of the detonator wire, jumped with the sudden jolt of an electric shock running through him like a bolt of lightning.

"Christ!" He dropped the wire, stunned.

He came to himself quickly enough, looking to Jaffey and Sam.

"Go!" Eli said weakly. "Go, I'll be all right. Get to the dynamo room." Amazingly, he picked himself off the promenade and walked to a bench to sit. His feet left red tracks on the wood decking.

Sam watched open-mouthed.

"What are you waiting for? *Go!"* Eli shouted.

Tom and Sam climbed down the trusses onto the train tracks as fast as they could. Sam started to chase after Sullivan but Tom stopped him.

"Forget him! The dynamo room!" he shouted. He was running before he finished.

"Jesus, look at the mob!" Sam panted as they ran.

"C'mon!" Tom didn't say any more. They dodged through the milling mass as best they could. Tom saw Charlie up on the top truss, helping people down off the promenade, still boiling and screaming. Suddenly one scream riveted him in his tracks. He skidded to a halt, scanning the crowd. He heard that scream again and a sickening chill ran through him. *Mary!* He saw her then, pressed against the railing, her hair wild, blood streaking her face, then she disappeared.

"Sam, it's Mary!" he shouted over the din as he tried to climb to her. The mass of people climbing down overwhelmed him, though. There was no way up.

"Charlie!" he called, his voice cracking and unnatural. "Charlie!" Heidelberg looked down at Tom, not sure what he wanted but not wanting to leave where he was desperately needed. Mary must have heard Tom too, for suddenly, over the tumult, a piercing, desperate cry rang above all others.

"Tommy!"

Sudden recognition registered on Charlie's face, and he turned back to scan the crowd. Tom saw him reach. Mary was being carried by the mob toward the stairs, like a river raging toward the falls. In slow motion she swept by Charlie, his hand thrown out like a lifeline. She grabbed and held on as he pulled with all his might to free her. Throwing everything into it, she reached with her other hand, grabbing his arm by the elbow. She was pulled off her feet. She felt her shoes being pulled off, her dress tear. She hung on. Suddenly, she was being pulled free. She clambered up on the trusses next to Charlie, who handed her down into Tom's waiting arms.

"Thank God you're all right!" he cried, hugging her trembling body against him. "Thank God." She clung to him limply, all energy seeming to leave her. Tom stood back and looked into her face. She had a wild-eyed, desperate look. Tremors shook her, and her knees went weak. She reached for support, clinging to Tom, her eyelids fluttering.

"Tom," Sam said. He didn't have to say more. Tom knew he'd have to leave her. The one chance they had of catching Sangree was slipping away with every heartbeat. He couldn't just drop her, though. She needed help. Tom looked around frantically. He spotted Pat Dolan in the crowd, helping people down off the trusses.

"Pat!" Tom shouted. "Take care of Mary. We've got to get Sangree!" He turned to her then and said softly, "Mary, I've got to go." She didn't seem to understand, and nodded distractedly. "Mary, you're okay. I'll be back."

She ran a bloody hand through her hair, looking about like she'd lost something. "Tommy, where's Chelsea?"

Tom handed her to Pat, saying, "Take care of her, Pat. Help her find Chelsea if you can. I'll be back."

Tom and Sam ran then, the cries and shouts from thousands of throats following after. Together they ran down to the street level and around to the left, toward the power house, where Tom stopped for a moment against the wall around the corner from the engine room door. Without a word, he took out the old Colt and tried to steady his breathing. Sam took the cue.

"Ready?" Tom panted. Sam nodded. "Let's go!" They rounded the corner of the power house. From there they could see the door to the engine room. Officer Monzet wasn't there.

"Shit!" Tom grunted. "I was afraid of that." They sprinted for the wall. Pistols held high, they flattened themselves against the brick on either side of the door. Sam nodded at the ground in front of the door.

"Blood," he whispered.

Tom nodded. "I've got the key," he said softly.

Jacobs had run in five minutes before, locking the door behind him.

"There's something going on up on the bridge!" he exclaimed, sounding perplexed.

"What? What do you mean?" Thaddeus shouted. "What the hell's going on?"

"I can't really see from this angle, but there's a lot of screaming and shouting. This sounds crazy, I know, but it looks like clothes are falling from the span, just beyond the Brooklyn anchorage." Jacobs didn't really believe it himself.

Thaddeus didn't hesitate.

"*Bart, I'm blowing her now!*" he shouted in the echoing room. Thaddeus Sangree gave out with a rebel yell at the top of his lungs. It vibrated off the brick and stone of the vaulted room like the ghosts of battles past. For an instant, in that stark, nightmarish vault, it could almost be imagined that the captain had conjured those ghosts and set them loose in an avenging tide. He slammed down the plunger on the detonator, making the small dynamo inside whir, as it sent a jolt of electricity out over the river . . . *Nothing*!!

The captain looked at it with wide-eyed disbelief. Jacobs stared, slack-jawed. They were frozen. Mocking seconds ticked off.

"*No! No! No! No!*" the captain screamed suddenly, slamming down the plunger again and again. Minutes careened by as they checked their wire connections, fumbling to find the reason for their failure. Sangree ranted, slamming the plunger down again and again.

Jacobs stood back, shock washing over him, draining his face of color. He checked out the window, then looked again. With unnatural calm, he said to the captain, "We'll be having visitors in a moment. Two cops; one of them's Braddock." Jacobs stood beside the door paralyzed. The sound of the door being pushed, then the rattle of a key in lock, brought him out of his stunned silence. "Thaddeus! Thaddeus!" The captain seemed oblivious to

Jacobs or to their danger. He worked in frantic haste, checking the wire connections and slamming the plunger. "*Captain Sangree! Captain!*" Jacobs shouted.

Thaddeus finally seemed to come to himself. He looked at Jacobs with red eyes, brimming with tears.

"You've got to go. Go now!" Jacobs said, waving toward the window in the opposite wall. "Go for Roebling! I'll hold them."

Jesus, you hear that?" Sam said, cocking an ear toward the heavy door. A moment after they had plastered themselves against the wall, they heard a savage, high-pitched yell inside, muffled by the brick and stone. Tom and Sam exchanged a worried glance.

"Never thought to hear that yell again this side of hell," Sam breathed.

Tom nudged him.

"Try the door." Sam shoved slowly but as hard as he could against the triple-thick yellow pine. "Locked."

Tom nodded to the key. There seemed to be more yelling inside.

"Get that?" Sam said.

"Somethin' about Roebling, I thought."

A worried frown creased Tom's forehead.

"Careful!" Sam whispered.

Tom's hand rattled the key around the keyhole before finally slipping it in. He turned the big key with a cautious hand, hoping to turn the tumbler quietly. They heard the lock click as the bolt slid back.

"On three," Tom said in a low growl. "One . . . two . . . *three!*"

Sam hit the door first and though he hit it hard, it opened no more than about two feet, with a scraping sound that told of something braced behind. Tom saw Sam duck to his right and bounce off the door. An instant later, a bright, bloody length of steel erupted from the collar of Sam's uniform. It appeared, then disappeared so quickly, Tom almost couldn't believe he'd seen it, flashing like an icicle from Sam's neck.

It was the bark of Sam's Smith & Wesson that made a believer of Tom. As Sam fell back against Tom, Sam fired through the gap in the door. Tom fired too from behind, the exploding pistols setting his ears ringing. Then Sam fired through the door, blowing splintery holes in the hard yellow pine. Tom caught him with one arm and emptied the Colt in an arc from door frame to door frame. The shots, deafening in the brick corner between the power house and the approach, sent splinters flying about their heads. Gunsmoke and the faint smell of yellow pine hung in the air. The sudden silence following the fusillade rang in their ears. Tom pulled Sam to one side of the door.

He gave a rasping cough and choked out, "I'm all right. It's okay, he just—" Sam held a hand to his neck, which leaked red into his blue coat in a widening purple stain.

"You see them? How many?" Tom asked his old friend.

"Just one I could see." Sam's voice sounded odd and strangled. He reloaded with a shaky hand, as did Tom. They positioned themselves on either side of the door once more. Sam looked pale but determined.

"I'll go low, you go high."

Sam nodded. They went through the door again, Tom diving through the gap and rolling, Sam wading in after. They swept the room, looking for targets among the dynamos, wheels, belts, and gears. Weasel Jacobs crouched behind one of the dynamos, a big cast-iron monster, hulking and sinister with threatening new power. Two bullets had caught him in the blaze of gunfire a minute before. One had carved a ragged furrow in his left arm the other had passed right through him from back to front. He looked down at the hole in his chest, amazed at the sight of his lung as it frothed through the silver dollar–size hole. His breathing was short, ragged, and unlikely to continue for very much longer, he realized. The knife was useless. It lay where he'd dropped it. He readied himself, his Remington .44 held tight in a shaking hand.

Tom saw the knife, a wicked length of bloody steel, sparkling on the concrete floor. He knelt to retrieve it, keeping his head up and eyes scanning. The almost imperceptible movement of a falling drop of blood caught his eye. He saw it fall and splash by a pair of feet on the other side of one of the dynamos. A hand was poised near the two feet. He was about to signal Sam when the hand left the floor. Jacobs popped up as fast as he could, but the sudden movement left him light-headed and reeling. He got off one shot at the sergeant before the man returned fire but couldn't tell if he'd hit his target. He was so dizzy it seemed like his pistol was firing all over the room and he wasn't sure if he hit anything. The .44 boomed like a cannon. To Sam, the appearance of Jacobs, the explosion of his pistol, and the angry buzz of the bullet were almost the same event. He fired back with no aim. Tom fired too, letting go three rounds at Jacobs's feet. Bullets slapped and ricocheted, as all three pistols blazed. Glass shattered, splinters flew. Jacobs felt as if a rug had been pulled out from under him. His left foot seemed to explode. He staggered from behind the dynamo, his pistol waving and belching sheets of flame in a deafening staccato. It was Tom whose bullet caught Jacobs in the neck. It must have hit the spine, for the spray of red seemed dappled with white. Jacobs's head lolled on his shoulder, a puppet's head with a severed string. He stood reeling, stunned and uncomprehending. Two heartbeats and two small fountains of deep red blood passed in slow motion as Jacobs's brain groped for the reason why the room was now on its side. He never got the answer.

Y ou okay, Sam?" Tom asked in a shaking voice.

"Yeah, okay . . . I think," Sam said uncertainly, looking down at himself. The front of his shirt was turning red at an alarming rate though. They checked Jacobs's corpse, then the rest of the room. The open window on the other side taunted them. Screams, cries, and the sound of running feet wafted in, a reminder of the disaster on the bridge. They looked out at the street but there was no sign of the captain.

"Christ! You see this, Tommy?" Sam pointed to the detonator, its plunger pushed all the way down.

An icewater chill rippled down Tom's spine. His hands trembled from excitement and fear. "This is what gave me the shock up on the bridge." Sam was shaking his head "Jesus H. Christ!" he said, his voice echoing faintly.

"Yeah," Tom whispered. "And where's Sangree?" He turned to Sam, suddenly remembering.

"Sam, you said you heard something about Roebling, right?"

Sam nodded. "Pretty sure, yeah."

A sudden realization dawned on Braddock, turning his face into a mask of horror. "Oh, God, Sam . . . The Roeblings!"

A light came on in Sam's weary eyes.

"Go! Go!" he said, waving at the open window. "I'll be all right. *Run!*"

Tom almost dove through the window, breaking into the fastest run he thought he could maintain all the way to the Roebling mansion. It was a good half mile to 110 Columbia Heights, mostly uphill. Tom dashed through the curious crowds, drawn to the cries up on the bridge. They slowed and tired him, forcing him to work even harder to keep up the pace. He hoped too that Sangree had been forced to walk so as not to draw attention to himself. He couldn't be sure, though. The image of the Roeblings and especially Emily shone like a beacon. He'd been too late to stop Sangree from pushing the plunger. If he was too late now . . . He didn't want to think of the consequences. He sweated up Poplar and Hicks streets, feeling he wasn't going nearly fast enough, gulping air like a drowning man. He prayed as he ran. "Dear God! After all they've been through, don't let it end like this." Tom pounded down Orange Street, Colt in hand, reloading as he ran. The Roebling house was right at the end. As he ran down the cobbles, his racing heart sank. The front door hung open.

Thaddeus hadn't hesitated. Jacobs was a soldier. He'd do his duty and die if necessary to slow the enemy. The captain ducked out the window and was gone into the crowd in seconds. He walked fast, trying not to draw attention to himself. At the sound of the muffled shots, though, he picked up the pace to a slow jog. No one seemed to notice. He kept up the pace, cursing all the way up Hicks Street. He raved continuously, cursing in disjointed bursts. The failure of all their plans, all their years of sweat and sacrifice had unhinged him. He felt it—knew that there was a part of him that had lost touch with reality. Another part seemed to observe, aloof and dispassionate, watching from some distant place as he came apart. Thaddeus knew it was happening but was incapable of stopping it. In fact, there was almost a pleasure in it, a mad exhilarating release from the world. He almost howled in his rage, putting back his head as he ran and letting forth a moaning, haunted sound that seemed to come from distant depths of loss and torment. He knew it was madness but it was beyond his control. He let it carry him, helpless yet exultant. He felt infinitely powerful . . . unstoppable. It was the power of madness, a voice said to him from somewhere back in his head. He rather liked the feeling. People he passed shrank from him. His eyes burned in his haunted face. He was frightening to look upon, he knew. He liked that too. He ran like a rabid dog through the streets of Brooklyn Heights with one goal in mind. Roebling. Fearful passersby stepped back but they needn't have. He was a man with one mission, one purpose. It was as if he were an angel of death, set down on earth to right an ancient wrong. No earthly power could stop him.

He crashed with incredible force against the heavy mahogany doors of the Roebling house. He hadn't remembered getting there, just the impact and the splintering of wood. Unstoppable! He stood for a moment in the foyer, casting about, sniffing the air for his prey. A sound, perhaps a footstep or the scrape of a chair, he wasn't sure what, drew him up the curving staircase to the second floor. He flew, bounding after the scent, sensing his quarry was cornered. In seconds the colonel would be dead. He could see it already, the glazed eyes, the pumping blood. He flung open the first door he came to, his pistol ready. The room was empty, save for a pretty beam of light flashing across the floor from the big front windows. A few steps down the hall brought him to another door, which he tried, but the knob wouldn't turn. No mere door could keep him out. He stepped back, then kicked it in with such force that it slammed back against the wall, splinters flying. Mrs. Roebling was there. She let out a small cry. He wasn't interested in her, though. She could live. It was the colonel who would do the dying. He could see the man across the room, standing framed against the window. Thaddeus stepped into the room and started to sweep Mrs. Roebling aside for a clear shot at the colonel. She had a determined look about her, though. He hoped he wouldn't have to kill her but he would if she forced him.

As he reached to push her aside, she brought her hand up and placed it against his chest. He couldn't believe she would attempt to resist him. Couldn't she see the inevitable? Didn't she know she couldn't stop him? *Nothing* could stop him. Too late he saw the glint of steel in her hand, felt the poke of it against his sternum, then the explosion. He heard it more than felt it, which amazed him. He wasn't hurt, he told himself, just off balance as he backpedaled, staggering out the door and across the balcony, trying to regain his equilibrium. He was brought up short against the balcony banister and put out a steadying hand to grasp it. He looked down at his shirt and smiled at the widening red stain. It hurt not at all. The temerity of the woman angered him. He brought up his pistol, a reluctant smile on his face as he brought it to bear. She stood blocking the door. He'd have to punish her now as well.

Tom heard the shot as he rushed up the front steps. The sound sent his heart to his throat. A sickening despair coursed through him. He was too late! The thought flashed through his mind as he burst into the house through the splintered front door, sliding to a stop on the marble of the foyer. He saw them above on the balcony! Sangree, his hand coming up, a pistol gripped stiffly, Emily standing still in the doorway, protecting the colonel to the last, the empty derringer hanging loosely in her hand. Tom didn't remember bringing his Colt to bear, didn't remember aiming. It bucked in his hand and what he remembered was surprise at how fast it had gone off. He saw Sangree buckle and twist toward him as a bullet caught him in the hip. Tom watched in slow motion as Sangree's pistol came around, swinging toward him. Tom fired again, seeing the impact, the crimson spray as the bullet plowed flesh and bone. Then Sangree was falling.

The slender banister wouldn't hold him. He crashed through it, tumbling twelve feet to the marble foyer. He blacked out for a moment from the impact but still he felt no pain, just a strangeness all over, a disembodied feeling, as if he were no longer in charge of himself. He could hardly move. His lungs wouldn't draw air. Where was his pistol? He'd need it to shoot the colonel. His hands groped for it. He'd have to get up now. It wouldn't do to let the bastard get away. But when he tried to move, there was pain—huge, billowing thunderheads of pain that stole his breath and shriveled his will. He knew now what Franklin had felt. The thought of his brother seemed to draw him farther from his body. It was not an unwelcome feeling. In fact, it was a warm feeling—almost sunny. He saw Braddock standing above him, towering, tall, and stern.

No need to be so stern, Braddock, he thought. Mrs. Roebling's done your work for you. He smiled up at the detective—a big warm smile, for that's how he felt now, warm. They were enemies no longer. He could afford to smile. He was going home.

Tom looked up at the Roeblings, standing at the head of the stairs. Washington's arm was wrapped about Emily, who still held the ivory-handled Remington at her side.

❋ Epilogue ❋

Tom and Sam sat in the front room of Tom's home on Lafayette Street. The evening was slipping in, as the day gathered her skirts to leave. It was June 2, 1883.

"Damn that woman's got sand!" Sam commented over his beer.

"Believe it! She has more tenacity than any two men I know, and she'd walk through walls for the colonel."

"Both barrels, point blank," Sam said shaking his head slowly. "Must've opened a hole big enough to put your fist through."

"He was not feeling well when I got there, I can tell you that. Drained out pretty quick. Didn't last more than a couple of minutes," Tom said. He took another sip of his stout, shaking his head slightly before he said, "Funny thing is—and I can't get this out of my head—he smiled at me."

"Sangree?" Sam asked, hardly believing it.

"Yeah. On his back, bleeding like a butchered pig . . . and he gives me this strange smile, like he was my friend or something. It was kind of . . . sad actually. I mean, for just a second there, he was . . . I don't know . . . human."

"He was a strange one," Sam said slowly. "Who can say what might come over a man at the end?"

"Strange, yeah," Tom mused, thinking of the scene at 110 Columbia Heights.

"Almost a shame it'll never get told," Sam said, shaking his head, wincing as he did and putting a hand to his bandaged neck.

"Nah, I don't think so. Better it's left to lie," Tom said, leaning down to scratch Grant's ear as the cat wound himself around Tom's feet. "The Roeblings have had all the stress they can stand. If I told it the way it was, there'd be an inquest, reporters, pictures in the papers. They deserve to go out in triumph, the world singing their praises. Why put blood on Emily's hands? Besides, Sullivan and Emmons could be just looking for an excuse to strike."

The two hadn't been found and as far as anyone knew, they were still a danger. Telegrams had gone out, of course, alerting police departments up and down the coast. Train stations were being watched. Still, Braddock figured they wouldn't be found. He had a feeling too that they'd never be back.

Sam held up his empty bottle. Tom got the hint and got up. Sam did have an excuse. The bandage that wrapped his neck and shoulder was stained a brownish-red again, though he'd changed the dressing this morning. Mary walked out of the kitchen then.

She pushed Tom back into his chair. "I'll get that. You two sit." She disappeared back into the kitchen, saying over her shoulder, "I've got something special cooking for you two heroes."

Tom grinned at Sam. She came back a moment later handing each of them a cold bottle. Tom got a small kiss with his.

"I am one lucky son of a bitch!" he said, shaking his head. Mary had been remarkably understanding of Tom leaving her as he had, once she found out what had happened. Chelsea had not been so lucky. She was in Bellevue, but she'd recover.

"By the way . . . you see Lebeau's body?" Sam asked. "Hell of a way to go—crushed like that."

"No sympathy for the likes of him," Tom's voice held a hard edge. "Eleven others . . . women and kids too, dead because of that mess. Who knows how many more hurt—hundreds probably." Tom took another swig of stout, adding, "The shit! Hope he had time to think about it before he went."

"Don't get me wrong, Tom," Sam said, holding up a hand. "Just a hard way to go is all."

Tom just shrugged. He didn't give a damn how hard Lebeau had it at the end. "The thing that gets me is the wires. Don't understand it," he said, looking up at the ceiling. "They could have blown the bridge easy."

"Hard to say what might take hold of a man," Sam observed. "If it was me, I'd cut the wires. Think of it. They'd worked on it for years, longer maybe than they've worked at anything else in their lives. Maybe it's the one thing that they ever really accomplished. And it's so beautiful that a hundred fifty thousand people come out on a sunny day just to admire it. I'm going to blow that to kingdom come?" Sam shook his head. "Killing wasn't the problem. It was the bridge made them give it up."

"When it comes down to it, I can't say I much give a shit why Sullivan did what he did . . . though I suppose you're right," Tom said. "I'm just glad he did it."

"Seems to me you had a hand in it too," Sam said. Tom just shrugged.

"You read the manifesto?" Sam asked. It had been found later in the dynamo room.

"The chief says it'll never see the light of day," Tom growled back.

Sam nodded at the wisdom of that. It would only open old wounds, stir things up, raise old resentments just when the country was coming together again.

"When you've been hating for so long, I guess it's hard to stop. Maybe you've got nothing else . . . I don't know." Sam said.

Tom frowned. "I suppose it's something that sort of defines you—like a job or . . . I know it would be hard to just quit being a cop, for example. Maybe it's like that."

"Yeah, exactly. Suppose being a cop was bad. Suppose you knew it but didn't know how to do anything else. You'd probably still do it," Sam reasoned.

"Interesting example," Tom said, looking at his friend directly.

They sat and watched the setting sun paint the top floor of the Astor Library in yellows and golds. The shadow of Colonnade Row crept up the front in a solid line. The bottom floors had lost their color, as if stolen by the fleeing sun. Tom and Sam drank their Clausen's in silence for a while. They were avoiding what they needed to speak of most. It was hard to break the silence. Tom finally spoke but still he didn't say what they both had been thinking . . . remembering.

"Fact is, I kind of hope we never find out," Tom said, getting up to light a gas lamp. "Sullivan may have earned a second chance. Speaking of second chances, I got a report from Doc Avery. I sent Mrs. Bucklin to see him. She's tubercular," he said grimly.

"Tough break. What about the grandkid . . . Mike?"

"That's what I'm saying about a second chance. Patricia asked me once, back when Terrence died, if I'd help with Mike if anything happened to her. Never thought I'd be in this position so fast. She hasn't asked yet, but the boy's got to get out of that shabby little tenement or he'll be sick too. Hell . . . might be already."

Sam didn't say anything. This was something Tom would have to work out for himself.

"He's a good boy, a real good kid. You'd like him."

Sam smiled. "I'm havin' trouble picturing you as a dad, Tommy-boy. Have you talked to Mary about this?"

"No." Tom shook his head doubtfully. "I just found out this afternoon."

Sam leaned forward in his chair. "So, what would you do, take him in?"

"I guess. Hate to see him in one of those homes for orphans or out on the street. Can't let that happen." Tom corrected himself almost right away, seeming to make up his mind right there. "*Won't* let that happen. Gave my word."

Sam looked closely at his old friend. "Seems to me you've made up your mind already. You're going to settle in with Mary now, right? Sounds like you got yourself a family. 'Bout time you settled down anyway. Been makin' all us married types jealous for too long," Sam said, grinning, his mouth full of stout.

"No apologies from me." Tom laughed. "Had my fun."

"I'll drink to that, Thomas." They slurped their beer together, the silence conspiring to resurrect the thing they'd been avoiding.

"Gonna be one hell of a funeral," Tom said finally. Sam looked at the mug of Clausen's in his lap, running his finger through the sweat on the glass.

"Never should have let him go first," he said softly, shaking his head.

"Not your fault, Sam. Nobody's fault. He was a good cop . . . wanted to do what he was doing. It was just—I don't know, it just *is*," Tom said, not knowing how to put it any better. "Could have been one of us just as well. Could've got shot when Jacobs opened on us. Could've been a lot of things," Tom reasoned, trying to ease both their minds.

Sam seemed to ponder this. He knew the truth of it, had seen it many times during the war. The war was history, though. It had been some time since he'd had to face a death like this, so close, so personal.

"Hate to lose the young ones," Sam said, regret and sadness coloring his words. "He just bled out. Couldn't stop it." He looked at his hands as if he could still see Jaffey's blood.

"Sam, it's not your fault, you—" Tom started to say. Sam had done his best, going back up on the bridge, injured and bleeding to see to Jaffey.

"Held him in my arms," Sam continued quietly. Nobody could have done more for him, Sam." Tom croaked, his throat tightening as he remembered how pale Eli had looked.

"I know. Tried to stop the blood but . . . he just slipped away." They sat in silence, remembering. It was a long silence. The night slipped in, stealing the last of the day while they sat. Tom looked up at the spot on the wall where he'd fixed the bullet hole. With a sad smile he said, "I'll miss him."

Emily watched the bridge as it slipped astern. She didn't think of the bridge, though. She had seen Tom Braddock for perhaps the last time the day before.

He had given them final assurances that the story of Captain Sangree and how he died would never be connected to her or Wash. Tom had buried it. There was nothing in the official police records, no mention of their ever having been there. As far as anyone knew, they were in Newport and Sangree was nothing more than a burglar, caught in the act. That was where they were finally headed, Newport. A long-deserved rest beckoned, a regrouping of body and spirit before life's second act.

Tom had taken care of everything that terrible afternoon. Shock had set in and she stared and shook, her ears ringing from the deafening report of the little gun. Emily couldn't actually remember firing. She recalled Sangree's face, though, the eyes fierce and wild as they looked through her to her husband. The hate shone there, the years of it, scalding and scarring from the inside. Emily could feel the heat of it, knew it would consume them both if she let it. She recalled too the surprise. He hadn't seen the small Remington in her fist. He hadn't expected a woman to stand in his way. He thought she could be swept aside. Emily had sensed that. It had angered her, a fatal error. She almost enjoyed his surprise now, though she hadn't then. She could see the mouth in an oval, the arms flung wide. But there was that fierce determination, the will that somehow kept the man on his feet. Then Tom, firing from the front door, and Sangree jerking like a puppet and falling. Next thing she remembered he was taking the pistol from her hand, telling them they should leave. Tom herded them out the back, down to their carriage house at the bottom of the hill. Wash drove. They took the ferry to New York, because he was afraid they'd be recognized at the bridge. From there they had taken the ferry to Staten Island and the obscure refuge of Wash's sister's home. Telegrams had come and gone to Newport and back, where Hughes covered for them completely.

Wash and she hadn't understood the need for such skullduggery at first.

"But I've done nothing wrong, Tom. I simply defended myself and my husband. Why should we sneak about like thieves in the night? We're not criminals!"

"Emily, first, we don't know how many more there might be. We can't take the chance that they may come after you and the colonel," Tom had said as he hustled them out of the house. "Second, if they think their captain's blood is on your hands, it'll make things just that much worse. Better they think I did it, and that's how it's going to look."

"But—"

"I'd give anything to undo all this, but I think at least I can contain it, keep your name out of it. It's best if we keep up the ruse of you two being in Newport. But you've got to go and go quickly."

They had agreed, of course, and the last she saw of Tom Braddock was a small wave and a grim smile, before he headed back up to the house. They'd driven away then and they hadn't gone back.

June 3, Braddock had been shuffling paper all morning, completing reports on the Bucklin case. Neither his head nor his heart was in it. He found himself staring blankly into space more often than not, reliving the events of the last few days. Nothing had gone quite as he'd planned. In fact, there'd hardly been a plan at all. It was all reaction—at least that's how it felt. He'd been frustrated at nearly every turn, staggering like a punch-drunk boxer from one blow to the next. Yet it was he who had won. There was no denying that. He had beaten them in the end. And though there were riddles yet unsolved and in truth probably would remain so, he was somehow satisfied. The bridge still stood. The Roeblings were safe in Newport. At least four of the conspirators were dead. Though he had regrets, he wasn't sure he'd have done anything differently. He'd done his best, as Eli and Pat and Charlie and Sam had done theirs. Braddock wished it could have turned out better, wished Eli was here to share a beer. He wished too that he could tell Mike who'd killed his father, but in truth he couldn't.

Hungry, Tom?" Byrnes asked, startling him. He'd been so buried in his thoughts he hadn't noticed the chief standing before his desk.

"Sure, I suppose," Tom said, pulling out his watch from a vest pocket.

"Good . . . join me?" the chief said, patting his stomach with both hands.

"You buying?" Tom asked with a grin. "I've never been known to turn down a free lunch."

Byrnes grinned back. With a successful case to his credit, Tom had taken a more confident tone with him the last couple of days.

"Sure, I'm buying. Let's go." Once they had gotten clear of the Marble Palace, Byrnes said, "Got a place I know on Mott . . . Used to go there once in a while with Coffin," he said with a strangled tone to his voice. "They make fried dumplings like you never tasted. Fabulous!"

"Sounds good. Mott, you say? Is it that little place, down a couple of steps from the street?"

"Yeah, right around the middle of the block. Ought to know it. Patrolled there nearly three years. Course that was quite a few years back."

"Don't know much about the Chinese myself," Byrnes continued. "Orderly people. Keep to themselves. They make a hell of a good dumpling, though." Byrnes laughed and Braddock laughed with him.

"Haven't been down there since Coffin . . ." Byrnes didn't finish. They knew how it ended. That observation cut the laughter short. "Closing the case," Byrnes said stiffly. "The press has been sniffing too close to that pile of offal." He shook his head. "Only reason they haven't been on it stronger is 'cause of the bridge thing. Goddamn Coffin. He left a tower of shit to clean up. The press sure as hell don't need to know. Nobody'd be safe." Byrnes looked to Tom for agreement and got it. "Don't want Nast drawing any more of his fucking cartoons," he said, making a sour face.

"I suppose not. Could be inconvenient." Tom understated the disaster potential by a mile.

Byrnes grunted agreement. "Better to shut it down. Bury it. Coogan, for example . . . he's off to Harlem."

Tom digested that tidbit.

Byrnes looked to Tom with an appraising, raised eyebrow. "Other changes're in the wind too. Lots of things are going to change around here, Tommy."

Tom said nothing, waiting for Byrnes to take the reins on that one.

They turned onto Mott, with Tom wondering if Wei Kwan would be in the little restaurant. He was certain that Master Kwan would be discreet, but mistakes were always possible. Byrnes didn't know that Master Kwan was the key to his Chinese connection. It was better that way.

"This is it," Byrnes declared, stumping his cigar out against a lamppost. Wei Kwan greeted them at the door with polite bows but no overt recognition of Tom. He led them to a small table by the front window, where they sat, ordered beers, and watched the legs of passersby on the street outside. The kitchen bustled and steamed in back of the small dining room, which didn't have more than twelve tables. It wasn't even a restaurant officially. It had no name, no sign on the door, no menu. Pots and dishes clattered, and Chinese rolled in unintelligible waves through the kitchen door as Wei Kwan and two other waiters brought the lunch crowd their meals. Tom and Byrnes were the only two white men in the place.

"Great place for a quiet conversation," Byrnes said. It was anything but quiet, and Tom raised a questioning eyebrow. "I should say a . . . private conversation, at least for the likes of us."

"Not likely anything said here will get back to the Marble Palace, that's true," Tom agreed.

"Exactly. I wanted to talk to you about something. Run it up the flagpole, so to speak."

"Oh?" Tom said, leading Byrnes on. By this time his curiosity was fully aroused.

"Yeah. You know . . . I liked the way you handled the Bucklin case. Stuck with it, kept your nose to the ground, dogged it till it paid out."

"Had some lucky breaks," Tom said. He was starting to say more when Byrnes broke in.

"Bullshit! No such thing as luck," Byrnes said, shaking a finger at Tom. "We mostly make our own luck one way or another. Your luck came 'cause you stuck close, followed through. That's all there was to it."

"Maybe . . . It was close. Can't exactly claim it was us who stopped them. Can't even claim to have shot Sangree first. Emily did that. Blew a hole in him he wasn't likely to recover from."

Byrnes nodded almost impatiently. "Yeah . . . with the gun *you* gave her."

Tom shrugged. "Mostly we were too late all around, a half step behind all the way."

"Again, bullshit! You're a goddamn hero, Tom. You've got to start acting like one. The only reason you were close at all was good hard work. For all we know, it was the chase of Lebeau that gave the others the chance to cut the wires. Ever think of that?"

"It occurred to me," Tom conceded, "but Emmons . . . who knows where the hell he is?"

Byrnes shrugged. "Some things we probably won't ever find out. Got to be content with what we can . . . move on from there."

"Well, we may not be able to ever prove some things—who killed Bucklin, for that matter—but we don't have to prove it to know what happened."

Wei Kwan came to take their order, standing patiently with pen and pad. He didn't even look at Tom directly, though he stood right next to him.

"I'm having the dumplings . . . steamed *and* fried," Byrnes said, making little dumpling shapes with his hands. "You understand?" Wei Kwan nodded but said nothing. His English was quite adequate.

"Sounds good!" Tom said. "I believe I will too." A tap of the foot under the table, a bow above, gave Tom his blessing. The dumplings would be extra-special.

"So . . . to finish what I was saying, you did well to handle the Roebling matter the way you did too."

"That I can agree with," Tom said with a satisfied grin. "No purpose served by letting them get plastered all over the front pages. Only make them bigger targets and tarnish a name that ought to be honored in this town."

"Couldn't agree more, Tommy. A little outside the standard police procedures, but that's what I liked about it. Shows initiative . . . ability to think on your feet, a willingness to bend the rules when you know it's right."

"Thank you, sir. I wanted to do good by them, just keep them from any more harm," Tom said honestly.

"Well, you know, with Coffin gone—oh here's the dumplings. Smell good, don't they?" Byrnes rubbed his hands together in anticipation.

Wei Kwan brought a steaming plate, piled with an assortment of steamed and fried dumplings, setting it before Byrnes.

"It's all I ever have here and they know to bring plenty."

"Mmmm." Byrnes savored the morsel. "So . . . like I was saying, Tom. With Coffin gone, I'd like to submit your name for the captaincy of the third. What do you think?"

Tom almost choked on his first bite, getting it down only with an effort.

Byrnes selected another dumpling, a fried one this time, dripping with fat as he hoisted it to his mouth. "Surprised, huh?"

"I . . . don't know what to say." Tom was at a loss for words.

"Say you'll take it," Byrnes said expansively. "There's no guarantee, mind you. I expect there'll be men pushed forward by every captain in the department." Byrnes held out a dumpling to Tom skewered on a fork Master Kwan had known to provide. He motioned to the dumplings. "They're *fabulous* today. Don't know what they put in them but they're better than usual. You deserve a rest too, you know," the chief said after a bit of thought. "Take Mary . . . and get away. Go up to the country. I hear the Adirondacks are wonderful."

He planned it out for Tom right then and there. "Take a couple of weeks . . . hell, take a month. You earned it. Let me worry about the promotion. You've built quite a reputation with this bridge business, even though it's all been kept quiet about the conspiracy. I quite agree with that, by the way. Bad enough to have that panic, but to frighten the public with crazy plots would ruin the bridge. Everyone would be scared to death to use it. Would have raised old ghosts with the South too. Best to let the whole thing fade away."

Tom, who was in midswallow, just nodded.

"But don't worry," Byrnes said, leaning closer to whisper across the table. "The people who count know what you did . . . right up through City Hall and all the way to Albany and Washington." He grinned. "If I have anything to say about it, you'll get your reward." Byrnes attacked another dumpling, lifting it to his open mouth.

Tom watched in morbid fascination. He cleared his throat with a little cough and said, "You know, a vacation doesn't sound bad at all."

. . .

Jumbo was the biggest living thing he had ever seen, and Mike wanted to see him again. Tom didn't mind. In fact, he enjoyed seeing Jumbo more the second time.

'"Even the Clydesdales that pull the really big wagons are tiny compared to that Jumbo," Mike had said with awe. He was eleven feet tall at the shoulder, with a trunk so thick and powerful it looked as if he could hoist a Clydesdale with ease.

"Does everything grow big like that in Africa?" Mike asked when they saw a white hippo, whose trainer walked him on a leash like some monstrous pig. I mean they got big elephants and big things with the long necks."

"Giraffes," Tom said.

"Yeah, and those camels with the humps are real big too. The only thing small is that baby elephant, 'Bridgeport,' but I guess he'll grow."

"I don't know, Mike. There must be some smaller things in Africa. They're just not as interesting as the big ones." What Tom seemed to like most was when a giant Chinaman named Chang paraded around the ring, all decked out like a Mongolian warrior with armor and a huge sword. Chang carried a midget named Major Atom on one shoulder.

"Holy mother o'God!" Tom burst out when the giant walked through the curtain at the end of the hippodrome. "That's an eight-foot man if I ever saw one. And that midget don't look any bigger than his head! I'll be damned. Wish Master Kwan was here to see that."

"Who's Master Kwan?" Mike asked.

Tom told him he was a friend, a very trusted friend.

When the last act had finished, a death-defying trapeze act with ladies in their underwear, they spent some more time in the menagerie, watching the "educated" kangaroos, the giant baboons, and a series of human oddities the likes of which had never been assembled before on earth.

Later they turned east out of the Garden toward Third Avenue to catch the El. Mike didn't mind when Tom put his arm around his shoulder.

"Mike?" Tom said, his voice sounding strange. He made a show of clearing his throat. "There's something I wanted to talk to you about . . ."

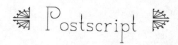

Postscript

Emily Roebling went on to become one of the leading socialites of Trenton. She studied law at New York University and received her degree, one of the first women to do so. She built a mansion in Trenton—near the Roebling works—which became a city landmark for generations. In 1893 she and Washington went to New York, where they walked out on the bridge together. No one recognized them. She attended the coronation of Tsar Nicholas and Empress Alexandra of Russia during a trip to Europe in 1896, one of the few Americans present. She died of cancer on February 23, 1903, and was buried in Cold Spring, New York. Washington, who was in Trenton at the time recovering from surgery, was too weak to make the trip.

Washington Roebling never built another bridge. As a stockholder in the Roebling Wire Works and an astute investor in the stock market, he became very wealthy. For many years he devoted himself to the study of geology, especially minerals. His collection, which included all but four of the known minerals on earth, is now owned by the Smithsonian Institution. In 1908 he remarried a Charleston, South Carolina, widow, and by all accounts it was a happy union. Washington, though in pain and discomfort virtually every day of his life, outlived all his assistant engineers. He outlived his brothers and his nephew, who went down on the Titanic. At the age of eighty-four, upon the sudden death of his nephew Karl Roebling, who had been running the wire making business, Washington took over day-to-day operations. He took the trolley to work each day with his dog named Billy Sunday and detested automobiles, refusing to ride in one. Not only did the business run, it prospered. In an interview, when asked how he was able to carry on, he was quoted in typical Roebling fashion: "You can't slink out of life or out of the work life lays on you." The end came on July 21, 1926, at the age of eighty-nine. He was buried beside Emily in Cold Spring.

Patrick Sullivan escaped to Texas, where for many years he rode with the Texas Rangers under the assumed name of Lester Cable. He was discovered and recruited by William Cody in 1891 and toured with his Wild West Show throughout the United States and Europe, where he routinely fought Sioux warriors, robbed stagecoaches, and hunted buffalo. Whenever the show came to New York, he always took time to visit the Brooklyn Bridge and was something of an authority on it. He died on his ranch in Texas in April of 1919.

Matthew Emmons was pulled from Buttermilk Channel by a passing fishing boat on the night of May 30. First thought to be dead, he soon recovered and spent the next few days at sea, fishing off the coast of Long Island. When he got back to New York, he eventually made his way to Coney Island, where he tended bar for nearly twenty years at a place not far from the boardwalk. He always boasted that he was actually the first man to successfully jump from the Brooklyn Bridge. Though he could never substantiate his claim, he insisted on it to his dying day and became a kind of Coney Island legend for it. He died in the fall of 1904 of liver failure.

Tom Braddock was awarded the captaincy of the 3rd Precinct in June of 1883. He and Mary were married in the spring of 1884 at the Church of the Transfiguration, on East Twenty-ninth Street. That same year they adopted Michael Bucklin and purchased a three-story townhouse on Willow Street in Brooklyn Heights. Tom took the train across the bridge twice a day for the next twenty-six years. He had a remarkable record of achievement, being decorated on eight occasions for heroism. Braddock never learned how to lead from behind a desk. He kept up a regular correspondence with the Roeblings over the years, but never saw either of them again. He attended Emily's funeral in Cold Spring, New York, a mystery to the other mourners.

In May of 1884, P. T. Barnum took a herd of twenty-one elephants, including the famous Jumbo, across the Brooklyn Bridge. It was one of his more inspired publicity stunts. The great showman thereupon declared that he was perfectly satisfied as to its solidity.